THE CONSTANTINOPLE TRILOGY

THE CONSTANTINOPLE TRILOGY

HAIG TAHTA

BLACK APOLLO PRESS

First published in Great Britain by Black Apollo Press

Copyright © Haig Tahta 2016

ISBN: 9781900355872

The four families in *April 1915*

The Avakians of Makrikoy

Karekin – Armineh
Deported 24 April

Sima (19) Olga (17) Nerissa (16) Haik (12) Seta (8)

The Asadourians of Cæsaria

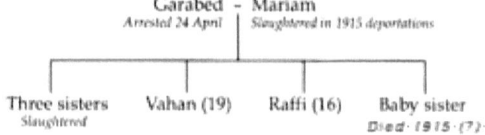

Garabed – Mariam
Arrested 24 April   *Slaughtered in 1915 deportations*

Three sisters   Vahan (19)   Raffi (16)   Baby sister
Slaughtered   *Died · 1915 · (7)·*

The family of Dr Nazim Kemal

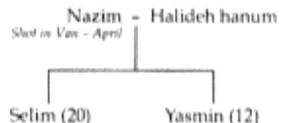

Nazim – Halideh hanum
Shot in Van – April

Selim (20)   Yasmin (12)

The Sarafians of Makrikoy

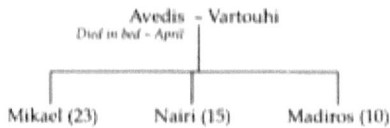

Avedis – Vartouhi
Died in bed – April

Mikael (23)   Nairi (15)   Madiros (10)

APRIL 1915

CONTENTS

Book 1: April 1915

PROLOGUE

1915 – the Ottoman Empire – so-called 'sick man of Europe' was not really as sick as the vultures surrounding it liked to make out. In this year, the reputedly moribund Empire was to inflict a major defeat on the proud British Navy for the first time in over one hundred years. The world would never be the same again.

1915 – the Austrian Empire – with more call to be considered the sick man of Europe, with its diverse and fascinating collection of peoples and cultures and ways of life. Throughout the Great War, it scarcely managed to win a single major campaign, except perhaps against the unfortunate Italians.

But were either of these two tolerant though inefficient, multiracial and multicultural empires the real 'sick men'. Hard and virulent unicultural nationalism was the growing creed in the world, and neither of these old and anachronistic empires sat comfortably with the seething tribal passions of the sovereign, territorial nation–state. But who in truth were the actual sick men? What reading of the events of the Twentieth Century, could point to the Hapsburgs or the Ottomans as hopelessly 'sick', next to their powerful neighbours?

Russia gave way to a materialistic Revolution, which within not much more than ten years resulted in the massacre, death and misery of mil*lion*s upon mil*lion*s of uncomprehending peasants. The German Empire – a much more efficient monocultural and monoracial society – gave way to a tribal nation–state in arms, whose hysterical demand for uniformity and racial 'purity' resulted in one of the greatest crimes in history. Other petty nation–states, springing up on the ruins of the old empires, produced tyranny, pogroms and, in the end, 'ethnic cleansing', far outweighing the inequalities and random cruelties of the old.

After the 1908 Ittihad Revolution in the Ottoman Empire, the Young Turks impatiently thrust aside the multi–national and tolerant legacy of the old Ottoman Sultans, substituting the narrow, prejudiced exclusiveness of the tribal nation–state. This resulted in the first of the great massacres leading to ethnic cleansing, for which this 'enlightened' century was to become notorious.

In August 1914, Europe entered into the destructive, European, war, known then, and for its first few months, as 'The Third Balkan War'. It was the entry of the Ottoman Empire into this war in November 1914 which turned it into the First 'World' War.

Finally – April 1915 – The Dardanelles campaign, fought within actual sight of that very first epic war of Western tradition – the Trojan War – was one of the great 'what–ifs' of history. It was also one of the greatest disasters suffered by the British Army until the fall of Singapore, twenty–five years or so later. Both defeats, ironically, were not at the hands of any recognised traditional European rival, but by a despised oriental foe. The world was changing, and here was the pivot.

Constantinople – Stamboul – Bolis ... The City.

Final note – In the Ottoman world people referred to their loved ones by many differing endearments which go far *be*yond 'my dear' or 'darling". These endearments, when translated literally into English, may appear somewhat stilted and artificial. Armenians, for example, use the word 'hokis', when addressing their children, or spouse. This translates as 'my soul', and has been used here throughout, as has 'my lovely father' or 'my little father' rather than always just 'Darling' or 'Dad', which would perhaps be the truer translations.

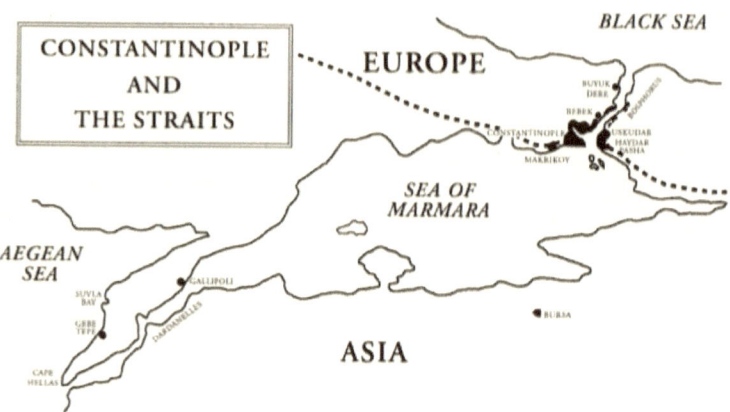

CHAPTER 1

Makrikoy, Breakfast at the Avakians

"I don't agree with you at all, Nerissa."

Sitting bolt upright at the breakfast table as she had been taught in a flowing white summer frock, Sima, 19 year-old eldest daughter of the Avakian family, haughtily addressed her younger sister.

"I see no reason at all why we ever came into this war in the first place, so why should the British, or the French for that matter, bother to attack us? Their real enemies, surely, are the Germans. What have we ever done to harm them?"

"But Sima, my darling," replied Nerissa, as she sipped her tea, "the bombardment by the British navy in the straits last month must surely be the preliminary to something – another attack – or, I don't know, – something?"

"For heavens sake, can't you two talk about something more interesting," said Olga, the family's second daughter. "I'm getting thoroughly bored with all this talk of war. It's happening so far away anyway. The only thing I've noticed is that there are no longer any decent clothes to buy in the shops."

Dressed simply in her college uniform, Olga nevertheless managed to display an elegance in the simple lines of her green skirt, which Sima, in her expensive white muslins, failed to achieve. Outstandingly pretty, Olga had a stunning smile, which, coupled with her large inquisitive brown eyes, she used shamelessly on all and sundry. Her charms were to no avail on her sisters, who ignored her comment and continued their discussion as if she hadn't spoken.

"Haik, will you please eat something. For heaven's sake, a piece of toast and honey isn't so difficult to swallow," snapped Armineh. She knew that continually nagging at her thin and wiry 12 year-old son about his stubborn refusal to eat at mealtimes was a totally pointless exercise, but she couldn't help herself.

Armineh was beginning, at last, to look older than the 38 years she was prepared to acknowledge publicly, and her noisy family was trying her patience more and more often in these difficult days. Her figure had always been round and short, but the birth of five children had made her increasingly dumpy. Armineh drew a deep breath, putting the sight of her son toying with his food out of her mind, and surveyed the rest of her family at the breakfast table.

Karekin, her husband, had not yet come down, and she glanced at the stairs that curved up impressively from the middle of the large hall where most of the family's activities took place. Here, in the centre of the house, immediately *bey*ond the main entrance door, stood the table and chairs where the family took all their meals. On one side of this great room, *bey*ond the dining area, was the door to the kitchens, and on the other side, doors to the formal sitting rooms. Dotted about the marble floor were settees and comfortable sofas and some large slightly faded but still beautiful Persian carpets.

The family's long-time nanny, Marie, whose large and comfortable figure bustled round the table, pouring tea and helping 8 year-old Seta, the youngest of the Avakian family. It was never entirely clear whether Seta was eating or talking as she seemed to be in a perpetual state of motion.

Breakfast at the Avakians was never silent, but, on this beautiful spring morning on the 1st day of April 1915, it was particularly noisy. Everyone was talking at once, when Karekin appeared at the top of the stairs.

It would be an exaggeration to suggest that his appearance was followed by a respectful silence as he walked purposefully down the stairs, though there was, perhaps, an almost imperceptible drop in the decibel level. Sima smiled up at her father, whilst Olga jumped up and gave her father a great kiss and a hug as he arrived at the bottom of the stairs.

Karekin was a tall and upright figure, almost always dressed formally in a grey suit of English cut. He was never seen in public, and indeed rarely even outside his bedroom, without an impeccably knotted tie. Every inch of his tall frame, with his prematurely bald head, was upright and dignified and he walked ramrod straight with his hands often clasped behind his back. Yet underneath all this formality, was an ultra-liberal temperament with forward looking ideas about education for girls.

It was very unusual for the daughter of an Armenian merchant family to be sent for her education to one of the Western schools in the City of Constantinople, and, in this respect, Karekin had always been considered eccentric by his business friends and neighbours.

Armineh, who was more traditional in her outlook, had not been happy about this book-learning, and was relieved that Sima had left school and was no longer exposed to temptation by daily trips into the city. By being at home, Sima could also help Armineh in dealing with Haik and Seta, and servants were getting more difficult to find.

That very morning, before coming down to breakfast, Karekin and Armineh had one of their discussions about the girls,

"Karekin, my soul, this war has dulled your responsibility to family matters."

"Oh, my love, are we going to have to go through all this again? You worry too much, and in any case …"

"Karekin, you must look at the situation here in your own home and stop spending your time with your political friends … and those …"

"Armineh, my love …"

"No, just listen. We have three problems. First you must consider Sima's marriage prospects. She's 19 and it is time you started thinking about this. Times haven't changed so much that you can shirk this duty, war or no war. Then there's Haik. He's 12, Karekin, and he's unusually naïve, but he's well into puberty – oh Karekin, pay attention – you know perfectly well what I'm talking about. He still runs about in the garden naked. You have to talk to him."

"You mean you want me to tell him to start feeling guilty about his body," replied Karekin, as he stretched his neck to knot his tie.

"Karekin, don't be obtuse. We're not talking philosophy here. We're talking about your son. You know exactly what I mean."

"Very well, Armineh, that's enough. I do agree with you, and I'll think about it, I promise. And now, my dear, what is your third problem?"

"I can't put my finger on it, but Olga is up to something – she is hiding something from us, but what it is I have no idea …"

"Armineh, my soul, this is you panicking as usual about everyone in your brood. Relax! There's nothing wrong with her. Look, Haik is my problem, I accept that, but you deal with Olga. She's getting a good education, and she knows wrong from right – which is more than can be said for most of the 17 year-old girls around here. As for Sima, we'll deal with her marriage prospects during the next month, so long as the British leave us alone."

"Karekin, honestly, you always …"

"Armineh, my sweet, don't stamp your foot in vexation. I'll be down to breakfast shortly, and that's an end to it."

On arriving at breakfast, Karekin sat at the top end of the table, and was immediately served with his usual light Russian tea with a slice of lemon by Marie, invariably followed by olives and white cheese, and usually ending with a slice of toast spread with the family's own honey.

"Baba, Nerissa and I were talking about the possibility of a Western allied attack here at Bolis. What do you think? Do you really think it likely?" Sima asked, as she passed the toast to her father.

"Sima, my soul – Marie some more tea please – I think Nerissa is right. Now that the British have failed to get their battleships through the Dardanelles, they're surely going to try something else, but don't ask me what."

"But, Baba, the French and English have always been friendly to the Ottomans and …"

"Yes, but they aren't now, and as they can't seem to get at the Germans. I'm afraid, girls, we are likely to be facing an attack of some sort sooner or later. Olga, where are you off to in such a hurry?"

"Oh father," Olga said as she rose from the table and gave everyone a quick kiss, "you know that I have to get an earlier train than you. Come, Haik, why don't you keep me company on the walk down to the station, then go on to school after the train goes."

Haik shook his head, while Armineh looked at Karekin meaningfully, as if to suggest that Olga's hurry to get away proved her point. Karekin merely waved his hand at her, making it clear that he didn't agree, and dismissing the subject. Meanwhile Olga, grabbed her bag, flashing a smile, and hurried out to catch her train to the city.

When Karekin at last rose to take his hat and stick, Nerissa and Seta came and kissed him, as always, before he went to work. Haik finally pushed his plate away, grinning at his exasperated mother, and went to give his father a hug.

"Baba – is there actually going to be any fighting – are we going to see British battleships firing their guns... can their shells actually reach us here ...?"

Karekin turned, returning his son's hug and replied,

"No, my son, that's pretty unlikely."

Having received a kiss from everyone, he straightened up even more, if that was possible, and walked out of the front door.

CHAPTER 2

The Asadourians of Caesaria

On this same 1st day of April, 1915, Vahan walked down the road to the Galata bridge, on his way to his classes at the Music and Drama Department of the University. Ever since his arrival in this wonderful city from his provincial home in Caesaria in Central Anatolia, he had been in a state of high excitement.

The Galata bridge!

This, one of the great bridges of the world, connected old Stamboul – the original city of Constantinople – to Pera and Galata, the original European trading suburbs. The crossing teemed with life. Turkish porters trotted past carrying huge loads on their backs, crying 'make way, make way'. A few gentlemen with Panama hats and walking sticks, strode along. One or two old-fashioned Ottoman gentlemen, dressed in the Stambuliya long coat with high collar walked slowly by. The occasional veiled lady passed from one side of the bridge to the other.

Then, there were the one-horse carriages, waiting to pick up passengers from the quayside under the bridge. The ferries themselves, hooting and jostling against each other as they drew up, trying to nudge into the quayside to discharge their fares coming in from further up the Bosporus, or across the straits from the Asian side. The ubiquitous red fez was everywhere, on Moslem and Christian head alike. Old and new, European and Asian, Christian and Moslem, Jew and Gentile, all thronging together in a noisy and jubilant mass. The only group underrepresented at this time in the morning, was women.

Vahan Asadourian was a stocky square-set young man. He had silky light brown hair and soft eyes with a permanently questioning look. Nine months ago, at the height of the summer of 1914, he had heard that he had won a scholarship to the Music Department of the University of Constantinople. His mother, Mariam, hiding her tears, had immediately started collecting all the things he would need when he left home. His father Garabed, bursting with pride, had taken him to the main bazaar of the provincial town – ostensibly to buy necessities for the journey, but really to show off his son's achievements to all his business friends and associates. Unaware of his mother's private tears, he had felt and even revelled secretly in his father's pride.

Just turned 18, Vahan had never been anywhere *beyond* the province of Caesaria. His father had travelled regularly on horse-back into the Eastern highlands to visit the many village families who produced the handmade carpets he commissioned; wonderful and intricate carpets, made with bright, vegetable-dyed wool. Garabed would sometimes take his second son, Raffi, with him on these trips, but his eldest son would always be left behind. Vahan could not understand why this was always the case and sharp words had been exchanged between them. Without much thought he had blurted out -

"Baba, it's not right – you took Raffi with you last time. It's my turn to go with you and meet the families with whom you do business. Look, I can take my violin with me, and I can play at night – they'll love it."

"My son, I need you to stay at home to look after your mother and sisters in case something happens to me on the trip. Vahan, life is hard in the highlands, these people have no time for music."

"Oh, father, believe me, you are wrong. Everyone appreciates folk music and melodies that help to relieve their worries and uplift their souls. In any case, both mother and grandma are far more capable than me of managing the house."

"You may be right about music, Vahan, but you don't understand the real issue," said Garabed, and Vahan recalled the mounting anger in his father's eyes at being contradicted.

"We live in a Muslim society. However competent your mother may be, a male head of the family is vital. Officials, or indeed anybody coming to this house, are trained to ignore the women – sometimes even to look away from them if they are in the same room. That's enough, Vahan, I will not listen to any more of your thoughtless nonsense. You will do as you are told."

Garabed Asadourian was a strict man liable to lose his temper easily and Vahan immediately acquiesced. Like most of his generation in Central Anatolia, Garabed had missed out on the great renaissance of Armenian culture and education of the late nineteenth century. He could only speak Turkish and whilst he attended Church and was an active member of the Armenian community, he had not been convinced by the nationalist fervour led by the teachers and academics from the great cities, who flocked into the local schools, teaching the language, culture, poetry and history of their people to their young pupils.

This strident ethnic nationalism appeared and flourished throughout the old, 19th century empires. Suddenly all over Europe, something unique and special was found in a 'German' forest, or a 'Czech' river. A Bulgarian poem became superior in some indefinable way to a Rumanian one. A Welsh song had a special quality, which other songs – particularly English – did not possess.

Garabed Asadourian's children had been educated by these new enthusiastic teachers. His children, even his daughters, all now spoke Armenian well. He was very proud of them, and he was proud in a rather offhand way of the architecture and poetry of his people. However, he was equally aware that, below the surface, nationalistic and ethnic passions could easily be aroused on both sides by all these well-meaning and enthusiastic educators, and that Armenian nationalism could easily arouse a backlash from a much more dangerous Turkish nationalism. For him, there was a lot to be said for the easy-going tolerance and stability of the old multi-ethnic Empires, and the Ottomans in particular.

Vahan's father had had no problem in acting as a 'Mukhtar' or local headman in the town and cooperating as well as he could with the Ottoman authorities. Like most educated Ottoman citizens, Garabed deplored the vicious and unstable character of the odious Sultan Abdul Hamid II. However, this did not prevent him from trying to work the system, or from cooperating with those of his Turkish Muslim neighbours with whom he had fairly good relations; relations, which admittedly did not extend to much family contact, but which certainly included having coffee and smoking a pipe together in the local street-cafe.

Garabed had welcomed the great revolution of 1908, which eventually resulted in the deposition of the paranoid Sultan, and he had been prepared to see Vahan – then only twelve – joining with the other boys dancing together in the streets in celebration. He had not objected or made any comment when Vahan had joined with his school friends – both Turkish and Armenian – to collect coins on street corners to help pay for the two great new Dreadnought-type battleships ordered by the government from the shipyards of Great Britain.

Garabed had known that Vahan's move to the University at Constantinople would almost certainly estrange him from his eldest son. The difference between life in the great cosmopolitan centre of the Empire and out in the remote provinces was enormous. But Vahan had reflected, with feelings of love, that this had been a price his father was prepared to pay for the inestimable benefits likely to arise in the future for his first-born.

He had left Caesaria early in September with 30 gold coins sewn by his mother into a belt he was to wear under his clothes. He had travelled on his own horse with a servant riding alongside, to the nearest railhead, which was some five days ride away. He had taken some books, his violin, some basic clothes, a bible his mother insisted upon, some ready money and his rolled up bedding.

At nights, he and the servant would stay at a *khan*, the traditional resting points for travellers, hardly changed since medieval times: large square courtyards, usually with a well in the middle, where the animals would be tethered, surrounded by low buildings. The balconies on the first storey looked down onto the courtyard below. There were no women to be seen. The washing facilities were limited, and the smells were strong and pungent – but the food served was usually surprisingly good. The atmosphere in these *khans* was nearly always aggressive and sexually charged. As a young lad, Vahan was well aware that he had to be very careful, eye contact being particularly dangerous.

On his arrival at Eregli, the railhead, his bedding and his horse were ridden back to Caesaria by his servant. Vahan had never seen a railway or a steam engine before, and when, after two days on the train, he arrived at Hayder Pasha station on the Asian side of Constantinople, he also had his first sight of the sea on the ferry ride across the Bosporus. He watched as the ferries chugged back and forth between Europe and Asia and all the shipping of the world passed into and out of the Black Sea. He boarded the first ferry going across to Europe with only the haziest idea of where his uncle's house was, too excited to care.

Then, as he passed Leander's Tower, the vista opened out to reveal the magnificent panorama of the Constantinople skyline, with its wonderful domes, minarets and palaces. Also visible were the two great German battlecruisers at anchor, grey and sleek in the water with the Ottoman flag flying from their mastheads. As the ferry passed nearby, Vahan saw the German sailors, wearing the red fez, but otherwise dressed in smart, white, German uniforms. He had noted the impressive 11" guns pointing unmistakably at the Byzantine shoreline and the Sultan's palaces. Both ships dwarfed everything else on the water.

In the late summer of 1914 the Empire was not yet at war, and all enlightened opinion was united in the belief that the Ottomans had to avoid another war at all costs.

On his first day in the city, eight months earlier, Vahan had eventually found his uncles, but it was soon apparent that he could not stay with either of them. Despite the paramount obligations of family relationships in Armenian culture, it was clear that Vahan's presence would be a strain. As finance was not a problem for Vahan – his father's contacts with the two or three carpet merchants of the city, with whom he did business, ensured that Vahan could collect the allowance arranged by Garabed regularly and without difficulty – he searched for alternate accommodation.

Accordingly, within a month of his arrival, Vahan had found lodgings on the Stamboul side of the city with a Greek family who were looking for a lodger. The family owned a small but delightful old Ottoman house set in a quiet cul-de-sac in old Stamboul. This house overlooked the railway line running round the old sea walls, below the Topkapi Palace and into Sirkeci station. Though unseen from the house, the Sea of Marmara could be heard below on quiet evenings.

All this had taken place during the crucial month of August 1914. Although Vahan was intelligent, well-educated and fully aware of what was then going on in Europe, it all seemed far away, and not half as important as the vital and absorbing matter of finding himself a suitable place to live.

CHAPTER 3

Karekin goes to work

Karekin usually caught the 8.15 a.m. local train from Makrikoy to the city. Before the outbreak of this war, he used to make a point of getting the later train so that he could stand on the platform and watch the slow passage of the magnificent train from Paris – the Simplon-Orient Express – with its long line of mysterious, dark blue, Wagon-Lits sleeping coaches. Trains and ships were often late or delayed in the Ottoman world, but it was rare for the Simplon-Orient not to be dead on time every day. The sight of the great train never ceased to give Karekin a frisson of simple childish delight, as the coaches passed slowly by the little station.

Karekin, whose main business activity was the importation of fine muslins largely from Lancashire in England, had once traveled to Manchester before the war to establish direct personal contact with his main supplier. His English was barely sufficient, confined to the few necessary words required for conducting business, but English was the lingua franca for all the great trading houses of Europe. Sima had attended the English High School for Girls and had gone on the trip with her father to help him with the language. The journey to Western Europe had been on this same inter-continental service, and on that same once-a-day sleeper coach that would be shunted across Paris, eased onto the train ferry across the Channel, finally arriving at Victoria Station in London, three days after setting out from the City.

But now, in April 1915, there were no more trains coming from Europe, with the exception of the occasional German freight train, routed through neutral Roumania and the wavering Bulgaria. So he had taken to catching the earlier train to town in order to get back to his family in the early afternoon while it was still light.

Karekin hadn't hesitated, seven years ago, in placing the then 12 year-old Sima in the prestigious English High School for Girls. However, Constantinople was a city in which the influence of the European Great Powers waxed and waned throughout these years. Wealthy Greek and Armenian families tended to put their sons into the schools of the dominant, and currently most highly regarded, European Power. The influence of France and England had been slipping, as they both got ever closer to Russia in their anti-German alliance. Russia was the permanent, age-old enemy of the Ottomans. The corollary of all this was a rise in influence and prestige of Imperial Germany in Constantinople, and the popularity of new German schools. Karekin was not enamoured of Prussian militarism and values, and had decided to place Olga, his flirtatious and sprightly second daughter, in the American School – Robert College – where she was still flourishing.

The long walk to the station was Karekin's main daily exercise and he strode along, occasionally raising his hat to neighbours and acquaintances. His large house, with its walled garden and orchards, lay just south of the new district of Osman Aga. He rarely took the short direct road alongside the Vali *Effendi* racecourse, preferring the longer road which went above the little town, past a vantage point where he could look down on Makrikoy – the ancient Hebdomen of the Eastern Roman Empire – seven miles from the city walls.

Here Karekin would sit on an old wooden bench for a few moments and muse on his family in the warm morning sunshine. It was not that he didn't discuss matters with his wife, Armineh; he did, but he was much older than her, and they had married in the old arranged style when she was barely sixteen. Sharp, intelligent and formidably strong-willed, her upbringing, in the Armenian heartlands of Erzerum in Anatolia, had been traditional, and she had little formal education. Within his own household, on the other hand, he had encouraged his four lively daughters to discuss and express their views volubly without fear. He had, as a result, paid the inevitable price of heading a fairly noisy and not entirely peaceful household.

Here, however, sitting on the bench staring down at the old Ottoman town houses, crumbling away among the ruins of the ancient Hebdomen palaces, he could let his thoughts wander in peace. Whilst musing, he could pick out the old Palace of Magnaurus and see the old granite column which had carried the statue of the Emperor Theodosius, and stood now in ruins right by the shore. All along the coast lay the ruins of more decrepit cisterns, ivy-creepered walls and the old Imperial Byzantine jetty, now almost entirely collapsed into the water.

Karekin's perspective wasn't dominated by a nostalgic view of the past. The old ruins were simply there forming a backdrop to his life. He had his own life to lead, his family to raise, and the fact that he was doing it in one of the oldest and most historically significant cities in the world, was coincidental.

So, he sat, his thoughts resting on other things. The question of a marriage for Sima was looming, and Armineh had been quite right to draw his attention to it this morning. Already two or three of his business colleagues had referred fairly openly to eligible sons, already in business with their fathers, and looking for another good merchant house with which to join forces. Yes, it was time that the proud Sima was introduced to some suitable young men.

The position with Olga was quite different. Vivacious, determined and self-absorbed, she was already meeting far too many young men at Robert College.

Karekin sighed. He had no real fears over the behaviour of his daughters. Under all the froth, even Olga, he was sure, knew right from wrong. However, Armineh didn't see it that way, and worried when Olga returned home on a later train than usual, having stayed on for tea at some friend's house in the city.

Karekin rose. Even in early April, the sun was coming up fast and he had little time left to get to Cobancesme station – the local station for this end of Makrikoy – to catch his train. He strode down, putting aside all thoughts of Olga and Sima, his mind now turning to the business needs of the day. He crossed the line and walked onto the platform. Amongst others waiting for the next local train, he saw his old friend Doctor Manuelian.

"Parev, Doctor," he greeted him, pleased, as always, whenever he met his friend Aram, with whom he regularly played backgammon on Sunday mornings after Church.

"What news, Aram?"

"Well, you know that concert of local culture that was held in Galata in the city a couple of nights ago. Both Talaat *Bey* and Djavid Pasha were there. The enthusiasm for the performance of our own Father Komidas was enormous, Karekin."

"No, I wasn't meaning that. I meant whether you had any news about the War."

"Oh, it's the same old stuff, large numbers of young men dying just to gain a few more yards for one side or the other. Let them get on with it. Ever since the failure of Enver's Caucasian campaign last year, even he must be sorry we joined in the War. No, no, my dear friend, all we need do is sit tight and let them all exhaust themselves. Don't worry man, you'll soon be getting your precious Lancashire cotton again."

At this point the local train pulled in. Nodding to each other, Dr Aram Manuelian clambered into his first-class carriage, while Karekin walked down and got into a second-class compartment. "Stubborn old bachelor," thought Karekin, "why won't he change his habits of a lifetime and join me on this short trip to town."

"What a ridiculously rigid fellow Karekin is," thought the Doctor at the same time, "he could easily afford to come with me and forget his egalitarian principles for once."

Stopping at every small station on the way, trundling along beside the Sea of Marmara, the train passed through the gap cut into the ancient great Theodosian Walls of the City, and, skirting round the Topkapi Palace, found its way into the European terminus of the railway – Sirkeci Station.

CHAPTER 4

Vahan settles in

So on the 1st April Vahan was on the Galata Bridge, looking out at all the hustle of the ferries coming and going from the quays under the bridge.

He was currently dressed in the uniform of the Harbiye military academy. He stood leaning against the iron railings, looking down at the ferries and the crowds surging up the steps. Staring across the water, he could just make out the looming, grey shapes of the two German battleships, towering over all the other ships. On his first arrival, Vahan could not have been aware of the menace implied by the guns of these two ships – but other more sophisticated observers certainly could.

Within three months of his arrival in Constantinople, the *Goeben* and the *Breslau* battle cruisers – now renamed the *Sultan Selim* and the *Medilli* – had sallied out into the Black Sea and had bombarded the Crimean coastline under the Ottoman flag, under the command of the German Admiral Souchon. The two ships had demonstrated their power by arrogantly sailing outside Sevastopol itself, daring the weaker Russian battleships to come out. Partly as a result of this, Turkey had been dragged into the war against Russia and the West – the entry of the Ottoman Empire into the Great War transforming a European war into the first World War.

Vahan finally gave up his musing, and ran to jump on a tram taking him to the University building to which he was heading. This was not the Music and Drama Department, but the military academy attached to the university to which he was now seconded. As a student in the university he had automatically become an officer in the Ottoman Army, and had to spend two mornings a week learning the theory of warfare, and the art of drilling. It was a lot of fun, and in stark contrast to the stories of what was happening in the trenches of France. If he found it a bit odd that he was a citizen of an Empire that was fighting a war against countries he had always admired, he certainly did not let it worry him and was prepared to fight, if necessary, like everyone else. Did he but know it, it was a feeling that applied to mil*lio*ns of young men throughout Europe on all sides in that year of 1914-1915.

He was unaware, even now, of the effect that the two battle-cruisers standing high and proud in the waters of the Bosporus had already had on his life and those of countless others.

The Patakis family consisted only of females: two daughters – Elena and Marisa, their heavy and overdressed mother Christina, and a formidable and sharp-tongued old grandmother. Christina's husband, the father of the two girls, had died recently, and it was his recent death, and the subsequent collapse of his retail business selling lokum and other sweets, that had resulted in the family taking in a lodger. Vahan had been brought up in a large, extended family with several sisters, but his provincial Armenian life in the country had left him without experience of dealing with girls of his own age.

Marisa Patakis was only fifteen, but she was a bright and lively girl, aware of everything going on around her. Elena, five years older, was quite different. She was a heavy, big-breasted woman with thick, sensual lips and hooded languorous eyes. She was dark, slow and ponderous, and acutely aware of her own sexuality, which was immediately challenged by the arrival in the house of this young, shy and reserved Armenian boy from the provinces. Vahan had arranged to take breakfast and the evening meal with the family, but that he would be out most of the day at the university. He was punctilious in letting Christina know when he would not be at home for the evening meal. Father Komitas was reciting and lecturing on Armenian liturgical music in the city during those months and Vahan often attended these evening recitals.

The day after his long reverie on the bridge, Vahan raced downstairs, late for the family breakfast. He didn't have to be at the university for a couple of hours, and relished, for once, a quiet breakfast by himself. Vahan sat and thought about the discussions that had taken place around the Patakis dinner table in the weeks before the Ottomans joined in the war. Marisa, always bubbling with questions about the momentous events taking place around them; Elena, who couldn't say anything at all without some sexual innuendo; Christina, who appeared to have her own agenda where the young Vahan was concerned; and the usually silent, but occasionally vituperative, old grandmother, always dressed in black, sitting at the far end of the table.

It was nearly always Marisa who would start up a discussion about something she had heard that day at school. He recalled specifically the day he first heard about the German battleship – *Goeben*:

"Listen everybody – did you hear that the *Goeben* raised anchor this morning, sailed up the Bosporus, and then stopped opposite the Russian Ambassador's new house – you know the one that used to be used as a summer house for the Khedive of Egypt. Well, it seems the ship turned round, broadside on to the road alongside. All the sailors stood in a line facing the house – took off their red fezzes – put on their German sailor's caps – and sang 'Deutschland uber Alles' at the top of their voices. We heard that the Russian ambassador was furious, and put in an official complaint to the old Grand Vizier. Isn't it all absolutely priceless?"

"Oh dear! What could the poor old man do about it anyway," Christina asked. "Enver and Talaat decide everything that goes on nowadays, and they aren't going to raise a finger."

Ignoring her mother, Marisa turned towards Vahan. "What do you think, Vahan? Will we go to war with Russia?"

"I don't know, Marisa, but it certainly looks more and more likely, though it would be a terrible mistake if we did. For centuries we've balanced Russia against France and Great Britain. Surely our present leaders wouldn't make the basic error of antagonising all three at the same time. No, no, not even our little Napoleon – Enver – would make that mistake, although heaven knows he has made just about every other one."

"Vahan," interjected Christina, "you really must be more careful how you speak about our current leaders, you can get into trouble."

"But, Vahan, if we don't have the French or English helping us this time, Germany will be with us, and they can deal with Russia far better than the others. With those two ships with their great guns sitting in the harbour – no stupid Russki is going to get past them," Marisa continued.

"But, for heaven's sake consider, Marisa! Why should Turkey go to war – what can we possibly gain?"

"Oh well, everyone else is tripping off gaily to war so why not us. The silly old Russians think that after this war, if they win, they're going to grab Constantinople – so wouldn't it be better to get the Germans to stop them."

"Vahan," Elena had interrupted, clearly bored by the discussion, "will you come with me to Church on Sunday? Afterwards, we can walk to the Square and have a sherbet or something."

Vahan, tried to ignore Elena's remark and continue the conversation, "Marisa – just think about it, the Russians would only be able to grab the City if we made the mistake of abandoning our neutrality."

"Vahan, you never answered – are you going to come with me on Sunday or not? You know you haven't even been to your own church once, since you've been here – so why don't you accompany me to mine?"

"I'm not much of a church-goer," he continued lamely, not having the courage to answer firmly that he was fast losing the simple faith of his mother each day that he remained in this town, the centre of so many different faiths.

Christina was well aware of Elena's interest in Vahan, and was happy to join her daughter in ensnaring this young man, despite her being at least two years older than him. With Elena now dowry-less, and getting on, she worried about her future. Here was a young man who clearly had a good allowance from his provincial parents, and who in any case was registered at the prestigious University. She pulled at his slender arm to get his attention and fixed her black eyes on him.

"Yes, Vahan, I would be most grateful if you could accompany Elena to church on Sunday, as I have to take Marisa to meet her aunt, and Elena must have an escort."

Vahan had sat there at the empty breakfast table knowing that he was beaten. He recalled that he had nodded, turned back to Marisa, and burst out with some political opinions about uni-cultural nation-states as opposed to multi-cultural empires which had been simmering in him for some time. He remembered how they had all looked at him, surprised at his vehemence. His feelings of inadequacy at having failed to parry Elena and her mother's manipulation, to which he had tamely submitted, probably prompted his outburst. At this point the old grandmother had got up and turned to Vahan.

"And that, my dear young man, is the view of a person who belongs to a people who have no hope of ever achieving a nation-state of their own in the first place. Sour grapes, my lad – sour grapes! It's the sort of talk the Jews here in this city indulge in."

Vahan watched the retreating back of the spiteful old lady and whispered, half to himself.

"Well, you never know, even the Jews might create a nation-state for themselves one day."

The old lady, capable of hearing even the quietest words when she wanted to, turned and snapped back at the increasingly anxious and confused Vahan –

"That comment, young man, applies equally to any tin-pot nation-state that your lot might one day manage to create." And with that she had sailed out of the room.

The very next day, Christina having previously announced that the other attic room opposite Vahan's had now been let, the new lodger – André Tarkowski – had arrived at the house.

André turned out to be a Pole from Germany. He was a slim handsome young man, five years older than Vahan, with fair hair and grey eyes, with a slight military bearing. Vahan never discovered what he was doing or where he came from. André never denied that he was a German citizen. Vahan presumed that he must either be in government employ, or a deserter or conscientious objector. He had turned up with two cheap suitcases, one of which remained locked and unopened under his bed. There was, in addition, an unusual tin case, also left locked under the bed.

Sitting alone drinking his tea, he laughed out loud as he recalled how Elena had almost immediately transferred her attentions to the confident Polish man. Right from the start this had let him off the hook. Even though he was presumably a Catholic, André had duly accompanied Elena that first Sunday to the Church, instead of Vahan, and continued escorting her on and off over the next few weeks.

André had exuded sexuality in every movement of his eyes and body. He and Elena, without any great objections from the complaisant Christina, often stayed out late. Their heavy flirtation took over the household, leaving Marisa confused and silent. For his part, Vahan was fascinated and overawed by André. He was the first Catholic and Westerner that Vahan had ever come to know at all intimately. He used to wander into Vahan's room across the corridor in the evenings and talked about general subjects, never politics or his own past. In particular he would chat about girls and life in the great European cities, while Vahan listened with rapt attention.

One evening, arriving late from a Komitas recital, Vahan surprised Elena and André in the little space between the two rooms at the top of the staircase. They were passionately embracing, and André's hand was hidden somewhere around Elena's dishevelled skirt. Both of them turned and stared at him as he came up the narrow stairs. Vahan had had no idea where to look or what to say and felt deeply embarrassed. They, on the other hand, did not appear to be the slightest bit put out and made no effort to hide the circumstances in which they had been found. Vahan had mumbled 'goodnight' and slipped past them into his room.

That night, as he was undressing, André had come barging into Vahan's room – his eyes alight with sexual mischief and violence. "You're a virgin, aren't you, Vahan? You've never been with a woman, have you? Good heavens, I bet you haven't even kissed a girl yet." André laughed out loud, whilst the half-naked Vahan stared back mutely.

"Oh, for heavens sake don't look so solemn – laugh, man, laugh. You're a good kid and I like you. You'll be all right one day. Look, have a look at this."

He pulled out two passports – both of which had recently been issued by the British Embassy. Still unsure what was going on, Vahan saw that one appeared to be in the name of André Tarkowski, and the other in the name of Elena Patakis.

"Elena and I are leaving very early tomorrow morning from Haydar Pasha station for Jerusalem, and then on to Egypt."

Vahan had just stood and stared at him – shivering slightly as he was without shirt or vest. André, eyes glittering with sly malice and a hint of sadistic pleasure, had suddenly grabbed hold of him and drawing him close, had kissed him fully, passionately and violently, on his lips, holding the astonished Vahan tight against him for several seconds. Then with a laugh he had pushed him back onto the bed, and strode out.

Vahan never saw either him or Elena again.

That next morning, after a night in which Vahan had scarcely slept, and during which he had heard his neighbour slipping downstairs, Christina, looking like an old woman, with her dark eyes red from weeping, had come up and cleared the room opposite, saying not a word to Vahan. She had broken open the cheap suitcase under the bed, and dragged it down, but the tin case had disappeared. Vahan had offered to help, but had been waved away. As he glanced at the half-open case, he had noticed that it contained a German naval uniform.

Three weeks later the *Goeben* and the *Breslau* had sailed into the Black Sea and Turkey had entered the War.

Vahan finished his tea, shouted 'goodbye' to the subdued figure of Christina in the kitchen, and left for the University.

CHAPTER 5

The family of Dr. Nazim Kemal

By 8 o'clock on this same early April morning, the Galata district was already teeming as businessmen and merchants walked briskly to their offices as they came off the ferries arriving at the quays below the bridge.

Doctor Nazim Kemal lived in a modern flat at the top of the road leading up from the bridge towards the Grande Rue de Pera. A sparse, thin man with a sharp, well-groomed moustache, he worked in the German Hospital at Siraselviler in *Beyoglu*, not far from Taksim and well within walking distance of his flat. This morning, as always, he was carefully shaving himself.

Nazim considered himself to be at the forefront of the modernising influences at work in the Empire. Like almost everyone else in the city – Turk, Jew, Greek or Armenian – he had welcomed the Ittihad Revolution of 1908. Nazim had not deemed it proper to join in with the public displays of dancing and singing, but he had not objected when his eldest son Selim – then 13 years-old – had asked to be allowed to join in with the happy crowds in the streets.

Things had gone badly wrong since that early, confident start. The detestable Abdul Hamid had been forced to abdicate, but not before there had been coups and counter-coups. The loss of yet more Christian provinces during the two Balkan wars, had resulted in an ugly and confused mood amongst the normally tolerant Ottoman elite of the city.

A month earlier, Nazim, with a group of his like-minded friends in a literary circle, loosely referred to as the Liberal Book Club, had decided to organise an evening of music and poetry, persuading his friends that this recital should not only include the great Turkish poets and singers, but should also be representative of the other minorities in the Empire – the Greeks and Armenians on the one hand, and the Arabs on the other.

The Club had contacted figures in the new government, who had all expressed enthusiasm. The new rulers saw this as a way of promoting specifically Turkish national identity, as opposed to the cosmopolitanism of the old Ottoman Empire – a multi-ethnicism which the new government were already in the process of repudiating. However for international consumption, the Ittihad leaders saw that a concert of this sort would be seen as a good example of the fresh modern outlook fostered by the new government. Ironically, modernizers like Nazim and his friends, were much closer in spirit to the tolerant Ottoman Sultans of the past than to the new nationalistic leaders..

Nazim stood at the entrance to the hall as the guests arrived, welcoming the many dignitaries of the Ittihad party, including Talaat *Bey* himself, in addition to two elderly Ottoman princes and numerous writers, poets and Muslim dignitaries. The Greeks were largely absent, but dotted around the hall were several Armenians, including the four current Armenian Members of Parliament, together with the Ambassadors of the allied powers of Germany and Austria.

One of the minority performers, whom it had been Nazim's task to persuade to attend was the Armenian priest – Father Komitas – who was currently working at the Armenian Church in Galata, where he was re-organising and improving the choir. Nazim knew that Komitas had for many years been working on the collation and transcription of Armenian folk songs collected all over the highlands of Eastern Anatolia. He had also worked on the core of Armenian medieval church music, rewriting a lot of the old musical liturgy in modern notation.

Komitas had only just returned from a trip to Berlin. There he had attended performances of Wagner's music at the Opera House. Komitas was unable to talk freely with other Armenians about such a secular preference as this love of Wagner. Already the Armenian National Church Assembly had published a biting criticism of the mild and gentle Komitas in a Constantinople journal for "commercialising and popularising sacred songs and dirges of the Holy Armenian Church."

Nazim was well aware of the ferment in the Armenian press, finding this all faintly amusing. Although he prided himself on his own secular attitudes, he was not an atheist and he admired and even loved the simple virtues of Islam.

For Nazim, the tolerant nature of the old Ottoman Empire, multicultural and open to all talents, was an ideal he would have liked to see the new state aspire. He despised both the passions aroused by religion on the one hand, and the nationalistic fervour of the teachers and rabble-rousers on the other.

The cultural evening had gone well. The presentation of Komitas to the audience had been a masterpiece of modern liberal Turkish sentiment, ended with the words:

"These are the people with and amongst whom we have lived for centuries".

Komitas sat down at the piano and sang and played his melancholy songs. Nazim recalled that the Hall had reverberated with ovations and applause. The old Turkish phrase – "May Allah save him from all evil eyes" rang out from all sides.

Nazim laughed at the recollection. Many of his Christian acquaintances had come up to congratulate him on the part he had played in arranging the evening. Nazim may have been a liberal intellectual, but he found it difficult to comprehend what he thought of as a typically Greek attitude to life and philosophy. His mind contrasted the subtle Greek concept of 'three-in-one' godhead with the simple pure tenets of his own father's faith. That the Armenians and Greeks should be separated by an argument, stretching back centuries, over fine points of biblical doctrine seemed to him utterly ludicrous.

He was interrupted in his thoughts as his son Selim, now a young man of 20, poked his head round the door –

"What's funny, baba?"

"Nothing, nothing my son – just a recollection. Are you ready?"

"Yes father – I'm just going. I will be home late this evening, as I'm doing some extra study with a friend. I've told Mama. Goodbye."

Nazim nodded. His decision not to send Selim to the old Sultan Abdul Mecit University in Bayazit, but to the American college – Robert College – in the north of the city seemed to him to have been a success. Selim was growing up with modern, liberal ideas, but did not appear to have rejected any of the old values which Nazim still felt were important.

Nazim finished his morning rituals and went down to join his wife Halideh for breakfast.

"Husband, come, your tea is ready. Selim has already left. I sent him upstairs to say goodbye to you."

Nazim grunted and began on his usual breakfast of thin Stambouli bread, olives and cheese and weak tea. He eyed Halideh, who was clearly anxious to tell him something important. He indicated that he was ready to listen.

"Husband of mine, I am worried about Selim. I do believe that your decision to send him to that infidel College was a great gamble. Who knows what immoral ideas he will pick up there. Yesterday he told me that he and a group of his friends had sat and had a little picnic in the College grounds with some of the young girl students. Nazim, it seems they talked together for about two hours. What self-respecting girl would stoop to such a thing?"

Nazim said nothing, continuing to eat his breakfast, and extending his glass for another tea. However, he was listening carefully. Halideh took a breath and continued,

"I understand that they all spoke together, seven or eight boys and about six girls. Can you believe it? He tells me they spoke about the war, and how badly Enver Pasha's offensives in the Caucasus had been managed. Nazim, listen, they actually openly criticised our government. But in front of girls, talking so freely with young men?"

"Halideh, my beloved one, once I made the decision to send Selim to a western-style College, I accepted that that decision must necessarily expose him to many different influences. I, also, believe that Enver and the others in the Ittihad party are driving this country in the wrong political and moral direction, so I really have no concern if this turns out to be the view held by Selim and his friends. However, my beloved, I agree that he should be more careful about publicly voicing his criticisms, and I will certainly warn him about this tonight."

"But Nazim, you have said nothing of this disgraceful mixing of the sexes."

"I agree that unsupervised contact between impressionable young men and women could be dangerous, but it is not our daughter who is involved, and I have every faith in the good sense and honour of our son. He will not be tempted into any wrong-doing, of that I am quite certain. Meanwhile, my beloved, please do not be anxious about our own daughter. I have no intention of sending her to any of these smart modern Western schools, and on this point I will defer to you, if I can."

Rising from his seat, Nazim saluted his wife, and stepped out into the busy street, heading for the Hospital.

Selim, Nazim's son, was a tall young man of 20, with broad shoulders and long powerful arms. He had black curly hair which he let grow long. He was dark and swarthy with deep-set black eyes, which looked out rather sleepily from under thick eyebrows. Like all the other students, he sported the usual Enver-style moustache. He never wore a fez or a hat.

Selim was aware of the enormous political issues facing the Empire in which he lived. Like any educated Turk, he resented the humiliations imposed on the Ottomans as a result of the recent Balkan Wars. However, he and his friends had not been directly affected. These wars had been fought as always by the patient long-suffering Anatolian peasants, led by inefficient and effete Stambouli officers. What could you expect?

Only the day before, Selim and his father had a long discussion over the direction the Turkish state was currently taking.

"Father, now that all our European Empire has been lost, probably for ever, there are no longer as many Christians as there are Turks. Don't you think that the state should now concentrate on its Turkish identity, rather than retaining its multi-national character?"

"My son, what you say sounds logical, but what about all the Greeks and Armenians still left in Anatolia, and who have been there as long as we have – what about all the Arabs who have lived under Ottoman rule for centuries. At least they haven't spent their time murdering each other while the Ottomans have been the dominant power."

"Oh, Baba – forget about the Arabs – they're not a problem, they're irrelevant as far as we're concerned. In fact it would be a good idea if we abolished the Caliphate. It's an anomaly in this modern world. We are a vibrant Turkish people – what need do we have for this ancient Arab institution."

"My dear boy, even if you are right about removing the title of Caliph from our Sultan, be careful what you wish for. Even if sometimes it has proved a broken reed, the Caliphate has acted as a restraining force on extremists, fundamentalists and crackpots, claiming some sort of divine revelation for whatever happens to be their current brand of murderous ideology."

"Well father, let the crackpots get on with it. What we want here is a Turkish state which happens to be mainly Moslem, rather than a Moslem state that happens to be mainly Turkish."

"Well put, my boy, well put. But the original Ottomans were not like either of those. What we had, until the odious Abdul Hamid ruined it all, was a universal empire based on geography and economic convenience, which tried to accommodate many different people, many different customs and many different religions. It may have been somewhat inefficient, but it did at least prevent people trying to eliminate each other in the name of some religious or national unity."

"Father, I know that you disapprove of the current direction that the Ittihad rulers are taking – I know you don't like their exclusive nationalism – but, baba, the Empire is dying, and we must start thinking of putting something new in its place. A state should be based on a 'people' – in this case Turkish."

"Beware, my son, of the passions of the 'people' when they are aroused as a tribal force. However, my loved one, you give me much to ponder and your points are well put." He disagreed with Selim, much more fundamentally than he had admitted, but he recognised in himself his own slightly world-weary conservatism, and above all he had no desire to squash the enthusiasms of his son.

As a young lad, Selim had joined enthusiastically with his friends in the streets, persuading passers-by to donate their paras and odd coins to the collection for the purchase of the two dreadnoughts, intended to recreate Ottoman seapower in the Eastern Mediterranean. But whether he was collecting for the glory of the multi-ethnic Ottoman Empire, of which he was a citizen, or for a new emerging Turkish nation state, he could not have said.

The people had raised the money by popular subscription to build these two ships in British shipyards. Agents had gone from house to house collecting small sums of money. There had been entertainments and fairs all over the country, and women had sold their hair for the benefit of the common fund. These two ships represented an outburst of popular feeling affecting every community.

The Ottoman Empire was not Turkish in the way that France was French or Germany German. The Ottoman ruling class, all born and bred in Stamboul, were Turkish only in that they knew and spoke Ottoman Turkish – itself a literary and upper-class language somewhat different to the common Turkish spoken on the Anatolian farms. The very word 'turk' was often used pejoratively by these well-born pashas, to refer to the simple Anatolian peasants of the interior, the cannon-fodder of the old Ottoman armies.

Yet in these proudly collected pennies, like everything in the last few years of the Ottoman Empire, there was a fatal paradox. For whom did all these eager people think that these two great ships were being built – the Muslim Caliphate – a nationalistic new Turkish state – or the old Ottoman Empire?

During August 1914, an immense anger had swept over Selim and his friends when they heard that the British government, far away on the other side of Europe, had impounded the two battleships. This confiscation had been carried out by an anxious British government at the very moment the bill for the ships had been fully paid with the hard-earned pennies of ordinary people, and at the very moment when Turkish crews had arrived in England to take over the completed ships. This had been a terrible miscalculation on the part of the British. The British fleet was immeasurably superior to the German, and two dread-noughts, more or less, could not have made any great difference. Yet, as always when war loomed, military concerns took precedence over what was likely to become a diplomatic disaster, and worse.

Unlike the masses throughout Western Europe, the young men of the Ottoman Empire were not bellicose nor did they look upon war with 'excitement'. Turkey had already been at war, on and off, for several years. Ottoman youths were much more aware of the dreadful side of modern warfare than their French, English or German counterparts.

On the 10th August 1914, just before Selim was about to start at Robert College, the two great German battleships - the *Goeben* and the *Breslau* had passed through the Dardanelles and anchored in the Bosporus opposite the Dolmabahce Palace. Selim could not have realised the profound effect these two ships were going to have on him and his contemporaries. Above all, when he heard that in order to maintain their neutrality the two ships had been "sold" by the German government to the Sultan, and had been renamed the *Sultan Selim*, and the Medilli, complete with their full crew, he fell about with all his friends, enjoying the embarrassed discomfiture and objections of the British Ambassador, all of which had been fully reported in the Press.

Actually for once, it did not matter whether you were a youthful

Turkish student, or a young Greek or Armenian one. The 'one in the eye' delivered by the government to the arrogant British Empire gave everyone immense satisfaction, the first time in years that Constantinople had dared to stand up to the Westerners. The fact that Turkey had virtually tied itself to an alternative Western power, Germany, was overlooked.

On the day of the announcement of the 'sale', the students flocked to the road along the waterfront and saw the German sailors parading, each with a fez on their heads, and with the Sultan's emblem at the masthead. They cheered and cheered, not knowing how or why the ships had got there in the first place, or what it would mean to them in the long run.

Selim knew that his father belonged to the school of thought which believed strongly that the Empire should stay out of the war. "Let them get on with killing each other – why should we care if one *giavour* beats up another *giavour*" was his continual refrain. Nazim's feelings were of course more complex than that, but it was what he said to his son, and Selim and his friends basically agreed.

In November 1914, whilst Selim was enjoying every moment of his new life at the College, the two great ships sailed out of the Bosporus, and into the Black Sea, where they totally dominated the old-fashioned Russian fleet which had no ship which could even match the *Breslau*, never mind the superb *Goeben*. The Crimean coast was bombarded, and the Ottoman Empire found itself at war with Russia and the Western Powers, and in alliance with Germany and Austria, pushed into a lethal death- struggle, which Ottoman statesmen had managed to avert for over a hundred years. The unthinkable had at last happened. The one fatal error that generations of old Pashas and Viziers – Greek, Albanian and Turkish – had studiously avoided, namely a simultaneous war against Russia and the western maritime powers, had come to pass. The ambitious, dapper Enver Pasha had gone off to the Caucasus, with an army still largely composed of Anatolian recruits and officered by the old Regular Army officers. The old Sultan, the German attaché and most of the Ottoman elite had advised strongly against a winter campaign in that terrible terrain. But the arrogant Enver had overridden them all, as he had at each critical step throughout the year, and had led the army to a major disaster.

But Selim's mind was on none of these matters as he ran down the street, having just left his father shaving. All he could think of was the meeting he had arranged with a girl from the American Girl's College whom he had met during a recent picnic. He simply could not get her out of his mind. He had been shy at meeting all these girls, several of whom were clearly not Muslims. But this girl – he only knew then that her name was Olga – had looked at him with her huge dark eyes, and had smiled so naturally and warmly that his heart had turned over, and he had almost cried out with a feeling of tenderness.

However, today on this glorious first day of April, he was going to ask her to meet him again at Tokatlian's for tea at the end of the usual college day – he, at any rate, proposing to be on his own. He didn't know how he was going to get through the rest of the day – though of course he did.

CHAPTER 6

Harry and his father

The whole question of the arrival in Constantinople of the two German battle cruisers at the start of the War, was at this moment at the forefront of Lieutenant Harry Bridgeman's mind. He was currently stationed at the Admiralty, employed in the process of analysing the reasons for the recent failures of the British Navy for the forthcoming court-martial of those commanders, who were ostensibly responsible.

Harry Bridgeman left his parents' house in Chelsea and strode off to his work at the Admiralty. Harry was a product of the public school system and Oxford, where the children of the English upper-middle classes were marked out for one of the Guards' regiments. However, his sharp mathematical brain, and his own inclinations, led him instead towards the Navy. He had tentatively put his views to his father – Colonel William Bridgeman – where he met considerable opposition.

Harry was an only son. The Colonel had harrumphed and blustered, around the breakfast table in their small suburban house in West London. His father maintained that the Bridgemans had always gone into the Guards. He declared that he could get Harry into any regiment he might choose – but it had to be the army, as he had no influence in Navy circles.

Harry would reply that he was not cut out to be a Guards officer, claiming that he was more of a technician, and his interests were more scientific. Above all, he knew he would be no good in the cut and thrust of army life.

And so the argument went on, over and over and round in circles. In the end, the Colonel had referred his problem to a member of his club, a respected acquaintance.

"Look, Smithson, I am at my wit's end with my son Harry. What the blazes are children coming to these days. I wouldn't have dreamt of contradicting my father on a matter of such importance. I really can't understand him at all. You know that the Bridgemans have always been in the army – now the little sod wants to go into the Navy – the Navy damn it – I've no influence there at all, and it goes against one hundred years of tradition."

"My dear Sir," the urbane Smithson replied, "you should consider yourself lucky. Harry might easily have ended up wanting to be a poet or to go into the teaching profession! Could you have coped with that? Look man, he does at least want to go into one of the services. Let him do as he wants, and be thankful."

William Bridgeman was an unnervingly direct man, without any doubts about his own opinions, but he was not stupid. He saw the sense of his friend's point of view, but he wasn't going to give in that easily, so their arguments continued for a little while longer, until he finally, and grumpily, conceded.

Harry was 24 years old, tall, somewhat angular, with rather dreamy soft blue eyes, which belied a sharp brain. He respected his father but he also feared him, and looked to his gentle, and somewhat careworn, mother, for expressions of parental love. Harry didn't have a sister, and like so many of his class and time, he had as little contact with the opposite sex as a young man of his age would have had in the Muslim East.

Harry was outwardly conformist. He had excelled at sports at his minor public school and had been fairly popular with his peers. He had often been invited to the large house parties of the period, and had little difficulty mixing with his contemporaries, but he never invited any of these friends back to his parents' own modest house. He knew how to behave towards others in the way they expected with impeccably good manners, though he could occasionally surprise his peers by quoting poetry or expressing some alarmingly liberal views. Lacking the arrogance to impose his own view of life on others, he simply did not have the confidence to act in any other way than to conform.

Harry was in awe of his father, plucking up the courage to contradict him as he grew older. It never occurred to him that what he craved, his father was incapable of giving. Harry was forever hoping for his father's approval, that he would be a source of pride to his father, but more than this, he wanted his father's love.

William Bridgeman, on the other hand, believed that bringing up a son required that the boy respect him and learn to be self-sufficient, and to that end, he should never show vulnerability. Over the course of his life, he had scarcely ever said the words "I love you" to anyone – not even to his own mother or his wife. Only his wife knew that secretly, and only on rare occasions – when Harry was a young boy – William Bridgeman would steal upstairs, stare down at his sleeping son, and give him a light kiss on the forehead and tip-toe away, fearful that Harry might wake, catching him in this moment of weakness.

On this bright spring day, Harry's step was brisk and his spirit was undimmed by the depressing news of the stalemate on the Western Front. He avoided the Underground, preferring to walk all the way to work. He recalled the crowds on this very route, on that gloriously sunny day in August 1914 when war was declared. The crowds had surged up and down in an ecstasy of patriotic fervour and delight. The war would be over in a few months. Meanwhile what a joy it was for all these eager young men to embark on the greatest adventure of the century – leaving behind the drudgery of their boring daily lives.

For once the ordinary people – the so-called man and woman in the street – were well ahead of their leaders in the cry for battle. It was all very well for Sir Edward Grey to stare bleakly out of the windows of the Foreign Office, and mutter about 'lamps going out all over Europe', but Harry and his friends had been in high spirits at the thought of flexing their muscles in a stirring camaraderie of danger and honour.

Harry grinned to himself as he strolled on to work – what was it that his friend, the young poet Rupert Brooke, had written. He considered and then recited to himself as he walked on –

"Now, God be thanked who has matched us with His hour,
And caught our youth, and wakened us from sleeping,
With hand made sure, clear eye, and sharpened power,
To turn, as swimmers into cleanness leaping,
Glad from a world grown old and cold and weary,
Leave the sick hearts that honour could not move,
And half-men, and their dirty songs and dreary,
And all the little emptiness of love." *

Harry was only three years younger than Brooke, and had himself met the young poet, having several friends who were mutual acquaintances. He had found Brooke to be not only an extraordinarily handsome young man, but also intensely witty and alive. Brooke had marked left-wing sympathies, and this had disconcerted Harry's circle. However, his youthful, exuberant patriotism had endeared him to all sections of the social class to which they all belonged.

Harry was not due at his office in the Admiralty before 9.30, even though there was a war on. He decided to sit for a few moments in St. James's Park and watch the ducks whilst he reflected on the report he was compiling on the unfortunate event that had occurred in the first few days of the War in the Mediterranean; a failure of the Royal Navy that was destined to become one of the few really decisive moments of the Great War. His task was to put the events into perspective from his own personal involvement and that of the central office of the Admiralty, for submission to the forthcoming Court Martial.

He was understandably nervous about this task, as he had come to the conclusion that his superiors at the Admiralty were themselves partly to blame for the predicament, which had been so badly handled by the men on the spot. He was reflecting, of course, on the escape of the two German battle cruisers – the *Goeben* and the *Breslau* – and the failure of the Navy to catch them before they finally arrived in Constantinople and by so doing, altered the course of the war.

On his arrival at the office, waiting for him on his desk, Henry found a copy of a memorandum – marked Top Secret – clearly written some weeks before by Sir Thomas Hankey, the Secretary to the War Cabinet, and addressed to the War Council.

Attached to this was a note scribbled by Harry's immediate superior in rather poor handwriting –

"Harry! Jack Fisher has asked me to pass this highly confidential memorandum on to you, as he thinks that you ought to bear it in mind when preparing your own report on the *Goeben* and the *Breslau*. The court martial proceedings are not of course interested directly in the far-reaching results of Troubridge's failure, but Jack thought you ought to be aware of the way current official circles are thinking so far as this area of the war is concerned. Incidentally, Harry, Jack has also indicated that he has had enough formal reports from many people in respect of this matter, and he would therefore like your comments to be entirely informal and a pure reflection of your own personal experience. Attach any other documents separately."

Harry cleared his desk – completed his monthly request to be posted back to an active station – then sat down to write out the final draft of his report on the decisive events of the previous August.

CHAPTER 7

Harry's Report

I was stationed on HMS Indefatigable, a cruiser commanded by Captain Kennedy, at the time of the events reported here. In those first few days of August 1914, we were all aware of the growing tensions in Europe arising from the assassination of the Archduke Franz Ferdinand in Sarajevo, but we were unclear exactly what our priorities were in the Mediterranean area. Indeed on that first critical day of the 4th August 1914, we were not even sure who we were at war with, if anyone at all.

What we did know was that the powerful German 'dreadnought' type battle cruiser, the *Goeben*, accompanied by its sister ship the *Breslau*, was cruising in the Mediterranean, commanded by Admiral Souchon. The previous evening, when we heard that an ultimatum had been sent to Germany, Captain Kennedy told me that the *Goeben* was undoubtedly the most powerful ship at present in the whole Mediterranean.

On the morning of the 4th August we heard that the *Goeben* and *Breslau* had appeared outside the ports of Phillipeville and Bone in Algeria, the embarkation ports for the French army stationed in Algeria, an army which was destined to be slotted into the Western front for the vital first two months of the War. Everyone believed that these first few weeks would be decisive, and the Admiralty had conveyed to Sir Berkely Milne – commander of the whole Mediterranean fleet – that his priority must be to give help to the French Fleet covering the crucial convoys of troops from Algeria to France.

So, that evening, commanded by Captain Kennedy, and with the *Indomitable* alongside, we were sailing fast due west, with orders to cover the French convoys, and later to block the Straits of Gibraltar to prevent the *Goeben* and *Breslau* from escaping into the Atlantic. As we sailed west into the setting sun, we suddenly sighted the two German ships sailing straight toward us due east. I was on the bridge, next to Captain Kennedy, and called out.

"Sir – My God, it's the *Goeben* and the *Breslau*."

To the cry of "Action Stations", the gun crews swung into position below us as the Alarm bells rang out all over the ship. The whole ship went into a heightened state of alert as everyone became aware that this might well be the first shots of the war.

Captain Kennedy waited calmly and we watched carefully as the two ships came closer. We knew we were now within range of the *Goeben*'s guns, while our own guns still required minutes to be effectively deployed. Neither flotilla altered their direction, and, on present course, would pass each other about half a mile apart.

"Sir, what are your orders? Shall I ready the Gunnery Master?"

"Lieutenant, this could be a decisive moment. We musn't take any action which could jeopardise government initiatives. The ultimatum delivered by the Foreign Secretary to Germany is not due to expire until eleven o'clock this evening – and whether that is London time or Berlin time makes no difference, there are still some hours to go. We cannot fire the first shot. Make sure, however, that everyone is on top alert."

The four ships passed each other at speed, but the immense firepower gathered on each ship stayed ominously silent. My binoculars were trained on the opposing bridge, and I clearly saw the little German Admiral staring straight ahead, and next to him, a lieutenant, my counterpart, who was staring through his binoculars at me.

The moment after we passed by, with both sets of crews standing on the decks staring at each other, Kennedy immediately gave the orders to turn around. Our ships swung round slewing over heavily at speed and we set off to shadow the Germans. Captain Kennedy ordered me to go down to the boiler room and inform the stokers of the crisis, but when I got below into the hot sweaty inferno of the boiler rooms, I saw the stokers were already frantically trying to raise additional steam to increase our speed. On paper, we should have been able to keep up with the *Goeben* – our respective top speeds, when fully manned, were the same. Only then did I discover that we were short of 90 stokers. I was not sure if Kennedy was aware of this, and hurried back up to the bridge to report on the position. I could already see that the two German ships – smoke pouring from their funnels – very slowly but surely pulling away from us.

"Sir, we are short of 90 stokers down below, and even working flat out those available won't be able to increase the present speed".

"Well, they've just got to do their best," replied the Captain.

Another of the other officers gathered on the bridge, suggested we deputise some of the gunners to go down.

"Sir, we should be able to keep up. Our boilers are in fairly good trim, and surely it's vital to keep the ships in sight".

"But what if they should suddenly stop and turn a broadside on us. If a shooting match was to start, and 90 of our gunners were down below shoveling, we are going to be caught with our pant's down for god's sake. I can't possibly risk it. The only thing clear is that rather than harassing the French, the bloody *Goeben* is currently going in the completely opposite direction."

All sorts of conjectures flew back and forth between us on the bridge. But, as we spoke, in the dying light of that summer day, we watched helplessly as the two German ships disappeared over the horizon, until at last we could not even see any distant plumes of smoke. Our Radio Officer had already signaled the news to the Admiralty, but by 23:00 hrs, we had to report that whilst the German ships were heading due east and thus away from the French crossings, we had, nevertheless, lost sight of them.

I am adding to the above personal account evidence obtained as to what was happening on the *Goeben* during these critical few days. This comes from a Polish officer, Lieutenant André Tarkowski, who was born in Miastiko in the German province of Posen. He came from a family which had lived in this part of Prussia for centuries, and to whom speaking German came as naturally as speaking Polish.

Tarkowski, who is the same age as I, was interviewed by our military intelligence officer in Constantinople about four weeks after the arrival there of the *Goeben*, and the following statement was taken down by the interviewing officer. The Ottoman Empire was then still neutral, and our embassy was functioning normally.

Tarkowski appeared at the Embassy out of nowhere, dressed as a civilian, and asked for an interview. He claimed that he was a Radio Officer on the *Goeben*, that he was currently on a week's official leave, but was intending to desert as a result of discrimination against Polish officers. He said that he was acting on his convictions as a Polish patriot.

In return for British travel documents, for himself and a certain young lady, he was prepared to give a series of interviews detailing as much information as he could about the *Goeben*, its systems and armaments. The Ambassador agreed, on condition that the interviews did not take place at the embassy, and that he had nothing to do with it, officially.

Our Naval attaché accordingly interviewed Tarkowski in a private house and obtained some information, most of which has been sent on to our technical department here in London. The following are those parts relevant to this enquiry.

I would add that I agree entirely with our attaché in Constantinople that Tarkowski's motivation had nothing to do with 'discrimination' amongst the other officers of the *Goeben*, and that his motivation was private and personal and apart from all considerations of duty and career. I would add that the travel documents and passports he requested were duly issued in his name, and that of one Elena Patakis, for travel to Egypt. I have no idea what happened to them. I do know that Tarkowski was posted as missing, and was being sought by the Turkish police as early as November 1914.

The evidence of Lieutenant Tarkowski.

My family come from Miastiko, a small town in the German province of Posen near to the Baltic Sea. As I saw it, when I was younger, my basic allegiance undoubtedly lay with the Imperial German government. My family had always been associated with the sea, so I had no hesitation in joining the Imperial German Navy. It seemed to me, a German-dominated Poland had a better future than a Russian-dominated one.

My Polish revolutionary hero was Pilsudski, but despite thrilling to tales of his exploits against the Russian state, I felt that my German identity was as important as my Polish, and when it came to ordinary everyday life, I saw my own future as a sailor in the Kaiser's new and growing Navy. I thought the sense of camaraderie amongst naval officers on a ship, overcame any feelings of racial animosity or superiority that may have existed elsewhere, and which I am told certainly made for tensions in the Imperial Army.

I was fascinated in the new technique of radio, and it was as a Radio Officer that I found myself on the *Goeben* at the beginning of August 1914, when war broke out with Russia and France. The commander of our little flotilla was Admiral Souchon. Souchon was a man of French Huguenot descent; a short, dapper, astute and intelligent sailor to whom his men were devoted. I myself saw and spoke to him frequently, as he would often come to the Radio room to check up on the latest messages from the Kriegsmarine Headquarters at Kiel.

On the declaration of war with France and Russia, we were cruising in the western Mediterranean, and were immediately ordered to approach the French Algerian coastline to disrupt the preparations for the convoy of French troops to mainland France, before the French fleet could arrive from Toulon. Whilst we all knew that the *Goeben* was more than a match for any single ship in the French fleet, in total their navy, particularly if reinforced by British ships, would be able to take us on with some possibility of success.

We bombarded the ports of Phillipeville and Bone, but sailed away as our engines were in poor repair. Furthermore we were already running out of coal.

Souchon informed us he was intending to make for Italy to take on more coal.

"Gentlemen, we will head for the port of Messina in Sicily, but I must warn you that I have no idea – nor yet has the Kriegsmarine – where Italy will be standing in this conflict. Above all we must avoid any enemy patrols at this stage until we can refuel."

In the early afternoon of the 4th August, as we slipped away towards Sicily, we encountered two British cruisers coming towards us in the opposite direction – the Indefatigable, and, I believe, the *Intrepid*. I came out of the Radio Room and stood and watched as the two sleek grey warships passed us steaming westwards at top speed, less than half a mile away. The tension amongst us was electric. I could see Souchon standing stiffly on the bridge, eyes firmly ahead, almost as if he was afraid to make eye contact with any British officer, though at that distance that was a ridiculous proposition.

An uneasy quiet hung in the air, though I must be exaggerating, as all ships ploughing through any kind of seas always generate background noise – but the tension created a strange feeling of stillness.

Nothing happened. Each ship held to its course without any of the usual courtesies or any guns booming in anger. However, within seconds of the ships passing, we saw the British cruisers swinging round without slackening speed, and start to follow us.

"Full steam ahead," was ordered from the bridge, as an Engineering officer came racing down to go to the boiler rooms to press for more steam. The ship seemed to shudder, as it strained to reach the top speed of 27 knots. I heard later that we never got above 24 knots, while, as the light began to fade, three of our engines failed one by one and our speed dropped even further.

Stokers began to fall unconscious from the enormous effort to raise enough steam, in a climate already heavy with midsummer heat. We were informed later that four stokers had died during this chase. We knew that the two British battle cruisers were perfectly capable of reaching 22 to 24 knots, but to our great surprise we saw that we were slowly pulling away, mile by mile, until we had got away from them completely.

On the 5th August, we steamed into Messina. Here Admiral Souchon went ashore to assess the situation. Although we had heard rumours of the pending Italian declaration of neutrality, nobody on board was at all clear what was going to happen.

Coaling was already taking place when Souchon returned and informed his officers that in accordance with the rules of neutrality, the Italian authorities had granted us only 24 hours in which to refuel, after which we had to leave. This was clearly not enough time to refill our bunkers. The combination of our leaking unrepaired boilers, and the burst of very high speed which we had raised to get free from the two British ships, had depleted our coal *bey*ond normal consumption.

I must say that neither I nor any of my junior colleagues had any idea what Souchon would do now, but we all assumed that we were going to make a dash for the Adriatic in order to join the Austrian fleet, where we could complete our repairs at leisure and refill our coal bunkers.

Souchon was informed by the Admiralstab that the Austrian Foreign Ministry, in a vain attempt to try and avoid war with Great Britain, if possible, had given orders that the *Goeben* and *Breslau* were only to be supported once they were actually under the protection of the Austrian fleet within Austrian territorial waters. However Admiral Haus, the Austrian Naval commander, indicated in a personal reply to us, that despite foreign ministry wishes, he was prepared to sail as far south as Brindisi, and would await Souchon there. We later heard that he did in fact sail out on the morning of the 7th, but by then we were miles away.

We sailed out of Messina harbour on the evening of the 6th, and I, for one, had no idea where we were going, but on the evidence of the radio messages going to the Austrians I assumed we were still heading for the Adriatic. As we pulled away from Italian territorial waters we did indeed seem to be heading for the Adriatic, but fairly soon we changed course decisively and began heading south towards Greece.

None of us had the slightest idea where we going ...

I am now attaching to this report a copy of a letter from a Mrs. Maurice Wertheim to her father Henry Morganthau, the American Ambassador in Constantinople. I have no idea how this copy got into the hands of British naval intelligence, but it is clearly authentic.

Dear Father ... We all went aboard the Sicilia, at Venice, as scheduled, on our way to come and see you. We had the most beautiful summer days as we sailed down the Adriatic. The company aboard was aware that there was a crisis developing between the European powers, but most of the passengers happened to be compatriot Americans, and we were all in cheerful mood. Entertaining our three little daughters took up most of my time, so I failed to notice what was happening around us.

We were lunching on deck somewhere between the coasts of Greece and Italy on the 6th or 7th August when I saw two strange looking vessels on the horizon. I ran for the glasses and made out two large battleships. We watched and saw another ship coming up behind them fast. She came nearer and nearer and then we heard guns booming. Pillars of water sprang up in the air along with puffs of white smoke. It took me some time to realise that we were actually witnessing a naval engagement. The ships were continually shifting position. The two big ones turned and rushed furiously at the little one, and then apparently changed their minds and turned away again. Eventually the little one, which turned out to be a British light cruiser, turned around and calmly steamed in our direction. At first I was somewhat alarmed by this, but all that happened was that she circled round us. exchanged converse with our captain, then turned and disappeared. The Captain told us that the two big ships were German, caught in the Mediterranean, and were trying to escape from the British ...

The rest of the statement of Lieutenant Tarkowski.

... Shortly after we changed course, we were spotted by a small British light cruiser, which I now understand was the HMS *Gloucester*. I was tapping away at my radio when I heard the sound of firing coming from the *Breslau*. I could not immediately leave my desk, but after a few moments I went up on deck and saw that the *Breslau* was in a furious engagement with the little *Gloucester*, which kept darting in and out until eventually turning away. It was clear that our change of course had been spotted and we assumed that the British would shortly be upon us.

Whilst we all knew by that time that the French fleet had finally arrived on the Algerian coast, and that it was now busy covering the crossing of French troops, we were also painfully aware that the British had several powerful cruisers in the vicinity. It was with a sense of mounting surprise to find ourselves in a calm and quiet sea, sailing unmolested round the tip of Greece, without sight of any other ship of any nationality on the whole horizon.

That day or the next – I begin to forget the actual sequence of days – we sailed up the Aegean and made a rendezvous with a German coaling ship, which met us at the little island of Denusa near to Naxos. I must say that we all felt proud of our fierce little commander with this turn of events. We spent almost three days coaling, with the three ships, our *Goeben* and *Breslau*, and the stocky little coaling ship alongside each other in the beautiful blue waters of the Aegean. Here, like everywhere else in Europe in that fateful month of August 1914, the sun shone from a clear blue sky every day. Looking over the side, we could see the little Greek island with its white villages and its timeless quality. Those of us not on coaling duty even had time to swim. The war seemed far away and no enemy ship appeared.

We set off on the evening of the 9th, this time on a northward course. I was on duty when we arrived at the start of the narrow Straits of the Dardanelles on the morning of the 10th. There was an enormous amount of coming and going – the arrival of Turkish officials ferried from the shore on small white boats, followed by the arrival of two clearly high-ranking Turkish naval officers, who were closeted with Souchon for hours. I spent the morning watching the shoreline on both sides through my binoculars: the Gallipoli peninsula – with its high cliffs on the European side, and the site of ancient Troy on the flatter Asian side.

To the north lay the historic waterway of the Dardanelles perhaps the most significant stretch of water in history, bristling with modern fortifications and guns on all sides. It lay just *bey*ond the tip of the bows of our two great ships, and we were all aware that behind us, the British fleet must surely be closing in fast. The Ottoman Empire was neutral, and we all knew that during times of war, by long-standing treaties, the state was not allowed to agree to any war vessels passing through these narrow waters. So where were we to go?

This ends the evidence taken by our attache from Lieutenant Tarkowski. I will now continue to trace the events as they appeared through the Admiralty records from the moment the *Goeben* docked in Messina. By the afternoon of the 5th August, Admiral Milne, commanding the whole British Mediterranean fleet, had a pretty good idea of the probable whereabouts of the two German capital ships in Sicily. However he had no idea of their intentions. Aware now of the declaration of Italian neutrality, the Admiral considered, and it seems to me a fair decision, that after leaving Sicily, Souchon would probably turn west again and resume his attempts to disrupt the slow French convoys carrying valuable troops across the Mediterranean to

Marseille. However, he was also aware of the other possibility – namely that Souchon might try to join the Austrian fleet in the Adriatic. Accordingly, he deployed his heavy battle cruisers west of Sicily, in order to prevent Souchon doubling back to attack the French convoys. At the same time, to prevent Souchon escaping into the Adriatic, Rear-Admiral Troubridge, with four armoured cruisers, would steam to the east, just off the island of Corfu, in case Souchon came out that way and turned north towards the Adriatic.

Just before the outbreak of the war, Churchill, the First Lord of the Admiralty, had signaled that Troubridge, in particular, was not to attack a 'superior force'. By this, the Admiralty had meant the combined fleets of Austria and Italy. At the same time, the Admiralty had made it clear that the *Goeben* was to be Milne's principal objective. Troubridge, who was in command of armoured cruisers, not fully capable of standing up to the *Goeben*, misunderstood, and assumed that the 'superior force' referred to by the Admiralty was the *Goeben*, particularly as he was now aware of Italian neutrality.

So, as the *Goeben* and *Breslau* steamed out from Messina the British fleets were positioned as follows –

Milne with the main Mediterranean fleet was west of Sicily covering the route to the Algerian coast:

Troubridge with his four armoured cruisers lay waiting near Corfu at the entrance to the Adriatic;

Several light cruisers, including the *Gloucester*, commanded by Captain Kelly, were patrolling between Malta and Corfu;

All were poised and ready to catch the two Germans between them.

When the Germans came out of Messina they were spotted by one of the light cruisers – the HMS *Gloucester*. Kelly immediately set off in pursuit, though keeping out of range of the *Goeben*'s guns. By nightfall on the evening of the 6th, it became clear that Souchon was not heading for the Adriatic at all, but had turned south. This news was duly radioed back to Milne sitting north and west of Sicily, and to Troubridge sitting to the east.

The gallant Captain Kelly could see that if he could delay the two German ships, Troubridge's squadron of four cruisers could sail down and join in intercepting them. Although enormously inferior in armament, though not in speed, Kelly engaged the *Breslau*, and undoubtedly this was the engagement witnessed by Mrs. Wertheim on the *Sicilia*. Like a gnat irritating a great beast, the *Gloucester* darted in and out, causing no damage, but holding back the Germans who twice turned back on him.

But Troubridge did not follow suit or come to his aid.

Worried by the Admiralty's slightly ambiguous instructions not to attack a superior force, he allowed prudence to override the Nelsonian principle – always to close with the enemy. Instead, at 3.47 on the morning of the 7th, he took the decision to turn away, and he signaled to Admiral Milne that he had abandoned the chase. It was said by one of his officers that he was in tears when these orders were given – and well he might be – as the consequences of his decision had the most far-reaching strategic consequences of almost any naval decision ever made.

The responsibility for stopping the *Goeben* now passed to Admiral Milne. He, however, continued in the belief that the greater danger was the possibility of Souchon doubling back towards the Algerian coast and the vital French troopships. But by the same night of the 6th and 7th, he was informed by the Admiralty that the French Navy were now, at last, sufficiently organised to counter this threat themselves, so he was free to single-mindedly pursue the *Goeben*. All his battle cruisers were fully coaled, and he could have set off in hot pursuit of the Germans without any difficulty, but once again the Admiralty intervened, warning that hostilities had now begun against the Austrians. Milne delayed, and once again the two ships were saved, by fortuitous coincidence, to make their decisive impact on history.

With the fairly recent advent of Radio, the desk men at Whitehall were suddenly finding that they could influence the fleet in a way that had never been possible before. In the event, Admiral Milne hung about at the entrance to the Adriatic, while Souchon enjoyed nearly three whole days quietly coaling in the Aegean. As British activity finally resumed, and Milne began moving to the East, Souchon sailed for the Dardanelles. He had nowhere else to go, but nevertheless he was taking a fairly major risk, as he had no idea what attitude the neutral Turks were going to take.

Admiral Milne was, of course, fully aware of the Treaty obligations involving any navigation by belligerents in the Straits, and he knew that the Dardanelles was heavily mined and barred to all warships. He might well have thought that Treaty arrangements would be honoured by the Ottomans, and that all he needed to do was to bring his own three battle cruisers into the Aegean, which, when added to Troubridge's four armoured cruisers, would be certain to catch and destroy the *Goeben*. So he did not hurry!

Thus, it was in the afternoon of the 10th August, that the two great German ships, still completely untouched by the British, anchored at the entrance to the Dardanelles. The British Navy, with seven large ships, was at last moving up fast behind them; ahead of them, was a barred and mined passage.

I have discovered in the naval intelligence archives a copy of a surprisingly uncensored letter from an unknown German sailor to a girlfriend in Basel, intercepted by agents, which, quite pithily, puts the situation as it seemed to an ordinary German sailor on that morning of the 10th August, which I attach here.

"On that morning of the 10th I was on duty on the deck of my ship – the Breslau – and I could see a hive of activity of small boats going backwards and forwards between the shore and the Goeben. My mates and I had no idea what our pipsqueak Admiral was up to, but we all had great faith in the little bastard.

We could see the big guns of the Turkish fortifications on the Asian shore. We also knew that the Brits could not be far behind. It looked to us as if we were between the devil and the deep blue sea. But just after midday, the Goeben began to steam slowly up the twisting Dardanelles, and I could see the Turkish pilots and naval officers on their bridge – and by now on ours as well. We moved ever so slowly right behind. These were narrow waters, which we all knew were heavily mined, and to begin with, we were all fairly tense.

We got through all right. We then sailed up to Constantinople.

Believe me, our arrival there in the late afternoon, and our dropping anchor at the entrance to the Golden Horn, just before that wedding cake seaside Palace – I don't know its name – with the sun beginning to set in the West behind the domes and minarets of old Stamboul, was a sight and experience I will never forget."

Finally, I have been given permission to quote from the diary of His Excellency Henry Morgenthau, the American Ambassador to the Sublime Porte, which deals with the events from the 10th August after the *Goeben* arrived in Constantinople:

10th August
I went to visit Baron von Wangenheim at the German embassy on official business. From his animated manner, edginess and excitement, it was clear he had something of importance to tell me. He rushed out, and came back a few moments later waving a wireless message.

"We've got them – we've got them, the Goeben and the Breslau have just passed through the Dardanelles."

I immediately understood his excitement. The voyage of these two ships was very much his personal triumph. By safely getting the Goeben and Breslau into Constantinople, he had all but clinched Turkey's eventual entry into the war as a German ally. I remain amazed that the large British fleet, dominating as it did the eastern Mediterranean, had failed to prevent this result.

16th August
The Ottoman government, that had earlier announced that it had 'purchased' the two ships, today hosted a formal ceremony in which both ships hoisted the Turkish flag with great pomp. The Turks announced that the ships were substitutes for the two dreadnoughts seized by the British government some 12 days

earlier. At a stroke, the Turkish navy had become stronger than the Russian Black Sea fleet, and the ultimate entry into war of the Ottoman Empire became almost inevitable. I, myself, doubt if any two individual ships have exercised a greater influence upon history than these two German cruisers.

CHAPTER 8

Olga

It was still early in April, on a bright afternoon, when Olga returned home to Makrikoy earlier than usual from the city. She and the young Turkish student – Selim Kemal – had had several further chance meetings and conversations at the College, though always in the company of others in their group. On the 1st April, Selim had finally caught her alone and summoned the courage to ask her to come out to tea with him after college. To her own astonishment she had agreed to meet him for tea on a day to be arranged at the fashionable Tokatlian Café.

Olga was much the most beautiful of the four Avakian girls, with a delicate thin nose, fine sensitive features, huge eyes, and a devastating smile. She was also socially composed and confident, but she was not entirely sure of her real feelings towards Selim. Selim was a good looking, darkly handsome, young man, without any trace of the usual flamboyant arrogance she'd seen in other Turkish males. But undoubtedly her interest was piqued by the excitement of doing something she knew was completely forbidden; not just a matter of ignoring parental disapproval, but going deeply against centuries old tribal and religious taboos affecting both communities. Olga was playing with fire and she knew it.

Her sexuality was aroused, but that had happened with her often enough before, and she had always kept it under control. However, she was sensible enough not to think of going to the proposed rendezvous alone. But if not alone, with whom? Who could she possibly ask to accompany her. If she went with any of her friends, it would be round the college in a flash. Clearly it would have to be one of her sisters.

As she sat in the train on the way home she thought of her three sisters, considering first her elder sister Sima. It did not take her long to dismiss that possibility.

'Oh no,' she thought, 'she's far too bossy, and over-emotional as well. Afterwards, she'll talk about it the whole time and take it far too seriously. No, it must be one of the others. Little Seta is only eight and obviously far too young and she is bound to blurt something out to mother – even if she manages not to shout it out from the rooftops.'

That left Nerissa – poor Nerissa – but yes, she would do fine. She hardly says a word to anyone, and she will leave me free to talk to Selim, without trying to butt in and take over like Sima would. But will she come – she's still far too shy with strangers – how am I going to persuade her.?

When the train arrived at the Cobancesme station, Olga alighted and hailed Abdul, the sleepy old driver sitting in his one-horse droshky waiting for fares. Not for Olga any hot dusty walk home like her father – it had to be the arrabiya. Her thoughts on the problem of a chaperone ran on as she clambered into the warm, horsey-smelling, carriage, asking Abdul to open the hood.

When she walked in at the front door and into the marbled hall, she found herself in the middle of a typical Avakian crisis. Her mother, Armineh, was standing in the middle of the hall holding a largish bottle of yellow liquid. She had on her outdoor clothes but was not yet wearing a hat, and she was looking rather vexed.

It only took a minute for Olga to recall that there had been talk earlier in the week that her mother might be pregnant and this must be the urine sample the doctor had asked for. For several days now, the whole household had been thrown into turmoil by this entire procedure, much to Olga's delight. At last all was ready – the urine bottle had been filled, a stopper had been fitted, and the *indomitable* Armineh was holding it in her hand outside the sitting room waiting to put on her hat ready to sally out into the street and face the world.

At this point, however, Armineh suddenly thought that she really could not be seen walking down the street with a bottle of urine in her hand. So, she had arranged to wrap the bottle in a newspaper. Then there was the question of which of the four girls should accompany her and carry the bottle. There they all were, excepting Nerissa, standing in the hall, when Olga walked in.

Seta was hopping about with excitement, assuring her mother that she would be more than happy to take the bottle and accompany her on this small, but significant, expedition. Neither Sima nor Olga were about to volunteer for such an undignified task Nerissa? – well, she was sitting curled up in the corner reading one of her books, and did not appear to have heard what was going on. So there Seta was – eager and willing – indeed jumping up and down in anticipation, whilst Armineh desperately sought some alternative solution.

"Oh mother," Olga spoke, once the matter had been fully explained to her, "for heaven's sake, get Marie to take it down – or even Abdul can take it, he's still outside with the carriage if we are quick about it."

"Never, you silly girl. You don't know what you are saying – I am going to see it safely into the hands of the Doctor or the Nurse at least. Come on Olga, do something useful for once and walk with me."

At this juncture, Armineh, who was about to lose patience stopped herself from making another caustic remark. She realised that it might be equally undignified to have one of her elder daughters do it for her in full public view.

"Well, well," she sighed, "Seta, you'll have to come with me after all," and still grumbling to herself, she handed the bottle to Seta and went to put on her hat. All were now in the tiled hall. The irrepressible Seta, clenching the wrapped bottle tightly in its discreet cover, waited patiently by the door for her mother to get herself ready, proud to be the one chosen to accompany her mother on this important occasion. Suddenly, to her horror, she felt the bottle slipping. The harder she clutched at the paper, the quicker the bottle seemed to slip through her hands until gravity took over, and it fell crashing to the floor. Armineh took one look – plonked herself down on the seat in the hall and wailed, "Oh my God, my God, even in my peepee, I'm not lucky."

In the chaos that followed, while the elderly Marie came bustling in out of the kitchen to help clear up the mess, Olga grabbed the surprised Nerissa who had finally left her book and come out to see what was happening, and dragged her upstairs, pulling her into her room.

"Nerissa, my love, I have arranged to meet a friend for tea at Tokatlians next week on the day the schools shut early – will you come to town and join us – it'll be fun for you."

"Why me, Olga, who is your friend, do I know her?"

"Oh, my dear, just come and have a nice afternoon – we can go to the Bedestan together before, and look at what's in the shops."

"Olga – you're up to something, I can tell. You know that I'd love to come, but you must tell me what it's all about."

Olga sat on her bed and thought a little. Although Nerissa was just 16, Olga knew she was young for her age and sometimes rather shy. She read voraciously, mainly English novels of the previous century, and had romantic notions, but Olga did not think that she had any real idea of what it was like to feel the thrill of courtship. She had never had any serious chats with Nerissa, so had no idea how Nerissa would react to the truth.

"Look – I'll tell you, but my darling you must keep it to yourself. I've arranged to have tea with a student friend – a young man."

Nerissa's already large brown eyes opened wide as she looked steadily at her sister.

"You mean, without anyone else there, just you and – er – him."

"No, silly, that's why I want you to come along too. We'll just have tea, listen to the music a bit, and come home."

"Olga, you can't – do Father and Mother know?"

"Certainly not – don't be a ninny, Nerissa – it will be an adventure. I'll tell mother that I am taking you shopping, and that we will stay out for tea together. She'll be well pleased that you're going out for a change – and with me. Come on Nerissa – there's nothing wrong with it. It's exciting – there'll be lots of army officers there."

Nerissa knew that her mother would be happy to let her go out for an afternoon with Olga. She had had a bad attack of rheumatic fever when she was eleven, and had had to stay at home for long months. As a result, she tired easily, and rarely went out, whilst her shyness with strangers left her somewhat isolated, even at the occasional dinner parties she attended with the rest of the family. She had been well looked after during her illness, secure in the knowledge of her parents' love for her, like all the Avakian children. Nevertheless, she felt that, with the ever-present excitement and exuberance that surrounded her sisters, her mother neglected her. She would probably be pleased to be told that one of her two elder sisters was proposing to take her out.

Between Nerissa and Seta came the only boy in the family – Haik – now twelve. It was natural that attention would focus on Haik, and then on Seta, the charming and easy-going baby of the family. This left the rather solemn Nerissa on her own, and this accentuated the introverted side of her character. However, although still rather shy with people outside the family, she was perceptive enough to know there was more to this matter than she was being told.

"Olga – have I met this young man – does he come to our church here, or does he go to one in town."

Olga, suddenly thoughtful, looked at Nerissa steadily. Here in Nerissa's simple, unthinking words was the first time that she was being confronted with the real issue. A little cold shiver ran through her, but it lasted only a few seconds. Then with a toss of the head and a smile, she dismissed the thoughts from her head, leant forward and planted a big kiss on the astonished Nerissa.

"Oh Nerissa, my soul, you're priceless – I love you."

"All right, Olga, all right – but you must sort it all out with Mother."

"I'll look after everything – you'll have a lovely day," Olga sang out, as she bounced out of the room, dragging Nerissa by the hand behind her.

CHAPTER 9

Garabed Asadourian

Garabed Asadourian was in every way a big man, both physically and morally. Though his marriage to Mariam had softened some of the rougher elements of his character, he remained a forceful man with a quick temper which he had difficulty controlling.

He had set his hand to many different trades and businesses during his life, but it was as an entrepreneur in the carpet trade that he was best known. At the turn of the century, Armenian and Persian carpets were still made by hand, with pure vegetable dyes, in the mountain villages of the Armenian and Persian highlands. They often took families more than a year to make; the really large ones, which would eventually grace public rooms in London or Paris, could take several years.

The loom would be set up according to the size required, built by the father of the family or male relative and were fashioned in the traditional form of the area, depending on the type of wood available. The basic design of the carpet would be drawn out and left alongside the loom, often only a piece of paper tucked into a crack in the wood. Then the slow, painstaking, task of weaving would be carried out, usually by the women and children, after returning from work in the fields, and all day during the winter, whilst there was light to work by.

The money to support the living expenses of the family and for preparing the cloth and dyes during the carpet's production was usually part of the arrangement between the family and their preferred entrepreneur-merchant. For his part, the merchant would commission a carpet according to his own idea of the market currently available; he would agree a price with the family and then pay sums on account as the work progressed, until the carpet was finished. He rarely discussed or questioned the design, unless there was a specific request from a client. There was often a close and mutually respectful relationship between the family and the *effendi* or *bey* from the city, who would often be consulted on other matters, when he visited, such as how to write a letter, or how to deal with an official. Problems with the growing children in the family were discussed between the *effendi* and the parents in the evening. Unlike the Christian families, the womenfolk in the Muslim families of the local Kurds and Turks, were not present, even though they may well have had the last word, once alone with their husbands.

"*Effendim* – please remain and accept my poor hospitality," would be the phrase which would signal the close of the purely business aspect of the meeting. Garabed, and latterly with his younger son Raffi alongside him, would then sit cross-legged on the villager's own faded carpet in their one big main room. Bowls of hot water would be brought in and hands and faces would be washed. The children would be introduced and led up to shake hands – it being known that Garabed was opposed to the more servile, hand-kissing.

Once the evening food was prepared and brought in, the women would join them – but unlike women in the city they remained silent. The night would be rounded off with the men smoking a communal 'narghilé', tobacco smoked through bubbling rose water. Raffi would try manfully to join in, but never really managed it, and would splutter and cough and only pretend to inhale. The guests would remain with their own bedding in the main room to sleep, and leave early the next morning with any completed carpets piled on the back of the donkeys.

The carpets, when finished and taken back to Caesaria, would then be sold at a fair profit to traders from Constantinople, who would often deal almost exclusively with their own favourite middle-man whom they might well have met at some stage. They would then send them to Western Europe with huge mark-ups. Needless to say, once the goods left the Empire, the biggest mark-ups of all would be added in the smart carpet houses of Paris and London.

One of Garabed's more carefully cultivated families was that of Sarkis, son of Shahan. Sarkis farmed land in the mountains near the town of Malatya, about a hundred miles away from Caesaria. He had a large family, large even by local standards, with two boys aged eight and eleven, two older girls of fourteen and twelve, and two more girls both under seven. The nimble fingers of his children, and the native artistic intuition of his wife, Adrineh, meant that the carpets commissioned from this family were of a very high standard, and Garabed paid accordingly.

The cash generated had put Sarkis in a favourable position as far as his land-holding was concerned. He had been able to purchase many of the tools and animals that his neighbours could not afford.

On the last occasion that Garabed visited the family, just before the outbreak of the war, he had stayed the night with Sarkis, who had now registered a surname – Shahanian. In the evening, after the other children had left, Adrineh had indicated to her eldest daughter, Anna, that she could remain with the adults. Despite having borne six children, Adrineh was still an attractive, buxom woman. Anna was thrilled at being able to stay and, nestling up to her mother, listened as Sarkis raised one of his concerns with Garabed.

"Garabed, agha, whilst our relations with the local Turks remain perfectly amicable, we are having more and more difficulty with the town officials. My neighbour, Mustapha Mahmud, and his family, have lived next to us all my life, working together at harvest time. However he told me that last month, when an Ittihad party official came on a tax assessment visit to our village, he said to Mustapha that we were not to be trusted, and that one day he hoped that we would no longer be here. What does it all mean, Garabed agha? Both my family and Mustapha's have been here living alongside each other for generations."

"What does Mustapha himself say?" asked Garabed.

"Oh! he just laughed and told me not to concern myself about what the educated city slickers said – they know nothing about the real way of life of farmers, and the way the rhythm of the seasons and nature shapes our lives."

"Well, he must be a wise man, this Mustapha. Keep him close to your heart, Sarkis *effendi*. What about the Kurds here."

"Ah, well, sir, they are a different matter, I'm afraid. Many of them are landless, and are easily persuaded to go about in groups harassing the settled population."

"I am afraid that I cannot give you much comfort my old friend. We are in the midst of a great crisis in the affairs of the Ottomans, affecting Turks and Christians alike. I can only advise that you try and keep a low profile and stay on as friendly terms as possible with all your neighbours."

Garabed had become a fairly influential man in Caesaria. During the pogrom in 1896, the mob, incited with full official sanction during the Friday prayers, rampaged through the town for two days killing as many Armenians as they could lay their hands on. Many local Armenians gathered in Garabed's house for safety. Garabed was the local mukhtar – headman – for the district. His house had two-foot thick walls, with only a few windows looking onto the street – and those had iron bars across them. Most of the windows and rooms, like so many of the houses in the town, looked into the inner courtyard, which was totally private and used very like a sitting room during the summer. The courtyard had a deep well situated in the middle, always providing clear fresh water.

This general massacre, ordered and arranged from the office of the odious and vindictive Sultan, Abdul Hamid, lasted only three days, during which time Garabed's house was full of women and children, together with a few well armed young men. The three larger churches in Caesaria were all also filled with people who had locked themselves in. These churches were solidly built, almost like castles, with large high walls, which could be entered only through one or two heavy iron-clad doors. The mobs attacked all three, but armed with only axes and sticks and stones, were unsuccessful. Nevertheless, many people, numbering in the thousands, were killed in Caesaria, and many more in other cities in Anatolia during those three days.

On the third day, the town crier began to go round the Armenian quarter shouting – "All slaughter and pillage must end on the direct order of the Sultan, our great Padishah – Abdul Hamid."

Then, within an hour, Turkish soldiers and gendarmes appeared on the streets for the first time. As always, this allowed Abdul Hamid's supine ministers to claim that the pogrom was spontaneous and ended only because of the arrival of the police. The crowds melted away even before the soldiers arrived, and thus the orders of the great and 'glorious' Padishah were *obey*ed, in all particulars.

Life in Caesaria revolved strictly round the seasons. The summers were very hot, without much chance of relief. The winters, on the other hand, were bitterly cold, and in the Armenian highlands to the east, it could stay as low as minus 40 ºC for long periods. There would be three months of heavy snow in Caesaria, and Garabed would often return home on winter evenings with icicles hanging from his moustache.

During the depth of winter, Garabed's two sons Vahan and Raffi would fill the large well in the middle of the central courtyard, which was about 25-feet deep, with snow, stamping down the snow until the well again became half empty – then calling for a ladder so they could clamber out. The next day, they would repeat the process, till once again they were below the level of the lip of the well. This would go on for several days until the well was full of hard packed ice and they could stamp it down no further. The well would then be covered up, and thus ice would be available for much of the summer.

Those long summer months were wonderful times for Garabed's two boys. The country villa was about two hours ride away from the town centre. Garabed would go in to work for two or three days a week, often taking one of the boys with him, riding on the back of the horse, holding tightly to Garabed's waist. There they would help – Vahan in the office with the books – Raffi, in the cloth mill. The cloth was woven on fairly primitive wooden machines run entirely by hand, and worked by a dozen men and boys – all Turkish. Raffi would join them on the days it was his turn to accompany his father, and work away with all the other young men who had become his friends.

The relationship between the Greeks and Armenians and the Turks, was quite different to that in the sophisticated city of Constantinople. In this provincial town, the Christian minority comprised, almost exclusively, the middle class of the town – both the professionals and the businessmen, while the governors and the political leaders of the town were exclusively Turkish, without any minority representation. The Turkish leaders here had a particular aversion to the Armenians, who were by far the largest of the minorities, whom they oppressed in minor irritating ways. There was an obvious irony in this, in that they often had more in common with the Greek merchants and Armenian bankers of the town, than with the Turkish underclass.

On this early April day, Garabed was becoming anxious about the developing political situation. A deep unease was in the air. The Russian army, supported by their own Armenian population, were moving towards the cities of Van and Erzurum. There was uncertainty in the official mind about the loyalty of the Ottoman Armenian population. Could the Ottomans continue to think of their Armenian subjects as loyal citizens of the empire, particularly after the failure of the previous Hamidian regime to accept them as such, or to give them the ordinary civil rights and protections afforded the rest of the population.

Garabed knew that another 'pogrom' could break out again, as in the 1890's. He thought he could take sensible personal precautions to protect his family but hoped that with the new modern attitude at the heart of the Ottoman government, he did not need to fear anything worse.

In the summer of 1914, Vahan had left for the city to take up his place at University. He had not returned since. Meanwhile, the rest of the family continued life as before – going to their summer house on the slopes of Mt. Erciyas at the height of the summer, and battening down the hatches for the bitter winters. They gave little thought as to how those two shots in Sarajevo were going to change their lives forever.

CHAPTER 10

Breakfast at the Avakians

On this clear and sunny April morning, as always, the Avakians gathered for the family breakfast in the great room in the centre of the house.

Nerissa, the third and most reflective of Karekin's four clever daughters, would listen to her noisy family, contributing an occasional comment of her own. She helped her mother with the younger children and she chatted to the servants.

She still attended the small Armenian school in the town in the morning. She was a voracious reader, particularly of English literature, Shakespeare and the Victorian romantic novelists. She had an excellent command of the language itself, which had not been missed by Karekin, who had already enrolled her in the sixth-form classes at the English High School for Girls in the city, where she would be starting in the Summer. Armineh, though, thought that Nerissa already wasted far too much time reading books and dreaming about impossibly romantic young male heroes.

Karekin was the centre of the household round whom everything revolved, but it was Armineh who dealt with the numerous problems of daily life, including all the stresses and emotional crises of her children, as well as managing the running of the house – all of which Karekin took for granted. Armineh felt that it was all very well for girls to have a liberal education, but what about husbands – and families!

Like all her sisters, Nerissa adored her father, though not without a small tinge of fear. She had just reached the age of sixteen. Still rather young for her age, she had a special affection for her younger brother Haik, with whom she played and chatted in the large garden at the rear of their house. Olga and Sima were too old and sophisticated and rarely talked seriously to her, and this had thrown her back on the unaffected love and simple affection of her young brother.

Haik, was a lively lad, as quick and responsive as his clever sisters. He was, however, physically delicate, and although now 12, he had re-tained his childishly pretty and delicate features, with his huge brown eyes, a clear pale skin and a thin, peaky nose. He had only ever known unbounded love and adoration from a household of women, and con-sequently he trusted everyone, almost to the point of naiveté.

Despite being the quietest and most introverted of the children, Ner-issa had a complex character. She was not conventionally pretty, having inherited her mother's rather dumpy figure. Her nose was a touch too large, her lips too full. She tended to be critical of what she saw as the social ambition of Sima, her eldest sister, and the shallow flirtatiousness of OIga, whom she regarded as a complete lightweight. Her assessment was fairly unjustified in both cases reflecting the intellectual arrogance of a clever 16 year-old, who had yet to learn that all people have both strengths and faults.

Nerissa was used to Olga's on-again, off-again ways, so never really expected to be called upon to fulfill the engagement to which she had tentatively agreed, so it was with real surprise when Olga reminded her that they were to go that afternoon to tea at Tokatlians.

"Nerissa, my love, there is no need for you to walk home from school this afternoon – I'm going to pick you up – and we're going to go to tea at Tokatlians'."

"This afternoon?" wailed Nerissa. "What shall I wear?"

"My dear – you'll be coming from school – just take a scarf or a shawl with you. We're only going to have some tea and cakes and a chat."

Nerissa looked across at her mother Armineh who was as usual fuss-ing over Haik, trying to get him to do more than just peck at his food.

"Mother, did you know that Olga has invited me to go to tea with a friend of hers at Tokatlians this afternoon, after school?"

"My girl," replied Armineh somewhat distractedly, "Olga has already told me – do go if you want to, it'll be a change for you. Now, Olga, mind you make sure that you are both back before seven o'clock, and don't walk up from the station, wait for Abdul or Mustafa, even if they are not there when you get off the train." Nerissa was half hoping that her mother would object. She had been careful not to tell a lie, but was aware that there was an element of deception in what Olga was planning, and it made her uncomfortable.

Karekin, as always already fully dressed for the outside world, came down and sat at the end of the table in front of his plate of home-made bread, cheese and olives, with a little honey.

"Haik, my boy – don't give your mother such a hard time – just eat up. Armineh, stop fussing over him – he's not going to waste away."

"Father," piped up Haik "when are you going to take me to the office as you promised."

"I told you – you'll have to wait until the summer holidays. In any case, with this dreadful war there is precious little to do. Armineh, did I tell you that I've had to let Leon and Berge go – there's just not enough work. In any case the government are tightening up on young men with deferment, and the army is certainly going to have them soon in any case."

"Is there any news in the papers of what is happening in Van and Erzerum?" asked Armineh.

"It's serious, my dear, that I can certainly tell you. I'm going to go down to the Patriarchate this morning to find out if there is any more hard news – but the regime is extremely jumpy, the general atmosphere is tense and I don't like the signs at all. I think for the next few days, Sima, you must take Haik to school, and either you or one of the servants must go in the afternoon to pick him up. There was an anti-Armenian demonstration yesterday outside the Bazaar. It was broken up by the police eventually – if only half-heartedly – and only after several shop windows had been smashed."

He turned to Olga – "Now Olga, listen, I must say that....."

"Oh father, Oh dear is that the time? I'm sorry I've simply got to dash – you know I've got to catch the earlier train than you." Olga jumped up before Karekin could finish, and ran out grabbing her coat and bags in the hall. She called back to Nerissa, "Remember Nerissa, I will be at your school to pick you up at about two o'clock this afternoon."

Karekin looked vexed, directing a comment at Olga's vanishing figure, when Sima forestalled him, rising from her seat.

"Come on, Haiky – finish up – let's go."

"But Baba – I'm 12 – I don't need to be taken to school any more.

The other boys will laugh at me," wailed Haik.

Karekin rose from his seat. His face darkened as he felt a deep anger rising in him, rooted in an indefinable disquiet he was feeling about Olga, coupled with nagging worries about the worsening political situation that threatened not only his family circumstances, but even their very existence.

Karekin had never raised a hand to any of his children, but when roused he exerted authority absolutely and automatically, tending to be very much harder on his only son than on his four clever girls. Nerissa, sensitive as always to the charged atmosphere, opened her eyes wide, fearful of the coming explosion. But Armineh and Sima were quicker and a good deal more practical than Nerissa. Pretending that Karekin had risen to prepare for his departure, Arminah handed him a list of things she wished him to fetch on his return from the market, whilst Sima tweaked Haik's ears and ushered him quickly out of the room.

"Come on, little man – let's get you ready. Don't worry, I'll leave you well before the school gates."

Haik had no idea that he had narrowly avoided his father's ire, due to the efforts of his mother and eldest sister.

Karekin quietly took his hat and coat from Armineh, who looked straight into his eyes, and gave him a kiss – to his surprise – right on his lips, in front of everyone. He knew that the tide of anger that had come over him had nothing to do with the boy. His worries and anxieties seemed to be multiplying. The news from the Caucasian front during January and February had been bad enough, but that coming from Van was devastating, if true. Karekin hurried out and walked straight to the station – no sitting on benches and musing these days.

He arrived at the city ignoring, as best he could, the tense atmosphere now ever present in the streets of Stamboul – as if the town was waiting for a storm to burst, and hurried to the quiet calm of the Patriarchate buildings. Crossing the quiet, tree- lined courtyard, he knocked at the door of Father Haroutune, one of the secretaries to the Patriarch and a personal friend.

"Hello my good friend – I am here for news."

"God be with you Karekin agha."

"Look, enough of these rumours, Haroutune! The patriarchate must know what is actually happening in Van and the Armenian vilayets?."

The little priest looked up – his eyes were red, and he was shaking and his voice quavered –

" My dear friend, I don't know for sure. The news from Van is clearly censored – but there is obviously either an insurrection or other serious trouble there and the army is involved. But Karekin it is not only Van. I do believe that something really terrible is about to happen in the interior, even if it has not already started. If the reports I am seeing are true, nothing like it has ever been seen before. Believe me, Karekin, we're going to look back on Abdul Hamid and his whimsical and random barbarities with nostalgia, when faced with what may be the beginning of a deliberate official policy of attacks against a whole population! The more I read of the decrees and proposals emanating from Talaat's office, the more I fear for for the future."

"For heaven's sakes, man, enough of these grand moral statements. Just give me the facts – I'll decide if we have anything to fear. For God's sake, Turks have been killing Armenians for centuries, and, for all I know, probably the other way round as well, so what's different now?"

Haroutune said nothing for a moment and lay his head in his hands.

"I don't know, Karekin, there's no word for it at the moment. Perhaps the world will make up a word for it, but believe me something evil is about to happen in the villages and little towns of the interior. Here, I have prepared a precis of the reports we have been receiving from our priests on the ground. But it is not only from them, but from German and American missionaries. Here, take the whole file, read it and let me know what you think."

Karekin always balked at the word 'evil'.

"Father, everyone is jumpy and nervous. With the failure of the British fleet to break through the Dardanelles a few weeks ago, we all know that they are going to try again with their army soon. So, of course we're all on tenterhooks. But, Father, this isn't the time to talk about 'evil'. We're at war, and panic and rumour abound. Living in a multi-national empire like ours, there is always the danger of racial tensions arising at moments of crisis. However, we have a duty to try and minimize it. Believing in evil can have the effect of making it happen."

"Karekin, I do hope you're right and I fervently pray that I am wrong. I know I'm a timid and fearful man, but I do sense something different about our new masters, something totally alien to the old Ottoman ruling class."

Karekin straightened up. He looked down at the little man and picked up the bundle of papers. Then on instinct he bent down and planted a strong and heartfelt kiss on the man's forehead, and walked out, deliberately ignoring the sign of the cross raised towards his retreating back by the nervous priest.

CHAPTER 11

The Siege of Van

I. The uncontested historical background

The much vaunted winter offensive by the Turkish 3rd Army into the Caucasus had been a complete catastrophe. Against the advice, of both the old Ottoman generals and the German military mission, Enver Pasha had overridden all opposition, and marched a badly supplied, and totally unmotivated army, into some of the most difficult terrain in the world. It had been a devastating experience for the Army, which had lost all its artillery and about 75,000 men, leaving only a small force of about 30,000 demoralised men, covering the whole of the Erzerum region.

Enver Pasha returned to Constantinople towards the end of January, his arrogance and Napoleonic pretensions intact. On his return, he made every effort to conceal the truth and to represent the catastrophe as nothing more than a local setback. He was totally indifferent to the dreadful suffering of the ordinary soldiers, huge numbers of whom died of frostbite. On the matter of the possible political fall-out, however, he was much more sensitive, and he immediately began searching for a scapegoat to take the blame for his own ineptitude.

In London, the Russian victory had strengthened the position of those who favoured an attack on Turkey. The scale of the disaster to Enver's 3rd Army seemed to make a direct attack on Constantinople more attractive in London, breaking the current stalemate. The fall of the capital would throw Turkey out of the war, whilst the opening of the Straits to allied shipping would aid the Russians and stave off internal unrest. By February, the British government was ready to take up an offensive option and approaches were made to the Russians for a diversionary operation – perhaps towards the Bosporus, the northern approach to the great city.

The Russians appeared ready to comply, except for the Russian naval commander in the Black Sea, Admiral Eberhardt, who remained cowed by the presence of the *Goeben* and the *Breslau* in the Straits. The Russians faced a dilemma. On the one hand, their obsession with Constantinople as the centre of their Orthodox faith, as well as the controller of the vital narrows which led to the only Russian outlet to ice-free, warm seas. On the other, was the threat that the two great battleships could cripple the Russian fleet. In the end, the Admiral's view prevailed with the continuation of a 'fleet in being' seeming of greater importance.

Meanwhile, back on the Caucasian front, as the harsh winter gave way to Spring, the Russians began a tentative advance towards the city of Erzerum, taking advantage of the much depleted Ottoman forces. This wild and inhospitable country, was farmed mainly by a tenacious Armenian peasantry settled there for centuries, while the main towns were fairly evenly split between Turks and Armenians. In between, lawless bands of nomadic Kurdish tribesmen roamed. As the Russians advanced, they naturally tried to exploit these age-old differences to obtain as much support as possible.

The Armenian situation in the high plateau heartlands of the Caucasus was very difficult. They were only in a clear majority in one or two of the great cities. The practice of Ottoman tolerance was merely a chimera here. For the peasantry in these regions, the situation was quite different. Here the mixture of races and religions, coupled to the poor soil and harsh conditions, had led to intolerance and tribal hatred and petty officials could and did stoop to trivial tyrannies against a generally peaceful minority. With the same peoples straddling the border of Imperial Russia, loyalties, impossibly strained by the terrible Hamidian pogroms of the 1890's, were much more complicated.

Early in April, the Turkish High Command, aware of the worst-kept secret of the whole war – namely the likelihood of an Anglo-French landing somewhere in or near Constantinople – realised that they needed to shore up the Caucasian front. The remnants of the Turkish 3rd Army were now being led by an irascible old Ottoman general – Halil *Bey* – not a member of the Ittihad, but connected to Enver by marriage. He led a scratch force of several batta*lion*s of regulars, some bits of artillery and a great mob of Kurds. He had already complained that the lack of proper medical services for his forces was threatening their effectiveness. Whatever the faults of the old regime – and they were many – the old Ottoman Pashas had understood the importance of adequately supplied and maintained armies.

By comparison, the Russian General Yudenich gave the greatest attention to the welfare of his troops. Supplies and sanitary and medical services were for the most part excellent.

In the area of Lake Van, and the valley of the upper Euphrates, the mob of irregular Kurdish tribesmen, ostensibly part of Halil's force, had put the whole countryside into a state of alert. No one – villagers, townsmen, tenant farmers, Armenians or even Turks felt safe, although it was the Christians who were the principle sufferers.

Meanwhile in the city of Van itself, a particularly vicious Ittihad Governor, Djevdet *Bey*, had been deliberately goading the Armenian majority. At last, the exasperated and increasingly desperate population of the city of Van, driven to extremity by the actions of the Ittihad Governor and the anarchy in the countryside around, rose in what appeared to be a revolt. Exploding out of the narrow streets of their quarter, young armed Armenian men commenced a fierce fight against the demoralised garrison and gendarmerie of the town. After only a day or two, the Armenians took possession of most of this ancient city and were in full control by the end of the second week in April.

This revolt was a spontaneous uprising of a population driven to despair. The different elements within the rising were as diverse as most unplanned revolts tend to be, but after its success, the professional nationalists and revolutionaries inevitably took over. The well informed General Yudenich, decided to take immediate advantage of the situation and ordered infantry units of his advancing 4th Caucasian Army group to turn towards the beautiful town on the lake, at the same time mounting a large Cossack cavalry raid through the Kurdish tribal areas to clear away some of the brigands in his path.

Halil *Bey*, hearing of the revolt, moved his 6,000 regulars up to take back control of the city before the Russians could arrive, starting the siege of Van, which was to last for weeks. By the time Halil's regulars moved up to take over the siege, his large contingent of Kurds had deserted. These Kurdish tribesmen were prepared to harry defenceless peasant settlers – a favourite pastime of nomadic people throughout the ages – but were not prepared to act as docile cannon fodder for the Turkish government. Accordingly, they had disappeared to join and profit from the general lawlessness as soon as they could.

Meanwhile, both sides dug into their fortified positions and began to fight it out.

II.   Doctor Nazim Kemal. The Turkish point of view.

Back in the capital, Doctor Nazim had continued his work at the German hospital. The closure of the French hospital had added to the workload, and he was in continuous demand. His criticisms of the Ittihad in general, and Enver and Talaat in particular, had not changed. However he came to modify his comments in public, although in private, he was more outspoken.

""Nazim," said Halideh one morning early in April, "I heard in the hammam yesterday that Enver is claiming nothing happened in the Caucasus during the winter."

"Well, my dear, that is clearly not true, as many of our soldiers died. The number of our men suffering and dying from frostbite was enormous, quite apart from the enormous number of men in terrible condition at the military hospital at Scutari."

"I've heard that he is claiming that Armenian irregulars gave a lot of help to the Russians, even those of Ottoman nationality, and that explains the defeats."

"Oh, mother," said Selim, "that sounds like pure propaganda, and even downright lies. In any case, hasn't he been saying that there were no major defeats?"

"Yes that could be so," said Nazim, who thought fleetingly that Selim seemed defensive these days whenever Armenians were mentioned.

"Frankly, I'm convinced that Enver made a real mess of the whole offensive. I think that General Yudenich out-manoeuvred him from the start. So now he's looking for scapegoats to blame for his own shortcomings. That's not to say that the Armenians, themselves, aren't making it easier for him by their ambivalence towards this war. My son, I believe that it was a fatal error to get into this war at all – but now we are in it, we must all rally round the only government we have. They are our soldiers – they must be supported. And that reminds me, son, we can speak openly at home, but you must learn to keep your opinions to yourself outside. We live in difficult and dangerous times. Abdul Hamid's secret police might have been disbanded, but instead we have a mindless mob, listening out for treasonous talk."

"Oh, Baba, you know I'm in favour of the Ittihad ideas in principle. I don't even think it was all that wrong to get into this war – we've been pushed around enough by the arrogant West. No, it's those idiots – Enver and Talaat!"

It was some days after this conversation that Nazim heard he was to be drafted into the Army as a Major; his medical and administrative services were going to be required on the Caucasian front. It appeared that the irascible Halil *Bey* – a Moslem gentleman of the old school – had insisted on an increase in medical services for his small force stationed near Lake Van.

There had been little time for Nazim to deal with all his affairs. Since receiving his commission, he had hardly been at home, while he gathered together, supplied and outfitted a scratch medical team to accompany him. On the day he left, he had hugged Halideh hard as they parted in the little hall of their flat in Galata. She had run to the window as the front door closed. She looked down into the street, as he emerged from the entrance of the building. Dressed in his clean new uniform, Nazim carried his own personal medical bag of surgical instruments, while Selim carried his father's bags.

Selim hailed a passing gharry, and stepped in, taking the bags with him. Nazim turned and looked up at the window, behind which he knew that Halideh would be standing. He made no grand gesture, save to ever so slightly raise the palm of his right hand in a discreet salute.

"The ferry station for Haydar Pasha station – driver," he called out.

They were both silent as they drove down the hill to the Galata bridge; remaining so as the ferry chugged its way across the straits and pulled up alongside the ferry landing stage for the Haydar Pasha terminus of the Asian railway system.

"My son, when we get to the station I will be distracted and busy, sorting out the doctors and several staff. We won't be able to talk. My boy, in case anything happens, your first duty must be to your mother and sister; however once that is done, your next duty is to fulfil yourself. Don't hurry to give up your deferment, my son – make sure you complete your education before rushing off to war – if you have the chance that is."

Selim shuffled. His heart welled up, and he felt a little sick as he looked at his dapper, well-groomed father.

"Baba, are we fighting a religious war... our enemies, Russians or … whatever … are Christians, aren't they. I mean …

"No, my son, not at all. This war is totally secular; it has nothing to do with religion. The Ittihad may have made a bad mistake in joining in – but there's no doubt that the Empire is beset by predators all round, and we simply have to defend our way of life."

"Father, are we obliged to hate as well? I mean, suppose I knew a Russian lady who was a friend, would it be. … I mean … I don't know, wrong to be friendly with an enemy of the state?"

"Don't be silly son, there's never anything wrong with friendship with anyone, so long as it goes no further than that. Life is changing, I accept that, and there's no reason why you can't converse with girls of your own age and class, and make friends. Don't repeat this to your mother, by the way! I know that you will always be honourable and just in your dealings, and that is all that matters."

"Major Kemal," a soldier addressed him, coming forward and saluting, as they stood in front of the station at the top of the steps up from the ferry station, "Your unit is awaiting on Platform 2. The medical supplies are currently being loaded at the freight depot, and your supervision is required, Sir."

Nazim turned to Selim, smiled and clasped his shoulder, and, without another word, turned and strode into the station followed by the young soldier now carrying the bag, reluctantly relinquished by an emotional Selim, who stood fighting back his tears as his father walked away.

The train made its way slowly to the east, where Nazim had been ordered to join Halil *Bey*, whom, he believed, was engaged in holding back the Russians moving towards the towns of Erzerum and Van.

On his arrival, Nazim reported directly to Halil *Bey*, whose HQ was in Bitlis, some miles away from Van.

"Your Excellency, I have the honour to present myself – Major Nazim Kemal, Doctor and Surgeon, with a small medical team raised in Stamboul about a week ago."

"Sit down, Major, sit down. I'm sure you would like to have a coffee." Halil called out to his orderly "Khaveh – shekerli?"

Nazim nodded and sat down.

"I am not sure, Major, how much you know of the situation here. I doubt if the government has been at all open in its reporting in the capital. In fact, I know the news has been carefully censored. The Provincial Governor here is an arrogant bastard by the name of Djevdet *Bey* – the new Ittihad breed you understand – who has made a mess of his relations with the infidel Armenians, who, incidentally, are in the majority in this town. Can't stand the fellow myself – but of course, this is no excuse for the cursed infidels to revolt. Infamous traitors the lot of them, when you think that the Russian army is close by and moving forward daily."

"What forces do we have available, Sir?" asked Nazim.

"Well, I have a military gendarme division, together with four battalions of regulars. Until a few days ago, I also commanded a mob of Kurdish irregulars: undisciplined and frankly pretty useless. For better or worse, they have all melted away and are over in the east pillaging everything they can lay their hands on, which at least gives the Russkis and the Armenians something to think about. This leaves me with about six thousand men, of which over a half are now manning the siege lines we have drawn round the city."

"Well sir, I'm amazed. I have some Armenian acquaintances in Stamboul, and I had always supposed them to be fairly loyal to the state, despite their awful experiences under Abdul Hamid. However, a revolt like this in the face of an invading enemy army is totally inexcusable whatever the provocation. I'm appalled. What numbers and strength are we talking about?"

"I don't know, Major. They certainly can't have much ammunition, and they must be using boys and old men. So far as my Intelligence officers have been able to gather, the actual numbers facing us with weapons are not much more than a thousand."

The next day, when Nazim arrived at the lakeside behind the Turkish siege lines, he looked across at the town, with its walled old city dominated by a castle on a rock, perched beside the beautiful deep blue lake, and bordered by magnificent mountains, still lightly covered with snow. He pinpointed the spot where he would set up his headquarters and went to work.

In his customary cool and efficient way, he busied himself with the setting up of his main tent as a military hospital, and spent the following day inspecting the Turkish front lines drawn around the Armenian quarter of the town. He made many recommendations as to the primitive sanitary arrangements, and slowly, by dint of persuasion, he managed to improve the conditions for the rank and file soldiers in many small but significant ways. The Turkish artillery, meanwhile, continued unleashing shell after shell into the old town below.

Nazim worked tirelessly – day and night – tending to the wounds of the Turkish soldiers. Unlike the Ittihad leaders, he slowly came to learn a new respect, which he had never felt before, for the illiterate and inarticulate Anatolian soldiers, who bore their pains so uncomplainingly. Night after night, the talk would turn on the question of when the city would fall, and how or why the rebels were still holding on, when their ammunition must surely be exhausted.

Punctilious as ever, Nazim shaved carefully every day. He spent his spare time writing letters home to Selim and his wife. He never complained of anything more than the days of boredom, punctuated with violent episodes. He did, however, sadly report to his son that the rebellion of the inhabitants of Van, right in front of the Ottoman's historic enemy, had soured his attitude to the Armenians. It was clear to him that there could be no excuse at all, regardless of provocation, for raising a revolt right in front of an advancing enemy army, when your country was in mortal danger.

III.   Clarence Ussher – A neutral position.

Van was one of the most beautiful cities in the whole Ottoman Empire, surrounded by well tended and prosperous gardens and vineyards. It stood on ground that gently sloped down to the deep blue lake – Lake Van – which is itself surrounded by gaunt and steep mountains. Some miles from the shore lies the island of Akhtamar, covered in greenery, with a serene and beautiful old Armenian church set amongst the trees in the centre, where families, Turks as well as Armenians, would go to picnic in the warm summers.

Just outside the old walled town, in the middle of the Armenian quarter, lay the American Protestant Mission. The buildings were surrounded by a high stone wall, and comprised a Protestant church, several schools, a hospital and dispensary, and residences for the staff. Five minutes walk away was the German orphanage run by two old ladies. All around them, were old Ottoman houses, in various stages of picturesque decay, with their wooden lattice bay windows, jutting out over the street.

The American Mission was led by Doctor Clarence Ussher, who was not only in charge of the hospital and the medical supplies, but was also in overall control of the whole Mission. He was helped by his wife, an elder sister, and several Armenian nurses.

Clarence Ussher was the son of a Canadian Episcopalian bishop from a family of devout Christians who had provided Church leaders for generations. A large bearded man with a soft round face and gentle eyes, he nevertheless possessed a clear, hard, inner core of moral certainty. Like so many in the missionary world, he was never at a loss as to what was the right course of action. Doubt never crossed his mind, and this gave him an inner conviction, which carried him benignly through circumstances which would have broken many others.

He was a competent general doctor with fairly good surgical skills and an efficient administrator. His wife, the daughter of a missionary herself, had been born in Caesaria in Central Anatolia. They both spoke Turkish fluently, and they both had a focussed intensity, so often seen amongst 'driven' 19th-century missionaries everywhere. Having failed to convert more than a handful of Turks, over the years, they turned their attention to good works and trying to convert one of the oldest Christian communities in the world to their own protestant beliefs. Ironically, this had not endeared them to Armenian clerics. Furthermore, it had contributed to the nationalistic fervour, which had been irresponsibly aroused in the vulnerable Armenian peasantry.

Dr. Ussher had been a fairly close friend of the previous Turkish governor – Ahmed Fari Pasha. Fari had been anxious to maintain good relations between all his subjects. Before the secular Young Turks had deprived him of his post at the start of the war, the old Vali, always interested in theological subjects, had delighted in evening dinner parties with the clerics of the various religious sects in the town.

The Ittihad leaders knew, without the need for spies, who would be reliable, if and when they decided to have a showdown with the minority populations. They knew they would first have to get rid of the old Ottoman ruling class. Accordingly, after the take-over by the Committee of Union and Progress, the old Ottoman Governor, Ahmed Fari, had been dismissed, and replaced by Djevdet *Bey*, a cold and arrogant official of the new nationalist school – and brother-in-law of Enver Pasha.

On his return from Enver's disastrous offensive, Djevdet *Bey* immediately began developing a confrontational policy towards the majority Armenian population. In the second week of April when disturbances broke out in a suburban part of the town, he arranged for four Armenian leaders to go and try to pacify the area. There, he had them murdered by a special police detachment under his direct orders, and he then arrested the Armenian Member of Parliament who was in the town, and sent him back under arrest to Constantinople.

At this juncture, the remaining Armenian leaders, desperately seeking a compromise, offered Djevdet *Bey* a large bribe to make up for the current shortfall of recruits from the city. At the same time, they approached Dr. Ussher asking him to intercede. He agreed to visit the new Governor, whose family he had known in happier days. Djevdet *Bey*, however, remained obdurate, and professing to be worried about the security of the American Mission, proposed sending eighty soldiers to occupy the American compound.

"Your Excellency," said Ussher, "I am greatly in debt to you for your suggestion, but I do feel that such a large force appearing in the middle of the Armenian quarter at such a tense moment would be a disaster and likely to lead to bloodshed. Perhaps if your Excellency sent a token force of say five askaris, this would be more than enough to guarantee the safety of the compound."

"I am sorry, but I intend sending a fully armed detachment to occupy the Mission for your own safety," replied the Vali coldly.

"Your Excellency, the American government is neutral in this war and I will be doing my utmost to make certain that we remain so. However, I would remind you that by arrangement with the Turkish government over many decades, the Mission here has full diplomatic status, as clear as a consulate: I cannot allow the entry of a large body of soldiers into what is technically American territory."

Djevdet Bet, clearly irritated, blurted out, "In that case, Doctor, I demand a written note absolving me of any responsibility for your safety." Ussher nodded, confirmed that he would be happy to provide a note to this effect and left the office.

During the previous winter's mobilisation, the Armenians had been relentlessly plundered under the guise of requisitioning. The rich had been ruined, whilst the poor, though willingly joining the Army, had been deprived of any arms, and had been forced into doing all the menial tasks for the military, resulting in a high degree of tension throughout the city.

On the day of the outbreak of the so-called 'rebel*lion*' – the excuse given by subsequent Turkish and other historians for this and all the later barbarities as well as for the new policy of total ethnic cleansing – some Turkish soldiers tried to seize one of a group of Armenian village women who were on their way to the city. She fled. Two Armenian soldiers came up to investigate, and at that point the Turkish soldiers opened fire and killed them. The Turkish entrenchments which Djevdet *Bey* had been drawing up round the Armenian quarter during the previous three days, then opened up an intense barrage of fire into the residential quarter. The old cannons on Castle Rock began pouring a slow but murderous fire on the houses below. The siege of Van, destined to last for several weeks, had begun.

During the whole of the siege, Dr. Ussher would not allow armed men to enter the compound. The Armenians, understanding this neutrality, gave orders, after the third day, that no wounded soldiers were to be brought to the American hospital. Instead, Dr Ussher would go down with the nurses to the temporary hospital, set up by the Armenians in the church hall, at least once a day. Even so, Djevdet *Bey* wrote to Ussher claiming that armed men had been seen entering the American compound, and as a result he would be opening fire on the hospital.

Djevdet *Bey* and Dr. Ussher corresponded with each other during the siege by sending letters to the Italian consular agent – Italy still being neutral. These letters were taken through the lines by old women carrying a flag of truce. At least four of these ladies lost their lives acting as postmen during the siege. It was a feature of the siege that a volunteer replacement was always quickly found. Ussher's note back stated clearly and explicitly -

"Your Excellency, I must make it crystal clear that at no time have I or any of my staff treated any armed, or previously armed men at my hospital. My mission is to preserve the neutrality of our premises by every means in our power. I accept that I have taken in refugees from the villages around, but not one of these villagers had any arms. Our hospital, with a normal capacity of 50, now accommodates 187. I remain Your Excellency's faithful servant."

Despite this, the direct bombardment of the American Mission started on the next day.

It was painfully apparent to Ussher, that in the event of a collapse of the Armenian defenders, the compound would be overrun, and that the chances of survival of his staff would be slight. Despite this, and despite the fact that he had a wife and young children present, who would inevitably be caught up in the slaughter, he remained absolutely steadfast throughout the siege, continuing with his humanitarian work. As always, he was totally confidant in the morality of his stance.

Ussher could have left, with his wife and three children, at any time during the siege. The Turks would have let them through their lines, while the Armenians often pressed him to escape. But neither Ussher nor his equally staunch wife ever wavered from what they considered to be their moral duty.

It has been argued that the terrible killings and massacres of the helpless Armenian population in Eastern Anatolia, which began soon after these events in Van, were triggered by what Doctors Ussher and Nazim saw from their different viewpoints. However, it cannot explain how the first ethnic cleansing of the 20th century came to pass. Djevdet *Bey* was unquestionably the wrong man in the wrong place at the wrong time, but his actions had in many ways been foreordained by factors which had shaped his formation as an adult, and which, by the coincidence of events, had placed him here.

Clarence Ussher had lived in Van many years before the siege. He had known Djevdet Bay as a growing boy, and had followed his development into an adult. He had seen the slow erosion of the old Ottoman values in this one individual.

First had come the paranoid suspicions and random cruelties of the odious and blood-crazed Abdul Hamid, whose incredible hatred towards the people who had lived amongst the Turks for generations, had deepened the distrust between the two ethnic groups to breaking point during his thirty year rule. Raised in the closed claustrophobic world of the Harem, there was uncertainty over the ethnicity of Abdul Hamid's mother and this may have aggravated his paranoia. As a young man he had an Armenian look about him. Normally the eunuchs in charge of the Harem were particularly careful to note the times and dates and pedigree of any girl who had shared the Padishah's bed. It was accordingly doubly unfortunate that there was a small element of doubt in respect of Abdul Hamid's conception.

Djevdet had been brought up in this atmosphere of suspicion and hatred and, from childhood, had witnessed the regular pogroms and humiliations visited on his Armenian neighbours. The harm Abdul Hamid had done to the minds and attitudes of his subjects, Christian and Moslem alike, was *bey*ond calculation, and that harm had penetrated the mind of the young Djevdet as much as any other.

Finally, to put the last touch to the development of Djevdet's character came the domination of the views of Enver, Talaat and Djemal within the Ittihad, all preaching a brutal nationalistic creed so alien to the great Padishahs of the past. The Western European style 'nation-state' with all its vicious hatreds and contradictions, had at last arrived in the Islamic world, and Djevdet *Bey* was the final political product of that movement.

Meanwhile, the siege, started in the second week of April, dragged on day by day without resolution, as Ussher went patiently about his work.

IV.   Nevart's situation.

Nevart, an Armenian born and bred in Van, was tired. Now a wizened shrunken old lady dressed always in black, she had lived over 70 years in Van, and apart from trips to the beautiful island of Achtamar in the Lake, had never left the city. Two husbands had come and gone, and her only remaining family was a widowed daughter, now living with her in her ancient Ottoman-style house in the garden city. The house, in the middle of the urban Armenian quarter not far from the American Mission, was cluttered with the detritus of a long life. The leaning and creaking wooden terraced building, with others of similar type on either side, with the ubiquitous latticed windows on the first and second floors. These bay windows stuck out over the street, reducing the view of the sun and sky from below, but giving welcome shade during the day in the hot summers.

Neither Nevart, nor her daughter Sona, ever really knew what was going on during those April days. They felt the tension in the streets, and they noticed there was less mixing between Armenians and Turks in the bazaars, hammams and cafés in the centre.

"What is happening Sona, where have all the young men got to? What is going on?"

"I'm not sure mother, but I have heard that our Governor is angry because the town hasn't produced its full tally of conscripts for the army."

"On top of all that," grumbled Nevart, not taking much notice of Sona's reply, "the price of fresh vegetables has gone through the roof. There must be fewer villagers coming in to town to sell their produce. The open markets are getting more and more bare. I had to traipse around for almost two hours yesterday just to get a few onions, and the price they asked was ridiculous. I walked back with old Yevret Hanum – you remember her, the wife of Agop's old Turkish friend and partner. She told me that bands of Kurds are roaming the countryside, disrupting the villagers' lives, killing and robbing, so the villagers are frightened to bring in their produce."

"Well, mother, no doubt it's all just rumours." Sona grabbed her hat and coat and hurried out of the house to work.

Nevart sighed, and picking up her big straw basket, she got ready to spend the whole morning, if necessary, trying to get some vegetables and replenish her stock of rice. She stepped out into the fresh morning air, hoping that she could make her purchases before the hot midday sun. The whole street seemed to consist of little old women, dressed in black, hurrying about chasing provisions of one kind or another.

She had just walked into the little square where the country folk usually came to spread their wares out on the pavements, when she heard the first shots ring out. These were quickly followed by a frenzy of shooting that were the opening salvos of the siege – the reasons for which she never came to understand, and which she never expected would go on for so long.

Suddenly the great gun on the Castle rock boomed out, and there was an explosion just ahead of her. Screams rang out, and people began scattering in different directions. Nevart stood quite still not knowing what to do. The other old women had mostly disappeared – though some were on their knees on the pavement crossing themselves and muttering prayers. Another shell burst very close by, and she felt the earth shake – and then a piece of masonry or something flew past her ear grazing her cheek deeply. Blood began to flow.

This suddenly woke her to the reality of her perilous situation. She started running – not exactly in a panic – but without direction. Within a minute or so she was already out of breath, and found herself outside the Protestant mission. The great doors of the compound were closed, as they usually were except on Sundays. Recollecting that there was an excellent medical clinic inside, she leant against the wall, gulping down breaths of air. She pulled the knob of the door-bell, and was immediately let in by the Turkish porter, who gestured towards the little hospital building across the court.

Here, she was immediately taken in by a nurse with the name Alicia pinned to her white coat.

"What's happening, mamoushka?" asked the nurse, and Nevart recognised the accent of an Armenian from the Russian side of the divide.

"I have no idea," replied Nevart, who by now had recovered both her breath and her senses. "There were a couple of loud explosions – some buildings were hit, and a lot of shooting. A stone or piece of falling masonry must have hit me. Then there were a lot of young men, who haven't been seen around town for some time, running about and shouting to each other."

While she listened, the nurse, who seemed to understand better than Nevart what was happening outside, continued calmly attending to the wound on Nevart's wrinkled cheek.

"Well, the whole town has been getting more and more tense over the last week or so. It will be a riot I suppose, though I did hear the boom of the castle gun, several times. You won't need any stitches, mamoushka, just be very careful and don't wash there for a few days," she went on, as she stuck a plaster on Nevart's cheek. "You better get home now, and try not to go out in the streets until whatever is going on, dies down."

Nevart walked out of the little hospital still bewildered, but more her usual self. She could still hear shooting, and the occasional boom of the bigger guns. The great doors of the compound were now flung wide open, and she saw the American Mission's leader standing by the gate. A small stream of women and an occasional old man, all with similar wounds to hers, were just beginning to walk or be carried in to the compound.

As Nevart passed by, she saw the American stop a young man who had been hopping in on an improvised crutch with a rifle in his hands. His leg was clearly badly crushed and incapable of supporting him. The American murmured a few words to the boy who nodded, and he then beckoned over one of the Turkish employees of the Mission. The young lad leant on the porter's shoulder and they shuffled away down the street. He had clearly been refused entry. Nevart stumbled home, still in a daze as the shooting was intensifying, and many of the old buildings which had appeared so solid only a few moments before, had crumbled to dust. She was totally disorientated.

Nevart had spent her entire life in the town, mixing with her Turkish neighbours, both as a girl and as a woman. In the Hammams – the baths – she had always joined in the usual rituals in the women's section of the baths. As a naked young girl she had duly scrubbed the backs of the older women, and listened to their gossip; she had endured and giggled as they made sly comments once she had reached and passed puberty. Then as an older woman herself, she too had had her back scrubbed and lathered by other young women in her turn, and she had indulged in the usual banter and gossip about young men who were available as husbands. Both of her own two husbands had been found as a result of discussions between mothers in these same baths.

The point was that there was no difference between a plump naked Turkish woman and an even plumper naked Armenian one. There might be tensions arising from time to time reflecting local political clashes in the outside world, but the women dealt with these sensibly, keeping apart for a few days until the tensions spent themselves and then drifting back to their usual comfortable tolerance of each other.

As she turned the corner into the street on which her house stood, she saw a knot of women clustered outside her house, the door of which was open. She knew. She knew instinctively what had happened. With a cry she ran forward. Sona's broken body lay where she had been reverently placed in the doorway – the victim of the very first shell of the very first day of the siege.

Nevart stood and stared, held up by the women. The sobs refused to come. Her last contact with life seemed to have disappeared. She allowed herself to be led into the house. Her neighbours took control of the necessary practical details. Nevart, herself, simply drifted into a state of numb indifference.

Once the siege got under way, the Armenians in Van were eventually gathered into a district about a mile square, with the American Hospital right in the middle. Protecting themselves against the entrenchments pinning them down, several of the old solid stone houses on the edges of the area had been turned into mined and barricaded defenses. Dr. Ussher's daughter had recounted to her father that despite the terrible shortage of all the material necessary for warfare, the young fighters, numbering about 1,400 men, were extraordinarily cheerful with very high morale. They were hopeful of being able to keep the 6,000 Turkish soldiers at bay. They were, after all, fighting for their homes and their very lives.

During those first few hours, as Nevart had stared at the body of her daughter, she was comforted and cosseted by those same black-clad women, all well versed in dealing with grief in all its forms. But Nevart had now finally lost everything that she had ever valued losing her capacity to deal with life at the same time.

However, eventually, a deep atavistic strength, emanating from generations of female ancestors learning to cope with tragedy, came to her aid, and overcame the apathy, which had gripped her. With no one left for her to feed or care for, she locked up her house, took her few saved gold piastres, and walked down to the American Mission.

On her way, she picked up a notice on the street printed on recycled paper, which appeared to have been issued to all the young men, which read –

"Keep clean. Do not drink. Tell the truth.
Do not curse or denigrate the religion of the enemy."

The doors of the compound were now permanently open, and she walked straight in. The formerly neat and tidy courtyard looked totally different from the day she had first visited the place. A large number of people were now sitting about, some under the shade of tattered umbrellas and some on faded carpets. These were mainly women and old men, although there was a sprinkling of middle-aged men, obviously villagers from the surrounding countryside. The women seemed to be coping fairly well, chatting and gossiping to each other, but the men looked listless and sad.

Nevart picked her way through to the hospital, where she saw several women in white coats bustling about. She sought and eventually found Alicia, the nurse who had treated her on that first day.

"Madam Nurse ..." she began, addressing Alicia, and then went on to explain the death of her daughter Sona, her last remaining relative.

"I would like to help you here. I can cook. I can help in treating wounds. I am prepared to do anything at all."

Alicia looked hard at her. "Mother are you sure, even if it was a question of risking your life."

Nevart smiled, looked straight into the young woman's eyes. "Yes! Yes! Anything at all. It would be a blessing."

Alicia looked a bit doubtful, but then smiled. "Well – I'll take you to see Dr. Ussher –he needs someone to deliver a letter to an address on the other side of the lines, as the last messenger hasn't returned. He cannot send a man. Nevart, you must understand, it is dangerous. Come, he can explain."

And so it was that Nevart became the last of Dr. Ussher's volunteer postal ladies, in his almost daily correspondence with the authorities on the other side of the lines.

CHAPTER 12

Tea at Tokatlian's

True to her word, Olga arrived early at the gates of Nerissa's school that afternoon. The longer she had been anticipating her meeting with Selim, the more thrilling it had become. She had seen and spoken to Selim many times at college since they first arranged the rendezvous, but the strong physical attraction she felt was augmented by an increasing certainty that this was a man of great personal honour and kindness, with whom she felt immediately at ease. They had never been alone together, but his smile, whenever he saw her, turned her feelings inside out.

Nerissa came out of school, ahead of any of her friends, wrapping a silk scarf round her neck, as she removed the rather dowdy round school hat, and put it into her bag. She too was excited. This was a major event for her, and she was looking forward to going to the Bedestan – the old antique bazaar. She wasn't worried about the rendezvous – she knew she wouldn't be called upon to say much, and she could simply sit back and listen to the little orchestra, and let Olga and the young man talk together.

As they walked along to the station, Nerissa realised that in all the excitement of planning this trip, Olga had never told her the name of the young man with whom they were about to have tea. Once on the train, Nerissa snuggled into her window seat, smiling at Olga, ready at last to enjoy this novel experience. Olga was looking so beautiful, she thought to herself catching her breath with a mixture of pleasure and sadness. She knew she could never aspire to Olga's beauty and social confidence.

"Well now Olga, my darling, – what is the name of your new friend – you know you've never got round to telling me".

The moment had come at last. Olga had always known in her heart that what she was doing would be unacceptable to her parents, as the mild deception she had been practising clearly showed. But she had not really considered the wider ramifications. For the first time in weeks, Olga was going to have to face up to the actual disclosure of the relationship.

"Selim Kemal," – Olga replied simply, saying nothing more.

Nerissa stopped smiling. She sat there, totally stunned. What could she say? Although only 16, she saw at once, with great clarity, all the implications contained in those two words. A Turkish boy! In the two minutes of silence that stretched between the two sisters, she analysed the impossibility of this situation – difficulties which Olga had obviously not even considered.

However shy and introverted Nerissa was, she remained the most studious, intelligent, and reflective of the four girls. Her native intelligence came to her aid. She sat in her corner seat, wondering what her father's reaction might be in such a situation. His principles were never to immediately reject any proposal, without first calmly considering everything from all angles. Once your mind was made up, you must not compromise or fudge the issues, but take your stance with courage and honesty.

"So, Olga, he is Turkish?" Nerissa, made sure that she did not look away from her sister's eyes, or appear distressed or anxious.

"Yes – he's a lovely boy, you'll like him Nerissa I feel sure. He's intelligent and thoughtful, and so gentle – not anything like all the other boys. My darling, when he speaks to me I feel so – so – warm and good and protected. Oh dear, it's so difficult to explain. He has none of that male arrogance which you see so often in the other Turkish students."

Suddenly Olga couldn't stop talking. All her pent-up feelings, which she had kept to herself, began pouring out, as she stared back into Nerissa's big brown eyes. But none of her explanations showed any awareness of the looming problems of such a relationship, neither to Nerissa directly, nor, more tellingly, to herself.

Nerissa listened, thrilled by being a party to the feelings of an elder sister, who, in the whirl of her active social life, had until then largely ignored her. At the same time, she found herself appalled at what she increasingly saw as a domestic tragedy in the making. She knew that her beloved sister was going to be badly hurt one way or another, whatever happened. She found herself thinking of the doomed Juliet and her love for Romeo. 'My God' she thought, 'Juliet's problem was nothing compared to the situation which Olga was going to have to face. Romeo was exactly the same race as Juliet, he spoke the same language as she at home, he belonged to the same religion and was from the same class.'

But did Olga realise what she was up against? Here was a young man, however gentle and pleasant, who nevertheless spoke a different language at home, was of a totally different religion, belonged to a different race, furthermore a race which had been locked in a fierce and, seemingly irreconcilable conflict with her own people for over 500 years, since the fall of the old Byzantine Empire.

What was the right thing for her to do and would Olga take the slightest notice? She could see that nothing she could say at this particular moment would make any difference. Meanwhile, now that the floodgates were opened, Olga chattered on oblivious to all but her own all-consuming feelings, and so Nerissa said not a word as the train slowly pulled into Sirkeci Station.

As they walked from the station to the covered Bazaar, Nerissa finally got round tentatively to raising the issue foremost in her mind.

"Olga, how far has your friendship with this young man gone?"

"Nerissa, listen, all I know is that this is a good man – a man of truth and honour whom I believe I will be able to trust, if necessary. But, Nerissa, I really don't know how deep my own feelings are, never mind being sure of his."

"But Olga, aren't you aware of the difficulties? What about when it comes to meeting his family?"

"Poof – who cares. For the moment all I want to do is to get to know him better. I don't care a hoot what other people may think. We're two individuals, why should we carry the weight of the past on our shoulders all the time? I am first and foremost a woman – not a representative of my ethnicity or religion. What difference would it make if we were on a desert island."

"But Olga, my soul, we are not on a desert island – nor in that metaphorical sense, could we ever be."

An hour or so later, after a short somewhat distracted visit to the Bedestan, which for different reasons, had lost its attraction, they came out of the Tunel and took the tram that deposited them at the front entrance of Tokatlians on the Grande Rue. Here a fairly brisk crowd of fashionable ladies and gentlemen, mixed with a good sprinkling of smartly turned out Army Officers and Cadets, were passing in and out of its Art Nouveau glass doors. Olga and Nerissa walked into the busy vestibule. Here, just inside the door, Selim was waiting, looking rather lost.

A sudden surge of excitement, coupled with a strong feeling of affection, sprang up in Olga, as she saw and appreciated his nervousness. At the same time, she felt a confidence in her own ability to manage the occasion. It was as if Selim's nervousness had sparked in her a calm certainty. Nerissa glanced at her sister and saw her face break into a really natural, warm smile; a smile unlike any of the superficial and consciously charming smiles her sister could so easily produce. Nerissa's heart lurched and nearly drowned in inward tears, as Olga stretched out her hand.

"Oh hello Selim. This is my young sister, Nerissa."

To which Selim, taking Olga's hand into his own, and holding it without making any attempt at shaking it, replied -

"Hello, Nerissa, Salaam! Shall we go in and get a table?"

It took several seconds before Selim became aware that he was still holding Olga's hand. By contrast, Olga had been aware of every second of his grasp, as had Nerissa. Selim, blushing deeply, let go as they moved, somewhat self-consciously, into the tea-room at Tokatlians.

Here, in the large and airy glass-roofed room, Nerissa stared at the noisy crowd of men with a surprisingly large number of women, chatting animatedly at small round tables dotted about the place. The room – or was it a theatre – was liberally sprinkled with potted palms and other plants placed strategically to shield the tables from one another. A huge chandelier, magnificent enough to have graced the new Paris Opera House, hung from the ceiling. The setting was grand, though perhaps not very tasteful. No Oriental opulence here, but dark mahogany walls, heavy green foliage, some tall palm trees at the side, small white wrought-iron tables and chairs, and the glittering chandelier hanging over all. A tiny stage at the side of the large hall held a small string orchestra, in front of which was a minuscule polished wooden floor for dancing.

The room was filled with Turkish officers. Nerissa wondered what they were all doing here in the City. Enver Pasha, despite the defeats on the Caucasian front, was clearly still the style of the day. The men were all clean-shaven, save for the same neat, clipped, moustache. They all affected a pose of nonchalant arrogance, with cold eyes and a supercilious regard. Male predators – all of them. As they sat down, Nerissa noticed a young man in the uniform of the officer-cadet school – the Harbiye – clearly an Armenian – sitting nearby with a small group of friends, who was looking at her with soft brown eyes, smiling when he caught her gaze, and then shyly turned away.

Nerissa smiled back and then tried to concentrate on what Selim and Olga were saying to each other, though it was quite clear that the real conversation was going on between their eyes. The little orchestra began playing a Strauss waltz with that absurd late 19th-century sentimental rhythm, and a few couples rose to dance.

To her dying day, and despite the drama of the tragic days that followed, Nerissa would never be able to forget the setting or to recall any of the actual words that passed between the three of them on that hazy afternoon in the old *thé dansant* room at the Tokatlian Hotel. She looked and listened, as Olga and Selim, chatted together inconsequentially, and touched hands under the table, with an innocent wonder at the intensity of their own feelings. The atmosphere was dream-like, hazy at the edges – a moment of complete calm, yet only a few days before the storm that was due to burst over them all.

Deeply anxious for her sister, but at the same time thrilled by the occasion, Nerissa sat and watched as this last bastion of the old and elegant Europe seemed to be dancing its last waltz; all these young officers and their companions unconscious that their world was about to die forever, as a result of the same two fatal shots that had assassinated an Archduke and his lady, only nine months earlier. Nerissa said scarcely a word, but she took it all in, and in those three magical hours, she moved inexorably from a shy 16 year-old girl into a young woman.

CHAPTER 13

André, Harry and the invasion force

When the wind blows from the north in Alexandria, blustery and damp, the old trams running along the Corniche clatter and shake about as they proceed from east to west and back again. All the weekend visitors from Cairo smile at each other and take bracing walks along the seafront, feeling pleased that they had taken the trouble to come. When, however, the winds blow from the south, they seem to bring with them the hot, enervating and sultry smells of the rest of Africa looming oppressively *bey*ond the town – a town turned firmly against the continent behind it. Then those same weekend visitors from Cairo wonder why they bothered to come at all.

André Tarkowski and his Greek girlfriend Elena Patakis had managed to get to Egypt before the Turkish entry into the war closed the frontiers. Arriving in Alexandria, André had somehow been able to lay his hands on more than sufficient funds. André's passport skirted over his German citizenship by referring to him as Polish. He proceeded to make great efforts to get work with the British naval administration as an expert in the relatively new field of radio.

André was getting more and more bored by Elena, who had to start creating her own entertainment. She had little in the way of intellectual reserves of her own; without much education, she had acquired few outside interests. André was always out at work or wandering round the town, and whilst their sexual relationship remained passionate and satisfactory, even the highly sensual Elena began to feel the lack of any common activity *bey*ond the bedroom.

As April advanced, Alexandria and Cairo began to fill with nationalities from all over the British Empire. André worked in the Navy's special Radio Telegraph room at the end of the tramline near the seaside Montazah Palace. He would often stand and stare at the bronzed and athletic young Australians, stripped to the waist on the sands by the sea, his perverse and brutal bisexuality never causing him a moment's thought.

André couldn't understand why these young men were here, and what they were doing in a war, which despite all the propaganda, was basically a European 'balance of power' contest, but he persisted in trying to find out, usually ending up getting details of their regiments.

He reflected on how his seduction of Elena and the affair that followed had already soured. Their only common language – the language they had all spoken together in the Patakis household – was of course Turkish. However André, though a natural linguist, was not all that comfortable in Turkish, and, in any case, it didn't seem worth the effort.

Elena was already enjoying the attentions of Greek lads she was meeting at the Church and in the wider Greek community and André showed no feelings of jealousy – much to Elena's surprise and irritation. Their little two-room apartment was at the top of a large 19th-century building standing opposite the Sports Club grounds, and whilst adequate, was constricting. The building itself housed Greek, Italian, French, and even an Egyptian family.

This was the middle of April – the landings in Gallipoli were due to take place within a week – and meanwhile André was flabbergasted at the total lack of security in Egypt. No military expedition since the Trojan War had ever been more loudly trumpeted and discussed. First the fleet had bombarded the Dardanelles Forts, pinpointing exactly where a future effort was going to take place. Then, news of the arrival and departure of all the great battleships and the hundreds of transports became common knowledge throughout Alexandria and Port Said, and was reported daily in Cairo. The names and numbers of all the British, French and Anzac divisions were freely referred to in the newspapers. There were even official references to "the Constantinople Field Force". The word Gallipoli was on everyone's lips. Everyone knew what was coming, as ponies, horses, camels, water lighters, shipping of all kind, were hastily purchased and gathered together in the Egyptian ports.

André simply could not credit this, in view of his experience of the secretive world of Prussian military security. In the end, he came to only one conclusion – they simply did not know what they were doing. Above all, it seemed their leaders had made the cardinal error of ignoring their history. They were failing to take the Turks seriously, or, indeed, to take any account of them at all.

The Turks, after all, had a long tradition of military prowess. Whilst they had long since lost the brilliance in aggresive offensive warfare of their nomadic ancestors, they had instead acquired a dogged, patient, stonewalling, defensive strategy that had always been their strength, even in the days of Byzantium before there were any Turks in Anatolia at all. The Anatolian peasants, who were the bedrock of the army, were mainly illiterate; they were misused and despised, and badly led by their Pashas and officers from Constantinople, but they were used to hardship. They could endure with patience and stubbonness in much the same way as the Russian mouzhik.

The Ottoman Empire, eventually including Greece, the Balkans, most of Hungary, and the whole of the Arab world including the holy cities of Islam, contained an enormous number of different races, creeds, languages and religions. By the 18th century, it had grown soft, and the question increasingly raised was what exactly united all these disparate peoples. The Ottoman Empire was the ultimate multi-cultural and multi-racial society, and despite some notably tragic moments, the Ottoman Empire had treated their many different minorities better than most of the so-called civilised nations to the north.

But as André could see, British officers were dismissive of soldiers who didn't dress like them or look like them. Who cares if the Turks know we are coming – 'our chaps' will still give the rotters a good hiding, was the unconscious thought of all of them, from the generals down to the ordinary Tommies.

Finally, and to cap it all, André knew something that, with all the intelligence at their disposal, General Hamilton and the planners at Whitehall did not know. The ridiculous and vainglorious Enver Pasha, would not be facing them at Gallipoli. He had only managed to emulate his hero Napoleon in one regard, by retreating in a winter campaign with only a tiny proportion of his original force left alive. The General who had hurriedly been placed in charge, and with almost a month to prepare the defences, was Mustapha Kemal. Enver was a gambler. Kemal, by contrast, was a cool chess player, who knew his men well, and who, whilst equally ruthless, never lost his essential humanity.

The flat was tiny, and sitting under the bed, up against the wall, taking up space which was in short supply, was a rather battered locked tin case, which André had brought with him, through all their travels, all the way from the house in Stamboul. Elena's references to it seemed to irritate André unduly, and unfortunately Elena had reached the stage where irritating him seemed to be the only way she could reach him. It would often end in a sort of ritualised violence, during the sexual act, in a way which seemed to satisfy both of them.

It was on that last night, at the start of the third week in April, before all the naval transports left, that Elena returned home unexpectedly early from supper with a Greek family she had met. André had been invited but had said that he was far too tired to go. On arrival, Elena found that the family were in a domestic crisis in regard to an elderly Aunt who had just died, and after giving her condolences and exchanging some polite conversation, she left. She walked into their little sitting room to see the tin case open on the desk, and Andre tapping at some keys on a machine, with what looked like muffs over his ears.

"Whatever is that thing, André – it's a funny kind of typewriter," said Elena, as she walked in putting down her hat.

André, who hadn't heard her coming in, carefully lifted off the ear pieces, and turned to face her – his eyes hard, glittering and full of that violence, which on this occasion suddenly caused her to feel a real stab of fear.

"Just one of my toys, Elena – come here," he answered, as he slowly rose from the desk and came towards her.....

Harry, too, was now in Egypt.

Within a week of submitting his report on the events which had led to the escape of the *Goeben* and the *Breslau*, and their arrival in Constantinople, Harry had got his wish and been posted to active duty on the destroyer, HMS *Leicester*. As the days drew on towards the end of April, the ship made its way, at speed, to Port Said. The *Leicester* was scheduled to escort the transports of the Royal Naval Division due to participate in the forthcoming landings at Gallipoli.

By the end of 1914, the war in Europe had already become an inferno of hundreds of miles of trenches: front- line trenches, transverse trenches, supply line trenches, rear- return trenches and others, where men lived and fought each other, like rats scurrying around in a maze. This was not a war of man against man, but man against the inexorable machine. One man's death, impaled on a bayonet or struck down by a sword, was an unbearable tragedy, but the death of 25,000 men, raked down by machine guns in the first 20 minutes of one of the great 'over the top' offensives, had turned these killing fields into industrialised slaughter, turning the deaths from tragedy to statistics.

The whole idea of a landing at Gallipoli started as an attempt to get round the awful stalemate on the Western front, by mounting a flanking manoeuvre as a purely naval operation, rather than as a direct attack on Constantinople. The plan was to capture Constantinople by a naval *coup-de-main*. It was the original intention that this would be a naval battle fought on sea. The navy alone, was going to force a way through the straits, and then appear outside Constantinople.

When the Navy finally sailed into the straits it had over 200 heavy guns, against a mere handful in the Turkish forts. The forts were silenced on the very first day. It was reliably reported that the rulers in Constantinople thought they were finished. Talaat is supposed to have had a car ready to take him into the interior at a moment's notice – the Balkan states suddenly thought of getting a bit of the action – the Russians talked of attacking Constantinople from the Black Sea. However, as day after day passed, nothing further happened. Somehow, the clearing of the old fixed forts didn't seem to prevent the hidden mobile guns of the coastal defences from opening up with accurate fire, whenever the minesweepers sprang into action during the night, trying to clear the mines to enable the great battleships to move on.

At last, the admirals decided to make an all-out effort. Seventeen battleships and a host of smaller craft, with a French squadron as well, moved forward. By midday most of the Turkish guns had again fallen silent. They were almost there. But then the mines began to take their toll. Three battleships were sunk and several others crippled – 700 sailors died – losses that were tiny compared with what was happening in the trenches every single day, but it was enough to finish off the admirals.

That evening they telegraphed the Admiralty to say that the plan had failed. They reported that they no longer believed that the Navy could force the straits alone. They confirmed that they would need the Army!"

Harry was in a state of intense excitement. He was sure that he had arrived at one of those great heroic moments in history. Even now, still early in 1915, despite the awful experiences on the western front, war was still thought of by all these young men as a glorious, exciting, adventure. Each of the European nation-states believed that their 'chaps' were plucky and gallant, full of honour and duty, ready to sacrifice themselves for their country, and, of course, for their particular God.

Harry's friend – the poet Rupert Brooke – had joined the Royal Naval Division (RND) scheduled to go in with the Anzacs. Brooke had written a letter to another acquaintance, a copy of which had been sent on to Harry, when he had been told that his division was bound for Constantinople. In it he had written –

"It's too wonderful for belief. I had not imagined Fate would be so kind... Will Hero's Tower crumble under the fifteen-inch guns? Will the sea be polyphloisbic and wine-dark? Shall I loot mosaics from Santa Sophia, and Turkish Delight and carpets? Should we be witnessing a turning point in History? Oh God! I've never been quite so happy in my life, I think ... I suddenly realise that the ambition of my life has always been since I was two years old to go on a military expedition against Constantinople."

"Oh no," thought Harry, "doesn't he realise that people are going to die? That there is going to be blood and pain, loss and horrific injuries, and most terrible and monstrous deaths?"

But even as he thought this, he still thrilled to the same passionate desire for heroic action.

As an intelligence officer who would be helping in the boarding and disembarkation, Harry went to visit the RND, camped on the other side of the Canal near Port Fuad. There he found the tents, all in neat rows, and eventually traced the one in which Sub-lieutenant Brooke was living. On arrival, Harry saw that clean-cut and handsome face, now swollen and puffed up – the lips thick and bloated – a wasted body lying in a muck sweat on the meagre camp bed in the dry Egyptian heat.

"Good heavens Rupert, what the blazes has happened to you?"

"Harry – Harry Bridgeman? It's those blasted mosquito bites – the blighters got me on the lip."

"Have you seen the medics? You ought to be in hospital. Rupert, frankly you look bloody awful".

"Harry – for god's sake, do shut up. It's only a mosquito bite. I'll be on the mend soon. Do you think I am going to miss a chance like this? This is the very battleground that Homer described in the first great epic of the Western world; Achilles, and Hector, Agamemnon and Priam fought only a mile away from where we are headed. Do you think I am going to miss out on the second instalment?"

"But, Rupert, you're not going to be seeing much in that awful mess. Look, let me arrange to send some RAMC orderlies round at least to have a look at you."

"Rupert," said the other young officer who had been standing rather helplessly by, "He's right– these things can get nasty – please just let someone have a look at you."

"No, Charles, if you want to do something useful, go and get some ointment and bring it here – there's a good fellow."

Harry felt that he ought not stay much longer. He had a word with the other young officer, said he would look out for both of them on board, clasped the poet's hand for a brief moment, and then left.

The very next day the RND packed up their tents and embarked on the little flotilla to the Aegean, which would be the kicking off point for the landings in Gallipoli. The harbour and roadsteads at Mudros, the main collection point for the invasion on the island of Lemnos, was, by then, totally filled with shipping. Harry's flotilla accordingly headed on for the island of Skyros, the alternative rendezvous point.

For some days the force – naval and military – remained on this delightful Greek island – all day the sun shown down from a bright blue sky. The whole island seemed to be made from great blocks of irregular white marble, piled up to 2–3,000 feet high and covered with masses of lilac, sage and purple thyme. The shepherds and villagers of the island carried on as they always did, ignoring the sudden arrival on their island of all these fair-haired, blue-eyed and impossibly young men. Harry found himself wondering whether they had acted in precisely the same way two millenia before, when Leander had passed by with another invasion force.

Two days before the force was due to move out, Harry was approached by a Petty Officer.

"I'm sorry, Sir, but could you please come to the division lines. I'm afraid that Lieutenant Brooke is dying."

Harry hurried on to the ship's cutter, reached the shore and raced up to where Brooke's tent had been, though it appeared that by then he had been transferred to a hospital ship. Several people were gathered round.

"He died a few hours ago, Harry," said an acquaintance, "he never got to witness the glory of war, which he so wanted."

The poet had died of a mosquito bite on his lips. It was as if Hector had slipped on a banana skin and infected his little finger, or Achilles had died of a bowel infection. They buried him that night under a few olive trees, and Harry helped carry his body slowly and carefully up the hill that evening.

Later that same night, back on board, writing to his mother, Harry described the difficulties in getting the coffin up the narrow mountain path.

"Mother, you would wonder at what a beautiful spot it was where we buried poor Rupert. It was at the top of a little stony hill surrounded by weeping olive trees, with the wonderful scent of Greek flowering sage, thyme and spring flowers. It was a beautiful moonlit evening. The path up was very narrow, and it was tricky going, carrying the coffin. A party of the others had gone ahead to dig the grave. We simply laid him in it, covered it with marble stones and piled on top all the flowers we could find. We then returned down the same narrow path, by which time it was completely dark, as the moon had gone behind clouds."

"Mother," he wrote, *"here is one of his last lines, in case you haven't seen it before."*

"These, laid the world away;
Poured out the red sweet wine of youth;
Gave up the years to be of worth and joy,
And that unhoped serene that men call age;
And those who would have been their sons,
Their immortality."

Two days later the Royal Naval Division embarked to join the Anzacs for the Gallipoli landings.

CHAPTER 14

Guests at the Avakians

Karekin stood in the bedroom, adjusting his tie carefully in the mirror. He asked Armineh to wait a moment before going down to see to the family breakfast.

"My dear, yesterday, Mr. Levonian – do you remember him, a textile merchant with business mainly in Germany and Vienna – offered me his seat in the tram going up from the bridge, saying that he was getting off at the next stop. Anyway, he never did get off at the next stop, but instead began talking about his son George. It seems that George has managed to get deferment for one reason or another, and has started working with his father."

"Karekin – for heaven's sake, do keep to the point of whatever you're trying to say. I haven't got all day." Armineh tapped her foot impatiently, and waited with her hand still on the doorknob.

"Ah – er – well, yes, at first I really wasn't clear at all what he was talking about. I must be getting past it, as I should have realised at once. Suddenly it dawned on me that he was talking about our Sima. I have no idea why it got into his mind at such a critical time, but he seems to be interested in a merger of our two merchant houses."

Karekin finished fiddling with his tie, now perfectly knotted, and turned quickly to face Armineh to stop her interrupting again.

"Sooner or later, Armineh my dear, this war is going to come to an end. Undoubtedly, he is right to believe that there will be room for expansion into Western Europe. Our cotton crop has not been affected, so, with me fully committed in Great Britain, and him covering Germany and central Europe, we could do very well in a postwar world. Armineh, I don't suppose life is going to be all that different in 1916 than it is today, if the war ends by then of course."

Completely missing the reference to Sima, Armineh replied,

"Karekin, I've had enough. I can't believe that you are asking me advice about a purely business matter. You know very well you'll do exactly as you want in that area. Now, unless there is something else you want to say, I'm going down. Please hurry, it's getting late."

"Armineh – some patience please my love. The question on which I need your advice is whether you think Sima is ready to consider the question of marriage."

Armineh, stopped, took her hands away from the door handle and stared, suddenly paying close attention.

"Of course she is ready to consider marriage – she's 19 and most girls of her age are already married and with child. She's always been a great help to me, and I'll miss her, particularly as Olga is so useless these days in the house – but it's time she was settled. Have we met this young man?"

"I don't think so, but we are going to meet him tomorrow, as I ended up inviting the family to tea," Karekin admitted rather sheepishly.

"Karekin – are you mad – you've lost your head. I'll simply never manage. You know how bad the situation is for entertaining. Really Karekin, how could you – it's going to be quite impossible – totally out of the question," said Armineh, as she stormed out, leaving the door ajar.

"There'll be four of them – the parents, the young man, and a younger sister," called out Karekin to the departing back of his wife. He grinned with satisfaction, being relieved that she had taken it so well. After over 20 years of marriage he was sure that Armineh was already working out how she was going to cope. He was also certain that she would.

Armineh, irritated as she was by having something like this thrust on her so suddenly, nevertheless knew perfectly well that she would manage. She could hardly not, after all the hints she had been passing to Karekin that he start bestirring himself where Sima was concerned. All thoughts of the war, the rumours of a possible Anglo-French attack on Constantinople itself, the awful news from Van, passed right out of her mind – not that such thoughts much occupied her, anyway. What was important was this first direct approach to be made on behalf of her first-born daughter. Oh yes! She would certainly do it right. Mentally rolling up her sleeves, she bustled downstairs for the daily tussle to get her delicate son to eat something before school.

Breakfasts at the Avakians remained noisy and full of life, as always – but there was an undercurrent of tension, noticeable to all, with the exception of little Seta. Although Haik had discovered that other boys at the school were also being accompanied to school by elder brothers or servants, this had not lessened the element of shame for him. Sima seemed sad and subdued, whilst Olga always appeared to be in a state of febrile excitement, quite incapable of sitting for long at the table. Nerissa, calmer and more reflective than the others, was sensitive to all the conflicting emotions around her, and was the only one aware of the reasons for Olga's animation. Though the family chatted on as usual, with the exception of Karekin himself, they didn't fear for themselves. Armineh continued to make sure that the everyday practical details of family life ran smoothly. By competently dealing with these, and despite all the problems outside her control, she gave the five children, and to some extent her husband, a firm anchor from which to contemplate the world's follies.

As Karekin came down to his glass of tea with lemon, Sima rose and said to Haik, "Come along young man, time for school." Haik, having avoided most of the food thrust at him by Armineh, and looking paler and more fragile every day, jumped up, hugged his father cheek to cheek as Karekin sat down, and went out. Karekin looked round at the rest of his children – Olga, Nerissa and little Seta.

"Tomorrow, my dears, some friends of mine will be coming to tea after church. I don't think you've met them – the Levonians – they live in Bebek."

"Gosh! That's quite far out, Baba," said Nerissa – "a long way for them to come."

"Yes, well, there'll be four of them – Hovannes and Yvonne Levonian, with their son George, and his younger sister."

"Father", Olga looked directly at her father, "how old, then, is this son – George?"

"Well, I believe that he's about 24. Anyway, I want you all to be well-behaved and careful. They are fairly old-fashioned, and we mustn't shock them – and that applies just as much to you Seta, my girl."

Seta looked up and grinned, undisturbed by her father's comment, and happy to be taken notice of.

Karekin rose – his breakfast these days was short and sharp – he couldn't wait to get back to the city to keep up with the latest conjectures flying around the coffee houses and the bazaar. For his family's sake, he knew he had to be ready for any eventuality, and to be alert to all the political possibilities. The three girls jumped up and kissed their father, who took his hat and coat and walked out.

"Seta, sweetheart, go and help Marie in the kitchen." Seta grumbled, but got up and went out. As soon as she had gone, Olga turned to Armineh and Nerissa, with shining eyes.

"Mother, I know something's going on – Father wouldn't comment about an ordinary tea-party. It's Sima isn't it. Nerissa, can you believe it, these Levonians are coming to inspect our Sima, and with a view," she giggled, "to matrimony, my dear." Olga wriggled with glee and laughed out loud.

"Oh no!" cried Nerissa, "it's disgusting, like a cattle market. Mother how can Baba even contemplate putting one of his daughters through something like that – I can't bear the thought – poor Sima."

Armineh, impatiently sipped her coffee, as Olga looked on with a mischievous grin.

"Nerissa – it's not like that at all. How do you think that Sima or any of you are going to meet pleasant young men, if we don't arrange meetings like this. No one, but no one, is ever going to make one of my daughters marry anyone whom they do not choose themselves – least of all your father. This is simply an occasion for two young people to meet – neither of them need take the matter a single step further."

"Oh mama don't get upset," said Nerissa, "of course I know that Baba wouldn't ever force any of us to do anything against our wishes. I don't doubt Baba's love for us, but that is not necessarily the same as trusting his judgement on what is right for us."

Suddenly Olga intervened, "Mother, when did you come to love father. You had only just met him when you married him, or so you told us. He was at least 15 years older than you – you yourself were scarcely much older than Nerissa here."

"Girls, life was very different in those days. Whilst I had brothers, I never met anyone outside the family. Life at home was constrained. There was no school. I never left the home except to go to Church. We never contradicted our parents, and frankly had few thoughts that weren't planted there by them. To be honest, I couldn't wait to get away and have my own home. I was ready to fall in love with the first young man to whom I was introduced. I was in addition used to doing what my parents wanted, unlike you lot."

"Yes, but when did real love arise," insisted Olga. "Was it on the very first night?"

Nerissa blushed deeply and looked away, although she was just as keenly interested in her mother's answer.

"Olga, my dear, I was only sixteen. Most of my real education came after I got married. I learnt more from your father in our first year together than in all my years of childhood …"

"Yes, Mother, but you haven't answered Olga, what about love?"

"What about passion?" Olga added.

Armineh sipped her coffee and reflected. Her husband had taught her to read and write. He had been gentle with her always, though he insisted on having his way in most matters. He relied on her to manage his home and daily life for him, which she did well and efficiently – and he was now 52 years-old! She realised that she could not even clearly remember that first night, but she could recall, with a sense of warm contentment, that very morning's act of love. That, however, was not what her daughter's wanted to know about.

Her relationship with Karekin: 'Contentment', certainly – 'Affection', oh God yes – but 'Love' …? Armineh gently put down her cup and rose as the two girls waited, watching her carefully for the different answers they each wanted for themselves.

"Come along girls – you'll both be late." Armineh got up, slowly and calmly, to check on the kitchen, get Seta ready for school, and make plans for tomorrow's tea party.

Hovannes Levonian was a fairly typical Ottoman Armenian businessman – corpulent and with a gold chain across a wide expanse of stomach. He wheezed and grunted as he got out of his first-class carriage, turning to help down his wife Yvonne. With his sharp and curious eyes, Haik picked them out at once. Yvonne Levonian was a thin, somewhat brittle lady, who had the habit of bursting into rather poor French, at every possible opportunity – no one knew quite why. Following her out of the carriage came a serious-looking young man – already beginning to become portly – sporting the usual Enver-style moustache, and looking older than his alleged 23 or 24 years of age. In his turn, he was followed by a pert young girl, with long fair hair and a bright grin.

"Karekin, my friend, meet my wife Yvonne. My dear, this is Karekin Avakian, of whom you have heard so much."

"*Enchanté – enchanté,*" said Yvonne, extending her hand, as if she expected it to be taken and kissed. Karekin smiled and took it into his own hand, for just the right amount of time, but making no attempt to bend down to kiss it.

Hovannes introduced his two children. "My son, George, and my daughter, Tamara." Karekin then introduced Haik, who was wearing long trousers for the occasion and who dutifully shook hands with everyone. They all strolled out of the station, and clambered into the two waiting carriages – the three parents in the bigger one, and Haik and his two guests in the other. George and Tamara sat in the comfortable carriage seats facing forward, whilst Haik had to sit opposite them, in the rather uncomfortable single seat facing backwards. He stared at Tamara, who stared back at him, swinging her legs beneath layers of Alice-in-Wonderland skirts. Although she was physically smaller than Haik, at 13 or so, she looked a good deal more mature. Whilst Haik was thin with his huge brown eyes dominating his face, Tamara was plump with full thick lips.

Tea parties of this kind, in these years in Constantinople, tended to follow a standard ritual. First, the guests would be seated in the main sitting room with all members of both families sitting in a semi-circle round the fireplace, without the presence of the girl whom everyone had come to meet. The inference was that she was out preparing the tea – although everyone knew perfectly well that the tea had been prepared by the servants long before.

Talk would be general, and would avoid politics or anything contentious. However, in the present political situation, with the war and rumours of a direct attack on the City by the Allies, Hovannes and Karekin were soon locked in a fairly heavy discussion on the subject. Armineh and Yvonne talked rather desultorily about the cost of vegetables, listening half-heartedly to their husbands. George said nothing. Haik, Tamara and little Seta fidgeted, whilst Nerissa and Olga, knowing that they were not supposed to say anything unless directly addressed, chafed under what seemed to them an impossible restraint.

"Karekin, my friend, what about the situation in Van? It's time we stood up for our rights. The day of the Ottomans is over – this is a hopeless ramshackle empire, and the best thing would be to have, as well as an independent Armenia, an independent Kurdistan, an independent Lazistan, an enlarged Greek state, and a Turkish Anatolian state. That's the way we can all become modern and westernised."

"And what will happen to Constantinople, with all your separate little nation-states. They'll all end up squabbling over it. For, Hovannes, it is this city and the Straits that is important to the world – not what is going on in the mountains of Anatolia or in the valleys of the Caucasus."

"Karekin, for heaven's sake – look what happened under the unspeakable Abdul Hamid. At least if we all had our separate states, no one would end up being oppressed by their own government."

"Don't you believe it, my friend. Exclusive one-nation states can be just as oppressive as any empire – in fact more so very often, as they consider themselves to have a legitimacy that the old multi-racial empires didn't possess."

So the conversation swung back and forth, with the corpulent Hovannes taking a more and more anti-Ottoman line, and Karekin mildly reproving him.

"In the end, Hovannes, this empire, however ramshackle, has been home to at least twenty different peoples and languages, at least five major religions, a whole raft of cultures and has kept a tolerable peace between them all for centuries. Do you really believe that the nation-states that might follow would be more tolerant of each other?"

The moment would then come, when the hostess would rise, excuse herself, and say she was going to arrange the tea – an unnecessary pretence – but there it is, it was the custom! Armineh rose and went out, returning almost at once, to be followed, in theory, by a discreet and demure Sima.

Sima, however, in true Avakian style, was in no way discreet or demure. She came in ahead of the trolley with a plate of cakes, and with none of those downcast eyes called for by the script for these occasions. Seta giggled at Marie, but was immediately silenced by a sharp look from Karekin. Sima, meanwhile, looked long and hard at George and his two parents, and went forward sociably to shake their hands. Karekin smiled to himself, saying nothing; Hovannes was slightly put out, but rallied; Armineh noticed nothing; and Haik looked on with pride at his statuesque and dignified elder sister, who had effortlessly taken centre stage without having said a word.

After a notional cup of tea and a cake, the young ones, if there were any, would be excused. So on this occasion Haik, Tamara and Seta got up and left. Nerissa had to stay with the grown-ups now that she was 16 although she would much preferred to have gone with the children. Seta led Haik and Tamara into the large garden at the back, but then excused herself to go and help in the kitchen where Marie was on her own. Haik was appalled at being left alone with this girl who looked at him appraisingly under thick eyebrows. He had no idea what he was supposed to do, and she didn't appear to be listening to anything he was saying anyway.

When he turned to look at his companion, Haik saw a young girl, fashionably over-dressed, with several skirts that came down below the knees. He saw her dark hair, her eyebrows, her lips and her large brown eyes. Tamara, for her part, saw a boy, who looked younger than his 12 years, with pale delicate fair features and a sharp pointed nose, unruly long hair, and big, bright inquisitive eyes – the whole having a somewhat feminine aspect.

"Come," she said taking him by the hand, "let's explore your orchard."

She led him down to the far end, as if it were her own garden, but he was glad that she had taken charge, relieving him of the obligation to initiate conversation. Wandering amongst the trees, they could not be seen from the house.

Tamara stopped, and began kicking idly at some dead branches on the grass. Haik leaned against an apricot tree and watched, fascinated, though uneasy, at the first young girl of approximately his own age that he had ever encountered alone. Tamara came up and facing him put her hands on either side of his face, then leant forward and touched his lips with her own. Neither of them really knew what they were doing – Haik certainly didn't, though he felt that the moment was important. He was surprised to find that the sensation was very pleasant. Tamara pulled back and their eyes met. She smiled.

Once again she leant forward, and once again her lips pressed against his. She held them there for several seconds – no more than the lips touching. Haik felt himself holding his breath and an unaccustomed erection rising, but he kept his arms firmly pressed back against the tree trunk. Unlike their first touch, their eyes were wide open as they looked at each other. The moment stretched into eternity.

"Haik – Tamara – where are you, come and join us," a voice called out from the house. Haik jumped, full of an inexplicable guilt. "We must go," and ran up the garden. Tamara stepped back, and walked calmly after him.

At the top end of the garden, Sima and George were standing awkwardly, waiting for Haik and Tamara to accompany them for a walk. There had been a moment of uncertainty when they walked out of doors to find the garden empty.

As she waited, Sima reflected on the young man standing by her side. She saw a man of about 24 – though he looked older. He was already turning to plumpness, with smooth, well groomed skin and a round baby-face. On his part, George saw a very proud, stiff and statuesque young woman, with the great Avakian eyes, but rather too talkative and direct for his taste. The irony was that whereas Haik and Tamara had been left free to roam as they wished in the garden, getting up to any mischief they liked – Sima and George had to be strictly chaperoned. Not all the social customs of the time made sense.

Both Tamara and Haik were aware of what was expected of them. Sima walked ahead with George, doing most of the talking, whilst Haik and Tamara, walked behind silently communing with their own thoughts.

George and Sima made polite small talk without communicating very much to each other. In an odd way, Haik and Tamara were communicating much more with each other without saying a word. Haik, who had already experienced nocturnal emissions, was nevertheless an innocent sexually. He had become erect immediately Tamara's lips had lingered on the second occasion, and he had felt both excited and guilty. Tamara on the other hand, had experienced exactly the sort of thrill that she expected, and there was no confusion in her mind at all.

And so the four of them walked sedately round the garden and through the orchard with George and Sima commenting on the flowers, Haik glancing anxiously at Tamara, reddening at the thought of her lips, and Tamara, walking demurely alongside.

That night Karekin knocked at the door of his eldest daughter's room, and walked in.

"Well Sima, what did you think of the young man?"

"Oh Baba, I don't think I could ever come to feel anything for him. There's no arrangement or proposal is there?"

"No, no, my darling, the important thing is to be clear right from the start so no one gets any wrong ideas. Don't worry, mother will see that it's all sorted out without any hurt feelings tomorrow."

The next day however was the 24th April – the day the Ittihad government was expecting the allied invasion, and also the day when it decided to begin the showdown with the minority in its midst ...

CHAPTER 15

The 24th April dawns

It was clear to the authorities both in Constantinople and Berlin, that having been defeated for the first time in a century, by the Turks of all people, the British Navy would attempt a landing of the allied armies somewhere along the Dardanelles. The Turkish High Command didn't need the spies to be aware of the approximate landing place. Even the date was fairly obvious, with the build-up of shipping gathered in the Aegean.

The British planned to land the elite 29th Division at the tip of the Gallipoli Peninsula on five separate beaches around Cape Hellas. From the outset it was a death trap. The small French contingent would make some feint landings on the Asian side. The Anzac, backed by the small Royal Naval Division, to whom Harry's ship was assigned, would land further north at the narrow waist of the peninsula.

The landing was fixed for the 23rd April. The armada grew larger every day with ships crowding the narrow harbours and bays of Mudros, Skyros and other islands. Then, just as the moment arrived, a fierce Mediterranean storm blew up, and the landings were postponed. The delay simply increased the readiness of the Turks. Their military dispositions were already in place in the peninsula. Anticipating the arrival of the invasion force on the coast, the 24th April was chosen to deal with the minorities in the interior.

Several days had passed since that dreamy tea party at Tokatlians. Over the next few days. Selim and Olga had continued to speak to each other at least once or twice each school day. All shyness and restraint between them had vanished. Olga spoke to Selim with a straight-forward honesty, which he found thrilling, as he came to a new level of understanding of the workings of her mind. Although not nearly so articulate, Selim bestowed on Olga an intimacy and warmth that she had never experienced outside her own family.

On the morning of the 24th, Olga walked slowly down to the Cobancesme station, past the open fields of the Vali *Effendi* racecourse, over the railway lines and into the little station, her thoughts on the coming meeting with Selim, but she could not ignore the intense conversations swirling around her as she waited for the train. Small groups of businessmen, split by ethnicity into Jewish, Greek or Armenians, stood huddled together on the platform. Snatches of conversation could be heard.

"Do you know whether they have landed yet or not?"

"I heard the booms of big naval guns last night coming from the Sea of Marmara. The British Navy must have broken through. I'm afraid there will be a bombardment of the City this afternoon."

"Have you heard that Enver and Talaat have fallen out, and that Talaat has left for Germany together with Liman von Sanders, who has been recalled to Berlin."

"I have it absolutely on the surest authority that the Greeks have declared war and are marching on the City to join an English force which has landed only 50 miles away in Thrace."

The voices and rumours, most of them well wide of the mark, swirled around her, and the fear was palpable. There was a sense that the whole of society was on the verge of a collective breakdown. Despite the failings of the Ittihad government, there remained a residual loyalty to the old Empire, in which they had all lived for generations. There was no historical imperative, rather it was the individual actions of men that would determine what happened.

Olga was only taking this in subconsciously. Her own thoughts were on the coming day at Robert College, and the delicious knowledge that she would be seeing Selim – and seeing him alone. Selim had made friends with the old caretaker in charge of the boiler room – Olga had no idea how, though she suspected the handing over of baksheesh. Over the past two days the old man had placed a couple of wooden chairs for them by the side of the enormous old boiler that provided heating for the buildings in the winter.

Twice now, Olga and Selim had sat on these two chairs, whilst the old man bustled about amongst the pipes in the dark depths of the basement room. A wonderful old man with a kindly creased face, a fez on his head, in old-fashioned baggy trousers, he was prepared to provide the chairs, but not to leave them alone. The chairs were placed close enough for them to touch hands for the 15 minutes or so they could afford to be together. Somehow it had not crossed their minds to draw the chairs closer than where old Mustafa had carefully placed them. She felt sure that as well as seeing his love for her in his eyes, their lips were surely going to touch today for the first time.

However, on reaching the College, it was simply impossible to ignore the sense of foreboding amongst her particular friends and the other girls. Once again she caught snatches of conversation as the girls talked with each other.

"My father said that the English and French landed today in the Gallipoli peninsula," said Angelina, her Greek friend. "But he says that it is quite untrue that Greece has declared war and is joining in the attack on the city."

"I heard that the old Sultan has called for a Jihad, but that Enver is opposing the idea, and a good thing too."

"My father's shop, which is just below our flat in *Bey*oglu was attacked this morning and the windows broken."

This last comment from another Greek girl, was dropped like a stone into the pool of anxious girls, causing an immediate, apprehensive hush. Even at 17, the girls were well aware of the difference between the ritualised violence of army manoevres in remote places and the uncontrolled violence of the mob.

"I must say, however," said the same girl after a pregnant pause, "the Police were there, for once, within minutes and they quickly broke up the small crowd that was forming."

A discordant voice called out from the back -

"You're all disloyal parasites. By God, you're all revelling in the difficulties we're facing. You'd love to have the bloody Greek army at our gates wouldn't you? Then you would treat with them and betray this country which has nurtured you for centuries."

This comment was followed by nods and vocal agreement by one section of the group of girls, and murmurings of dissent by another group. Racial tensions, dormant, and usually well below the surface in this great polyglot city, were clearly rising to the top as the city waited breathlessly for news of the foreign invasion, replicated here in the small world of the College.

Olga looked over to where a much noisier group of boys were shouting at each other. She could not see Selim. There was a fairly significant gender difference at the college. Amongst the boys, in the separate building they occupied, there were a majority of Turkish students, reflecting the fact that liberal Turkish parents were willing to send their sons to the progressive American college; in the girls' building, there were far fewer ethnic Turks, as such liberal attitudes did not extend to their daughters. Accordingly, amongst the girls, there was a higher proportion of Greeks, Armenians and Jews.

The tension in the college grounds was conspicuous. A group of young men called out, taunting the girls, something unheard of in normal times. Olga, was not oblivious to the sense of menace in the air, becoming increasingly nervous and emotional.

The class was already smaller than usual – some of the students had already gone home or been fetched. Olga could only think of the moment she would be in Selim's presence. The interminable hours did at last pass, and then without looking left or right, she hurried through the corridors, into the courtyard and down the stairs leading to the basement room.

Like everyone else that morning, Selim had been caught up in the rumours of a landing by the enemy in or near the Straits. Unlike Olga, he was able compartmentalise his feelings, so was able to concentrate on the political situation, entering wholeheartedly into the debate amongst his classmates. Selim found himself discussing current events almost entirely with his Turkish friends.

"My father said that the Russians had landed at the Black Sea entrance to the Bosporus," said one.

"The Greek army has entered Adrianople, and there has been a terrible massacre of Muslims. The great mosque has been burned down."

"Did you hear that the French have landed at Bursa?"

Selim smiled at the last one – how did the speaker imagine that the French had got through the Dardanelles, when the British had failed so signally a few weeks before. Selim had not forgotten Olga and the coming lunchtime rendezvous, and was well aware of the deeper issues and dangers involved. He was simply gripped by the unfolding drama of the events unfolding around him, as were most of the other young men.

Selim was looking forward to his third short meeting alone with Olga. What neither he nor Olga were aware of, was that their interest in each other had not gone unnoticed by some, at least, of their fellow-students, although nothing had actually been said.

Selim hurried out after class, avoiding any further discussions, which were growing uglier by the minute, as the young men began to mirror, in microcosm, all the worries of the adult world. He raced into the courtyard and down the stairs and called out to Mustapha as he arrived.

Mustapha was a calming influence. He knew that Olga was a *giavour*, but this had made it easier for him to accept Selim's tips, as he expected no better from infidel girls. He salved his conscience, which had indeed given him a few moments guilt, by making sure that he always remained within sight and earshot of the young pair. Selim waited.

"Oh Selim, Selim" cried Olga as she ran into the room.

Selim grasped her hand. Even now, despite all the emotional turmoil, their upbringing and cultures made it impossible for them to clasp one another. It was not simply Mustapha's presence. Both of them were aching for physical contact, but, in its absence, everything had to pass between them through their eyes and their interlocking hands.

"Selim, my soul, what is happening? It's all so awful – some of these girls seem to hate me. Oh Selim, it's so wonderful to see you, but what are we to do – Selim, what are we to do?" For the first time in their short relationship, she was afraid and confused.

"Sit down here Olga, my love – calm yourself, my loved one. The world is certainly turning upside down, but it won't affect us, Olga. Oh! Olga, please don't cry. Who cares what the other girls say – it will all pass – it will all pass. Today the Germans – tomorrow the British – it will pass."

Olga felt her heart bursting with an emotion that she had never felt before. She knew that what she was doing and feeling was not only rash, but also positively dangerous. For the first time in eight weeks she felt the cold touch of fear – not fear for herself – but fear for the love that she felt for this man. Selim did not share her fears. Whether it was the gender difference, or the fact that, as a member of the majority, he had never felt what it was like to be the member of a minority group. Either way, where previously Olga had always been the stronger in their relationship, her fear now gave him more strength.

There was a moment of silence between them as they stood facing each other, but then Olga turned away. She could bear it no longer.

"Selim – we have to part for the moment. I don't know what's going to happen, but oh Selim, I love you – I love you," she cried out for the first time, through tears of joy and fear.

Selim's mouth went dry as he stepped forward. He grasped Olga for a brief, fleeting moment round the waist as she looked up at him. Their lips touched for just a moment – just a touch – then Olga turned and ran up the stairs, as Mustapha coughed loudly in the darkness behind them.

Upstairs in the courtyard, the atmosphere had turned ugly. Rumours of arrests and worse were circulating amongst the students. Something was happening that the two halves of Robert College – the

Mens department and the Girls School – had not witnessed before and the student body was fracturing into its ethnic constituents. Already the place was thinning out – but it was the minority students that had been hurrying home, whilst the young Turkish men and women in their separate groups, stood about discussing the situation loudly and aggressively. The boys, in particular, were all goading each other on into more and more extreme positions. It was into this whirlpool of undirected passions that Olga suddenly emerged from the stairs leading down to Mustapha's basement.

"What were you doing down there, hanum," called out Leila, whose envious personal feelings about Olga and her relationship with the popular Selim, could at last be given free rein, masked behind a political fervour that had suddenly become acceptable. "*Giavour* – why are you still hanging about – don't you know all your infidel friends have gone home ready to welcome our enemies," called out another one of the group of girls milling about in the courtyard, and now pressing forward.

"You and your lot are all parasites waiting for the Empire to fall – you can't wait for the enemy to get here," shrieked Leila, as the other girls spurred her on.

Olga tried to walk away. She had no fear of the young men – though they might jeer, she knew they wouldn't touch her. But the girls were a different matter. For these Turkish girls, Olga was a scheming slut of the worst kind, who had contrived to ensnare one of their own boys. Little had Olga realised that while she had been able to keep her relationship with Selim hidden from her parents, this had not been the case in the closed, gossipy world of the college. Furthermore, they all put the worst and most lurid construction on it.

Olga was a spirited, lively girl, who could stand up for herself in most matters, but the threatening atmosphere in which she now found herself was tipping her into a state of extreme distress. Her lips quivered as she tried to elbow her way through the girls as they taunted her and pushed her about. These girls were only channeling the views of their parents as the war came ever closer to their doors.

No one was going to hurt Olga physically – there were enough level-headed students around to prevent any real violence – so it was unfortunate that Olga finally broke down into tears of frustration and anguish just at the moment Selim appeared in the doorway at the head of the stairs. He couldn't see much – all he took in was the sight of Olga sobbing in the middle of a crowd of girls, most of whom were now pulling back, suddenly appalled at their own behaviour. The sight of the girl in tears had brought most of them back to their senses. But this was not clear to Selim.

"Olga, Olga," shouted Selim and began running toward her without thinking. Several young men, good friends of Selim, grabbed him and held him tight.

"Yok, Yok," they gently chided him, without rancour, but nevertheless holding his struggling form tight to make sure he didn't get himself into real trouble by having a go at the girls.

Olga looked up at his cry, but through her tears saw only that Selim was struggling and being restrained by some of the other young men. She looked round at everyone staring at her, and then with a strangled cry, she turned and ran blindly out of the school gates.

CHAPTER 16

Karekin

That very same morning Karekin had arisen early.

"My soul," he said, as Armineh bustled about behind him, "You must be careful. The town is in a very excited state; rumour is that the Allies were landing somewhere along the coast yesterday."

"Karekin, what does it all mean? Is there going to be a pogrom or killings in the streets?"

"No, no my love, the presence of the German and Austrian legations are probably a guarantee that the government is not going to let the mob get out of hand. But that won't stop individuals bent on violence. It's best to keep a low profile."

"Karekin, my darling, leave me to manage the house and the children – you be careful yourself and try to come back early if you must go to work today. Karekin, are we going to be affected by this?"

"My soul – if the British do break through to Bolis, our whole world will change for ever – of that I have no doubt. Anything could happen and we must be prepared for all eventualities."

"But we've had rumours and crises like this before. Perhaps it's all just idle chatter. We've heard it all before."

"Armineh, my dear, a British landing within 50 miles of Constantinople will happen. It's no secret. Ever since the British Navy failed to break through to the Marmara, there's been no attempt by them to hide the fact that they are preparing for a major invasion."

Breakfast that morning at the Avakians had been as lively as ever, but surprisingly there had been little discussion about the war.

"Sima, my dear," said Armineh – "I think it would be a nice gesture if you called on Yvonne Levonian this morning. Take her a bunch of those lovely spring flowers that have just come out in the orchard. Don't worry, George and his father will be out at work. Your father has plans for a possible merger with Hovannes' business after the war and it would be a nice way of keeping friendly relations between us."

"That's fine, Mama – I'll go straight after breakfast, so I'm back in time to pick up Haik. Honestly, though, I find her switching in and out of French speaking half the time quite wearing. She really is a bit silly! Does anyone want anything by the way, whilst I'm in town?"

"Oh! Olga, are you off?" asked Armineh. "Can't you wait for Sima and go in together?"

"No, I'm sorry, but I really mustn't be late today – we have a test this morning."

"Listen, Mama," Sima interrupted as her mother began to protest, "Olga's right, I have to wait for Haik anyway. Look I'll go and pick some flowers now. Tell Marie to prepare some nice wrapping paper, and then I'll go on to the station after leaving Haik at school. Nerissa can come with us if she doesn't mind waiting a few minutes."

Olga had left the house first, but very soon after, Karekin strode out, immaculate as always, in his grey suit. Nerissa, with her despised school hat in her hand and a smart leather bag, waited for Sima and Haik. Finally Sima was ready to go, clutching a glorious bunch of Spring flowers.

Karekin arrived at his office determined to try to get some business dealt with for once. He felt that he had had enough of political alarms and turmoil, as day after day had passed with excited café talk between his friends and business acquaintances, to the exclusion of almost everything else. News from Van seemed to have disappeared from the papers, and his friends – the Armenian deputies in Parliament – had given no hint of impending trouble. Karekin sighed and considered the good sense of his wife's comments that morning – it was certainly a time for a low profile.

The young men who had been his assistants had departed – one to the army, the other to who knows where; Karekin had had to employ two elderly men, one Jewish, the other a Turk, to do some typing and deal with enquiries in the outer office. Karekin was working at his desk, when there was a knock at his door.

"*Effendi*," said the old clerk "there is a policeman at the door asking to see you."

"Well – show him in, show him in," Karekin rose to his feet. An elderly Turkish gendarme from the local police station, whom Karekin recognised, came diffidently into the office, and bowing respectfully, said-

"*Effendi* – Karekin *bey* – I have been instructed to ask you to come down to the station please, to answer some important questions that have arisen."

"What! Right now?"

"*Effendi* – yes please. I understand the matter is urgent, and my commander has asked me to impress this upon you. It will only take a few minutes. Perhaps you could accompany me."

Karekin was not completely surprised. These summonses were happening more often, and he didn't suspect any ulterior motive. Karekin nodded, and picked up his hat, but left his stick. He gave some instructions to his two clerks, and left the office – the elderly policeman politely making way for him at the door. On the way to the local station, through the busy and crowded streets, the gendarme kept a discreet step or two behind Karekin. Karekin felt the air of restlessness and excitement on the crowded pavements. He raised his hat to the occasional business acquaintance. Everything seemed perfectly normal.

On arrival at the station, the elderly gendarme disappeared. Karekin was asked by the Clerk at the desk to go in, and then conducted into a large bare room at the back of the station. Already seated at the tables, looking puzzled and disconsolate, were a group of about seven other gentlemen, amongst whom he immediately picked out his old friend Doctor Aram Manuelian.

Karekin felt the first little butterfly in his stomach, but went forward smiling.

"Aram, my old friend, whatever are you doing here – and what the blazes is going on?"

"Karekin, I have no idea, and neither have any of the others," said Aram gesturing to the others in the room. "All I can say is that we are all Armenians, but there seems to be no rhyme or reason why we should be here. We now have in this room a doctor, two lawyers, a journalist, and now you, a prominent businessman."

At this, everyone suddenly started talking at once. This chatter continued unabated for some moments, until the door opened again, and the local commissioner ushered three other people into the room.

"Gentlemen, I have to inform you that you are all under arrest," the commissioner stated. Karekin recognised the man who had called regularly at his office, year after year, during the time of the Bairam festival, to extend the compliments of the local Police force, and to collect the charitable contribution that Karekin offered to the local police fund. This announcement was met by a babel of comments, objections and questions from the eight people now in the room. The commissioner raised his hand and called out – again looking no one in the eye,

"I can tell you nothing except to inform you that last night Talaat *Bey*, from the Interior Ministry, ordered the arrest of Armenian leaders suspected of having extreme nationalist sentiments, and of aiding the Allied war effort."

Amidst an ever-increasing tide of objections and cries, he turned and walked out – the gendarmes closing the door behind him, and they heard for the first time the ominous turning of the key.

Karekin sank into one of the chairs and began to reflect, though his thoughts did not get him far, except to increase the creeping unease in his stomach.

As the morning progressed, more and more people were ushered into the room – all as bewildered and annoyed as those already present. There was something particularly odd going on. It wasn't until fairly late in the morning that four of the Armenian Parliamentary deputies were brought in. By then, the room contained around 50 people and was becoming crowded. The group was now made up of scholars, musicians, a large group of lawyers, a couple of doctors and even some clergymen, none of whom, by any stretch of the imagination, could be said to be connected with political events in the city.

This was more than a round-up of what might be termed 'the politicals'. It constituted a microcosm of the prominent men from the whole Armenian community.

By midday, the group had become too large to be accommodated in the hall and they were all led out to the courtyard in the centre of the station. Once in the courtyard, yet more people began arriving. One of these, a certain Doctor Allavertian, was known by Karekin to be a well- known member of the Ittihad party itself. He had raised considerable funds for the CUP, and was supposed to be well in with Enver and Talaat – indeed to be one of their friends.

"Dickran, whatever is going on," asked Karekin, when he had the chance to get to his side.

"Oh God! I don't know, I don't know," wailed the doctor. "I said to the Commissioner when I arrived that I would be grateful if he could ask his questions as soon as possible as I had to get back to my office quickly. But he merely smiled and said 'soon, soon' and left me. I just can't understand it."

"But, Dickran, don't you realise that we are under arrest – this is not a matter of answering a few questions. That was just an excuse – it's much more serious."

"Nonsense, Karekin, and I would ask you not to say these things out loud – bad for morale you know. It's all a mistake – someone is carrying out improperly issued orders. They are being over-zealous. I've asked the Commissioner to send a message to Talaat."

"Dickran, Dickran – what's the matter with you – can't you see what is happening?"

"Oh tush, Karekin, leave me alone. We are at the start of the 20th century for god's sake – this is not the days of some crazed medieval Sultan." With that parting shot he walked away, unwilling to continue a conversation he found distasteful.

Karekin shrugged, but now began thinking of how he could get a message to Armineh to tell her what was happening. He could see the signs of something a lot more sinister than Dr. Allavertian would allow. His friend Aram, though equally at a loss, was also beginning to see a pattern as more and more people were herded into the courtyard. The mood however was still, for the moment, anxious and troubled rather than frightened and panicky. There were even jokes, as people assured each other that somehow, somewhere, the whole thing was a mistake. Several people had been accompanied by sons or servants who had entered, but were then required to leave by the guards now permanently stationed round the walls. Names would be ticked off by the clerk at the door – and those not on his list would be asked to leave. Karekin sidled up to the doorway set in the wall leading back to the main station, and waited for his opportunity as midday passed. There was, by now, less movement in and out of the courtyard, and the numbers of people milling about had already risen to over one hundred and fifty. Suddenly there was a sort of gasp from those standing near the door as, the familiar figure of Father Komitas – the acclaimed musician and moderniser of the Armenian liturgical Mass, was ushered into the courtyard. He was looking as bewildered as everyone else on their arrival.

Accompanying him was a young man – clearly a student and registered at the Harbiye in his cadets uniform – though clearly an Armenian. He was holding the cleric and steadying him as he was obviously distressed and finding it difficult to walk. Karekin recognised that the arrest of this man confirmed his burgeoning suspicions, as Father Komitas could never be described as a political risk. This was a man who had studied in Germany, and whose life and passion was ancient music. What was happening was something totally new and very dangerous.

Karekin edged up to the young man, who had now let go of Komitas, as the clerk ticked his name off the list. Father Komitas moved on into the courtyard to join the other two clerics already there.

"Young man – my name is Karekin Avakian." He then gave the man his address in Makrikoy. "I desperately need to get a message to my wife telling her what has happened. I know it is a lot to ask, but would it be at all possible for you to do this for me." Karekin then felt in his pocket and produced a silver Lira and proffered it as delicately as possible. The young man looked at him and glanced quickly at the clerk, who was still checking his list. He shook his head at the proffered coin, and smiled.

"Sir – it's very tricky in the city at the moment, but I will certainly do my best to try to get to Makrikoy, though to be honest, I have no idea what is going on myself."

"Never mind that – just let them know where I am. I am really most grateful to you."

The young man then went over and kissed the good Father, and turned and walked out, nodding at Karekin as he went past, reiterating with his eyes that he would not forget.

The arrival of Father Komitas, for some reason raised the spirits of the group. Komitas now radiated optimism, claiming like Allavertian that the whole thing had to be an administrative error, and would shortly be sorted out. There was the approaching Allied intervention on the one side, and there were the foreign ambassadors still in Constantinople on the other. Karekin was not so sure, but wisely kept his own counsel. Some of the men were now clearly frightened, depressed and close to tears.

It was in this way that the greater part of Constantinople's prominent Armenian citizens were rounded up during the course of that day. These were not just the politicals , but a whole cross-section of a community, under arrest, not for any specific misdemeanor, but simply because they were Armenian. Gathered in three separate police stations, they numbered almost four hundred men. Meanwhile, an enemy army was approaching scarcely 100 miles away.

CHAPTER 17

Sima

After Olga and Karekin had left the house that morning, Sima and Haik had walked down the hill together as usual, save that they were accompanied on this occasion by Nerissa. Once Sima had left Haik at the school gates, they walked on down to the little station of Cobancesme. Nerissa proposed keeping Sima company while she waited for the next train. No one was waiting on the platform; the station being almost empty. The sun was up in a beautifully clear blue sky. Sima felt good and was glad of the calm presence of Nerissa, as they sat together on the bench.

"Nerissa, this introduction to George Levonian was very confusing. Although I didn't have any feelings for him, shouldn't I be more thrilled by the fact that someone has shown some interest in me as a woman?"

"Sima, my love, you're not 'thrilled' as you say, because, in truth, it was not that sort of interest that was being shown. This was a social occasion only – neither of you had the slightest chance to explore the possibility of deeper feelings."

"Nerissa, my soul, you're really rather wise for your age, where does it come from?" asked Sima, not thinking for a moment that she was being patronising. "What do you think of this way of meeting a husband?"

"I'm not sure how I feel about marriage as a business transaction – making a commitment to live with another person for the rest of your natural life. What a decision! It's frighteningly vital that you get it right isn't it?"

"Yes, Nerissa, but what other way is there? Would we be more successful if we chose ourselves – based on what? It would, I suppose, have to be purely physical attraction. What would that be founded on? Conversations hurriedly held in school or university corridors, rendezvous in crowded coffee houses, unsatisfactory clandestine meetings, perhaps, like those novels you're forever reading. Would that be any better? Mother and Father's marriage seems to be fine enough isn't it, and they had only met once before they married."

Nerissa didn't answer. She thought of Olga and Selim, and wondered whether Sima had any idea of Olga having the sort of relationship to which she was referring. Nerissa thought back to that tea party at Tokatlians.

'Unsatisfactory clandestine meeting' – was that a fair description of that dreamy afternoon, and that look in the eyes of her sister and the young man as they discreetly held hands under the table and stared at each other? This was certainly not, she supposed, anything that Karekin and Armineh had experienced in their younger days   On the other hand, was it a reasonable basis for a life-long marriage? Even she, who was normally so self-possessed and clear in her opinions, felt confused.

The whistle of the local train sounded from down the line, and the girls stood up. Not a word had been said about the war, largely because here on this little suburban station on a glorious spring morning, there appeared to be nothing to disturb the peace – an exquisite moment of calm.

Sima kissed Nerissa, who turned to trudge back towards school, whilst Sima settled down in her corner seat, clutching her bunch of flowers. She sat back to enjoy the short journey to the city.

The moment Sima arrived at Sirkeci station, however, the whole atmosphere of the day changed for her. Despite this, there was an unusual undercurrent, which the more sensitive Nerissa would have noticed at once. Clutching her flowers, Sima threaded her way alongside the trams to the Galata bridge, down the steps to the quays, stepping on to the right ferry. The ferry departed, chugging up the Bosporus, swinging from the European shore to the Asian and back again. The ferry station for Bebek, the home of the Levonians, was not far down the straits. Soon Sima stepped out onto the landing stage, and made her way up to the Levonian house. She had been given clear directions how to get there, and on such a lovely morning, there was no need for a carriage.

On arrival, Sima was shown into an ornate, baroque sitting room with imitation gold-legged Louis Quinze chairs, where Yvonne Levonian was regally ensconsed. Yvonne graciously accepted the simple spring flowers, which suddenly looked a bit bedraggled next to the great blossoms of hothouse concoctions gracing every corner of the room.

"*Enchanté, ma cherie,*" said Yvonne. "*Assayez-vous, s'il vous plait.*" The '*tu*' originally utilised by Yvonne in Makrikoy, suddenly becoming 'vous' here in sophisticated Bebek, thought Sima. After some banal exchanges of compliments in French, Sima changed to Armenian and launched into a description of the unusual atmosphere in the city. Yvonne was not unsympathetic. Even to her shallow mind, centred, as it was, round her house and her social pretensions, there had come a realisation that the crisis was of a more serious nature than she had thought. The decision, by Hovannes, to keep Tamara at home that morning, had come as a greater surprise to her than all the newspaper reports, which had mostly gone in one ear and out the other.

Once Yvonne ceased speaking in formal French, conversation with her was not too difficult. Sima only needed to sit back and let her prattle on about the many friends and recent social occasions she had attended, expressing some surprise that Sima had never been present.

It was in the middle of this, the unusual sound of a telephone came through the open door. The Levonians, like several households in Bebek, possessed a private telephone. There were still none in Makrikoy. Within a few moments, young Tamara came in, looking prettier and more natural – Sima thought – than when she had visited them at Makrikoy.

"Mama, that was father. He and George are coming home right away. There's a lot of trouble in town. He says that there's nothing to worry about, but it appears there have been a few arrests, and there is a mob throwing stones and getting excited in the Grande Rue de Pera. Tokatlians' windows have been broken. He says that we must put up the shutters. He'll be back soon."

"*Mais c'est affreux – qu'est que se passe?*" wailed Yvonne, reverting to her execrable French. "Why the panic? Tokatlian's windows get broken regularly don't they. I wonder they ever bother to repair them…Oh my dear, don't go."

But Sima, recognising a crisis, jumped up, assured Yvonne that she would be quite all right, kissed Tamara on the cheek, and hurried out walking briskly down to the Bebek landing stage.

Here, all still seemed to be as it was in the morning. As always, there was hardly a moment before the next boat pulled alongside. Everyone waiting pressed onto the ferry, which, so close to the terminus, had no seats left. Sima stood watching as the ferry weaved near the battleships in the harbour, crossed once to Asia and recrossed, before approaching the bridge.

Once here, however, all had changed. Sima looked at the bridge above. This was filled with a large mob of excited and gesticulating men, milling about and totally blocking the road. The jetties below the bridge were also full of people, as the crowds already on the bridge made it impossible for the passengers coming off the ferries to get up the stairs. Several ferries, unable to dock, were milling about, unable to get in to discharge their own passengers. In all the shouting and excitement, Sima could not hear what the mob was yelling.

Suddenly, in the midst of all the noise, there came the unmistakable, loud foghorn blast of one of the two great battleships in the Straits. Like almost everyone else, Sima turned, and saw the *Goeben* and the *Breslau* belching out great spurts of smoke from their funnels. Even as she looked, the majestic *Goeben* began to slowly move forward turning heavily on its axis, until it had completed an 180 degree turn. The battleships began steaming south towards the sea of Marmara and the Dardanelles. It was a majestic sight, and Sima was rivetted by its metallic grandeur. However the whole manoevre had taken well over half an hour, and meanwhile here she was still stuck on the ferry-boat, admittedly with hundreds of others in the same predicament.

As Sima stood waiting for someone to do something, she suddenly realised she was not going to be able to get back to pick up Haik from school. Whilst she felt a bit guilty that she had not thought of this before, there was nothing she could do about it. After all, nothing had happened in the days since Karekin had first insisted on Haik being picked up from school, and surely he would make his own way home, once he realised that she was not coming.

By now, it had become clear that the demonstration involved a Turkish gutter mob. They were yelling the usual stuff about *giavour*s, Greek pigs, Armenian parasites and Jewish scum. Sima did not feel any personal fear. Quite apart from the fact that the passions were not at this stage directed against individuals, she felt secure in her experience that a woman, whatever her race or religion, if dressed discreetly and demurely, would not be touched in the Ottoman Empire. Meanwhile, time was getting on, and here she was still stuck on the ferry trying to get onto the bridge.

It was less than an hour before the arrival, at last, of police reinforcements. Then with yells, whistles and a bit of pushing and shoving, the mob began to thin out. All the people still on the wharves were able to climb up the stairs and go on their way, whilst those ferries which had been waiting, were able to move in and discharge their passengers.

Sima began to make her way back up to the station. A train was already waiting. She climbed in and sat down thankfully, having been on her feet in the boat now for almost two hours. Her mind turned back to Makrikoy, and she hoped that Haik had already reached home. Arriving at Cobancesme station, she crossed over the footbridge, and was just coming out of the ticket hall into the dusty entrance to the station, when she saw a very flustered looking Armineh alighting from a gharry. Armineh came hurrying up to Sima who was standing, mouth agape, wondering what was going on.

CHAPTER 18

Vahan in Makrikoy

This same morning of the 24th April, Vahan was due to go to his weekly singing classes with Father Komitas. Father Komitas gave music lessons not only in the Armenian church liturgy which he had already done so much to modernise, but, also, much to the disgust of the traditionalist clergy, in secular classical music. These lessons were a collective affair of at least twelve pupils.

That morning Vahan had received a letter from Caesaria from his mother, Mariam, which had jolted him out of his carefree student life. He was aware of the tensions in the city and the rumours of the allied landings due to take place on the Gallipoli peninsula, however, he had not been following the growing concerns of the Armenian community about the events in Van, and the implacable movement by the Ittihad government towards a 'final solution' in the Armenian highlands. Life was really too good and too exciting for him to allow external political events to effect his current way of life. So it was that he read the letter from his mother with ever-increasing dismay and incomprehension.

"My dear son,
May God bless you, and may you walk with Christ beside you all the days of your life. I kiss your brow and pray for you every day. God be praised, we are now all well, but I must inform you of the shock which we suffered recently. A week ago a police officer came to our house asking to see your father. We knew the policeman, who had come to our house on previous festival occasions collecting for the station, so had no hesitation in summoning your father. Garabed came down

and the policeman simply addressed him in the usual way -

'Garabed effendi, the Chief Commissioner of Police has asked me to request you to accompany me to the station to ask you some questions.'

This Commissioner was a man who had eaten at our house. Your father, went with him straightaway.

Before you were born, we had trouble under the old Hamidian regime, and it was known then that your father's house was a refuge which would have been stoutly defended with firearms if attacked by the mobs. It seems that the authorities had not forgotten this in all these years. For some reason they are now looking for any firearms that the Armenian population might still have.

But, my boy, there were no firearms left in the house at all. Garabed had handed all of them in at the start of the war, when the order was first given that all firearms were to be brought to the police station.

I am sorry to have to tell you that your respected father was roughly inter-rogated, and was beaten throughout the day. It seems they did not believe his assurances that there were no more guns in the house. They hit the soles of his feet repeatedly with an iron bar, and kicked his face with their boots. I must say, my son, I had heard of such things being done at the police station to rogues and thieves, but I never thought it could happen to us.

Your father was returned early in the evening, like a piece of baggage hang-ing over the back of a donkey, an animal that belonged to a local Turkish carpen-ter who knew your father and happened to be passing when father was dumped outside the police station. My darling boy, I worked for almost a week to restore his ravaged face and to get his swollen feet well enough to walk on. You wouldn't believe the state he was in when he was returned. I had a hard time calming your brother down. But you know your father, he is getting better fast and has become impatient already to get back to work. I suspect he will go back tomorrow regard-less of what I say. I have found the time to write to you. Father ordered me very strictly that I was not to worry you about what has happened, so please don't write to him about any of this, but both I and Raffi thought you should know.

I pray to God to keep you safe and in good health, my child. Your loving mother."

Vahan felt a surge of anger. He knew that this outrage must clearly have been carried out by men who had come to his father's house many times on official business. Hospitality had always been offered to them. But he had been told in an earlier letter that the old Ottoman Com-missioner of Police had been replaced by another of those hard-faced nationalists of the Ittihad party some months ago, who were no doubt carrying out orders emanating from Constantinople.

He wondered how his emotionally volatile younger brother Raffi was coping with the clearly deteriorating situation in the interior. For the first time he felt the political situation affecting him personally. However, with the thought that there was nothing he could do about it for the moment, he put on his Harbiye uniform, and walked to the house of Father Komitas where the classes were due to take place.

On his arrival at the house, he found a scene of some turmoil and confusion. Most of the other students had already arrived and were milling about in the small hall at the foot of the stairs. Sitting in an upright seat by the front door, looking a little uncomfortable, was an elderly police officer. Father Komitas himself was standing on the bottom stair expostulating with one of the students, Kegham.

"What's going on?" Vahan asked one of the other young men.

"This police chap has just arrived and asked the Reverend Father to accompany him to the police station to answer a few questions. You know how jumpy everybody is these days. He says that they'll only need him for about five minutes. But you know Kegham; he has got excited and is telling the good Father not to go."

"Hi, Vahan, we need your good sense. Tell Kegham to calm down," called out another of the students.

Vahan suddenly thought of his mother's letter that morning, and felt a surge of fear. To everyone's astonishment he remarked: "I agree with Kegham. There's no need to go. They can either talk to him here, or issue a proper official request for him to attend at the station."

This prompted another uproar, which was only dealt with when Father Komitas himself, already dressed in his long black clerical gown, raised his hand.

"My children, I am going with this officer. We don't need any trouble. I am not going to change my habits of a lifetime now. Vahan, my son, if the authorities want to ask me some questions why shouldn't I go and help them – I have nothing to hide."

Kegham, still holding on to the Father's black sleeves, spoke urgently.

"Don't go, don't go. At least if you do, let me come with you."

This was met by a chorus of approval from all the waiting students.

Father Komitas looked round. It was the good Father's own inclination to accompany the policeman to answer whatever questions might be put to him. To calm everyone down he agreed to take one of them with him.

"Very well, Vahan if you don't mind, I would be happy if you would accompany me with this officer," indicating the unhappy police officer who now rose from his seat. "Gentlemen," he turned and smiled at everyone, "although he said only five minutes, we all know how long these formalities can take, so I am afraid this morning's class must be abandoned. Come Vahan, let's go."

Then, smiling all round at his pupils, and gesticulating at the gendarme to go ahead, he walked out, with Vahan trailing alongside. Vahan had called out in support of Kegham largely as a result of his mother's letter, but he had no real anxiety for Father Komitas. What might happen in provincial Caesaria surely could not happen in sophisticated Constantinople. However, he felt honoured that Father Komitas had chosen him, out of all the others, to accompany him.

Once at the station, everything began to turn into the surreal Kafkaesque nightmare which had already overwhelmed Karekin Avakian. Vahan stood by the side of Father Komitas, both of them becoming more bewildered. Komitas was a man who could not cope with harsh words or treatment, so when the desk Sergeant brusquely ordered them to go through to the courtyard, without answering any questions and without the usual politeness, the Father's steps faltered. Vahan linked his arm with the priest's and supported him through to the courtyard at the back of the station. Here, as they arrived, Vahan gave the Father's name to the clerk at the door.

Vahan heard a gasp from those nearest the door as he and Komitas walked in and the priest was recognised. There appeared to be a crowd of a hundred or more men – all Armenian - milling about in the courtyard. Vahan recognised one or two, such as the well-known parliamentary deputies. As it happened by then there were some clergymen there also, and Father Komitas walked across to them and began conversing earnestly. Vahan stood at the door uncertain what to do next, when he was approached by a tall distinguished-looking gentleman in a grey suit who introduced himself as Karekin Avakian.

"I know that you don't know me and I'm sorry to have to request a favour from you, but as you can see I can do nothing here myself. I must get a message through to my wife as to what has happened. It is a lot to ask, but could you possibly get the information to her."

At this point he fumbled in his pockets, and muttering something about expenses, produced a coin. Vahan, still with his eyes on Father Komitas, shook his head declining the tentatively offered coin.

"Sir, I will of course do my best. I will certainly get a message to your family one way or another. Could you give me your address."

Karekin was ready and gave him a card showing his private address. Vahan took this and said again that he would do his best. He then strode forward, embraced Komitas warmly and left the courtyard.

Vahan was not insensitive, but Makrikoy was a fair distance away, and it was not certain that he would have gone himself, though he would always have at least sent a messenger. As it was, with nothing much else to do now that the class had been cancelled, he wandered down towards the bridge, deciding as he went through the narrow streets to go to the station and take the next train himself. The tense atmosphere in the city was pressing on his nerves, and the thought of a stroll in the leafy suburbs of Makrikoy had its attractions. The rounding up of over a hundred prominent Armenians in that police station courtyard had still not quite penetrated his thoughts.

When he got to the bottom of the Pera hill, he saw that quite a crowd was gathered on both the bridge and on either side. This consisted of the usual riff-raff yelling about *giavours* although Vahan was surprised that the emphasis seemed to be particularly against Armenians on this occasion. "Shoot them all" rang out the cry from the crowd and although Vahan did not fully realise it at the time, it was clear that news of the arrests was beginning to seep out.

The crowds were not too dense as the first police reinforcements had just arrived. Vahan slipped through and walked up to the Sirkeci station. He noticed that some ferries were milling about below the bridge trying to discharge their passengers, who were only just beginning to trickle up the stairs from the jetties.

Vahan had been to Makrikoy before, to the racecourse, but he had no idea where the address given to him by Mr. Avakian was. Accordingly, when he got to the little station he felt it essential to get a gharry, and a carriage was in fact waiting in the dusty station courtyard when he arrived. He gave the driver the address, and the old man replied: -

"Ah yes, the Avakian house," and named his price for the round trip. Vahan climbed in and they trotted up past the fields bordering the Vali *Effendi* racecourse.

Vahan breathed in deeply, enjoying the green fields and the fresh air, and even the horsey smell of the carriage. They soon passed the fields and almost immediately stopped outside a substantial house, having the usual blank wall with few windows looking onto the street. Not expecting to be more than a few minutes, Vahan told the driver to wait and knocked at the door.

Meanwhile the fleeing Olga had caught one of the last trams to get across the Galata Bridge before the crowds gathered blocking the bridge. She, of course, noticed nothing through her tears. She had stopped running almost immediately after leaving the college – girls did not run through the streets of Constantinople, however upset. She kept shaking her head, trying to clear the fears and impressions running though her mind. She was oblivious to all the tension in the streets; everything centred round her own feelings. She walked on automatically.

As she sat in the tram, and later on in the train, she became more and more distressed. She had no idea that the young men forcibly restraining Selim were his friends, anxious that he should not get himself into trouble by lifting a hand against any of the girls tormenting the unhappy Olga. It seemed to Olga as if he was being attacked because of his friendship with her. Furthermore, although she had been blithely carrying on over the past eight weeks without a thought for the possible consequences, at a subliminal level she knew that at the very least she had been deceiving her parents. Her supreme self-confidence had for the first time been shattered, and she now swung to the opposite extreme of despair, and a feeling that she was being punished for the relationship.

The fraught political atmosphere in the city, and the inevitable fears for the future that now lay in the hearts of most residents as a result of the arrival of an invading army, was totally banished from her thoughts. She could only see everything in terms of Selim and herself, and of their love for each other.

So, on her arrival at the Cobancesme station, seeing that no gharry was currently waiting outside the station, she immediately made the decision to walk home. She knew she would not have the patience to wait for one of the carriages to turn up. She crossed the lines and began hurrying up the hill a little further on from the racecourse to get home as fast as possible. She was not exactly running, but was walking very fast, and in her distress she found she could not stop crying.

When in her anxious emotional state the distinctive yellow silk scarf she often wore slipped off her shoulders, she never noticed the loss. If she had only turned round at that point, she might have seen the two rough looking louts, who had been trailing behind her all the way from the station, pick up the scarf where it had fallen on the road. She might then have turned back and retrieved it from them. But that last heart-rending cry of "Olga" as she ran away - was churning around in her head, driving everything else from her mind. So it was that a chain of events began with the mere dropping of a yellow scarf.

She tried to collect herself when she reached the door of the house. She pulled the bell knob and wondered suddenly and with more rising feelings of panic what she was going to say to her mother. She need not have worried. Instead of Marie at the door or one of the kitchen maids, there stood Armineh. Armineh knew at once, within a second, what this tear-stained girl standing fearfully at the door needed. Armineh simply and instinctively opened her arms wide and with a great heaving sob Olga threw herself into those arms in a way which she hadn't done for years.

"Oh mother, mother," cried Olga as she was quickly drawn into the house and then into the sitting-room. Marie who had heard the sobs came out and closed the front door, and the door to the sitting-room, leaving mother and daughter alone. At last Olga began pouring it all out - her love for a young fellow-student at the College, the meeting at Tokatlian's with Nerissa present, the taunts and threats this morning and finally a somewhat exaggerated version of the young man in question being attacked by the other boys.

Armineh, continuing to hold Olga tight as they sat together on the sofa, was more and more confused. The name 'Selim' had not as yet been mentioned, and so, seeing little to worry about, she remained fairly calm. In any event it was clear to her that for the moment she did not need to say anything, but only continued to stroke Olga's beautiful hair, as she sank down with her head in Armineh's capacious lap. Armineh was thinking hard, but she had still not cottoned on to the real problem.

As nothing but encouragement seemed to be coming from her mother, Olga began feeling better and better, as her rambling discourse went on. After about fifteen minutes of this, the front door bell rang again. The door was opened and the welcome tones of Nerissa rang out from the hall -

"Mama, Mama, I'm home."

The sitting-room door opened, and Nerissa walked in, throwing her school hat onto the chair in the Hall.

"Mama, we've been let out early, as there is trouble and demonstrations in the city, and even here. Oh! Olga! What are you doing home?"

"Nerissa, come and sit down," said Armineh, as Olga finally lifted herself and sat up, dabbing at her eyes with the lace handkerchief always kept up her sleeve. In true Olga fashion she had already convinced herself that all was now well, and that her problem had somehow miraculously disappeared.

"Oh, Nerissa - come and give me a kiss," she gestured gaily and sat upright. "I've been telling mother about the tea-party we went to at Tokatlian's, and all about my feelings. She's been so understanding. It's been an enormous relief to get it all off my chest."

Nerissa stood totally amazed. She loved her sister and had a great faith in her mother, and it simply did not cross her mind that there might be any misunderstanding between mother and daughter. She rushed forward, hugged the two of them, now sitting up next to each other.

"You mean Mama now knows all about you and Selim? Oh I'm so glad my darlings."

The confusion in Armineh's mind suddenly and sharply cleared with a snap.

"Selim. Selim. What's this about Selim?"

At exactly the same instant, both Olga and Nerissa realised that Armineh had had no idea that Olga had been talking about a young Turkish boy, and not some Greek or Armenian Romeo. There was a dreadful silence. Then Olga jumped up and ran out of the room upstairs to her bedroom.

Nerissa was about to follow her, when Armineh, in a voice Nerissa had rarely heard, ordered her to sit down.

"Now, Nerissa, I want no lies or half-truths, no attempts to hide anything. I want the whole story. Who is this young man for whom Olga appears to have lost both her heart and her head?""

"Oh mother, honestly, I don't really know too much, believe me. All I know about him is that he studies at Robert College, and is the son of a doctor, who I think is employed at the German Hospital. I did go to tea with them at Tokatlian's a few days ago you remember - to be a companion for Olga, and he seemed a nice boy. But oh! Mama, you should have seen them - they are truly in love"

"Love - tush!" snorted Armineh, as she began to contemplate with some trepidation the awful and tricky explanations with which she was going to have to cope, when Karekin got back in the evening. "What do they know about love - the ninnies. How old is this boy, Nerissa?"

"I think he's about nineteen - certainly not more than twenty. Oh, mother, what is Baba going to say."

"Your father is not going to say anything, as he is not going to know about it for the moment. He has enough problems on his mind without having to worry about his daughter's stupidity. Nerissa, my dear, can't you see the impossibility of the situation. I'm really surprised at you. Haven't you thought for a moment how unhappy this is going to make your sister sooner or later. This whole nonsense would have been out of the question even during normal times, but now with all this tension it's ... Nerissa really!"

"Oh! Mother, of course I saw the problem even before I met the young man. But, Mama, how could I have put it to Olga. You know she still thinks of me as a little girl. Then when I first met him I could say nothing. Mama you haven't seen them together. It's something beautiful, but you wouldn't be able to see it I suppose."

Armineh sighed, and looked sadly at Nerissa, who blushed deeply. It suddenly struck Armineh that she had not spoken in any serious and meaningful way to Nerissa for a long time, and that this had been her own fault. However, she mentally braced herself. She now had to face up to a showdown with Olga. However, it was better by far to deal with it here and now before Karekin got home and matters inevitably became more complicated.

She went to the bottom of the stairs and called up loudly and firmly, trying to keep any anxiety or anger out of her voice :-

"Olga, my daughter, you must come down, and you must come down now. You know we have to talk."

The door to Olga's room opened, and she came down the stairs, pale and anxious, but with all evidence of the tears washed away, her hair brushed, and with two high spots of colour on her cheeks. Nerissa came out of the sitting-room, unsure whether her mother wanted her to stay or not. Armineh's calm nearly wavered when she saw the stubborn determination on Olga's face. Armineh's own emotions were now in turmoil.

"Olga, my love, it is vital that there are no lies or any hidden agenda between us now. Please tell me again what you ..."

Just then, there was a knocking at the front door, clearly a stranger who as so often happened hadn't seen the bell knob. All three glanced at the little window by the door which looked out at the street, and saw outside old Abdul sitting in his gharry, obviously waiting for whoever was knocking.

Nerissa hurried forward to open the door. Standing somewhat anxiously in the door, dressed in the uniform of the Harbiye military college, with his cap in his hand, stood the young man who had smiled at her in Tokatlian's - could it only be a few short days ago. A moment of silence stretched out as the three women stared at the stranger, and he with a shy smile looked back.

"I am very sorry to disturb you like this, unannounced. My name is Vahan Asadourian. I have come on behalf of Mister Karekin Avakian - I trust that I am at the house of the Avakians."

Vahan continued to stand at the door. He had not recognised Nerissa, the eye contact at Tokatlian's had been so fleeting, and it had not been such a memorable afternoon for him as it had been for her. Armineh, whose mind had been entirely on the problem posed by Olga's infatuation, turned sharply at the mention of Karekin's name and came forward.

"What are you thinking about Nerissa, standing there staring like a silly goose. Come in, my boy, come in. Yes, we are indeed the Avakians. This young lady staring is my daughter Nerissa, and my daughter Olga." She waved back vaguely towards Olga still standing on the stairs.

Vahan came into the hall, and wondered where to start. Largely as a result of his mother's letter which he had received earlier that morning, he was aware, more than many others that day, of the increasingly dangerous situation.

"Madame Avakian, I am afraid I have some bad news."

"Oh my God, my God - Karekin - his heart."

"No, no," said Vahan quickly. "He's in good health so far as I could see. However, I am sorry to have to tell you that he has been arrested this morning, and he's currently in the main prison in *Bey*oglu."

"Arrested!", all three women burst out together.

"Yes. I don't know the circumstances in which he was taken. I myself had gone this morning to Father Komitas for one of his group music lessons. When I arrived, I found that he had been invited to go down to the police station to answer some questions. I went down with him, and when we arrived we found that there were about a hundred Armenian gentlemen there all in the same predicament, all under arrest without any idea why. Whilst there, I was approached by your husband, Madame, who asked me to do him the favour of coming to tell you what had happened. He gave me this address."

"Oh my God - why? What's it all about? You said there were others there – do you know who they were?" Armineh spoke disjointedly as she tried to grasp what was being reported to her.

Vahan felt distressed that he was unable to give any real comfort or hard information to these three women. "I can tell you nothing for sure, Madame, but my opinion is that it's political. I saw two of the deputies there, and the rest also appeared to me to be men of some importance in the community. There was, unquestionably an official list, from which names were being ticked off."

"I must go to him - I must go at once," Armineh's practical mind already beginning to plan what she was going to do.

"Madame, I must warn you that there is a lot of tension in the City. It isn't entirely clear at the moment whether the British have landed or not, or indeed whether there's been any Greek or Russian involvement. The streets are full, and there are the usual mindless mobs milling about and shouting anti-Greek and anti-Armenian slogans."

"Thank you, young man. Olga, I suggest you go up and have a rest, you look all done in. Nerissa, this gentleman - Mr. Asadourian isn't it? - has come all the way from the city to give us this news; the least you can do is to close your mouth - it's been wide open now for at least a whole minute. Please arrange for a coffee and some refreshment to be served to him at once."

Vahan began demurring, but Nerissa had already hurried out to the kitchen. Armineh meanwhile grabbed her coat, stuck a sensible hat on her head, and said to Vahan -

"Mr. Asadourian, I wonder if I could call on you for one more favour to the Avakian family. May I take your carriage outside to go now to the station."

"Madame, of course. Indeed I'd have walked up anyway if I had known the way. Please take it - I'll go and tell the driver."

"No need, no need. It's old Abdul, I'll deal with it. Mr. Asadourian I don't know how to thank you for all the trouble you have taken. I hope we will meet again in happier circumstances, but meanwhile do please sit down - please".

Armineh bustled out of the front door with her mind now cleared of everything beside the situation facing her husband. She stuck a pin firmly into her hat, as she clambered into the gharry. Abdul immediately roused the dozing horse and started trotting down to the station.

CHAPTER 19

Armineh and Sima

As Armineh settled back in the carriage, she started calmly working out what to do. There was a ritual for this sort of emergency, which womenfolk through the ages had learned to cope with. She checked in her bag to make sure that she had the key to Karekin's office safe, his official papers, her own nufus, and a roll of low denomination currency notes. The road, as always at midday, was deserted save for two rough looking youths chewing stalks as they lounged on the grass on the other side of the fence.

On arrival at the station, she clambered out, handing Abdul some money.

"Madame Avakian hanum," Abdul waved aside the coins. "I have already been paid by the young gentleman for the round trip."

This was honesty of the old school and Armineh did not want to insult him by pressing him to take the coins. As she hurried into the station, she suddenly saw Sima coming out – obviously returning from her trip to the Levonians. Armineh had lost all sense of time, and it didn't register how late Sima was in getting back, nor the thought that she hadn't been in time to pick up Haik. She made up her mind immediately.

"Sima, my darling, well met. Father has been arrested. I don't know why exactly, but I am going to find him. Can you come with me – two heads are better than one in these circumstances?"

Sima turned back without a word, assuming that by now Haik had already returned home, and went with her mother to get the train back into the city. On the way, Armineh explained as much as she could of the circumstances, becoming ever more fearful as she did so.

On their arrival in the city, they went first to the office, where the old clerk recently taken on by Karekin was still sitting at his desk. Armineh hurried in, as the clerk rose and bowed to the wife of his employer. Armineh didn't mean to be rude, but her mind was now racing ahead of her body. She hurried into Karekin's back office, indicating to Sima to shut the door. Opening the safe, she extracted the little velvet bag of gold coins kept there for emergencies, ignoring everything else. She counted out the coins, amounting to around forty, and popped the bag into her own handbag.

Then, they hurried out, nodding again to the clerk, but making sure not to enter into any conversation with him. Their first object was the main *Beyoglu* police station. The police station was totally quiet, and for a moment Armineh wondered if she had come to the wrong place.

"I would like to see my husband – Karekin Avakian – who was detained here earlier this morning," she said to the desk sergeant. The officer rummaged about with some papers on his desk.

"Dear ladies, we no longer have any detainees at this station. More than one hundred men were arrested this morning from this area. About half have been sent to the Yedikule Police station, which has a large gaol, and from where, so I understand, they'll eventually be going to the Sarayburnu boat station to be deported to the interior. The other larger group has gone direct to Haydar Pasha station, where they will be boarding a train this very evening for the interior."

"But why – what's the charge?" asked Armineh.

"Madam, I don't know but I suppose wartime espionage may cover it. Either way they are destined for internal exile. Now, ladies I must ask you to leave. I cannot help you further, as I have no record as to who went where."

Armineh and Sima walked out and stood on the pavement uncertain what to do next. Sima found herself unable to think clearly. The effect on Armineh, however, was just the opposite – whilst obviously on edge, she was now thinking very clearly.

"Sima, my dear, we have to assume what the policeman said was accurate – his words are all we have to go on. Those who were sent to the Yedikule local prison are going to spend the night there before going on to Sarayburnu – but those sent direct to Haydar Pasha may be leaving tonight. It's no use trying to find out who was sent where. We must be off to Haydar Pasha now, and see if Karekin is in that group – we can always try Yedikule later if he's not there."

Taking the tunel back down to the Galata bridge, they had no difficulty boarding a ferry to Haydar Pasha station. Sima sat with silent tears running down her cheeks – not just of sorrow but from physical and emotional exhaustion. Armineh just stared ahead, with pursed lips, trying to work out what she was going to do when they arrived.

On their arrival they saw that the station was brightly lit and full of soldiers and policemen. A flight of white marble steps swept up from the open area between the ferry station and the grand façade of the railway station. The main entrance was blocked off and no civilians were being allowed in without showing valid tickets for trains departing that evening. Armineh thought fast. She turned on her heel, and went quickly to a ticket booth round the corner outside the station itself and asked for two single tickets to Eskishehir. She cheerfully paid for first class, as she realised that for her and Sima to produce cheaper class tickets on this line would undoubtedly look suspicious.

Back at the front entrance, she and Sima worked their way to the front of the queue waiting to get into the station. After a careful scrutiny of their papers, and tickets, they were let in to the main hall. Here, there were no crowds milling about. In their place were large numbers of fully armed soldiers standing guard. Over in the far corner of the hall, outside the station restaurant, was a particularly large group preventing entry. Inside the restaurant, a group of respectable looking gentlemen could be seen through the windows behind the pillars standing or sitting at the tables. Armineh, holding Sima firmly by the arm, manoevred herself closer, but she could not see Karekin through the windows.

Clearly, getting inside the restaurant just by asking was going to be quite impossible. The last scheduled train of the whole day was due to leave in about an hour, and Armineh reckoned that once this train left, the station would be cleared of everyone. She turned and facing away from the guards, she whispered to the white-faced Sima.

"My darllng, take this bag of coins and slip it into your bag, then move across a little and stand with me near to that young officer over there. You must be brave, and pretend to faint or feel the heat or something. Just close your eyes, drop down and let me do the talking. If you get inside, try to see your father, and if you do, give him the bag. Just do your best. If you find out he is there, but you can't get to him, give it to anyone to pass on to him."

Sima, whose heart was bursting with anxiety for her father and a deep fear, did as Armineh had directed. They stood for a moment together, then Sima gave a strangled cry, closed her eyes and fainted into her mother's arms. It required scarcely any acting on her part.

It worked. The young officer came forward "What's the matter, Madam?"

"Oh, officer, we are waiting for the next train. There's nowhere to sit, and my daughter here is not well. Can she go in and have a glass of water and sit down just for a few minutes. I'll stay out here," she added as she saw him hesitate. Sima opened her eyes and began to try to struggle up, as Armineh produced her tickets.

"Perhaps this soldier can go in with her," she indicated the young soldier who had come up with the officer – "I'm sure he can make certain all will be well, and he can escort her back here."

Saying this, she produced two notes – both generous, but carefully graded in her mind. The officer had already half made up his mind to let them in, and he took the notes, pocketing the bigger one, and giving the smaller to the young soldier standing alongside. Sima, now recovered, but still looking very white, was permitted to lean on the soldier, and the two of them walked through the glass doors and into the *fin-de-siecle* dining room.

Inside, amongst the dark mahogany tables, potted plants and dusty chandeliers, the cream of the Armenian community of the city was standing or sitting in varying attitudes, from boredom to near panic. Sima and the soldier went to get a glass of water from the bar, which was doing a roaring trade. Sima's eyes roamed round the room anxiously, as the young soldier sat her at a table near the door – the occupants hastily being waved away. Sima was the only female in the room, and she had no idea what to do next.

As it happened, Doctor Manuelian was wandering about and was the first to spot her. He had the sense not to call out, but immediately went to fetch Karekin. Sitting in the far corner he had not seen Sima's arrival. Aram warned Karekin that Sima was here, but that she was accompanied by a soldier, and that it was clear that she was here under false pretences.

Karekin strolled over, and then saw her, sitting white-faced, and with a tearful expression. His heart turned over at the thought of his daughter in such surroundings, and he had to make a real effort not to run across and comfort her, as she was clearly distressed and close to tears.

They sauntered over, planning how they would tackle the situation. Aram came first, making clear with his eyes to Sima that she should not show any sign of recognition. He ordered up two 'rakis', and offered one to the soldier, with whom he began an animated discussion about a recent wrestling match which, against all the odds, had gone against the favourite. Karekin moved and stood behind Sima's chair, touching the back of her hair with his chest, but making no other sign. Sima whispered to him -

"Oh Baba – we've only got a minute or two. I am dropping this little bag under the chair. It has gold coins in it for you – you are going to need them. Oh baba, baba, what is going to happen."

"My soul, it's in the lap of the gods – I don't know. Tell everyone that I love them all, and don't weep my love, don't weep."

"Baba, mother is outside. When I leave, go to the window so she can see you; but don't wave, don't make any sign. We are supposed to be travellers on our way to Eskishehir on the next train."

Even in that dire and critical moment, Karekin grinned to himself at the thought of Armineh's deception. Having finished the glass of raki, the young soldier bestirred himself and got up, asking Sima if she was feeling better. Sima, through the tears she could barely restrain, smiled at him and said she was. She then rose and walked out through the glass doors with the young soldier behind, but not before seeing out of the corner of her eye, her father bending down and picking up the little velvet bag.

For twenty minutes Armineh stood *bey*ond the line of soldiers as if waiting for the next train, glancing every few minutes at the figure of Karekin in the window. For his part, Karekin stood there staring at her fixedly without moving. She and Sima had to leave before the last train was called, to avoid any suspicions. Armineh took one last look at the man she had married, knowing that it was most unlikely that she would ever see him again. He raised one arm, and held it palm forward by his ear in salutation, as she and Sima turned to make their way out of the station to return home.

CHAPTER 20

Raffi, and the arrest of Garabed

The same scenario was unfolding throughout the Empire on that morning of the 24th April and Caesaria was no exception.

Raffi had been deeply shocked at the sight of his father when he had been brought home on the back of the carpenter's donkey from the Police station, two weeks before. It was not just the trauma of seeing his father's condition, there was a feeling of shame and fear at the thought that this figure of authority, whom he had looked up to all his life, was as vulnerable as he was himself. On Garabed's return, Raffi had had the presence of mind to find and throw away the old Mauser pistol left over from the 1895 troubles.

Garabed had recovered remarkably quickly from the beatings and had been going back into work for the last few days, despite all the efforts of his wife to dissuade him.

Apart from the extraordinary violence meted out to Garabed, there had been no other open attacks on the Armenian minority in the town. By the 24th April the siege of Van had been going on for almost two weeks, together with the slow advance of the Imperial Russian army towards that town. Neither had provoked street violence or demonstrations. As the Ottomans had been fighting the Russians in the remote mountains of Eastern Anatolia for centuries, the current Ittihad leaders looked on that front with some equanimity. It was the arrival of a Western army within striking distance of their ancient capital, which triggered the paranoia, and led to the terrible events of the next few months.

On this morning, bright and sunny everywhere in the Empire, except ironically on the shores bordering the Aegean Sea, Garabed had decided to stay at home and rest. Raffi and his father were sitting together at breakfast when a policeman again came to the house and, being known to the maid, was immediately let into the breakfast room.

Raffi's mother – Mariam – hastened in as soon as she heard that a policeman had arrived.

"Garabed *effendi*, I have been asked to come and request you to attend at the police station this morning, in order for you to deal with some official business in your capacity as Mukhtar of the district."

"Baba, baba – don't go – let them deal with the business with you here," cried out Raffi, whilst his mother stood quite still, covering her face with her hands.

Garabed looked at the policeman, who stood diffidently to one side. Raffi, getting more and more excited and emotional shouted again, -

"Baba, you don't have to go – we'll deal with it together," and he jumped up with clenched fists, tipping over his chair.

It was fairly clear that Garabed would have to comply with the polite request of the policeman, but this outburst from Raffi, and the threat that he might easily knock the policeman down, decided him. All he could think of was shielding his family.

He rose from the table, put on his hat and coat, kissed his wife and strode out with the policeman following politely behind. For a short time there was a silence in the breakfast room. Raffi simply could not credit that his father, this strong-willed big man of whom he was both in awe and a little afraid, had meekly gone to the police station, when he had had such a terrible experience only ten or so days before.

"Mother! Mother! Why didn't father object more strongly? Mama what will happen if they beat him again? I can't bear it. We must do something. Why did he go so meekly?"

"My son, my son, calm down. Getting excited isn't going to help your father. I think he knows that there won't be a repetition of what happened a couple of weeks ago. Several Turkish business acquaintances of your father, old and respected Ottoman families, raised the matter with the Governor. But I don't know why he has been asked to report again. Tensions are running high, ever since the Van situation broke out. If I had to give you a reason, I suspect that they are going to go for another forced loan from the Christian community."

"If they beat father again – I'll – I'll kill them," yelled Raffi, who had scarcely taken in a word his mother had said, while jumping up and down, unable to keep still.

"Raffi, you must calm down. The situation in the town is very difficult. I want you to finish your breakfast, and then go up to the bazaar and see if you can find out anything. You must promise me faithfully, that you will avoid speaking to anyone that you don't know. Don't go to school today, but come straight back to me."

"I promise, mother," Raffi was suddenly sobered by his mother's calm but beseeching tone of voice.

Wolfing down the remainder of his breakfast, Raffi left the house and walked through the narrow streets, eventually coming out into the square in front of the main Armenian Church of St. Gregory. To one side of this was the Kapali Charshi – the covered bazaar – in which most of the merchants were Greeks or Armenians. Raffi went in and was immediately met with an uproar, quite unlike the usual hustle and bustle of the market. He did not have to speak to anyone – the gist of what was happening soon became clear. It appeared that that morning there had been arrests of about a hundred of the more prominent Armenians from all over town. He gathered that most arrests took the form of polite requests to come to the station to answer questions, although it also appeared that some had been more violent.

Raffi went from group to group gleaning all the information that he could, and eventually came across Ismet, his father's Turkish foreman. Ismet looked at him sadly.

"Ah, Raffi, I'm sorry but I've just found out that Garabed *effendi* is one of those who have been arrested. He's been taken to the Town Hall, where they're all gathered at the moment in the gardens. I am sorry that I haven't got any more hard information – but, my boy, I believe that they're going to be sent out of the town into exile."

"But Ismet, why?"

"My boy, I've no idea. All I know is that bad things are happening, things I never expected to see in all my days. Please tell your mother Mariam Hanum to be very careful. She can call on my help at any time. I'll try to keep the business going until, ishallah, Garabed *effendi* returns."

Raffi touched his forehead and bowed and was about to race home when he recalled his promise to his mother to remain calm. Instead, he sauntered out, hands in pockets, and strolled back.

On his arrival he found the house in upheaval. His old grandmother was roaring at his elder sisters. It appeared that the Turkish wet-nurse, recently taken on to look after the newborn baby of one of his married sisters, had suddenly given notice that morning, and had fled from the house not even waiting for her wages.

Raffi took his mother aside and told her all that he had discovered. Mariam stared at him as despair flooded over her. This was something new and sinister, and she had had no previous experience of how to deal with it. One thing was clear – it was still April, and here on the Anatolian plateau it could get cold again, very suddenly. She took Raffi by the hand and led him into her bedroom. There, bending down, she pulled out from under the bed, the heavy old strongbox. Raffi moved to help, but was waved aside.

Taking out a key from her belt, she opened the box. Inside were the deeds of the house and other properties, together with various documents that Raffi could not distinguish, some baptismal and other certificates, and finally in the corner some paper money and a bag of gold coins. Ignoring the paper money, Mariam took the bag of coins and pouring them out on the bed picked out most of them, amounting to about thirty, and handed them to Raffi. Then going to the large wardrobe in the corner of the room, she lifted out the warm sheepskin coat that Garabed used to take with him on his trips into the highlands, and handed that too to Raffi.

"Now Raffi, take these coins – hide them carefully – and the coat, and give them all to your father, if you can get to see him. Raffi, make sure that he takes them all. He'll make a fuss about the coat, I know him, but say I insist. Once done, hurry home. Don't loiter on the way back. I know by experience that the mob will soon be out on the streets, excited by these events and looking for trouble."

She looked carefully at him, and then suddenly put out her hand.

"My son – give me that cross you're wearing round your neck."

Raffi pulled it over his head and handed it to her without a word. Then taking the coins and the coat he hurried out. Once again, heeding his mother's words, he sauntered through the streets, though he badly wanted to run. He draped the coat over his shoulders, and put the coins in his pockets.

When he reached the square in front of the Town Hall, Raffi saw a large detachment of gendarmes who were guarding the steps up to the entrance of the building. Raffi strolled round to the road leading away from the square alongside the gardens of the building. Here, looking through the high iron railings, he saw several well-dressed men, walking amongst the trees. Now out of sight of the guards at the front, round the corner, Raffi pressed his face up to the bars and waited. Shortly, three of the men came past, talking animatedly, and Raffi called out to them.

"Gentlemen, please can I talk to you – do you know my father – Garabed Asadourian – a big man? Do you know if he is here?"

"Asadour *effendi* – yes, yes, he is here somewhere,"

"Could you please ask him to come here. Tell him his son is waiting."

"Why certainly. Look, wait here, but stand away from the railings until he comes – it will be safer for you." The man turned away and, joining the others, walked back towards the Town Hall building, which could just be seen through the trees.

Raffi moved away to the other side of the street, and leaned against the wall. His heart began beating fast.

"Raffi, my soul," came a quiet voice.

"Oh Baba, Baba," cried Raffi, racing forward and clasping his father's outstretched hands through the railings.

"My son, my son, calmly, calmly. You must be strong for your mother's and sisters' sakes. No tears now – nothing has happened yet – all may be well."

He smiled at his second son. But Raffi was no longer a child; he knew that death was probably just round the corner, and that his father was trying to comfort him. However, he gulped down the tears that had been threatening to flow, and pushed the coat through the railings.

"Look, for heaven's sake it's hot, I don't need this".

"Baba, mother said I was to insist that you take it, she knew that you would probably refuse, but it's still only April, and heaven knows where you'll be at night."

Garabed grinned.

"Well, we must do as your mother commands."

He took the coat, shook it out, and then draped it over his own shoulders.

Raffi then handed him the thirty gold coins. Garabed took them and looked down thoughtfully at the coins in his hand. There was a moment of silence. He carefully counted out five of them, slipping them into the pocket of the coat now draped over his shoulders. He then took another hold of Raffi's hand and gave him back the other twenty-five.

"Raffi, take these back to your mother. You'll all need them more than I will."

The inference was very clear. Garabed knew it, although he did not at this moment realise that Raffi understood too. No one could be sure what was going to happen, but one way or another, the likelihood was high that within a few days, Garabed would be dead. Raffi had no idea what to do or say. All his life he had looked to his father for comfort. He knew only two things for certain – firstly that he must follow his mother's wishes and insist on his father taking all the coins, and secondly, that he must not under any circumstances give way to any tears.

"No, Baba, I can't. Mother said I must make sure you took them all." Raffi hesitated, even in this terrible moment, he reflected that he had never before had the courage to contradict his father.

Garabed looked at his son, and a short moment passed as they looked into each other's eyes. Then in a stern hard tone, and gathering together all the moral authority he could muster. "Raffi, you will do as I say, and you'll do it now and without any question. Take these coins home and leave straight away, right now. Tell your mother not to despair, and remember, remember that I love you all."

Garabed dropped the coins into Raffi's hand, which he had been holding with his other hand all this time, and then without another look at him, without a kiss, without a sign, he turned on his heels and walked away through the trees.

With the departure of his father, probably forever, Raffi could no longer control his emotions. He walked to the other side of the street, leant against the old stone wall, and gave way to floods of tears, but the tears gave him no release at all.

Eventually he gathered himself together sufficiently to walk back through the streets, with the 25 gold coins clutched in his sweaty hands, thrust deep into his pockets.

CHAPTER 21

Van. The last effort

The rebel*lion* in Van was almost into its third week. Halil *Bey*'s Turkish regular troops were increasingly frustrated at their inability to dislodge the 1,500 or so Armenian irregulars holding on in their square mile of fortified enclave. Meanwhile, General Yudenich and the Russian army was approaching Van from the north. Turkish families in the smarter suburbs were beginning to leave the town, many in boats crossing the lake to the northern and western shore.

Halil *Bey* decided to mount one final offensive before the arrival of the Russians. Aware of the poor morale among his 6,000 men, he realised that his only hope was to clear the enclave, turning the town into a proper defensive bastion. Unlike the smart new Turkish officers of the nationalist Ittihad party, old Halil *Bey* did not despise his Anatolian peasant troops, ensuring adequate medical support for the offensive. Dr. Nazim and his medical team were ordered forward into the front lines facing the makeshift barricades at the perimeter.

The final push began a day or two before the 24th April. The strength of Turkish military arms had always lain in their capacity for dogged defence, rather than in their offensive ability. The ordinary young men carrying out their orders did not lack courage, but they had died in their hundreds for minimal gains, as thousands did on other fronts.

On the other side of the barricades, similar young men, anxious for their families, defending their own homes, fought back tenaciously, with nowhere left to retreat to. The cleared ground around the perimeter became filled with the dead and the dying. By the morning of the 24th April, the repeated attempts to break into the enclave were abandoned, and both sides took a breather.

Within the American Mission compound, Dr. Ussher continued his medical work, careful not to let any armed men into the main hospital grounds. Despite this, the hospital was still being shelled from the Castle Rock. He prayed ever more fervently with his small group of Protestant converts, avoiding any display of political bias.

On this morning of the 24th April, Clarence Ussher went down to the church hall where the Armenians had set up a temporary hospital for their own wounded. He saw the dead and dying in the no-mans-land between the barricaded stone houses of the perimeter, and the surrounding Turkish entrenchments. He noted with horror, the hovering vultures, and the moans of the badly wounded unable to crawl forward or back.

Dr. Ussher hurried back to his office. Sitting at his desk in the gloom of his cool, windowless office, he hastily composed the following letter to Djevdet *Bey*, whom he imagined was still in charge of the operations round the enclave:-

'Your Excellency, having seen the awful slaughter of many young men on both sides, and the plight of the wounded in no-man's-land between the forces, I would like to respectfully suggest a twelve-hour ceasefire to enable both sides to bury their dead and tend to the badly wounded. I am sure I can prevail on the Armenian leaders here to agree to such a proposal, and to allow your men to remove their dead and wounded. Perhaps you could signify your agreement by giving your answer to this messenger, whom I will instruct to remain at the Italian consulate to receive your reply. I remain, with the greatest respect, your humble servant."

After signing the letter, Dr. Ussher called for nurse Alicia, and handed her the note.

"Alicia, could you give this note to the good lady who has been carrying letters to the Italian consulate for me. She must stay there until she receives a reply from Djevdet *Bey*."

Alicia looked at the doctor, whom she deeply admired, without saying a word. She wondered if the man knew that three of these elderly ladies had already died in this regular exchange of messages. Had he simply chosen to ignore the deaths in the interest of the greater good of God's work, or was he simply unaware. She would never know.

"Yes, very well Doctor. I'll deal with it." She took the sealed letter and hurried out to seek out Nevart, who had already delivered four messages across the lines since she had first arrived to work at the mission.

"Nevart, mother, I have another important letter from Dr. Ussher for you to deliver as usual to the Italian Consulate. After delivering it you must wait at the consulate, inside if the Signore will allow, for a reply before returning yourself. Be careful, make sure that you hold the white flag up high at all times. Go now while there is a lull in the fighting."

She kissed old Nevart's creased brow, and handed her the stick with the bedraggled white flag of truce.

Nevart touched the ground and lifted her hand to her brow and crossed herself, took the flag and the letter, and walked out of the compound and along the now quiet cobbled streets to the spot between the demolished stone houses, where she had set out on previous occasions.

This was a sector of the line commanded by one of the revolutionary nationalist leaders thrown up by the conflict. This youth was impossibly young, fair-haired and blue-eyed, with a look of fanatical zeal in his smiling eyes that left little room for ordinary human compassion. His name was Aris, and he had already, on two previous occasions, shown impatience at Nevart's simple, old-fashioned, blessing whenever she went past him.

He stared dumbly at her as she came up to warn him that she was going into no-mans-land with a flag of truce to deliver a message to the other side.

"May Our Lord Jesus Christ protect you," Nevart tentatively raised her hand to bestow a blessing and her lips to offer a kiss but Aris rebuffed her advance. Confused and hurt, she lifted the flag high, waited a few seconds so that it could be seen by both sides, and then walked between the rubble of the demolished houses and out into the area between the two forces.

Right opposite her, and sheltered behind another stone house on the other side of the no-mans-land, stood Dr. Nazim Kemal, temporarily unoccupied now the offensive had petered out. He was exhausted after two days of non-stop work, when he had spent hour after hour patching up horrific wounds, removing embedded bullets, cutting off shattered limbs, until he was acting on autopilot, but, despite this, remained sharp and alert. Even in these difficult circumstances, he had managed to have a shave that morning, much to the amazement of the men around him.

Nazim could see the badly wounded and dying men lying between the Armenian barricades and the Turkish entrenchments. He contemplated going out, protected by a Red Crescent banner but then wondered whether it should not be under a Red Cross banner. His mind went round and round on the point, questioning whether the irregular guerillas on the other side would respect such rules of war? He stood there in a state of uncertainty, wondering what to do.

Nazim was the first to see the white flag waving on the makeshift stick and moving out between the two crumbling houses in front of him. The men beside him stared with tired and lack-lustre eyes, as a small, old woman, dressed all in black, shuffled out of the gap between two buildings and began advancing across the dusty corridor between the two lines. The old lady gingerly stepped round the dead bodies in her path. She had just about reached half-way, when Nazim saw one of the Turkish soldiers, lying with a leg almost off and dried blood covering his face, raise his hand to the old woman as she passed and call out in a harsh strangulated cry -

"Mamma! Oh my god, Mamma! Mamma!"

Nazim watched and saw the old lady start and look down. She dropped the white flag, bent down and took the man's head into her arms. Just then a shot rang out from the Turkish lines and the old lady staggered forward and dropped to her knees, blood spurting from her side. As she fell she cradled the young soldier's head and then sat up holding his head in her lap. Another shot rang out from the Turkish lines kicking up dust at her feet.

Nazim sprang out from his position shouting, "Cease fire – cease fire you louts," to the men around him, and raced over the dusty uneven ground. There, alone between the two lines, Nevart was rocking back and forth, blood pouring from her side, with a trickle now from her mouth, cradling the young Turkish soldier's head in her lap, stroking his brow and his black hair, and crooning an old Turkish lullaby.

Nazim had run out without even an armband. As he ran up to the pair, he was already fumbling for the dressings and antiseptics, which he had instinctively grabbed. As he arrived a shot rang out, this time from the Armenian side. Nazim stood clutching his breast as blood spurted out. Nevart, for the first time looked up. Nazim and Nevart stared into each other's eyes for a split second – an eternal moment – and then Nazim died, fatally shot through the heart by Aris, who had seen everything, and who had inevitably understood nothing.

Immediately, the whole sector became a maelstrom of shots as both sides began blazing away at each other. In the middle of it all, Nevart continued to rock back and forth cradling the dying soldier, her own strength slowly ebbing away. Finally, in the midst of a fusillade of shots, Nevart bent down and kissed the lips of the son she had never had –

"May your Allah receive you into your heaven, my son," murmured Nevart as she slumped forward, dead, across the breast of the unknown Turkish soldier.

"Mother, oh mother," groaned the young man, as with the ghost of a smile on his face, he too finally expired.

The aimless shooting went on in this sector for several more hours, as the carefully composed message from Clarence Ussher to Djevdet *Bey*, now torn and blood-spattered, fluttered away in the wind.

Later, in the course of clearing up the Doctor's effects, his orderly discovered the last letter written by Nazim to his son Selim, which he had not had time to send. This was sent on to the family in Constantinople with his other personal effects and together with a letter of commendation from Halil Bay himself. The letter to Selim read –

'My incomparable son,

I am writing to you from my camp bed on the shores of the lovely Lake Van. The nights here are bright and clear and fresh, though very cold. When the moon is full and high, the lack of any artificial light makes for crystal clear visibility and you can almost see across the lake to the high mountains on the other side.

I have been moved up to the front with the whole of my medical team, as Halil Bey is proposing to mount a full-scale major offensive to clear the town of the rebels before the arrival of the small Russian force currently advancing towards us.

My son, I have had a lot of time on my hands which I have spent thinking about our lives, the Empire, and what it all means. War often consists of days of intense and terrible activity with not a moment in which to catch your breath. But there are also long periods of utter boredom, when there is nothing to do but think about one's loved ones and write letters like this one.

I remain rather sad at the way the Armenians have treacherously risen against the Empire at this moment of crisis in our history, but perhaps not quite so incensed as I was when I first arrived here. The intensity with which they are defending the perimeter of the town does indicate at least a certainty of their moral position, which I had not expected.

Part of the problem, I believe, is the rise amongst them over the last 30 years of 'nationalist' ideals about the creation of a one-nation 'state'. I am sorry to add these same beliefs are growing now amongst the Turks of Anatolia. It is precisely what I object to in the current Ittihad government – the urge to create a single exclusive nation-state, intolerant by definition.

But, my son, it is not preordained or inevitable. It is possible, my boy, to love one's own religion, one's own language and literature, the ethnic food you have eaten all your life, the dance, the music and the theatre you have enjoyed, yet still be content to be part of a country that may not celebrate these things, but takes no part in suppressing them.

Ah well!

My darling boy – I know that you have been brought up with truth, and that your heart is strong, and your convictions firm and honourable. Always consider all sides of any position on which you are obliged to make a stand, but act decisively once your mind is made up. Look after your mother and your young sister in case any accident may befall me. You will recall the details of the savings box in my study of which I told you before leaving.

My respectful embraces to your mother, Your ever-loving father – Nazim

CHAPTER 22

Haik

Haik's school was not let out early that day. The age of the boys at this school was significantly lower than the school Nerissa attended further away in the little town. They kept them in a little longer to allow plenty of time for those coming to pick them up.

Haik was a little surprised when he got to the school gates and found that Sima was not there waiting for him. He sat with some of his friends on the grass but as time passed, the others were either picked up or went home on their own until Haik found himself on his own.

"Hello, Haik, what are you still doing here," one of the teachers asked as he passed out of the school gates on his way home, "Are you all right?"

"Yes, sir, I'm waiting for my sister. I'll go on home if she doesn't come soon."

"Well, don't wait too long – she might be delayed in the city, you know."

The sun was hot, but it was a beautiful fresh clear day so finally, he decided that he had better get on home. After all, he had been walking home by himself now for well over a year, before his father's recent decision. He hoisted his worn-out old satchel, and sauntering along to the road, he began the walk up the hill.

He was about half-way up the slope, past the racecourse, when he first noticed the two rough-looking men staring at him. One was wearing baggy trousers with a dirty green shirt, the other with an equally dirty old-fashioned red blouse. Turks? Albanians? Gypsies? Haik had no idea, and never found out.

The boys at the school didn't have any real idea what was going on. They were conscious of the raised temperature and their parents generalised fear. Accordingly, as he had never seen these men before, he instinctively avoided any eye contact and trudged on – though no longer with quite the same abandon. All might have been well, if he had not glanced over as he passed, and saw one of the louts sniffing at a distinctive delicate yellow silk scarf. Haik stopped, turned and stared. He immediately recognised it as belonging to Olga; there simply could not be another like it.

"Hey!" he shouted, pointing, "that belongs to my sister. Where did you get hold of it?"

"Does it indeed – squirt," jeered one of the youths, waving the scarf like a red rag to a bull.

Surrounded as he was by a houseful of loving women, Haik had led a very sheltered life. The only violence he had ever experienced was the rough and tumble of boys of his own age at school. As a result, he failed to recognise the menacing danger in the eyes of the two men.

"If it belongs to your dear sister – why don't you come and take it. I'm sure she'll be overjoyed," the other sneered. Haik failed to understand the threat in their words.

Instead, he came and clambered over the wooden fence and onto the grass verge running alongside the road, where the two youths stood, laughing at him. Haik walked up to them and held his hand out for the scarf.

"And what are you going to give us in exchange," said green-shirt with a dangerous glint in his eye.

"Look – this scarf belongs to my sister, and I haven't anything to give you anyway. She must've dropped it on her way home. I bet you found it on the road."

"Well – I'll tell you what – you give us your nice clean shirt and pants in exchange and we'll give you the scarf – that's a fair exchange," red-blouse answered, grinning.

Haik stared at them both. He hesitated, not entirely sure what to do, but began to lose his patience. Thin and delicate though he appeared, he nevertheless had the Avakian spirit, as well as the healthy energy of any 12 year-old boy. What he lacked, was any sense of self-preservation.

The physical aggression of the two youths was fairly clear to Haik, but what he failed to see was the sexually-charged, sadistic threat in their jibes. The scarf was now lying on the grass in front of green-shirt. Haik bent down and grabbed the scarf, then straightened and turned to walk away.

Like a flash both youths were up, and to Haik's genuine surprise, he was grabbed by red-blouse from behind and his arms pinioned to his side, whilst green-shirt came in front of him and punched him several times in the face and stomach. Haik began struggling and yelling, out of a mixture of both fear and anger.

"Shut your gob, you little pig," whispered red-blouse right into Haik's ear. It was unlikely that Haik would have stopped yelling, except that green-shirt gave him a really vicious punch right across his mouth. Haik's nose now began to bleed, together with his cut lip. Even this might not have stopped Haik's spirited yells, if green-shirt had not produced a long knife from the depths of his filthy trousers and held it firmly to Haik's throat. This, even Haik could understand. Two things then happened – firstly he stopped wriggling or making any noise, and secondly real fear as he had never felt it before gripped his guts, and a trickle of urine involuntarily escaped into his pants.

Tears of fear and frustration began to flow, but without any sobs. Blood was streaming from his nose and mouth, and his huge eyes for the first time searched the face of his tormentors. What he saw gave him no comfort.

"This is one of those damned *giavour* kids from the school in that town down below – I'm sure." Red-blouse was still holding Haik tight, whilst green-shirt held the knife steadily at Haik's throat.

" Yeah – you're bloody right – and you know what, they've all been shouting in the city that all *giavour*s are traitors, and should be slaughtered like the pigs they are."

"So, how are we going to make sure that he's a damned *giavour*."

"Well, we'll soon be able to tell, won't we," greenshirt laughed and with one hand still on the knife, he fumbled at the buttons of Haik's trousers with the other and yanked them down. They both looked down as the pants fell to the ground, then both laughed –

"There, you see, I knew he was a filthy Christian pig." "Not a pig – he's a sow – let's show him."

For the first time Haik realised what they had been doing; they had pulled down his pants to see if he was circumcised or not, and therefore if he was a Muslim or not. The knife, as it happens, had also gone back into green-shirt's baggy pocket, and unfortunately with the disappearance of the knife, Haik found the courage to start yelling again and struggling to get out of red-blouse's grip. He was yelling and sobbing at the same time, and it was this that finally tipped the balance of violence from mere aggression to a perverted, lustful and sadistic attack. These youths had spent the whole morning milling around with the mob in the city; listening as adults denigrated and cursed the members of this boy's race and religion. The crucial tipping-point had come when the gutter is persuaded to stop thinking of the denigrated people as humans. And here they were now, holding a young *giavour* boy totally at their mercy.

Suddenly, Haik found himself thrown down onto the grass, his face thrust into the earth, his shoes and pants pulled off and his shirt torn from his back. Then Haik felt his genitals pulled and pinched, and felt one of the youths falling down on top of him. Something was happening to him that was causing a terrible pain. He lifted his head, kicked his feet, which connected violently with the youth on top of him and at least relieved the pain. He cried out loudly for help, before his face was thrust back down into the earth. He began suffocating, and again green-shirt fell down heavily onto his back. Once again the knife came out, held against his cheek and a complete terror gripped him. He heard the sinister voice of red-blouse as he almost passed out.

Back in the compound of Robert College, shortly after Olga had run out of the school gates, Selim was released by his friends. "Don't go after her, my friend," Nurhan counseled, "she's already left, and consider, at this moment it might be worse for her if you were to chase after her."

Selim, whose body was quivering with repressed emotion, shook himself free. His friends stood back, watching him carefully, some with sympathy. The girls looked away and one by one hurried off, many in shame at what they had done, but some in exultation. Selim smiled at his close friend Nurhan, and the others around him.

"Thank you," he said quietly, but without really meaning it. "Hopefully I'll see you all tomorrow." He went in, collected his things and walked calmly out of the College gates.

Once outside, however, he began hurrying down to the Galata bridge. He knew that Olga would be making for Sirkeci station and the train home to Makrikoy. By the time he got to the bridge, however, it had filled up with the crowds that were preventing Sima from disembarking from her ferry.

Almost at once, Selim made the mistake of trying to push his way through the crowds. His emotional state prevented him from considering the situation logically. Had he waited, even for a moment, he would have seen the impossibility of trying to push his way through, in which case he might have thought of other ways of getting across to the Stamboul side. As it was, he plunged impetuously into the milling crowds.

The shouts of "*Giavour*s to the gallows!" and "Death to the traitorous pigs" and "Down with the British dogs" and so on – the usual mindless yells of the gutter – passed right over his head as he struggled to get through. Eventually it got to the point that he could go neither forward nor back. He roared with sheer animal frustration, but no one took the slightest notice of him, because of course everyone else was also shouting.

Whereas Olga's tram had been one of the last to get through, and climb up on the other side, Selim, who had walked down from the College, got there in the middle of the demonstration. Nevertheless, police reinforcements arrived and, slowly, the crowd began dispersing.

As the crowd thinned, Selim finally pushed and shoved his way across the bridge, and up to the Sirkeci station. No train was in, and he had to wait impatiently on the platform, by which time he had been joined by many others, waiting for the next train.

When Selim got to the Cobancesme station, he jumped out. He knew exactly where the Avakian house was. In all their conversations together, Olga had spoken at length about her house and the daily walk down to the station. As he left the little dusty square beside the station he saw a dumpy middle-aged lady getting out of a carriage, but he was far too nervous and excited to contemplate sitting in a carriage for ten idle minutes. Selim crossed the railway line and began walking rapidly up the road beside the Vali *Effendi* racecourse.

He was about halfway up, when he heard the piercing scream of what sounded like a young boy, crying for help. Ahead and in the field to the left, there appeared to be a boy, almost naked, being set upon by two rough men, both of whom Selim immediately recognised as city street thugs. In other circumstances, Selim might have acted a little less precipitously, but in his fraught emotional state, he did not hesitate for a second – taking the fence at a running jump he charged into the little group. The youth who had been on top of the young boy rolled off and began fumbling at his dirty baggy trousers as he stood up. The other heavy who had been kneeling by the boy's face also jumped up, and Selim saw for the first time the knife in his hand.

Selim had had no more direct experience of street violence than Haik, but he was eight or more years older, and was much more street-wise. Above all he was in a rage – an inchoate anger at everything, and this gave him a momentary advantage over the two ruffians. Had he stopped to remonstrate with them, he would probably have lost the initiative. As it was, with fists flailing, he knocked down the green-shirted youth who was still fumbling with his trouser belt. Then he turned to face the man in the red blouse who was circling round with his knife, ready to lunge.

The young boy on the floor, clearly traumatised, had lifted his head from the grass, and was trying to sit up, his face a mass of blood, and taking in great gulps of air. Selim jumped at the red-bloused man and they rolled onto the grass. For a moment all seemed well as Selim ended up on top, but then Selim felt the cold steel of the knife bite into his side. He jumped up and felt his bleeding hip, and then he sensed rather than saw the green-shirted tough circling round to his back, as the man with the knife got up, ready to strike again.

Meanwhile, back at the Avakian house, after Armineh had left in Vahan's carriage, Vahan had settled in the sitting room, no longer in a hurry to leave this charming house. Olga, though still distraught and red-eyed from weeping, had not gone to her bedroom as had been suggested, but sat on the other couch waiting for Nerissa to return with the coffee. Vahan felt surprisingly at ease, while Olga only had thoughts of her last desperate view of Selim, being manhandled by a group of College bullies. They sat silently, but comfortably, waiting for Nerissa to return.

Nerissa, who had finally come to her senses, returned very quickly with strong sweet Turkish coffee, and some 'courabides' biscuits, which Vahan politely declined.

"Where are you from Mister Asadourian?" Nerissa asked, as she sat down next to Olga,

"Caesaria – but I have been living in Constantinople now for over eight months. I'm studying music and drama at the Stamboul University, although as you can see, I'm also enrolled at the Harbiye military academy."

"And what of your family, Mister Asadourian?"

"Well … er … by the way, my name, Miss Avakian, is Vahan – er, do you think you could call me that?" Vahan glanced at Olga who, truth to tell, was not paying much attention.

Nerissa did not blush – she was not that kind of girl. She simply looked at Vahan, and said without any hesitation.

"Why, yes, Vahan it is – and my name is Nerissa."

"I have a brother about your age Nerissa – Raffi – and three elder sisters back in Caesaria."

Who knows how long this ever so delightful and totally unrevealing conversation might have meandered on, if Olga had not at that moment extended her hand and said -

"Oh, goodbye, Mister Asadourian – I'm sorry, Vahan, of course – if you'll excuse me I'm exhausted. I'm going up to have a lie-down. Please do feel free to remain and finish your coffee."

It was a decisive moment. It had only been about 15 minutes or so since Armineh had left. Vahan could see that Olga meant what she said, and that there was no objection to his staying and chatting with Nerissa – an increasingly pleasurable temptation, but after shaking hands with Olga, he finally turned, smiled at Nerissa, and indicated that he would be on his way. She accompanied him to the front door. and he turned and started walking briskly down the hill back to the station.

He had just reached the view of the racecourse below when he saw the fight going on below. He could see the two youths and a young man standing in a posture of defence but holding his side, which was bleeding profusely, and a young boy who was almost naked, with blood running from his mouth and nose, struggling to rise from the grass. The boy was being ignored, whilst the two toughs were circling round the bleeding young man each with knives in their hands. The young man was shouting something at the top of his voice, but he could not distinguish the words.

Vahan, too, was unused to violence, but his own experience in provincial Caesaria had taught him to differentiate between poor peasants dressed roughly because they couldn't afford better, and city ruffians. He too did not hesitate, but raced down the road shouting out at the top of his voice – "Stop, stop, police, stand back, stop …" He had immediately realised that he would be unable to reach the fight before the knives could do further irreparable damage, and hence his instinctive decision to try and advertise his impending arrival.

Everyone looked up at the approaching figure of Vahan hurtling down the road. Whatever gave Vahan the brilliant idea of using the word 'Police', it did the trick. First green-shirt, and then red-blouse took to their heels and ran down the road and away.

Selim, still bleeding from his right side, but now pressing his left hand over the wound in an attempt to staunch the flow, sat down heavily on the grass. Haik, now knelt, looking first at the bleeding Selim, and then at the panting Vahan, as he arrived at the scene.

"What's going on, what's going on?" panted Vahan as he ran up.

"Heaven knows, *effendi*," said Selim, "All I know is that this young lad was being attacked when I intervened."

Haik, for the first time aware and ashamed of his near nakedness, scrabbled about in the grass for his torn pants and shoes, both of which had also been wrenched from him. He began to tremble in reaction to the fear which had devastated him. He imagined he could still feel the knife on his cheek. There were no more sobs, the tears had dried up, but he could not control his trembling.

The two young men, however, understood at once what had either happened or was about to happen, and despite Selim's bleeding side, where the knife had clearly penetrated between the ribs, they both instinctively thought first of the young boy's distress. Vahan went to pick up one of the shoes and brought it back to Haik, who was in the act of pulling on his torn pants. Selim, releasing for a moment his grip on his own wound, fitted the other shoe as tenderly as he could on Haik's other foot. They were careful not to question him, or even to touch him. They had no idea how far the assault had gone.

It was as Haik finally struggled up, with a tentative smile at the two young men, that Selim saw and recognised for the first time lying abandoned under where Haik had lain, the yellow scarf. He gasped as the memories of the day came flooding back. Meanwhile Vahan bent down and grabbed the scarf, tearing it down the middle. He tied the two parts together. He then picked up Haik's shirt, still lying torn on the ground and stuffing it over Selim's wound he bound the scarf very tightly round Selim's waist to hold it in place and to stem the flow of blood.

Selim thanked him with his eyes, but his mind was on the scarf.

"Where did you get this, lad" he addressed Haik and indicated the yellow scarf, as Vahan tied it tight.

"It belongs to my sister" said Haik. "These two men were trying to make off with it, when I tried to take it back."

The two young men stared at Haik, wondering at the foolhardiness, and sheer stupidity of this frail boy in risking himself for a mere scarf.

Haik's nose and mouth were still bleeding as he stood in his torn pants and muddy shoes. Selim was swaying with weakness from the loss of blood. Vahan too felt tired as the adrenalin drained away. It was Haik who broke the moment of silence.

"My parents' home is just up the road. My name is Haik Avakian – do you think, sir, we could go there now. I'm sure that my mother will look after this gentleman."

Neither man had the energy nor the wish at this stage to question what appeared to be an extraordinary coincidence. With both Vahan, and now Haik, supporting the ever-weaker Selim, they clambered back over the fence and shuffled slowly up the road, eventually reaching the Avakian front door, which Vahan had left only a few short minutes earlier.

CHAPTER 23

The last hours of the 24th April

After the departure of Vahan, Olga had finally gone up to rest, while Nerissa moped about downstairs. Following the drama of Olga's confession to Armineh, and the devastating news of her father's arrest, Nerissa felt the need to think of calmer things, her thoughts turning to her younger siblings. So far as the rest of the family were concerned, she had been the one who had always been responsible for seeing to both Haik and little Seta. Seta, she knew, was being collected from school for her weekly piano lessons with the elderly Madame Chatelle. This would last for the rest of the afternoon, as she always took her tea there as well. However, she was just beginning to wonder what had happened to Haik, when the doorbell rang.

Nerissa ran to the door, opened it, and met there a scene she would never forget. Standing there, clearly short of breath and not gabbling away immediately as usual, she saw her young brother with his nose bleeding, dressed only in torn pants and shoes, his chest bare and dirty and with his mouth covered in dried blood. Leaning against him was an incredibly pale Selim, clutching his side, with Olga's distinctive yellow scarf tied round his waist, and with blood seeping between his fingers. Taking almost the whole of Selim's weight on the other side, was Vahan, who had left the house only 15 minutes previously.

For once Nerissa did not just stand there open mouthed. She immediately beckoned them in, yelling for Marie and Olga to come help. She took Haik's free hand and gently drew him towards her. At the tender touch of his beloved sister, Haik at last, and for the first time, burst into heartbroken sobs – no longer the sobbing of anger and fear, but the despairing cries of a child, needing comfort.

Nerissa could see at once that Selim's physical condition was much worse than that of Haik, but she felt instinctively that Haik's hurt, whatever it was, was ultimately more serious. She held him tight, as the other two entered behind him. Marie, who had bustled in from the kitchen on hearing Nerissa's shout, took one look at Selim and ran back to collect what was needed. Olga, bleary-eyed, arrived at the top of the stairs, took one look at the melodramatic scene in the hall, and almost fainted there and then, unable to make any sense of what she was seeing. However, when it came to the crunch, Olga had more than enough of Armineh's practical good sense and *indomitable* will. Recovering her wits she immediately ran down the stairs, asking no questions, but taking the weight of Selim from Vahan, she led him to the chaise-longue in the sitting room and got him to lie down. Selim himself by now was dizzy and almost on the point of fainting from loss of blood, incapable of saying or feeling anything other than the pain in his side.

Marie came bustling in with a bowl of steaming hot water, a bottle of bright purple antiseptic, and a roll of linen dressing. Nerissa held on tightly to the quietly sobbing Haik who had buried his face in her breasts, while Vahan stood panting and getting his breath back.

"Miss Olga," Marie explained, when she saw that Olga was not going to relinquish her position by the side of the wounded young man, "You must wash the wound carefully all round – then you must apply the antiseptic and make sure it goes well into the wound. Don't worry, my dear, he's in no real danger – he'll be fine – the only danger is if the wound gets infected, and that we must be prevent."

Olga nodded, and delicately undoing and removing the scarf and shirt began, efficiently, and with a surprising calmness, working as Marie had directed. Without any hint of embarrassment or uncertainty, she lifted Selim's shirt and pushed down the top of his trousers to reveal the full extent of the wound – her mind totally on the purely nursing task required.

Meanwhile Haik had finally cried his fill. Some brightness had come back into his previously dulled eyes, and Nerissa decided that it was time he was cleaned up and she persuaded him up the stairs to the bathroom. Marie moved to follow, but before she started up, Vahan suddenly bestirred himself and came over signalling her to wait a moment. Marie looked steadily at the anxious brown eyes of this stranger. Vahan was deeply embarrassed, but he felt the situation concerning Haik should be made clear and that an effort be made to find out exactly how far events had gone before Selim had turned up.

He outlined the facts as he knew them and which had been quietly confirmed by Selim, making certain that Marie understood that one of the toughs appeared to have been on top of the half-naked Haik when Selim had arrived. Marie nodded – she was well versed in the ways of the world – particularly the Turkish world.

"Madam," said Vahan who was not quite sure of the position Marie had in the household, "I do believe that you should try to find out the basic facts now, so that you can inform his mother and father when they return, without involving him directly. Er

... Madam ... I hope that you will be careful, and er ... also not involve Miss Nerissa at this stage ... I mean ...," as Vahan's faltering words dried up under Marie's penetrating stare.

"My dear sir," Marie haughtily replied, "I have nursed these children for 20 years, do you think I don't know my job? Really!" and she marched upstairs. Vahan reddened even more than before, and withdrew, wondering if he had gone too far.

Marie arrived in Haik's bedroom with yet another bowl of hot water. He was sitting up on his bed, shoulders still drooping, but his eyes more alive. Nerissa was simply sitting on the bed, holding him tightly, without doing anything about the still bleeding nose or the cut lips.

"Now then, Miss Nerissa, run along and help your sister downstairs. We need to get this young man tidied up, and, my dear, you're a little in the way here."

Nerissa nodded, gave Haik a tender kiss and went out. At the touch of her lips, Haik was almost about to start crying again, but was stopped by his old Nurse's stern look.

"Now Haik," Marie carefully wiped away the blood from his nose and mouth, "this is not too bad a cut – go and change into your pyjamas, hold your head right back pressing this cotton wool to your nose, and then have a good wash all over."

Marie knew that Haik had to be left alone to change – the latent shame in his semi-nakedness being fairly clear to her experienced eyes.

Haik returned in about five minutes in his pyjamas, cleaned up at least to the somewhat half-hearted point natural to a 12 year-old boy. His injuries now washed clean, did not look at all bad. Above all the eyes had brightened even further, and there was a new alertness in the way he was holding himself.

"Haik, you better get into bed and have a rest."

"But I'm not sleepy Marie, and I want to know what the others are doing."

"I know, dear, but it's all been a bit of a shock and you need the rest. Don't bother to try to sleep, you can read until Mummy comes back. Would you like to tell me now what happened?"

Haik told Marie about the walk back from school, the two youths lounging on the grass, Olga's yellow scarf, their sudden attack as he tried to take the scarf, the knife, their inspection to see whether he was circumcised or not, his torn shirt and the assault, all without any embarrassment – after all Marie had bathed and dressed him as long as he could remember, until the last few years.

Marie listened, then chose her words carefully.

"Did you feel any bad pain down below when you were thrown to the floor."

"Well, yes, I did feel a sudden pain starting, Marie, but I kicked out and yelled at the top of my voice. The pain stopped, and never came back again, as it was just about then that the first gentleman came running up when he heard me shout."

Marie registered these facts carefully, ready to be able to pass them on to Armineh when she returned, and otherwise sighed in relief at Haik's words, spoken totally innocently and without guilt. She knew it would be for Karekin to deal with on his return that night. Indeed Marie had always felt that Karekin had been neglectful of his son's education in this field.

"Call me, my love, if you need anything."

When she got downstairs, she found Selim still lying stretched out on the chaise-longue, with Olga still kneeling alongside putting the final touches to the new clean dressing round his waist and tightly bound over the wound. Nerissa standing behind Olga waiting with scissors to cut the end of the linen. The bleeding had stopped. Vahan was still standing, looking dumbly on. Marie went over to him.

"It's all right, sir, the other gentleman seems to have caught the situation just in time, thank God. No permanent damage seems to have been done, and I don't think it will haunt his memories. Either way, it is a matter for his parents now when they get back this evening."

Vahan nodded and smiled at her, probably the first smile that had crossed his face that whole day. With that, Marie left the room, saying that she would be back shortly with some coffee and biscuits.

Selim was already recovering, and some colour had returned to his face under Olga's careful ministrations. Having worked like a professional nurse ever since Marie had gone upstairs, she suddenly became aware of Selim's body – bared to the chest, and with his trousers right down to the hips. She also became conscious that her fingers had worked over this male body. Their eyes met, both of them aware of the swiftly changed mood that had arisen between them.

Olga stood back indicating to Nerissa to finish the work. All of a sudden she felt faint again as different, though welcome, emotions flooded over her. It was clear that Selim was not going to be able to move for some time, so they all settled themselves in the sofas and chairs round the chaise-longue, as Marie came in with a tray of coffee and some welcome food.

Somehow the drama, which they had all just been through, had removed most of the normal social constraints between them. The girls, aged 16 and nearly 18, and the young men – 19 and 20 – at last drew a sort of collective breath. Vahan and Selim, already experiencing a bond, having shared and overcome danger together, at last introduced themselves. The coincidence of the events unraveled, even including a guess at the hitherto unexplained failure of Sima to turn up at Haik's school.

It was clear that Selim could not leave for another hour or two while he recovered his strength. None of them were in a mood for inconsequential chit-chat. It was Selim, who, now hearing for the first time of the arrest of Olga's father that morning, raised the issue behind all the current problems of the Empire. He turned to Vahan and commented -

"Here I am amongst an Armenian family for the first time in my life, although I have always lived next to Greek or Armenian neighbours. What an experience! Tell me Vahan, my friend, do you feel more Armenian, more Christian or more Ottoman."

"I feel all three," replied Vahan. "Our identity isn't exclusively one thing or another, but includes all our different affiliations, interests, cultural activities, even the type of food we eat – indeed we're a mixture of many elements, all of which make up our own unique identity."

This kicked off a long conversation, mainly between the two men, about the issues of identity and the current course of the Empire, listened to avidly by Nerissa at least, while Olga looked on with wonder at the strength of her feelings for this man.

"Good heavens!" Nerissa interrupted, "you're both beginning to lecture each other, but neither of you have referred to your identity as a male, which after all gives you an affiliation – I think that's the word you used – with half the human race. I have a female identity, which, Selim, is surely just as important as my being an Armenian."

"Well, I don't know," Olga spoke for the first time, "I only know that my own identity has changed over the last eight weeks."

"Oh Olga," said Nerissa impatiently, "can't you ever think of anything but your own feelings. We are discussing something serious here."

Selim looked down at Olga at his side, and winced as he moved slightly closer to her on the sofa, while Vahan looked on vacantly and said -

"Hang on Nerissa – let's hear what Miss Olga has to say."

"Come, come, Vahan, surely 'Olga' by now."

"I'm sorry, 'Olga' of course," replied Vahan with a smile.

"Well, what I suppose I meant was that had you asked me a mere eight weeks ago where my main allegiances lay, I would have said – I am an Armenian, and a Christian, and above all a member of a close family unit, and that my principle 'deep down inside' identity was as an

Avakian daughter. Now, eight weeks later, I am not so sure anymore – my sense of my own identity has suddenly become bound up with the identity of someone else."

Selim squeezed her hand hard.

By now all four of them were thoroughly engrossed in the discussion. Vahan was enjoying immensely a fascinating argument with a man for whom he was beginning to feel a great affection. Nerissa, because she had never felt so accepted before in what she thought of as a grown-up exchange of views. Selim, by the continuing throb of the wound in his side, but more by the whole atmosphere of friendship and affection which boded so well, or so he thought, for his love. Olga, by the simple proximity of the young man by her side whom she imagined that she might have lost for ever only a few hours previously.

Time was getting on, and it was clear that Armineh would not be returning for some time. Nerissa suddenly spoke in some distress -

"Oh, Olga, I forgot mother, and probably Sima too, if they met at the station. What can be happening?"

The mention of the arrest, and the departure of Armineh to find her husband, brought all four of them back to the present. Nerissa, recalled that Haik had surely now been left upstairs on his own long enough. Olga began worrying about what was to happen to Selim. But it was Vahan who then rose and asked Olga how he could arrange for a carriage to the station, as clearly Selim ought not to walk back. A servant was duly dispatched to go down and come back with one of the gharries.

The doorbell rang again. Nerissa ran to the door.

"Hello everyone – it's me, it's me," called out a breathless Seta as she ran in, not even acknowledging Nerissa, who slipped outside and waved a thank-you at Madame Chatelle's maid hurrying away down the hill. Seta stopped at the sight of the two young men, but showed no shyness.

"Hello, I'm Seta – who are you?" holding out her hand and not listening to anyone's reply. "Where's Haik? Did you all hear that great foghorn of the big ship in the harbour this morning? We saw it from the windows, out in the sea. Where's Mummy? Madame Chantelle was all excited today – it must be her birthday or something."

This was not by any means all that she said, but by now the party was breaking up.

Selim and Vahan departed on the carriage when it arrived, with Selim leaning heavily on Vahan. Arriving in the City, Vahan saw Selim into a carriage prior to trudging home himself to his lodgings in the now much quieter streets. Selim trundled home, unaware of the telegram awaiting him informing him of his father's death that morning. Vahan, too, walked home, equally unaware of the letter winging its way to him from his brother as to his own father's arrest and disappearance from home, that very same day.

It was the last hours of the 24th April. The City brooded, as the great western armada finally began arriving at the fatal entrance of the Dardanelles.

CHAPTER 24

Harry at Gallipoli

No one could have called General Hamilton, the British Commander in Chief a "donkey commanding *lions*." He was a kindly gentleman of impeccable breeding and manners, a poet manqué, with a lyrical turn of phrase, very popular wth all the troops However he was simply not ruthless enough to take command of a whole army. From the very start, he had been unable to stand up to Kitchener and Churchill, two far more forceful characters, so he failed to insist on those matters of detail, vitally necessary if the coming operation was to have any hope of succeeding. He was simply the wrong commander in the wrong place at the wrong time.

> "'Good morning, good morning,' the General said
> when we met him last week on the line.
> Now – the soldiers he smiled at are most of 'em dead,
> And we're cursing his staff for incompetent swine,
> 'He's a cheery old card' grunted Harry to Jack,
> As they slogged up the hill with rifle and pack …
> But he did for them both, by his plan of attack."

The contrast with Mustafa Kemal, the Turkish General in command of the defences of Gallipoli, was enormous. Inevitably, Turkish accounts of the Gallipoli operations have concentrated on the part he played in the defence. But this is, for once, a justified piece of hagiography. Despite the contribution of General Liman von Sanders, the German military advisor, in the early stages, in the end it was the dogged defence of the high ground – the spine that ran down the centre of the peninsula – by the patient Anatolian peasant-soldiers, inspired by the personal leadership of Kemal, that 'did for' Harry and Jack and the entire allied operation.

Back on the beachhead, the ship on which Harry was stationed lay close in to the shore as the infantry disembarked onto the beaches.

Believing the arrangements for the wounded to have been totally inadequate, the commanding officer of Harry's ship instructed him to go ashore with the second wave

"The chief RAMC officer told me yesterday they were only expecting a ridiculously small number of casualties. I blew up, as you can imagine, There doesn't seem to be any real provision for taking off the wounded. We could help out a bit with basic first aid. I'll send Seamen Jim Conrad, and Jack Jones with you – they're good strong lads. We are not leaving till tomorrow morning, and we could help out by taking off a few of the wounded. But look Harry, whatever the situation, I want you back by daybreak as we must leave by 0700 hours."

So, an hour or two after nightfall Harry, and the two seamen, landed at Geba Tepe in the dark, and in a miserable sleeting rain. As they neared the shore, bullets and shrapnel were splashing into the water, with some thunking into the boats.

"Hey, mate, how far are we from the shore," asked one of the soldiers.

"I'm not at all sure," Harry replied, "but it was deep enough here for the ship to come quite far in. Maybe another 10 minutes." He was trying to sound as off-hand as possible, though he was in a fair state of panic himself inside.

"I bloody well hope so – I'm getting fucking sea-sick, much worse than when we were at sea. Oh. bloody hell! – I'm going to throw up."

"Hey, Jacko, if you're going to be sick come here and stick your face over the side, bullets or not," called out another.

"Don't be daft. I can't bloody well move."

"Christ, you fucking old gumsucker – for god's sake belt up and save your breath. You'll be all right lad – just think of how wonderful that hard solid ground is going to feel once we arrive," called out the old Sergeant at the front of the tossing boat.

Harry looked round at all these young men, none much more than nineteen; excited, deadly frightened, but still grinning, carefully hiding their real fears from their companions.

Once the boat crunched onto the sand, they jumped out into a scene of indescribable confusion. On the narrow strip of sandy and stony beach, at the foot of the hills, which rose ridge after ridge above them, men were moving about in all directions. Troops marching west, troops marching east; mules and horses – some stationary with their heads drooping, some carrying stores to god knows where; water barrels dumped haphazardly; and, above all, stretcher bearers coming down the cliffs with wounded and dying men.

The next day on the ship, as it ploughed its way back to Egypt, Harry sat down and wrote to his mother –

"Before half an hour was over, my work began, and after that I never had a moment. It went on till about three in the morning. One wounded and dying man after the other. Poor fellows, with wounds of all kinds, disfigured and caked with blood and dirt; some totally unrecognisable. But, mother, within minutes, I found I was ceasing to feel the terror and horror of the situation. Sights that ordinarily would have upset me, seemed to pass over me without any feeling at all. I closed the eyes of one young lad, he couldn't have been much more than eighteen, who had been moaning for his mother for two hours. I did it almost absentmindedly when he died, whilst I was bandaging up someone else.

Mother, dear, it was bitterly cold all night, but one of the desparately few ambulance men around, lit a fire. There was still the sound of sniper shots coming from the hills above us, but even this sound died out as the night wore on. At about four in the morning, the noise started all over again and we suddenly found ourselves being shelled by the *Goeben*, which had crept up during the night and began lobbing shells at us from the other side of the peninsula, anchored as she was safely in the Straits. I thought of the Report I had written, and the dramatic sight of the *Goeben* on that very first day of the war, whilst I stood on the bridge of the Indefatigable, and saw the great ship slowly slipping away from us in the dusk. Now here she was again, hurling shells at us. At times I fancied that she was aiming at me personally.

The confusion remained incredible. Eventually, we followed the stretcher bearers, working their way down to the beaches, which were again being raked by rifle fire from the heights above. Jack and I helped to put some of the wounded into our pinnace which was waiting, and we set off for the ship. Jim was no longer with us. Shrapnel fire from the *Goeben* had done for him only minutes before. Love Harry"

On the other side of the artificial line separating the two bodies of men, there was similar activity, but not quite the same confusion. As the line solidified during the night and the next day, Kemal Pasha set up his headquarters right on the front line.

And so another stalemate of the Great War began. After some six months, out of about one mil*lion* men drawn in to the conflict in the Gallipoli peninsula on both sides, about a half became casualties of one sort or another. Of this half mil*lion*, about a quarter were dead.

The effect of the whole campaign from a military point of view was negligible. But, politically, the operation was undoubtedly instrumental in triggering the massacre of the Armenian people, the first of the many attempted ethnic cleansings which have so disfigured the rest of the 20th century.

CHAPTER 25

Garabed's escape

The next day, Raffi went out again to see if the arrested men herded into the town hall gardens were still there, but the place was empty. The news of the landings at Gallipoli the previous evening had been filtering through all morning on the telegraph line. Fearful for his father, Raffi walked back through the narrow streets without daring to make enquiries as to what had happened to those arrested. He returned home to his grieving mother without being able to hold out any hope.

In fact, that very morning before dawn, four decrepit lorries had arrived at the town hall. The whole group, including doctors, lawyers, businessmen and some district heads, had been herded into the back, where there was only standing room. There were very few lorries in Caesaria, but this group were considered important enough to warrant transport and guards.

The government had released criminals from the prisons, and the whole countryside around Caesaria was to become a killing ground for people about to be deported from this and other like towns on foot. This was the policy of 'ethnic cleansing' now being planned in Constantinople by Talaat and the others. But for this group, the leaders of the community in the first of the deportations, there were lorries! And significantly unlike the later mass deportations was that each lorry was accompanied by two or three armed Turkish soldiers at the front and back.

Although there were some petrol cans slung along the sides, Garabed believed that the lorries were only going a short distance, after which they would drop their human cargo and turn back.

Everything that was happening was entirely outside the experience of these men. There was no precedent, no point of reference to inform them how they should act. Between them, they had a wealth of experience in managing the affairs of their local communities, businesses and churches, but the violence and intimidation of their present treatment, had sapped their collective will. Not one of them would have hesitated to act decisively if one of their children had been threatened, yet now, fully cognizant of the danger of their situation, they took no action at all.

The lorries trundled on over rough roads winding through the wild mountains into the countryside. Little was said by the men squeezed together, standing and swaying as the trucks jolted about. Garabed reflected that he had perhaps made a mistake in not taking all the gold coins. He had been under the impression that he was not going to survive the night, and any coins he might have on him would surely have been quickly stolen. However, surprisingly, none of the deportees had even been searched, and many of them had managed to retain some cash.

As they passed through the poor impoverished villages, those with money purchased bread and other provisions from the villagers whenever the lorries stopped.

Eventually the group came to a halt in a narrow valley, with bare moss-covered hills, rocky and strewn with boulders on either side. Running down the middle was a little stream with rubbish and the bones of dead animals alongside. In the middle of the valley there was a small *khan* – a local wayside inn – a ramshackle building with rooms for travellers and a large kitchen. This was a barren desolate spot, and had clearly been chosen as the first night's stop as it was well away from any inhabited area. Standing in the dusty area in front of this building were eight or nine high-sided ox-driven carts; the oxen grazing on the sparse grass nearby.

Everyone got out of the lorries, and some of the prisoners wandered into the *khan* to purchase food, encouraged by the guards who now distributed loaves from several bags of unleavened bread stowed in the back of the carts. There was little sign, at this stage, of any racial tension between the prisoners and the local soldiers. This was early days, before the grim machinery of the deportations had been devised and implemented. The prisoners shared their purchases of boiled eggs, onions, olives and cheese with each other, and with the guards who had accompanied them from Caesaria.

It was still light when the starting handles of the lorries were turned and they drove off back to the town. At almost the same moment a further cart, holding a dozen smartly uniformed soldiers, appeared over the hill behind them and drew up in front of the *khan* alongside the other carts. The men all piled out of the cart and formed rank. Garabed saw that they were a detachment of gendarmes and were led by a hard-faced officer – an Enver look-alike with the unmistakable stamp of an Ittihad supporter. The atmosphere darkened immediately.

A few bedraggled tents had been in the back of the carts when they had arrived. Some of the prisoners now set about, somewhat inefficiently, putting them up in the grass around the *khan*. It was not a particularly cold night, although at this altitude anyone without a good coat would have been in real difficulty. Garabed chose to sleep outside, wrapped up in his good sheepskin for which he blessed his wife. Before settling down, he smoked a cigarette with an old acquaintance.

"Garabed, agha, what in heaven's name is really going on. Are we facing another pogrom?"

"My dear Levon, I've no idea, but I fear the worst. We seem to be a very carefully chosen group. This is not just a round-up of *giavours* to satisfy the gutter instincts of the mob, but a carefully selected list prepared by the authorities."

"Nonsense, Garabed, the regime isn't clear-minded or efficient enough."

"Levon, it might not be clear-minded, but it's certainly efficient enough. Think about it! In the old days of Abdul the damned, there would have been screaming and shouting, bullying, blood-lust and death, but not this awful cold Prussian efficiency. I fear we could be facing imminent execution at any point, somewhere remote on the way, – maybe even here."

"But Garabed, why would they go to all this trouble, for heaven's sake, when they could simply have had us all shot in the town hall gardens yesterday?"

"Because, Levon, they still have European allies and they daren't risk the adverse publicity. Quite apart from the unrest that would be aroused in the Armenian population if there were open shootings in the town, it is likely that there would be a few influential Turks of the old school who would object and report to Constantinople."

"Well, even if you're right about that – why are they doing it? What's the point of this carefully drawn-up list?"

"First, Levon, they get rid of the natural leaders of the community. Most of the young men are gone already, either in the army or in labour battal*ion*s. They can then deal with the old men, the women and the children as they want."

"My God, Garabed. Aren't you being over-pessimistic? Nothing like this has ever happened before. Go to sleep, my friend, you'll feel better in the morning."

Once wrapped up and alone, Garabed began considering his position further. On the one hand, although he was not an intimate friend of any of the others, he knew most of them, and they knew him. He felt the warm camaraderie of men sharing the same discomfort and danger.

On the other hand, Garabed was one of the few prisoners who was aware of the changed political situation within the empire. This awareness was as a result of the beating that he alone, apparently, had suffered two weeks before at the police station. He recognised a sinister under-current, camouflaged by the basically indifferent attitude of the Anatolian peasant soldiers guarding them, but which was not manifest in the new guards who had just arrived, or in their officer. In the last few weeks, officials had become curt and evasive. Garabed knew that this was not just some war-time emergency measure. Death was present, group or no group.

The choice was clear. Did he stay with the group, sharing its fate, one way or another, or did he try to make it on his own? If escape was to take place, it had to be done this very night. Would survival be more likely if he struck out now on his own into unknown territory in a wild countryside, or if he stayed instead with the group being led like sheep to God knows what fate?

He did not know where he was, he had no food apart from that one loaf of bread, which the guards had handed out. He lay awake, turning it all over in his mind. In the end it all came down to the fact that by slipping away, if he could, he would at least be taking his fate back into his own hands.

Gathering up his coat quietly and wrapping it round the loaf, he began crawling slowly along, avoiding the tent pegs and the sleeping bodies. He had noted the exact position of the two guards on night watch. Both were dozing and he knew that he must get away before the second watch.

"Good-bye Garabed – good luck – may God be with you," whispered one of the sleeping bodies as he slithered past. An elderly voice, Garabed never knew who it was or what became of him. Slowly and stealthily he drew away from the light of the two fires burning away near the two guards.

Once out of sight and across the stream, Garabed rose, stretched and began striding away up the hillside northwards. He reckoned that this would be in the opposite direction to that taken by the group, which would presumably be going to the south towards the Arab provinces – if it was going to go anywhere at all. He planned to be several miles away, well into the hills, long before the camp rose in the morning.

He stumbled on, heading northwards guided by the stars. As the sun rose the next morning, he found himself in the middle of mossy, rocky hills with no sign of life anywhere. Garabed, a leader of the Armenian community in the city, a father of six children, a respected merchant dressed in a dark town suit already crumpled and totally unsuitable for the countryside, found himself in the middle of the Anatolian wilderness, alone, afraid, unable to return to his home. This enormous change in his life had happened in a mere forty-eight hours. For the moment, putting all thoughts of his family and former life out of his mind, he strode on.

Two days later, his eldest son – Vahan – received the news of the arrest and immediate deportation when he returned home from his day with the Avakians. The news arrived in a letter written to him by his brother Raffi –

My dear brother,

I know that mother wrote to you a week or so ago about the awful experience our father went through at the Police station. I was so mad, Vahan, when I saw father slung across the back of that bloody donkey, like a sack of grain, I simply couldn't keep still. Once we had got father inside I left him to our mother and sisters' capable hands, and went running out into the countryside, I was so charged up. I am afraid, Vahan, that this was not the end. Yesterday something terrible happened and we are all afraid that it is only the beginning. Father was arrested and taken to the town hall. Mother gave me some money to take to him once we got over the initial shock and knew where he was. There were about eighty other Armenians arrested with him. I saw them all milling about in the town hall gardens. Vahan, I was scared stiff – the news of the allied landings only arrived later, but the general feeling in the town was awful. The news of the Van rebel*lion*, and the killings in the East, are all over town.

I went again to the town hall this morning, but they had already been taken away. Oh, Vahan, father made it clear that he didn't expect to survive. I knew that I ought not to let him see me cry, but I couldn't help it. He held my hand tight, and looked hard into my eyes, and then spoke quite sharply, telling me to go home and look after his wife and daughters. He would not even lean forward to kiss me through the railings – I couldn't bear it.

We keep hearing terrible rumours of what is being prepared for the Armenian community here. My dear brother – if it is at all possible, could you send urgently to our mother a copy of your commission in the Harbiye Military academy. I am not certain, but I feel that now most of the leaders of our community have gone, the authorities are planning something awful for the women and children left behind. I believe it may be very helpful to mother if she can show that her eldest son is an officer in the Ottoman army – even if only a student. Please don't worry if what I ask is impossible. Vahan, look after yourself.

Your loving brother.

CHAPTER 26

Karekin's escape

Karekin remained at the window of the station restaurant for several minutes staring at the spot where Armineh had been standing, long after she and Sima had departed. Although few of the group had any real idea what this was all about, Karekin didn't rate his chances of survival very high. Slowly, after the last scheduled train of the day left, the station emptied until there were not even any railway employees present. In the concourse, groups of soldiers stood about bored and disconsolate, whilst in the restaurant, general conversation had dried up.

In due course, after it had grown dark outside, the special train ordered by the government finally arrived. The prisoners were shepherded out, counted, and ordered into the coaches. No one had any idea what was happening; even the officers in charge seemed unclear about what was going on. The doors from the corridors into the compartments were all open. An order was given that all doors must remain open at all times. Three or four armed guards were allocated to each coach, sitting at each end and patrolling up and down the corridor at regular intervals. Otherwise, the prisoners were free to sit wherever they wanted and to talk amongst themselves. Some bread was distributed. Many of the group had purchased cheese, olives and fruit in the station restaurant, all of which was shared in each compartment. There were those among them who were resigned, those who were in a state of denial, those who were calm and those who were in a state of complete panic.

Karekin noted that only a couple of officers boarded the train. Both were in the front coach. The rest of the officers and remaining soldiers lined up on the platform waiting for the train to leave. Eventually, to the accompaniment of whistles and yells, the train let off steam and began pulling away. The officers left on the platform saluted.

"My, my," muttered Aram to Karekin with a wry smile "what an honour".

"*Morituri te salutant*," murmured Karekin, getting his quote totally the wrong way round.

Karekin and Aram had managed to get a compartment to themselves and were able to lie down, sleeping on and off during the night. Within an hour or two of leaving the lights of Haydar Pasha station behind, most of the passengers were sound asleep, exhausted from the physical and mental strain of the last 12 hours.

During the course of the next day the train trundled on, passing through Eskishehir and turning south to take the line leading to Eregli, and the as yet unfinished tunnels through the Taurus mountains. It appeared that their eventual destination was to be the Vilayet of Aleppo in the Arab province of Syria.

"Karekin, what do you think this is about?" asked Aram Manuelian.

"My dear Aram, I've no idea, but I suppose it's all tied up with the allied invasion in the Dardanelles. You can see that they haven't just arrested the 'politicals' – the deputies or the journalists or the activist lawyers, which the government might regard as the troublemakers. It includes all the leading elements of the community, religious, artistic and social as well as political."

"Well, Karekin, that means – doesn't it – that it is not simply a 'security' issue in the face of an enemy invasion, but an attack on the whole Armenian community."

"I'm afraid that is exactly what I do think. What we have to face up to right now is whether they intend to shoot us all somewhere, or whether they genuinely intend to send us to Aleppo."

"My dear Karekin, what the blazes would they do with us all once we got to Aleppo anyway? Are they going to put us in some sort of camp – I doubt it? That would mean having to feed and shelter us. No, no this train has to be emptied soon after Eregli, whatever their present intentions, because the tunnels through the Taurus are not completed yet, so we will have to walk or ride. At that moment, my friend, some story of a breakout, or of marauding Kurdish brigands, will be concocted for foreign consumption, and the entire group will disappear – murdered – while the authorities wring their hands and talk about the impossibly difficult conditions in the interior."

"Well if that's the case, Aram, why don't we just try to get out of the window next time the train stops."

"Sheer inertia, and the fear of the unknown, Karekin. At the moment we still remain in touch, however tenuously, with civilisation and the way of life we've always known. This is a train, it's fairly comfortable, the soldiers belong to our government, and we can't believe in our hearts that it has changed so drastically. Out there, we would be on our own in the middle of a near desert, with no experience of how to survive. So, we sit where we are, heading for god knows what, but afraid to do something about it."

"Yes, I understand. But we're free agents, we can surely think it out, one way or another," Karekin mused.

Night came again – more dry bread was distributed, and the passengers settled down for a second night as the train trundled on slowly through the desolate Anatolian countryside. Eventually, early in the morning as the sun was rising, the train arrived with much shunting and hooting into a goods yard alongside the main station of Konya. Konya, a larger town than Caesaria, was the capital of the Vilayet of the same name.

Karekin woke with a start – it was about six o'clock in the morning. Checking that there was no guard in the corridor outside the compartment, he opened the window and leaned out, taking a deep breath of the cold fresh air with great satisfaction.

"For God's sake, shut the window, it's freezing cold out there," snapped Aram, turning to find a better place to put his sleepy head, and stretching his legs out.

Karekin grunted and continued to look out. Directly in front of him, on the other side of the railway line, was a platform, not intended for the travelling public but for freight handling. Over to his left was a marshalling yard with several lines of railway trucks, either waiting for despatch, or to be unloaded. In the middle of the platform were some railway employees, dressed in brown overalls, ready for track mainenance work.

Seeing Karekin leaning out of the window, one of them – a young man scarcely more than a teenager, jumped down from the platform and sauntered over.

"Hello, *effendi*, this is unusual, to have a passenger train stopping in this goods yard."

Karekin, recognising at once by his accent that he was probably Armenian, switched to Armenian and gave a short account of what seemed to be happening.

"*Effendi*, there are no guards here on this side of the train – you must get away. We have been hearing all day of arrests and deportation orders all over Eastern Anatolia. Your lives will be in danger if you stay on this train."

Just then, there was a whistle and a small engine came into sight pulling several flat trucks, loaded with tools and sleepers and rail lines, together with some high-sided closed trucks.

"That's our work train," the young man pointed. "Good luck, *effendi*, my name is Aram," saying which he saluted and ran across the line to join the others on the platform. The train now pulled up, with the closed high-sided trucks standing between the deportation train and the platform.

Karekin did not hesitate. Whatever it was that triggered his decision he would never know.

"Wake up Aram, wake up" he whispered, shaking the dozing doctor violently but quietly.

"What is it, what is it?"

"Quick, Aram, now's our chance – probably our last one. We've got to get away. We can easily get over the window and jump or fall out. There is a train right alongside. Come on, come on."

Karekin began pulling himself up onto the lowered window, squeezing through and ready to drop out on the other side.

"I don't know, Karekin, I don't know," wailed Aram in a state of frightened indecision, although now fully awake.

"For God's sake, Aram, the worst that could happen at this stage is that we'll get a very painful beating if we're caught. Look, I am going – are you coming."

"Yes, Karekin, yes – go – go!" and Aram jumped up, and with a quick look at the still empty corridor, clambered onto the window as Karekin dropped down to the ground between the two stationary steaming trains.

They both stood there, crouching and panting, not so much with exertion, but from the rush of adrenalin. Then running between the trains, bent almost double to avoid being seen from any windows, they sprinted along until they passed the last coach. Trying to act nonchalant, they began walking slowly across the rail tracks to the left, towards the marshalling yard. They felt that by walking slowly they might be taken for native inhabitants. This was ridiculous as they were fully dressed in smart city business suits, even if now soiled and crumpled. Fortunately, they were not spotted before they reached the first of the waiting goods trains. They ran up and down between the trucks trying out the great metal doors. Most were locked, or wide open, showing empty holds.

Eventually they found one that was closed, but not yet locked. With some effort they managed to pull the door open enough to allow them to squeeze inside. They found they were sharing the freight car with a cargo of hazelnuts. The space was filled almost to the top, and already the action of pulling open the door had dislodged the cargo and many nuts had trickled down into the grooves of the sliding door. They hauled themselves up and in, and then spent the next five minutes straining and pulling to close the door, dislodging more nuts, which split and cracked as the door slid over them, never managing to close the door completely. Then they burrowed into the pile of nuts at the far end of the truck – dislodging yet more.

Back on the deportation train, the open window and the empty compartment had been discovered and a search of the station precincts was ordered.

Aram and Karekin heard the soldiers calling out to each other when they finally arrived at the several freight trains waiting in the marshalling yard. With pounding hearts, and unable to say anything, Karekin heard them moving down between the freight cars, trying each door. Eventually one of the soldiers arrived at the hazelnut car. Grunting with effort he tried to open up the door, which was now completely wedged. Karekin, out of pure nervousness, began chewing a previously cracked nut. The guard continued to strain at the door. He then stopped and called out to his mates –

"This one is either locked or rusted, so there can't be anyone in there," and he moved on to the next car.

The search went on all over the station for another hour, until at about 8.00 Karekin heard the shriek of the train's whistle and the welcome sound of the pounding of the rails as the deportation train pulled out of the station, with its load of passengers either on their way to safety in Aleppo, or to their doom somewhere before.

The two friends now had to decide what to do. Their quick look at the area had already revealed that the station yard was surrounded by walls and fences. Yet whatever happened, they would have to open the truck door sooner or later. They scrambled out of the pile of nuts slowly and using only their pens and their fingers, they started to prize away the nuts stuck in the grooves. By midday, they were able to move the door sufficiently to allow them to squeeze out whenever they needed to. But they had nowhere to go, with the goods yard buzzing with employees going about their business.

With no food, they munched away at the hazelnuts and waited.

Suddenly in the late afternoon, after boredom had driven them both to distraction, they felt the jolt of an engine being connected to the head of their train. Karekin got ready to jump out, almost in relief, but Aram put his hand on his arm –

"Karekin, my soul, don't move. This is one certain way out of the yard. It's only a goods train, it will travel very slowly. We'll jump out once we're free of the station."

Karekin nodded, and they waited tensely.

Within minutes the coaches shuddered, jolted back and forth, and then began slowly trundling out of the station – through the great gates, and into the outskirts of the town. The hazelnuts were thrown about haphazardly all over the car. The two friends stood and slithered about as the train jerked and stopped and started again.

Eventually, the train began running alongside a beaten dusty path, with houses and sheds on the other side, moving very slowly. Karekin stood by the door with Aram behind him, waiting for a moment when nobody was around. Suddenly it came –

"Now, Aram, now," he cried and jumped out – followed immediately by his friend. They sprinted across the path the moment they landed, and melted away into a narrow street between some houses. They stood panting a moment, leaning against a wall. They had escaped but now found themselves in the middle of a hostile world, where they were now outlaws. The train moved on out of sight, They grinned nervously at each other, catching their breath.

CHAPTER 27

Mikael and his father

It was a fine warm day on the day after all the dramatic arrests – the 25th April - that Mikael Sarafian stood on the Galata Bridge leaning on the iron railings. It was already almost six months since the Empire had entered into the great European war in the winter of 1914, changing Mikael's life as drastically as it had changed that of so many others. He had joined up in the Ottoman army the previous year in November, 1914.

At 24 years of age, Mikael was a tall, thin young man, with flashing black eyes and straight dark hair, sporting the standard black moustache of Ottoman young men of the period. He had a superiority of expression that marked him more as a Turk, than an Armenian.

Like most young Ottomans, he had originally welcomed the revolution of 1908, which was supposed to have established the principle of equality before the law. This meant that both Christians and Muslims were required to serve in the military. Reciprocally, the Muslims were supposed to pay the special tax, previously levied on the Christian millet, in lieu of military service.

Mikael, from a poor family and unable to get any deferment, had been one of the first of the Armenian youths to become a private in a Stambouli army unit training outside the city. He recalled the conversation with his father, Avedis, on the day he registered at the government office in the suburb of Makrikoy, where the family lived.

"My son," his father had said, "you know my views. I am against all these changes that are being forced on the dynasty. We were always prepared to pay the exemption tax instead of bearing arms – why change now?"

"But father, only by enforcing absolute equality before the law will the Empire stand any chance of survival. After all, you would feel differently about forceably taking the first-born sons from Christian families as janisseries, just because it worked so well years and years ago. "

"Come, come – don't be sarcastic with me, son, I'm not arguing against change *per se*, I'm simply pointing out that mimicking all Western European practices isn't correct in all circumstances. I don't believe that the Army will treat Armenian and Greek recruits in the same way as it treats Arabs and Turks. Decrees, my boy, don't change people's basic attitudes that easily."

"Father the right and duty of all citizens to bear arms is a fundamental principle for any nation. That's what being a citizen is all about."

"Yes, yes, my boy, that may indeed what we are all being taught by the West, but all that matters to them, son, is their nation's capacity to impose its will on other nations, by force if necessary. Oh dear, don't mind me, my son, go and fight for the Padishah if that's what you want."

"Father, it has nothing to do with choice – I have to, in these days of conscription."

Mikael watched as two ferries almost collided trying to get to the next space on the quayside. He reflected that four months in a Turkish regiment had shown that his father had after all been right. Mikael hadn't experienced any overt racism from the other soldiers, most of whom were from Stamboul, and used to the rich racial mixture of the city. However, the attitude of the officers was different. The Armenian and Greek soldiers were given the more menial tasks, and Mikael had been fortunate to escape being sent to the interior in the labour battal-ions to repair roads.

After the many months of training, Mikael's unit was about to be assigned to a front, and there had been much speculation among the soldiers whether this would be against the British in the Sinai, or the Russians in the Caucasus. It was on the 18th April that he was sum-moned by the duty officer. He had rushed off to the office of the young lieutenant, currently the duty adjutant. Mikael had saluted and, stand-ing at attention, waited for the officer to speak.

"Private Sarafian, I must tell you that this morning we received a note from your mother informing us that your father is dangerously ill, and unlikely to survive for more than a few days. Under the circum-stances, soldier, I am issuing you with a week's pass to go home. I trust all will be well. May Allah protect you and your family."

With that, Mikael had saluted and turned away. He had packed his very meagre belongings and hurried home. The Sarafians lived in a modest, ramshackle, terraced house in the middle of the small town-ship of Makrikoy. Mikael, in his ill-fitting uniform of a private in the Ottoman army, was entitled to free railway travel, just as well, as he had hardly a piastre on him. He had walked quickly and anxiously through the quiet dusty streets.

On reaching the house, after embracing his mother at the door, Mi-kael had raced upstairs, his mother having indicated with a nod that his father was in their bedroom. Avedis lay propped up in bed. He was unshaven and looked pale and sickly.

The bedroom, at the back of the small house, was dark and had a faint smell of mothballs. There was a large, heavy, dark mahogany wardrobe, which took up the whole of one wall of the room. Always locked, as well as the linen it held all the secrets of the household, the family savings, the documents and all their more important possessions.

The small window on the other wall looked out onto the back alley and was always shuttered. On the wall behind the bed hung old sepia photographs, heavily touched up, of the four grandparents who Mi-kael had never known – except through these old highly posed photo-graphs. Finally, against the fourth wall there was an old French dressing table, probably the only valuable piece in the whole house.

"Baba, Baba, what's the matter" stuttered Mikael, running forward to his father's side as his mother stood at the door looking on.

"My son, my son, welcome," whispered Avedis as Mikael embraced his father.

"Father, what's wrong?" he asked, after drawing back from that first embrace.

"My son, it's a mixture of old age, and something going wrong with my breathing."

"But Baba, come, come, you're not even 60 yet. What does the Doctor say?" Mikael, turned to his mother as he spoke. His mother looked hard at him, without tears or emotion, but said nothing and turned away.

All that week, Mikael spent his days sitting next to his father, by the side of the bed, in the dark and enclosed bedroom. In the afternoons, his young brother and 15 year-old sister would return from school and come to join him. Mikael would leave for an hour or two and talk to his mother. Mikael always saw his mother as a dry and dissatisfied woman, with thin disapproving lips and an unhappy disposition, while his father was an expansive, jolly man, filled with bonhomie. When guests had come to the house, he was always the life and soul of the party.

After an hour or two of desultory conversation with his mother, Mikael would return to his father's bedroom. His sister and young brother would leave, and Mikael would spend the rest of the evening chatting and playing interminable games of backgammon with his father.

Avedis was clearly getting weaker by the day, but was hanging on, and he had remained interested throughout in what was going on in the wider world. In fact it was on this 25th April that he had asked Mikael to go into the city and purchase the latest newspapers – Turkish as well as Armenian.

The British had landed in the Gallipoli peninsula that morning. There were rumours that the Russians were going to invade from the north, and perhaps that the Greek army was also approaching. The Greeks in the city were in a state of excitement. The Turks were anxious and angry. The Jews were worried for the long-term future of the Empire, which had sheltered them for so long. The Armenians were in a state of total panic. Mikael had arrived in the city just as the news of the arrest of over four hundred prominent Armenians the day before had become common knowledge. It appeared clear that they had either been deported to the interior or had been liquidated.

After staring at the busy shipping for over half an hour, Mikael at last sighed and turned away. He hurried across the bridge towards the Armenian Patriarchate compound, where he prayed for a few minutes in the church. He went round to the office to ask if a priest could accompany him home to perform a final blessing for his father, who was not expected to survive for more than a day or two, but no Priest was immediately available, as too many had been called out to give comfort to families distraught at the loss of their men folk. However, the staff on duty told him to leave his address, and return fare, and a priest would come as soon as possible the next morning.

When Mikael got home that evening, he reported all the news to Avedis.

"Father, the really devastating news is the arrest of over four hundred of our people, simply because they were Armenians. Even our gentle Father Komitas was among those deported. This is pure racial persecution isn't it? It makes me hopping mad."

"I'm sorry, my son, truly sorry," whispered the ever weaker Avedis, whose eyes remained as bright as ever. "This sounds like state repression of the worst kind. I really fear for the future of our community."

The sheer effort of speaking, gave rise to a fit of coughing from Avedis, and a hug, and a 'hush, hush' from Mikael. There was silence for a time before Mikael spoke.

"Father, I heard that my army unit has already left for Gallipoli – I will have to go soon. My leave runs out in a day or two."

Avedis had given no reply to this, but had sunk back onto the pillows, already exhausted by the few words he had spoken.

In the morning a priest arrived. On entering, he blessed the house, and extended the blessing to Vartuhi, who knelt and kissed his hand as he came in. Mikael himself came down, crossed himself at the sight of the priest and also knelt and kissed the priest's ring. He then escorted the priest upstairs to the bedroom. Vartuhi did not follow.

"My name is Father Haroutiune" the priest said to Avedis, who had struggled to sit up a little in his bed. Mikael's sister, who had stayed at home that morning, plumped up the pillows and held her father up as the priest took out his oil, put the sign of the cross on Avedis' forehead, and began reciting prayers in a quiet sing-song voice, finally giving a blessing to all in the room. Mikael brought forward a chair, and the priest sat down by the bedside and stretched out to hold Avedis' hand.

There was then a long period of silence. His father turned his increasingly feverish eyes on the old priest, managing to whisper.

"Father, my son is a conscript in the army. His unit has been sent to the Gallipoli front. Armenians are being arrested and deported all over the Empire for no other reason save they are Armenian."

He began coughing and gasping for air. They all urged him to stop talking, but he raised his hand making it clear that what he had to say was important to him.

"You know, Father, I've always been a believer. I've also always supported the Ottoman state. I have never had any patience with the nationalist revolutionaries. But, Father, where the state has deliberately turned against a part of their own people, do those people still have a moral duty to support that state?"

"Render unto Caesar that which is Caesar's and unto God that which is God's," Haroutiune intoned a little sadly. "That is the Christian teaching, my son. The Muslims of course say that it's one and the same. The head of their state, the Sultan, is for them the same person as the head of their religion, the Caliph." The three Sarafians stared at him uncomprehendingly.

Haroutiune sighed, belatedly realising that the family were not interested in the theological difference between the Christian and Muslim attitudes towards duty to the state. He paused and thought for a moment before starting to speak again. He cleared his throat nervously.

"Avedis *effendi*, a month ago my answer to your question would have been that loyalty to the state that nurtured you was all-important. However, the reports that I have been getting from the interior, the deportations that have begun all over the Empire, the terror that is being turned against our people by the state itself, has unquestionably altered the situation. Your son must, of course, act according to his own conscience. However, I now believe that the moral authority of the state has been compromised by openly picking out our young men to be sent to the most dangerous sectors of the front or to labour batta*lion*s in the interior, like convicts. I fear that the deportation of whole families, whole villages, to God knows where, Avedis *effendi*, is the beginning of a great evil the like of which has never been seen before."

There was a long pause – a moment of silence that hung heavily in the air between them all. Then Father Haroutiune stood up, raised his hand high above the bed to make the sign of the cross, and spoke in a loud and firm voice.

"Whatever may befall … May the blessing of God almighty, the love of his son Jesus Christ, and the spirit of the Holy Ghost be with you all in this room, now and for evermore and to the end of time."

Mikael, whose head had been bowed, looked up and saw the little priest bend down and kiss his father on the forehead. The priest then turned and walked out of the bedroom.

Mikael remained in the room all day, rejoined by his sister Nairi, once the priest had left. His father was clearly sinking; as the afternoon wore on, his breath became more and more laboured. In the evening, Avedis, in a hoarse whisper, spoke his last words to them both, sitting by the bed on either side, whilst Vartuhi stood silently in the doorway,

"Mikael, my soul, I have thought hard about what I am going to say. I've thought of all the possible consequences. My advice to you is not to rejoin your unit. Don't go back, Mikael, my son, don't go back. My son … my son …"

He then looked up at Vartuhi, standing in the doorway. They stared at each other for a moment of eternity. Avedis then closed his eyes and died.

On the death of his father that April, Mikael had been involved in arranging the funeral. He was already two or three days overdue from the expiry date of the pass issued by his superior officer. Mikael did not worry too much about this as, first and foremost, he had to fulfil his duty to his family and ensure his father was honourably buried. He knew that he would be in some trouble when he finally did return, but Muslim officers would appreciate the overriding requirement to see his father properly buried.

Father Haroutiune had agreed to conduct the service, and Avedis was to be buried in the cemetery at Sisli. Mikael, Nairi and Vartuhi set off early in the morning; Mikael's younger brother – Mardiros – was left with a neighbour at Vartuhi's insistence. Mikael, could not understand his mother's response to the death of her husband. She shed no tears, seeming detached and distracted.

At the little church in the cemetery officiated by Father Haroutiune, there were only about thirty people present – friends of Avedis, and some cousins and other relatives whom Mikael scarcely knew. The ancient rituals of the Armenian Orthodox burial service were observed, beautified by the music of Father Komitas. Mikael felt a welling of emotion as the liquid notes of the "Sourp, Sourp" rose from the voices of the small choir. At that moment there was a slight disturbance, as three more people entered at the back. Mikael, intent on his memories of his father did not look back. However, he saw his mother Vartuhi glance backwards and for the first time he saw she was distressed. She sat down on the hard pew, as everyone remained standing and as the music soared.

Mikael sat down beside her and took her hand.

"Mama, Mama – cry – cry." He mumbled. She looked at him and then away, pale and trembling. Nairi on the other side took Vartuhi's other hand, while tears did at last appear in Vartuhi's eyes.

Father Haroutiune finished a short homily and blessed the coffin. The bearers moved up solemnly and bore it out down the aisle to the graveyard led by the priest. As was the custom, Mikael, walking alone, went immediately after the coffin, followed at a short distance by Vartuhi and Nairi. As he got to the door, Mikael heard a short cry, and a gasp from the small congregation behind him.

He turned. Vartuhi was standing stock still, her face flushed, staring at a woman, considerably younger than herself, who was standing at the back holding the hands of two small boys. His mother appeared to be breathing hard, while Nairi grasped Vartuhi tightly round her waist. There was a moment of silence. Meanwhile, the coffin bearers, with Father Haroutiune ahead of them, were walking on through the cemetery, having noticed nothing.

"I am going home," hissed Vartuhi, handing Mikael a brown envelope for delivery to the priest and the small choir. Then, without another word, pulling herself roughly away from Nairi, she strode past Mikael and down the path out of the cemetery without a backward glance. Mikael, in a turmoil of emotion and confusion could only stand and stare, as the rest of the congregation waited for him to move on.

Mikael hurried after the coffin in a daze, followed by Nairi and the rest of the congregation, catching up with the cortege at the open grave. The bearers laid the coffin in the grave, Father Haroutiune gave the final words and the blessing, and the grave-diggers began filling it in.

Everyone moved up to shake hands with Mikael and Nairi, and at that point Mikael saw the young woman begin to walk away holding the hands of the two small boys. Making his excuses to those who had not yet come forward to offer their condolences, Mikael hurried after the trio as they walked towards the gates of the cemetery. He walked briskly past them, and then turned and faced them. The trio stopped and stared at him.

"Madame," Mikael began, "my name is Mikael Safarian. I am the eldest son of Avedis Safarian, whose funeral has just taken place … May I thank you for attending my father's funeral, and ask you why you have come?" He extended his hand towards her.

The woman ignored the proffered hand and said nothing, while the two boys stared uncomprehendingly up at Mikael.

Mikael was totally thrown by this. He had no idea what to do. Mikael tried to catch the young woman's eyes to no avail. There appeared to be a deadlock, but then Mikael squatted on his haunches, bringing himself down to the level of the two boys. He faced the elder of the two, and smiled.

"Hello! My name is Mikael. What's yours? How old are you?" For a moment there was no response – but then the boy piped up, pulling himself away from his mother's grip.

"My name's Mardik, and I'm seven years-old".

"And you, my lad?"

The other boy, looked with curiosity at Mikael.

"My name is Ardem, and I'm already five years-old. I'll be six soon. What are you doing at my daddy's funeral. Are you his brother?"

"Well, you must be my uncle then," said the elder boy Mardik.

The young woman grabbed at the two boys and began dragging them off. But Mikael was having none of it. He stood firmly in their path making it quite clear that he would not allow her to leave. He saw the other mourners walking away from the grave in the distance, and Nairi slowly making her way towards him through the cypress trees.

Mardik, who had clearly had enough of being held by his mother, again wriggled free of her grasp, and looked at Mikael, to whom he had obviously taken a liking.

"Why did that old woman you were with spit at me, sir?"

Mikael could only stare in confusion. Nairi approached, curiosity overcoming all her other conflicting emotions. Mikael had turned again to the woman –

"This is my sister Nairi. Could you please give me an answer now, Madam. You must surely see that neither I nor my sister can leave here without knowing who you are."

"Mikael, my dear brother, what do you ... " "Nairi, quiet! Madam, please ..."

At last the young woman turned and, sitting down heavily on the grass alongside the stone path just inside the gates, she indicated to her two boys that they could go and play.

"But, Mardik, don't go out of the gates, and always keep an eye on Ardem. Don't pick any flowers anywhere, and stay in sight."

The boys ran off, glad to be let off the leash.

"My name is Katya," the young woman said. Mikael recognised a fairly heavy Russian accent – or could it have been Greek – in the Turkish words.

"I can't say anything to you to make this any easier for you, so I will say it simply and directly. Your father and I have lived together off and on for many years. The two boys are your half- brothers. Oh my God, my God, we should never have come, we should have kept away, I didn't mean ... ," and she burst into tears.

Mikael, although something close to the truth had already started to occur to him, was stunned into silence. As the weeping continued, Nairi spoke.

"But, how is that possible? I've scarcely ever known my father to be away for any length of time. At most, he was away for a day or two every so often when he had to stay in town for work."

"Yes ... well," mumbled the fair-haired Katya almost under her breath. "We live in Yedikule, in a tiny house near the station. On days when your father stayed in the city, he would stay with us. As you know, Yedikule is only a few stops away from Makrikoy. My boys knew that their father had to stay away at nights and could only be with us occasionally. Mardik has recently been getting curious, as he sees how other families live. I've been begging your father to clear up the position one way or another for some time – but you know Avedis – oh my God... so charming, easy-going and such fun, but never decisive."

At this point Katya began quietly sobbing again, hiding her face from Mikael.

"But, my mother ..." Mikael asked.

"Well, she knew all about us of course," Katya wiped away her tears. "She came once to my house. She stood at the door, and we stared at each other for what seemed like an eternity. I knew at once who she was. My boys were much younger, and they came and stood beside me holding my skirts. Your mother stared at the boys and then, without a word said by either of us, she turned and walked away. I have never seen her again until this morning. Avedis told me that on that very day she moved her bed out of the marital bedroom."

Nairi got up and moved away. She joined the two small boys who had been playing with stones, and squatted beside them. Mikael watched her talking quietly with them, while he sat, absolutely shattered, by the side of this young woman, probably only some four or five years older than himself.

Mikael discovered that Katya's parents were originally from the Crimea, and that she was half Greek and half Russian. He must have sat there some time before he realised his mind had completely blanked out. He rose and as they parted, she gave him her address. She and the two boys hurried away as if they were being chased.

As he and Nairi took the train back home from Sirkeci station, he found that despite the revelation, he was unable to change his feelings towards his mother. Suddenly, the reasons behind his mother's feelings had been thrust brutally upon him. All he had room for in his heart was his father's friendly, open-hearted attitude to life as against his mother's repressed and disapproving character.

Neither Vartuhi nor Nairi said anything to Mikael about his continued failure after that day to report back for duty. Day after day passed, and Mikael stayed on in the ramshackle old house. He would take his seven year-old brother Mardiros to school in the morning, and then take the train up to town to work in the great covered bazaar with a Turkish friend from school, who had purchased deferment, and was currently working for his father at their shop.

Twice he went to consult Father Haroutiune about the discovery of his father's secret life. On the second of these occasions, he had referred to his inability to feel for his mother, or wholeheartedly to condemn his father. Haroutiune had replied –

"My son, you don't have to condemn your father in order to feel sympathy for your mother. Avedis undoubtedly sinned, but he seems to have tried to keep his original family together as best he could. Your mother could not forgive him, and that was her prerogative. In repressing her natural instincts for the sake of her three children, she became bitter and destroyed herself emotionally."

"I don't know what to do, Father. I've become a deserter, and I wander about all day without purpose. I can't get the thought of those two little boys, my half-brothers, out of my head. Oh God! I'm so mixed up... What shall I do?"

"Mikael – you have their address – why don't you go and see them?

They're only children. It might do you good. Above all, my son, try to make an effort to understand and comfort your mother."

Fateful words. Mikael felt lighter and more at ease with himself after this conversation. The very next day, on his way up to town, he suddenly took it into his head to alight at Yedikule. He began wandering around the back streets of the poor working-class area near the old fortress, looking for Katya's house.

He had just turned into the little street that he was looking for, when he ran into a patrol of three burly policemen. None of them recognised him as a resident and immediately demanded to see his papers, surrounding him and making it impossible for him to flee. Mikael at first bluffed and said he hadn't got them on him – already an offence. Holding him, however, they took his wallet. Inside were all Mikael's papers, which confirmed his name and religion and the military pass for a leave of absence until the 27th April, which had expired weeks before.

"*Giavour!*" the burliest of the policemen had spat out. "You're a bloody deserter. You're under arrest."

Then with a mighty blow he struck Mikael across the face, followed by a punch in the stomach. Mikael was dragged off to the dreaded Yedikule police station, retching from the blow to the stomach, with a cut lip and bleeding nose.

CHAPTER 28

Garabed in flight

Garabed spent his first morning trying to get as far away as possible. He walked high up in the hills, avoiding the occasional villages, over desolate ground covered in green scrub grasses, dotted with rocks and stones.

This was an area of sheep farming. Garabed gave them a wide berth. When a flock moved straight across his path, he stopped and rested until the way was clear again.

As the sun came up and it got warmer, Garabed looked about him for a spot to lie down and sleep. He decided it was better to sleep during the day, while it was warm. In this treeless landscape, shelter, if only from prying eyes, was difficult to find. There were several tiny streams running down the hillsides. He knelt and drank whenever he had the chance.

Eventually, he came across a spot where several large rocks were clustered close to each other. Here he found a position where he could lie down out of sight. Garabed blessed his wife for her foresight in sending his warm coat, wrapped himself up and tried to sleep. He was a man who rarely spent time worrying or analysing his feelings. However, here was a situation the like of which he had never experienced. He wondered what was happening to his family? His stomach rumbled with hunger, but he eventually drifted into a deep sleep.

He woke just as dusk was falling, and the chill of the night was beginning. He chewed slowly on his loaf, eating about half. His clothes were sufficiently soiled and crumpled to appear somewhat less conspicuous in this remote countryside. However, he knew that he would have to try and get a change of clothes soon.

Garabed rose, splashed his face in a stream and walked on, guided by the stars in the mercifully clear night. He passed more and more villages as the area began to become more cultivated. There were no lights or fires to be seen in the darkness, and he was often only alerted to the fact that he was approaching a habitation by the barking of dogs. He would retrace his steps until he found a way to skirt round the farm or hamlet.

By now he was getting more and more hungry, but the risk of trying to steal food, was too great. Every farm and village had dogs, who started barking the moment he got near. His one asset was the precious five gold coins in the pockets of his sheepskin coat. However he could not be sure if a coin of such value would be accepted here in the countryside. Furthermore, if offered, it would certainly arouse suspicion, and could alert the authorities.

Garabed was getting increasingly tired from lack of food and the exertion of walking over rough ground. He stopped well before dawn was breaking and ate the last of his bread. With no idea where he was, he lay down to sleep on the bare grass of a hillside.

The sun was already quite high when he next awoke to the sound of cow's bells. Garabed struggled up, immediately alert. He was on a gentle slope, lying on the coarse grass. At the bottom of the hill were a few rough houses. Coming up an uneven path, was a young boy, with a small dog running alongside, driving about five meagre cows up the hillside.

Garabed rose, picked up his coat, and draped it round his shoulders. He tried to compose his features into a friendly smile. The cows wandered up the gentle slope, but the boy stopped. He called to his dog to come to stand by him. The call was in Turkish.

Garabed moved forward and spoke in Turkish, the only language that he knew anyway.

"Good morning, young man. I've lost my way. Could you tell me where I am."

"*Effendi*, our village is called ...," and the boy mumbled something rather quickly, which Garabed did not catch, and which, on reflection, probably wouldn't have meant anything to him anyway. At least he had made contact, and whilst the boy remained suspicious and alert, somehow the fact that this apparition had spoken, in a language he understood, had reassured him.

"Do you know the name of the nearest town?" asked Garabed hopefully.

"Do you mean ...," said the boy, and he came out with a name which sounded like 'kutchuk bagh', and meant absolutely nothing to the well-travelled Garabed. Garabed changed his strategy.

"Perhaps you could tell me whether your father is at home, so that I can speak to him and ask him my way."

"*Effendi*, I'm sorry but my father is away in the army. He is a corporal, serving in a group that is defending the big city," the boy answered proudly."

"You mean Stamboul?"

The boy looked at him blankly. Garabed again changed tack –

"Young man, could I speak to your mother? Which house is yours? What is your name?"

The boy hesitated, but eventually pointed to one of the four houses at the bottom of the hillside.

"That's my mother's house. My name is Achmet. I must go now, *effendi*."

Saying which, he whistled at his dog and ran off after the cows, still plodding slowly up the hillside, waving back at Garabed as he ran. Garabed wished that he had some sweets or a small coin to give the lad, but he had nothing. He nodded at the wave, and began walking down the path to the house the boy had pointed out.

As always, dogs started barking as Garabed approached the hamlet and walked into the beaten earth courtyard of the dwelling the boy had indicated. The path ended at the houses, and there was no road or track between the farms. However each farm had a rough wooden fence around it, and one of them even had a gate. Garabed saw that after the furthermost building another track started and continued down the valley.

He approached the faded and rather worn out front door, the top half of which was open, coughing as loudly as he could, and then knocked at the closed half of the door. He could hear a baby crying inside, but his knocking aroused no further reaction.

Garabed called out loudly,

"Hanum – I'm sorry to disturb you."

He then stepped well back from the door and out into the yard.

A strong-looking and weathered woman appeared at the door with a baby on one arm and a small girl, clinging to the woman's long multi-coloured skirts, peering at him over the top of the half-door. On seeing Garabed, the woman raised her free arm and put it across her face covering her mouth and the lower half of her face below the eyes. She did not appear alarmed, much to Garabed's relief.

"Hanum, I must apologise for disturbing you. May Allah protect you and your family. Your son – Achmet – directed me to your house. I have lost my way. Could you tell me the name of the nearest town?"

"Malatya," replied the woman. "It's about a days walk from here."

Garabed could now see into the house as the woman swung open the bottom half of the door. It was stone built, and as was familiar to Garabed from his travels, it consisted of one large room with a fireplace at one end, with a small fire at present burning in it. There was a door at the other end leading into a small, second room. The cool mud floor was hard and clean. Iron pots hung from the walls, together with a couple of faded carpets. There was little furniture, save a roughly made table, several solid, wooden chests, and a wooden crib with soft, clearly new, straw, without linen coverings. The baby was wearing a long white smock.

There was a rich variety of smells coming from the dwelling, from the faint smell of a baby's urine to the musty smell of a rich, bulghur porridge with spices. Garabed's mouth watered, but he realised that a gold coin here would be quite useless.

"Which is the way to the town, hanum?" asked Garabed.

The woman pointed to the track going down the valley at the other end of the little hamlet, and said shortly –

"That leads along the stream to the river – and follow that as it goes all the way to the town."

Garabed wondered how to proceed towards asking for some food. Anything was of some value to these people. He slipped off his sheep-skin coat and then offered his smart, but crumpled jacket which he offered saying -

"I am hungry, and have a whole day's walk ahead of me before I can reach Malatya – can you give me some food?"

This the woman understood at once. She motioned to Garabed to squat where he was. She then disappeared into the house. Shortly after, she re-appeared, still carrying the baby and the little girl beside her. In her free hand she had a bowl of the bulghur porridge, out of which stuck an old, and not too clean, wooden spoon.

Garabed did not rise from his cross-legged position on the ground. She came forward and handed the bowl to Garabed. He took it in both his hands and raised it to his forehead in thanks. He then began eating it quickly, nodding at the jacket which he had left draped on the swinging half-door. The woman left Garabed to eat and went inside again, whilst at long last the little girl left her mother's skirts and stood just inside the door, sucking her thumb, and staring with huge eyes at the strange man greedily wolfing down porridge.

Garabed had just finished when the woman re-appeared. The baby had at last been put down. She had in her hands two large onions and a rough loaf of bread. Garabed now gently rose, leaving the bowl on the floor and salaamed. Silently she handed the food to him, and then picked up the dusty jacket, smelling it. She smiled. Garabed smiled back and bowed deeply.

"May Allah, the all-merciful, protect you and your family and bring your husband back home to you soon, safe and sound."

"Inshallah," replied the woman.

Garabed slipped the food into the capacious pockets of the sheepskin coat, then turned and walked out of the yard, following the track down the valley, as the woman had indicated. He could see where the stream reached the river below and recognised the river as the one he used to follow on his trips to the home of Sarkis, the son of Shahan, whose family made such beautiful carpets.

"Yes!" thought Garabed, almost shouting out the word aloud in glee and triumph. "That's where I'll go – it's obvious. My god, it's a good thing I came in this direction. I'll certainly be safe with them for a while."

Armed with that thought, and with hot food in his belly, and some reserves in his pockets, Garabed's confidence began to return, for the first time since the arrest. He took a long drink at the stream before it reached the river, and strode out with purpose and renewed hope.

By the time Garabed finally arrived in Malatya, the town was in turmoil. There had always been a large Armenian community here. Once again there were no longer any young men in evidence. The arrests and exile of the leaders of the community had already taken place, while the younger men were away either in the army or in labour battalions. Accordingly, the general population was helpless and unprotected, facing hatred and a murderous official policy.

The town of Malatya had been designated by Talaat as one of the main gathering points for the Armenian deportees driven out from the interior further west. Already people were arriving and assembling in the rocky fields outside the town, where a ramshackle shanty town of tents, broken down old carts and makeshift shacks, was growing.

Garabed eventually managed to exchange one of his gold coins with a local money-changer, and found a cheap *khan* in which to stay whilst he worked out his best course of action. The increasing lawlessness in the countryside outside the main towns was already apparent here.

Kurdish tribesmen were regularly attacking the slow-moving lines of Armenian refugees, as they were forced out of their homes. Turkish criminals had also been released from the prisons, and they, too, were roaming the districts around the towns, terrorising the helpless deportees.

Reports of the unfolding catastrophe were being sent by the few conscientious Ottoman officials who were still in place, but all such reports were studiously ignored by the new masters in Istanbul. The dregs of town and country, deliberately freed by the government from their normal restraints, was beginning to attack and pillage even those Armenians who were not yet on the roads.

Garabed stayed in Malatya over a week before he decided to make his move and attempt to get to Sarkis' farm, some days ride from Malatya in the mountains to the east. He needed to be armed, but pistols would be hard to obtain, and dangerous if he was stopped by soldiers and ammunition would be impossible to find outside the city. In the end, he opted for a long wicked-looking knife. He did not expect to have to use it, but he hoped that the sight of it, coupled with his determination, might deter someone bent on violence. He did not imagine it could save him from a gang attack, if one occured.

He had got rid of most of his clothes, except of course the wonderful sheepskin coat. Now, blending much better into the local population, he at last set off up the hills. He decided to wear a very simple turban wrapped round his head, a headgear still regularly worn in the remoter rural areas. This advertised to the world that here was a pious Muslim walking home. Of course it would not suffice if there was a direct confrontation, but it might just prevent such a confrontation taking place.

Moving slowly but steadily, avoiding contact as much as possible, it took Garabed several days to get to the area where Sarkis Shahanian had his farmstead. This was an area with which he was familiar as a result of the many trips he had made both alone, and latterly with Raffi.

All along the way, Garabed passed burning farms, corpses and old men, women and children, looking lost and helpless – most of them already at the end of their capacity to survive. There were too many such sad sights for Garabed to take in, so he steeled himself and walked on.

He was becoming anxious, with his food provisions beginning to run low. It was now well into June, and whilst the nights were cool, he had been able to sleep outdoors without too much discomfort. On the last day, he pushed on as fast as he could to get to Sarkis' farm before nightfall. He was relieved to see that he was passing houses and farms that he recognised and which did not appear to have been touched, but their doors were bolted, and a number of the Turkish farmers were standing at their gates, with their sons alongside, holding rifles ostentatiously at the ready.

Garabed hurried on as the sun began to disappear below the horizon. Everything seemed quiet as he approached the farmhouse of Sarkis. Further down the valley – quite a distance away – Garabed could just make out a group of men, some on foot and some on horseback, who appeared to have surrounded a farmhouse and were milling about, yelling and gesticulating, punctuated by the sound of gunshots. He hurried up the track, once again and stopped dead.

There in front of him, with the doors and windows smashed and hanging loose stood Sarkis' neat farmhouse. The outhouses, the stables and the henhouse were all burnt and still smouldering, but the stone house itself seemed intact. Garabed ran forward with his heart pounding. What met his eyes as he approached was more horrific than he could ever have imagined.

Hanging from the eaves of the roof, just by the space, which had been the front door, swaying gently in the breeze, swung the body of Sarkis. Blood, now dried, had flowed from a deep gash in his side. His face was battered, his eyes open and staring, and his tongue hung out, purple and bloated.

Garabed sank to his knees from the shock of the sight, putting his hands on the floor in front of him, and kneeling like a dog, his whole body retched. He knelt like this for several seconds, until he became conscious of a low moaning coming from inside the farmhouse. He arose and went tentatively into the main room of the dwelling. At this point, as his eye took in the scene inside, he was violently sick. His whole stomach heaved and he had to run back outside.

Eventually, he lifted his rough pullover over his nose, and went back into the room. In front of the fireplace, lying face up on the stone floor, with her clothes almost completely torn off, her legs wide apart, lay Adrineh. Blood and semen seeped from the bruised and battered area between her legs. She was clearly unable to move, and it was from her lips that the low animal noises were coming.

To one side of her lay the bodies of the two little girls, covered with flies, their legs and arms hacked off. In a state of shock, he heard a movement coming from the small bedroom. He staggered over and went in – the door having been torn from its hinges. In the room the sight was even more shocking. Spread-eagled across the bed were the two older girls – Anna and her younger sister. Both had been violently raped, probably by several people, like their mother outside. Anna's lips were moving but making no sound; her younger sister was already dead. In the far corner was the younger of the two boys whose body was covered with sword or knife cuts, also clearly dead. Next to him, whimpering with fear and shock, with huge staring eyes, huddled the eleven-year older boy, his naked body a mass of stripes and weals.

For what seemed like eternity, Garabed was unable to move, his mind refusing to accept what he was seeing. Then he took the hand of the eleven-year-old lad. The boy screamed and shrank back. Garabed stopped and backed away, lifting Anna in his arms and taking her out into the yard, laying her body gently near the well.

Then he returned, picked up the little bodies of the two girls by Adrineh's side and took them into the bedroom. He tried once more to coax the boy, who again shrank from him in terror. Overcoming any scruples, he grabbed him, put one hand over his mouth to stifle the screams, and bore him struggling and kicking out of the room and outside, leaning him against the wall of the house. Finally he went back in to deal with Adrineh.

This was much more difficult, but he had to get her out of the charnel house which the building had become. He could not lift her properly as every movement caused her to cry out in pain. In the end he half carried and half dragged her out of the house. He lay her down next to Anna, who was still lying muttering to herself. Garabed could do nothing about the boy, whose name he could not even remember, but he could try to do something for the two women. Fortunately, the pail and the pulley, above the well in the yard, had not been destroyed. He drew some water, and came and knelt by Adrineh, murmuring words of comfort, unsure whether she heard them or not.

He needed some cloths to clean them up but there were no clothes or linen to be found. Swallowing hard, he cut away the cleanest strips of the dead children's clothes and hurried back outside, his gorge rising again.

As gently as he could, he dipped the strips of cloth into the water and gently wiped away all the blood and filth in and around Adrineh's vagina, and then turned to do the same for Anna. He kept drawing up clean water, giving each of them a sip or two before continuing the cleaning process. The water at last revived Adrineh, who nodded at Garabed in a sign of recognition. Anna, however, was completely traumatised.

All this time, the boy stared at Garabed saying nothing, lying naked against the wall. And shrieking every time Garabed moved towards him. Garabed gave up and concentrated on the two women. It was already beginning to get darker, when Adrineh at last lifted herself up, at least sufficiently to lean back against the low stone wall of the well. The full realisation of Garabed's presence came upon her suddenly, and to his relief this brought back some sense of modesty, and she wrapped her torn and bedraggled clothes around her legs.

"Garabed agha?" she said, looking directly at his face for the first time.

"Adrineh, hanum, yes it is I."

"Where is Sarkis, sir?"

"Madam Adrineh, you must be prepared for the worst."

"I know, Garabed *effendi*, my Sarkis must be dead. Oh my God, my two little ones too – my two little ones – oh God my two little ones." She brought her hands up to her face, and at last, to Garabed's relief, she began sobbing deeply.

Garabed pointed to Anna and the boy, still huddled against the wall. Adrineh looked round and stopped sobbing. She staggered upright and shuffled over to Anna, keeping her legs apart in an odd crab-like movement. She fell alongside the girl and took her head in her arms and began rocking back and forth murmuring words Garabed could not follow. Garabed tried to adjust what was left of Anna's clothes, but Adrineh waved him aside. Then she looked up.

"Garabed *effendi* – could you please fetch some clothes – they will be in the big wooden chest in the back bedroom."

"Adrineh, hanum, there is nothing left in the house – no clothes no linen nothing."

There was a long silence in which the only sound was Anna's unintelligible muttering. Then Adrineh spoke.

"Garabed, *effendi*, would you please go and ask Nefise Hanum to come. She is the wife of our neighbour Mustapha Mahmud. Their farm is the first house as you go down the hill."

Garabed hesitated.

"But they are Turks. Will they help you? Are there no Armenians nearby."

"Please, Sir, do as I ask. I know what I would do for her, and what she would do for me."

Garabed looked about at the devastation around him and nodded. Once he saw that Adrineh was again absorbed in crooning to Anna, he took out his knife and moved quietly to the front door. He was just able to reach up to the rope from which Sarkis was hanging. At full stretch, he sawed away at the rope and held tightly onto Sarkis' body. Eventually the rope gave way, and Garabed gently put the body of Sarkis down – all the time conscious of the young boy's eyes staring at him as he worked.

Once completed, he raced off down the hill to deal with Adrineh's request, with a guilty feeling of momentary relief in escaping from the horror, if only for a short time.

As he approached the first farmhouse, he saw a man standing at his door with an old but serviceable looking rifle held up in his arms. Beside him stood a boy of about 12 years-old, holding an old hunting rifle. Both looked very grim. Garabed slowed down, made sure that they could see his hands were empty, and walked up to the fence and called out to the two who were staring back at him -

"My name, sirs, is Garabed Asadourian. I am a friend of Sarkis, son of Shahan. There has been a terrible tragedy at their farm. Adrineh, his wife, has been -er -er – molested, but she is still alive. She asked if Nefise

Hanum will come to her. There is no more immediate danger, as there are no intruders left."

Garabed gabbled all this out in a breathless rush. Before he had finished, a large well-bosomed lady, dressed in several layers of black skirt, pushed past the man, and ignoring him, the boy, and Garabed, began hurrying up the hillside – taking no notice of the restraining hand which the man had extended as she swept past him. He shrugged.

"Burhan, my son, go with your mother and follow any instructions she may give you."

As the boy ran off after his mother, the man turned to Garabed.

"Yes, I have heard of you from my friend Sarkis. You are the merchant from Kayseri who buys his carpets. My name is Mustapha Mahmud. I must remain here, there are small children inside. But please know that my house is your house. What has happened to the Shahan family?"

Garabed, still catching his breath told him of the death of Sarkis, and a short description of everything else he had seen. Mustapha, a grizzled weather-beaten man, whose age Garabed could not judge, hung his head during Garabed's recital – then raised his hands palms up to heaven and cried out some words to Allah in a dialect Garabed could not follow. Then he turned back to Garabed.

"I saw these men passing my house earlier. They were led by an official from the town, and I was relieved that there were two soldiers with him. However, most of the rest were a drunken mob. I am ashamed to say that there were also many Turks – scum from the town. You know, *effendi*, that a decree has been issued that all Armenians were to leave the area to go to the Vilayet of Syria."

Mustapha paused, and Garabed could see that he was clearly in some distress.

"Oh, my God, my God – I advised my friend Sarkis to stay put for the moment and see what might happen. What have we done, what have we done. I should have realised that the official from the town was one of those godless Ittihad devils."

He sank to his knees – but then jumped up immediately as Garabed, too, turned and saw the boy running back down the hill. Garabed noticed Mustapha hastily arranging his features so as not to alarm his son.

"What is it Burhan – what is it?"

"Oh Baba – it's terrible. My friend Ara won't talk to me. He is lying there naked, and when I went up to him he screamed and turned his face away. Mother says I am to bring some of my clothes for him, and also some of Hikmet's dresses. She also wanted some of that soap you made recently – oh, and something else – oh yes, a cup."

"Quickly, then, Burhan, bring everything out and we'll make a bundle."

Mustapha nodded at Garabed and went into the house, leaving Garabed standing outside. Garabed had deliberately not returned to the stricken farmhouse straight away with the boy, in order to give Adrineh and Nefise some privacy. However, when Burhan came out from the house staggering under an armful of clothes, he took some of the clothes, and the soap and a cup from Mustapha, and wrapped them up with the clothes. He then turned to the weatherbeaten man.

"Mustapha, *effendi*, I salute you. May your Allah reward you for all your kindness, and for the risk I know you are taking in helping your neighbour."

Garabed then bowed and touched the floor at the man's feet, then straightened up and touched his forehead. He did not, however continue with the sign of the cross on his chest. Then he turned and hurried off after Burhan, who had already begun climbing up the path to the Shahanian house.

CHAPTER 29

The Avakians

Even though neither Robert College nor the attached Girl's school closed its doors after the outbreak of the Great War, Olga decided not to go back. With the events of that dramatic day of the 24th April, she had simply outgrown any desire to remain a student.

This feeling was of course partly induced by the arrest and deportation of her father. Had he been present, Karekin would undoubtedly have urged Olga to continue her studies. Armineh, however, gave her no such encouragement. Indeed she welcomed Olga's decision not to go back. In Armineh's opinion, she felt that separation from Selim, for a time, might also be helpful.

When she and Sima had finally returned from Haydar Pasha station, Armineh was incapable of taking on board any additional problems afflicting the family. In fact, the whole family, all physically and emotionally exhausted, had collapsed into bed at the same time as little Seta, much to her surprise.

The next morning, Armineh had to deal with all the vital matters that had arisen the previous day, but first she was confronted with a new problem.

"Madam Armineh, I am most sorry to hear the terrible news of Karekin *effendi*'s arrest. I will pray to the Virgin Mary every night for his safe return. But Madam, something else happened yesterday which you have to deal with immediately."

"Oh Marie – I know about Olga's unfortunate infatuation with a Turkish lad. Come, it's not all that difficult – she is not a complete fool. We'll sort something out."

"No, Madam, I am referring to Haik."

"Haik! Heavens, woman, what are you talking about? What's happened? He seemed fine to me, fast asleep, when I popped in last night."

Marie carefully explained exactly what had occurred: Haik having to return home on his own after school – Olga's lost scarf – the assault – the arrival on the scene of Olga's boyfriend Selim, and then Vahan. Marie explained she had tried to find out from Haik what exactly had taken place. Armineh sighed. She knew that she was going to have to cope with everything: the house, the business, the children's education, everything, but this particular problem should have been Karekin's task. The chances were she would only make things worse by talking to the boy.

"Marie, is he all right for the moment?"

"Madam, I believe so. But you know Haik. He is so naïve and trusting that he doesn't realise the danger he was in. But what about later? He is at a very sensitive age, and this is an experience which must be discussed and exorcised from his mind."

"Oh Marie, forget it – he's a healthy boy. Let's just thank God that nothing happened. Too much talk can only do harm, especially if it comes from me."

In a corner of her mind, Armineh knew that Karekin would have taken Haik into his full confidence and would not have let the matter go. Now, only 24 hours after his departure, she was badly in need of her husband. She could cope with nearly anything, but on this one matter, she felt paralysed. She was trying to convince herself that it was right to do nothing.

"Marie, thank you, I think we'll take the whole matter slowly. We'll wait and see. I may try to have a word with him, but he is unlikely to be any more forthcoming with me than he was with you. I believe it will go from his mind soon."

Marie looked hard at Armineh, then nodded and turned back to the kitchen.

Nerissa had been the first down after that, and Armineh found out the full details of everything that had happened whilst she and Sima had been gone. Armineh probed gently, but Nerissa hadn't appreciated the possibility of what might have taken place during Haik's assault. In the midst of all her other problems, Armineh put the matter out of her mind. Once out of hers, it went out of everybody's, including Haik's.

In explaining to her mother everything that had happened, Nerissa showed a new, appreciation of Selim as a person, and a more mature awareness of his relationship with Olga. Armineh turned almost thankfully to the problems of her daughters and away from the experience of her only son.

"Nerissa, my soul, I accept your appraisal of this young man. How can I be indifferent, after all, towards a man who may have saved my only son's life. Olga is a silly goose, but I never feared for a moment that she would ever fall for a bad man.

But Nerissa, my dear, we don't live on an island; love isn't enough in these troubled times."

"Oh mother – I've already said I'm sorry for what I said yesterday. I understand the situation perfectly, and I daresay that Selim does too. Neither of them are going to act precipitately. I feel sure that you can rely on that."

Sima was the next one down. That long hour or two in Haydar Pasha station had brought home to her, more forcibly than to her brother or sisters, the possibility that she might never see her father again. Her eyes were red with weeping all night.

After the others had come down, they had a somewhat subdued breakfast. Marie took Seta off to school. Immediately after she left, for the first time ever, an Avakian breakfast conclave took place without the all-powerful presence of Karekin. It had been remarkably efficient. It was as if the removal of the patriarch of the family had brought out the competence of the women. Some of the decisions taken on this very first morning, after his disappearance, lasted for the whole of the next year. Armineh was the first to speak.

"With your father away, children, I must go to the office, if not daily, at least once or twice a week, to see to his investments and other business interests. I think Sima, you must accompany me so that you can pick up the threads. Eventually I'll expect you to deal with most of the routine matters there."

"But mother, what about my taking Haik to school," said Sima, who had not yet got over her feeling of guilt over her failure, the previous day, to arrive in time.

"Mama," Haik pleaded, his bloody lip and nose having almost cleared up overnight. "Yesterday was a one-off. I know I shouldn't have tried to get that scarf of Olga's back. I'm sure, Mama, that I'll be fine now. You must trust me to be more careful."

There was a deep silence as all the women reflected, then everyone began talking at once. Armineh held up her hand and eventually, reluctantly, there was a silence again. Armineh regarded her son, who was not only eager, but in whose eyes she saw, for the first time, an anger at what was happening around him.

"Yes, Haik, I agree with you, but we will all have to take more responsibility for each other now. From now on I want you to be responsible for taking Seta to school, even though this means that you'll get to school yourself earlier and will have to wait. I'll instruct Seta's teacher that she must be kept at school till you arrive to pick her up in the afternoon. Remember, Haik, you will be responsible not just for yourself, but for your little sister as well."

Haik's eyes shone with pride, and he nodded.

Olga then stated firmly that she was not proposing to go back to college. Even at that early stage, at that first morning's meeting, she indicated that she would be trying to get work at one or other of the city's hospitals. She went on to say to her somewhat startled family,

"Don't stare at me like that. You saw how well I coped yesterday with Selim's wounds. It's work I think I could do well, and would enjoy doing, if people will let me.

"But Olga, hospital work isn't all tending the wounds of romantic young men. There is filth and excrement to clear up and potties to empty and heavy lifting," Nerissa pointed out.

"Nerissa – you have never ever considered that I might have any common sense. For God's sake – sorry mother I know I'm not putting this well but I have to say it – for once have some confidence in me as a person." The blood rushed to Nerissa's head and she went a deep red.

This was the second time within 24 hours that she had been guilty of intellectual arrogance.

"Oh my darling Olga, I'm so sorry, I'm so sorry."

Nerissa rose, took a step towards Olga, dropped to her knees by her chair and buried her head in Olga's lap. At this turn of events, Olga suddenly laughed out loud – the first laugh in the house in what seemed like days – patted Nerissa on the head, and, still giggling, shooed her off. Nerissa and Haik then got ready to go out to school. In the midst of all the drama, and the devastation of their father's arrest, somehow, carrying on everyday routine seemed to be the best way of coping.

Armineh made no comment on Olga's declaration. Like Nerissa, she doubted that Olga would have the resolution to go through with this current obsession. Although Nerissa was now careful not to say so to anyone, this was surely, she felt, just another bit of Olga whimsy.

As it happened, however, within a few weeks of that morning's discussion, Olga had indeed found a job. She deliberately avoided going to the highly prestigious and efficient Armenian Hospital – Sourp Pirgitch – and had instead picked on the Turkish military hospital in Uskudar, even though that entailed a much longer daily journey. Her interview with the administrator of the nursing staff, had been a great success. She was already learning how to temper her outgoing nature and superficial charm into something more sincere and mature. She arranged to do shift work, so she could stay in the hospital for four or five days at a time, and then return, for her days off, to Makrikoy.

Of all the children, it was Nerissa who had the most difficulty in adjusting to the changes wrought by the arrest and disappearance of Karekin. The English High School for Girls had finally closed down for the duration of the war, and without Karekin's guidance and encouragement, Nerissa had no idea what to do when she finished at the local school that summer. She ended up by giving English lessons to the sons and daughters of well-off Makrikoy families, Turkish and Greek as well as Armenian, and this had helped to bring in yet more welcome ready income to the family. The proximity of an English- speaking army, within a hundred miles, stimulated the wealthier residents of Makrikoy, most of whom already had a smattering of French, to tackle this new language.

And so the family struggled on reasonably comfortably. Sima began going regularly into Karekin's office in the city. Whilst there was not much to do, she was able to keep up the correspondence with agents and old customers. This at least maintained the belief that the business was still alive. At the same time, Olga brought in a small income from her job as a nurse, and eventually even Nerissa was bringing in some money.

About two months after that terrible day on the 24th April, Armineh received an unsigned postcard – postmarked from Konya – with the single word "GABRIMGOR" written on it in Latin capital letters. It was this unsigned postcard with its single word – "I am living" – which gave the whole family an enormous boost and will to carry on.

It arrived at just the right moment. For over a month, Armineh had driven the family. She had encouraged Olga in carrying through with a project for the first time. She had taken Sima to Karekin's office, dealt with the departure of the old Turkish clerk, whom she could not afford to pay anymore, and instructed Sima in the basic tasks. She had dealt with all the rest of the family problems. But at the end of the month, as the little practical matters began falling into place, and she had some spare time on her hands, despair began to eat into her heart. Nothing had been heard from any of the deportees, and several more arrests in the city had aggravated the situation. Rumours went round from one family to another, but there were no real hard facts. Then out of the blue came the postcard. Suddenly it all became worthwhile, and Armineh bounced back, redoubling her efforts.

The first thing that the two friends Karekin and Aram had done after jumping out of the train, reaching the shelter of the houses and collecting their breath, was to wander down to the clothing bazaar of the town, still open in the late afternoon. The town of Konya was fairly well known to both of them from previous visits. They had no difficulty in finding their way to the bazaar.

There, as hurriedly as possible, they bought thick, rough pullovers, strong and equally rough trousers and some local shoes. Fortunately Aram had a little small cash on him, which they were able to use. At the same time Karekin, wandering round the market, found a money changer and managed to change a couple of the gold coins at his little desk. This was a simple old wooden table covered with many different currencies, and scales for weighing gold and silver. The grizzled old man sitting at the desk had looked sharply up at him when offered the two heavy coins, but, making a substantial profit, he said nothing. Finally they also purchased a cheap leather suitcase.

Leaving the bazaar as quickly as possible, as their city clothes, were already attracting some attention, they found a sheltered spot between high blank walls down a side alley. Whilst Karekin mounted guard, Aram changed into the shabby, ill-fitting, newly purchased clothes. Aram then took up the look-out position, while Karekin changed. They then stuffed their city clothes into the case. Feeling much less conspicuous, they walked out of the alley and wandered down to the old square of the food vendors. With night falling, and hour by hour feeling more confident and anonymous, they sat on the rickety bench of a kebabji and ate a couple of the surprisingly tasty shish-kebabs.

"My God, Aram," said Karekin, with meat juice running down his face, "What an enormous difference some decent hot food makes to the way we feel about the world."

Aram edged along the bench towards the little charcoal grill on which the kebabs were cooking, and warmed his hands.

"You're right Karekin – but I'll tell you what, I'm beginning to get a bit of a reaction. Look, I'm shivering and feeling cold. It's all been too exciting – and we're not out of the woods yet. It's going to get cold tonight and where the hell are we going to stay."

As it happened both of them knew that there was a small Armenian community in the town, most of whom lived together in one of the suburbs, which had even become known locally as Ermeni-mahallesi.

"We certainly won't be able to find anything tonight," reasoned Karekin, "but I suggest we walk out of town in the direction of the Armenian quarter, and see what we can find tomorrow."

The two men were replete with bread and kebab. They were enjoying the feeling of wellbeing, resulting from the meal they had just eaten in the friendly noisy atmosphere of the dimly-lit eateries in the square. They were still euphoric from the adrenalin rush of their escape, as they walked through the suburbs and into the farming area outside the town. Here they eventually came across an old ruined barn, not too far from the road, where they fell fast asleep.

The following morning, once again nervous as they considered their next step, they walked over to the small Armenian quarter. Sitting in a miniature coffee-house, smoking a narghileh, and speaking as little as possible, to hide their distinctive Stambouli accents, they sipped their coffees and began enquiring as to possible lodgings. Someone told them of a young Armenian couple, who owned a modest house nearby. They left the coffee-house and went to the address given. A friendly woman, who was just about to go to work, came to the door, agreed to take them on immediately, on payment of a good deposit. She explained that she and her husband ran a little sweet shop in the centre of the town.

For several days, Karekin and Aram hardly stirred from the house, feeling somehow more nervous now that they were more settled, than they had been when they were on the run. But they could not avoid thinking of the future, and how best to survive the situation. In any case, they soon became bored of their interminable games of tavloo, in which mil*lion*s were won and lost each day.

The situation in Konya was somewhat unusual at this time. The then Governor of Konya – Djelal *Bey* – was still the old Ottoman appointee. He had little sympathy for Talaat and the Ittihad gang in Istanbul. He was not a liberal, and not even particularly sympathetic to the Armenians. Nevertheless, he had ignored, and continued to ignore the spate of vicious decrees and widespread deportation orders emanating from Talaat's ministry, which required all people of Armenian origin to leave Anatolia and move to one of the Arab vilayets.

At this early stage in the unfolding catastrophe, the severity of enforcement of deportation orders varied from vilayet to vilayet, according to the disposition of the Governor. The general pattern was that the further east in Anatolia, the more severe were the effects of the decrees. In the eastern-most vilayets, bordering on, or close to, the Russian frontier, where the Armenian rural population was at its densest, long lines of women, children and old men, had trudged through the countryside in the general direction of Aleppo. Set upon by released criminals, Kurdish tribesmen and Turkish riff-raff, including some soldiers, large numbers were dying on the roads. The women were being raped and the children abused. Those that managed to leave Anatolia, were then dying of starvation, in their thousands, in the Syrian desert.

During these early days, as Karekin was coming to terms with his situation, he had plenty of time to watch, listen and reflect on what was happening in the Empire. It became obvious to him that the whole terrible catastrophe had been carefully stage-managed. It was not unfolding spontaneously. It had begun with the rounding up of a carefully considered list of the community leaders. The young men were mostly in the army or in the carefully policed labour batta*lion*s. With the leaders arrested or killed, and the young men disarmed and out of the way, the stage was thus set for the removal of the whole Armenian population.

Karekin and Aram survived those first months due entirely to the invaluable gold coins that Armineh and Sima had brought to Haydar Pasha station at such risk to themselves. Once settled in their lodgings, and ready at last to venture out, Karekin began looking about town for some opening. Eventually his natural entrepreneurial instincts led him to use a good part of the coins to buy up the stock and shop of a dealer in that thin diaphanous material from which the better-class yashmaks were made.

At some time during those first two months, Karekin, fearful of giving himself away, or endangering his family, nevertheless contrived to send an unsigned postcard to Armineh – a postcard, which had given such comfort at home, and which had been so instrumental in helping to keep up their spirits in their own efforts at survival.

Once purchased, Karekin threw himself wholeheartedly into improving the shop layout, using his natural talents to make the decoration and atmosphere of the shop welcoming. Having only ever been a doctor all his life, Aram found himself working enthusiastically in this new trade, and getting considerable pleasure out of it. With Aram helping in the shop, and with their unfailing courtesy to all, they had not only kept going, but were indeed doing quite well. In the course of time, with a bit of bribery, and using some connections they had made, they both got false papers – though they retained their identity as Armenians.

Life soon settled into a steady routine. The friends would leave early in the morning, passing the local villagers bringing their produce into town to sell in the food markets. The shop opened early and remained open all day until the bazaar closed in the early evening. Lunch would be provided by the itinerant vendors who went round all the stalls and shops, and would be eaten at the back of the shop. The two friends would then walk home at night to their lodgings, where their evening meal would be taken with the young couple.

However, as the summer was just beginning to fade, the even tenor of their fugitive life was about to disintegrate.

As the weeks had passed, the Armenian population in Konya had continued to hang on, keeping a low profile, but unharmed. But Konya was not Constantinople or Smyrna. Sooner or later Talaat and his cronies were bound to step in and enforce their policy. It was only in Smyrna, or Bolis itself, that the old Ottoman ruling class, backed by the presence of foreign ambassadors, was strong enough to successfully resist Ittihad pressure. As the summer of 1915 began to turn to autumn, the moment finally came, when orders for the dismissal of Djelal *Bey* arrived from Istanbul. His replacement was to be an Ittihad appointee – yet another 'one-language, one-folk, one-culture' nation-state fanatic. It was clear that, shortly, a man impatient to have done with Ottoman diversity, would arrive in Konya.

That evening, as the posters announcing the deportation orders went back up on the public notice boards, the mood in the town began to change. Karekin and Aram began to discuss their next move.

CHAPTER 30

Raffi faces life and death

It was still early in May in Caesaria and the days were getting perceptibly warmer. Almost two weeks had passed since the arrest and deportation of Garabed, together with most of the other leaders of the local Armenian community.

Cries of "*Giavour asiliyor – giavour asiliyor*," "an infidel is to be hanged," rang out in the meat market, as Raffi stood waiting to be served in the butcher's shop.

Since that terrible moment when his father turned and walked away, Raffi had had to come to terms with the knowledge that they would probably never see him again. Raffi had increasingly taken on the role of his father as a support to his mother and the other women in the household. Thus it was that on this particular morning, he had come out to the market to buy some fresh meat – a task formerly carried out by Garabed, as he returned from work in the evenings.

"An infidel is to be hanged … Quick – quick – let's go."

Raffi found himself pulled along helplessly as everyone in the shop, and, it seemed in the whole market, began running excitedly to the nearby main square in front of the town hall. There, pressed in by the crowd all around him, unable to get away, Raffi watched as he saw his gym teacher frogmarched down the road between two policemen, swinging his arms vigorously in the characteristic manner that he had, and that the boys had cruelly imitated in happier times.

Raffi's immediate neighbour in the crowd – who was to his surprise a fairly well-dressed man – laughed and dug Raffi in the ribs saying,

"See, the *giavour* pig – swinging his arms like a soldier. Doesn't he know that he is going to be hanged. They won't be swinging like that when he's swinging from the gibbet – the bastard."

Raffi had aged by years in the weeks since his father's disappearance and he had no difficulty in stifling the tears that might have raised suspicions in the crowd.

A great roar arose as the man's body was raised, kicking and swinging, and with the noose tight round his rather scraggy neck. The gym teacher was still swinging and jerking there, when only a minute or two later, Raffi saw his headmaster escorted down the road in the same way – with a policeman on either side. Raffi had always been particularly fond of this man, whose name was Vahan, like his brother's. The headmaster was young for the seniority of his post. He was an inspiring teacher who had a way of rousing enthusiasm in his boys.

Raffi found that he could not prevent his body trembling. He shrunk down behind the men in front of him. He knew that he had to hide his feelings and not attract attention to himself, but he could not stop trembling, and he was beginning to feel dizzy and hot. Fortunately, no one seemed to notice his distress, and Raffi kept his gaze firmly on the ground.

As those at the front kept up their hate-filled chorus, the edges of the crowd began to drift away and the crush eased. Raffi was free to move. He looked up and at that moment, he almost fainted away, for there, swaying in the breeze, swollen tongues purple and hanging out of their mouths, eyes staring and bloodshot, were the six principal teachers from his school. For a moment he almost vomited, then turned and hurried home.

At the sight of his mother, when she opened the front door, he burst into paroxysms of tears.

Very shortly after this incident, the deportation orders from Talaat's ministry in Istanbul, were posted all over town, and reinforced by the town criers calling out in all districts. All Armenians were to leave town within a week. There was to be no selling of any goods, no drawing of any money – everyone simply had to leave and make their way to the Arab vilayets. Supposedly there were to be guards posted along the way.

The only exceptions at this stage, were to be families of officers serving in the Turkish army, and those few who could show that they were Catholics or Protestants, rather than Orthodox. However, even this latter exception lasted only a week, as soon as it became clear to the Ittihad leaders in Stamboul that their Austrian and German allies were not, after all, going to raise anything more than a formal protest.

Raffi had written many weeks before to Vahan, asking him to send some evidence as to his officer status. Vahan had immediately contacted his superior officer at the Harbiye military academy. An upright old Ottoman official, he had promptly furnished a stamped and signed copy of Vahan's commission. Sensing the possible importance of this document for his family back in Caesaria, Vahan had written to Raffi immediately, confirming that he had passed on the document to a trustworthy Turkish merchant, who had known and done business with Garabed, and who was travelling to Caesaria within days.

Raffi received the document within a day or two of the public hangings in the town square.

The emptying of the Armenian quarters now began. Raffi had purchased a large tent and a couple of donkeys ready for the journey, but was in a state of panic-stricken indecision. Despite the document, he did not know what would happen when the local commissioner finally arrived at their house. In the last resort, Vahan's commission was only a piece of paper. There was nothing he could do if it wasn't accepted. Meanwhile, he would have lost his chance to sell some of the contents of the house. Suddenly those 25 gold coins which Garabed had returned into Raffi's care, became vital to the family's survival.

Too soon, the day came when their little street was ready to be emptied. Accompanied by some local policemen who knew the district, the local commissioner came down their little cul-de- sac. Almost everyone was ready, and began moving out. Like all his neighbours, he knew the dangers; nevertheless, neither he nor his neighbours, were aware that not one Armenian from this street would survive the killing fields which stretched all the way to the Syrian deserts, where almost all of those who made it that far, would die of starvation.

In the last house before that of the Asadourians, the family was ready, as they all were, but they asked to be exempted at least for some time. It appeared that their old grandmother could not walk at all – indeed could not be moved from her bed. They had no cart to carry her. Raffi watched as the old man explained all this to the commissioner. It was to no avail. In the end they were forced out, and the whole family trudged away, leaving their sick grandmother in bed in the house. They left some food and water by her bedside, and the main door open. Raffi watched as they walked away, eyes downcast.

At last, the police group came to the Asadourian house at the end of the street. Raffi had prepared the tent and all the other items on the backs of the two donkeys, which were still inside the courtyard standing patiently and fully loaded by the side of the old well. He now stood, trembling with anticipation at the door, with his mother a step or two behind him, as the commissioner approached.

"Come, come, you must leave now – everyone in the house must be gone today." The official had repeated these words all day to a series of desperate and confused people.

"Commissioner *bey*, my brother is an officer in the Ottoman army," Raffi answered, as confidently as he could manage. He handed over the Harbiye Commission. The official turned to the local policeman standing beside him.

"Whose house is this?"

"It belonged, *effendi*, to one Garabed Asadourian, who has already been deported."

"Well – did he have an elder son called Vahan or not?"- asked the Commissioner.

"Yes, your Honour," said the policeman.

There was a long pregnant silence as everyone waited for the commissioner's verdict. Even at that moment of stomach-churning panic, Raffi reflected in a corner of his mind that this was the true definition of tyranny – the totally arbitrary nature of a society, where a decision of life or death, could depend on the whim of a single unaccountable person.

The moment stretched out, as Raffi waited. Then the official took a piece of chalk and wrote in large letters on the front door – 'Zabit ailesi' – 'officer's house.'

Without a further word he turned, and he and the other policemen walked out of the now totally empty street. Raffi, whose nerves were stretched to the limit, almost fainted as his mother came forward and held him tight.

Three days later, an old Turkish lady who lived on the next street, came knocking on the door, and asked to speak to Mariam, reporting that there was an old lady crying, abandoned and unable to move in the house next door.

Mariam said nothing but immediately called out to Raffi, who was listening in the corridor behind her, as the old lady walked away.

"Raffi, listen, did you hear that? I had no idea. You must go right away and bring her here."

"Mother, my soul, mother, listen – we have grandma already in bed here. We have sisters and a baby. Also, your old bedridden aunt will come when she hears that we've been exempted. How can we look after anyone else?"

"Raffi, please, we must. Neither of us is going to be able to sleep if we don't act"

Raffi felt guilty that he had forgotten the plight of this old woman and left immediately.

The woman was lying on her bed, covered with her own dirt and urine, abandoned, weeping softly and unable to move. He lifted her, carried her to the street, and put her on the back of the donkey, bringing her back to the house, and then into the bathroom, under Mariam's direction. Without embarrassment, Raffi helped his mother carefully wash the old woman, and took her to a bed.

The house now held six women, including two helpless old ladies who had to be fed, bathed and changed. In the midst of it all, half-boy half-man, the hapless 16 year-old Raffi, had to do all the lifting and carrying. Fortunately he found himself too busy to think too much. Meanwhile, the whole of the rest of their little street stood completely forlorn and empty.

As the weeks passed, two further old women were brought round to the Asadourian house on the back of Raffi's donkeys. Within a few weeks of the day that the little street had been emptied, there were eight women living in the house: Mariam, Raffi's two elder sisters, probably widowed by now, the two bedridden grandmothers, and the two newcomers.

The whole of the Armenian quarter around them had become a ghost town. The streets were quiet and empty, and the atmosphere was eerie and oppressive. One or two displaced Turkish families, from the areas currently occupied by the Russians, had moved into a couple of the empty houses, but the majority lay quiet and abandoned. Indeed the whole town was subdued. Most of the remaining Turks found, to their surprise, that the forced departure of the hated Armenian minority was not, after all, as welcome to them as they had imagined.

The government was now calling up 17 year-olds for military service. It had therefore become dangerous for Raffi to wander the streets. Whilst there were still a few Armenian families left in the town, none of these were young able-bodied males.

Mariam and his sisters did most of the pure nursing work, but it was Raffi who had to carry them to the toilet and turn them over in their beds. Mariam had paid heavily to get some false papers for Raffi, which gave his name as Soliman, his religion as Muslim and his age as sixteen.

Raffi's grandmother, his father's mother, was sinking the fastest. Her condition had been deteriorating from the moment Garabed had been arrested, and it was fairly clear that she would die soon. She was a particularly pious old lady, who had been with her husband on a pilgrimage to Jerusalem many years before and while there, she had purchased a specially blessed and holy burial shroud. This garment was a beautiful white linen cloth, embroidered with angels and crosses, resplendent with the whole paraphernalia of Christian iconography. Raffi had often seen her take it out of the wooden chest, hang it up and contemplate it with great satisfaction.

The day eventually came when Mariam and Raffi sat by her bedside as she slowly slipped away.

"I will be buried in my shroud, won't I," she whispered to Mariam.

"Yes, yes, I promise, mother. Don't be anxious."

Raffi said nothing, but continued to hold his grandmother's withered old hand, as with a sigh the old lady finally expired. There was no priest left in the town so far as Mariam knew, and the Armenian churches were all closed and boarded up. Mariam and Raffi sat together whilst the others in the house came, kissed the old lady and left. Mariam rose, called her daughters, and as Raffi looked on they bathed the body and brought out the burial shroud and began putting her in it.

"Mother, for heaven's sake it's far too dangerous," said Raffi urgent-ly. "How can we take her down to the cemetery in this climate, with that garment calling out our race and religion to all the world."

"My son, it was her last wish – I promised, I promised. I'll suffer years of guilt if I don't fulfil it now."

"But mother, it's just superstition – what does it matter what she's buried in?"

"Please, son, I'll find a blanket to wrap round her whilst you take her down – but you must remove it before you bury her. Raffi, don't shake your head like that. I know it's not a religious duty – but I couldn't live with the thought that we didn't do our best. It was such a source of pride for her."

Racing through Raffi's mind was the thought – 'for god's sake she's dead, nothing can affect her now,' but what he actually said was

"Very well mama, get her ready, I'll do it this evening."

So that afternoon, Raffi went on one of his rare trips into town to seek the help of old Hassan, the local rubbish collector who had always been a friend of the family. There were no Armenian males left in the town to whom Raffi could turn for help, at least as far as he knew. Has-san blinked and hesitated when Raffi explained the task he required, but he did not refuse. Hiding their spades in bags, they carried the old lady's body, wrapped in the blanket, laid her across the donkey and set off.

The gates of the Armenian cemetery were open, but Hassan drew the line at going inside. He and Raffi began digging a grave just outside in the grass by the gates. They had not gone far when an army officer came by on a horse. Leaning down he said to Hassan, whom he recog-nised,

"*Giavour* or Islam?"

Hassan was tongue-tied and speechless, but Raffi quickly answered in his place –

"We don't know, sir, as we found her already dead in one of the empty Armenian houses."

"Well, take her down to the Muslim cemetery just in case," suggested the officer. He then lit a cigarette and trotted off. Hassan stared at Raffi, and there was a long moment of silence between them.

"Hassan, I can't do it – I simply can't."

"Look, I have every respect, as you know, for Mariam hanum – but just don't tell her. I can't take the risk, if he comes back and takes a look under the blanket and sees the shroud, we're in for it – you're dead, and I'll be badly beaten."

Raffi was momentarily lost, not knowing what to do. But he was growing up fast. He grabbed one of the spades.

"Hassan, my good friend, start walking the donkey and the old lady away towards the Muslim cemetery as you are supposed to do. Go in a circle. I'll finish the grave here. When you get back it'll only take a moment to tip her in and bury her."

It was of course a totally unnecessary risk. However, Hassan did as suggested and when he returned, it did indeed take only a moment to bury the old lady. Raffi pulled away the blanket, as the first clods of earth were hastily piled back onto the resplendent shroud.

When in due course he recounted these events to Mariam, Raffi somewhat mischievously paused at the point that they had been ordered to bury the body in the Muslim cemetery. Mariam paled and almost fainted. Raffi knew, then, that he had been right to take the risk, seeing his mother's face clear, as he hastily proceeded with his narrative.

It was not long after this incident that the police arrived at the house. One of the new neighbours, a displaced Turkish family who had moved in from Russian-occupied Erzurum, had seen Raffi on the roof and denounced him to the police.

Quite by chance, that same morning a Turkish family, the wife, sisters and elder daughter of a certain Major Suleyman – an old acquaintance of Garabed – had come visiting Mariam and her two daughters, whom they knew well. They were all sitting in his sisters' reception room taking coffee, when there was a knock at the front door.

Raffi never answered the door, but would make himself scarce whenever there was a unexpected knock. The policemen at the door explained to Mariam, who had hastily covered her face with a yashmak, that they had been informed that there was a young man in the house. Mariam spoke loudly to make sure that Raffi could hear.

"Yes, it's true. My second son was here recently. However he demanded money from me, and when I told him that I didn't have any – he hit me here and ran away. I haven't seen him since."

"Madam, we intend to search the house. Please stand aside." Raffi had long since slipped through into the private women's area of the large house. He walked into his sister's room. The Turkish ladies all began hastily drawing down their veils, looking at Raffi curiously. Raffi immediately faced the wall so as not to look at them. Under his breath, he told his sister, Sira, what was happening. She bundled Raffi into the next room as the Turkish women looked on excitedly. Shortly after this the police,having searhed the rest of the house, appeared outside the door to the area that would normally be 'haram' – forbidden – for any honest Muslim.

"Madam," the senior policeman addressed his remarks to Mariam, who was still with them, "we have to search the whole house."

"But officer, we have the family of Major Suleyman here visiting my daughter. They are inside, unveiled."

"Madame. Certainly, of course we cannot go in while they are unveiled. However, please ask them to veil themselves and then come through to the other part of the house where we have already looked."

Mariam knocked at the door, not knowing that Raffi was inside, and told Sira what was to happen. The ladies quietly donned their veils, while Sira went hastily to the next room where she bought out a feradjeh, and some ladies shoes, and quickly dressed Raffi in the loose gown and veil, whilst the ladies of the Major's household, now fully veiled, waited to be escorted out. Sira then opened the door, and she and the ladies walked out – each lady carefully looking down at the floor as they passed. However, the policemen also avoided looking at the ladies as they passed. They were already uncomfortable enough in that part of the house which would normally be *'haram'* for any strange males. Raffi, in a state of terror and scarcely able to walk, shuffled past the policemen with downcast eyes as Sira waited behind to show the policemen round.

The lovely ladies of Major Suleyman's family said not a word, neither then nor later when they left the house. When it was the policemen's turn to leave, the officer told Mariam,

"We know full well that your second son is somewhere around. We'll be calling again we can assure you."

That night Raffi packed a small bag and took out his false papers. He kissed his mother passionately and said his farewells to everyone. All Mariam's men were now gone. She took out the gold coins, now down to 15, and wrapping them up in a cloth gave them to him with her blessing. Raffi, with deep pride in his heart, mixed with the pain of parting, carefully counted out five, as his father had done, and returned the rest to her.

Raffi left early in the morning while it was still dark. He spent the whole morning in the dusty square, where the carriages and lorries set off for other towns, watching out all the time for police presence, and waiting for his chance to board something.

CHAPTER 31

Garabed drives on

When Garabed arrived back up the hill accompanied by Burhan, the 12 year-old son of Mustapha, the situation had not greatly changed. Adrineh was now looking somewhat less dishevelled. Both she and Nefise Hanum were gathered round the still recumbent figure of Anna.

Neither woman appeared to have made any attempt as yet to deal with the problem of Ara, who was still crouched naked against the old wall of the farmhouse.

Burhan handed over the women's clothes to his mother. Garabed looked away and moved over to stand near the boy. Dusk was falling and Garabed felt that the first priority, was to start a fire somewhere. No one was going to go back into the slaughterhouse that the farmhouse had become, and so, with Burhan's help in bringing twigs and wood, he prepared and lit a fire in the yard. The flames immediately began to add a touch of warmth to the scene, as the darkness cloaked the sight of the devastation all around. Continuing to ignore the two women still fussing around Anna, Garabed motioned to Burhan to fetch the pottery cup. Garabed filled it from the well and then went over to Ara, who had been watching the activity taking place around him. He crouched beside the boy and tried to hold the cup up to his lips. But Ara, though now no longer screaming, turned his head away.

At this point, Burhan, who had been watching this latest attempt to get through to Ara, came and took the cup. Burhan walked over and, for the first time, a tiny flicker of recognition came into the dulled eyes of the young boy.

Burhan offered Ara the cup.

"Ara, my friend Ara, please drink some water."

For the first time Ara did not shrink back, but took the cup from Burhan's hand and began drinking. Once started, he asked for the cup to be refilled and drank and drank, as Burhan ran happily back and forth to the well.

Burhan watched with satisfaction as his friend became increasingly aware of his surroundings and, shortly after, took up the clothes Burhan had left by his side. Standing up, he began to dress himself.

It was a warm evening, and Garabed asked Burhan to go down to his father and bring back a spade. Nothing had been left intact in the Shahanian farm, and there were no tools anywhere. While Burhan was away, Garabed carried out the bodies of the four children, and lay them down side by side on the grass outside the courtyard. As he did this, Nefise looked across every so often in sorrow and sympathy, but Adrineh looked away continuing to ministrate to Anna. She could cry no more.

Garabed tried to be as discreet as possible, dragging the body of Sarkis across the courtyard to be laid alongside the children. When Burhan returned with the spade Garabed started digging. The bodies were buried in two shallow graves, Sarkis in one, and the four children together in the other. Anna had by now been washed and dressed by the two women, and Nefise persuaded Adrineh to come and stand by the mounds, as with arms outstretched and palms up to heaven in the fashion both of the Muslims and the Christians of the area, Garabed mumbled some words which at least sounded like prayers. To everyone's relief, Adrineh began crying again, but now softly and copiously, whilst Nefise hugged her close.

Gathering together the remaining clothes, Nefise squeezed the hand of the still weeping Adrineh and bowed to Garabed saying -

"May Allah preserve you, sir."

Garabed raised his hand to his forehead and bowed in his turn without saying another word. Burhan and Nefise returned home, taking the remaining clothes and the spade, but leaving the cup. Garabed tried to wrap his sheepskin coat round Ara, but the boy flinched away from his touch, clearly he could not accept the presence or touch of an adult male. Adrineh and Anna huddled together and fell asleep by the fire.

Though completely exhausted, Garabed could not sleep. He stared at the flickering flames, every so often throwing more wood on the fire. What was he going to do now? From being an active, strong middle-aged man on the run with good prospects for survival, he was saddled with a whole family: a woman who had just been raped, and who had lost her husband and four of her children; a totally traumatised young girl; a young boy, fearful, and looking upon him with suspicion. Despite this, of all the courses of action open to him, one was quite impossible – there was no way he could now abandon them.

Garabed looked round, and there, wide-awake and staring at him with the intensity of madness, he caught the eye of Ara, lying nearby. Garabed shuddered a little, turned on his side, and eventually dropped off into a troubled sleep in the early hours of the morning.

The next morning, with no food available and just some water, Garabed had to start making some decisions. Adrineh clearly looked to him, as she would have done to her husband. It was impossible to stay – sooner or later, the authorities from the village below would catch up with them.

Garabed finally decided. He strode down to Mustapha's farm in the hope of catching him before he started work in the fields. "Mustapha, *effendi*, I will have to leave today, and I must take Sarkis' remaining family with me."

"You are right, Garabed *bey*. It is not safe for you to remain here. I have spoken with my wife, and we are prepared to take in the boy Ara. We don't require him to take up Islam, but we will want to have him circumcised, both for his and our own protection. It has already been decreed that anyone harbouring Armenians will be punished."

"I will put it to Adrineh hanum. I thank you, but I don't believe that she will want to break up what remains of the family. May I propose that Adrineh formally gives you all her husband's farm. If you have some paper – any paper will do – I will write out a formal gift and get her to put her mark. Perhaps in return you might be in a position to let us have two of your donkeys."

Garabed knew it was not a fair exchange. After all, once gone, Mustapha could have simply taken the land. However, it might be of help to Mustapha in the future to have some evidence of formal ownership. Garabed then produced one of the invaluable gold coins, deciding to keep the already changed notes. He handed the coin to Mustapha saying –

"Mustapha *effendi*, I would request you to load one of the donkeys with any spare rice or provisions you can manage. Perhaps your son, may Allah be with him always, could walk them up the hill. We will be leaving as soon as possible, but will be going on up the hills and away from the valley."

Mustapha took the gold and nodded. The two men looked at each other for a long moment, and then without a further word, Garabed turned and walked away.

When Burhan arrived later that morning, Adrineh and Garabed put her silent and distracted daughter astride one of the donkeys. The other donkey was laden with a bag of rice, a pan, a bag of onions and two squawking hens tied by their legs. Burhan tried to embrace Ara, but stopped as soon as he felt Ara flinch. He salaamed Garabed and stood watching as the little party trudged away. Garabed led the laden donkey in front, followed by Ara walking firmly alongside his sister, making sure that she did not fall. Adrineh brought up the rear.

Garabed had decided to make for Diyarbekir and Mardin, which were on the way to Aleppo, but to keep away from the recognised roads and tracks. On the first night, he discovered that the admirable Mustapha had hidden at the bottom of the bag of onions an old but usable pistol, with some ammunition. Not much use against a band of determined men, but maybe enough to ward off the individual robber.

Day after day passed as the little party walked on, avoiding any towns or villages, and, indeed, any human habitation. Garabed moved along in a sort of daze, but he knew the country well and managed to avoid the bands of Kurds and lawless men roaming the countryside and looking for *giavour*s to rob and murder. They had been travelling for about two weeks, when Garabed became aware that they were coming out of the bare mountainous terrain, into a more populous area. He began to see the occasional camel, and the days were getting warmer.

One night, Garabed awoke in the early hours of the morning and lay staring at the stars above him. He became aware of the sound of weeping. He turned quietly onto his side and looked at the form of Adrineh lying beside him. Garabed pushed off his sheepskin coat and moved over wrapping his arms round the silently weeping woman. Adrineh herself responded immediately, though her weeping continued. Her arms came up to envelop him. Garabed moved gently across her and their lips sought each other with tenderness, but without a sound.

Garabed fumbled with his trousers, whilst Adrineh did the same with her rough and tattered skirts. Silently, and scarcely moving at all, Garabed and Adrineh made love with a desperation that had little to do with affection.

As they continued to move down from the Anatolian plateau towards the Syrian desert, their nightly encounters became more and more passionate. They were still very cautious as they travelled, with their eyes peeled for strangers and possible robbers, yet they scarcely said a word to each other during the day, and certainly there was no acknowledgement of their night-time trysts. The physical comfort they gave each other in the middle of the nights, was a simple gift after the rigours of the days.

It was probably about five days later that the daily rhythm of their travels came to an abrupt end. Garabed and Adrineh's coupling had become more passionate and less silent. So it was that on this occasion, in the midst of his passion, Garabed felt a sudden presence, a warning, a sixth sense of danger. He stopped and looked up. Staring down at him with mad, inflamed eyes, stood Ara. Held in his hand was the long knife originally bought by Garabed in Malatya.

The tableau of this threesome – with Ara glaring at Garabed, with Garabed keeping his eyes warily on Ara, and with Adrineh staring up at Garabed – held for a long, impossible moment. Then with an almost insane scream, Ara lifted the knife and shouting incoherently – "turk – kurd – beast – murderer" he struck down at Garabed with all his boyish force.

With all his considerable strength, Garabed rolled the two of them away as the knife came down, but he felt it slice through his arm. With all passion spent, and now free of Adrineh, he jumped up, blood pouring from his arm.

Ara screamed again, dropped the knife and turned, running off into the night. Anna awoke, gibbering and mumbling, but for the first time there was a sign of a reaction in her eyes. As Garabed sat heavily down on the ground holding his bleeding arm, the thought came to him that either Anna had gone completely insane, or she had been jolted out of the dazed trauma of the last few weeks.

"Garabed, Garabed," said Adrineh, addressing him familiarly for the very first time in their relationship, "What happened? Your arm is bleeding – come let me see it – what happened – was that Ara? Oh my God where has he gone?"

"Adrineh, my love," Garabed responded with affection to her first words of intimacy, "Ara must have woken up and was watching us. What he saw tonight must have brought his mind back to … Well you know … and how could he tell the difference at his age between the violence he saw then and what he saw now?"

Garbed stopped and then called out, "Ouch – that hurt," as Adrineh poured some precious cold water over the wound and tied a rag tight above the wound to stop the flow of blood.

It was pitch black, and impossible to look for Ara before morning. Anna, still muttering, moved over to cling fiercely to Adrineh. This was the first positive emotion that Garabed and Adrineh had seen, since that terrible day. Adrineh held her tight, and they all sat quietly together as they waited for the sun to rise from the east.

At first light, Garabed rose, splashed his face, took up his knife, and with one of the donkeys, set off to look for Ara. They were in a fairly populated area, and before leaving, he carefully took out the old pistol, loaded it and handed it to Adrineh.

"My darling, you know how to use this I'm sure. If anyone approaches, point it and first fire away if they look like molesting you. It might be some time before I get back, but don't worry, I'll find him, I promise you."

This was a countryside of scrub and low hills, interspersed with cultivated fields that were surrounded by small boundary stones. There were no woods, but only the occasional single tree and no bushes at all, so there was no cover anywhere. Garabed walked round the campsite in ever increasing circles until he was fairly sure which way the boy had run.

It was two hours or more before he finally saw the huddled form of the young boy, fast asleep, nestled up against a solitary rock. Garabed stopped, leaving the donkey, and considered the best approach, without alarming the boy unnecessarily. He slowly shook the boy by the shoulder.

"Ara, my son, Ara, my soul, my son Ara."

The boy still half asleep stretched up his hands as Garabed, straining with the effort, picked up the boy in his arms.

"Father, father," Ara cried and clung on tightly to Garabed, laying his head on to his shoulder, with his cheek firmly against Garabed's.

Garabed walked slowly back to where he had left the two women, followed docilely by the donkey. He held Ara tightly in his arms. The boy was heavy, and the wound in Garabed's arm began bleeding again. But short of food though he was, exhausted, desparate and short of sleep, Garabed never faltered, never once contemplated removing the boy from the position he had adopted to sit him on the donkey, but wove his way back, feeling a sense of triumph that he had not felt for weeks.

There was less than a kilometre left to go when, in the clear morning air, two gunshots rang out ahead of him.

CHAPTER 32

Selim and the Arab dimension

After the funeral service for his father, Selim decided, without much hesitation, that he could not return to Robert College to resume his studies.

Although he had never been very close to his father, his death had inevitably come as a shock, and he felt that he needed to make a clean break with his past. He had known his father, Nazim, as an educated, honourable and dignified man, always carefully correct in his dealings with everyone. However, Nazim had always kept him at arm's length, believing, somewhat like Colonel Bridgeman, Harry's father, that sons should not be shown too much affection by their fathers. Unlike his mother, Selim felt no bitterness towards the men who had caused his father's death, but they had inevitably become the enemy, and this in turn coloured his thoughts of Olga. Finally, like all the young men in these years, Selim felt the need to be part of the historical drama unfolding around him. He could no longer remain a student.

He wrote a short note to Olga letting her know that he had decided to abandon college and was considering joining the army.

Despite his mother's appeals, Selim went to the local Army Board and handed back his deferment papers, asking to be placed on active service. Like Vahan, Selim had been seconded to the Harbiye officers' training establishment and had been attending regularly; to the Army he was, to all intents and purposes, fully trained. Selim expected to be sent to the Gallipoli front. He was therefore surprised and excited to hear that he was to be posted to Damascus, where he was to join one of the three Arab divisions stationed in Syria.

Before leaving, Selim wrote another short letter to Olga. She had replied to his earlier letter telling him that she too was not going back to College. The death of Selim's father and the arrest and deportation of Karekin, had left them both anxious not to upset their families further. By mutual agreement, they had taken the decision not to meet. So, apart from telling Olga that he had been posted to Damascus, Selim made no further attempt at contact, and left from Haydar Pasha station to link up with the troop train to Damascus.

The triumvirate who ran the CUP and the Ittihad party consisted of Talaat, the sinister Minister of the Interior, Enver Pasha, the flamboyant Minister of War, and Djemal Pasha, once military governor of Istanbul, but now in charge of the whole Arab front. Just as Enver fancied himself as a great general, so Djemal Pasha also believed himself to be a great leader of men. Enver's absolutely disastrous campaign against the Russians at the start of the war, was mirrored in the south, when Djemal took command of the Ottoman Fourth Army and made a wild stab at crossing the Sinai desert to take the Suez Canal. He had been decisively defeated by the British in Egypt, since when he had settled in Damascus as Governor of Greater Syria, ruling the whole of the Arab vilayets of the Ottoman Empire, almost as a private fiefdom.

Once he had arrived in Damascus, Selim reported direct to Djemal Pasha. Djemal was a large jolly man, the son of a respected army officer. Due to his large, corpulent frame he was known – to his great secret pleasure – as 'Buyuk Djemal'. He was a clever and ruthless man in his forties and had been an early adherent to the Ittihad. Djemal, had been partly educated in Paris, and of all the Ittihad leaders he was the only one committed to the continuation of the multi-culturalism of the Ottoman Empire. He kept himself well informed of the various Arab nationalist movements – and the ferment amonst the other minorities, in particular the Armenians.

For a few weeks, Selim was put on Djemal's personal staff. At one point he found himself escorting, clandestinely, a couple of members of the Armenian revolutionary party the Dashnaks to secret meetings with his superior. Eventually, he was promoted to full Captain on Djemal's recommendation, and posted to the garrison at Baghdad.

Within days of his arrival at Baghdad, Selim was sent to his new unit on the Tigris as part of the Turkish forces stand against the Indo-British army, commanded by General Townshend, advancing up the river heading from Basra.

The Ottomans had been unable to do anything about the initial British landing. They had only a few Arab units, operating at the end of a long and tortuous supply line. However, Townshend's troops were also strung out 50 miles south of Baghdad, with equally long supply lines.

Selim joined an Arab unit, and found himself overseeing a slow retreat, as the British were drawn further and further away from Basra. This was a war being conducted by Indian soldiers officered by British, fighting against Arabs officered by Turks. Selim was in the middle of a countryside of swamps and deserts, without roads of any kind. Everything – men and materials, arms and even basic food – had to move up and down the meandering and shallow River Tigris. The conditions were terrible with pestilence and fever in the air. The climate was lethal for the Turks, used to the more equable north, while the Arab soldiers were immune. The British too were losing more men to disease than to military action, while the city-bred Turkish officers, were also succumbing.

Fighting was continuous, and Selim always in the forefront. While commanding a Company holding back a British patrol, he received a bad wound in the lower part of his left arm. After the skirmish died down, he retired and had the wound patched up at the main camp. There were no sedatives, and after drinking a half bottle of raki, he went to his tent to rest.

The next morning Selim awoke with his face swollen, unable to open his eyes and with a raging fever. Delirious and often unconscious, death in these circumstances tended to follow within days. His arm was infected and was poisoning his system. As the British were advancing more slowly each day, Selim was immediately evacuated back to Baghdad. There, in the still incredibly primitive conditions of the makeshift military hospital, Selim, was operated on. His increasingly gangrenous arm was roughly cut off just below the elbow.

More dead than alive, it was decided he should be sent back to Constantinople. If he survived the journey, he could be treated at the military hospital at Uskudar.

So it was that in the company of a coach-load of other wounded and dying officers, Selim was transported across the whole of Anatolia, with his wounds continuing to fester. In reality, he was being sent to die at the hospital at Scutari, where Florence Nightingale had first done so much to raise the vocation of nursing as a respectable profession.

CHAPTER 33

Harry and the Arab Bureau

The ship on which Harry had been serving, had made several further journeys to and from the Gallipoli staging areas, escorting supply vessels on their way out to the peninsula, and then hospital ships returning, crowded with the wounded..

Sooner or later, it was almost inevitable that Harry, a bright and knowledgeable regular officer who had already worked for several months in the Admiralty, would be transferred back to an Intelligence job. Despite his request to be left on active service, he found himself working at the Administrative Naval headquarters in Alexandria, a building situated near the Montazeh Palace at the far end of the corniche tramline.

Harry watched as the horrific death toll of the Gallipoli campaign got higher and higher. Nothing seemed to go right. Harry wondered how many of those eager young Australians on the landing craft with him in April were still alive.

It was well into the winter of the year 1915 that the Gallipoli campaign was eventually wound up. By dint of a brilliant strategy, almost a quarter of a mil*lion* Allied soldiers were evacuated in the very face of the enemy, and hardly a single life was lost. It was the only moment of glory in the whole mishandled campaign. Harry had long since lost any illusions in the glory of war, but he was thrilled by the sheer military brilliance of this event, though he was aware that wars are not won by brilliant evacuations.

A group of young Englishmen, imbued with romantic ideas about Arab sheiks in flowing robes, obsessed with trying to engineer an Arab Revolt against the Ottomans were organised in what was known as the 'Arab Bureau' in Cairo. Their chosen method was to act through Sheriff Hussein, nominee ruler of the Hejaz, which included the two Muslim holy cities of Mecca and Medina.

The Ottoman governor in the firing line of such an uprising would be Djemal Pasha – the governor of Greater Syria. As it would be the Navy's task to give whatever logistical support was necessary, Harry was instructed to undertake a study into the character of this man, one of the three principle leaders of the Ittihad. Harry also began a detailed consideration, of the Arab situation on behalf of Naval Intelligence.

Harry had had the same educational background as these young officers of the Arab Bureau, all products of the English upper-middle class educational system – Oxbridge and public school boys with strictly classical educations. However, Harry was somewhat different, having studied science, which gave him a different outlook from those eager young officers of the Bureau. He had also rebelled against his father's desire to push him into the army and since the war began, he had also become disillusioned by his experiences at Gallipoli.

Harry found himself questioning the romantic visions of these young men. As he researched their position more thoroughly, he saw that what real strength there was amongst the Arabs, lay in the great Arab towns of the fertile crescent – not in the flamboyant Bedouin tribes of Arabia. He also understood that in the last resort, the Arabs would always tolerate a foreign Muslim Imperial ruler above a foreign Christian one.

In the midst of this ferment of ideas passing between the young Oxbridge officers of the Arab Bureau in Cairo, and the Naval Intelligence Services in Alexandria, Harry was informed that a representative of the Armenian Revolutionary Federation in Cairo – the Dashnak party – had contacted the High Commission with an extraordinary proposal emanating directly from Djemal Pasha himself.

As the Navy's expert on Djemal Pasha, Harry was invited to go to

Cairo for the meeting with the Armenians, Army Intelligence, officers from the Arab Bureau and other experts on the future of the Ottoman Empire.

On the day of the meeting, Harry took the three-hour train journey through the lush Egyptian delta to Cairo. He stared out of the windows, watching the ancient panorama of fellahin working the fields with their patient camels and donkeys, the   picturesque water-wheels tended by a small boy with a stick. A few looked up as the train passed. 'What great War?' they might well have asked.

A most extraordinary meeting took place in a room at the British High Commission. There were several young English officers, all ready to carve up the Ottoman Empire in their own image. Lord Kitchener's current favourite – Sir Mark Sykes – was also present.

Harry knew he would have to give a written report of the proceedings to his superiors on his return to Alexandria. This, bereft of the necessary formalities is the gist of his report-

"I went straight from the station, with its usual bustle and pandemonium to the High Commission building. There were several people in the room when I arrived. I remember in particular the three young men from the Arab Bureau – an Oxford Archaeologist, Philip Graves a journalist from the Times, and another young officer – Thomas *Lawrence*. However the most important person there was Sir Mark Sykes – a Tory MP – who was probably the oldest person there, though not much more than 35. While he is a good and amusing talker – he has an easy and fluent turn of phrase that I envy – he is impatient of any opposition. He is a committed Roman Catholic, a convert, which is an important part of his make-up.

After introductions and some general discussion, two Armenians were brought into the room, and given seats at the end of the table. One was a young man – a hostile, dark-haired individual who introduced himself as Aris, from the city of Van. Throughout the whole of the proceedings, he looked as if he was about to explode. The other, the only man present over 40 years-old, was a tired-looking, grey-haired merchant who introduced himself as Sarkis Papasian. It was he who opened the discussion, informing us he had been told, in great secrecy, by party members in Damascus, that Djemal Pasha had indicated a willingness to overthrow the current government, if he could count on the support of the Allies.

"How did you get this information?" asked one of the officers.

"We were regularly taken to see him in his private office by a Turkish officer, a member of his staff," Aris replied.

"It appears," continued Sarkis, "that Djemal wishes to distance himself from the massacres and deportations of Armenians taking place in Anatolia and is prepared to act to save those surviving Armenians, still in the area, with allied support."

One of the Arab Bureau's delegates looked directly at Sarkis.

"So, why should we be that interested in saving Armenians. Djemal's got it all wrong if he thinks that is a priority in Allied thinking. In fact, it is providing amazingly good propaganda for us against the Central Powers."

While I did tend to agree with what the delegate man said, it wasn't very tactful in the circumstances. After this comment, the scowling Aris jumped up and was about to say something when Sarkis pulled him down telling him to keep calm in Armenian.

The old man continued, "The same suggestions have been passed on to the Russian foreign ministry, and Sazonov has indicated that the Russian government are interested. Djemal has proposed, with allied help to march on Constantinople, depose the Sultan and install a new regime."

The young foreign office official, who to my mind had been looking more and more ill at ease, nodded his head at this.

"Yes I can confirm that we have heard something along these lines from the Russians. The proposal is to create a new Empire, including a Turkish Anatolia, a greater Syria, an autonomous Christian Armenia, and a Kurdistan, all under a new Imperial dynasty – I suspect Djemal himself."

At this point, Sykes, rapped on the table, and spoke for the first time. "Our political masters would not agree. Our friends, the French, will insist on taking most of Syria, and I am already in negotiation with Monsieur Picot on that. Also, frankly, we have our own eyes on Mesopotamia at the very least. Forget Djemal's proposals – we can finish off the Ottomans without his help."

Sykes stood up and surveyed us all, totally ignoring the two Armenians, sitting disconsolately at the other end of the table, and announced, as indeed I'm sure he will report later in writing to Kitchener, and as I have carefully noted –

"Never mind all the natives, Armenians, Jacobites, Maronites, whatever. This ramshackle middle-eastern Empire must cease to exist. Smyrna can become Greek, Adalia – Italian, Cilicia and Syria – French, Filistine and Mesopotamia – British, and everything else can go to the Russians – yes even including Constantinople itself. Gentlemen, I shall sing a Te Deum in Constantinople in the Santa Sophia, and a Nunc Dimittis in Jerusalem in the mosque of Omar. We'll even be prepared to sing it in Polish or Armenian or Welsh, in honour of those gallant little nations, bless their bleeding hearts."

I have to say that I was frankly surprised – not by the lack of empathy or rudeness, but by the fact that it was so unnecessary. Simple silence would have sufficed. In any event, I looked round and it didn't seem to have worried any of the others round the table, who smiled, but did have the grace not to look at the two strangers at the end of the table.

Aris stood up, fists clenched and eyes smouldering, but once again the elderly Sarkis was too fast for him. He too stood, and holding Aris by the arm tightly, in order to make sure that he said nothing, turned and said to everyone in the room –

"Gentlemen – we have carried out our task – no doubt you will have your own ways of communicating with Djemal Pasha if you want to. For us, the priority was to prevent the continuing murderous and genocidal death of our people in central and eastern Anatolia. I see that, sadly, your priorities are different. But gentlemen, bear in mind that you have not as yet conquered the lands you are busy dividing up amongst yourselves. Beware, of the quagmire you may be creating for future generations to deal with."

The two Armenians left without another word.

I returned on the 7.00 pm train."

Harry did not record that after the Armenians left, Sykes and the young men of the Arab Bureau spent the next hour dismissing Djemal's proposals, followed by a further happy hour which they spent drawing lines across the map of the Ottoman Empire, as their young fancies led them. For all of them, this land was a completely blank playground for their romantic and heroic impulses, not a place where people had lived and died for centuries and who were as different from each other racially and culturally as anywhere in Europe.

CHAPTER 34

Mikael and Olga

The police station in Yedikule was at the southern edge of Stamboul, right up against the great Theodosian walls of the city as they came down to the Marmara Sea. Mikael, was dragged, rather than walked into the station.

"Name," rapped out the sergeant at the desk.

Mikael did not reply, but looked up at the officer with the dark look that was his unfortunate trademark.

"His name, sergeant, is Mikael Sarafian, and he's a fucking *giavour* deserter," said the policeman, putting the papers down on the desk, and indicating the out-of-date pass.

"Put the bastard in the cells," said the sergeant dismissively.

"One of the public ..."

"No," interrupted the sergeant, looking meaningfully at the three policemen, "in one of the single ones down below."

Mikael was taken down to the basement. He was thrust into a dungeon without a window, and a single, dim electric light swinging from the roof. There, nonchalantly, he was punched, thrown to the floor and kicked as a matter of course. He lay there, spitting blood and imagining the punishment that would be awaiting him when he was returned to his army unit.

However that night, the desk sergeant accompanied by a couple of guards, came into the cell, where Mikael sat on the bench, propped up against the wall and, without a word, was systematically beaten for half an hour, repeatedly punched in the face and stomach until he collapsed on the floor. The men never said a word, and the only sound was Mikael's screams. The screams soon became moans until, mercifully, he finally passed out. There he was left for over 24 hours, lying in his own urine.

Early the next morning, having been reported to his regiment, three soldiers and a lieutenant came down to the cell to take him back to the unit headquarters.

"Good God! What the blazes has happened to him?" the officer asked the guard who had opened the cell door.

"I believe he tried to escape and had to be restrained," replied the guard.

"For heaven's sake! Some restraint!," said the lieutenant. "What do you say soldier?" he addressed Mikael.

"Water, water please," Mikael managed to croak through cracked and bloody lips.

"Bloody hell! Take him out, wash him down and give him some water, and let's get going.

Mikael was carried out into the courtyard where he was undressed, hosed down, and after lying on the floor naked for a few minutes, was given a blanket to wrap round himself. He was incapable of standing on his own, so he was carried out of the police station and put into the army carriage waiting outside.

Mikael kept sliding in and out of consciousness. He barely registered what happened to him during the next 48 hours, and was only able to piece together events much later.

Driven back to the city headquarters of his unit through the streets of Stamboul and out through the gates, he was eventually seen by an army doctor, who thought him much closer to death than had appeared at first sight. After careful examination, the doctor diagnosed that apart from the bruises and outward damage, Mikael had a ruptured liver, and his kidneys were not functioning properly. Either way, the army could not possibly have him back on active duty as he was.

The administrative officer of the regiment decided he should be sent immediately to the military hospital at Scutari. It was there, some days later, that Mikael regained consciousness and opened his eyes.

Bending over him, looking anxious, was his old boyhood friend, Loris, dressed in a once-white, coat, obviously a hospital orderly of some sort.

"Loris – oh my friend Loris – did you manage to get the apricots," murmured Mikael with a smile of recognition, and then drifted off into oblivion again.

Mikael recovered very slowly as the weeks went by. His friend Loris visited him everyday and made sure that he got all the attention and medication prescribed. Without his personal care, Mikael would have been neglected, and would most probably have died.

Mikael later discovered that on being called up, Loris had claimed to be a qualified Vet. He had hoped thereby to be put in charge of the Army's horses and mules – and it was true that he did know something about animals, as his father kept a small herd of cows in their ramshackle old house on the outskirts of Makrikoy. When he was not at school, Loris often went with his father delivering milk to the terraced houses in the town, and the grander houses up the hills above the Valli *Effendi* racecourse.

However, in true army style recognised in all armies, this claim had resulted in a posting as a hospital orderly attached to a certain Doctor Turhan, who practised at the military hospital in Uskudar. Here, Loris had been allocated a tiny room of his own at the back of the enormous barracks.

As Mikael's health slowly improved and he was able to shuffle about, he began to spend more and more time in Loris' tiny den. He spent his time trying to improve his hitherto rather cursory education. He began reading voraciously any book he could lay his hands on.

As there were not that many Armenians working at the Barracks hospital in Uskudar, it was inevitable that Loris would eventually come across Olga Avakian. Olga used to stay in the nurses' dormitory at least four or five days every week. She returned to Makrikoy for her days off, but even when on duty, there were many moments when the staff interacted. Loris had indeed seen Olga several times, but they had done nothing more than nod at one another.

There was a considerable shortage of female nurses. Normally, these would have been provided by the minority populations – the Greeks, Armenians and Jews. Turks of the old school did not encourage their daughters in this sort of work, and this feeling had not changed much even for the modernisers. However, the news filtering in throughout the summer of the killing fields in Anatolia had left the Armenian community fearful and wary of courting attention, so there were no other Armenian nurses left. This meant that all the girls were overworked, and that Olga had only Greeks and Jews as colleagues.

It was Dr. Turhan who drew Loris' attention to Olga –

"Loris, my boy, did you know that one of our most conscientious nurses here is an Armenian girl. She's really very good. Every time she works with me, she seems to have learned more than the last time. I understand that she often stays at the hospital in the female staff dormitory. You should make an effort to meet her."

"Certainly, sir, thank you, I'll make a point of it," answered Loris, without any intention of doing so. All his spare attention was given over to Mikael, whose condition remained critical, even though he had now begun to regain some mobility. Every movement was still painful.

Loris and Mikael had been close boyhood friends in the little Armenian school in Makrikoy. They had clambered over the walls of the wealthier houses, in the Osman Agha area of the town, above the racecourse, and stolen apricots and peaches from the ample orchards there. They had kept watch for each other. They had wrestled together in their early teens, combats inevitably won by the bigger Loris who would demand an abject surrender, which was never given.

Loris had spent Mikael's first month at the hospital feeding him, bathing him, ministering to him on an almost hourly basis. There was not a spare moment that he did not spend with Mikael; first by his bedside, and then as Mikael began to shuffle about the corridors, alongside each other on the bed in the little room. Here they would reminiscence about their past, and make rather impractical plans for the future. Whenever Loris finished work, he come back to his room to find Mikael had been there most of the day reading.

Soldiers from the Gallipoli campaign kept pouring in every day with the most horrendous wounds – a new and terrible reality. Everyone was overworked and overtired, and thus it was that one day Dr. Turhan and Olga had worked together since early morning on the emergency cases flooding into the hospital. All were stretched to their limit. The doctor's hand slipped for the second time as he and Olga began stitching up a wound. There was a gasp from Olga and the other nurse as the doctor hastily corrected himself, and finished the task.

"Yes … Yes … All right Nurse Avakian. We're both exhausted. Neither of us can do any more good here. Nurse Avakian, please go and tell Loris to report to Doctor Fadil immediately. Then you must go and get some sleep yourself – that's an order."

Olga washed up, took off her white apron, dressed and went off rather reluctantly to find Loris' room. Contrary to what the good doctor thought, she had never spoken to Loris except for some cursory professional pleasantries. She thought he would already be on duty in view of the current state of emergency in the hospital. So she didn't hurry as she trudged up the stairs and knocked on his door. Somewhat to her surprise there was a call from inside –

"Yes. Come in, the door's open."

Olga walked in. She saw a thin, frail man, dressed in regulation py-jamas and a threadbare dressing gown, lying on the bed, reading a slim book. He had dark and feverish black eyes, with a haughty look about him. Mikael put down his book, and looked up at the exhausted nurse. He noticed her reddened eyes, that still retained a sparkle in them, and whose dress uniform seemed to hang on her effortlessly, with elegance and grace.

Mikael struggled to stand up, and at that point his whole life changed yet again. Olga's face softened, and she gave him a warm smile, putting forward a firm restraining hand saying,

"Please don't, sir. Lie still. Can I see what book you're reading?"

She leant forward and took the book from his fingers as he sank back on the bed.

"Ah. Namik Kemal – the early poetry. You admire his work? Are you a friend of Loris or a patient? My name by the way is Olga – Olga Ava-kian." And she held out her hand to the supine Mikael.

Mikael had none of the shyness with girls usual in the young men of his generation. He sat up on the bed, shook Olga's hand, and moved his feet off the bed inviting Olga to sit next to him.

Without any embarrassment, Olga sat down.

Working flat out since the early morning, Olga was tired. For his part, Mikael, though on the mend, was still in pain, particularly towards the end of the day. Nevertheless they talked together in Armenian for two hours. Only once did Olga get up and go and fetch some water, but she hurried back immediately. They soon discovered that they both lived in Makrikoy. They had even attended the same early primary school, though of course at different times, he in the boys section and she in the girls. As Olga described her house and her life, Mikael thought to himself that she probably lived in one of the grand houses that he and Loris had raided for illicit fruit when they were young.

This inconsequential chat, which they were both enjoying, could have gone on all evening, until, that is, the moment when Loris finally walked in – himself exhausted. Mikael tried to rise, experiencing an odd feeling of guilt.

"Hello – what's going on," said Loris as he took in the sight of Mikael trying to get up, and Olga sitting on the bed, smiling, with her eyes alight.

"Oh, Loris, I've been reading in your room. Er ... I suppose you know Miss Avakian ... er ... my friend Loris Temazian ... er ... you must know each other surely."

Olga remained seated on the bed between them as Mikael finally managed to stand up facing Loris.

"Are you well, Mikael, you look tired. Can I help you back to the ward?" Loris asked, ignoring Olga.

Olga scarcely had room to stand – but she did so at this stage, and faced Loris.

"Oh, Mr. Temazian, Dr. Turhan sent me up here to ask you to go on duty early, but you were already on duty when I got here. I've been chatting with your friend – we've discovered we are from the same town – isn't that a coincidence? Anyway, I must go now. Goodbye."

She flashed Loris a smile and went out.

Loris looked at Mikael. He, too, saw a frail vulnerable body with the far too large black eyes; he too saw the shabby regulation pyjamas and the meagre gown and the fact that this man was still very ill. But Loris was also seeing something more. He sighed and clasped Mikael round the shoulders.

"I'll walk you back, Mikael. I hope that girl didn't exhaust you. Please be careful of her, she has a bad reputation, and I believe she's a hopeless nurse – one of those rich spoilt girls playing at nursing. I'll see she doesn't worry you."

Then, he helped Mikael back to the crowded main ward.

Olga could not get the frail and rather prickly Mikael out of her mind. As the days passed, she often encountered Loris in the long, dreary and increasingly dirty wards of the old hospital. Any cleaning that went on was not very effective, and the hospital probably looked little different from the days of the Crimean War.

Olga sensed very quickly that Loris did not approve of her. To her surprise and irritation, no amount of stunning smiles or sympathetic eye contact made any difference. Loris remained indifferent, indeed even hostile, towards her. He never volunteered any information about Mikael, and made a point of telling her that Mikael remained very ill, and needed to be left alone.

Nevertheless, Olga took the trouble of regularly going to the enormous ward in which Mikael languished. She would sit by the side of his bed and chat to him, whenever she had the time. When she was with Mikael, she felt no need to exercise any artificial charm, but chatted freely and with spirit, enjoying the pleasure of mutual discovery. Slowly Mikael began to recover his strength, although Dr. Turhan said that his kidneys had been permanently damaged. Whenever he felt stronger, and if Olga had any free time, they would walk together along the hospital corridors, she in her ugly, regulation uniform, he in his threadbare dressing gown.

A rather unlikely affection began to grow between this aggressive but insecure, lower-class Armenian young man, and the confident, sophisticated girl from the upper-middle class. Class distinctions in the Ottoman world were never anything like those in the much more class-conscious West. The Turks never had an entrenched, hereditary ruling elite. Indeed, until the 18th century, most of the Turkish Viziers and ruling Pashas were technically 'slaves' of the Sultan and rose and fell, independent of family background.

However, there was a considerable difference in education and sophistication between the wealthy professional and merchant classes of the City, and the porters, workers and small shopkeepers, though neither side took much interest in the hard-working Anatolian peasants of the countryside, of whichever race.

Day by day, Mikael and Olga became more and more friendly and intimate with each other. Olga, lonely at work, and with the rest of the family at home more and more involved in their own affairs, found a great source of strength in the growing relationship.

It was well into the winter when Loris told Mikael that he would be going to stay for a few days at the house of Dr. Turhan in Stamboul. It appeared that the doctor was due to attend a conference of army medical officers at the War Ministry. He had been asked to bring with him a secretary to take notes of their discussions. He had asked for Loris to undertake this task.

Mikael had continued to use Loris' little room as he grew stronger, although he was more careful to use it only when Loris was on duty, so it was free when he got in from work, but on this particular occasion, Loris came in early. When Mikael rose from the bed on which they were both sitting, Loris too rose to say goodbye. Loris embraced him fiercely, cheek pressed to cheek. Mikael eventually had to make a physical effort to pull himself away. Slightly taken aback, Mikael opened the door to leave.

"Well Loris – goodbye till next Sunday. Do you realise that we've seen each other at least once, almost every single day for several months. It'll be nice for you to have a change from my incessant company."

"I don't want a change," replied Loris rather sharply, his eyes smouldering emotion.

"Come, come. Good God, you must surely be fed up with this bloody building. Just crossing the straits is going to be great for you. Right – well then – till you get back." Mikael smiled, walked out and went back to his ward.

It was two days later that Olga, off duty for a few hours at last, came to Mikael's ward early in the afternoon for their usual stroll and found him already dressed and sitting on his bed.

"Well, well, Mikael – how are you feeling? No dressing gown today – you're dressed. You need new trousers, you know, they're pretty scruffy. Actually Mikael, my dear, forget what I just said, you look better than I've seen you for some time. Your cheeks have colour, and your eyes seem brighter. What has the doctor told you?"

"Hey – Olga hanum – come and sit on my bed for a change," called out the soldier in the bed opposite, who had only one arm and one leg.

Olga flashed him her wonderful smile and turned back to Mikael.

"Well, let's go, or do you want to sit here?"

"No, no, I've got a surprise for you – let's go and have a chat in Loris' room."

"No thanks," replied Olga with a flash of anger. "you know perfectly well that he can't stand me – and for my part, I don't want to have to face up to his snooty disapproval."

"No, Olga, Loris has gone away for a week … we won't be disturbed, we can have the room all to ourselves."

Startled, Olga looked at him long and hard. Mikael stared back at her – eye to eye – with that slightly dismissive stare of Turkish young men everywhere in the Empire. This was the look which Olga had found so refreshingly absent in Selim. There was a long moment of silence between them, though all the noise and hubbub of the cavernous ward continued around them. Olga thought back to her actual words to Nerissa when she had said of Selim, that he had none of that hard arrogance of most educated Ottoman young men.

Olga would be 18 soon – she saw a tall and thin man, slightly stooped due to the effects of his injuries. His moustache – Enver style – was not now so cock-a-hoop, and his black eyes looked sadder, and had deep lines at the sides. However they still flashed with pride and a latent violence. Olga felt aroused.

"Very well, Mikael; but look I can't be away too long. I have to be back on duty again soon," she lied, without any qualms at all.

Mikael was cursed with an expression that somewhat belied his real character. He was a good deal more insecure than appeared on the surface. When they arrived, Mikael shut the door behind him as they walked in. Olga turned and found herself clasped urgently and fiercely round the waist. She felt Mikael's thin lips passionately pressed against her own full ones.

This was Olga's first real kiss. It was totally different to that wonderful moment when her lips and those of Selim touched and quivered for a second in the basement boiler room at the College. This was passion – she knew it – her body flowed with it, and she wanted Mikael to continue, to force her, to press harder. This was not Mikael's first kiss, nor his first sexual experience – but the emotion accompanying the moment was new for him. His body stirred with urgency, and he felt he would burst with desire. He had experienced these feelings before, and recognised them – but he also felt a tenderness and affection which had not accompanied any of his previous experiences.

They sank onto the bed, there was no place to stand in any case. Olga shifted and Mikael naturally came across her. Olga was fully dressed in her Nurse's uniform, and Mikael was wearing a shirt and his own shabby trousers, for the first time since coming to the hospital.

The kiss continued, as Mikael got more and more excited, but as Mikael's hands strayed, and as he began fumbling both at his clothes and hers, Olga came to her senses. A part of her was desperate for Mikael to go on, to loosen her clothing, to impose his will. Another part of her knew it was impossible. She had to hold back – urgently and at once. Already she had allowed matters to go far *bey*ond any reasonable level. A kiss was permissible; anything more was out of the question.

Olga moved her free hand, and held the busy hand of Mikael hard and tight. Mikael responded at once to her unspoken command. They remained clasped together. They continued to kiss, and explore each other's lips – but it was not going to go any further. Olga felt both relief and frustration simultaneously.

Eventually they lay side by side on the bed, and talked about the war, about nursing, about Olga's family, and about Makrikoy. Mikael's feelings got deeper, centred more on Olga, and less on his own desire. They remained together far longer than Olga had envisaged – she seemed to have forgotten having said that she had to go on duty again..

Meetings in Loris' room at the top of the hospital began to take place daily – often for as short as half an hour. Mikael now came looking for Olga, while Olga began trying to cool down the relationship.

After several days of increasing contact between them, Loris returned. The meetings ceased abruptly. For many days there was no question of any meeting between them – even the previous walks together stopped. But Mikael became more and more obsessed with the desire to speak to Olga and touch her – if only just to hold her hand. At last, one day, he caught her in the corridor outside his ward.

"Olga, you've been avoiding me."

"Not at all, Mikael, my dearest. But look, Loris is back and I know I am not welcome –you know that."

"Olga, my love, my soul. I think of you all the time. I want you – you must know that I love you. I'm getting better day by day. I'll be able to walk out of here soon. Heaven knows what is happening around us, or where we're all going to be when this bloody war ends. But sooner or later it will – sooner or later we'll be picking up our lives again. Will you wait for me Olga – will you marry me when I am in a position to marry? I want to live with you always, Say something Olga – for heaven's sake say something!"

Olga looked at this man. She thought of her family – of her par-

ent's reactions. She reflected on her own feelings – on the good qualities of this man almost five years older than her – of those moments of
thoughtless anger and violence she knew he was capable of. Then she
remembered that no thought of her parents, or her situation, had ever
entered her head during the relationship with Selim.

"Mikael, I don't know what to say. We're living in such uncertain
times, and in such uncertain circumstances. Is it right to enter into
long-term commitments while the war is on? All I can say to you is that
I have no feelings today for anyone else other than you."

Olga leant forward and gave Mikael a warm kiss on his lips, then
turned and walked away without another word.

That night, as she lay awake in the nurse's dormitory, she reflected
that even at that moment, when a young man had bared his soul to her,
and begged for a word from her, she had still failed to speak the words
– 'I love you'. Why not? Wasn't that what she had felt during that first
passionate kiss? Olga turned over and fell into an untroubled sleep.

It was on the very next day that Olga's situation became even more
complicated. On that day, she was on duty doing the rounds of the officers' wards with the duty doctor – Dr. Fadil. The officer's wards were
both smaller and cleaner than the dirty, white-tiled wards of the ordinary soldiers. They moved slowly from bed to bed, as the doctor inspected each man, and Olga took notes or administered the doctor's
recommendations. The doctors were efficient, but had no time to speak
to the patients *bey*ond asking the usual questions – most of the nurses
did try to say a few words before moving on.

Olga suddenly stopped as they approached the next man. She found
herself staring at an officer with one festering and badly bandaged half
arm, and whose whole body was shaking with what appeared to be ma-
larial fever. It was Selim Kemal.

CHAPTER 35

Raffi hangs on

When Raffi left his home early in the morning, after passing directly in
front of the police dressed as a woman, he had no idea where he would
go. He knew the areas west of Caesaria had not been as badly affected
by deportation and killings as the lands to the east up to the Russian
frontier. At the back of his mind was always the thought of his brother
Vahan, apparently safe in Istanbul. So his first thought was to go west-

wards to Konya, which also had the advantage of being on the railway line to the capital.

As so often happens, a minor and purely accidental incident changed this plan. Raffi was 'streetwise' when it came to the customs and habits of the town and knew how to avoid the unwelcome attentions of policemen and officials, so when he got to the dusty square, he knew how to keep a low profile as he milled about amongst the crowd.

Even at this early hour, the square was filled with horse dung. There were almost as many animals as there were humans – chickens trussed together, donkeys carrying heavy loads, lambs and goats, about to be loaded on carriages that would accompany villagers on their trips home. There were also old, badly maintained, petrol lorries, carrying passengers and animals to destinations further afield. Everything and everyone were mixed up together in an atmosphere of noisy but friendly confusion.

Raffi pinpointed exactly where the four or five policemen on duty were standing. He also noted, thankfully, that he did not recognise any of them. They were ignoring most of the villagers with produce, but Raffi could see they were looking at the papers of anyone dressed smartly, or any young men who might be of military age.

Raffi drifted, checking on the destinations of the lorries and coaches going westwards and saw another young man ahead who looked familiar. As Raffi came closer, he saw a thin and very frail-looking young man – scarcely more than a boy, with a pale, almost consumptive, look. The lad was clearly nervous, and sooner or later, thought Raffi to himself, he would catch the eye of one of the policemen.

Raffi was just about to turn away when he heard the boy ask the price of a 'simit', the round hard bagel which was a speciality of the town. At that same moment he also recognised the boy as one who had attended the same school. This lad was, if anything, older than he was, despite his appearance. As he walked forward, he saw the boy's eyes go up under his upper eyelids, and he began to sway, clearly about to faint. Raffi did not hesitate but grabbed him as he fell, holding him up and calling out so that at least all those in the immediate neighbourhood could hear -

"Abdul, Abdul – stand up – are you all right. Allah be praised, he's only ill – he just needs a little air."

The simit vendor, who thought he was just about to make a sale, was anxious to help. Holding him on the other side, they carried him and sat him down on one of the rickety chairs outside an old café on the edge of the square. Checking carefully that the commotion had passed unnoticed, Raffi paid for a couple of simits, and handed one of them to the young man who was recovering.

"I am sorry to be such a nuisance, *effendi* – I do thank you – I will be all right now, and on my way," said the boy rising to go. Raffi now recognised the lad as Armenian, the lighter hair, wavy rather than straight and black, the large round eyes, and the long face gave it away. There was also a haunted expression. Raffi leant forward.

"Hay-yem (I am Armenian)," he whispered – whereupon the lad collapsed back onto the old cane chair, and covered his face with his hands.

Raffi called out for a large coffee, and passed both the simits to the young man, who began eating them eagerly. After a short exchange, Raffi learnt that the lad was already 16 and his name was Dikran. He had left the town with the remaining members of his family many weeks before under the first deportation orders. The guards allocated to this particular group had melted away after the first few days, and the wretched column of women, children and old men had been attacked, hunted down, robbed and killed as it made its way slowly through the desolate countryside. In one particularly vicious encounter, Dikran had lost the last of his family, and had decided to escape.

Once on his own, Dikran realised that they were not far from the town, although they had been walking for days, so decided to make his way back. He had been sleeping in cellars and the empty houses of the old abandoned Armenian quarter for the past weeks. However, he had no money, and he had been slowly starving, living off what scraps and rubbish he could find. He had not dared to try and get any work as he didn't have any papers.

It turned out that Dikran had been told that well to the south of Caesaria, where the main railway line to the Arab vilayets passed through the Taurus mountains, the German company building the unfinished Berlin to Baghdad railway, were taking on workers, no questions asked. The Turkish government was anxious to have the railway line completed; all that remained were the tunnels through the Taurus and the connection would be made between the great Arab cities of the Levant and Constantinople. Raffi knew the government was even allowing Army deserters to work there unmolested, so important was the project to the war effort. From Raffi's point of view, it was completely in the wrong direction, but as the boys talked, Raffi became more enthusiastic about the idea.

Raffi felt excited and ready for danger. While not a great thinker like his brother, the situation in the house over the past weeks had made him depressed and nervous. Now, for the first time, he had found a male friend of his own age and they bounced ideas off each other in a childish, but natural, manner.

The first task was to get to the railhead. Raffi changed the first of his precious gold coins, and the boys paid a lorry driver who was carrying passengers to Ulukishler railway station. Buying some bread and kebabs for the journey, Raffi and Dikran stood the whole way in the back of the lorry along the terrible pitted roads to the railway line. Without thinking, they found themselves chatting together, laughing and gig-gling, reverting, if only for a moment, to the boyhood ways they had lost for ever.

When they arrived outside the station, they clambered down from the lorry with most of the other passengers. Raffi looked carefully around, but there were no more than a couple of policemen, leaning against the low stone wall separating the railway line from the road. The atmosphere here appeared much less charged, but it was not go-ing to be easy getting on to a train going to the strategically important Taurus tunnels.

It was Dikran who came up with the bright idea of getting one of the many troop trains, posing as 'simit' sellers, going on to the next station.

"Look Raffi, we go to that bakery over there, and buy up all the simit they've got. We get a pole of some sort – you know the way they do it – get on the train and walk up and down the corridors selling, like all the other kids do."

"It's all very well for you Dikran, you could pass for 13 or 14. But look at me? I won't pass for a child."

" Right – we've still got some cash left. We've got lots of time. We go into the town and buy a pair of dark black glasses that people with poor eyesight wear and a stick, white if we can find one, and you can hobble along behind me holding tightly to my shoulder."

This seemed a ridiculous plan but, after all the horrors and tensions of the past weeks, he couldn't come up with anything better.

After they had stocked up with the bagels, putting them along two poles, they waited on the platform for the train due from the capital and were not challenged. When the troop train arrived, all the wagons were full of soldiers – all the seats were taken, and young, shabbily uni-formed soldiers were leaning out of the windows laughing and joking. There were military police everywhere, who got off the train and stood about on the platform by the doors of the carriages as the train came to a hissing stop.

There were scarcely any 'civilian' passengers getting on the train, and those that were, had their papers carefully checked. Raffi had his papers in the name of Soliman ready, and his heart was pounding with excitement as he and Dikran approached one of the carriage doors. But Dikran, frail and consumptive though he might be, was a natural ac-tor. He grinned cheekily at the two military police at the carriage door, made a breezily ribald remark, offered them each a simit, which they declined and walked boldly onto the train calling out "Simit! – Simit!".

Raffi scrambled up after him with his hand tight clasping Dikran's shoulder, in a state of fear and triumphant excitement, in equal parts. While the train stood, hissing and steaming in the hot and dusty sta-tion, Dikran sang out his goods, exchanged rude and sexually explicit suggestions with the soldiers, and made a play of having to hand over the bits of cash to his older, and surlier companion. Then at last, with a great jerk, the train hooted and set off. It was only then that Raffi relaxed, as the presence of the boys, now rather desultorily selling pastry, was taken for granted for the rest of the journey.

On arrival at Belemedik – the end of the line where the tunnels were being constructed – the boys tumbled out with all the soldiers, who cheerfully wished them well as they made ready to march off.

Raffi soon got work with the German engineers building the railway line, but Dikran couldn't get employment with his frail and youthful looks, quite apart from the fact that he had no papers. On top of this he looked sickly after the weeks of near starvation he had endured.

Raffi found work as a brakeman for the construction gang trains going through to the tunnels. This was a hard, back-breaking job, which really needed a man's strength and physique. Fortunately for Raffi one of the German engineers asked him if he could read and write in the Turkish–Arabic script. When Raffi said he could, he was removed from his first job and taken to work in the engineer's office. Meanwhile the boys lived in the makeshift shanty town for the construction gangs, alongside the little town in the valley, in a shabby room in a hostel.

Dikran had changed. All those high spirits – that flash of inspired adventurousness when they had first met – had gone. A feverish, red colour had come into his pale cheeks. He ate badly and became querulous. He stopped going out to buy the food, his only task, and began staying in bed all day. At night, Raffi would be woken with sighs and whispers as Dikran suffered from terrible nightmares, which he could never recall the next morning.

It soon became clear to them both that Dikran was seriously ill, and might be dying. Asking around, Raffi discovered that Dikran appeared to be suffering from cholera, or a severe form of dysentery. Without doctors or medical services available, he went down to the town one day and sought out an old woman, recommended by one of the maids at the hostel, who came up one evening and muttered some imprecations over the dirty and sweating Dikran. She boiled up some foul-smelling herbs and roots, which she forced Dikran to drink. Dikran vomited it all up almost immediately after she left. He had not eaten for days by then. At least Raffi knew how to look after the sick and dying, and he fell back into this routine, but it was much more difficult here – for a start, there was never enough water to keep Dikran clean.

Dikran simply wasted away, until the day Raffi returned from work to find he had died. Raffi sat up all through the night by Dikran's body and reflected that they had never talked much about his family. While Raffi had chatted on about his own life, his big brother in Bolis, his mother and father, his trips to the farms in the highlands, he realised that he was not even sure of his friend's surname. Dikran had become simply one of the awful statistics of these events. He held the boy's lifeless hand, and in the early morning, the tears came as he slept with his head on Dikran's unmoving chest.

All the joy that Raffi had got in Dikran's cheeky behaviour during the trip from Caesaria, and for some time after they arrived, had evaporated. Though now safe enough and able to wait out the end of the war, Raffi became restless. He missed his new-found, and now lost, friend, in turn, his family. Living alone was not natural to his character, and the death of Dikran began preying on his mind – the room seemed cheerless, and the unmarked grave of the boy, so close by, began to upset him. Even though he was not particularly imaginative, Raffi decided to leave. He left that very night, writing a careful crafted note to his master, who was absent again for a second night working at the far tunnel, explaining that he had had to return home quickly as his mother was gravely ill.

This time he was determined to revert to his original plan of heading back towards Constantinople. Already, there were few Armenians left east of Caesaria, except individuals surviving alone and in hiding. The main danger was whether he was liable to military service. Either way, if his true identity was known as an Armenian deportee, death would inevitably follow. But Raffi was now experienced in the art of survival. He decided that arriving in the capital suddenly was too risky. Instead, he would go to Konya, where it was known that the current Ottoman governor had not applied the Ittihad deportation orders stringently.

When, after the usual difficulties and adventures he finally arrived in Konya, Raffi decided to retain his identity as Soliman. Only two of the precious gold coins were left. Raffi decided to go into business for himself. He found lodgings with a respectable, Turkish family on the outskirts of town. He invested in a large wheelbarrow, and, getting up very early in the mornings, he would go round to the local farmers who lived closest to the town. There, he would buy their fresh vegetables at a good price as they knew it would save them a long trek into town. He was a good judge of fruit and vegetables and was rarely cheated.

Then he would trundle his wheelbarrow,filled with fruit and vegetables to the central market, where he hired a small wooden platform to lay out his wares like those around him. He was usually sold out well before the end of the day, as his fruit was always fresh. This allowed him to go home in the afternoon with a small, but perceptible, profit on which he could live.

He avoided going to the public baths, where the fact he wasn't circumcised would be noticed, and was always very careful to maintain a strictly Turkish appearance. Soon after he arrived, the old Ottoman governor was unfortunately replaced by another fanatic Ittihad appointee, and once again, the remaining Armenians had to leave. Raffi found that he had done well not to change his habit of hiding his origins. There were Armenians who still remained, but they were there only on sufferance, and he pretended not to understand the language, even when, as happened once, he was accosted by two men calling out to him in Armenian.

Raffi was lonely – that was his main problem. He couldn't afford to have friends, and kept himself to himself. As the Armenians even here in Konya began to disappear, he knew that the only way to survive was to wait patiently for the war to end. He survived, but that was the best that could be said. He survived.

CHAPTER 36

Olga and Selim

Olga stood transfixed, and stared at the young man lying in the bed as Doctor Fadil began gently to remove the dirty bandage inexpertly tied round the stump of the arm. Turning to Olga, he said impatiently,

"Nurse Avakian, what's the matter with you for heaven's sake? There's a job needing to be done here. This bandaging is terrible – it will need to be replaced immediately, though I suspect the arm is again infected."

Selim was still suffering from the effects of the awful seven day journey by coach and train from Baghdad. He had been lying feverish and disoriented for days, and was barely conscious. But the words – Nurse Avakian – shouted by the irritable doctor – penetrated his hazy consciousness, and he opened his eyes. There, standing behind the doctor was the girl who had never left his dreams. Olga gave him a quick, harassed smile of recognition, as she hurried round to help the doctor gingerly separate the bandages from the pus and dried blood of the wound, which had not been cleaned for days.

Since he was first wounded, Selim had lived a sort of half-life until this moment. But now, for a moment he forgot everything – his father's death – the war – his pain and the lost arm. He simply gazed at Olga as she came round to his left side, managing to give her a great, heartwarming smile. Nothing else mattered. Out of the blue, life had suddenly become worth living again, at the same time that it had appeared to be ebbing away.

"Good God, this is getting infected and gangrenous all over again.

Nurse – a sedative for this officer right away. Young man, I see you are awake. I'm going to have to cut away some more of the re-infected area and clean up the original wound properly. It's best done right away. It will be painful and Nurse Avakian here will give you a heavy sedative which will send you off to sleep."

The fussy little doctor moved on to the next bed, while Olga took the ether bottle and a fresh gauze mask from her trolley and moved to Selim's side.

"Olga – Olga my love, what are you doing here? Oh, my God, how wonderful just to see you. Let me touch you," gabbled Selim hysterically.

"Hush Selim, my soul, hush. Your arm is really bad, even I can see that. We've caught it only just in time. Don't move my darling."

Olga gently put the gauze mask over Selim's nose, holding his arm tight. Looking carefully at what she was doing, she began to drip the ether bottle onto the mask. She was aware all the time that his eyes were burning and staring at her, trying to make eye contact, which she carefully avoided.

The doctor came back to the bedside as Olga finished and closed the bottle.

"Come, my boy – look at me, let me see your eyes – good. Now start counting – yes, yes, just counting."

"One, two threeee, frr …" and Selim was gone.

When Selim woke again several hours later, his arm was throbbing with pain – but he had been washed and he had clean white bandages over his stump. Above all, the fever seemed to have passed, though he remained very weak. He knew that he would not be able to stand up on his own two feet. He waited with increasing impatience for Olga to come and visit him.

Olga got through the rest of her working day by mechanically performing her tasks, knowing that she was not giving of her best. Everything that had occurred a year ago came back to her vividly as if it had happened yesterday, but it was not just the memory that returned. That smile – the look in his eyes – when Selim saw her in that first moment, made her heart leap with a joy that she had not felt for a year.

She was due to return home that evening after work, but she knew that this evening would be for Selim, when he awoke.

The moment that Olga arrived and sat down on the bed beside Selim he grabbed her arm with an intensity that almost hurt her. Olga smiled, leant forward and kissed him on his cheek.

"Oh Olga – Oh Olga, my loved one. What joy, what joy, just to see you. Allah is merciful. I can't believe it. Tell me, my love, tell me what are you doing here?" Selim spoke in a hoarse whisper, aware of the other patients around him.

Several hours passed as they sat like this, with Selim holding Olga's arm tightly the whole time. Olga talked quietly and told him all that had happened to her since their parting. Food came and went – nurses on duty moved around – conversation hummed amongst the other patients around them – there were even some visitors, whilst the two talked on and on.

Selim soon began to feel sick – the usual effects of ether. What with that, together with what almost amounted to a re-amputation, he kept breaking out in a sweat. However, he would not let go of Olga's arm and she did not want him to. Olga took a cloth from the side of the bed, and kept mopping his brow, and occasionally touched her cheek to his.

It was during this period of intimacy – deeply private, even though they were in the middle of a large ward – that Olga felt someone was staring at her. She looked up and saw the figure of Loris by the door, looking at her with an expression of hatred mixed with triumph. When he saw her look up, he walked away. Olga didn't really care – but it suddenly reminded her, she had promised to call on Mikael before going home that evening. Selim, meanwhile, was still talking urgently and disjointedly. His fever seemed to have returned.

"Enough, my darling, enough. I'll have to go now. Tell me, do your mother and sister know that you're here?"

"Oh, Olga, yes of course. In all my joy I forgot about my poor mother. She may not even have heard about my being wounded in Mesopotamia. My darling – could you possibly let her know? Heavens, they could even visit me here. That would be wonderful – wonderful."

"Of course, Selim, of course. Look, it's my day off tomorrow. I'll go into Bolis, and visit your mother."

"Olga – that would be really kind. But listen, do you know where she lives?"

"Come, Selim, of course I do. I passed it every day before the British arrived in Gallipoli. I would look up and think of you inside. It's that big, modern block almost opposite the Galata Tower, isn't it?"

"On the fourth floor – rather a climb, my sweetheart – Flat 8."

"Selim, my soul, sleep now – sleep. I'll come and visit you again tomorrow, as soon as I get back from seeing your mother. I'm sure she'll make an effort to visit you herself very soon."

Then Olga carefully withdrew her hand from Selim's. She leant forward and gave him a light kiss on the lips. Already the war had changed everything. Only a year had passed since that precious moment when their lips had touched ever so lightly in the basement cellar, but now, even in the midst of a ward full of other men, neither Olga nor Selim thought twice of a kiss, unimaginable only a year before.

The next day, Olga took the ferry and crossed over to the Galata bridge on the European shore. She was dressed simply as always, but she knew she was looking her best. Mounting the stairs in Selim's building, she knocked on the door of Flat 8. The door was opened by a young girl with wavy black hair, who looked to be about 12 years-old. She was wearing the uniform of the German Gymnasium, and she looked at Olga questioningly.

"Hello – I am Olga Avakian. I am a nurse at the Uskudar barracks hospital. Is you mother in? I've some news for her."

"Mama," called the girl, and opened the door further to let Olga into the compact hallway.

A woman dressed in black but with a beautiful, diamond brooch on her left shoulder came out of a door. She did not offer to shake hands in the modern style, but bowed her head and nodded, saying -

"I am Halideh – can I help you?"

"Yes, I am sorry to disturb you. I am a nurse at the Uskudar military hospital. I have brought news of your son – Selim."

The excessive and somewhat strained politeness and formality vanished from the woman's demeanour. She took Olga's hand and led her into a small, but neat and tidy, sitting room, with potted plants, two exquisite Turkish carpets, some low coffee tables, two pouffes, a sofa and a settee. She called out – 'coffee' to the maid who was hovering at what Olga assumed must be the entrance to the kitchen. "Shekerli?" she asked Olga.

"No thank you, I have to return soon," replied Olga, warming to the sign of anxious love in Halideh's eyes. They sat, side by side on the settee.

"I've come at Selim's request to tell you that he is here at the Hospital and that…"

"What's happened, what's happened – is he all right?" interrupted Halideh.

"Yes, yes – he's improving. He has been wounded, but his life is in no danger. However I …"

"Allah be praised, Allah be praised. Now, my dear, tell me more. I won't interrupt again I promise you," and Halideh laughed out loud in relief and touched Olga's hand.

Olga told her quietly all that she had heard from Selim – his experiences in Damascus and along the Tigris facing the British Army. Halideh winced and looked down as Olga came to the wounded and amputated left arm – but she continued to listen carefully to all the news.

"When can we see him, Nurse, when can I go to him?" his mother asked as soon as Olga had finished.

"Well, you can visit officially during the afternoons – but many relations bring food to the men at other times as well, so it is all rather informal."

"Thank you, thank you. May Allah preserve you for ever. What is your name, my dear, I did not catch it when you first came in."

"Olga Avakian."

There was a long moment of deep silence. Olga felt the woman draw back and freeze. Olga realised then, that knowing this to be a Turkish Hospital, Halideh had assumed that she was Turkish.

Halideh stood up from the settee in emotional turmoil. Still not a word was said. Olga sat with her hands clasped together on her lap. Now, for the first time since she had first seen Selim again, all the old problems which had driven them apart came back to her. She suddenly recalled the circumstances in which Selim's father had died at the siege of Van and this was why the lady was dressed in black. Nazim Kemal, for whom this woman was still in mourning, had died at the hands of Armenian rebels, and Halideh hanum was clearly still bitter. Furthermore it was not entirely clear whether she was aware of the relationship between her son and Olga.

The silence was broken by the voice of the young 12 year-old girl who had been listening intently throughout in the corner.

"Mama – Mama – Selim is here, Selim is here. Let's go and see him now right away," and she jumped up, eyes aglow.

Halideh, with tears appearing in her eyes, which now had a hard glint in them, turned away, as Olga rose in some confusion. Carefully avoiding looking at Olga, she walked to the window, with her back to the room, whilst the young girl looked on in some puzzlement.

"Yasmin – yes of course we will go soon. Meanwhile please show Nurse Avakian to the door as she is leaving."

"But, Mama, what ..."

"Yasmin! Do as I say. Please tell her, as she goes, that we are grateful for the trouble she has taken in coming here to give us this news."

Yasmin took Olga's hand – totally innocent of any problem, though she couldn't help but feel that her beloved mother had acted in an unusually rude manner. For the first time since she had seen Selim again, Olga now became prey to all the doubts that she had had a year ago. She squeezed Yasmin's hand, walking out into the hall and out of the front door without saying another word.

Olga was less prone to tears than she had been before entering the hospital, but the humiliation to which she had just been subjected now hit her, and she felt tears trickling down her cheeks. All the unalloyed joy that she had felt with the return of Selim, evaporated completely. Selim appeared to have resolved his own doubts, and that had given her enormous satisfaction, but she saw that the problems of a love between her and Selim had not gone away. In many ways they had become even more intractable. Fitted into the equation were now two mothers – Halideh and Armineh – both of whom had lost a husband in circumstances which made it impossible for them to face up to any emotional ties Olga and Selim might feel for each other.

On her arrival back at the Hospital, she recalled her promise to Selim to go to him immediately, but she had no idea what to say.

"Olga, my love, tell me, tell me. How was it?" said Selim as she came along the ward and sat by his side on the bed.

"Selim – yes – yes – calm down my love. I saw your sister, Yasmin. What a lovely girl she is, isn't she? She was really happy to hear that you were here, and they are going to try and come to see you very soon."

Olga held the hand that Selim stretched out to her, but said nothing more. Selim looked questioningly at her.

"Yes – yes, Olga, yes?"

Olga knew that he was disappointed at her failure to say more – to speak more warmly about his mother, his home. However, the days when Olga could cheerfully make up stories and white lies, were over. Olga felt silence about that morning's events was better than giving some false impression – though she saw and felt his hurt.

Olga chatted on about all that she had seen at his home, but she kept silent as to how Halideh had reacted. She saw that Selim sensed she was holding something back. To her deep sorrow, she also saw that Selim believed that it was she who had taken a dislike to his mother. A year ago, Olga would not have accepted that double humiliation, but today, she was prepared to take the consequences of appearing in a bad light, in order to save this young man a greater pain.

She felt her tears coming, so she leant forward, kissed Selim on the lips, smiled and got up to go. Selim grabbed her arm, but she moved free. I'll see you again soon, Selim, but first you must be ready to welcome your mother and sister. I'm sure that they'll come this afternoon."

As Olga walked out of the ward, she suddenly felt incredibly tired, and made her way up to the nurse's dormitory. As she arrived in the corridor leading to it, there, waiting for her was Mikael, fully dressed with a cheap cloth bag by his side.

CHAPTER 37

Vahan survives

It was one of those wonderful fresh spring mornings, with a crystal clear blue sky and a weak sun shining on the dark waters of the Bosporus; the kind of day so beloved by the people of Constantinople – the Bolsetsi.

Vahan sat at his desk in the offices of the main Electricity Company of the town; originally a Belgian Company, now being run by German directors. His job was to go through the electricity consumption accounts for most of the city, work out the totals and type up invoices on an old typewriter. The accounts were then delivered by the Company's messengers. These messengers milled about the offices all day, coming and going and animating the surroundings.

The offices, situated on the Pera side, were modern and airy. Every day, Vahan walked from the Patakis house down to the Galata bridge, across and up the hill on the other side. The work was easy, and, in its way, quite satisfying, giving him a sense of steadiness and routine, which prevented him from worrying too much about his current circumstances. However, it was hardly mentally challenging, and he would finish his assigned tasks quickly, and leaving too much time to stare vacantly out of the window, into the courtyard gardens.

That extraordinarily packed day of the 24th April, now over a year ago, had changed the whole course of Vahan's life. The arrest of Father Komitas, the arrest and deportation of Karekin Avakian, the assault on the boy Haik and his meeting with the Avakians, had affected him profoundly. However, it was not until he got home that evening and received the letter from his brother telling of the arrest and deportation of his own father – Garabed – that the situation finally struck home with full force.

The news filtering through from the interior, and the reports of the appalling events taking place in the eastern vilayets, made it almost certain his father was now dead. Despite the occasional postcard, he didn't know how long the rest of his family back in Caesaria, would survive. He was particularly worried about his volatile and emotional younger brother, Raffi.

Vahan had continued drilling at the Harbiye Military Academy and learning the business of being an officer in the reserve.

Like everyone else in the dying days of the Ottoman world, Vahan was politically confused – though from a different viewpoint than his Turkish colleagues. On the one hand, the success of the old Empire, in holding at bay the arrogant self-confident Westerners in the Dardanelles, was a great source of pride to the Ottoman youth –whichever racial divide they came from. Suddenly, their despised country was fighting back against people who looked down on them, regardless of their cultural identity.

On the other hand, the minority peoples of Bolis were learning of the horrors being inflicted upon the Armenian peasantry of the interior. It might be that those horrors were exaggerated – truth being the first casualty of war – but the Armenian community in Bolis, had

experienced, at first hand on the 24th April, the arrests and disappearance of their own leaders, giving more credence to the news filtering
out. How then, could an Armenian Ottoman citizen remain loyal to a
state which had so clearly turned violently against its own people, and
directly against members of his very own family?

. The ordinary soldiers in the army facing the British in the Gallipoli peninsula were becoming less and less ethnically Turkish. Large
numbers of Arab soldiers were being sent to plug the gaps in the ranks
of the original divisions, which had fought with such distinction under
General Mustapha Kemal. Mixed in with the Arab cannon-fodder were
young Armenian men from the labour batta*lions*, fed into the front lines
and dying in their thousands. On the other side, the English and Aus-
sie soldiers shouting – "Hey, Johnny Turk!" were unlikely to be facing
Turks at all.

The Harbiye military barracks was quite distant from the Patakis
house, and Vahan recalled that he would spend many nights, illicitly, in
the little sick room at the barracks, to save the long journey home and
back again each day. As it happened, just across the fields at the back
of the barracks was the house of his violin teacher – a certain Madame
Yalbak – a widow of French extraction, who had been the wife of an Ottoman Turkish army officer. Vahan would keep his violin in his locker
at the barracks and occasionally creep out in the evening to call upon
the old lady. She was delighted to feed the young man, who seemed to
be perpetually hungry and play duets together in her cluttered, velvet-
upholstered sitting-room, before he clambered back across the wall into
the barracks.

Madame Yalbak loved Stamboul and was deeply immersed in Ottoman culture. Vahan had come, not just to admire her, but to love her.
She provided an emotional anchor of inestimable benefit to him. Sitting
at his desk in the office, fiddling with his pens and staring out of the
window, Vahan broke into a smile at the mere thought of her.

The good lady pressed him, on a daily basis, to leave the University
and the Harbiye, and hide out until the war was over. She would regularly say,

"My boy, this government has exiled, if not murdered, your father.
They are carrying out a deliberate policy of murder against your unprotected people in the east. Your family are barely surviving, living
in terror, while all their neighbours are mostly dead. Why – oh why –
would you fight for them?"

"Well, because – for better or worse – it is my state and ..."

"But, Vahan, that state has turned against you. You haven't turned
against it – nor have most of your people."

"Yes, all right Madame, but what you are suggesting is desertion,
however you dress it up, and deserting is a hanging offence."

Vahan recalled that the day had come when he had again stayed one night illicitly in a bed in the sick bay. He had shaved that morning, had given a fond, quick kiss to the night duty nurse who had let him stay, and ran down to have some breakfast in the canteen, prior to joining the morning's first drill in the parade ground. A fearsome drill sergeant had come up to him and barked out -

"So, trainee lieutenant Asadourian – you so love the army you stay with us all night do you? The Captain wants to see you – at the double!"

Vahan remembered the sick feeling of terror he'd felt at that moment. The Sergeant had shouted and sworn at him, but then he had just walked away. His punishment might have been severe, but it was not a life or death matter.

He realised that he had not actually made a conscious decision; all the madness of those past weeks: the terrible news and rumours from the countryside; the barrage of words from Madame Yelbak; the probable death of his father, all seemed to have congealed in his mind at once. Pushing aside his meagre breakfast, he had stood up as the sergeant moved away, and without saying a word to those around him, he had gone straight to his locker. There he had taken his rifle, as if he was going out on parade. He also took down his precious violin, and his few personal belongings. He left all his books. Then, with a beating heart, he had gone down to the armoury, handed in his gun, and had walked, not run, through the fields at the back of the barracks, and clambered over to Madame Yelbak's house on the other side of the road.

As he thought back on it, Vahan marvelled at what he had done. Without any real thought, he had cut himself off from all the comforts of comformity, and put himself into the utmost danger – all without plan or foresight.

Madame Yelbak, however, had not hesitated for a second when she opened the door to him at that early hour of the morning. She knew at once what was behind his sudden arrival at her door. She waved away the Greek maid, and took Vahan into the kitchen. She went upstairs and sorted out some of her husband's old clothes, while Vahan sat at the kitchen table, shivering with fear and excitement.

"Take off that uniform, Vahan," the old lady had commanded, handing the clothes she had picked out. She took the uniform and pushed it, item by item, into the kitchen range, the burning cloth making a terrible smell, as he dressed in the clothes that had once belonged to the long-dead Major.

"Have you finished with the first lot of invoices," piped up one of the messenger boys, standing at his desk with hands outstretched. Vahan came to the present with a start. He had actually already completed the whole lot of his assignment for the day, but he carefully picked out about half of them and handed them to the boy. He kept the other half on his desk as if he still had to deal with them, and called out to one of the other office boys,

"Kahve – Osman – kahve. Shekerli please"

Vahan sipped his sweet black coffee as he continued to ponder his situation. He had been lucky to get this job so soon after deserting the Harbiye, and for over a year, he had survived just one step ahead of the police.

Vahan sighed and turned his attention back to his work.

In the evening, he walked home, down to the Galata bridge where he stopped, as always, for a few minutes and watched the ever-fascinating boats trafficking up and down the Horn, and onto the quays under the bridge. Then looking up at Stamboul hill, to the sun setting behind that incomparable skyline of domes and minarets, he walked home.

On the very next day, after breakfast, Vahan walked out of the Patakis house into the little street. He saw immediately that it was cordoned off at the far end, and that the police were examining everyone's papers. Another group of policemen were moving down the street searching the houses. Vahan turned to go back into the house, then reflected that there really was nowhere to hide, and he did not want to get Christina into any trouble. He could see that the police were searching pretty thoroughly, and that this was not just a question of bribing a single policeman.

He walked boldly to the end of the street and handed his papers to the policeman at the gap, who studied them closely.

"*Effendi*'s name is Sami – and you are Ermeni and not yet eighteen."

"Yes officer"

"Join that small group of men over there."

Vahan moved over and joined a group of young men, some boys and a couple of older men guarded by yet another policeman. They were a totally nondescript and disparate lot, with no particular identifying characteristics, save being males.

Eventually the whole group were herded off to the local police station. Here, Vahan found himself locked into a small room with all the others. There was nowhere to sit, and there was a smelly open bucket in the far corner for urinating. No one spoke to each other, and no one knew why they were there. The door was regularly opened, as one-by-one they were led out and away. About half had gone when it was Vahan's turn.

He knew that they had neither believed his papers, nor that he was under 18 years of age. With his heart pounding, and in a sweat of anticipation, he stumbled after the policeman who had picked him out, and found himself in another white-washed room which was much cleaner, and in which there was a doctor and a male assistant standing by. Here, he was told to take off his upper clothes. The Doctor carefully examined him, and, in particular, his mouth and teeth.

"This man is probably 20, but is certainly over 19," then, marking something on the card given him by the policeman, he called out, "Next".

Vahan said nothing, though he was surprised by the accuracy of the doctor's comments. He was taken to the lobby of the police station, and told to sit down. The desk sergeant laboriously wrote out the details of the arrest, and indicated to the numbed Vahan that he would have to go to Court the next day. It was at that low point that he heard a cheery voice call out,

"Hello Vahan, what's going on?"

It was Marisa Patakis. The sergeant noted that Marisa, who was now nearly 17, had transformed the atmosphere of the station by her cheerful salutation. He smiled at the young girl who smiled back. It appeared that Marisa had seen the arrest of Vahan from her window and persuading her mother, Christina, to give her some money, she had hurried down to the station.

"Sergeant, this young man lives with us at this our address nearby," and she handed over her own papers, which the sergeant carefully perused.

"He won't run away – can we please bail him in the usual way?"

The sergeant considered.

"Very well, mamzelle. He must report here tomorrow morning early to go to the Court in *Bey*oglu. The bail will be set at two hundred piastres – you better make sure he comes."

Marisa who had brought just enough, handed over the money and they both waited whilst the sergeant wrote out the bail papers, a copy of which he gave to Marisa. When Vahan and Marisa walked home, Christina, who had never really recovered from Elena's sudden departure, said nothing.

Vahan now wrote out a letter of resignation to the Electricity Company, explaining that due to a complication in his affairs he was going to have to resign. He arranged for a messenger to deliver it. He spent the rest of the day in a state of fear and anxiety as he tried to imagine what would happen to him at the court hearing the next day. Vahan was unable to sleep the whole of that night.

The following day, Vahan took the copy of the bail documents and arrived at the police station early. Here he waited for almost two hours, sitting on a stool by the reception desk, prey to a host of fearful presentiments. Eventually the moment came when a new desk sergeant called over a bored policeman, handed him the documents of the arrest, the doctor's report and the original bail papers, and ordered him to escort Vahan to the district court in *Bey*oglu.

There was no handcuffs or other restraints. The bail papers guaranteed by Marisa Patakis were still in the hands of the policeman, so Vahan couldn't do a disappearing act. Once again Vahan walked across the Galata bridge by the side of the policeman, this time looking at the scene with a weary eye. How different the vivid scene seemed to him this morning. He had no wish to linger – he just wanted to get it all over with.

He had forgotten that the Court was on the same street, a little further along from the Electricity Company offices. They walked into the large and once-imposing marble hall of the Court. Vahan stood well back as the policeman walked up to the busy reception and handed over the bundle of complaint documents, Vahan's papers and the bail papers. Vahan was standing back, still contemplating his likely future.

He watched as the policeman took out his duty book and got a signature from the man at the desk for the papers. Then to his surprise and increasing delight, he saw that the policeman, having completed his duty, his task completed, without saying another word, turned on his heels and walked out. Vahan suddenly realised that the clerk had no idea that Vahan had arrived under arrest. Vahan joined the queue, and eventually said to the Clerk when he reached the front.

"Ah, *effendi*, I believe that these papers apply to me. Can you tell me where I should go, and to whom I should report?"

The clerk motioned that he was busy and was dealing with several matters. He then gave a quick look at the headings of the papers on the desk.

"Look – take these papers and report to Chavik *Bey*. He will see to the matter. He's on the first floor, along the corridor to the right as you go up the stairs – the last office at the end."

In disbelief, his heart now pounding, he took the papers and turned to walk up the grand but dusty marble stairs. Once at the top he saw a long corridor with office doors on each side, and many clerks and messengers wandering up and down, smoking and chatting. No one was taking the slightest notice of him. Vahan stopped, surreptitiously taking deep breaths to calm himself down. He looked over the balustrade down into the entrance hall, which had become increasingly busy as the time for the morning petitions and hearings drew closer.

Vahan waited, and then at a moment when the reception clerk was busiest, he walked back down the stairs and straight out of the building. No one challenged him, and with the bail papers and his own documents firmly in his hand he walked back along the street. He knew there was no other documentation evidencing his arrest with the possible exception of a note in the local station records, so he walked along taking great gulps of the suddenly wonderful Bolsetsi air, and turned into the Electricity Company offices.

His boss still had his letter of resignation on his desk when Vahan walked in. Vahan explained that his affairs had all been satisfactorily arranged, and he would therefore like to withdraw his resignation if that was possible. Vahan's boss sighed with relief – finding sufficiently educated young men was becoming increasingly difficult. He told Vahan that he had not as yet taken any steps on the resignation letter, and that Vahan could simply go to his room and carry on working – the previous day's absence to be treated as illness.

Vahan sank onto his chair, called for a coffee, and spent a good half hour trying to control the trembling, which had taken over his body. He then threw himself into his work preparing invoices, in order to catch up on the previous day's workload. It was nearly lunchtime when one of the old porters came up to him.

"Sami *effendi*, there is a soldier outside who has given us your description and who is looking for you."

Vahan, who had thought himself safe, suddenly felt sick with apprehension all over again. He assumed he had been caught out. There was, however, nothing to be done, his colleagues were looking at him curiously as sweat broke out on his brow. The porter waited courteously –

"Ahmed, can't he come up to see me here?"

"No, *effendi*, he insists you come down, and, truth to say, I can see that he can't come up – he has someone with him."

Vahan couldn't make head nor tail of this, but nevertheless, he arranged his desk – most of the work had been finished, took some personal items out of the drawer and followed Ahmed down to the front door. Through the door, out in the street, waiting on the other side of the narrow road, he saw an elderly-looking, unshaven and badly turned out soldier, whose arm was in a sling, standing alongside a young country boy.

Vahan walked across, no longer concerned that this had anything to do with the morning's events, and approaching the soldier, stopped and stared –

"Oh my God – Father – Father, my beloved father – Baba, Baba ...," clasping the malodorous Garabed in his arms and, oblivious to the surrounding crowds, began at last to cry softly.

CHAPTER 38

Garabed finally arrives

Vahan rarely wept openly. But this day's events had finally been too much for him. He had been on a roller-coaster of emotions from deep fear and anxiety to moments of euphoria on escaping from the Court building. The sudden appearance of his father, whom he had believed was dead, was the final straw. There and then, standing on the pavement, Vahan wept.

It was Garabed who first pulled away and kissed Vahan on his cheeks, as Vahan swallowed hard and composed himself. Almost immediately, they both started talking at once, and stopped and started again together, and then finally stopped again, laughing with the release of tension.

"My son – we came to try and find you the moment we arrived in the city and were told where you worked by the quiet Greek lady at your house. We've only been here a few hours."

"Father – look, we can't talk here on the street. Wait a moment. I'll be back in a minute. Are you all right, baba? Is your arm badly wounded?"

"No, son – don't worry – it's just a disguise. Off you go, we'll wait here."

Vahan ran back across the street and into the building asking leave to take the rest of the day off. Then he rushed back out again, marvelling at how his life had been turned upside down twice that day. Garabed was still there, with a young boy standing alongside him, holding tightly on to his free hand. Vahan felt that this was not the moment for explanations. His main concern was that his father stood out rather more than most.

Vahan had spent a lifetime looking up to his father, following his lead and decisions in almost everything. Suddenly, the tables were turned. Without hesitation, he motioned to his father to follow him down the street. Then, looking at the young boy, he asked,

"Well, baba, who is this young man?"

"His name is Ara," said Garabed simply. "Ara, say 'hello' to my eldest son – Vahan."

"Parev, Barón – hello sir," Ara responded, speaking Armenian, the first time the language was used. Vahan was startled, knowing, as he did, that his father could not speak Armenian. However he held out his hand – then seeing that Ara did not know what to do with it, he took the boy's free hand and shook it.

"Welcome Ara, welcome to Bolis. Come, father, the first thing we are going to do is to get you both cleaned up."

Vahan put his arm round his father, noting that Ara on the other side did not once let go of his tight grip on Garabed's other hand. Strangely connected like this, they walked rather awkwardly down the street. Vahan went straight to the local small hammam, where fortunately it was the day for the men. He ordered and paid for a private room.

This was one of the more opulent of the city's baths. Having picked up their thick, warm white towels, and with their white dressing gowns in hand, they went through into the marble courtyard inside. This had a large tree growing in the middle. All round the court were small but comfortable rooms, each with a rattan table and chairs, with lockable doors and a small window looking into the courtyard. There was a small, inner staircase which led up to a first floor balcony running all the way round the court.

Ara, eyes wide with wonder, stared and stared, and clung on even more tightly to Garabed. Vahan got to their room, tipped the attendant generously and ordered kebabs and bread.

"Come, baba, get out of those awful clothes, and take off that sling. Father, I've forgotten, what's your chest and leg size? Oh ... yes, thank you. Look, you and Ara go into the baths. Have a really good scrub down. Take your time, baba, go into the steam rooms, and when you are in the hot water rooms, make sure that they use one of those really harsh loofahs on you. You too Ara – come on, get undressed, don't be shy – have you never been to a hammam before?"

"No, Vahan," Garabed said rather gruffly, "he's lived in the country all his life – leave him to me please."

"Fine, fine, baboushka. Now look, I'm going to go and get some clothes for you both. They'll be pretty rough, baba, but they'll be better than what you've got on at the moment. We'll burn this lot. I'm amazed that you got this far in Pera without being stopped by the police."

Vahan was all hustle and bustle. Suddenly he felt in total control and it felt good. He watched for a few moments as Garabed gently disengaged Ara's hand. Vahan felt a surge of warmth for his father, though he also noted that Garabed had been far gentler with the boy than he would ever have been with his own two sons. Had Vahan or Raffi hesitated to do as he ordered, Garabed would have commanded immediate obedience. Here, however, to Vahan's surprise, Garabed gently urged Ara to get undressed and to put on his dressing gown and follow him into the baths. Vahan, hurried out into the streets looking for the cheaper clothes shops in the back streets nearby.

With Garabed washed and shaved, and Ara, too, scrubbed, and both as pink as babies, they dressed in the clothes Vahan had purchased. They all walked back across the Galata bridge and to the Patakis house. There was no sign of any police, and, in any case, all the trauma of the day had passed out of Vahan's mind in the joyful activity of seeing his father. Christina was at home when they arrived. She had already seen Garabed that morning when he had first arrived asking after Vahan. After a slightly sticky start, Garabed turned on all the charm he could muster. This was a side of his father that Vahan had never seen. Indeed, Garabed was usually reserved and upright in front of his children. But in these circumstances, he knew that he needed to get on the right side of this lady, and he was accordingly very gallant towards Christina, who lapped it up.

The arrangements were soon made. Garabed was to take the old attic room which André had used, and which had never been re-let after his disappearance with Elena. Ara was to sleep with Vahan, whose room opposite was a little bigger and could take an extra bed.

After an early supper eaten mainly in silence, Vahan gave a brief account of what had happened to him at Court, and gave the bail papers back to Christina, promising to repay the bail money as soon as he could. He did not elaborate on how they had come back into his possession. Garabed took Ara up to bed. There, to Vahan's astonishment, he sat with him until the boy fell asleep. Vahan meanwhile sat on the bed in André's old room, waiting for his father to come in.

It was still fairly early, and it had only just got dark, when Garabed finally began recounting everything that had happened from the moment that he had been arrested at home. He passed fairly quickly over the things he had seen and done at the farm of Sarkis, and then went on to the difficult and tiring days when he and Ara, together with Ara's sister Anna, and his mother Adrineh had plodded with their two donkeys through the desolate countryside after leaving the farm. Garabed finally came to that last night when he had been attacked by Ara. Vahan noticed that at this point Garabed, who had been pouring out all his feelings as he relived those moments, hesitated, and clearly was not disclosing everything.

"Well, my son, on this particular night, perhaps I was more relaxed as we were getting closer to the Vilayet of Syria, and I could feel that the evenings were getting warmer. Anyway, I awoke … er … I had not been in a deep sleep, to find that Ara had got my knife and was … er … looking around wildly. I thought he must have seen or heard something, so I too sat up and looked around. What then happened … er, in all the confusion in the darkness … was that Ara almost hit his mother with the knife, and wounded me in the arm."

"Good heavens – how extraordinary and what was it that caused all this?" Vahan was plainly puzzled.

"Yes, well anyway, realising his mistake and feeling upset … you must remember, Vahan, he is only 12, and think of what he had seen and lived through, the trauma and the nightmares. Anyway, as I say, he dropped the knife and ran away into the dark. Well, Vahan, you know how pitch black it can be on moonless nights in the country. So all we could do was to wait until dawn. I built up the fire, so he could see it if he wanted to come back, and we settled down until first light."

"Whether it was the light of the fire, or whether it was fate but at the crack of dawn, I left the old pistol with Adrineh and went off to find Ara ... Oh God, Vahan, I had so many things to think about all the time. It just seemed to me that the needs of the boy, out alone in that wilderness, frightened, were more important at that moment than the two women."

"I should have thought more. I could have packed everything up and taken them with me but I thought, in the pitch dark, the boy couldn't have gone far. Anyway, after about three hours I found the lad curled up fast asleep against some rocks. He was bruised and dazed – he must have wandered for hours. I picked him up and we started back to where I had left his mother and sister. I don't believe that I was even one kilometre away, when I heard the sound of shots in that still morning air. Oh Vahan, my son, I knew that the worst had happened. I tried to put Ara down and told him to follow me, but he clung onto my neck so hard I couldn't shake him off. I began running as best I could, before I came in sight of the dying fire. Oh my God, my God."

At this point Garabed buried his head in his hands. Vahan rose from the bed, stepped over and went onto his knees and hugged his father. Vahan felt awkward trying to give such comfort to the strong authoritative figure of his father. He rose, stepped away and flopped back down on the bed.

"Continue, baba, what had happened?"

"Well, my soul, I will never know for sure, of course. Lying dead by the side of the remains of the fire was the girl Anna. She looked fairly tranquil. She had been shot at fairly close range by one shot in the heart. Away from her, there was more blood on the ground and signs of a scuffle. The donkeys, our provisions and Adrineh were all gone. I believe what must have happened is that a party of men came upon these two. Anna was already hovering on the brink of madness. I think that after Adrineh fired off her warning shot to no avail, she shot Anna before they could get to her, and then probably tried to shoot herself before she was grabbed. Vahan, I saw no body anywhere. She's gone – gone for good. Who knows where, or what became of her?"

"And what about Ara in all this, in view of what you told me about his reaction to the awful events in the farmhouse?" asked Vahan.

"Well, my boy, whatever the reason may be, Ara was fantastic. It was almost as if this last horror kicked him back to reality, whereas until then he had been in denial. Vahan, I had no spade, nothing. We had nothing left – only two gold coins left in my pockets, and the knife that

I had picked up quite by chance before setting off to find Ara. Yet we had to bury the poor mad girl somehow. Vahan, my love, it took us the whole of the rest of that day – and even then it was more of a mound than a grave – but we did it. It was a very bare hillside, but we just managed to keep the fire going. That night, Ara crept up after I had gone to sleep, and curled up into my arms. He's still a child, Vahan."

"That was in the summer – what happened over the winter?"

"My son, I could go on for ever. The details will have to wait for another time, but I decided that we had to press on into Syria. There was no point in turning back, now that we had come that far. I'll tell you something Vahan, poverty and deprivation in the city is degrading and squalid, but, my soul, poverty in the countryside is worse – desperate. It may be cleaner, but you will starve more quickly.

Ara may be a naïve country boy – did you see the wonder in his eyes when we went into the baths – but he was good at scavenging and finding edible things. You wouldn't believe the things we got round to eating. We were hungry all the time. Well, we got to Aleppo eventually, and there, at least, things began to improve. Here I came into my own, and whilst currency is collapsing in value all around us, gold pieces were doing well – and I had two left. This was just enough to get us started. I was able to get a job humping cotton bales and other goods for a shop in the bazaar. Knowing the trade well, I was able to give the Arab shopkeeper a lot of help. Eventually he agreed to take on Ara as well – for just the day's food of course – to run around getting coffee and tea, which he would bring on a brass tray for the customers.

I saw many Armenians in the town – almost all poor peasants – and many of them simply collapsed and died in the streets. But the richer merchants and professional people who made it that far, moved on to Lebanon or Damascus. We heard, however, that most of the population had either died on the way or died in the desert in Syria.

Vahan, my boy, this was no life, and when the summer came I decided I would try to make my way to Bolis, knowing that you were here, and that most of the Armenian population had not been touched. Caesaria was out of the question. We spent months slowly collecting everything we needed – a soldiers uniform for me, false papers, that bloody sling and, most difficult of all, a medical pass for a broken arm. Once ready, we travelled by train, walked and more trains. But, my boy, my soul, we made it. We made it! Then to cap it all, you tell me that Mariam, my sweetheart, and my darling daughters are still alive, so far as you know. The Lord Christ be praised, Vahan, we're through. We're here. Who knows, if what you say is true, then maybe even Raffi might still be alive somewhere."

"Father – calma, calma. This war is not going to end just like that. We've got a lot to get through yet. But yes, baba, yes, I think we've a good chance now. Ara is young, and now that he's here, he is out of danger. You too. I will just have to be more careful.

Oh father, father how good it is to have you here by my side. We're going to make it. My God, I do believe that we're going to make it!"

CHAPTER 39

Karekin and Aram return

Seated at a coffee table in a shabby run-down part of Stamboul, close by the Grand Covered Bazaar, was a tall, middle-aged bald-headed gentleman. He was dressed in good clothes, which had obviously seen better days

Karekin Avakian sat, eking out his one tiny cup of coffee to make it last, and waiting for the return of his friend Doctor Aram Manuelian, who had left him only an hour ago. He sat pondering the events since he and Aram had jumped out of the train in Konya. It had been a time punctuated by moments of high tension interspersed with long periods of intense loneliness and boredom. He fiddled with his teaspoon as he thought of the last few weeks before they left Konya.

Karekin was beginning to get anxious about Aram's failure to turn up as promised. The news filtering through was bad. Sivas, it seemed, had been emptied of Armenians. Erzurum had become a ghost town. Everywhere, the news had been of the dead and dying on the roads going south and east.

The Russians had finally arrived in Van, relieving the encircled Armenians, but within the year they were in retreat again. Meanwhile, tens of thousands of Armenians had died in the deportations and death marches.

As soon as Djelal *Bey*, the old Ottoman governor had been dismissed, and the new governor was on the point of arrival, Karekin had realised that their refuge was no longer secure. In their interminable discussions over alternatives, Aram had thought the best place to go was Smyrna, but it was Karekin who made the startling suggestion that they should return to Constantinople, under their new assumed names. Karekin recalled the decisive conversation. "Look, Aram, neither of us have ever been to Smyrna. We don't know our way around, and it won't be as easy to meld into the local populace as we have here. Of course we can't go to our old haunts, but we're probably safer there than anywhere else. It's a big city, we know how to avoid the police and where to go, and, above all, there are no deportation orders there."

"You're crazy, Karekin. If we were recognised it would be immediate imprisonment or worse."

"But Aram, we won't go anywhere near Makrikoy. In the city, we'll hardly be strolling into Tokatlian's for lunch, or going to places where we would meet business friends."

In the end it hadn't taken much argument to persuade Aram on this course of action. He knew that everyone from Constantinople – the Bolsetsi – always retained a love of the city, whatever the circumstances of their departure.

With a sizeable amount of cash, reconverted into gold coins, and with battered old suitcases still holding their old city suits, Aram and Karekin got seats in a carriage going to Bursa, travelling on to Yalova and then by boat to Bolis. Karekin had to persuade Aram not to get on the train running directly to Constantinople, which would have been much quicker and a good deal more comfortable, because the trains were always patrolled by efficient police guards, whilst the gendarmerie on the roads were lax and always open to a bit of financial persuasion.

"Well, well, Karekin, now that we are here," said a voice, "what are we going to do? Our cash isn't going to last for ever, and one thing is obvious – there is no way that you are going to be able to open up a little business here."

Karekin looked up with relief as Aram sat down at the table. The waiter, with his dirty white cloth over his arm, hurried up, thankful for a further order from this table at last.

"*Effendim?*"

Karekin ordered two coffees – one sweet and one without sugar.

"First things first, Aram. Did you get to see your partner at your old surgery?"

"No, Karekin – it's boarded up with a closed notice on the door. The note looks fairly new, so I suppose Avedis couldn't manage on his own and has sold up. I went off to the library to take a look at a list of current medical practitioners but Avedis is not listed anywhere. I'm supposing that he has either retired or perhaps even died – he wasn't that young – and his flat above the practice is empty."

Karekin nodded and said -

"You know I do agree with you that we're not going to be able to attempt in Bolis what we managed in Konya. Sooner or later, I would be recognised if we opened a shop."

"Yes, but look here, Karekin, what about your family and the business. If I know Armineh, she might well be managing to keep your business going. Now that we are settled in, what about contacting her discreetly."

"Aram, whilst the present situation continues, I simply can't take the chance of putting my family at risk by appearing at home. If they are discovered harbouring a fugitive, they will all be thrown out, imprisoned or worse. Armineh knows I'm alive and somewhere in or near Konya – that's enough. I must pick the moment carefully to make myself known to them, if that moment ever arrives, and only when I know they won't be in danger."

"All right, I see your point, Karekin. However, honestly, while it seems that the days of our poor old Empire are numbered, the war could still last another year or more, and meanwhile how are we going to manage? Living here in Bolis is a good deal more expensive than it was in Konya, and, sooner or later, our cash is going to run out."

"What about your flat in Makrikoy, Aram. Surely no one will have taken that over. Do you still have your key?"

"Yes, as it happens, but Karekin, isn't that a ridiculous risk? We can't possibly live in Makrikoy."

"No, probably not – but you must have some valuables in the flat, things we might be able to sell. Your spare cash might still be there. We've been here a week already. I've grown a moustache and my wispy beard is coming along nicely – I doubt if anyone in Makrikoy would recognise me. I never had more than a few acquaintances there."

"Karekin, the position is quite different for me. Any of my old patients in the town would certainly recognise me, even if I grew a beard. Being arrested a second time would almost certainly mean death for either of us. Think about it – escaped deportees – false papers – there would be no hope at all. Good heavens, the caretaker alone will be enough to ruin us."

Karekin considered for a moment,

"All right – here's the plan. We buy some flowers from one of those smart shops on the Grande Rue de Pera which do personal deliveries. We get them sent to one of the ladies in your block – I'm sure you remember the name of one of them. When ordering, we ask to speak to the delivery boy – say we need to give him special instructions – it's often done. Then, here's the tricky bit, we ask him to find out the name of the caretaker who lives in the basement – and to give us a description if he sees him. We tell him that he'll get a good tip, and that we'll call the next day."

"Where does that get us?"

"First it tells us whether the same caretaker is still there. If it's the same man it will have to be a more risky night job. But if it's a new man, we can bluff our way in during the day. We might even be able to use the flat again if we play our cards right."

"Karekin – do you know you've got a criminal mind? I think it's terribly chancy, but then so has almost everything else we've been doing. All right lets do it. I do have some money hidden under a loose floorboard, which might well still be there. Look – I know that I'll start worrying and thinking of everything that can go wrong if this drags on, so lets start this very afternoon, before I start getting cold feet. I know the right flower shop, and the lively Jewish widow on the floor below mine will adore getting the flowers. She won't be the least surprised to get some nice flowers delivered from a secret admirer. Come on – pay up, let's go!"

The plan had worked perfectly. Karekin and Aram had waylaid the flower delivery boy on his return to the shop, having already promised him a large tip. The lad had given them the name of the caretaker at the block. As Karekin had thought likely, the previous young concierge was no longer there, probable called up for military service. There was a new elderly man, who, if the boy could be believed, was so old as to be almost senile.

Karekin had already grown a fairly respectable beard by the time that they plucked up their courage to make the train ride that had been Karekin's daily trip in happier days before the war. This time, they both travelled third class without argument. Aram muffled himself up in a thick greatcoat despite the warm weather. Karekin laughed at him, and took nothing but an old scarf.

It was only a few minutes before the train was due to steam into the Cobancesme station that Karakin suddenly thought of a problem, that he had overlooked.

"Oh, my God, Aram, I've forgotten old Abdul and Mustapha – the gharry drivers at the station. They'll recognise me for sure whatever I do. I've used them almost every day for years."

"Ah ha, Karekin my dear fellow, so you're only thinking about this now. For once I'm way ahead of you. When I bought the tickets at Sirkeci, I got tickets for the main Makrikoy station in the middle of the town. It's only a bit further to my flat from that station, than from Cobancesme."

"Well done, Aram, good thinking. You owe me two mil*lion* or thereabouts so far – I'll let you off a straight mil*lion* for quick thinking. I'll soon get it back anyway."

Karekin sat back in his seat as the train stopped at the familiar station. They had chosen the middle of the day for their trip, so there weren't many people in the train or on the platforms. Three minutes later the train stopped in the main Makrikoy station.

Karekin was not given much to introspection. He tended to get on with life as it arose, enjoying without guilt its many pleasures, and facing up to its many difficulties, without complaint. But, now, he found himself contemplating the little town with a warm emotional attachment he had not felt before. This was the town in which he had lived and brought up his family – the town which he had feared he might never see again.

Both Karekin and Aram were nervous as they made their way through the main street. They walked past the shiny new shopfronts, alongside the old-fashioned, tiny shops, where people still made, at the back, the goods they sold in the front. Nobody took the slightest notice of them, and they arrived outside the modern block of flats, where Aram used to live.

It was an awkward and decisive moment for them. To get into the block, the caretaker had to open the main door after dark, but the door was usually left open during the day, as it was on this occasion.

"Karekin – I think we should contact the fellow now, whilst it is broad daylight and in less suspicious circumstances than if he accosts us coming out," said Aram, knocking at the door of the caretaker's little room which faced onto the courtyard, just past the main door. The door opened.

"*Effendim?*" said the man who came to the door, nothing like as old as the flower delivery boy had made out.

"Porter *bey*," said Aram, "I am Doctor Aram Manuelian. I live in Flat 7 on the third floor. I don't think we've met before, I believe you are fairly new. I've been away at the front, and have only just been released. Here is my 'nufus'. And your name is?"

Aram handed the old man his original internal passport papers, which he had been careful to bring with him.

"Ah yes. Er ...my name is Murad, Doctor *effendi*. I've been here three months, and this is, indeed, the first time we've met, though I do have your name on my list," said the caretaker looking at the nufus and handing it back to Aram, whose confidence was increasing with each word.

"Well Murad, my good fellow, I'm a doctor and in these difficult wartime conditions I have to spend a lot of time at the military hospital in town. I've been back a couple of times in the last two months, but haven't seen you before. This is my good friend – Mahmud Acimoglu – who will be staying at the flat for a few weeks whilst I am away."

At this point, Aram handed the old man the false papers of Karekin, which they had obtained in Konya. Confidence was what mattered, and Aram found himself oozing assurance. He then clinched the situation by showing the man his keys,

"I have my keys with me, Murad *effendi*, so I can go straight up as always. Has my cleaning girl been coming?"

"Oh no, *effendi*, she hasn't been here at all as far as I know."

"Ah well, never mind," said Aram, holding his hand out for the papers, "I'll find someone else. Meanwhile, Murad *effendi*, this is for all your trouble, and I hope you will be helpful to my friend if he needs anything." Aram gave the man, whose face creased up into a large grin, a big tip. He and Karekin then walked up the stairs in a mixture of triumph and excitement.

The keys still fit – there had clearly been no official entry.

Karekin and Aram walked into the empty flat. It was almost a year since anyone had lived there, and although the flat was clean there was a musty, damp, odour about the place. Aram went straight to the main bedroom. Here the bed had been left unmade – the blankets and new sheets folded at the end of the bed. Aram pushed the bed to one side, while Karekin stood at the door watching hopefully. Aram knelt down, feeling the boards, and called out to Karekin,

"Karekin, my soul, go and get me a knife from the kitchen." When this arrived, Aram began working away at one of the wooden tiles forming part of the modern parquet floor – digging the knife in between the cracks. Eventually he prised it up, and felt down with his hand, and very gingerly brought out a vicious looking mousetrap, which sprang shut as he put it down. He then felt down further, lying flat on the floor. "Karekin, it's still here!"

He carefully pulled out a largish cloth bag, upended this on the floor and out poured some coins, mostly gold, and some wrapped large denomination notes.

"Hey! Well done Aram. My God! What a lot you've managed to save. I didn't know that you doctors did so well."

"No, no Karekin – this is money left by my father for my mother – which she passed on to me just before she died. Good God, I couldn't have saved anything like this on my fees."

The two men had discussed for hours exactly what they would do in the event of accessing the flat and finding the money intact. It was far too risky for Aram to be seen in Makrikoy. Quite apart from the other residents in the block, who would be certain to recognise him, he had many personal patients in the town, so it would in danger of discovery on the streets as well. For Karekin it was different. Almost all his friends and business acquaintances were in Bolis and not in this district. Whilst he had indeed lived in the Osman Agha area for years, he had rarely come down into the little town. He never did any shopping here. He never accompanied the children to school, and he never used the main station, always travelling from the Cobancesme halt.

So it was agreed that Karekin would stay in Aram's flat, while Aram would take most of the money, and go back to the city and find some lodging where he could have his meals prepared, and be less likely to attract police attention, particularly as neither of them were eligible for military service.

The two friends arranged to meet regularly, twice a week on Mondays and Thursdays at a particular cafe in the Stamboul side of the city. This rendezvous was sometimes changed, but usually it was a dilapidated spot beside the old Moslem cemetery above Eyup. This was a quiet area right at the end of the Golden Horn inlet. Just as Aram could not be seen in Makrikoy, Karekin couldn't wander about in the Pera side of the city.

Karekin's moustache and beard had soon grown to a respectable size. He fell into a hazy dream-like existence as the spring ended and summer arrived. There was far too little to occupy his mind, and, he was constantly aware that he was within a few miles of his family and all that he loved in the world. When he and Aram met at the café agreed the time before, they played innumerable games of tavloo, and slowly Aram's debt mounted into many mil*lion*s of gold or sovereigns – they never specified what currency it was. Aram would always be waiting for him at the same rickety table, outside the old coffee house above Eyup.

Bored to tears, Karekin began taking risks that he had promised Aram he would avoid. Anxious to have a glimpse of some of his family, he began to make a point of hanging about outside the little primary school for girls that Seta attended. On the first occasion, pressed back against the wall of one of the houses across the square from the school, he saw Haik walking hand in hand with Seta. His heart lurched as he saw his only son, laughing and restraining Seta, who was skipping rather than walking, and never once stopped talking. Karekin wondered why it was Haik who was bringing Seta to school and not Marie or one of the maids. After seeing Seta into the school gates, Haik would turn and sprint away, and Karekin realised that he wouldn't have much time to get back to his own school on the outskirts.

Karekin began making a point of wandering past Seta's school in the afternoon to watch Haik arrive to pick her up. Karekin could see that Haik was very careful to take Seta by the hand, and he noted that they immediately went off together up the hill past the racecourse without saying a word to anyone. He ached to press them to his chest, and envelop them both in his arms. However they appeared cheerful, and he knew that appearing suddenly before them, would be difficult for them, and dangerous in the extreme for him.

It was well over a year since his arrest, that two events occurred that would once again change Karekin's life. Already several weeks had gone by since he had moved into Aram's flat. That morning Karekin took the late morning train into the city, and stepped out at Sirkeci station. There were always police about at the station, stopping people at random and asking to see papers as they showed their tickets at the exits. Karekin had been stopped before – his tall bearing tending to stand out. However, as he was clearly well *bey*ond military age, and his new grey beard made him look even older, their inspection of his papers was fairly cursory. On this occasion he was again stopped, and their inspection was a little more thorough, although they soon waved him on.

Karekin felt an atmosphere of suspicion in the city, and for some reason there were more policemen about. These days of added tension happened fairly often and were usually associated with some news from the front, or scare-stories about spies or riots in the city. He took the tram that went to the suburb of Eyup. On arriving he walked past the remains of the old Blachernae Palace of the Byzantine Emperors, through the little streets surrounding the Eyup mosque and on up the tiny cobbled street that led up along the old Muslim cemetery. He passed by the old tombstones slewing to one side or the other at crazy angles, and walked round the corner which brought him in view of the simple old round wooden tables with rickety chairs, where Aram would sit in the sun and wait for him to arrive.

The moment he turned the corner, Karekin saw four policemen, all with their backs to him. One had a gun in his hand, and another was waving some papers and shouting. Standing, staring straight at him as he appeared, was Aram, with blood coming from the side of his mouth and from his nose. Karekin saw one of the policemen give another vicious punch to Aram's stomach. Aram doubled up but his face must have shown the light of recognition or something, as two of the policemen began turning to see what Aram was looking at.

The next moments happened in a flash – scarcely more than a few seconds – but it was as if time slowed down as each action and reaction took place. Aram, even in his physical distress, seeing the two policemen beginning to turn toward the corner of the lane behind them, suddenly yelled at the top of his voice into the air, "Pakheh' – pakheh – get away." He then straightened up and struck one of the policemen who was turning – a heavy push really rather than a strike – and began to run away in the opposite direction. He couldn't get far because of all the tables and chairs around him.

Karekin stared for one second, then turned and strode back round the corner, and started running. Despite the panic and the rush of adrenalin, there was little doubt in his mind that he heard the sound of two gunshots ringing out behind him. He stopped and there was a long moment of silence. For another second he hesitated, but then began walking down the lane and into the busy bubbling streets of Eyup.

He thought of walking straight back to the station. But his legs felt weak, and he had to stop. He wandered into a rather rough and ready eating house, ordered he knew not what, and sat staring into space, piecing together in his mind what had just happened. The scene ran over and over in his mind in cinematic detail. He had no idea what the police were looking for, but the blood pouring down Aram's face showed that he had been arrested and repeatedly struck. It slowly dawned on him, that his old friend had deliberately shoved the policeman away in order to distract them from turning towards him. And the two shots ...

A wave of despair swept over Karekin, and tears came into his eyes as he thought of Aram and all that they had meant to each other over the years. Karekin never wept in front of his family, but here, in the midst of a huddle of uncaring strangers, he silently sobbed, impatiently wiping away his tears as they sprang from his eyes.

Once again, riots were erupting in corners and alleys all over the city. Once again, the mindless cries of 'giavours this' and 'giavours that' were being shouted by crowds milling about, whose real problem was not the infidels in their midst, but the lack of reasonably priced food and the other deprivations caused by the war.

But ultimately this was not Eastern Anatolia. The government was aware of the presence of their Allies' embassies in the city and knew that the Empire could not afford to be seen to be complicit in ethnic or religious killings. Hence the police were out in force with direct orders not just to stand by, as they usually did, but to control the mobs. The churches, Greek and Armenian, and the synagogues, were well protected and the centre of the city saw no deaths or looting.

Karekin was unaware how long he sat at the table. Eventually he rose, having eaten or drunk nothing, left a payment and made his way on foot to Sirkeci station. Feeling guilty at not having stopped or returned to share his friend's fate, and still in deep distress, he got on his train.

Sitting in a corner seat, he stared out of the windows as the sea walls passed, and the train went through the gap driven through the great walls of the city. Still not entirely conscious of his surroundings, he got out, without thinking, at the Cobancesme station, instead of continuing into the town. He was lucky – neither of the carriage drivers were present. However, the mistake suddenly brought him with a snap out of his reverie and back to the dangerous present, as he began walking into town.

It was then that he first noticed that there was a mob of gesticulating and rough-looking men running past him up the road. Turks, Albanians, riff-raff of one kind or another – where they all came from he could not tell. They were certainly not local Turkish townsmen. He walked on paying little attention, but then he suddenly became aware of what they were shouting. His heart missed a beat as he heard -

"Allah be praised – Allah be praised – the bastards are burning. The filthy *giavour* school has been set on fire. They're going to rot in hell. Come on, come on."

CHAPTER 40

Olga decides

Mikael scrambled up from the floor where he had been squatting as Olga approached down the corridor.

"Olga, I'm leaving the hospital today. I've been given a medical discharge. That's the positive side. The negative side is that Dr. Turhan has told me that my kidneys will never recover."

She was still upset at the outcome of her last brush with Selim, and looked at this man, and realised that he wanted more from her than she could give. With Selim, there was an ethnic and historical divide, whilst with Mikael, the divide was one of class and education. Also she simply did not feel the same strength of feeling towards Mikael that she felt for Selim.

"I expect, Olga," continued Mikael, "that you knew this when you told me to forget our feelings. But Olga, the doctor said that I could have years of fairly healthy life, and that in all other respects I am cured. Olga – I intend to go far – I know it. Please, Olga, don't shut me out."

"Oh Mikael go home, my dear. Of course we'll meet again, we live in the same small town for heaven's sake."

Mikael's face reddened.

"I'm sorry Olga, my soul. Listen, I'm going to go back to Yedikule to finish what I started – and then I am going to look for some work in the city before I even consider going home."

Olga leant forward and gave him a gentle kiss, by way of a goodbye. But Mikael was having none of it.

"No, Olga, we can't part like this. I love you – you know I love you. It has only been your presence here that has kept me going. You are going to be mine. Just say it!"

Olga looked at him – hesitated for a moment – and then speaking softly, without smile or encouragement, she said,

"Go carefully, Mikael my soul. We will surely meet again whether you are in Makrikoy or Yedikule – I know it, but my dear there can be no commitment."

Mikael lifted his hand and touched Olga's cheek, shook his head, and turned and walked away.

Olga soon heard that Selim's mother and sister had indeed turned up, and had sat with Selim several hours that afternoon. Selim was to be discharged as soon as the stump of his left arm had fully healed. The departure of the British and Australian forces from Gallipoli had slowly eased the pressure on the military hospital and Olga found more and more time to spend with him.

Shortly after Mikael left, Selim had been getting up and about, and now it was the turn of Selim and Olga to walk up and down the corridors and outside in the fresh air. Olga worked hard at lightening the atmosphere of their meetings. Under her careful and attentive nursing, Selim began once again to take an interest in the difficult and confused politics of the dying days of the Ottoman Empire. Most people appreciated that even though the Empire had done remarkably well against the Western Allies, the Empire as it was currently constituted, was doomed.

For Selim, for the first time, an Arab dimension had been added to the political mix. During his few months in Damascus, Selim witnessed the latent intellectual ferment amongst the Arab intelligentsia and middle classes. This awareness had been broadened by his experiences on the Tigris, south of Baghdad, where he had commanded ordinary Arab peasant conscripts, whom he had come to like and respect. He poured out his ideas on the future of the Empire to Olga.

"Olga – you wait and see – we do have a future. Djemal has some great ideas, and he's going to be very influential once this war ends – as it will, my love, as it sooner or later must. It was a revelation to me how loyal and reasonable my men in the Baghdad vilayet were. The British can intrigue as much as they like, but the Arab populations would still prefer to be ruled by Turkish Muslims, than by the Christian West."

"But Selim, my love, a revolt was declared by that man who was put in charge of the Hejaz – what was his name?"

"Yes, yes – Hussein. He is a Qureshi of course, of the tribe of the prophet, but he is a mere nominee appointed by Constantinople. He revolted because Djemal was about to depose him, and appoint one of his rivals. What matters to the Arabs is what goes on in the great Arab cities; in Cairo, Damascus and Baghdad. There is no real Arab revolt – it's a figment of the over-wrought imaginations of young British officers in Cairo. When it comes to the crunch, you will see that not a single Arab soldier from our regular army will desert. The British don't give two hoots about the Arabs – all they bloody care about is their precious route to India."

Olga put her arm on Selim's shoulder to urge him not to get too excited.

"Oh Olga – I do love talking to you. You've changed, you know. I wouldn't have gone on like this a year ago. I suppose we've both changed. Olga – forget the politics – we do have a future together don't we, despite the loss of my arm?"

"Selim," said Olga, speaking very carefully, "we can't forget the politics. Your father was shot by an Armenian revolutionary in Van and ..."

"Yes, but ..."

"Let me finish, Selim my love. A year ago, you wrote me a letter warning me of the insuperable difficulties we faced in developing a lasting relationship. I had to agree, and I tried putting you out of my mind. I have to tell you that I never succeeded and ..."

"Olga, darling, I ..."

"Selim, listen. It isn't only you who've lost a father – your mother has lost a husband. We both of us live in a society where family ties are vitally important. Have you ever considered what your mother might think of an Armenian daughter-in-law?"

"It's the loss of my arm isn't it?"

"Selim, how could you! You know that isn't true," and she walked off in a real temper.

"Olga – I'm sorry, I'm sorry," Selim called out after her. Nevertheless, he couldn't suppress the thought that his disability had affected their relationship.

It was soon time for Selim to leave and return home. Meanwhile, Halideh and Yasmin were now making regular visits to the hospital, and walking out with him into the grounds.

On the day before he was due to leave, Selim had some further minor surgery to his stump, which was otherwise healing well. He was confined to bed when Halideh and Yasmin appeared with a set of clothes he could wear when he left the hospital the next day. It so happened that on that day Olga passed through the officer's ward while on duty. Selim saw Olga passing and called out to her,

"Nurse, hello, – you remember my mother and sister?" Olga stopped and came over.

"Hello – it's Olga isn't it? See I remembered your name – what a wonderful job you do. I'm going to be a nurse when I grow up," gabbled Yasmin, smiling up as Olga approached.

"Hello, Yasmin," said Olga, then turned to smile at Halideh. Halideh nodded, but turned away. Olga blushed, then said to Yasmin,

"Would you like to come along with me for a few minutes whilst I do my rounds? You must promise just to watch and not to say anything."

"Oh yes please, yes please. Can I?" she turned, not to Halideh who was about to say something, but to Selim, who was oblivious to Halideh's quiet rejection of Olga's advance.

"Yes, of course, off you go Yasmin – be good now."

Olga took hold of Yasmin's hand and they walked off out of the clean and neat officers' ward. They went through to one of the soldiers' wards, where Olga usually worked. Here the atmosphere was quite different. There were scarcely ever any visitors – most of these men being from the Anatolian interior – so Olga was an attraction for these men, though all of them had been brought up to show a deep respect towards her.

The presence of Yasmin – a friendly, pretty 12 year-old, brightened up the whole ward. She walked solemnly behind Olga, but she could not suppress her natural bouncy spirit and soon broke her promise to Olga, and started chatting with everyone.

On their return, Halideh was standing waiting for her.

"Where have you been, Yasmin? We're very late. You should have been back ages ago."

"But mother I ..."

"Not another word, my girl," and Halideh grabbed Yasmin by the hand. Turning to Selim she said,

"The military are sending a car – yes, a motor-car – for you tomorrow. We'll see you at home – good-bye till tomorrow."

Halideh walked out without another word, and without a glance at Olga, who stood by and gave a sad little wave to Yasmin. Selim, sitting up in bed looked at the back of his retreating mother, then at Olga, who looked back at him for a second then turned and walked away. She knew, and she knew that Halideh knew, the source of the bad temper.

That night, before she went to the dormitory, she came and sat for a few minutes by Selim's bed. He had been lightly drugged in order to give him a good night's sleep before leaving the hospital the next day. Accordingly, he was only half awake when Olga came, sat by the side of his bed and held his good hand tightly for several minutes. He murmured at Olga, and then fell back into a sleep.

Olga leaned over him and whispered,

"You were right, my darling, you were right after all. We're going to have to part again. Your mother has to be given more time to grieve. It's all too soon for her. I love you, Selim – Oh God how I love you – but there is really no hope for us!"

Olga leant forward and gave a long lingering kiss to Selim's forehead, and then rose and left as Selim stirred, murmured something, and then turned over onto his other side.

The next day, Selim dressed and waited and waited for Olga to come and see him off. She never came. No one knew where she might be, and eventually Selim left to go home. That same day Olga applied for and was given a week's leave to return home to her family in Makrikoy.

CHAPTER 41

Makrikoy. The Avakians

Haik had been taking Seta to school and picking her up for months. He was now 13, and the memory of the assault on the 24th April the previous year had faded into the welter of all the other dramatic events which had occurred. While in many respects he remained innocent and naïve, he had certainly become more streetwise. Too young to take on the role of male head of the family, Armineh's decision to make him responsible for the safety of his little sister had been brilliant.

On this summer afternoon, Haik felt the atmosphere was much more tense in the town than normal. His teacher had let them out early due to rumours of riots in the city. The riots were about the price of food, but this only aggravated existing tensions.

During these last days of Empire, riots aimed at the Jewish and Christian communities, sometimes spread to the suburbs. Haik was now much more attuned to these matters, and he was alert and ready for all eventualities as he trudged into town to collect Seta. As he approached the square where the school was situated, he saw the running crowds and shouting going on around him.

This was the same day that Karekin returned from his last fateful rendezvous with Aram at the old cafe in Eyup. As Karekin heard the words the crowds were shouting, he joined them, running as fast as he could into the town. There was only one *giavour* school inside the town, and this was Seta's.

As he ran, he saw the smoke rising over the roofs ahead of him and in his fevered imagination he thought that he could smell the fire. Panting, he arrived in the little square – the Nusretiya – and saw smoke and flames billowing out of the centre of the school building.

There was a large crowd standing around the sides of the square. The police were out in some force, and the crowds were being pressed back, away from the fire. Karekin was in a state of extreme anxiety. His only thought was – 'first my best friend and now my youngest daughter'. He thrust himself forward, edging people out of his way, but avoiding the police, and arrived directly in front of the entrance to the burning building across the narrow street. The large main gates leading into the courtyard within, were wide open.

Haik, meanwhile had arrived some minutes earlier. He had no idea what to do. He saw the crowds and policemen standing about. He remained calm, and noticed that many of the teachers were already outside, with their young pupils gathered around them on the side street. They were counting their charges over and over again, and handing over the children to distraught parents. As Haik wriggled forward through the crowd, he recognised Seta's teacher, and pushed his way through towards her.

A strange change of roles was taking place between father and son without them even being aware of each other. Haik with his new-found responsibility, was calm; Karekin's emotions, usually so cautious and controlled, were at fever pitch. He stared in a dazed manner at the burning school, as the flames licked round the sides and began to burn the high wooden fencing, which came right up to the main gates.

Then, at the far end of the courtyard, to the right, by the side of the main school building, out of sight of anyone not standing directly in front of the gates, he thought he saw a little girl coming out of the out-door toilet building, standing confused and too terrified to move. Any restraint Karekin could have mustered evaporated at the sight. He ran forward across the street, and stared into the school courtyard already filled with smoke.

Meanwhile, Haik had finally made his way to the group standing around Seta's teacher. She had stopped her frantic counting, as all her class was accounted for. Seta ran round on seeing Haik and grabbed his hand.

"Oh, Haik, I'm so glad you came early and you're here. Isn't it exciting? There's no danger, we're all out. There was a shout of 'fire – fire' in the school and we all ran outside. I wasn't frightened, Haik, while we were inside. I didn't really see anything until I got out. But when we got out and I looked back and saw all the flames – well that did make me a little scared."

Haik squeezed her hand, and they sidled forward to the front of the little group, which was getting smaller and smaller as more and more parents came running to pick up their little girls. It was then that Haik saw a tall man with a grey beard and moustache run forward towards the gates. Seta did not see the man from the front. She looked up only as he stopped, for a moment, with his back to her and pushed aside the policeman at the gate.

Under almost any other circumstances, she would never have made the connection. However, for some reason she thought she recognised her father. She screamed out – "Baba – Baba."

At this precise moment, Karekin reached the gate, and heard a voice, a little girl's voice – Oh God, his daughter's voice – cry out, "Baba – Baba!". To his disturbed mind it seemed to come from the terrified little girl that he could see by the outbuilding. With another cry, covering his eyes, he ran through the wooden gates and into the courtyard, where burning beams and other debris were beginning to fall.

Nerissa was also in Makrikoy that morning, giving one of her English lessons to a Greek lady in the town. They didn't hear any of the shouts in the street, but through the window, Nerissa saw the smoke coming up above the roofs a couple of streets away.

"My, my, that's coming from the Nusretiya Square, said the women."

"Oh Madame," said Nerissa, "That's where my little sister's school is. I must go and see she's all right."

Nerissa hurried out, arriving at the Square to find the town's old fire engine trying to bring the fire under control . To her relief, she immediately saw the remaining knot of pupils by the side of the square, with Haik and Seta, hand in hand, staring at the front gates. The flames had taken hold of the wooden posts, and the gates themselves were beginning to smoulder. A group of three or four policemen were standing close together, staring into the smoke-filled courtyard.

Nerissa worked her way round the square to Haik and Seta, and had almost reached them when suddenly there was a shout from the policemen at the gate. The firemen began training their leaky old water-pump hoses onto the gates, and Nerissa saw a young policeman run into the courtyard between the flames. Through the smoke, a middle-aged man with a singed grey beard, and crazed and bloodshot eyes, was staggering out from the flames, holding a weeping child in his arms. He staggered forward and handed the little girl to the young policeman.

To her utter amazement, she saw little Seta, now just ahead of her on the pavement, pull her hand away from Haik and run forward towards the gate. The man, badly burnt, had sunk to the ground outside the gates, as the school's headmaster came running forward to take the weeping little girl from the policeman's arms. Nerissa instinctively moved forward to try to grab and restrain Seta, when she heard Haik, behind her call out,

"Nerissa – leave her, leave her."

Nerissa stopped and turned,

"Whatever are you talking about, Haik?"

All this happened in a flash, within the time it had taken for Seta to reach the man, who was now sitting, legs outstretched, with his head buried in his hands. Nerissa saw Seta go down on her knees alongside the man, and put her arms around him, and press her cheek to his. At that point Nerissa suddenly saw. It was her father. Neither she nor Haik moved, as Karekin hugged Seta fiercely to his chest.

The next moments were chaotic and noisy, but indescribably poignant. The little girl Karekin had rescued was reunited with a grandmother, as Karekin, picked up Seta, and seeing Nerissa and Haik standing side by side across the road, staggered over – putting Seta down – and said urgently,

"Come, my lovely ones, come. Let's go before anybody starts asking questions."

He took Seta's hand and began walking away as an elderly woman approached him. He turned and said to her,

"No, no Madam – that young policeman over there. Yes, he was the man who saved your ... Yes, Madam, do, do ..."

Karekin hurried them all out of the square, and away down the street. Haik and Nerissa were both in a state of shock and bewilderment at the sudden reappearance of their father.

Once they were out of the town and on the road by the Valli *Effendi* racecourse, the questions, the love, the worry, poured out. Being Avakians, they all talked at once, with much stopping and starting, touching and holding, so little sense was made. It was also a very inefficient way of making any progress up the hill. Every so often, Seta would demand to be carried by Karekin, and he tried – but was defeated by the rawness of his exposed and inflamed skin. In the end, Haik squatted down, and Seta was hoisted onto his spare but willing shoulders, though she still insisted on holding on to her father's hand, and in this way they continued up the hill towards the house.

The burns he had sustained were causing Karekin spasms of pain, while Haik, with Seta on his shoulders could only walk slowly. Nerissa began to worry how Armineh would react to their sudden, dramatic arrival. Karekin also knew that the dangers, which had kept him away from his family for these past few months had not gone away. For the moment he was so full of joy – so completely overwhelmed by this unexpected turn of events, that nothing else mattered.

The noisy party walked straight into the hall of the Avakian house as Nerissa opened the front door. Haik dumped Seta somewhat unceremoniously onto the sofa, from where she immediately jumped up and ran to fetch Armineh shouting – "Baba's back – Baba's back!"

Armineh came running in, then stood stock still, drying her hands on a hastily swept up tea towel. If Nerissa had expected her to faint or do something equally melodramatic, she was disappointed. Armineh just stared at Karekin, and he stared back, both suddenly oblivious of the noise around them, and the arrival of Marie and Sima in the hall.

Slowly the chatter died away, as the family stood quietly, each with their own thoughts, frozen by the immobility of Armineh. A rare moment of silence suddenly descended over the household.

No one afterwards remembered how long this lasted, but the spell was broken as Armineh walked forward and took Karekin by his hand, noting he winced as she touched his skin. Without another word, without waiting for explanations, she led him up the stairs. Half way up, she turned and said,

"Salve, and the burns ointment, Marie please, from the medicine chest. Haik and Seta get a move on – start laying the table for tea. Nerissa, my soul, for heaven's sake close your mouth. See that extra places are laid – remember Olga is back this evening. Come Karekin, my husband, welcome home my darling, let me see to these awful burns."

She lay her hand gently on his cheek, smiled, for just a moment at the children staring up at them from the room below, and then turned and they both disappeared from view at the top of stairs.

The British Occupation 1920

CONTENTS

Book 2: The British Occupation 1920

CHAPTER 1

Nikolai

Defeated armies are the same everywhere and throughout all time. The uniforms and weapons might be different, the modes of transport might change, but the atmosphere and faces of the men are always the same. Napoleon's Grande Armee retreating from Moscow, surviving Roman legionaries after the battle of Cannae, Sir John Moore retreating to Corunna, all trudging on hopelessly, eyes fixed on the road ahead, concentrating solely on moving on.

So it was with the White Russian army commanded by the larger-than-life General Wrangel, after the Red Army had at last broken through their defences in the Crimea and inflicted a final defeat.

Nikolai stumbled along with everyone else – exhausted, lice-ridden and hungry – along the treeless, dusty roads that criss-crossed the Crimean countryside, making their way to Sevastopol. Sevastopol and what? Nikolai had no idea. Only recently out of his teens, he had fought for nearly two years in the vicious civil war raging across Russia, following on the coup in St. Petersburg. The Tsar had died and everything was in the melting pot.

Alongside the troops was a stream of refugees – peasants, merchants, and the odd aristocrat. The only sign of privilege was those who rode and those on foot.

"Hey Androv – what are you dreaming about now?"

Nikolai looked up from his contemplation of the dusty road at the squat compact figure of a Circassian infantry officer sitting astride a pony.

"Ah, Captain Tombak. I'm not dreaming, I'm simply concentrating on the road."

Captain Tombak leant back and got out a bottle from his saddlebags. Pulling out the cork with his teeth, he handed it down to Nikolai.

"Take a swig of this. It'll give you courage even if it doesn't give you strength. I intend swinging off to the east soon. The Reds are right behind us and what the hell is Wrangel going to do! There's going to be a massacre here if we don't get out of their way."

Nikolai, assuming the bottle to contain vodka, upended it and took a great gulp. It turned out to be a bottle of fiery Caucasian brandy. He choked and tears burst from his eyes as Tombak, again roaring with laughter, reached hurriedly down from his pony to grab the bottle back.

"Why don't you come with me? I'm taking the road to the Kerch straits. We'll get a boat and cross over to the Kuban. You're going to die if you remain with this lot."

"I can't, my friend. My mother and brother came down to stay in the Crimea near Sevastopol a year ago when we first took Rostov and I am hoping to find them when I get to the port. I'll try my luck in Sevastopol. Could I perhaps hold on to your pony's bridle as we go, until you turn off."

So Nikolai lumbered on – only an instinct for survival keeping him putting one weary foot in front of the other, as at last his fellow soldier waved his hat and rode off to the east a few miles before Sevastopol.

Nikolai looked down from the hills on the large enclosed harbour of the city as they finally arrived at Sevastopol from the north. He could see that the great harbour was crowded with ships: sailing boats, steamships, old-fashioned caiques, yachts and, in the distance, the warships of the old Imperial navy. He stumbled on down the hills, through the streets and finally arrived at the quayside, where he joined the crowds milling about on the seafront.

Family groups were sitting about on wooden cases and shabby leather luggage; blankets of all shapes and sizes draped around them against the cold. Rumours – tangible like fog – were passing from one group to another. The Reds are coming … The Reds have turned back … The Reds have issued a declaration that they are going to kill everyone, military or civilian found in the city … The British and French have sent a fleet and are going to land an army … Lenin has been assassinated … Lenin is alive and well and has decreed that Sevastopol will be utterly destroyed … Trotsky has stated that Sevastopol will be declared an open city and everyone who wears a red badge will be spared.

There was desperation, hunger and, incredibly, even laughter in the midst of it all. The crowds shifted about as the waters lapped against the quayside. A continuous murmuring noise! Merchants in fur coats haggling quietly in corners with sailors, captains or owners of any kind of boat; a dishevelled officer bending low and kissing the outstretched hand of a lady who looked more like a gypsy than a former princess of the Court; children everywhere – running about, some barefoot, some in good but soiled clothes, irrepressible despite their situation; Imperial Russian navy officers in neat white uniforms looking smarter and more composed than everyone else amidst the melee of civilians, shouting, gesticulating, crying and even laughing. Noise, bustle, and some welcome food for a few roubles of continually diminishing value.

Nikolai knew nobody. It was his birthday. He was just twenty-two – alone in a world he could not recognise. The Revolution had saved him from the trenches but had thrust him into this maelstrom instead.

For two days Nikolai wandered up and down the quays and along the boulevard fronting the bay, staring into the eyes of the huddled groups of refugees, searching desperately for his family. And then at last on the third morning after another almost sleepless night on the quayside, as the atmosphere of crisis thickened –

"Nikolai, Nikolai, oh God my brother – Nikolai!"

Alexei, a boy of fourteen but looking a good deal younger with his sunken cheeks and huge black eyes, dressed in an odd assortment of clothes, topped by an army greatcoat which reached down almost over his feet, came running up and clasped Nikolai, tears of joy running down his cheeks, resting his head on Nikolai's chest. They stood there for a full minute pressed tightly against each other, oblivious for the moment of everything else around them.

"Oh my God, Alexei ... at last ... Thank God! Where's mother?"

"There – there, over there. Oh, Nikolai, you're alive!"

Dragging Nikolai along by the hand, he pulled him over to where a lady with white hair, bright blue eyes and a heavily lined anxious face sat on a rolled up carpet – the Countess Natalya Androva. Nikolai fell to his knees and hugged his mother without a word.

"My dear Nikolai – oh, my dearest boy ... my son – thank God you are well ... thank God!" There was a long silence as she clasped Nikolai round his shoulders and stroked his dishevelled hair.

"My son, your father is dead – oh heavens! my memory – you were still with us when we heard. Our house has been burnt down, the servants have all fled and the estate is ruined. There is really nothing more to keep us here. We have to leave if we can ...."

They sat together for two hours informing each other all that had occurred during the past terrible years of upheaval and civil war. Then, urged on by the countess, Nikolai began to consider what options were left to them. He paced up and down finding difficulty in concentrating, conscious all the time of the eyes of his young brother, trusting that now his elder brother was here with them, they would be saved.

"Alexei, you see that soldier over there handing out leaflets – go and get one."

Alexei jumped up and ran off as fast as his clumsy greatcoat would let him. Nikolai turned to his mother – "Mother, did you manage to save much in that bundle?"

"Yes, son. I have most of the family jewellery and some other bits and pieces which should get us by for some time if we can get away from here."

Alexei came running back with a roughly printed leaflet in his hand. On this was printed a declaration under the name of General Wrangel confirming that the army had been defeated and that the Reds

were now scarcely more than a day or two away from the city. The declaration then went on to state that he gave all his officers and soldiers
and any civilians a completely free choice whether to go with him into
an unknown exile, or remain and risk the coming Soviet occupation.
A quiet wail and a murmuring arose from the crowds as the leaflets
passed from hand to hand. Nikolai was in a state of total indecision,
conscious again of Alexei's eager eyes on him. Although two years of
horrific civil war had matured him – the responsibility for a family relying totally upon him, unnerved him. He thought of his father so much
stronger and more decisive than himself – and dithered.

Then at that moment, his life took a new turn. A somewhat exasperated voice called out in English – "Does anyone here speak English?" A
young officer in a smart British naval uniform was looking about him in
some bewilderment at the crowds.

"Yes sir, I do."

Nikolai's English governess had taught him excellent English, so
that unlike most of the Russian governing classes Nikolai spoke better
English than French. She had also instilled in him not only good manners but a certain un-Russian reserve as well.

"Ah! Great! I see that you are an officer in the Volunteer Army. I
need an interpreter quickly. Could you please accompany me, I have to
report to General Wrangel and I don't even know where he might be."

"Certainly, sir," said Nikolai, whose brain had at last clicked into gear.
"But my family, sir, the evacuation is about to begin and I daren't leave
them here alone. I have not as yet organised our departure."

"Let them stay right here – we won't be long and I will help you as
soon as we are finished. By the way, my name is Harry – Lieutenant
Harry Bridgeman – and yours?"

"Nikolai Petrovitch Androv, sir, at your service."

And so it was that Nikolai found himself in the company of this
cool Englishman some four or five years his senior, weaving their way
through the crowds to the further end of the quayside. Eventually, they
came into the presence of the tall and commanding figure of General
Wrangel himself, standing with his staff in a tent erected on the quayside. Wrangel was dressed in full uniform with his high Cossack fur hat
making him appear even taller. The Englishman saluted and, through
Nikolai, reported the arrival into the harbour of a British destroyer and
a coaling ship under his orders, and with Admiralty sanction to take off
a limited number of refugees. Wrangel conveyed his thanks in French
and asked the English Lieutenant how many he could safely take. Looking at Nikolai, he mentioned he was already committed to taking three
– this gentleman and his family. Wrangel looked at Nikolai, asked him a
few questions as to his military service to date and then, turning to the
English Lieutenant, said –

"Lieutenant, we are going to Constantinople. There, I understand, the city is currently under your occupation. I would like this officer to accompany me as a temporary member of my staff on the *Kornilov* as an interpreter. I would be grateful, however, if you could as arranged include the rest of his family on your vessel."

After Nikolai had finished translating all this in some surprise, Wrangel turned to him and said,

"Lieutenant Androv, go and see to your family, but I want you back here within four hours to join my staff, at least till we get to Constantinople."

Nikolai and the English Captain struggled back through the milling crowds, now beginning to move onto the various launches of the bigger boats out in the harbour and the yachts and steamboats already alongside. There was a rising tide of hysteria as people remembered the stories of the terrible scenes that had taken place at the evacuations of Odessa and Novorossiysk.

Alexei and the Countess were waiting patiently and arose as soon as they saw Nikolai approaching. Nikolai picked up the bundle, and led by the Englishman they pushed their way to the quayside where a British naval launch was tied up alongside.

The crowds were pressing up against the quayside but there was no movement as the English officer jumped into the launch and turned to help the Countess. However, as the crowds saw a fellow Russian beginning to clamber into the foreign boat, there was a wail and the crowd surged forward in a threatening and aggressive manner. Nikolai pulled out his revolver. Acting fast and decisively, he swung round from helping his mother, shot three or four times into the air, then levelled his pistol at the front of the crowd. The crowd fell back while others around ran up to investigate the shots.

"Careful there, mum," said a cheerful English voice as the countess made it into the swaying boat, followed by Alexei. Nicolai kissed them both as he bent down to say goodbye.

"We'll meet again in Constantinople soon, Mother. I'm on the General's boat and won't have any difficulty finding you."

"God be with you, my son."

The launch moved away from the quayside, and Nikolai hurried back to join Wrangel's staff. Shortly after, General Wrangel and all his staff, now including Nicolai, were stepping into the launch of the Kornilov.

Fires could already be seen in the suburbs to the north of the city. As the general's launch – one of the last boats to leave Sevastopol – pulled away from the quayside, the sound of gunfire and explosions could be heard.

CHAPTER 2

The Androvs arrive in Constantinople

The shabby grey battleship belched out thick black smoke as it left the Black Sea and entered the Bosporus. The narrow straits separating Europe from Asia were bounded by beautiful and uncluttered wooded hills close by on both sides. At the head of a great line of ships, the battleship steamed slowly down the historic waterway, passing between the two old Ottoman castles guarding the straits on each side.

Nikolai, still bleary-eyed from lack of sleep and food, was leaning on the ship's rails watching intently as the shore slipped by. His uniform, though no longer dusty, was encrusted with dirt and stains that he had been unable to remove. His knee-high boots had seen no polish for weeks. In the scramble on the docks at Sevastopol, not much more than 24 hours before, he had lost his officer's cap, revealing his thick black hair, uncombed or washed for weeks.

Although only 22 years-old, his sunken cheeks and his lined, unshaven weather-beaten face made him look older. His cheekbones were high like most Slavs, with fair skin and wild, unruly hair, rather than straight. However, Nikolai's nose was squat and small and his eyes were a deep black. It seemed likely that there had been some Tartar blood in the family somewhere in the past. The Androvs were from the south of Russia and owned – or rather once owned – a large estate on the lower Don.

He scratched himself absently. He knew he was covered in fleas of many different species – Caucasian fleas – Crimean fleas – Red fleas or White fleas – but he had survived, and that was all that mattered. Furthermore, so had his mother and his young brother. Having found them on the quayside at Sevastopol, he had at last acted with calm resolution, in ensuring their safe passage to Constantinople.

His musings were cut short as the battleship – the *General Kornilov* – began to slow down. The chocolate-box frontage of the Dolmabahce palace came into view on the European shore and passed on their right. The ship drifted on into the main anchorage of Constantinople where there was already an immense amount of shipping lying at anchor. Here stood the warships of the western allies – British, French and Italian – and in the distance, lying forlorn on its own in the waters, was the great German battleship *Goeben* now renamed *Sultan Yavuz*. The *Kornilov* had survived several encounters with this historic ship throughout the past war, and now here they both lay, silent, facing each other across the harbour.

Nikolai looked up and saw a fast motor-pinnace racing across the water towards them, coming out from the quays under the great bridge crossing the Golden Horn. In the cold clear morning air, the rising sun picked out the rounded domes and high thin minarets on the low hills right ahead of him. Nikolai stared at the great city. Constantinople!

Polis to the Greeks – Bolis to the Armenians – Stamboul for the Turks – Byzantium to the ancient world; an architectural jewel set astride two continents, dominating the most important waterway in history. The world's desire!

Nikolai looked again at the approaching motorboat manned by smart white-uniformed sailors, and saw the British Union Jack at the masthead. Standing upright on the deck was a smartly uniformed senior officer. Nicolai knew that the western allies had taken control of the great city – the only enemy capital to be occupied by the victorious allies after the War – but the sight of the British flag brought home this reality.

"Lieutenant Androv! The general wants you in his cabin, sir, right away."

Nikolai hurried through the untidy ship, which in all its voyages had never quite seen anything like this one. There were exhausted men, women and children, dotted about the decks, clutching bundles of what might be clothes or just rags. Some had expensive furs and shawls wrapped around them. Others sat dressed in extraordinarily mismatched outfits. All had haunted hollow eyes with desperation and deep sadness lurking in their depths.

Nikolai picked his way round the recumbent figures. He avoided the children, some of whom, unfazed by their parents desolation, were already beginning to run about. He looked back from the rear of the ship and saw the long line of ships – over eighty he had been told – which had been following the *General Kornilov* all day and night, and on one of which, he recalled with some satisfaction, he had managed to put his mother and little brother.

"Ah, Androv, come in! I am about to receive the British General commanding the allied forces of occupation. It is important that we get on good terms with him right from the start. Lieutenant, where the blazes is your cap." Wrangel snapped at him as Nikolai entered the main cabin.

"I'm sorry, sir, but it was lost in the confusion of getting my family away in Sevastopol."

"Anton, see that he gets another – right now. I don't want my staff looking scruffy. Also see that the British General is welcomed and brought here. Admiral Kedroff, can we put on some drinks?"

Everyone stood as a distinguished-looking British General in high knee-length boots, with regulation Sam Browne belt and full uniform, came into the ship's boardroom: a handsome face with a perfectly groomed white moustache, almost as tall as Wrangel and with smiling eyes. The two generals saluted each other, with Nikolai translating.

"Tim Harington, General, commander of the allied forces of occupation. Welcome to Constantinople."

"Pyotr Wrangel – but I fear, sir, no longer commander of anything except a party of refugees."

And so the meeting began.

"General, I am instructed by my government," began Harington, "that you and your men are to be given every facility in our power to grant. We must stick together against the Bolshevik menace. The Ottoman government here have already agreed with me that they will cooperate as best they can, but General, we were under the impression that we would be dealing simply with the remnants of your army. We now understand that you have with you thousands, perhaps hundreds of thousands, of civilian refugees."

"I am afraid that that is indeed the situation," replied Wrangel. "I am hoping to keep my men together – at least those who want to stay with me. However, I have no authority whatsoever over the civilian refugees. Until they can disperse under their own volition, they are, in a sense, at your mercy."

"Well, well, we'll see. For the moment I must ask you to exercise what authority you have left to make sure that no one, soldiers or civilians, disembark. Meanwhile I will see what pressure I can put on the Sultan's government to do something about accommodation. In any event, wherever we place your men, rest assured that no one will starve and my government will provide some sort of aid."

At this point, with Wrangel clearly relieved at the tenor of the General's words, drinks were produced and the conversation became more wide-ranging, with Nicolai going from group to group to translate where needed. Harington was eventually solemnly saluted and piped off board.

After the English party had left and Nikolai had been dismissed, he strolled to the rear of the ship and looked back at the long line of vessels strung out behind the *Kornilov* – all now stationery, searching unsuccessfully for sight of the destroyer with his mother and Alexei on board.

Nearby, he saw rowing boats and small caiques, laden with bread, cakes, nuts, sweets and fruit brought by enterprising Turks for sale. Nikolai could see women, once elegant ladies of privileged families, leaning over the side of ships and offering fur coats and jewellery in exchange for the bread and other food piled up on the little boats lying alongside. Down would go the fur coat or a small carpet or whatever on a long string. The boatmen would feel it, weigh it, scrutinise it carefully, and would then fill a basket with fruit or bread, holding up his offer, usually accepted with a shrug. The jewellery or cloak would be whisked away and the basket of food would be attached to the string and drawn up.

Nikolai turned away to stare again at the shoreline of the great city where he would start his new life. There he saw the wonderful rounded domes of the mosques on the low hills to the south, with their graceful white minarets rising up, silhouetted against the deep blue sky. In the foreground, the bustling activity of the waters, filled with ferries, and small boats, busily chugging about, was mirrored by the jumble of houses and streets running up the hillside. His basic situation might be hopeless, he might be hungry and dirty but, by God, it was all very exciting!

CHAPTER 3

Vahan and Nikolai

Prinkipo – the island of the Princes – was a fairly short steamer ride across the Marmara Sea from the Galata bridge. The island was covered with tall pines, which tumbled down from the hills and came right up to the seashore. Hidden amidst the trees, usually near the beaches, were the summer houses of Ottoman pashas and wealthy Greek and Armenian merchants. There was a little port – Buyukada – with a few shops where the steamers from Bolis stopped and where somewhat shabby carriages waited for the frequent arrival of the ferries.

Only two days after the meeting between General Wrangel and Tim Harington, all the Russian refugees had been efficiently absorbed into the already rich mixture crowded into Constantinople. The soldiers of the White army, together with all the unattached males, were housed in a teeming, overfilled, tented camp outside the walls on the European side; the civilian families were largely quartered on the island of Prinkipo.

The Ottoman authorities, prodded by the Allied administration, had commandeered many of the rich houses owned by wealthy Bolsetsi for the use of the refugees. After two years of dreadful civil war Nikolai felt that he had arrived in paradise. He and his mother and the young Alexei had been allocated a small room in an outbuilding set in the yard of a lovely white villa bordering the sea. Food was being provided by the British administration, which had set up soup kitchens at strategic spots throughout the Island.

"Mother, now we are settled in, at least for the time being, tell me exactly what did you manage to salvage when you left home?"

"Not much, son – but Alexei has been wearing a belt under his tunic into which I managed to sew about forty gold coins," the countess replied as she rummaged into the bundle of clothes still sitting on the only table in the room.

"I have jewels, including this diamond star – supposedly a gift of the Empress Catherine to your father's grandfather – and this icon. I don't know if it's as valuable as the jewellery, but it is reputed to be a Rublev."

"Mother, we don't know what is going to happen to us, but we must try to hold onto these things. The British won't carry on feeding us for ever. But first, I should go into the city to look for work – anything to earn a few piastres."

"But, Nikolai, what can you possibly do?"

"For a start, I can speak English well, that must count for something, seeing that the English control the city at the moment. My written French is fairly good and I learnt to do petty accounts in the army. But look, maman what may be more useful is the violin. Our music tutor claimed that I had real talent. I haven't played for nearly two years but I don't think I've lost my technique. Give me some gold coins and I'll see if I can buy one. I'm told that all the bars, restaurants and night clubs are doing good business with so many foreigners in town – the sailors and the occupying forces."

"Well, if you're sure. We'll have to wait for Alexei. I told him never to take the belt off."

"Ah yes, mother, and that reminds me. We have only been here a few days, and already he is wandering all over the island with his new friends, but what about his education. He's fourteen and he's just running wild."

"I am aware of this, Nicolai, but you must back me up and use your own authority. He adores and looks up to you, whilst I seem to have lost my ability to discipline him since your dear father's death. I can teach him myself, but you must enforce some structure and daily routine."

When Alexei returned, he thankfully handed over the heavy belt, which had been wrapped, round his waist, relieving himself of its weight for the first time for weeks.

That same day, armed with ten of the precious gold coins, Nicolai took the midday ferry to the city. There, hooting and tooting, pushing and shoving, the Buyukada ferry touched in at the moorings underneath the Galata bridge.

Nikolai got off, indeed was swept off, the steamer and was pushed up the iron steps leading from the quays to the bridge above. He stood bewildered by the huge crowds – a jumble of noisy humanity going up or down, over and across the bridge.

The Galata bridge!

In reality this bridge only joined old Stamboul to Pera across the Golden Horn – but Nikolai had the impression that it was joining Europe to Asia. Turkish and Kurdish porters half trotted across –with huge packs on their backs attached by a thong across their foreheads, calling out "Make way! Make way!" Veiled Turkish ladies passed towards Stamboul to go shopping in the great bazaar or towards Pera for the Taksim gardens. Portly Greek or Armenian merchants, some wearing the Ottoman fez, but now many sporting panama or trilby hats, strolled across. Allied seamen of all kinds swaggered past. Peasants from the nearby fields of Thrace or from the Asian side riding on their donkeys or a shepherd from the hills driving a flock of sheep, even here in the city. Modern electrified trams clattered by and, plodding behind them, a camel loaded with goods. Amidst all of this, Nicolai saw new-fangled motor-cars.

Nikolai recognised compatriot Russians of all types – émigrés, refugees, well dressed ladies and smart officers and broken-down soldiers interned outside the walls, preferring to take their chances in the city, most of them evidently living rough.

Nikolai had never seen anything like it – but then neither had the elderly Turks sitting at the cafes on the shore at each end of the bridge puffing on their narghilehs and watching the invasion of their ancient city – a city now occupied by the troops of a Christian power for the first time in over 450 years. The Armenians and the Greeks were beginning to 'swagger' a bit themselves. No one gave a thought to the rumours of a Turkish revival in the Anatolian interior – after all the British were here and the Greek army was close by in Smyrna. The old Turks sat watching and smoked in silence.

Nikolai had to catch his breath. Leaning against the iron rails, he looked out at the harbour and all about him. On his right was Stamboul – the original city – sheltering behind the great Theodosian walls still largely intact, was Turkish despite containing both the Greek and Armenian Patriarchates. Dominated by the great mosques with their wonderful shallowly-rounded domes and pencil-like thin minarets, it contained the great covered bazaar where most of the business of the city was carried out. On his left was Pera, founded originally as a suburb by the Genoese but now the centre of the modern city. Pera was populated by all the races of the Empire, but the Turks were the minority. Here lay all the bars and restaurants, the hotels and all the burgeoning nightlife of the city, and it was to this side that Nikolai turned.

He turned and walked up the hill to the Grande Rue de Pera, and strolled along the main road towards Taksim. Near Tokatlians tea rooms, he found a music shop. He spent the next hour trying out violins, both new and secondhand. He wasn't entirely sure that using their precious capital on this purchase was going to be well spent and whether there would be any work available? None of the instruments was less than six of his precious gold pieces. So he dithered, while thinking what his father would have said. "Any decision, my boy, is better than no decision at all. Now snap out of it – and get a move on, lad!"

But those days seemed a world away. A wrong decision by the old count was never likely to be fatal, but for Nikolai … .

Nikolai was feeling faint and he could tell that the Armenian salesman was getting impatient. Over in the corner another young man who had a violin case under his arm was fingering some sheet music preparatory to making a purchase. The salesman muttered some clearly disparaging remarks in Armenian to this young man, in which Nikolai heard the word 'Russner'. He sat down dejectedly on the only chair in the shop. The other customer snapped at the salesman, who blushed deeply and retreated behind the counter. The young man came over, looked down at Nikolai and said, speaking in French,

"Good morning, monsieur, are you not feeling well?"

"I'm fine, thank you monsieur – I've just come over a little faint. I'll be all right in a moment."

"Let me introduce myself, my name is Vahan – Vahan Asadourian." Smiling broadly the young man extended his hand warmly. Nikolai immediately jumped up, bowed and shook his hand.

"Count Nikolai Androv, at your service," he said in English, without thinking.

"You appear to have a problem in choosing a violin. Perhaps I could help, I am myself a violinist," Vahan replied in English.

Nicolai immediately warmed to this young man who appeared so sympathetic, without even knowing what problem was exercising his mind.

"Well, sir, the fact is that my means are limited and I do have a problem, but it is not a problem of choice of instrument."

Vahan Asadourian was a music student from the University of Stamboul, who had never completed his degree due to the war. He was an Armenian from Caesaria who had managed to survive those traumatic years. He gave the young Russian a shy smile and said –

"Count, my dear sir, problems are always worth sharing with others, perhaps I might be able to help. Would you accept my invitation for a coffee together. I can't find the Haydn quartet sheet music I am looking for in any case."

Curtly nodding at the assistant, he led Nikolai out of the shop, and they went down the road to the Tokatlian building and into the front cafe, by the main door.

"*Iki kahve – shekerli* – is that all right Count Nikolai?"

"Fine, but please I am Nikolai Petrovitch."

And the two young men, carefully appraising each other, entered into a long conversation with easy familiarity as if they had known each other for a long time. Nicolai saw a short rather squat figure sporting the ubiquitous Turkish-style moustache, dressed fairly formally in suit and tie, but without a fez. Strong features and big brown eyes, like most Armenians Nicolai had ever encountered. Vahan, for his part, saw a young man, clearly younger than himself and conventionally good looking. Wild rather unruly hair, but with very black eyes – could there be a touch of Mongol blood?

They talked and gradually Nicolai's problem became clear.

"Well, Nicolai, my friend, I understand your problem completely. Obviously you cannot apply for a musical post without having your own violin, but you are worried at spending such a large proportion of the family money in case you can't find a job. And you are right to worry, as I'm afraid Russian musicians are two a penny here at the moment. We are inundated with Russian orchestras, Russian folklorists, Russian tearooms ..."

Vahan paused for a moment then continued.

"The answer is simple. You take my violin. Do the rounds. If, after doing so, you still can't find any work, at least you will have held onto your precious gold pieces. I'll give you a week, and when you do find work you can come and use your money wisely."

"Vahan, my friend, that is wonderful. But what will you do meanwhile?"

"Ah well, you see, while I have kept up my playing – I have a circle of friends and we meet and play chamber music together – I have not carried on with music as a career. I had to give up my studies as a result of the terrible events that took place in Anatolia five years ago. My father, one of the first to be arrested and deported, survived and in due course turned up here and opened up a small business. I now help him. I am afraid that the world has changed and a career in music is no longer an option for me."

"And the rest of your family?"

There was a short silence as Vahan looked at Nikolai, not quite knowing what to say.

"My younger brother – Raffi – ran away and managed to survive. He is also now here and working with my dad. He's about your age, I think."

Nikolai said nothing, waiting.

"Yes – ah well – my mother and my sisters with their children were all forced onto a deportation march despite all my efforts. They were never heard of again, like so many others."

"I'm so sorry – I shouldn't have pressed you."

There was another short silence, and then Vahan jumped up and said, "Look, I have to go. Here is my violin. We live up near Taksim, just round the corner from the Park hotel. Here is the address – please come tonight in any case and meet my family. We are an all-male house-hold. Anyway, by all means try the manager here, but they tend to take only Armenians. There are émany night clubs around in this area, but your best bet is the Pera Palace hotel further down. Make absolutely sure that they know that you have a wide repertoire and not just Rus-sian folk music."

Vahan pressed the violin onto Nikolai, paid the bill and hurried away. Nikolai stood outside for a moment and watched as Vahan walked briskly up towards Taksim. He pondered on the fact that his only ex-perience of Armenians in Russia was as merchants and shopkeepers. In aristocratic circles they had a reputation as petty bourgeois money-grubbers. Yet, here he had been trusted with a fairly valuable object, despite an acquaintance of only a few hours. Nicolai felt this encounter was unusual and wondered whether this new friend was a touch naïve. He turned to go back into Tokatlians to see the manager.

Meanwhile, Vahan hurried home. He had a rendezvous for tea at the *Thé Dansant* room back at Tokatlians. The war had changed every-thing. It was now perfectly acceptable for a young man and a young girl from good families to go out together unchaperoned. However, even so, there was no question of young Nerissa Avakian being allowed to stay out late. Vahan never questioned this as the city was full of foreign-ers – French, British and Italian soldiers of the occupation forces. They were relatively well-disciplined, but the town was also full of seamen of all nations and refugees of all kinds. The American fleet was in port and fights were regularly breaking out between the British and American sailors.

That absolute certainty which had existed under the old Ottoman culture that no lady walking in the streets, veiled or not, would ever be molested, no longer applied as the brash values of the West began to intrude into the city.

Vahan had said nothing about his meetings with Nerissa to his old-fashioned and puritanical father, despite the fact that he knew that his father would probably approve of any developing relationship with the wealthy and highly respected Avakian family. His younger brother Raffi, tougher and more worldly-wise than him, had however been told all about it. He was at home when Vahan arrived.

"Hey Raffi, my soul, please tell Siran I won't be here for dinner to-night."

"Well, well, brother, going out dancing again. What you need is one of those painted ladies in the Bayram Sokagh."

"Don't be coarse, Raffi. Look I'm in a hurry – the university classes will be closing soon. Come up and chat while I change."

And he hurried up the steep stone staircase to his room at the top of the tall narrow house. Raffi came up after him. He made a point of disagreeing with almost anything his elder brother said, though he would then often adopt those views later, as if they were his own. He deeply admired his brother, but didn't want to show it. However, Raffi considered he had his own feet firmly planted on the ground, while his brother was a mere dreamer – an intellectual – a musician for heaven's sake.

Raffi thought that Vahan was still a virgin, whereas he himself... Nevertheless, life was considerably more interesting when Vahan was around. He sauntered into Vahan's room and leant against the door.

"Vahan, why don't you tell baba about your meetings with that Avakian girl?"

"Miss Avakian to you, my lad."

"Yes – well whatever. If you're serious, and you certainly seem to be, you'll have to let him know – and anyway why not? She sounds very suitable."

"Oh Raffi, shut up. I can't possibly make a serious proposal. Her father is one of the wealthiest merchants in town and I haven't even a home I can bring her to. He's already looking around for suitable young men – I know. I would need my own home, and we can't afford it. After all she couldn't come here – there is no woman in the house."

"Have a pleasant afternoon, brother, but I still say that the ladies in that street behind ..."

"Raffi, you have a one-track mind. I've got to go."

Vahan embraced Raffi as he hurried past him and down the narrow stairs. At the bottom, in the tiny hall before the front door, stood yet another young man leaning against the door of the sitting room. Thin, looking permanently under-nourished regardless of how much he ate, he smiled up at Vahan.

"Vahan, my brother, my soul, where dost thou go?" he said in his old-fashioned accented Eastern Highlands style – an accent now rarely heard.

"Ara, you little pipsqueak, don't ask – you're not old enough to be told where Vahan is going, and Vahan is too prim to tell you anyway," said Raffi, grinning as he came down the stairs behind Vahan.

Ara, the traumatised orphan lad rescued by Garabed, Vahan's father, from the horrors of the deportations five years ago, looked back at Vahan questioningly.

"Ah well, Ara, my soul, I am going dancing at Tokatlians with ... er ... well, yes ... I'll tell you all about it when I get back. Goodbye, everyone."

Still adjusting his tie, Vahan hurried out.

CHAPTER 4

Breakfast at the Avakians

Meanwhile, that morning, the Avakian family gathered for the only meal of the day at which they were all certain to be present – breakfast. The task of serving at table had been taken over by a young girl – Talin, who had been orphaned by the catastrophe overtaking the Armenian people of Eastern Anatolia in 1915. She had been just ten years old when her parents and all the rest of her family had been slaughtered. The family never ever knew the full details, but could imagine the even worse possibilities that may have befallen her. Talin herself never spoke about her experiences.

Karekin Avakian, the head of the family, had returned to Constantinople almost two years after his arrest and deportation in April 1915. As soon as the war ended he had helped to set up an agency in the city, which tried to make arrangements for the many Armenian orphans still milling about in the Syrian deserts, or eking out a living in the cities of the Arab vilayets, now under British or French control. There were a large number of these children, the survivors of the thousands of Armenian families slaughtered or starved to death during the year of forced deportations.

Karekin himself took on personal responsibility for a couple of these children. Those chosen by the agency representative in Beirut were Talin and a boy of seventeen, Paramaz – who had been under twelve at the time of the death of his parents and family. He had given them each a job and a home, Paramaz to work with him at the office, and Talin in his family.

As usual, neither Karekin himself, nor his only son – Haik – was yet down at breakfast. But all the women were already seated at the table in the great hall where most of the Avakian family events took place. Armineh, Karekin's short and rather dumpy wife, was presiding at the end of the table nearest to the kitchen door. The four daughters of the family were seated on each side.

"Sima, my adorable sister, you can't really be meaning to marry that George Levonian man. Why? Why? For heaven's sake, you told me only last year that you could not love him."

Olga, an elegant twenty-two year old, well dressed and confident, said this chirpily and without any intention of upsetting her statuesque elder sister. Armineh herself replied for her eldest daughter, saying sharply –

"Oh, don't be obtuse, Olga. People's opinions and feelings change. Love is something that comes and sometimes goes. Love in a marriage can come later as you get to know your spouse better and come to appreciate his or her virtues."

"Well, I know that's what you always say, mama," said Nerissa, who had not yet quite reached her twenty-first birthday, "but I agree with Olga for once. When people marry without that spark of love, it's bound to end in disaster."

"You're both talking a lot of rubbish," Sima suddenly burst out, "What has marriage to do with love. It is a contract organised by society. Hopefully love may happen as a result, but it is possible that it may not."

Olga and Nerissa stared dumbfounded at their elder sister, open-mouthed, saying nothing for once, while she looked away from them in some embarrassment.

The fifth person at the table was little Seta. Seta was the baby of the family, who was not only little in the sense that she was the youngest, but she was also petite for her age. She had already tried to interrupt several times but had been ignored. She now stood up in an attempt to get some attention.

Seta was fourteen and was still as irrepressible as ever, however, even standing, she was totally ignored and sat down again. Instead, Nerissa, finding her voice said, "Sima, my darling sister, marriage without love is utterly wrong. The War has changed everything and we ..."

"The War has changed nothing," snapped Armineh, "at least nothing that's really important in human relationships, my girl."

At this point Haik came clattering downstairs two steps at a time in shirtsleeves – his hair all over the place, his tie still hanging halfway round his neck and with his coat over his shoulder.

"Sorry mama, I dropped off again."

"Yes, yes, my boy, very well, but you're lucky that your father is still not down ..."

"Hello, girls. A kiss please Seta, my soul – yes right here – that's good. Talin, a bowl of yoghurt please. No mother, I'm not going to eat anything else so please don't look at me like that." And at last Haik sat down at his place and grinned at everyone.

"Well, what is all the chit-chat about?"

Now seventeen, Haik was no longer quite so naïve and innocent as he had been in April 1915 at the time he had been assaulted on the road up to the house from the railway station. He was still thin and wiry and had not as yet fleshed out – looking more like a boy than a young man. The unstinting love of a mother and four doting sisters, coupled to his father's absence for two highly formative years, had not been helpful in developing the more robust, or masculine, side of his character. He was convinced that everyone automatically loved him. He was aware of the terrible events that had taken place in the Anatolian interior to the bulk of his people, but was unable to identify with this himself. The Turks whom he knew and associated with – his fellow students at Robert College – his sister Olga's special friend Selim – were all friendly and he liked them all.

Armineh had done her best by way of discipline during those two years when no one really knew what had happened to Karekin or whether he was even still alive. But it was not discipline that Haik had lacked, it was a male role-model. By the time Karekin had returned when Haik was fourteen, the habit of confiding in and talking with his father had gone for ever. Haik remained confused as a result of the attempted rape and by the failure of Armineh to have addressed the matter immediately. That day had after all coincided with the arrest and deportation of her husband Karekin.

"Well, come on, what are you all talking about?"

"You're too young Haik," said Sima a little stiffly.

"Nonsense," said Olga gaily. "We were talking about Sima's proposed engagement to George. You remember George – the older brother of that little minx Tamara who's always making sheep's eyes at you."

Haik blushed, but in true Avakian spirit rallied at once in counterattack,

"Well, I don't see why you're all going on about it. It's up to Sima isn't it? What's it got to do with the rest of us?"

"Good boy, that's quite right," said Armineh nodding her head vigorously.

"Haik, you're so simple, of course it has to do with all of us – though the decision is Sima's naturally. Why shouldn't we give our opinion? After all, it affects us all much more than most of the other matters we incessantly argue about."

At this comment everyone began talking at once, with Olga and Nerissa sticking to their romantic notions of marriage, Sima and her mother disagreeing, Seta jumping up and down and demanding to be heard but being ignored as usual. Haik, having opened a hornet's nest, grinned and said nothing but winked at Talin, who had been hovering round the table.

Karekin at last appeared at the top of the stairs, but the argument continued as Karekin, tall, balding but still imposing, dressed immaculately as usual, walked slowly down the stairs and round to his place at the head of the table. By the time he sat down, the talk had finally somewhat died down. Only Seta said, as her father bent down for a kiss –

"Baba, they won't listen to me – they never listen to me. I'm nearly fourteen and I know as much as Haik about all these things anyway."

"Well, well, my girl – Talin, a tea please and some of that honey, thank you – what have you to say then, we're all listening."

At this there was indeed a silence as Karekin looked sternly at everyone and they all then turned to look at Seta, who, suddenly the centre of attention, became confused and forgot everything she had been wanting to say.

"Oh! – Oh! – I don't know – I mean – I just don't want anyone to marry anyone and go away – no, I mean – oh Sima, I do love you, and I want you to stay with us for ever and ... oh dear ..."

Everyone roared with laughter as Seta blushed at her own incoherence, but smiled bravely as Haik said –

"What do you mean, little mouse, saying that you know as much as me. Let's see – do you know for instance who Nerissa is going to meet this afternoon after she leaves the university?"

"Haik, you little devil!"

"Oh, come on Nerissa," said Olga. "We all know. It's that solid peasant boy Vahan that you keep seeing and who runs off before any of us can get to the door when he brings you home."

"Olga!" said Armineh, "that's cruel and unnecessary. I really won't have a word said against the young man who saved my son and is always so polite and agreeable – though – hm, yes, er – perhaps a little too much so – er – yes where was I? Oh yes that reminds me! Nerissa, you are getting back later and later. I know that Bolis has become much safer since that new British commander took over – but there is still a lot of riff-raff roaming the streets. Some of them look pretty desperate, and the allied soldiers can't be everywhere. So please get back whilst it is still daylight."

"Very well, mama, I'll do my best, though to be fair, mama, I think those Russians are often better behaved than some of the allied soldiers," said Nerissa, thus immediately starting up yet another Avakian argument and neatly avoiding any further discussion about the lateness of her return.

Karekin looked with pride at Nerissa – one of the few girls to be enrolled at the University of Stamboul. All his daughters had been particularly well-educated: indeed so much so, that his more old-fashioned neighbours and business acquaintances looked at the family somewhat askance. But despite Armineh's comment, the War really had changed everything. Suddenly it had become fashionable within wealthy Greek and Armenian circles for girls to continue their education after high school, instead of immediately getting married. Karekin knew that Nerissa, with her impeccable English, learnt both from the novels she read and from her attendance at the English High School for Girls, was exceptional, but sometimes he wondered whether she was a little too clever for her own good.

"Come, Haik, it's time we were off. Talin, my lass, go and tell Paramaz to get ready. I don't want to miss the 8:20 train. Haik, for goodness sake tidy yourself up a bit. We are meeting one of our more important English suppliers from Lancashire this afternoon, and you will have to be present. There is a possibility of our picking up a contract for supplying linen to the British forces here. Anyway – get on, comb your hair and smarten up. Really Armineh, can't you get him to dress better?"

"Karekin – what are you saying?"

"Ah well – ah well – never mind. Hurry up!" he shouted as Haik ran up the stairs.

Paramaz, a tall young man with the signs of a slight moustache appearing on his upper lip, heavy cheeks, small brown eyes, and a dark look, came in from the kitchen side of the great room and waited respectfully at the front door as Karekin got ready. Paramaz looked hard at Seta as she got up to place a kiss on her father's cheek, as he stooped down smiling. Seta saw Paramaz staring at her from behind her father. She blushed deeply and looked away, stammering a farewell to Karekin, covering her blushes well.

Haik was already rushing downstairs – hair combed, tie straight and with his coat now properly on. Only he, from halfway up the stairs, had noticed Seta's unhappy confusion at the staring of Paramaz. He paused for a moment, then came on, joining Karekin who was already on his way out.

Haik passed out of the front door behind his father ahead of Paramaz, who waited and followed after him. Their eyes met as Haik passed; Haik's eyes angry and worried; Paramaz's eyes looking right at him, dark and smouldering.

CHAPTER 5

Mikael

Mikael Sarafian had been discharged from the hospital in Scutari nearly two years after his near-death experience, the result of the vicious beating he had endured in the Yedikule police station in April 1915. After having said farewell to Olga, who had gently rejected his ardent advances, Mikael had returned home to Makrikoy to live with his sister Nairi and his disapproving mother. The war, meanwhile, had dragged on. Mikael had been given a specific date on his discharge papers from the hospital for reporting back to the army. Although the deportations in the eastern interior had slackened off, largely because there were now few Armenians left, service in the Ottoman army was still very dangerous for an Armenian, and Mikael had had no intention of returning.

Mikael had gone regularly to see his father's mistress Katya and her two boys in their tiny house in Yedikule. His mother, Vartouhi, knew where he was going and she made her disapproval very clear. She would never forgive her deceased husband's betrayal. Nairi, Mikael's sister, would have liked to meet her half-brothers, but loyally supported her mother. Mikael did not feel the same way and refused to give up the relationship he had forged with this second family.

Away from Makrikoy, Mikael was not known to the local policemen, and as a young man obviously of military age he had already been stopped twice by police patrols in Yedikule. On the second occasion, Mikael had recognised one of the policemen who had beaten him up so savagely two years previously – and saw the glint in the man's eye showing he had also been recognised, but the date for his return had not yet arrived.

Some weeks after that second confrontation, in November 1917, the Bolshevik coup had broken out in St. Petersburg – and in that same month, Mikael had managed to get a lowly job as a deckhand on a Bulgarian freighter docked in Bolis, and had crept on board just before she sailed. The captain was short of men and had asked no questions. He carried coal from Zonguldak for the Turks, grain from Odessa for the Russians, arms from and to everywhere for everyone, hoisting whatever flag took his fancy. Mikael jumped ship in Odessa and then onto another freighter to Rostov on the river Don, where he disembarked.

Russia was in a complete mess. The Cossacks of the Don had set up a separate administration, but there were no police, no identity papers needing to be shown, and the value of gold and roubles fluctuated wildly. Mikael knew only a few words of Russian. On his arrival in Rostov he had to find work fast. On the very first day of his arrival, he found himself in the centre of a riot. He was simply walking along when he suddenly heard a great deal of shouting. He turned and saw a crowd of industrial workers, still in their factory clothes, come running down the street. Mikael found himself caught up in the wild enthusiasm, though he had no idea what was going on. The crowds yelled and lifted their arms high, so Mikael did the same, though he understood not a word.

Mikael wandered round the town and eventually found a cheap lodging house, paying in advance and using up one of his last gold coins – Turkish gold, more valuable than Russian, was in high demand.

He wandered back onto the streets in the evening and watched the crowds milling about, and stopping to listen to speakers who were spontaneously haranguing the crowds. Though he understood nothing he had picked up a word or two – enough to order a bowl of greasy soup.

A few days later, Mikael had still not found any work, and he was again in a street in the town centre when for the first time he heard organised shooting. Some Cossacks on horseback came round the corner at the far end of the street riding straight towards where he was standing. Firing broke out behind him and then began coming at him from all sides. Mikael just managed to slip inside a shoe shop before the shopkeeper locked the door and began hastily closing the wooden shutters.

The shopkeeper let Mikael out at the back into an alleyway, and he began working his way back to his lodgings on the outskirts of town. There was firing coming from all sides now as Mikael sidled along, keeping close to the walls. In several places he saw that the Cossacks had dismounted and were firing from the pavements and in doorways. Mikael had just passed near the railway station, where there appeared to be a concentration of firing, when he saw for the first time some regular soldiers on the street behind who started firing up the road on which he was standing. Mikael realised later that they must have been 'White' army soldiers. No one on either side had any discernible uniforms, with the exception of the Cossacks who Mikael recognised from pictures he had seen. Mikael dropped to the ground and crept along the wall to where a little old lady was cowering in a very narrow doorway. The woman was clearly terrified. She was carrying two loaves of bread and immediately began hysterically gabbling at Mikael, but he could only nod his head. His position was dangerous as the doorway was too narrow; there was only a foot or two before the shelter gave out and the pavement began. But he was confused as to which way to go. There was one lot of soldiers – or fighters – at one end of the street and another lot at the other. He had no idea which were which nor what they were fighting about. But he had to move. He went on to his hands and knees and began inching his way along the wall, instinctively away from the soldiers he could see, towards the corner ahead where there were others behind a makeshift barricade across the street. The old woman held onto his shirt and crawled after him. The shooting continued and he heard a moan behind him and, turning his head, saw the woman collapse, blood pouring out from an undisclosed spot. Her eyes turned up and she was dead. Mikael acted fast, grabbed the two loaves and rose and began running, crouched as low as he could get. More shots flew from behind him; the barricade of old furniture and an upturned cart ahead of him. He reached it gasping for breath, dodged round and made it behind the barrier.

"Well done comrade," said a young Russian who had a cloth cap on his shaved head. Sewn rather roughly onto the peak was a stubby red star.

Mikael handed the young man one of the loaves, but could say nothing of course. The young man pointed down to a dead body slumped up against the barricade – was this a soldier – a boy – could it even be a woman? Mikael realised that he was expected to take up the rifle. He did so, peered through the barricade and began firing at the crouching figures running towards them. His early training in the Turkish army came in useful and he had always been a good shot, though the rifle was dirty and not very accurate. His new friends grinned at him as he picked off several of the enemy, whoever they were.

Then at the other end of the street a ramshackle lorry appeared with rough iron plating hanging down its sides and with sheets of iron over the top of the driver's cab. It began slowly clattering up the street towards them followed by soldiers sheltering behind.

"Come, comrade, we can't hold this position any longer," said the young Russian, putting his hand on Mikael's shoulder as the others started to scramble away down a side-street. Mikael didn't have to understand the words – the situation was clear.

Still holding the rifle, Mikael began moving back following the others. He had no idea who his new friends were or who he had been firing at. In fact, Mikael had blundered into the start of the Russian Civil War. He had just witnessed how Rostov had changed hands from the Reds to the Whites. During the two years Mikael remained in the town, it was to change hands more than seven times. Chance had put him with the Reds and Mikael, who had at least six months military training in the Ottoman army, was immediately accepted in the group, on the assumption that he had volunteered to join the Red Army.

The group he had joined – later becoming a formal brigade – were mainly young workers from the local factories with a leavening of Lettish riflemen left over from a regular Latvian unit in the old Imperial army. They were full of enthusiasm; long discussions went on night after night wherever they were hiding out in the town, most of which Mikael did not follow until several months had passed. He only understood that the enemy were considered vicious counter-revolutionaries – landlords, aristocrats and capitalists determined to exploit and grind down all his new friends.

However, looking down the sights of his rifle, they did not look to him to be that much different from the lads alongside whom he was fighting. He found he no longer exercised any personal initiative. He lived from day to day in the company of other young men with whom he felt a camaraderie, which was enough for him.

A few month's later, the enemy began evacuating the town. Mikael and his group emerged from their hiding places, though they didn't fire as they were out of ammunition, and he watched as the White army marched away in fairly good order. Rostov had changed hands again.

Mikael, now an accepted member of the Bolshevik party, found a job in a munitions factory, but he was also a soldier. As his Russian improved, he found that most of his new comrades had no better idea who they were actually fighting against than him. The war had not officially ended and the Germans were approaching. A state was set up in the Ukraine. Where had the Cossacks got to? Mikael had no idea. He went to work day after day and joined his own group for some desultory military training, and for long rambling debates at night about politics, land, and socialism.

Mikael had discovered an Armenian church in a village containing several Armenian families not far from the city, and being a devout believer, was there on the Easter of 1918. That day, White Russian troops moving out of the way of the German army had entered Rostov from the unexpected western side. Mikael, still in the village of Nakchivensk nearby, had no idea what had happened. However, the Reds in the town had woken up to find the White forces in control of the railway station and the rest of the city. Rostov had changed hands.

Mikael stayed for a few nights at Nakchivensk. Within a week, the Reds launched a counter-attack. The Whites left, but this time there were killings and brutality as they burned and looted indiscriminately before retreating. Mikael returned to the town just in time to face yet a further change. This time it was the Germans who marched in and Rostov changed masters once again.

Mikael's health was all the time deteriorating, though he remained surprisingly cheerful in spirit. In the midst of all the turmoil there was little fresh food and typhus and disease was everywhere. Why did he continue? Mostly because there didn't seem to be much else he could do on top of the sheer inertia of just carrying on doing what he had started. However, as he came to understand more of what was going on around him, he did feel that he had inadvertently joined the right side. He saw the horrific brutalities of the 'enemy' whenever they appeared. He did not take the same account of the similar brutalities on his own side, as he never saw them in quite the same way.

He remained emotionally unattached. Others took the decisions; he simply fought whenever required and to get more food for himself when he was not so required. What he did see was that the vast majority of the ordinary Russian people around him were totally unenthusiastic about both sides. It was a civil war, but it was one between two small parties.

The Germans left Rostov after the Armistice of the 11th of November, and the Reds came back. Some months later in the winter the Whites recaptured the city yet again, and the Red Army, of which Mikael's group had become a regular unit, was defeated and surrounded. Some ten thousand soldiers were captured with a great deal of equipment and almost one hundred abandoned railway locomotives. Mikael found that he had become a prisoner.

The Red prisoners were paraded in a large open area of the town near the river. Mikael stood there in line with about 9,000 other men – all shivering with cold and fear. He wondered what was he doing there and what had all this to do with him?

Mikael watched as every commissar attached to the Red army was removed from the ranks and shot there and then in great batches – six hundred men. The demoralised Red soldiers, both the regulars and the volunteers, like the Rostov group, looked listlessly on. After the killing of the commissars stopped, the rank and file were given a straight choice – join the White Volunteer Army or be shot.

Four thousand men joined the Whites. Mikael was one of them.

While fighting with the Reds, Mikael had been a civilian volunteer who trained with a group and fought only when he was called upon. However when he joined the White Volunteer Army he became a full-time soldier. For the first time he learned the name of the White general who had re- taken the town for the third time and who was now his commander – General Denikin – under whose orders his new unit moved out.

Mikael never returned to Rostov, nor was he present when the Reds eventually stormed back into the town. Nor did he witness the new brutalities as hundreds of uncomprehending people were shot or bayoneted in the streets alongside the few White soldiers who were found in the city. He had marched out with the army, fighting different enemies – sometimes Reds – sometimes independent Cossacks – sometimes units of the tottering state of Ukraine. His clothes were in tatters, his boots were those taken from the bodies of other dead soldiers. His health continued to deteriorate.

It was known that there were huge quantities of uniforms, headwear and boots sitting in warehouses, at several ports in the Black Sea, provided by the British and French governments, but nothing ever got to the front-line soldiers, fuelling instead a thriving black market run by speculators of all kinds. Knowing this the morale of the White army began to falter. Like so many other soldiers around him he marched, counter-marched, advanced and retreated, without the slightest idea where he was or what were the real issues. But he slowly became an experienced soldier.

Somewhat surprisingly, now that he had become a cog in the machine of a regular army, however bedraggled, he began to lose the apathy and fatalism of the last two years. Camaraderie and the joy of fighting with friends shoulder to shoulder, which had sustained him before, was suddenly no longer enough. He began to look carefully about him and to think about his chances of getting away. Mass desertions and switches of side were the norm rather than the exception throughout the civil war, but one had to be careful. Reprisals were swift and terminal. In any event Mikael now had no desire simply to exchange one army for another.

The White army was in the Kuban, steadily fighting rear-guard actions as the Reds began closing in. The only safe area left for the Whites was the Crimea, which was held by the efficient General Wrangel. With Rostov now finally in the hands of the Reds, the only way to the Crimea was across the sea from the port of Novorossiysk. Mikael found himself retreating with the rest of the army to this small port. Although it was already March, it was still bitterly cold. Freezing winds tore over the mountains and made the passes down to the sea icy and treacherous.

The Reds were not far behind them, though a Cossack rear-guard unit still tried to protect the army's flanks as it marched on. The roads coming down from the mountains heading to the little port were packed with a stream of humanity, most of whom had no idea where they were going or why. Of course, those who were relatives of White officers or landowners knew exactly the fate awaiting them if they were taken, but most of the rest were simply affected by blind fear and panic.

Apart from the remains of the army itself, there were many others hoping to be evacuated – bands of Cossacks who had fled from the collapsed Free Republic of the Don, Muslim nomad families from Daghestan, Chechen refugees, the fleeing middle classes of Ekaterinodar and other urban centres.

Mikael marched along, still part of a recognisable military unit. The gravel and mud roads were lined with bodies already stripped of clothes and shoes, lying frozen alongside abandoned heavy equipment and overturned carts. Neither Mikael nor his current companions were yet aware that Denikin had lost all semblance of control over the situation. The numbers of ships in the port were nothing like enough for the numbers now converging on the town, all looking to flee across the sea. Mikael marched on, assuming that the senior officers had made the necessary arrangements.

When Mikael's brigade reached the town, it was already crowded with refugees and other army units. Denikin had contacted the British Black Sea squadron. The Admiral in command, had already received London's decision to pull out, together with clear orders that any further intervention or help for the Whites should be strictly avoided. Nevertheless, turning a Nelsonian blind eye to his orders, he got together as many ships as he could find and sailed to the little port. The Bolsheviks continued to advance, but were held back, for a short period, by the army's Cossack rear guard. The whole army, and not just the officers who would certainly have been shot, wanted to leave. Mikael stood with the rest of his unit and waited.

The Red artillery finally made it to the mountains overlooking the town. Shells began falling in the streets, though the range was too far for them to reach the ships. Panic took hold, communicating itself to the hitherto disciplined soldiery. What with the wailing and crying of women, the screams of children wounded or separated from parents, the whine of the incoming shells and the explosions, and the now obvious fact that not everyone was going to get away, the people milling about in the little town were stunned and in a state of shock.

However, the army remained fairly steady amidst the chaos. The Cossack units now clattering into the town shot their beloved horses and turned their faces away as parties of refugees ran forward to hack away pieces of flesh. Small fires sprang up along the quayside. As the last hours arrived, it became clear that only those army units still armed and organised were being taken aboard. Officers and sailors were guarding the gangplanks of the ships moored alongside. Increasingly shots rang out as desperate people were turned away or were killed trying to rush the barriers. Desperate deals were being done with the few private boats and fishing vessels. At last it was the turn of Mikael's brigade. It was made clear that any soldier who wanted to stay and take their chances with the approaching Reds was free to do so.

But Mikael shuffled aboard with the rest of them. As the army units left the quayside there were less men capable of holding the barriers. Mikael watched as a party of men finally broke through and rushed at the gangplanks. Shots rang out, and men and women fell into the sea. In the midst of the noise and chaos, the remaining ships began pulling away, often abandoning the gangplanks that were full of men trying to force themselves onto the boats. In some cases, a part of a family was already aboard as the other part tried to clamber up gangplanks which were slipping away from the quayside.

In the distance, the Reds were now sweeping down the hills, firing as they came into the outskirts of the town. Fires had already broken out in the suburbs. The ships, loaded with humanity but with no stores of any kind, slipped slowly away from the quayside. All told, about 50,000 people, the bulk of the broken remnants of the Army, together with about 20,000 civilians who had somehow got aboard.

On arriving at the port of Sevastopol in the Crimea, Mikael had managed to slip away in the chaos of the disembarkation. The rest of the brigade had paraded and marched off to the defensive positions in the north – currently under the command of General Wrangel. Mikael was now a deserter from both sides.

For some time he led a hand-to-mouth existence in Sevastopol while trying to get another job as a deckhand on a boat or freighter heading for another port in the Black Sea. But all to no avail. The only major shipping was allied controlled and, for the moment, fishing boats and small yachts were not prepared to go any distance. Eventually Mikael managed to get a loading job on the docks. Here, once again he found himself amongst men sympathetic to the Reds.

The moment came when General Wrangel was finally defeated and the last White army still left in Russia came pouring back into Sevastopol. Mikael and his delighted fellow-workers watched as the quaysides filled with despairing multitudes of fleeing families, merchants, peasants, and individual soldiers long since separated from their units. However, this was not Novorossiysk and Wrangel was not Denikin. There were an enormous number of ships in and around the harbour, and on land there were armed guards everywhere. While there was fear and despair, there was also more discipline.

Mikael waited, making sure first that the fleet would indeed be heading to Constantinople. As the days passed and the quayside filled up, Mikael separated himself from his new companions. Reds or Whites – it made no difference to him. It was time to get home. The war had been over now for almost two years. Constantinople was occupied by the Allies so he had nothing more to fear from Turkish police.

Mikael continued to wait and watch. He would surely be able to get onto some ship one way or another. However he had to be careful not to end up simply as a White soldier being evacuated, with the danger of being recognised as a deserter. On the other hand he also had to be careful to avoid his latest Red companions who might have taken him as a spy if they saw him slinking away.

The atmosphere of crisis thickened as the evacuation started, and the crowds remembering Odessa and Novorossiysk began to panic, though held back by the military. A British launch from one of the destroyers in the harbour pulled up near Mikael as he wandered the quayside on the lookout for a chance to slip away. A smartly turned out naval officer stepped off it and into the crowds. He stopped and began talking to a young White officer whom Mikael had noticed before, a typical cold and supercilious type – the sort of desiccated White aristocrat Mikael had learnt to despise. The two disappeared into the crowds.

Mikael had his eyes on the small freighter nearby that he was going to board if he got the chance. There were two gangplanks but only one sailor guarding, standing in between them. Whilst nothing like the desperate atmosphere at Novorossiysk, there was, nevertheless, a certain amount of anxiety and panic apparent as the realisation sunk in to the milling crowds that the choice was between Russia under the Reds or complete and irrevocable exile.

Mikael, his whole nervous system in a high state of tension, watched the return of the British naval officer and his young aristocrat companion who had with him a young boy and an elderly lady. For some unaccountable reason of mob hysteria, as this Russian family reached the British launch and prepared to embark, the crowd nearby began yelling and pushed forward, putting everyone in danger. Mikael saw the young Russian officer pull out a revolver and fire three shots into the air, and then turn and level the weapon against the crowd.

The crowd shuffled back, as others nearby, hearing the shots, came to see what was going on, including the guard on the gangplanks of the ship next door. Mikael did not hesitate for a moment, but took immediate advantage of the incident. He pulled back from the crowd and walked calmly up the far gangplank, and onto the deck of the boat, already filled with families and assorted refugees, though without soldiers. No one questioned him. Mikael slumped down next to a small family consisting of a woman, leaning back against the bulwarks, with two small children by her side. The woman sat with staring eyes, but the two children were fast asleep, lying restlessly on the deck. Mikael sat himself down, gave a beaming smile at the woman and gently took the little boy's head and placed it on his thigh comfortably.

The sailor-guard returned from his inspection of what was going on in the commotion alongside, and came back up the gangplank, never giving this 'father' a second look.

Within a few more minutes, the gangplank was lifted, the ship hooted and pulled away from the quay to move into the bay and allow another boat to take its place. Only a few hours later, the huge convoy of ships began leaving the great harbour as the sound of gunfire was heard coming from the hills to the north.

CHAPTER 6

Mikael and Elena

The long line of ships that had followed the *General Kornilov* across the Black Sea from Sevastopol and into the Bosporus anchored in a great mass opposite the Haydar Pasha station, where the straits opened out into the Sea of Marmara. At the time, Nikolai had been told that there were at least 80 ships in the convoy, but there were, in fact, over 120, when all the private yachts and small fishing boats were taken into account. One hundred and fifty thousand souls, including almost the whole of the remnants of Wrangel's South Russian White Army, had been crammed on board this extraordinary fleet.

Mikael Sarafian, lay exhausted on the deck of the small freighter he had boarded. The boat was anchored just opposite the Seraglio Point, but the great panorama of the Stamboul shoreline at which Nikolai had been staring with such fascination from the deck of the General Kornilov, aroused only a melancholy sigh of satisfaction for Mikael returning home after three years, for he had lived in this great city all his life and the wonderful views of the hills, mosques and palaces were simply a backdrop to his daily life..

Nobody was moving – nobody was going anywhere for the moment, as the officialdom of four nations contemplated the great exodus and wondered what should be done.

Mikael had aged; the terrible beating he had suffered at the police station in Yedikule five years before had resulted in a ruptured kidney. He had not been formally discharged from the army, but had spent the next two years in the Turkish military hospital at Scutari, where he had met and fallen in love with a nurse – Olga Avakian – during his convalescence. His health had deteriorated further during the three years he had spent in Russia. He retained a hardened arrogant look that was so uncharacteristic for an Armenian. He looked more Turkish than Armenian, with black eyes, straight black hair and the ubiquitous Enver-style moustache. But his cheeks were now sunken and his wiry athletic body had become sparse and frail. Hungry and weak, he drifted back to sleep.

He came to with a start as the little boy stepped on his foot as he struggled to pull away from his mother's grasp. Mikael found himself looking straight up at the small kiosks and gardens of the Seraglio Point on the other side of the bay.

"I'm so sorry sir, I hope you weren't hurt." The woman alongside him spoke Greek with an unusual accent, but as a streetwise Bolsetsi, he knew Greek well enough to converse easily.

"No, no, please don't worry. Are you from Polis?"

"No we are from Odessa – at least we were."

She sighed, and Mikael recalled that there was a sizable Greek community along the northern shores of the Black Sea.

"So, will you be staying here?"

"No, sir. We are going on to Smyrna, where my husband... er... yes, my husband ... has a brother. I have his address and I know he will be expecting us, as he wrote after the war advising us to join him there where he said we would be safe."

"And your husband?"

"Oh God, I don't know. He failed to get away from Odessa when the

Greek and French army evacuated the town and the Reds entered the city."

"And you and the children?"

"He had already sent us to the Crimea before the evacuation. He himself never made it but I have no idea what really happened to him."

Mikael reflected that this conversation could have been repeated with only small variations a thousand times. Mikael and the young woman – whose name was Elena Pantelis – talked together for hours, as he waited to disembark.

Elena was small, blue-eyed and surprisingly fair for a Greek of the Black Sea coast. She told Mikael she didn't know what had happened to her own family, who had lived in a village fairly remote from Odessa itself. She thought that her husband was probably dead. With considerable foresight he had sent her to the Crimea, promising to follow as soon as he could gather together more money for his property.

Once in the Crimea, she had heard of the collapse of Odessa. The Greek and French military forces had re-embarked in frenzied haste and left for good, as the Bolsheviks poured down into the town. She had heard the description of the devastating scenes on the Odessa seafront as the panicked population pushed and shoved and died in their attempts to board the ships.

As the day slowly passed, without food and only a little water, Elena continued to talk, rarely interrupted by Mikael. Too long on her own, with only childish chatter to sustain her, she could not stop herself enjoying a conversation between adults, even though it was more of a monologue.

Elena explained that she was staying aboard the ship and had boarded it in the first place because it was bound for Smyrna. As governments crumbled all around them, everybody came to rely more and more on their extended family networks and she was relying on the support of her late husband's brother, her children's uncle, in Smyrna.

Late in the afternoon, those passengers bound for Constantinople were finally given permission to disembark. Mikael took note of the uncle's address in Smyrna and kissed the boy Andreas and his sister Anya goodbye. Elena was almost in tears as he left them.

Early in the morning, while it was still dark, the shabby old freighter pulled out of the line of ships and began moving away into the Marmara Sea on its way to Smyrna.

CHAPTER 7

Three young men at the Avakians

Some weeks after the arrival of the White Russian refugees in the city, Vahan and his Turkish friend Selim were sitting together in the coffee lounge of the Pera Palas hotel, watching the fascinating pot-pourri of races passing through the public rooms in the hotel.

"Selim, my dearest friend, it's not just a question of Turkish honour. Sooner or later these British and French soldiers are going to leave this town. They have no permanent place in our culture. The question is – who or what is going to replace them?"

"Vahan, my brother, it's no use trying to persuade me to stick to the Ottomans; the days of that dynasty are completely over. We have to move into the twentieth century and that is why the news from Anatolia must be welcomed."

"Oh dear, we never seem to agree on this matter. The Ottomans represent five hundred years of Turkish influence and prestige. How can you repudiate them so easily? It's only in the past sixty or seventy years that they have fallen so dramatically into dishonour and decadence. What do the Kemalists represent? – nothing but a narrow exclusive single-nation state. What do the Ottomans represent? – a great multi-cultural, tolerant all-embracing power respecting many races and faiths. Why would you want to substitute for this ideal, a one-faith, one-party, one-culture, one-people state, intolerant of anyone or anything that might be different?"

"Oh Vahan, shut up – you do go on a bit! There is no empire any more. I don't want to be brutal or insensitive, and I don't need to tell you how much I deplore what happened to your people in the interior four years ago – but it happened ... it has happened. My friend, what we have now, after 500 years, is a state with only one people left – the Turks. We are therefore at last in a position to create a western-style nation-state."

"And the Kurds?"

"Poof ! – what do you care about the Kurds? They're illiterate savages, as your own people found out to their cost five years ago."

"And your own religious leader – the Sheik-ul-Islam – who last month denounced the Kemalists as 'traitors to Islam.'"

"Equally – poof! I have always said that the Arabs were a drag on the Turkish state. God! Vahan, you sound just like my old dad who was a great reforming Ottomanist. But he was wrong, my friend, quite wrong. Now that we have lost the Arab part of the state, we can get rid of those old-fashioned concepts. Let it go – let it go – it was always an Arab thing, not Turkish at all. We must now embrace the modern nation-state with its efficiency and unity ...”

"And with all its intolerance of diversity, and its exclusion of other peoples, other faiths, other ideas. Selim, my friend, beware – never mind the ideology – you are proposing to substitute the power of Anatolia and it's illiterate dumb peasants for your cosmopolitan Constantinople and its international culture and its old traditional power."

"Well – to hell with the Ottoman Empire – to hell with Stamboul and fifteen hundred years of Imperial power. I met the people you call illiterate dumb peasants during the war, as did my father, and both of us found them honest and loyal fellows. Let Anatolia take over. Enough of Byzantium! Come Vahan, it was after all Constantinople which spawned the odious Abdul Hamid and the horrors of Yildiz Palace."

"Yes, but ..."

This conversation, one which Selim and Vahan had had with suitable variations ever since the Armistice of Mudros, would have continued without resolution for the rest of the afternoon if the little orchestra in the next salon had not finally stopped playing. Almost immediately, a young man in a worn evening suit appeared at the entrance with a violin under his arm and strode towards Vahan with a smile and an outstretched hand.

"Selim, I want you to meet my new friend Nikolai."

"Nikolai Petrovitch Androv, at your service. I am pleased to meet you," said Nikolai in his poor, heavily accented Turkish, as he took the empty seat at the table and ordered a coffee.

"Nikolai has got a job with the Pera Palas orchestra," said Vahan.

"Thanks to some invaluable help given to me by the good Vahan," Nikolai said, smiling at the two of them.

Nikolai turned to look at Selim. He saw a tall young man, older than himself, with thick black hair, wavy rather than the usual straight hair of most Turks. Swarthy and with a heavy stubble, he must have recently shaved off a moustache, as his hand kept wandering to his upper lip as if to stroke where it had once been. It was only then, Nikolai noticed that Selim's left arm was cut off at the elbow.

The three young men, all in their twenties – a Russian, a Turk and an Armenian – sat, surrounded by British officers, American sailors, Greek merchants, elegant Frenchwomen and many others, all of whom seemed to be talking about what was likely to happen here at the navel of the world. Vahan was happy to find that after introducing his friends to each other, they immediately got on so well together. Finally, the conversation changed to another topic ...

"Selim, listen, Nerissa has invited you and I to visit the family this afternoon. You haven't seen Olga for weeks. Let's go – now – and take Nikolai. Can you come? You're not on duty again until this evening, are you? Come on, let's go! You'll find them a fascinating family."

"My darling sisters, you have to stop all this nonsense about love and chemistry. What chemistry are you on about? There is obviously chemistry in all relationships – fathers and daughters – between sisters – even between strangers. George is a good man, my parents approve of him and his family. He is Armenian and we have a lot in common. Above all, he will be a good father to my children. He is kind, gentle and courteous. That's enough for me."

Sima, the eldest Avakian daughter, was sitting more primly than usual, sewing a pair of Haik's woollen socks, eyes bent on her needle, and a flush in her ivory cheeks showing how long they had been arguing – Avakian fashion. Neither Nerissa nor Olga were going to give an inch as the argument raged on.

There was no pretence here; all three girls had definite ideas. Sima thought that her mother was right. You picked your man by his virtues, by the position or potential position he held or would attain, by the things that you could share together. In those circumstances, there would be affection and 'love'... well, it might appear in due course. Olga, for her part, did not think at all; she believed that you simply went with your instincts and, if not, you had better let it remain as a flirtation. Nerissa, of course, was at the other extreme. She understood the dangers of picking your man without any thought of social and long-term consequences. However she was also convinced that 'love' or 'chemistry' had to come first and not later.

The bell at the front door rang.

"Oh dear, that must be Vahan and Selim already," said Nerissa.

Nerissa and Olga stood up as Talin opened the door of the sitting-room, and Selim, with a great grin on his face, walked in holding a large bunch of flowers in his good hand.

"May Allah be merciful to this house and all in it," he said, eyes lit up as he handed the flowers to Olga with a short bow. Olga took the flowers and stretching forwards her other hand, she touched Selim lightly on his right cheek, and held it there for a moment. They could not of course kiss, but the intimate gesture had an even greater intensity than a peck on the cheek.

Selim was followed into the room by Vahan and another young man who stood silent at the door as Vahan came and shook Olga's and Nerissa's hand. Both Selim and Vahan then went and bowed to Sima who had remained seated, though she had put aside Haik's socks.

"Miss Sima," said Vahan, speaking in English, "may I present my new friend – Count Nikolai Petrovitch Androv, who has arrived from the Crimea."

Nikolai came forward, shook hands with Sima, and then with the other two girls.

"Talin – put Olga's flowers in water, and then bring some tea," said Sima to Talin who was still hovering at the door. "Come gentlemen, let's all sit," she continued in English, having noted Vahan's switch to that language, second nature to the cosmopolitan, multi-lingual citizens of Bolis.

"Selim, welcome, we haven't seen you for some time. How is your mother?"

It sounded like a natural rather formal opening for a conversation. It was however loaded with a meaning that everyone except Nikolai understood. The continuing impossibility of the simmering relationship between Selim and Olga – Turk and Armenian – Moslem and Christian – was a festering sore in both families. The bitterness towards Olga of Halideh Khanum, Selim's mother, whose husband had died at the hands of Armenian rebels at the siege of Van, was as determined as ever. Nor could the passing of time erase the memory of the terrible events that had occurred during 1915 for Armineh and Karekin.

But Selim had persevered, and Olga had let his persistence gradually override the caution she had felt when confronted with his mother's hatred. And it was in this constrained way that three years had passed. Ironically, while it was now acceptable for Vahan and Nerissa to meet in the afternoons, dance at Tokatlians and have tea together without any third party present, it was still quite impossible for Selim and Olga. Neither community would accept it – but still they persevered – and neither had thoughts for anyone else, despite all the efforts of their respective mothers.

On the arrival of tea, the conversation became less general. Selim and Olga sat on one armchair and whispered together and Nikolai found himself seated next to Sima. He saw a tall woman sitting very still with her hands resting tightly together on her lap. However reserved Sima might be, she was still an Avakian daughter and her conversation was direct and well-informed, quite unlike that of the great majority of women of her age and station in the city. The nature of the Russian civil war was considered, the Red victory analysed, and the plight of the White refugees discussed.

For the first time since the great evacuation from Sevastopol, Nicolai launched into a recital of his own experiences during those troubled two years. He found himself confronted by the unspoken but understanding sympathy of his listener, and to his surprise saw tears in the eyes of this cool and controlled woman as he described the suffering of so many ordinary people.

The arrival of Armineh with her shopping, heralded by a loud commotion in the great hall of the house, immediately broke up the party. The three young men stood up – as did Olga who had been holding Selim's hand. Armineh bustled in and took in at a glance the six young people in the sitting room. Vahan, who should have spoken at once did not say anything, and it was left to Nerissa who said – turning to Armineh, and switching to Armenian – "Ah, mama – you know Vahan and Selim of course – and this is Count Nikolai Androv – a new friend of Vahan. We've all just had tea. Would you like me to ask Talin to make a fresh pot?"

"Thank you, no, my soul. Gentlemen you are welcome," said Armineh in Turkish, not moving to shake hands with anyone, and avoiding looking at Selim. "Where is Seta?"

"I think she is upstairs. She was going to continue the reading and writing lessons for Paramaz," said Sima.

"What's this – why isn't he at the office with Haik and your father?"

"Baba is anxious for him to improve his reading and writing and sent him home when Seta got back from school."

"Very well," said Armineh, turning to Talin – "Please, my girl, call her down and then make a fresh pot. I will have a tea after all."

Some minutes of desultory conversation later, the normally bouncy Seta walked rather than ran into the room. Her hair was all over the place and she had a high red flush in her cheeks. Haik would have noticed that there were tears in her eyes. When introduced to Nikolai, she shook his hand and gave a small curtsey, but did not look into his eyes, nor did she kiss either Vahan or Selim. All rather unusual!

Shortly after her arrival, the three young men left and returned to the city.

CHAPTER 8

Paramaz and Seta

Karekin paid a subtle price for his advanced liberal and tolerant views. Living in a culture where women and their opinions were disregarded, at least publicly, he had nevertheless educated all his four girls to the same level as his only son. But, as a result, people were wary of him and his family, feeling there was something unusual and slightly disreputable about the Avakians. The social climate at the end of the war had loosened the strict codes of conduct that had existed between the sexes before the war, but while this western freedom was all very well for the Christian upper classes in Bolis, or even for the Ottoman elite, it held real dangers for the more generally uneducated population of the countryside – Greek, Armenian or Turk.

After his return to his family, Karekin came to terms with the almost impossible situation created by the love of Selim and Olga for each other. As he saw it, this was a price he was willingly prepared to pay for the benefit of a good education and enlightenment. He was still loyal to the Ottoman empire. He was committed to living in a multi-racial, multi-cultural society in which, despite recent events, there was a basic tolerance for each other's beliefs. Of course, he might have preferred his own family not to be a testing ground for his views, but in the last resort he accepted where they lead, even to intermarriage!

But it was Armineh, as always, who had to cope with the practical details – the tears of Olga – the refusal of Selim's mother to have anything to do with Olga or her family – the nasty rumours in the community as to why her beautiful 22 year-old daughter was not in the marriage market, and why Olga continued to work in the Turkish military hospital rather than at Sourp Pirgic, the Armenian hospital.

But all this passed over Karekin's head. He strode through life, head held high, believing in the rightness of his liberal and enlightened views and that all the traditionalists, conservatives, and religious enthusiasts were just plain wrong – and that was that.

But all was not well in his own home. Seta, at fourteen, was being overcome by feelings with which she was unable to cope, and there was no one available to help her.

Seta was not conventionally beautiful like her sister Olga. She was also not as commanding or as forceful as her eldest sister Sima, nor as intelligent as Nerissa. However she had a vivacity which gave her features a sparkle that was extraordinarily appealing.

Ever since the recent arrival in the household of the two survivors from the Anatolian catastrophe – Paramaz and Talin – Seta had been drifting further and further towards a fatally confused fascination for the young man. Haik, also seventeen, could still be described as a boy, whereas Paramaz, though younger, could only be described as a young man.

Seta was not stupid, she knew she had to keep these new feelings to herself. She poured them out in page after page of her carefully locked diary, and so by analysing them each evening and indulging her romantic notions, they took on a greater significance than they otherwise should have.

Paramaz stared at me all morning today as we were getting ready for church. I looked back at him out of the corner of my eye as I didn't dare to look at him directly. When he stares at me like that I get confused and I can't help thinking of his lips. I'm sure that I shouldn't be having such thoughts. I told Araxi at school a few days ago, but she laughed and said it was perfectly normal – but then she is already fifteen and I'm sure knows much more than me about such things.

Yesterday Paramaz and Haik got rather sharp with each other. I had no idea what it was all about, but they ended up challenging each other to a race in the garden. I went out from the French windows at the back and watched as they both took off their shirts, shoes and socks. Paramaz turned and looked hard at me with those dreadful black eyes of his. I felt dizzy and wanted to touch him. Then Haik suddenly pushed Paramaz, making him turn away, and ready himself for the race. Paramaz won of course – he is bigger and stronger than Haik.

Today, baba asked me if I would mind giving Paramaz some lessons in the evening after I get back from school. I was very excited but rather nervous. Paramaz talks much better Turkish than Armenian, though of course the Arabic script is well *beyond* him. He tells me that his parents never learnt to read or write Armenian, and that his own education was cut short when he was driven out of his home and onto a death march with his mother, after his father was killed. It seems he was picked up by some Kurds, after his mother died and he was wandering alone. He was living on the streets in Aleppo, when daddy arranged for him to come here.

Baba is getting a bit impatient that Paramaz is not learning his letters as quickly as he should. He was sent home earlier this afternoon so that I could give him an hour's lesson. It seems that Haik had a row with Baba. I think Haik wanted to come back with Paramaz, but Baba needed him and got very angry and almost struck him in front of Paramaz, which he told me about rather gleefully. I could see how his eyes glowed when he told me how Haik had retired crestfallen after Baba told him off. I don't know what I wanted, or why I wasn't more upset at my poor brother's humiliation.

Today we were working at the desk and Paramaz was reading aloud, though very slowly. He is quick and clever, so I thought that he should have been doing better by now. But baba did say yesterday he was pleased that his reading was improving. His knees and legs were pressing against mine. I think it was lovely, but I knew it was wrong and I tried to move away, but his legs seemed to follow. I got rather hot and I could feel the colour in my cheeks as I tried to concentrate, but he didn't seem to notice. I heard Talin call upstairs that Mama had returned and wanted me to come down. I got up at once. I was about to turn to go down when he suddenly pulled me towards him so that I was pressed against his chest and couldn't move. He then leant forward looking straight into my eyes. I pulled out of his grasp and saw him smiling as I ran out to join the others downstairs..

Even if Paramaz had been able to write, it would never have crossed his mind to keep a diary. One thing was clear to him as he took up his exercise book and the reader from Seta's desk and walked down the back stairs to his own small room behind the kitchen; he had no feelings for this pert and silly girl – the spoiled child of a family he could not understand and did not want to. What sort of family allowed a nubile girl to be alone – even for an hour – with a young man? He dumped his books on the shelf and stretched out on his bed. His mind raced back to his own strict father and pious mother, neither of whom would ever have allowed his young sisters to be left unattended when another male was present, even for a second, and he thought of his life in those days.

The mountains and valleys of his homeland had been harsh and the environment cruel and unforgiving. In summer the dust and heat were unbearable; in winter the snow piled up metres thick and the temperatures plummeted. Paramaz had now lived in Karekin's house long enough to know that the area in which he had been brought up had several names – the Armenian plateau – Eastern Anatolia – Northern Kurdistan – the name given dependent on politics rather than geography. The farmers had been mainly Armenian; the villagers a mixture of Turks, Armenians and Assyrians, while around the villages and farms, were large, nomadic, Kurdish families.

Paramaz recalled the last time he had seen his father. He was ten years old – or had he been nine? His family of two younger sisters, lived in a tiny ramshackle mud-brick house consisting of one large room, in a small village largely Armenian, with only one earthen street and perhaps twelve houses ranged on each side.

There were no shops, government buildings or officials. Some of the larger houses had gardens and orchards behind them. Paramaz knew that his father had no land and hired himself out to the local farmers when they needed extra hands, having to compete for the work with itinerant Kurds and poor Assyrians. He also did odd jobs in the village for tiny sums or extra provisions.

The family were deeply religious, but it was a religion of superstition and rote. His mother would cross herself at any opportunity. She knew the Lord's Prayer, and the highlight of her year was the days of

Easter when the whole family would walk to the nearest church which was about a day's journey away, and spend the three days of Easter in someone's barn. However she understood little of what it all meant.

Here in the deep countryside there was no easy mixture of races and cultures so dear to the Ottoman ideal in Constantinople. Here was hatred and a dislike of neighbours who did not have the same beliefs. They spoke each other's languages but understood little of their own religion let alone that of their neighbour's. There was neither church nor mosque; yet the villagers seemed to cling ever more passionately to their differences, even though there was so little dividing them.

Paramaz's thoughts were not as clear as this of course, though ever since coming to the city these questions had been troubling him. He conjured up in his mind the last time he had seen his father.

He and one of the other village boys were bringing the village sheep and goats back down from grazing in the hills in the late afternoon. When they arrived back in the village they saw some rough-looking bearded men in the street with rifles over their shoulders and belts of ammunition draped round them. They were holding down a man on his knees whom Paramaz recognised as one of the wealthier villagers. Standing to one side were a few old men and all the women of the village, amongst whom Paramaz saw his mother. As the boys stopped to stare, a shot rang out and the man sank to the ground with blood pouring from his head. The women screamed. Paramaz and his companion began to run up, but his mother, Zabelle, saw him and shouted at them to go and hide. Any young male, even a child, could be killed in such situations.

Paramaz ran off and hid in one of the orchards – the sheep and goats, left abandoned, simply milled about bleating. There were more screams and shouts but no more shots, and Paramaz, whose curiosity far outweighed any fear, crept out, came between the houses and looked out at the street. He now saw that several men of the village, including his father, were standing on the other side of the street, watched – or was it guarded – by another bearded man carrying a rifle and wearing a Russian fur hat. Everybody, including the women, was listening to a man who was standing on the decrepit old horse trough in the middle of the street.

Paramaz drew closer, fascinated. He had never seen a man quite like this before. He had a little goatee beard and wore rimless spectacles. The man wore a smart buttoned-up cotton shirt with what looked like a bit of patterned cloth hanging from the neck and clean breeches tucked into high leather boots. He also wore a Russian fur hat rather than a fez.

Paramaz knew Armenian though he and his parents usually talked Turkish together, but this man was talking in a strange Armenian dialect, which even at that young age Paramaz recognised as Russian Armenian just over the border. He picked out many words and phrases as the interminable speech went on.

"Thus will die any other ignorant traitors to the great cause... sacred motherland and the right ... justice for all ... act as one and take our future into our own ... liberty, equality and ... better to die as free men than live as slaves ... brothers, join us in ......"

They stood and watched silently, careful to avoid looking at their dead neighbour, or the woman still weeping beside him. Paramaz crept up closer. Then the man raised his hand and the whole troop of armed strangers burst into a rousing song, quite unlike the gentle crooning songs Paramaz usually heard from the women, or the lyrics sung by the men.

There was another silence as Paramaz made his way to where his mother and two little sisters were standing. At this point, Paramaz recalled how his father had crossed the road and had come up to the family group and said –

"I'm afraid, Zabelle my soul, that I will have to go with them. Paramaz, bring me my rifle."

"If that's what God wills," were the only words his mother said, bending her head.

Paramaz came back from collecting his father's rusty old rifle and handed it to him. His father gave one look into Zabelle's eyes, turned and without a word or any other sign, or even a touch, joined the strangers who were already beginning to file out of the village. Paramaz never saw his father again.

Two years later – or was it three – a small contingent of Turkish soldiers appeared in the village. There were again screams and shots, but this time the few remaining males over fifteen were immediately shot and the village had to be cleared of Armenians within two hours. Paramaz recalled the terror – the screams and wails of the women – the decisions over what should be taken – bread or valuables. Paramaz's mother was spared that problem, at least, as they owned nothing of value. The soldiers were already escorting a sad and bedraggled group of women, children and old men who stood silently in a long line, holding their sacks, bags and luggage.

There was nothing to take – a few pots and pans, some threadbare cloth and their bedding. The house was simply abandoned. Those few neighbours who were not Armenians stayed shut up in their homes with their window shutters closed as the Armenians trudged away. Paramaz didn't have any idea what was happening.

As Paramaz lay thinking about it all, he realised that he might have been killed there and then. There were no young men left in the village, and those who were fourteen or more had all been shot. At the age of twelve, robust and well-developed for his age, he was lucky to be passed over.

The march started, and the crowds struggled over the harsh terrain; other small groups joined the long line of hopeless people as they passed through villages on the route. People died by the wayside from lack of food and above all fresh water. His little sister Yester, by then eight, was the first in the family to fail to awake in the morning after a night on a bare hillside.

They had been walking for about ten days, and it was already early evening when a marauding band of men on horseback came galloping up, yelling and shouting. Kurds? Turks? Paramaz had no idea. Some of the men jumped off their horses and grabbed his other sister, ten-year-old Maneh. Paramaz recalled with a mixture of hate and deep shame that his mother had screamed and ran back but was immediately held and thrown down. The few Turkish soldiers who were still with this group bringing up the rear, simply grinned as they passed Zabelle, who was being continuously raped by the side of the road in full view of everyone who passed, and of Paramaz himself, cowering hidden behind a bush.

After a time of horror – twenty minutes or was it twenty years, the men rode off with Maneh slung across a horse, and with a last burst of shots into Zabelle's bleeding body, leaving Paramaz alone behind the bush as darkness fell. Paramaz had done nothing. He had not even shouted. He had been twelve, he could surely have done something. He lay on his bed hating himself rather than those unknown men. Why him? Why his poor family? Why not these pampered rich people in their city? Why not the man with the goatee beard who had spoken about some great cause for which his father had been made to fight? What harm had his family ever done to anyone? What had caused such a horror to be visited on them, and not on others?

Paramaz shed no tears as he lay on his bed in the Avakian house. He was grateful to Karekin for having rescued him from the back streets of Aleppo and from his perpetual hunger. But, perhaps it had come too late to save his soul as well as his body. Mixed in with the gratitude, and already beginning to overwhelm it, was a hatred and envy of the comfortable bourgeois existence of this family. He overheard their conversations, the political discussions about independence, about the Armenian political parties, their pity for the orphans and their slaughtered parents, and he thought why not them? We could only think of where our next meal was coming from. What had any of this got to do with us? Yet it was we who had had to pay the price.

Left alone in that wilderness as the pathetic line of women and old men moved on, he had not even been able to arrange a proper burial for his mother's broken body. He had covered it with some stones and set off at random away from the march. Within a day, with the beginnings of delirium setting in, a nomadic Kurdish family, on their way towards new pastures, came across him lying exhausted without the will to go any further.

Paramaz was saved by that family, but he became their servant. Being uncircumcised, it was clear that he was an Armenian survivor and he was abused and treated badly by the men from the start. But there was a rough 'campfire' tolerance of him so long as he did what he was told and went nowhere near the girls and the women.

But after escaping from them and arriving in Aleppo, he was no longer able to differentiate between a kind act and a cruel one.

In another part of the house, Seta was still thinking confusedly about Paramaz, while Paramaz lay thinking about his own family. His simple kindly father, having to abandon his family for some great cause; his two little sisters whom he had failed to protect; his raped and slaughtered mother whom he had abandoned without raising a finger. He should have wept, but the tears would no longer come. He thought of these city people, who were so indifferent towards the simple villagers who had only wanted to get on with their lives. He rejected them all – the intellectuals, the political leaders, the teachers, the revolutionaries and all those who had wanted to change his life without any real feeling for him or his family. Finally, he hated this cosy family with its thoughtless free-thinking tolerance, their intellectual superiority and their elitist life. He could not forgive them for the horror inflicted by evil and thoughtless men on his family, and not on theirs.

CHAPTER 9

Smyrna – the Quaysides

Elena was hungry like everyone else on board the ship that had brought them all from Sevastopol. She had no money and nothing to offer the men in the little rowing boats, loaded almost to overflowing with fruit, nuts, bread and cheese, crowding round the refugee ships in the anchorage off Constantinople. She had watched as well-dressed but exhausted passengers in the ship immediately behind them shouted down over the side, haggling with the Turkish rowers in different languages.

Elegant-looking ladies lowered fur coats and wicker baskets containing jewels and gold pieces in exchange for food. But neither she, nor anyone else on board her vessel appeared to have anything to barter.

Her two small children, Anya and Andreas, were famished, but they had passed *beyond* the stage of complaining and sat listless and apathetic, leaning back against the bulwarks with their short legs outstretched on the deck. The ship's captain was a Greek, but the sailors were an amalgam of other races from all over the Eastern Mediterranean and *beyond*: men who were arrogantly referred to by western Europeans as 'Levantines.' These mariners were harassed and had been in a state of anxiety since their experiences in Sevastopol. There were no welcome sweets, or pieces of shared bread being offered on this boat to the children.

After Mikael and all the Russians on the vessel had disembarked in the evening, Elena was left very much on her own on the deck, with only some other Greek refugees who were also going on to Smyrna or even Athens. Early in the morning, the ship gave out a long mournful hoot and finally swung away from the line of ships stationary in the sea lanes off Constantinople, and steamed away into the Sea of Marmara. It was only then that the captain saw her on his rounds. Some food was at last provided for her and the children, which at least revived her body.

The ship steamed carefully through the narrow Dardanelles, past the site of the recent Gallipoli campaign on the right-hand side, and the ancient siege of Troy on the left, and moved into the open sea of the Aegean.

Eventually the ship slowly swung into the great inlet of the bay of Smyrna, and approached the long coastal stretch of the city. Elena saw a small harbour area, defined by an enclosing stone sea wall. It was crowded with small freighters, cargo vessels, rowing boats, boats with tall masts, tugboats and fishing boats, all jumbled together such that you could walk out quite far from the quayside into the centre of the sheltered part of the harbour, jumping from boat to boat. Elena wondered how boats in the middle wanting to leave the harbour managed to get out.

On either side of the harbour walls, a long extended corniche ran north and south right next to the sea. The sea lapped right up against the road, only six inches below the road surface. Bollards placed at intervals were the only visible sign separating it from the road. Other boats, small and large, were moored here and there along the whole stretch, on either side of the harbour itself. With low hills in the background and the ruined Byzantine fort sitting high on a pinnacle to the south, the view was dramatic. The main stone buildings of the town lay along the seafront on the other side of the road, facing the sea, with a line or more behind, while all the residential quarters, still mainly wooden, clustered up the hillsides behind the town. Church spires and the minarets of the mosques rose from the middle of these tangled buildings. Dramatic – but of course nothing to match the great architectural wonders of Constantinople.

Elena only absorbed this in a superficial way. She was, naturally enough, in a state of anxiety. She had little idea of the history of this town or of the continuity of Greek life and culture in the region. All she knew was that here was a place they would be welcomed into a new family. But if this failed and her husband's brother no longer lived here, or did not want to help, what would she do then?

The ship nosed its way into a spot within the harbour, and finally tied up against the quayside. The wide quay was a continuation of the same corniche on either side, but with rails laid into the road and horse-drawn trams moving up and down. Some carried passengers, but most were flat cars carrying goods of all kinds. On the other side of the quay, there were low stone buildings running all the way along, with great green and white awnings stretching down at an angle from below their first floor windows and balconies. These went out over the road, covering almost a third of it, and were then attached to poles set into holes in the street. Under these awnings passed a continual stream of people. Set back against the buildings were tables and chairs, weighing machines, scales for gold – a whole outdoor office where business transactions were constantly taking place.

Elena stood up and moved over to the side as the ship berthed. She held on to her worn suitcase while each child hung on to her skirt. Dirty and dishevelled, the children stared with huge famished eyes. They clutched their mother's skirt with one hand and their own little tin suitcases with the other, as they had been doing for days. Elena tried to focus on the crowds on the quay.

Several large family groups were waiting there on the quayside, staring up at the ship as it docked. This ship was one of the first boats to arrive from Sevastopol, almost a week ago. The news had flashed round the town, and those families expecting friends or relatives among the refugees had come down to the harbour quays.

Elena had no idea what to expect or whether any of these family groups waiting and looking up at the ship were her children's relatives. She had written from Sevastopol in the Crimea, but who knew whether her letters had reached their destinations in the current chaotic conditions. The gangplank finally came down.

While there were a fair number of Greek refugees from Odessa and Crimea on the boat, Elena was the only single woman with two small children. As she stepped off the gangplank, there was a rush towards her by a family group. Young boys in ragged shorts grabbed her suitcase, women dressed in black dresses embraced her indiscriminately, chattering away in a Greek dialect she could scarcely understand, while other women picked up the bewildered Andreas and Anya, passing them from one to another, smothering them with wet kisses.

It was all too much for the children. They had been scared and hungry for too long to be able to distinguish quickly between good events and bad ones. They suffered the emotional attentions, the kisses, the minty bad breath, getting more and more apprehensive. Andreas was old enough to cope, but Anya had difficulty holding her urine, separated as she was from both her brother and her mother. For Elena too it was almost too much. She burst into floods of tears, but they were tears of deep relief, enveloped as she was in an emotional welcome, which she had never expected.

For this Greek family in Smyrna, Elena was not just a member of the family in distress, she also, personified the whole unfolding Greek tragedy overtaking the widespread communities surrounding the Black Sea. Already Pontine Greeks, as well as the Greeks of nearby villages, had been trickling into the Smyrna region – and everyone in the town knew of the tragedies hitting so many of these Greek communities. They all wanted to give her the warmest possible welcome – genuinely felt – knowing that she had come through a crisis and survived. It never occurred to them that they too might soon be facing a similar situation.

The harbour road was a confusion of bustling activity. There was no moment of stillness anywhere in the scene. A few Turkish women, more fully dressed in long layered skirts, sat selling fruit and nuts from great baskets were perhaps the calmest element. Interspersed among the office buildings were cafes and restaurants with trees at their front; under the shade of these trees, men played tavloo at the tables with great spirit and gusto, lifting their hands to heaven as they threw the dice, yelling out imprecations at the wrong numbers turning up.

Elena stared as she walked, surrounded by the smiling, laughing family all talking at once. She saw the Greek flag everywhere on the main buildings. There were Greek soldiers strolling in the streets, completely relaxed, even those on policing duties, giving an air of permanence and safety to the urban scene. The produce on sale at the market showed there had been an abundant harvest in the Autumn. The weather was benign, even though it was so late in the year.

The family party turned off the sea road and began walking towards the centre of the town. They began to pass the great open markets of the bazaar area of the town as they headed on towards the Greek quarter. These markets exuded wildly varied smells – the aroma of the plump Smyrniote grapes, the famous fresh figs of the area, the apricots and all manner of other fruits and cheeses. Then, as they passed along the narrow streets, they were enveloped by a strong smell of roses. This was where the sweet somewhat sickly rose jam, so well-known through-out the Empire, was made.

Smyrna was always known to the Turks as the '*giavour*' city. This was not only because there was a majority of Christian Ottomans in the town, but because of the large number of European foreigners who had settled there as well. These foreigners were merchants and busi-ness men who had gravitated there from all over Europe, for, until the Great War, Smyrna had been the main exporting seaport of the whole of the Ottoman Empire. This area of western Anatolia was very fertile and well farmed, and all the copious goods of the interior had poured into the city, largely carried in on great camel trains, which made their stately way through the town to the warehouses of the merchants, right opposite the place the ships were moored on the other side of the wide quays. The caravans arrived daily, some from further locations, carry-ing fruit, tobacco, silk, carpets and sometimes spices. Furthermore it was a two-way process, as the same ships that took away this produce to Europe, returned with luxury goods and practical industrial tools from Europe. Those same camels then carried these, as they plodded back into the interior with their loads.

As Elena soon discovered, the whole region around Smyrna was a wonderful area, without many roads, but with shaded paths and lanes which wound their way through lush valleys, past prosperous villag-es – some Greek, some Turk – over beautifully arched Ottoman stone bridges, eventually ending at a road leading to the town. And everyone – Greek, Turk, Armenian, Jew and foreigner – made money, played cards, danced, gambled and laughed, as the trade went on and Smyrna prospered in the sun.

Of course, Elena did not take all this in at once, but she felt the warm and tolerant atmosphere of the city, starting with the warmth of the wel-come she had received from her children's uncles and aunts. After all the months of living hand to mouth, of anxiety and suppressed panic, she felt, from the very first day, that at last she was at peace.

As the days passed, Elena began to smile again – the new Year of 1920/21 arrived and passed and all was well. Andreas began to attend local boys' school and Anya, to flesh out. Elena settled into this large bustling family; she made friends and a few enemies; though these were short-lived. She began at last to believe that her wanderings were at an end, and that she and the children would not face any further upheav-als.

CHAPTER 10

Harry Bridgeman

Harry Bridgeman, the English naval captain who had appeared so fortuitously in Sevastopol and had taken the Countess Androva and her son Alexei on board his destroyer, duly disembarked all his Russian civilian passengers and reported to the British naval authorities in the city. There he learnt that the Admiralty had instructed him to take his flotilla home and report to London.

After landing and handing over his command in Portsmouth, Harry went home for a few days leave. His father had visibly aged and appeared to have mellowed. He was clearly proud of his son's achievements in the navy, a pride he tried but failed to hide, while Harry was no longer quite so anxious to gain his father's approval, so their relationship improved. In due course Harry reported at the Admiralty, where he was directed to the intelligence section and was interviewed immediately by an administrative officer.

"Ah – Captain Bridgeman – I'm afraid that now that the war is over, your talents are going to be needed elsewhere than on board a fighting ship. We need you back in Naval Intelligence."

"Yes, sir – well I can't say I'm happy, but I do understand."

"Good. I think you'll find it fairly interesting. You have been seconded to the Imperial Occupation Forces at Constantinople as naval liaison officer to the current British commander of those forces – General Charles Harington."

"Sir. Yes ... well, I saw him during the few days I spent in the city, after Sevastopol."

"Right Harry, you'll get all your travel documents from my secretary. We have already booked you with a sleeper on the Simplon-Orient Express, and you leave in a couple of days. I think you are going to find that you will have a lot to do. We have several ships now based in the Straits. Harington, needs to keep in close touch with the navy. We have all our usual problems with the French. On top of that our Welsh wizard Lloyd George is falling over himself to cosy up to the Greeks who can't make up their minds what they want either. It's a mess over there. On the other hand, the Turks are totally cowed, and you are going off to what is undoubtedly the quietest part of the British Empire at the moment."

"The British Empire?"

"Well, not technically of course – but this is how it usually starts. First, a so-called temporary occupation, backed up by continual statements about how we wish to leave as soon as possible."

Both men laughed as Harry rose, put his cap on, saluted and turned to leave.

Back home, as he watched Harry packing, William Bridgeman ordered his wife to prepare a small trunk of tinned provisions, which Harry protested was unnecessary.

"Look Harry, I was chatting with some army friends in the Club, and it appears the Orient Express is still not running with its old efficiency as it goes through the Balkans. There are frequent breakdowns and hold-ups. Neither this new country – ah, yes, Yugoslavia, nor Bulgaria, are settled. People can say what they like about the Hapsburgs, but they did at least provide some sort of stability to that powder keg of a region."

"Ah, father, you are an incorrigible old romantic – pitying the plumage but forgetting the dying bird. We need thriving new nations now, not the old failed empires."

"Oh yes! – where the hell is the nation-state in this new Yugoslavia? Never mind, my boy, just take it from me, we are all going to be sorry that the power of Vienna has gone, at one end of the Balkans, and that of Constantinople may well be going at the other end."

And so, armed with some gold sovereigns, a small trunk packed with tinned food and several bottles of wine, Harry got onto the coach at Victoria station which ran all the way to Constantinople, first attached to the Golden Arrow express to Paris, and then shunted round to join the Simplon-Orient. The journey, which before the war took only three nights was now taking six days or more.

Harry knew there were some experiences you had to have on a trip like this. That included dinner in the famous art deco restaurant at the Gare de Lyon before the train left for Milan. Harry was still in a bit of an alcoholic daze when he awoke the next morning. Having forgotten to pull down the heavy green blind, he looked straight out of the window onto snow, mountains and pine trees, as the train wound its way slowly down through the Alps and into Italy. What a wonderful way to wake up, he thought.

Breakfast that morning in the dining car was in the company of a Levantine merchant – at least that was how Harry thought of him – still retaining the racial prejudices of his class – but he found the man interesting – chatting fairly freely to him about the trip, a journey he had already done several times since the line was reopened a year ago.

"And have there been any problems on the line?" asked Harry.

"Certainly, my dear sir, I believe that in the first few months there were several attempted attacks on the train by brigands in Bulgaria –

rather like those wild west films."

"Come, that sounds unlikely in this day and age."

"Well, I haven't had first hand evidence but I was on the train myself a few months ago, when the engine ran out of coal somewhere between Belgrade and Sofia. The staff on the train had to trudge to the nearest God-forsaken village; it was in the middle of winter and in heavy snow. They didn't have enough ready cash to pay the villagers, and the train just sat there in the middle of nowhere while they went round collecting money from the international passengers."

"Good heavens! Did you get your money back."

"Well we were all given receipts of course, but frankly I didn't bother to collect my contribution, which ... er ... was rather small as I didn't have much on me. Anyway it took a further six hours whilst the villagers brought wood on what seemed to be their only cart. Some of this wood had to be chopped there and then by the side of the rails. However, we made it to Sofia, through the spectacular defile, you are going to see soon."

A few days later, Harry was up early in the morning as the great train moved through the empty treeless plains of Eastern Thrace and approached the capital. Some thirty miles before they reached any substantial buildings of any kind, the train steamed alongside a military camp – lines of white tents neatly laid out with the blue and white flag of the Kingdom of Greece flying from the main flagpole.

When the train was not much more than fifteen minutes from the gap cut into the great city walls for the railway line, Harry was still standing at the windows of the corridor facing the inland side. He saw small villages, and soon small towns, as the train passed by platforms already filled with passengers waiting for the next local train. Most of the men still wore the fez, but some were sporting trilbys and panama hats. Harry got excited and his heart beat that little bit faster. He was at last arriving by land to the city which heralded the approach of the Orient, and which had defied every attempt at invasion by his military colleagues five years before from the peninsula of Gallipoli.

Sirkeci station – the terminus of the European railway system and the final destination of the coaches of the Compagnie Internationale des Wagons-Lits et des Grands Express Européennes. Porters bustled about – whistles – loud noises – crowds and shouts – enormous noise, more than seemed reasonable for what was a fairly small station. Harry was momentarily anxious and disorientated as several porters offered their services. For a moment he thought of Sevastopol – and then a quiet voice – "Excuse me sir, Captain Bridgeman?"

The British Empire, with that inimitable cool efficiency and equally inimitable arrogance, suddenly manifested itself on the platform.

Harry turned to see an impeccably neat British naval rating in a spotless white uniform, who saluted as Harry nodded. The young sailor called up two porters, standing to one side, whom he had already engaged. Harry, despite the layers of irony behind his feelings, felt highly relieved by the presence of the Empire at work.

The weather was cold but bright and clear as Harry looked back as he crossed over to the Asian side in a naval launch. Since the end of the war, his boat had passed through the straits into and out of the Black Sea several times, but the great view of Stamboul with its domes and minarets against the light blue sky had never ceased to move him. And so he arrived in Moda – the European quarter of Uskudar on the Asian side where the British 28th Division had its headquarters, and where he was to be stationed temporarily, though the division's offices were already moving to the European side.

The next day Harry, now in full naval uniform, re-crossed the straits and made his way to the old Turkish military academy – the Harbiye – where General Harington had his headquarters and which ultimately was the base for the whole allied operation in what was left of the Ottoman Empire.

When Harry was let in to General Harington's office he saluted and motioned to sit down, as the General looked up and said politely – "Ah! Captain Bridgeman of the navy – Colonel William Bridgeman's son I believe. I trust, sir, you can wait a moment, while I finish this report. Won't take a minute."

Harry sat and looked at the man sitting in front of him and saw almost a caricature of a Great War general, with highly polished knee high black boots, a Sam Browne belt, leaving a clear space for medals and ribbons on the left, the high flat cap with the gold braid round the peak and, above all, the impeccably brushed white moustache.

"Well, Captain Bridgeman, I understand you are to be my liaison officer with the Admiral. I would like to start by putting you fully in the picture as to the situation here in Constantinople. Have you been following what has been going on?"

"Not really, sir. Although I have been in and out of the straits several times since the end of the war, my station has been mainly in the Black Sea."

"Well, it's difficult for anyone to encapsulate in a few sentences the last two years since the armistice of Mudros ended our war with the Ottomans, but I'm going to try. Did you have a good trip, by the way? You will have a coffee – we all drink it Turkish style."

After ordering coffee, the general continued –

"The first point is that in October 1918 the Ottoman Empire was completely defeated. There was no army left at all. Those scoundrels Enver and Djemal fled, while that sinister bastard Talaat escaped to

Berlin."

Harry shifted a little in his seat. There was something a little didactic – schoolmasterish – about this man. He felt he was going to be in for a long lecture, and wished he could have lit up a cigarette.

"Anyway that left only the new Sultan Mehmed VI, who had just succeeded. By God – I saw him then, and I still see him from time to time. He's an ugly, sad old man and one senses the weight of the ending of the 500 year-old dynasty on his stooped shoulders. But it's an interesting situation here. In Vienna and Berlin, the Hapsburgs and Hohenzollerns collapsed immediately, blamed by their native populations for leading them into the Great War. Here in Constantinople, however, people knew that it was the Young Turks, and specifically Enver and Talaat, not the dynasty, which had acted so unwisely. I'm not saying, Bridgeman, that the dynasty has survived intact. The splendour of the Ottoman throne has gone for good. The great Bayram receptions at the Dolmabahce palace are a travesty. Few people attend. Poor Mehmed, even though the sick man of Europe has outlived the Austrian, Russian and German empires, he has no army left and relies totally on cooperation with us and our allies. Meanwhile Turkish nationalism is on the rise in the interior."

"Well sir, this is all very clear and understandable, but what about the Christians and all the other minorities. The Jews, I know, were always deeply loyal to the Ottomans. Surely the Greeks and Armenians too could rally to the throne." Harry said.

"My dear Bridgeman, I was here when that cocky French general – Franchet d'Espery – arrived in that first year. You know the chap, the one all the Tommies on the western front used to call 'desperate Frankie.' He landed at the quay below the Galata Bridge in a great fanfare of Christian triumph. Some bloody Greek idiot arranged for a white horse to be brought down to the quayside – and he, poor simpleton, mounted it and rode that white horse through the streets all lined by cheering Greeks up to the French embassy in *Bey*oglu."

"Well, sir, what of it?"

"Bridgeman, my good fellow, it was a clear reference to the entry of Mahmud II, the conqueror of the city in 1453, who rode to the Byzantine Palace on a white horse. People in this city have long historical memories, and everyone – Greek, Turk, Armenian and Jew – understood perfectly well what was being suggested."

"Yes, very well sir, I understand, but I ask again – knowing what could be the alternative, why don't they rally to the Ottomans?"

"Well, that's what this briefing is all about. The Greeks are mesmerised by the idea of an enlarged Greek nation-state. The new Greek Patriarch has decreed that there is to be no more cooperation with the Ottoman state. You will see the Greek flag everywhere in the city – it's like a bloody great party going on. Being short of British or French troops, I am myself in command of a few Greek brigades to help me out. The compromises and cooperation of centuries have been entirely forgotten by everyone, with people saying that it is impossible for Turk and Greek to live together – what the hell do they imagine they have been doing for the last 400 years?."

"And the Armenians?"

"Yes, well, they follow the Greeks like sheep. But for them, there is the experience of the terrible events that befell their people in Eastern Anatolia in 1915 and 1916, which has soured them, understandably, to the dynasty. In fairness most of their intelligentsia, at least those that are left, are perfectly well aware that the culprit was the small group of Young Turks and not the dynasty. However, they remain a deeply confused people who have been led astray for twenty years by western-educated nationalists, clamouring for an impossible to achieve Eastern Anatolian independent state, all in areas where they were never in a clear majority. Look, it is my opinion that their best interests would have been served, and would still be better served, if they had rallied behind the dynasty."

"It sounds a bit too neat, and not something that ordinary people would think of, sir. After all, didn't their troubles all start with Sultan Abdul Hamid."

"Yes, well you're quite right, Harry, I have gone a bit over the top and digressed a bit. I have, however, at last got to the point. I am going to ask that, as well as your naval duties, you live in the city and report to me on a monthly basis on the support or otherwise amongst the Turkish population for the Kemalists."

"And who are they, sir, are they the followers of that general in the interior who did so well against us at Gallipoli?"

"That's right, he's our baby. Harry, we have two great games going on here in Constantinople. First there is the great game of nation-states. Who is to control this city and all that it stands for? This city and the waterway it controls has cost the world more trouble and more blood and passion over the last thousand years than almost any other spot on earth. And now suddenly we are in control – we, Harry, we, the British Empire. What couldn't we do if we wanted.

However there is a second game going on – the conflict between the Ottomans and this city on the one hand, and their purely Turkish subjects in Anatolia on the other. We can well leave the game of nation-states to our own Lloyd-George and Curzon, but on this second matter we need to keep our own local eye on the problem. Harry, this is where you come in, as I need, discreetly, to monitor the situation all the time.

If you've finished your coffee - it's an absolutely essential part of any meeting or discussion in this city by the way – I'll cut this short. Since we took over control of the police last year, and since the Turkish National Congress was convened in the interior, there has been a steady trickle of defections of Turkish officers and statesmen joining Mustapha Kemal in Ankara. Meanwhile the 27th Division has been recalled and I am losing men daily to this hasty demobilisation, and am having to rely more and more on Greek troops. It is a recipe for disaster and we have to be vigilant. So I want a monthly report from you on the atmosphere in the city."

"Very well, sir."

"Right – well now, go and see my adjutant, and he'll discuss accommodation with you. I don't want you either with the 28th in Moda, or on the *Iron Duke* with the Admiral, but here in the city. He'll also organise a desk for you here at headquarters. Good luck, Bridgeman."

And so it was that Harry went to take up accommodation in an apartment arranged for him in Pera near Taksim Square. From this base he entered into the fabric and life of Constantinople – a colourful, vibrant, fascinating city as it stood balanced on the edge of a number of a number of possibilities for its future, while facing the end of almost 2,000 years as a great Imperial capital.

CHAPTER 11

Sima at the Pera Palace

Whilst Olga continued to work at the Turkish Military hospital in Scutari, Sima stayed at home, occasionally going with Karakin in the mornings to help in the office. However, with Haik now able to do the translating and working daily throughout the holidays and Paramaz also available to help around the place, her services were no longer really needed, even though Karekin's business was booming. Imports of Lancashire cottons and muslins were in enormous demand, and the presence of all the allied forces added to the amount of money flowing into the economy. The office, in a small street parallel to the Grande Rue de Pera, was always a hive of activity.

But even though she no longer needed to work, Sima would often go into town to go shopping for Armineh and to meet friends. She would then usually call in at the office to be welcomed enthusiastically by Haik. With old social restraints breaking down, it was also possible for her to call at the Levonian offices that were nearby and go out for a coffee with George, who would give up whatever he was doing whenever she turned up.

The subject of a formal engagement would often arise, but was somehow always put off. Sima knew that the proposed marriage was right; she was already over twenty-three and past the age that most girls in the city were already married. She recognised that George was a reliable man and would prove to be a good father. Her mother was always at her to take the decision. So she even surprised herself by never finding the right occasion to agree to a formal engagement.

On this particular morning, some weeks after the afternoon when Vahan and Selim had turned up with the young Russian, Sima had arranged to meet an old school-friend – Kohar – for lunch, who was now married. The two friends were having a very pleasant afternoon window-shopping in the lower Pera area when it began to rain. Sima never knew why the thought occurred to her, but on the spur of the moment, she suggested that they walk to the Pera Palace hotel for some tea, though it was still quite a way, and Tokatlians would certainly have been closer and more convenient.

The little orchestra was playing as they entered the tearoom, filled as always with everyone in the world. British officers with wives or local girls, always Greek or Jewish; Frenchmen and Italians all part of the occupation forces; American, but not British sailors, who couldn't afford the prices; Greek ladies out shopping for the day; Armenian merchants and businessmen without wives; and the occasional Russian aristocrat and his party. However, amongst all this cosmopolitan throng, there were very few Turks.

The whole hotel was a kaleidoscopic spectacle in itself. In the tearoom and dining rooms at least twenty different languages could be heard at any one time, and the atmosphere was noisy and confusing.

Somewhat to her friend's surprise, Sima chose a table near the orchestra. Sima smiled broadly when she recognised Nicolai, and gave a shy half-wave when he looked up and caught her eye.

"My darling, who is that man you just waved at."

"Kohar, my soul, he's a Russian whom I met at home in Makrikoy a few weeks ago and who ..."

"How did he turn up – he looks interesting."

"He's a friend of Vahan Asadourian and ..."

"Who? Oh, you mean that boring young musician from the provinces. How are they connected?"

"I don't know. For heaven's sake, Kohar, don't keep interrupting. Shall we order tea?

"No cakes for me, my gorgeous girl, just some toast. I'll have to be going soon."

It was at this point that the little orchestra stopped playing, and some minutes later Nicolai arrived at their table, bowed to both women and took and kissed Sima's hand. Sima, so cool, so stiff, so carefully controlled, felt herself blushing and saw that Kohar – now a Mrs. Melkonian – was looking closely at her. She introduced them.

Nicolai immediately took Kohar's outstretched hand and kissed it. Conversation was a little formal and stilted until, somewhat reluctantly, Kohar rose, saying she had to go.

After Kohar left, a surprising change came over both of them. Nicolai opened up in a way that he had failed to do with anyone for the past two to three years. He talked about his father's estate in the Russian countryside – about the wide, slow-flowing river Don which was within walking distance of their house – about his English governess who had taught him English and good manners until he was twelve – about the military school he had been destined to enter had the Revolution not intervened. Sima too seemed to lose all the usual reserve she would normally feel with people outside her family. She found herself talking to this young man, who was almost a stranger, in the same open way that she chatted at home.

For Sima it soon became a wonderful liberating experience and an emotion she had never felt before overcame her. At first, it was the simple pleasure of communicating with someone outside the family as fully as she could do at home, but then she found the added pleasure of being free of family constraints in her conversation with this young stranger.

When Nicolai took breath and at last gave up on his nostalgic description of life on the Shevarno estate, Sima took over and spoke with feeling and warmth about her own family, about her trip to England with her father before the war, and about the current situation in Russia and in the Ottoman Empire. Nicolai listened in wonder. He had lived the fairly sheltered life of a minor Russian landowning family in the depths of the countryside, his days revolving round tutors – neighbours – the estate – and the village. Without any sisters and in a particularly remote part of the country, he had little experience of girls of his own class.

He had expected to acquire social skills once he arrived at the military academy in Kiev, however the February Revolution in 1917 had changed everything. Nicolai had stayed in Shevarno excitedly watching events unfold like most Russians. Then after the Bolshevik coup in October the situation changed yet again, and Nicolai's sympathies swung away from the Revolution. His father had died in the last doomed offensive against the Austro-German front mounted by the Provisional Government under the excitable but peculiarly ineffective leader – Kerensky, and Nicolai had craved action after the Bolshevik coup. He joined Denikin's Volunteer Army, followed by two years of vicious, civil war.

So Nikolai was having the totally new experience of sitting in a civilised atmosphere, talking easily with affection and warmth to a woman of his own age as educated and articulate as he was. As they spoke and listened to each other, he found his feelings increasingly engaged and a good deal deeper than simple admiration for an intelligent woman with whom he had such empathy.

Sima, meanwhile, to her own surprise, found that she was no longer concerned with the time or whether it was proper for her to remain in such intense communication with a young man in a public place for so long. She did not look round once to see if others were looking at them or consider whether she was compromising herself. For the first time, perhaps, she was totally and thoughtlessly enjoying herself. It would never have occurred to her that her own excitement might be the initial stirrings of 'love'. She was far too sensible. This meeting was simply a pleasant late afternoon encounter with an agreeable person of the opposite sex.

And so the afternoon wore on. Like all the citizens of Constantinople, the ability to make one tiny cup of coffee or one small tulip glass of tea last for hours was a common trait. The Turks raised this to an art, sitting almost the whole day with one cup of coffee before them, puffing occasionally at a narghileh. In any case, waiters throughout the city were used to tables being utilised like this all day.

It was the occasional silences which now began to arise between them that Sima found so confusing. She was not used to silences like this. For a start, silences in the Avakian family were very rare, but these silences were somehow different. Over the whole three hours that they were together, Sima and Nicolai never touched after the first formal kiss of the hand when they met, but there wasn't a moment that they had eyes for anyone else in the room, so they missed the arrival of a small party at the other end of the room.

Karekin walked into the large public tearoom, accompanied by his new business associate – Hovannes Levonian, George's father, followed respectfully a pace or two behind by Paramaz. The three of them sat down at a table and Karekin ordered coffee.

The two merchant houses of Avakian and Levonian were working well together in the thriving commercial atmosphere in the city. Karekin Avakian had his long-standing connections with Lancashire, and solid outlets here in the city. Hovannes Levonian complemented this with his connections in Germany and Central Europe, and his outlets in Smyrna and with the rest of the Greek community in Ionia. Everyone was expecting this purely business association to be cemented in due course by the marriage of Sima and George. The gossip factory of the Armenian community reckoned it was only a matter of time, but could not decide who was making the better match. The Avakians were of course the more old-established Bolsetsi family, but on the other hand there was something a little odd about them, something unconventional and a little weird – all that education for girls!

That afternoon, having finished their discussions on a proposed trading venture earlier than expected, Karekin had suggested repairing to the Pera Palace hotel to have a coffee together before they all went home. Haik had been deputed to close up the office, while Karekin decided to give Paramaz a taste of an interesting atmosphere outside the office environment. The tearoom orchestra had stopped , and the evening orchestra had not yet started – which is exactly how Karekin liked it.

"Well, well, Hovannes, enough of muslins and cotton sheets. We can leave your George to sort out the details of the contract with the British military. He can always get Haik to give him a hand if there are any translation difficulties."

"Ah, Karekin, my friend – Haik's a bright young lad. Perhaps we might consider a double connection sometime. My daughter Tamara is eighteen after all."

"Hovannes, my good fellow, whilst Tamara may indeed be ready to start thinking about marriage, Haik is much too young. Look, it must be more than five years before he can contemplate anything like that – and that will be far too late for Tamara."

"Well, you are quite right of course, Karekin, it was just a thought. Listen, did you hear that since the fall of Kars and the defeat of the Armenian republic army, the Kemalists have begun talks with the Soviets. You know all about politics – what does it all mean?"

"Yes I did hear it, and I believe it is quite true. The situation is extraordinary. We have the Ottoman government still functioning here in Bolis, while a totally separate government led by Kemal seems to be functioning quite openly in Anatolia, having repudiated the Treaty of Sevres which the Ottomans have signed, cosying up to the Reds and getting armaments from them. The Greeks could be in trouble."

Paramaz of course said nothing as the two elders chatted, bouncing between them all the current ideas about what was to happen to the city. Looking on at all the fashionable customers of the hotel around him, he had not failed to see Sima and the young man with her. He watched, saying nothing, until the moment came when a waiter came up to the young Russian and whispered in his ear.

"Look, my father," Paramaz interrupted the conversation as the young man stood, "Isn't that Miss Sima over there?" Karekin and Hovannes turned.

Summoned to resume his task with the evening orchestra, Nicolai had reluctantly got up.

"Miss Sima, I have to rejoin the orchestra, but I will insist on accompanying you home – it is already getting dark."

Sima rose, leaving a banknote on the table,

"No, Nicolai, I am quite all right. Despite everything, Constantinople is still a very safe city. I will be fine, it is really quite early. Please go – I too must leave and go straight home, so don't worry."

Sima extended her hand. Both of them were conscious that Sima had said 'Nicolai,' and not addressed him more formally. Nicolai took her hand in both of his. Then – at that moment - to his own surprise and to hers, he did not bend to kiss it, as they both expected, but instead held it in both his hands, tightly, for a moment of time that was perhaps short, but also far too long for anyone watching.

Nicolai looking directly into Sima's eyes bowed and turned away towards the kitchens. Sima collected her bag and walked out to the front hall. Karekin and Hovannes stared. Paramaz sat silently, saying nothing.

CHAPTER 12

Mikael and Nairi

After Mikael's return from Sevastopol, he went home to his mother's house in the back streets of Makrikoy and proceeded to drift for months, unable to settle down to anything. His experiences in Russia had matured him. He had become a little more tolerant, and this was reflected particularly in his relationship with his mother. However those experiences had also unsettled him; regular civilian life now seemed to him to be dull and insipid, and he could not decide what he wanted to do. He and his mother, Vartouhi, were never going to be close.

She carried in her heart a deep resentment of her former husband's second family in Yedikule, and could never be reconciled and, indeed, as Mikael now realised, why should she? For his part, Mikael had renewed the friendly relationship with his father's half-Greek, half-Russian mistress, and mother to his half-brothers, and visited them fairly often. He never sought to hide this from his mother and Vartouhi saw this easy relationship as a further betrayal.

Vartouhi could never change in this respect and Mikael saw that she revelled in it; it had become a vital element in her sense of her own identity – the wronged, betrayed Vartouhi!

Mikael had a lot of his mother's harsh character and little of his father's easy-going and cheerful temperament. He also had his full share of her spiky pride. He desperately wanted to see Olga again but could not bring himself to walk up the hill and knock at the door of her house. She had made it clear she could not contemplate a long-term relationship with him. He imagined her house – surely brimming with superior servants – where he would only need to open his mouth to be despised and spurned by everyone.

There was no way that Mikael could have confided all this to his mother Vartouhi, but his young sister Nairi was different. She had refused to accompany him on his visits to Katya and the two boys in Yedikule. She had no objections for herself, but felt she owed at least this much loyalty to her mother. In almost all respects her character was closer to that of their father Avedis – tolerant and easy-going – though with an integrity which he had lacked. Reserved though he normally was, Mikael finally confided in her – in fact on the very same morning of the conversation he had had with his mother exploring the possibility of contact with the Avakians.

"But Mikael, my lovely brother, why don't you just go up to the house, ring the doorbell and ask to speak to her? If she's there, she'll come down and talk to you, and you can take it from there. If she is not there, you can leave your name and address, and ask her to drop you a note."

"Oh my God – impossible, Nairi – she said she didn't want to see me again."

"Nonsense, Mikael, my soul! You're simply crucifying yourself unnecessarily – that's not what you told me originally when you first came out of that hospital three years ago. Look, fine, if you don't want to go to the house – it's only fifteen minutes away for heaven's sake – then go and see if she is still working at the army hospital in Scutari."

"Nairi, my darling, if I go all the way to the Asian side just on the off-chance of seeing her it'll look as if I am desperately chasing after her."

"Well, brother, the fact is that you are and why should that upset her in any way. I should be so lucky to have such a wonderful man chasing after me."

"I can't do it. She's a wonderful girl – but she's an Avakian daughter. I can offer her nothing. Oh God, it's all so hopeless."

"Right! I think you're talking utter rubbish – its inverted snobbery. If she's such a nice girl, as you've always claimed, she'll love seeing you again and to hell with her family if that is worrying you. Look – listen, I've got to go to work now in *Beyoglu*, but this afternoon after work, I'll pop over to Uskudar, and see if I can meet her at the hospital."

"Nairi – that's ridiculous – you'll do no such thing, I absolutely forbid it."

Mikael squirmed with embarrassment at the thought of the humiliation for his beloved sister, of a brush-off from Olga. But Nairi had a mind of her own. She was nearly twenty. She had learnt to type and was now working in a typing agency which had daringly started employing girls for the first time. They worked in a small office just off the Grande Rue de Pera under the eye of a severe madame, strictly segregated from the men, of course. Nairi felt it was time that her gloomy brother had some outlet outside the family. She was aware of his restlessness, and believed that his obsession with Katya and their two half-brothers was unhealthy. She left for work quite determined to act.

The defeat of the Ottomans and the arrival of a western Christian army of occupation in Constantinople had totally changed the culture of the city. This was particularly true for the Greeks, Armenians and Jews. Girls, though not perhaps those of the best families, were now taking up office work in the Pera district, though the more old-fashioned families made sure their daughters avoided situations where they might be alone with men. As a result, typing agencies employing girls were proliferating. These establishments paid badly, as they had a large captive labour force. There were far more people wanting this sort of all-female environment for their daughters than places available.

That afternoon after work, Nairi strolled down to the Galata bridge. The old Ottoman sense of security – that certainty that no woman would ever be molested in the streets of Bolis – had gone for ever. British and American seamen, often drunk, staggered about in the streets. Soldiers from the Occupation forces swaggered arrogantly, often accosting single women. Impecunious and desperate-looking Russians were everywhere. The Ottoman police, now managed by the British, were powerless. So Nairi kept her eyes down as she walked to the bridge to take the ferry across.

As she stepped off the ferry at the Uskudar station, she wondered at her decision to go. She had never met this girl, she didn't even know if she was still working at the army hospital. It had been nearly three years since Mikael had last seen her. Even if she was still there, people in this profession worked in shifts, and she might not be on duty.

However, it was a beautiful afternoon. The boat ride past Leander's Tower to the Asian side was an abiding wonder. Unlike Mikael and most other Bolsetsi, Nairi never lost the thrill of seeing that incomparable panorama, that superb skyline. Nairi took deep breaths as she walked up to the rather forbidding hospital building, determined to enjoy the afternoon regardless of what might transpire.

As it turned out, Olga was 'on duty' and, unusually, she was not currently in the operating room or very busy, so far as the receptionist knew. The receptionist was a stunning Turkish girl – Nairi had a good eye for feminine beauty. Turkish girls of good families, while still not prepared to be nurses, were beginning to work in administrative capacities in the hospital. She asked no questions and arranged for one of the attendant messenger boys to go and fetch nurse Avakian.

Olga, who hadn't immediately connected the name 'Nairi Sarafian' with Mikael came into the visitors reception room in which Nairi was the only occupant. Olga immediately saw the resemblance and recognised that this must be Mikael's sister. For her part Nairi looked up and saw a beautiful woman in a nurse's uniform which somehow looked more elegant and stylish than everyone else's. She also saw a beautiful warm smile emerge, as Olga walked up to her with her hand outstretched.

"You must be Mikael's sister – I'm Olga Avakian. Will you have a coffee? My, I haven't seen Mikael for three years. How is he? What is he doing?"

There was no hesitation, no awkwardness, no uncertainty. Olga rattled on in great Avakian style, as Nairi managed to get in the occasional word as to Mikael's current welfare. Nairi was charmed and overwhelmed. And then, without a word or any suggestion from Nairi, Olga invited Nairi to come to tea at home that very next day and to bring Mikael with her.

"I haven't seen Mikael since he left the hospital three years ago. What has he been doing with himself? You must, both of you, come to tea tomorrow. It's a Friday so even if you work, you'll surely be off in the afternoon. You know our house don't you – it's only a short cab ride away up the hill ..."

"Well that would be lovely, but you know I'm not so sure that I shouldn't first ..."

"No, no, I insist. Tell Mikael that I miss our long chats – no excuses – I insist, any time after three. My mother will be there, but I doubt if there will be anyone else other than the family. I look forward to it."

Not long after all this, Olga had to return to work. Nairi, suffering badly from the full blast of the Avakian personality, and Olga's own extra brand of breathless charm, took the ferry back to the Galata bridge. Instead of staring and enjoying the views as she usually did, she mused on her experience. Nairi was not naïve, she saw the beauty and the elegance, but she also saw that while Olga might have a depth *bey*ond the surface charm, it was not focussed on her brother. She knew, also however, that he would not be snubbed by this girl, she was not that sort.

She took the train home, determined that she would send Mikael on his own to tea the next day, and really feeling rather pleased with herself.

CHAPTER 13

Breakfast at the Avakians

"Armineh, my soul, I have to tell you something but I want you to listen, my love, before you say anything," Karekin said to his wife the next morning as she got ready to go down to preside over the family breakfast,

"Well, get on with it, husband."

"Yesterday, Hovannes came to see me about some business matters – establishing ourselves with a branch office in Smyrna actually, and ... oh, yes ... after finishing our discussions we went to the Pera Palace to have coffee. There I, er ..."

"Yes, Karekin, what is it – you sound upset my dear."

"Well, I had not seen previously – but my attention was drawn to the other side of the tearoom. Sima was sitting there at a table with a young man – I think it was the young Russian you described to me who came here some weeks ago with young Vahan and Olga's Turkish friend."

"Karekin, Olga's friend's name is Selim as you well know. If you had the courage of convictions you are always impressing on me, you would refer to him by his name. Impossible as any future relationship might be, he is a good man. Now, as to your seeing Sima – what of it? Even I know that a young man and a young woman having tea with each other in public places is no longer something to be worried about. For God's sake, Karekin, you're the one who goes on at me about how things have changed. Look, Sima is much the most sensible of all my silly daughters. Now if that's all, I'm going down."

"Oh ... well ... er ... if you are sure that ..."

"Karekin, my soul, I'm so sorry my love, there's something more isn't there. I can see you are upset – I'm sorry, I won't interrupt again."

"Armineh, I watched them saying 'goodbye' to each other, as did Hovannes. This young Russian took her hand ..."

"And he bent down and kissed it – they all do that Karekin, it's quite normal they don't mean ... oh, sorry."

"Yes – well it's difficult for me to explain it so that it makes sense – but instead of shaking hands or bending and kissing as they do, he held them and they stared at each other for a very long moment. Armineh, I would probably have dismissed the whole thing without a further thought – but Hovannes was sitting next to me and I could see that he was shocked. After Sima and the other fellow parted, he made it clear that he expected an explanation."

There was a short silence between them as Armineh, no longer impatient, waited for Karekin to continue.

"I felt awful. I didn't know what to say. I mumbled something about a passing acquaintance. Hovannes might have been ready to pass it all off at that stage – but that simpleton Paramaz, who was with us, remarked that the young man had indeed come to our house with Vahan and Selim some weeks ago. It was like a red rag to a bull. Hovannes sort of bridled – anyway he was upset not only at the revelation that this was a young man who appeared to have been invited previously to our house, but even more when the name Selim was mentioned. You know how rumours go round the community about him and Olga. He was really most distressed, Armineh."

"How did your attention get drawn to them in the first place."

"It was Paramaz, you know how good his eyesight is, at least compared to mine."

"Oh – right, it was Paramaz was it? And it was he who mentioned the earlier meeting with this young man at our home."

"Yes – he really has no idea of diplomacy or tact."

"That's how you see it, do you? Well we'll discuss that later perhaps. Meanwhile, Karekin, I don't think you need to worry too much. Sima knows exactly what is necessary when it comes to relationships with young men. For the moment, I wouldn't worry. Believe me, Hovannes won't mention it to anybody – neither to George nor to his silly wife. On the other hand, I do think we need to bring this whole ongoing situation between Sima and George to a close. Sima must commit herself one way or another – this unmentioned understanding has gone on far too long. I'll speak to her."

Armineh hurried downstairs as Karekin, uncharacteristically, failed to tie his tie exactly right on the first attempt. He generally left these sorts of situations to Armineh, but on this occasion he recognised that he had felt humiliated in front of Hovannes and he wondered whether it was that humiliation that rankled, rather than a genuine worry for his daughter.

The usual Avakian noise no longer abated, even for a moment, as Karekin walked down the stairs. He walked round to his place and sat down.

"My tea please, Talin."

"Listen father," said Nerissa. "Every day we hear some new rumour. Everyone is in a permanent state of excitement. I have seen more Greek flags on the streets in one day than I've ever seen before. The University is permanently buzzing with all sorts of theories – what do you think?"

"I told you there is no ..." said Haik.

"Haik, be silent. You must learn not to interrupt. It is a form of bullying always to imagine that your view, whatever it might be, must be heard immediately. Listen to your elders and betters for once," snapped Armineh.

There was a short silence, as Haik nodded with a guilty smile, accepting the rebuke and turning to look at his father expectantly.

"Well – funnily enough I was just thinking about this as I was getting ready. I agree with you Nerissa, it is a very tricky and yet important situation. There are I believe four possibilities as to what could happen here. Talin, the white cheese please.

First – the British could revert to their centuries-old traditional policy of supporting the Ottomans. This would allow the Ottoman state to revive with a close alliance with the British Empire, and with a liberal constitution. Mustapha Kemal would represent the principal political party in the state. Now that Constantine is back in Athens, all that 'megali idea' of Venizelos could well be abandoned. I don't know what the eventual boundaries of the state would be, but Bolis would remain the capital of a new liberalised Ottoman state. This solution would be very acceptable to me."

"And what about Thrace and Adrianople," said Nerissa.

"I have no idea what the actual final boundaries would be. I'm just giving you possible options. Now, the second possibility is that the British switch their policy and go for a greater Greece and control of the area through a close alliance with them. If it worked, this of course would end up making Bolis a Greek city. I think this would be a more difficult solution for the British – firstly because Constantine is back in charge in Athens, and the English are suspicious of him, and secondly because the Greeks are not reliable allies and quite incapable of working co-operatively. I would not be quite so happy with this solution – for a start, if the recent events in Smyrna are truly as reported, I would fear for the remaining Turkish population here."

"Well, the Greeks taking over here would be fine for us wouldn't it?" said Olga.

"Yes, I suppose so, though the problem would then be what happens in Anatolia – some sort of Kemalist republic perhaps."

"All right baba, so far we have two possibilities – the capital of a liberal Ottoman revival, or a Greek city. And the third possibility?" said Nerissa.

"Well – a British protectorate over the city and the straits areas. You know how good they are at getting something for themselves out of these situations – like how they picked up Cyprus. This too would be great for us, but it is unlikely. I heard the French military attaché remark to a Turkish friend of mine at a reception that both he and his Italian counterpart had already warned their governments of the creation here of what he called a new 'Constantinobralter,' and would both work hard against that, even to the extent of supporting Ankara."

"Constantinobralter ! Oh God I just love that – that's great," said Haik.

"Finally, probably even less likely, but in my opinion a great alternative would be to make Bolis the capital city of the new League of Nations. A lot of people have been suggesting it. It would make an ideal international city. The only city in the world that is both in Europe and Asia. What a great solution – but somehow in this Eurocentric world, those westerners won't see it that way – so it will probably end up being Geneva or Brussels or somewhere equally boring."

"It's all speculation baba isn't it?" said Olga. "Whatever happens, we ourselves can't do anything about it, so our own ideas are immaterial."

"No, no, not at all Olga," said Nerissa. "Public opinion is beginning to count more and more these days, so the sum total of all our opinions will have an effect."

"Yes, and look Olga, with our new connection with the Levonians, we are getting deeper into business relationships with merchants and buyers in Smyrna, so what finally happens both here and there is important to us," said Haik. "You haven't been saying anything Sima, what do you think? Oh, by the way, that reminds me, Paramaz tells me that you met that Russian guy at the Pera Palace yesterday. He seems to be a pleasant chap – any friend of Vahan must be a good guy."

"Haik," Sima finally said, "I was indeed having tea with Kohar yesterday when Count Nikolai turned up. He plays in the orchestra there, you know. He joined us and made quite an impression on Kohar, I must say. You are right Haik, he is an interesting character – he told me a lot about the Russian civil war, for the couple of minutes that we talked together after Kohar had to leave."

Everybody started chatting again. Karekin relaxed – his flash of gloomy thoughts peremptorily dismissed. Paramaz came in from his room behind the kitchen, summoned by Talin that breakfast was ending and that Karekin was about to leave.

Armineh bustled about automatically, making sure that Seta was ready to go off to school. She had carefully avoided looking at Sima as she had spoken, and had made no comment. She knew her eldest-born better than she knew any of the others. She had not believed a word that Sima had said. She knew, with some sense of alarm, that Sima had not been telling the truth.

CHAPTER 14

Smyrna – the politics

The Greeks had done well out of the First and Second Balkan Wars, which had preceded the Great War. Having done the least fighting and lost the least numbers of men, they had taken the greatest prize – the important cosmopolitan city of Salonica. But romantic nationalism had taken over Greek public attitudes. This new religion of the sovereign, unrestrained, nation-state, as first envisaged by the Treaty of Westphalia, took over the public imagination in Greece, as it had throughout Europe.

The nation-state! The union of all people who happened to speak the same language wherever they may be – one people, one flag, one race, one religion, one nation – no minorities or cultural diversity to be tolerated. How could the ramshackle Ottoman Empire, with its centuries-old tradition of tolerance and acceptance of many races and religions all living together under one authority, stand up against this overwhelming idea.

Several accidents of birth and death conspired to create a typically Greek fracture within the Kingdom. The first of these accidents set the new King Constantine on the throne in Greece, as a result of the assassination of his father, George I, while on a great triumphal state visit to the newly-acquired town of Salonica.

Salonica was a cosmopolitan city, where a great many of Turkish leaders, including Enver, Talaat and Mustapha Kemal himself, came from. The largest group in the population of this fascinating town were Sephardic Jews, originally 16th century refugees from Imperial Spain. Turned away bt the rest of Europe they had been welcomed by the Ottomans, settling in Salonica, protected by an empire that accepted cultural diversity. The next largest group were the Turks – and well behind came Bulgarians, Greeks and many other interesting ethnicities and nationalities.

When, as a result of the assassination of his father, Constantine came to the throne, he took the title of Constantine I, to the great disappointment of a large section of Greek public opinion. The last Byzantine Emperor, Constantine XI died in 1453 defending the great walls of Constantinople from the huge Ottoman armies, and those Greeks, filled with visions of the glories of the ancient past, wanted the new King to take the title of Constantine XII. It was an important symbolic decision, as rather than creating a 'Greek' empire in place of an 'Ottoman' one, the new king was simply interested in an enlargement of their little Balkan nation-state into a somewhat larger one.

The talk of a revival of the Byzantine Empire under a Constantine XII became a smoke-screen for a narrow national agenda, which wanted to bring the Greeks of Smyrna and the Ionian coastline into a Greek kingdom, while ignoring the Turks and other nations living there, and turning Constantinople into a purely Greek city in a purely Greek state.

This was the exact mirror image of the equally narrow agenda emanating from those Turks who were slowly building up their power in Ankara. Constantinople, for them, was to become a Turkish city in a Turkish state. The great imperial city stood squeezed between two narrow, provincial, one-people towns – Athens and Ankara – determined to fight it out. But it was wonderfully heady stuff. The old saying resounded, "A Constantine built the city – A Constantine lost it – A

Constantine will recover it."

At the same time, a dynamic leader from Crete had emerged – Eleftherios Venizelos, who had been the prime minister throughout the Balkan Wars and had been instrumental in bringing Greece to its high point just before the outbreak of the Great War.

Venizelos was an enigmatic larger-than-life figure who liked to tell stories of his exploits during the Cretan insurrection against the Turks. He had escaped to the mountains and taught himself English by reading the Times, with a rifle across his knees. He was a heady mixture of a man of great charm, a brigand, a man of courage with an intellectual literary background but also something of a showman. Above all, he was a consummate politician; a large, muscular smiling man, with eyes that glinted through his steel-rimmed spectacles.

Energetic, persuasive and with a charm that had won over every important delegation at the Versailles conference, Venizelos was Greece's greatest asset in the turmoil in the aftermath of the Great War. Without him, Greece could never have achieved what it did at the conference tables in Paris. But, alas, without him Greece might not have tried to swallow so much and to choke almost to death in the attempt.

Venizelos was a great believer in what became known as the 'Great Idea' – the resurrection of a Greater Greece to include all the Greeks living throughout the Ottoman Empire. To this end, Venizelos had wanted Greece to join the Great War on the side of the Entente powers against the Ottomans. But Constantine, the new king, saw the position differently. He was far more realistic than Venizelos about the 'Great Idea,' and he also believed that Germany would win the war. Married to Sophie, a sister of the Kaiser, he was an honorary field marshal in the German army.

The British and French distrusted him and saw him as pro-German. Nevertheless, he stood up to the pressure exerted by his brother-in-law, the Kaiser, to join the Central powers just as strongly as he stood up to his prime minister's wish to embroil Greece with the westerners. He distrusted the British, whereas Venizelos had a strong emotional attachment to Britain and France.

These two personalities were set for the great national schism which split the country into two rival and warring camps. During the War, this resulted in two separate governments – the Royalists in Athens and the Venizelists in Salonica. As matters developed, the two factions were more concerned with fighting each other than with the foreigners, with often fatal consequences for the parties.

The complex vagaries of Greek politics eventually ended with the triumph of Venizelos as German defeat loomed. Constantine, pressured by the British and French, left the country, without formally abdicating. He was succeeded by his second son Alexander, in every way a more successful monarch then his father, whose evasions had been so catastrophic, quite apart from his unconstitutional meddling in the country's politics.

All seemed to have turned out for the best. Venizelos now returned in triumph to Athens to become the prime minister of a united Greece. But the bitter divisions had simply gone underground. The first act of the new government was to order the immediate dismissal of all the Royalists they could lay their hands on, however efficient and useful to the state they might have been.

The whole of Venizelos' political ethos revolved round the one idea, that by joining the war Greece would be allowed to 'liberate' from Ottoman rule the whole Smyrna region on the other side of the Aegean with its majority Greek population, along with the rest of Ionia. By the end of the war, Venizelos, now in total charge, led the Greek delegation to the Paris peace conference, and sought to reap his reward for his steadfast support of the allied cause.

Supported by the young King, Venizelos seemed to be in a strong position. He became a close personal friend of Lloyd George, one of the three vital figures at the Conference. Lloyd George was an old Gladstonian Liberal whose knowledge of the Near East was based on the Bible rather than an understanding of geography or culture. He was deeply, indeed passionately, anti-Turk. He thought of the Ottoman Empire as a 'prison of nations.' His Tory coalition partners, despite their centuries-old support for the Ottomans, were blinded by the fact that they had just fought a war against this empire, and let him have his way.

In Paris all the delegations tried to reconcile a whole gamut of contradictory promises and principles covering the region. Firstly, to resolve the conflicting promises regarding the Ottoman Empire made by the French and British governments. Then there were the secret treaties dividing up the Empire, Wilson's fourteen points, Italian greed, British and French imperial rivalry. As time went on and there was still no peace agreement with the Ottomans, Italian troops landed at Adalia in an area promised to them in the secret treaties and began creeping up the coast towards Smyrna. To avoid a *fait accompli*, Lloyd George wanted Greek troops to be sent to occupy Smyrna. There was no question of sending British troops, who were being hastily demobilised; this was to be imperial control on the cheap. Venizelos, surprised by Lloyd George's suggestion, but highly elated, took the plunge and sent a substantial Greek force escorted by British destroyers to occupy Smyrna, landing in the town in the summer of 1919. Smyrna – the alleged home of Homer – the principal trading port of Roman Asia Minor – the chief trading port of the British Turkey Company – *'giavour'* Smyrna – was to be Greek at last.

It was just like the arrival of 'desperate Frankie' in Constantinople six months before. Huge crowds of Greeks gathered on the quayside as the Greek transports led by a British destroyer steamed into the great harbour. The Greek Archbishop Chrysostom stood there, surrounded by all his clergy on the quayside in his full white and gold ecclesiastical ceremonial vestments. As the first soldiers arrived on the quayside, he raised his arms and his golden cross high in the air and blessed the troops as they landed. The crowd burst into a roar of approval.

The troops marched up towards the Ottoman governor's residence – the Konak. What happened then was to become the subject of countless witness reports, discussions and bitter arguments from that day onwards. As the Greeks passed near the Turkish barracks, shots rang out and the whole triumphalist spectacle dissolved into chaos. The crowds following the troops scrambled for safety, whilst the Greek soldiers began firing indiscriminately in undisciplined panic. Several of the Turkish soldiers were dragged from their barracks and were killed, and some Turkish civilians found near the area were murdered.

It mattered not a whit whether the numbers that died – Greek or Turk – was forty or four hundred or that Venizelos moved fast to restore order; that the military authorities tried and sentenced Greeks who had been active in the disorders; that the Greeks arranged for restitution to Turks of a large amount of stolen property. All that mattered was that the reports of this day's events spread through Anatolia like wildfire. Seized on by the nationalists in Ankara and exploited throughout Turkey, the numbers killed at the docks and in the streets of Smyrna on this day reached the unbelievable figure of ten thousand. The occupation of Smyrna by the Greeks, urged on by the British, became the single most important event leading to the rise of Kemal and the nation state of Turkey, and the ultimate fall of the Ottoman Sultanate.

The new Sultan – Mehmet VI – wept when he heard the news, as well he might, for ultimately this Greek invasion spelt the end of his dynasty. The exclusive Greek state was now in direct confrontation with the new nationalists in Ankara. Neither of these states had any desire to accommodate each other's minorities, but the Kemalist nationalists had a much larger population base as against the   better-equipped and officered regular army of the Venizelists.

Then fate again intervened – incredibly, in the shape of a monkey's bite!

Venizelos, riding high on the success of the Greek army throughout ancient Ionia up to the Marmara Sea, and his undoubted diplomatic successes in Paris, called for an election in November 1920. He expected to be swept to power on a wave of nationalist euphoria. However, five weeks before the actual elections were due, King Alexander suddenly died.

Alexander had been taking a walk in the gardens of the Tatoi palace in Athens, when his dog jumped into a clump of bushes. Hearing the sounds of a scuffle, Alexander parted the bushes and saw that his dog had grabbed a pet Spanish monkey in its teeth and was shaking it vigorously. While trying to free the monkey, the young King was bitten by the monkey's male mate, and died a few days later.

The king's father – Constantine – had never formally abdicated, and returned to take up the crown again. The Venizelists, who had undoubtedly persecuted supporters of Constantine while in power, were now swept out of office. The grim cycle of the persecution of political opponents began all over again. Venizelos was forced to retire from politics and Greece lost for the moment its greatest statesman. More to the point, all the principal, experienced army commanders were dismissed at a stroke, replaced by inexperienced officers, whose only qualification was that they were Royalists.

There was an opportunity at this point for the Greeks to have settled the whole problem reasonably, but when it came down to it, Constantine did not have the courage of his convictions. Now back in power, he could not bring himself to give up the gains which appeared to have been made by Venizelos. The short fleeting chance that the change of regime gave Greece to retire gracefully, disappeared for ever.

The two nation-states faced up to each other for a final shoot-out, both determined that the provinces of Thrace and Ionia should now to be either exclusively Greek or exclusively Turkish.

The stage was set.

CHAPTER 15

Some encounters in the city

In approaching Olga and accepting her invitation to tea, Nairi had acted in all innocence, motivated by her love for her brother. But she had no idea what she was letting him in for when she quickly accepted Olga's enthusiastic invitation. Unfortunately a series of coincidental meetings and further invitations which followed, conspired to make the next day's tea party at the Avakians a major crisis in the lives of four young men.

Harry had been found accommodation in a small flat just off Taksim

Square near the up and coming Park Otel, a younger and more modern hotel than the old Pera Palace and fast becoming just as fashionable. Harry often strolled in the park, directly opposite the hotel beside the
square. Here, British and occasionally French regimental bands would
play airs and marches on weekend afternoons. The Stambouli weekend
lasted three days, with the Moslem Friday, the Jewish Saturday and the
Christian Sunday.

Harry listened carefully to all the gossip of the city during his chance
encounters in Taksim park, and while in the lounges and public rooms
of the Park Otel, noting all the varied views of the different subjects of
the Empire. The Greeks – waving their national flag and speculating on
when they would take over the city; the Armenians – cowed and traumatised by the terrible events of 1915, keeping a low profile but hoping
for an international city under western control; the Jews – discreetly
but persistently arguing for a continuation of the Sultanate; the Turks
– heavily split between those supporting the old Ottoman system, and
those who increasingly looked to Mustapha Kemal and the Nationalist
rebels of Ankara.

One by one prominent Turkish political figures departed to the interior, by train to Izmid and then slipping through the lines and on to
Ankara; others by embarking on fishing boats or coal freighters and
then through the Black Sea to Zonguldak. It was Harry's rather unhappy task to report on all the different attitudes to this exodus and to
hand in the names of these political 'deserters' to the British occupation
authorities.

Neither Harry, nor his immediate superior – General Harington –
liked this aspect of their work. But London was insistent that the local
British authorities make more of an effort to stop the seepage of politicians and young men out of the city.

Few arms of any kind had been left in Anatolia after the end of the
war. The Armistice of Mudros stated that all arms should be handed in
to the occupation authorities. But, just as the British had departed from
the spirit of the agreed terms by occupying Constantinople, so during
1919, successful raids on the depots gave the Kemalist forces more and
more military equipment. On top of that Harry reported that ordinary,
educated young men were increasingly drifting away to join the forces
in the interior.

Then, with the final defeat of the Whites in the Russian civil war,
Russian arms began trickling across the Black Sea to bolster the Ankara regime. After the capture of Kars from the small Armenian force
desperately attempting to hold on, the Turks and Bolsheviks achieved
direct land contact with each other and yet more armaments poured in.

However, the British authorities still felt that the Kemalist movement
could be ignored. Even Tim Harington, despite his increasingly gloomy

reports to London, indicated to Harry that the allies still had the initiative.

The Greek forces in Smyrna and throughout the Ionian region amounted to about a hundred thousand men, backed by all the resources of a functioning state apparatus. Furthermore, the allies still controlled the person of the Sultan who was here in Constantinople. Despite the Sultan's hatred of the old Ittihad party, Mustapha Kemal, who had distanced himself from the old triumvirate, still paid lip service to the Sultan's authority.

It so transpired that on the day before the Avakian's tea party to which Olga had invited Mikael, Harry had decided for the first time to stroll down the Grande Rue du Pera and take a drink at the Pera Palace, rather then his usual haunt at the Park Otel. He was standing at the Orient Express bar, chatting to some Greek army officers, not of course in uniform, when he saw a young man in a rather threadbare evening suit passing through the salon on his way out, with a violin case under his arm – obviously a member of the little orchestra which had just finished playing in the adjoining tea-room.

"Nicolai! It is Nicolai Androv, isn't it?" he called out, going forward to meet him with a smile.

"Why ... yes sir," said Nicolai hesitantly, clearly not quite sure whom he was addressing. But then, shaking Harry's outstretched hand, he said, enthusiastically, "Oh, yes. Of course. Captain, er ...... Bridgefield."

"No, no ... Bridgeman." Harry laughed. "But you must call me Harry. How very nice to see you again. Are you on duty? No, well come, let's sit and have a drink together, and you can tell me all about what you've been doing since you disembarked. And how is your mother and your little brother?"

And so it was that the meeting of Harry and Nicolai on the quayside at Sevastopol, led to this further meeting some months later in a luxury hotel in Constantinople, and that in turn .....

Harry was in a particularly good mood. Here in Constantinople he was a representative of the principal occupying power. He reported direct to Tim Harington who, to all intents and purposes, now ran the city. It was the British who controlled the police, and not the Sultan and his government of aging Ottoman statesmen. Everywhere he went, his uniform afforded him a natural respect and deference, which was not at all like the fear that might be shown to an enemy occupier. Over half the population of the city welcomed his presence and the sense of security offered by his uniform, whilst the Turks, split as they were by their own political ferment, were not cowed. This allowed him a confidence and a relaxed attitude to communicating with others, which he had never experienced before.

As their conversation wore on, Nicolai, for his part, warmed to this Englishman who exhibited none of the class arrogance that he was beginning to associate with the British officers with their haughty swagger sticks whom he regularly saw in the hotel bars. Stories were continually going round the city about the British officers. The issue was not whether the tales were true or not, it was the fact that such was the general demeanour of these arrogant westerners that the stories were believed by all sections of the population, Christian or Moslem.

At his meeting with Sima Avakian the previous day, at this very same hotel, Sima had invited Nicolai to come to tea on the next Friday afternoon and to bring Vahan with him. Nicolai had immediately accepted, but remembered that Vahan could not come as he would be working all day with his father. Without really thinking, Sima had suggested he bring along another friend instead. Meanwhile, of course, unaware of these invitations Olga had invited Nairi and Mikael for the same afternoon.

"Harry," said Nicolai as they chatted. "I am invited to tea at the house of friends – the Avakians – in Makrikoy tomorrow afternoon. I was told to bring a friend. Would you like to come? They are a delightful family. Have you ever been in an Armenian home?"

"No, actually I haven't, and I would love to, but are you sure it isn't a problem?"

"No, no, it will be interesting for you, and I believe interesting for them too. They all speak excellent English – er well the young ones anyway. Look, meet me at Sirkeci station tomorrow – Platform 2 – at three o'clock. What about it? It'll be great!"

"Very well, Nicolai, I'll be there."

But that wasn't the end of it. When Sima had left the Pera Palace on the previous day, she had been in a state of considerable confusion. She forgot, or rather ignored her throwaway suggestion that Nikolai could bring a friend with him, and was not aware that Olga was that very same evening inviting Mikael and his sister for tea with the family. She began to worry that Nicolai might, after all, come to tea alone.

The invitation wasn't improper – not any more, anyway. If Sima had simply looked upon Nicolai as a new, interesting acquaintance, it would not have crossed her mind to be concerned whether he came alone or not. But, those moments when they held hands, just too long for a goodbye, the pleasure she had felt in his company took on a significance in Sima's mind which suddenly made the prospect of Nicolai arriving at her home on his own, alarming.

Yet the Levonian offices were just round the corner. It would only have needed a short detour for Sima to have gone round and invited George as well. It was the sensible solution, and Sima was undoubtedly the most sensible of the Avakian sisters. But strangely enough she did not go to the Levonian offices, but walked on down towards the Galata bridge towards the station, and home.

And then, by chance, by the Grande Rue, at the point where the road swings down to the left to descend to the bridge, she passed Selim and his mother as they emerged from the block of flats on the corner and Selim called out in salutation.

Sima turned and smiled as she saw Selim with a lady clinging to his good arm. Although she had never met Halideh Hanum before, she immediately recognised this must be his formidable mother.

"Oh – Selim *effendi* – I'm so sorry, I didn't recognise you. Greetings!"

"Miss Sima, may I introduce you to my mother – Halideh Hanum. Mother this is Miss Sima Avakian from Makrikoy."

Sima saw Selim's mother stiffen as he gave her name. But she was in a public place, and would not, could not, shame her son with a snub. She smiled, for her son's sake, and extended her hand for a European handshake, but she said nothing.

"I am most happy to meet you Halideh Khatun," said Sima.

Then, as the silence between them lengthened, Sima came out with the words which finally set the seal for the next day's events.

"Selim *effendi*," she said, carefully keeping to the old formalities in deference to the presence of Selim's mother – "We are having tea to-morrow at Makrikoy. If this good weather holds we are hoping to be able to have it in the garden. My father will not be present, but my mother and the rest of the family will be there with perhaps another guest or two. I wonder if you would honour us by coming – nothing formal."

At this point Sima felt rather than saw the disapproval of Halideh. She suddenly felt awkward and wondered whether she should extend the invitation to her as well. Instead, she added, turning to address the mother rather than Selim – "Perhaps others in your family, your sister for example, might care to come also."

"Certainly not – Yasmin will be engaged," snapped Halideh, struggling to keep calm, but nevertheless bordering on rudeness, until Selim said, ignoring his mother –

"Why certainly Miss Sima, I would love to come. Will Vahan be there?"

"No, I'm sorry Selim *effendi*, he will be working with his father. We will expect you then – any time after three o'clock."

Looking at Selim's mother she began – "Allaha Izm ..." but failed to continue as Halideh turned away. Selim smiled and bowed as Sima said goodbye, and began walking back down the road to the bridge.

"Nairi – how could you? What did she say – what did she look like?

No, no it was wrong. I don't want to push myself on her. But listen, sister, what were her actual words? How did she look when she spoke them? How did ..."

"My darling brother, I've already told you three times. She spontaneously asked me to ask you to come to tea tomorrow at about three o'clock. She was very friendly – it is absolute nonsense to suggest that she was in any way snooty."

"Yes, Nairi, but you know how far out of our league they are. Her father is one of the wealthiest merchants in the city - the girls all go or went to posh, western style colleges. Olga went to Robert College, you know."

"Oh, Mikael – what does it matter these days. You're always such a pessimist – what's the matter with you? For heaven's sake, just go and see if you still have the same feelings for each other. If you do, just get on with it. She seemed to me to be a very genuine and honest girl – and believe me she was really keen to see you again. Anyway, ever since coming back from Russia you've been mooching about not knowing what to do with yourself. You have to get down to doing something soon."

"Oh God, you sound just like mother – you'll be saying that I need a good woman to be my wife next."

"Well, my soul, it's absolutely true. You've always been restless, big brother, but since you went away – my God, Mikael it's almost a year since you got back – you can't even sit still when someone talks to you ... look at you."

"Sorry – go on I'm listening."

"Mikael, I know I'm younger than you, but listen you must make an effort. You couldn't do much better than to recapture the heart of that Olga girl. Forget the class difference – just go for it. One rejection isn't the end of the world."

"Well I'll certainly take the plunge and go to this tea, but, sister, I am not sure that I would be able to survive another rejection. Do you know if anyone else will be there?"

"No, no, Mikael – I am sure that it was all on the spur of the moment. Even if her sisters will be there, it should be easy for you to have a private talk with her – and for goodness sake Mikael be charming to the mother."

And so it was that on the next afternoon – a Friday – four young men, Selim and Mikael, Harry and Nikolai, converged on the Avakian house. George Levonian was not amongst them.

CHAPTER 16A

The Avakian tea-party – in Armenian

"But Sima, my soul, I don't understand you at all. You have invited some impoverished Russian soldier to tea. Then, on top of that, you tell him by all means to bring along any other friend with him, someone we don't know and have never met before?"

"Yes mother, but ..."

"On top of that, my dear, you then happen to meet Selim and invite him as well. My soul, you of all people must be aware of how impossible this whole business between Olga and Selim is – and you make it worse? What would your poor father ..."

"Oh no, mother, don't give me that. At least baba would not ..."

"Sima, you know perfectly well what I mean. Look, don't get me wrong, my dearest girl – I don't mind at all – it's always nice to meet new people. What I find the most surprising in this whole matter, is that you made no attempt to invite George, even though you have managed to ask three young men to come and have tea with you."

"Well, mama, I'm not sure myself how all this came about, to be honest, but anyway Count Nicolai is probably unlikely actually to invite anyone else. Then, after ..."

"On top of all this, we have a fourth guest turning up, as Olga has sent me a message to the effect that she has invited another young man we don't know, a Mikael Sarafian, who is actually from Makrikoy, I believe. Do you know them by any chance? Ah well, it doesn't matter, it keeps us all on our toes I suppose. But Sima, why didn't you invite George?"

There was no immediate reply.

Armineh was always ready to cope with anything that her family threw at her, but she did like to know what was going on. Karekin had of course already discussed with her the meeting he had witnessed in the Pera Palace hotel between Sima and a member of the tearoom orchestra. Before they had both gone down to breakfast after that discussion, they had agreed that, curious though the incident was, there was nothing to be concerned about. Nevertheless, as Armineh now pondered Sima's invitations, she found it odd that Sima had not offered a similar invitation to George.

It was already past midday on a wonderful hot spring morning. There was no wind, not a breath of the usual cooling breeze that normally blew down the Bosporus from the Black Sea, keeping the city fresh and cool during the summer. The Avakian women had all instinctively agreed, without a word being said, that their afternoon tea would be taken in the garden for the first time that year. The two round white iron tables had already been set up just outside the French windows of the sitting room, on the large marble-floored veranda that ran the length of the back of the house overlooking the garden. The steps leading down to the lawn had been brushed clear of any remaining leaves. The large orchard at the end of the lawn was covered with spring blossom. There was a pristine freshness in the air. It was, in short, a beautiful day, with Constantinople showing itself off at its best.

Even though it was a Friday, Karekin had taken Paramaz and Haik off to work, and had indicated that they were unlikely to be back before the late afternoon. Armineh and Sima had been out on the veranda, helping Talin lay the tables. Seta and Nerissa had just come down into the garden and overhead their mother's final remark. Armineh's query about the failure to invite George hung in the air and there was a silence as everyone looked curiously at Sima.

"Oh, mother, you know I just didn't think about it at the time. As for inviting Selim, it just came out of the blue. I happened to meet him in the street as I was coming home, and it just came out."

This seemed a reasonable explanation – a typical Avakian situation, with which they could all sympathise – and they all began chatting at once. Armineh was dressed in her normal sensible clothes, dark grey skirt unfashionably down to the ankles. Both Sima and Nerissa had chosen to wear their thin white muslin summer dresses. Only Seta was in colour, with a bright blue dress, billowing out just below the knees, and wearing white socks. The talk turned to domestic issues – what cakes to order up from Makrikoy – what time people would come – whether the men in the family would arrive in time – and above all who was this Mikael that Olga had invited. Olga herself was at the hospital and was due back shortly.

But Sima was still worrying at the original question posed by Armineh. She knew that her reply had been glib, and not entirely true. There had been no formal engagement between the Avakians and the Levonians, but it was accepted by everyone that a proposal was near. Sima and George had been going out together for some time, and while strict chaperoning was no longer necessary, it was accepted that there was an understanding between the families, if nothing else.

So why had she not taken the trouble to walk up the street to the Levonian's office? As she stood there watching everyone bustling about, getting in Talin's way, she unaccountably blushed, recalling the wonderful afternoon she had spent the previous day at the Pera Palace with the young Russian. Sima shook herself, impatient at her own thoughts. What nonsense! An impoverished Russian aristocrat, no future, no passport, no prospects. She knew little of his background or of his family or of his religion. However it came to her that she did know 'him' in a way she had never known George. On the other hand she knew everything else about George – his prospects – his culture – his religion – his family. And that surely was another way of knowing 'him', wasn't it?

Once again Sima shook her head, as if to clear her thoughts – and at that moment Olga finally arrived, rushing out of the sitting-room and calling out – "Hello, everyone, hello. No one here yet – thank goodness. I was worried Mikael might have turned up before I got home – and that would have been terrible. Look everyone I must run off and change."

"Olga, sister, who is this Mikael?" said Seta.

"Just a young man I met at the hospital during the war a few years ago. He's an interesting guy. Listen, Seta, come up with me and chat while I get dressed. Tea in the garden, is it? Lovely! Come on Seta, my soul, keep me company."

Olga ran breathlessly back into the sitting room, beckoning Seta to follow. It was at this point, as Olga disappeared back into the house that Sima suddenly recalled that Olga had not as yet been told that Selim too was coming to tea that afternoon. She made a grab at Seta, who was about to dash after Olga.

"Seta, my sweet, go and tell Olga that Selim is coming as well this afternoon."

The afternoon had begun. A hot sun shone down from a clear blue sky. All the domestic arrangements had been sorted, with baklava, corabides, and various cakes already on their way up from town. Talin hovered. Nerissa sat next to Armineh as they both lazily stared out at the garden. Seta came running back – after all she rarely ever walked anywhere – and said, "Oh, Sima, Olga is a bit upset that you invited Selim."

"What! I don't believe it. Why?"

"Yes, well, she seemed to be very vexed, and almost started crying. But you know Olga – she suddenly started laughing instead. She'll be down in a moment."

"Well, I must say that's a bit of a mystery – she usually likes to see him."

Armineh heard all this but said nothing. The warm sun and the fresh air made her feel drowsy. She reached out and held Nerissa's hand for a few moments as they both sat contemplating the garden and their own thoughts.

There was a loud knocking at the front door.

"That must be this new chap Olga invited," said Sima. "Everyone else knows where the bell is. You know we really must..."

"... do something about the ivy covering it," called out Nerissa and Seta together, giggling.

Seta jumped up and went into the hall to welcome their first guest of the afternoon.

Mikael did not know quite what to expect. Although his relationship with Olga during his time in the hospital had been close and within the conventions of the time, fairly intimate, he was not sure how she would view a renewal of their friendship. They had talked quite a lot about her family but he still felt awkward. He had always been highly sensitive about the difference in their class and background.

As he had walked up the hill past the green grass of the Vali *Effendi* racecourse, he reflected that this house he was visiting for the first time might well have been one of those he and his boyhood friend Loris had stolen fruit from those many years ago. This in turn brought his mind back to those months in the hospital at Uskudar when Loris had single-mindedly nursed him back to health. Certainly he would try to find out from Olga what had happened to him. Mikael had fought both with the Red army and with the White army during the Russian civil war, though he had felt more at ease with his Red comrades than with the Whites. In the end he had understood the Red cause better than the White. What was the use of having individual liberty, and a large plethora of human rights if you didn't know where your next crust of bread was coming from?

Mikael was not, by nature, envious. He got angry at suspected slights to his pride, but he did not covet or resent other people's property. So, as he stood at the front door of the Avakian house, he did not reflect on his parent's shabby town house in the run-down quarter of Makrikoy, Katya's tiny house in Yedikule or the sordid accommodation that he had had to put up with during his three years in Russia. He just stared at the door set in a small porch totally overgrown with ivy. Seeing no bell, he lifted and banged the large bronze knocker three times with quite unnecessary force.

When the door opened, he entered a room which was perhaps the largest in any private house he had ever seen; a beautiful marble floor liberally dotted with worn but gorgeous Persian carpets of rich reds and blues; and an elegant staircase in the centre of the room to an upper floor with balconies overlooking the room itself. The room looked comfortable and well-used. Mikael did not know quite what to make of it – too grand for him to take in, but too homely to be treated with derision.

Out from a room on the right side hurried a young girl in a light blue billowing dress, who ran forward without any shyness or artifice, extending her hand, as he stood uncertainly in the middle of the room.

"Hello – hello – I'm Seta. You must be Mikael. How nice to see you, we've heard a lot about you."

She smiled and taking hold of Mikael's hand, said "My, you look so serious, sir, come and meet the family. Its such a lovely day we're all going to have tea in the garden. Come and say hello to Mama. Olga has only just got back from the hospital, she won't be a moment."

Seta pulled Mikael into the sitting room and then, quite unselfconsciously holding his hand, took him straight through and out of the French windows, into the garden.

Even the dour puritanical Mikael was enchanted. Two young ladies – that is how Mikael thought of them – both dressed in flimsy white muslin stood up, turned and smiled at him. The garden looked larger than he would have thought possible from the outside. The spring blossom was in full array on the trees of the orchard at the far end. Sitting rather squarely in an easy chair on the veranda in front of two tables already covered with lace cloths, was a dumpy woman dressed in a long dark grey skirt. She was looking at him with cool appraising eyes. He felt a little awkward. He felt as if he wanted to wipe his hands on his trousers before extending it. Seta led him up and said "Mama – this is Mikael – he's very serious, he hasn't smiled once yet."

"Seta! – that's rude," said one of the ladies in white.

Mikael took the mother's hand and shook it as introductions were made all round.

"Come, sir, come and sit by me," said Armineh indicating the chair Nerissa had just vacated. "Don't mind my youngest daughter, she hasn't learnt good manners yet. Olga will be down in a moment. Now tell me all about yourself, and how you and she came to meet."

Despite himself, despite his determination not to be taken in by their bourgeois charm and breeding, he found himself sitting at his ease and enjoying himself. Nerissa joined them with another chair and Mikael found that he was talking freely about the events of 1915 and his meeting with Olga at the hospital, and what had happened to him at that time, finding himself coming out with views about the Russian civil war that he didn't even realise he had.

Though it was not apparent to him, Armineh, disoriented at first by Mikael's somewhat brusque manner and rough background, was becoming more and more interested by what appeared to have been a close friendship between this man, who was at least Armenian, and Olga.

And then the bell rang! The conversation stopped as everyone waited to see who it might be. Within a short moment Talin appeared at the French windows and showed Selim into the garden.

"You see, you see – I found the bell," called out Selim delightedly, as he bowed over Armineh's hand. "How lovely to see you all again."

The talk, which until this moment had been in Armenian, immediately and seamlessly, resumed all round in Turkish, in that instinctive way only the Bolsetsi knew how to manage so effortlessly.

CHAPTER 16B

The Avakian tea-party – in Turkish

Selim was in a good mood. How could one fail to be, on such a marvellous day. He loved this garden, and quite apart from his relationship with Olga, he enjoyed the company of all the Avakian girls. He had a good relationship with Karekin, but he was always a bit chary of Armineh. He was aware that she was working hard to put as many obstacles as possible between himself and Olga.

Selim was not a fool and understood that both mothers had a very reasonable case in acting as they did. He could see, himself, the difficulties in matters going any further between them. He was conscious of the immense social obstacle in trying to establish any permanent relationship, if they wished to live together in the city, but thought they could ultimately get around parental opposition. Olga saw the problem entirely the other way round. She could not care less for the 'social' difficulties, but she could not contemplate taking the relationship further without the ultimate sanction of both mothers. In particular, she had been quite unable to cope with Halideh Hanum's hatred.

Mikael was introduced to Selim as an old friend of Olga from five years ago. No reference to Olga was made at all when Selim's name was given, but Mikael immediately recalled from his hospital days that there had been some gossip linking Olga with a wounded Turkish infantry officer. Nerissa and Sima came and sat down as Selim was motioned to a chair, and the conversation became general. At a sign from her mother, Seta slipped out to see to the preparations in the kitchen and to tell Olga to get a move on.

"What news from the city, Selim," asked Nerissa.

"Well, our conquerors swagger about as always. For the first time in centuries, Pera has become quite unsafe for women – certainly after dark. The Greek flag is everywhere. I sometimes feel a stranger in my own city."

"But, Selim," said Nerissa, interrupting, "the diversity of the city hasn't really changed, just new faces and ideologies. Of course, it's not just you, we all look a bit askance at our conquerors. Many of them are rude and uncouth and have little idea how to behave. I must say, though, that when drunken British and American sailors start fighting in the streets, I wonder where their vaunted superiority lies."

Mikael, no longer at ease and surprised by Nerissa's outspoken intervention said, much too sharply for such an occasion –

"And what is the difference between your feeling a stranger here in Bolis, now that it is held by the British, and an Armenian feeling a stranger in Kars now that it has been captured by the Kemalists. Kars – a city which has been Armenian for centuries." Selim's good humour vanished in a flash as he stared in surprise at this arrogant young man, but before he could reply Armineh quickly intervened –

"Gentlemen, please, this is not the time or place to talk about Kars. I'm sure there will be an accommodation soon, and anyway this is really far too nice a day to start arguments of that kind."

Both young men immediately began talking about something else, turning away from each other. They may have taken an instant dislike to each other, but they both had enough sense to see that their hostess would be upset if they continued to discuss the issue. Furthermore, Armineh had that old-fashioned capacity to exercise her will on obstreperous young males who needed to be reined in.

Talk once again became general, somewhat to Nerissa's disappointment, when Olga finally appeared in the doorway to the sitting-room. Both Nerissa and Sima immediately recognised that she had gone to greater lengths than usual to appear at her best. Unlike them, she was not wearing white but wore a simple green dress, with a wonderful old Turkish shawl round her bare shoulders. She was not only very beautiful, she was elegant and fashionable in a way that neither Sima nor Nerissa could ever achieve. However, Nerissa alone in the whole party, could see that she was nervous. She was pulling at the shawl and her eyes were not very focused, moving nervously between one person and another.

Social training came to her aid, and she stepped forward and shook hands with Mikael – nodding at Selim, who had also risen from his seat.

"Mikael, how wonderful to see you again after all these years. Where have you been? What are you doing now?" Olga babbled on as the original circle broke up, and she sat down on the chair by Mikael's side.

Selim's good humour had already gone, but in its place was now an inchoate irritation which he could not express or understand. This young man's reference to the Turkish capture of Kars from the hands of the crumbling Armenian Republic over four months ago had surely just been designed to raise tensions in an otherwise pleasant family atmosphere. On top of that, why was Olga sitting next to him? Although, they were talking in Turkish, he did not try to listen in to their conversation. The fellow was making sheep's eyes at her, and twice he had leant forward in his chair and taken Olga's hand, as he bored everyone by chatting on about his Russian experiences.

The man had been a deserter from the Ottoman army, that was surely clear enough. He must have fled to Russia to avoid going to the war, as was his duty. Nothing like his friend Vahan – oh no, Vahan's situation had been quite different. What could Olga see in him? And yet she sat there, ignoring everyone else.

Selim suddenly became conscious of his lack of a complete left arm – amputated as it had been at the elbow. Somehow, whenever this happened, the stump of his left arm would begin to ache. Meanwhile Nerissa had been talking to Selim, although he had only been half listening. Nerissa was aware that she did not have his full attention, and suddenly stopped. In the silence everyone began listening to the words coming from Mikael as he eagerly turned to Olga and said "Do you remember Loris, Olga, could you tell me, is he still at the hospital – where is he?"

"Oh, Loris left last year. The last I heard of him was that he had gone to Bursa, and joined the Greek army as an auxiliary nurse, when they entered the town in July."

At this comment, reminding Selim yet again of the humiliations being heaped on his country, his irritation had boiled over. Standing up and ignoring Nerissa, he rudely interrupted what had until then been a private conversation, and said sharply –

"And who is this Loris?"

Olga looked up, surprised at the anger in Selim's voice, and saw a passion in his face that she had not seen before.

"Oh, Selim – he was a great personal friend of Mikael, who was an orderly at the Uskudar military hospital during the war when I was there."

"Yes, I see – an Ottoman citizen who has gone to join the Greek army as it begins to bite into Ottoman lands. Bursa, the old capital. It's a disgraceful sign of ..."

Mikael now himself stood up. Clearly the word 'Kars' was about to erupt from him again, and his eyes were now on fire. Selim said nothing more, but did not back down. The moment stretched. Olga looked down at the ground, her heart aflame. She had never seen such anger in Selim's eyes before. She could not cope with it. But she realised that she had sat talking to Mikael too long. It was all very difficult – she had invited Mikael, she had had to make him feel at home. Selim was in the wrong to have blazed up like that, however her heart was with Selim and she had no idea what to do next. She continued to look down.

Armineh, who had not been paying much attention to the conversation, now became angry at the aggression palpably emanating from the two brash young men, both of whom were acting badly, and began to rise from her chair.

And then the knocker on the front door banged again very loudly. Everyone stood silent in an almost operatic moment of tension. A few moments later, Seta stood in the French windows – on one side of her stood Nicolai with a beaming great smile on his face, and on the other was a cool-looking British officer in an outfit which was slightly strange, not the usual British army uniform. Everybody stared for a single moment of time that was too long.

Then, Armineh, having stood up from her seat, said in her rather poor English – "Welcome, gentlemen – please come in."

And the talk immediately, effortlessly and seamlessly resumed all round in English.

CHAPTER 16C

The Avakian tea-party – in English

Harry was not sure what he was expecting from this visit. He met Nicolai on Platform two at Sirkeci station for the twenty minute stopping service to Makrikoy. He had decided to wear his formal naval uniform instead of his civilian clothes. They hailed a cab from Cobancesme station to the Avakian house. Knocking on the door, it was opened almost immediately by Talin.

Harry had little time to look around, as a lively girl in a pretty blue dress came running out to collect them. Seta was old enough to recognise a British military uniform, though it looked different to those she normally saw in the streets. She could see that Nicolai was neither Turkish nor Armenian, failing to notice she had already met him.

"Hello – I'm Seta – are you friends of Olga?"

"Hello Seta – don't you remember me, Nicolai. I came here with Vahan and Selim some weeks ago. We ..."

"Oh, yes of course, I'm so sorry. I remember now – come in, come in, they're all out in the garden".

Harry found himself being ushered through a formal sitting room and out through French windows onto a wide veranda that ran along the back of the house. Steps led down to a large lawn with evergreen trees and high bushes at each side. At the end, was an orchard of various fruit trees, most in full spring blossom, past which he felt, rather than saw, was an old stone wall.

His eye took all this in at a glance. He also saw a small lady in a long dark dress, with sharp questioning eyes, who appeared to have just arisen from a cane chair. She turned toward them and said in heavily accented English – "Welcome, gentlemen, please do come in."

Nicolai immediately went forward and took the woman's out-stretched hand, bent down and raised it to his lips, saying "Madame, I am most grateful for your kind invitation. May I present my friend Captain Harry Bridgeman of the British Navy, currently stationed here in Constantinople."

Armineh nodded at Nicolai and then turned to Harry. She looked up at him, and held out her hand, carefully changing the position of her palm to show that a handshake was perfectly sufficient.

Harry felt a tension in the atmosphere as he shook hands with Armineh. He could sense that she was angry at something, although she responded politely to his formal thanks for the invitation.

Armineh did not smile. She was still seething with anger at the two young men, and, forgetting that it was Sima who had invited Selim, she was also angry with Olga, who in her opinion had gone *beyond* the bounds of hospitality in spending so much time talking exclusively to Mikael. Her pleasure in seeing that Olga had another relationship with someone other than Selim was spoiled by her behaviour.

Nevertheless, the arrival of the two newcomers to the party accompanied by the cheerful and irrepressible Seta, did defuse the awkward situation that had arisen, and conversation again became general, as everyone was introduced to each other. Nicolai sidled across to Sima as soon as he decently could, and Harry saw them wander down the steps into the garden, talking together with animation.

Harry, himself, had been living in Constantinople now for over four months. His duties took him round the city, listening out for all the political opinions and cross-currents swirling about the town. He analysed these for General Harington in his weekly written reports, and then discussed his judgements with him in conferences at the office. However, nothing quite like this had come his way and he sat and chatted with interest and fascination. After a short time, Armineh, whose command of English was poor, excused herself, ostensibly to go and see to the tea. Nicolai and Sima had disappeared into the orchard. Harry saw the strikingly beautiful girl to whom he had been introduced as Olga, take the Turkish lad and lead him down onto the lawn, where they walked up and down talking with great urgency. Harry found himself chatting with the surly looking Mikael and Nerissa in a little group of three. Somewhat to his surprise the talk quickly turned away from the usual frivolities to current politics. He did not realise that it was Nerissa, who had manipulated the two men by asking,

"Well, sir, are we to become an adjunct of the British Empire then."

"Please, Miss Nerissa, call me Harry."

"Yes, certainly, but then I'm Nerissa, not Miss Nerissa. Our city has been an Imperial city for over fifteen hundred years. It has to be part of someone's empire, even if it ceases to be a capital."

"But why for heaven's sake," said Mikael. "The day of empires is gone. No, sir, don't look at me like that – this applies to your empire as well. How much longer do you have – twenty years – forty years? We are moving into the age of triumphant nation-states."

"But Mikael, which nation-state is to have Constantinople – nearly a mil*lion* people and not one completely dominant racial group."

"Well, not the Turks, anyway. The allies will see to that. On the other hand, the Russians are out of the picture now too – though ironically there are more Russians living here since the departure from the Crimea than ever before," said Mikael.

"Wait a moment," said Harry, "Are you so sure that the Turks won't win out in the end. After all they ..."

"Which Turks do you mean," Nerissa interrupted. "The Ottomans are still ruling here, but day after day we hear of the successes of the Kemalists in Central Anatolia."

"Yes, by God," Mikael raised his voice. "They're just a band of brigands and guerillas, yet they have already held back the Greeks, captured Kars and ..."

"Mikael – no more of Kars. You heard mother. Please." Nerissa glanced over at Olga and Selim, still striding up and down on the lawn, talking urgently together. She continued –

"Mikael, you can't have it both ways. If you believe that the day of multi-ethnic empires is over, and you welcome nation-states, you have to decide about this city. You reject the Ottoman Empire; you sneer at the British Empire; you denigrate the brigands of Ankara; then who?

"The Greeks – the Greeks – let them have it back and make it their capital instead of that tin-pot jumped-up village they call a capital at the moment." Mikael was getting excited, and he glared at Selim and Olga walking together, though his voice did not carry.

"Steady on, steady on Mikael" said Harry, not quite sure why this aggressive young man was getting so het up. "I should tell you that despite Lloyd George, no one is going to allow the Greek army to walk into Constantinople. Believe me, if necessary we will move British troops to prevent it."

Now it was Mikael's turn to get upset and angry as he watched Olga and Selim. The long conversation he had had with Olga had made it crystal clear to him that she had no intention of renewing any deeper relationship with him.

Olga may have been shallower and less intelligent than Sima and Nerissa, but she had a good heart, and she knew that she must make her position clear to Mikael right from the start. She had not been the one to invite Selim, and there was absolutely no intention on her part to play one young man off against the other. This was why she had talked so long and earnestly to him earlier.

She felt that she had done her best – after all it was she who had invited Mikael to come here; she therefore had to make him feel welcome. But now, having done so, she had to make it up with Selim. Her heart ached at the anger she had seen in his face and heard in his voice. She was well aware of his sensitivity about his amputated arm, and she needed urgently to set his mind at rest. But, as a result of this, it was now Mikael who was seething with inchoate anger.

Tea at last arrived. Seta and Talin laid the table – the baklava and kadaif – bread and thin slices of soudjouk and pasterma – cucumbers, tomatoes and slices of cheese. Seta called out – "Tea everyone!" Selim and Olga came up the stairs. Olga looked depressed and nearly in tears. Nicolai and Sima emerged from the orchard. Sima, looking flushed and oddly anxious, clutching a bunch of bedraggled flowers in her hand. Nicolai walked a pace or two behind her, and he too looked a little flustered, but his eyes were shining.

Everyone sat round the two tables, most facing the garden. Armineh had returned and poured out the tea, which Talin handed round. Everyone was hungry, except for Olga who ate nothing but nervously plucked at her shawl. As the food disappeared, the conversation, still in English of course, became general and bland. As the cakes were at last finished, Armineh, who at one stage had almost dozed off, excused herself and left. It was once again Nerissa, impatient with pleasantries, who was the catalyst for the final explosion.

"Selim, we were talking about what is going to happen to this city of ours and the Ottomans. We are all friends here aren't we? We can surely be open about our views. Do you think that the Ottomans can hold on here, and if so what is to be the relationship between them and the Kemalists in Anatolia?"

"Nerissa – it's all very difficult. However I have to say that I believe the Ottomans are done for. Who now supports them? Some old-fashioned Pashas with summer palaces along the Bosporus – the elite classes of Constantinople – the Jewish community – some romantics – a few …"

"Well, Selim," said Harry seduced into an uncharacteristic interruption by the openness of the discussion. "I think you will find that the Allies too are coming round to the view that the Ottomans are worth supporting."

"They're finished – they're finished!" Selim, who for various reasons had not been satisfied by Olga's urgent representations, was getting excited again.

At this point, Mikael, unable to suppress his anger, entered the debate.

"I agree with you, Selim *effendi*, the Ottomans are finished and good riddance to them. What, then, do you suggest should take their place?" Mikael was smiling, but the words came out harshly and the smile was not in his eyes.

"A new sovereign Turkish state," snapped back Selim, perhaps stating the proposal more strongly than he had first intended.

"And the minorities here and elsewhere? No, by God, in this city they would be the majorities. I suppose in your solution they are going to be deported, like happened elsewhere? 'Relocated' I believe you call it. Oh yes – very neat, the usual Turkish solution."

The women looked helplessly on as the two young men smouldered and glared at each other. Both men had arisen from their seats. Nicolai, still sitting, looked at Sima and smiled reassuringly at her, but said nothing, not really knowing what it was all about. Nerissa, who had imagined that they were all about to have a cosy Avakian-style intellectual discussion, was completely appalled. Sima, who should have intervened, seemed lost in her own thoughts, staring all the time at the wilting flowers in her lap, and occasionally glancing at Nicolai, then quickly down again as she saw his eyes fixed firmly on her. Olga, now with tears beginning to flow said "Mikael, please, please, you must know that Selim has never ever for a moment supported ..."

But Selim interrupted her, shouting, "You, sir, are a brash ignorant peasant! You hypocritically agree with me that the Ottomans are finished – so what do you then want to happen to Stamboul. Are you saying that the Armenians should take over. You stupid, uneducated oaf. You must be ..."

"Not the Armenians, you fool, the Greeks. This was always a Greek city – even at the height of the bloody Ottoman Empire. It remained culturally a Greek city, and Greek it will become again."

At this point, Harry, the oldest person present, aware of the increasing distress of his female hostesses, stood up and said,

"Gentlemen, please, can't you see that you are distressing the ladies. Please calm down – you're both getting over-excited." Had Harry, at this point, said nothing more but just smiled, the incident might – just might – have ended there. Unfortunately, he added, "I'm sure the Allies will sort it out. Neither the Greeks nor the Kemalists will be allowed to take Constantinople, we'll see to that."

At this, both Mikael and Selim began shouting, and both reverted to Turkish, while Harry stared at them in amazement. For Harry, his quiet comments were intended to calm the situation. For the two young men, it was the last straw – a proof of the contemptuous arrogance of the western Europeans. Mikael so forgot himself as to start swearing, both at Selim and Harry. Selim, much more controlled but equally furious did just have enough of his father's coolness and politesse not to give way to swearing, but he too told Harry, who didn't of course understand a word, what he thought of the dithering Allies in general, and Harry's commanding officer Harington, in particular.

Within a few moments, as Harry gazed in disbelief, Mikael and Selim turned back against each other and were shouting out things that they were going to rue for the rest of their lives.

"Uncivilised Turk! All you know is how to kill women and children ... barbarian who needs to return to the steppes ... bourgeois exploiter ..." and so on from Mikael, pouring out all the anger and humiliation that had been smouldering under the surface ever since his arrival in this elegant elite home.

"Uneducated peasant ... terrorist traitor ... bloody Greek lover ... illiterate porter ..." and so on from Selim, smoother and without swearing, but equally aggressive and malevolent. He knew in a remote spot in his mind how much his father would have disapproved, how he would have admonished him, not only for the excess of his feelings, but for the sheer bad manners he was displaying.

Olga, now in tears, twice raised her hand to Selim's good arm to try and restrain his anger. Selim, to his lasting horror and shame whenever he recalled it, shook it off in impatience.

Sima, at last fully alive to the awful situation unfolding, stood up as the two young men looked as if they were actually going to come to blows. Nicolai, also understanding little, but seeing her distress also got up and moved alongside Selim. Harry instinctively moved towards Mikael. Olga now in floods of tears and sobbing quietly remained seated looking lost. Who knows what might have happened as the two men continued to shout at each other – when suddenly Karekin appeared at the French window, flanked by Paramaz and Haik.

Karekin could not credit what he was seeing. Selim and a strange young man shouting at each other, and he could actually hear swear words. A British naval officer – he recognised the uniform immediately – moving towards the stranger as if in anticipation of something. His daughter Nerissa clearly in distress looking at the floor, and by God his daughter Olga in floods of tears.

"Silence! Silence!" he thundered in Turkish.

There was, in fact, an immediate silence as everyone on the veranda stopped whatever they were doing or were about to do and turned towards the house. Only Olga's quiet sobs could still be heard, though now more subdued. Selim, suddenly brought up short, blushed red. Deeply ashamed and embarrassed, he tried to touch Olga, but this time it was she who cringed away. Selim could do nothing as he cursed himself for so forgetting his manners, if nothing else. Mikael, however, felt no shame. He knew exactly who this impeccably dressed merchant was, and he refused to lower his eyes.

"You and you," said Karekin, indicating Mikael and Selim, "swearing in front of ladies, will kindly leave this house immediately. Paramaz, please show them to the door."

He stood aside as Mikael, head held high, and Selim, almost in tears himself, moved out. No one said a word. Then Karekin turned to Haik.

"Haik, take your sister to her room."

Haik walked over, gently touched Olga, who at his gentle and caring touch, burst out again in noisy sobs. However, she got up and went into the house with him.

There was a further short silence. Then, Karekin finally walked out into the garden, and turning to Talin, who was still hovering about white-faced behind the tables, said "A fresh pot please, Talin, and some lemon."

He turned and shook hands with Nicolai, who bowed and muttered – "Count Nicolai Androv, *effendi*, at your service."

He then looked round and shook hands with Harry who also introduced himself. Sitting down, he motioned everyone else to do so. He looked completely calm and at ease, but Nerissa noticed from the corner of her eye that he took out his beautiful amber beads and began clicking them, a habit he rarely ever did in public.

"Now, Nerissa, my soul, pull yourself together, we still have guests here. We will have some more tea together and you will all tell me what has been going on here. Where is Armineh for heaven's sake!"

CHAPTER 17

Selim and Mikael

Selim could not think about what had happened at the Avakians without a deep sense of shame and loss. He recalled the anger he had felt for that awful man. He remembered he had almost shouted out, "You filthy *giavour* pig!" As he lay in his darkened room he swallowed back his tears. His father would have been appalled. How much better it would have been if he had kept his cool.

He wasn't concerned about what Mikael might have thought. He had realised almost immediately that Mikael came from a poor, uneducated and under-privileged background – an anomaly in the Avakian household – but that made his own outburst and lack of restraint even worse.

He went through every word, every nuance, and suddenly remembered, with horror, how Olga had taken him into the garden and begged him to calm himself, explained why she had spoken so long and earnestly with Mikael, how she had pleaded with him to be tolerant.

What had he replied? How had he reacted to the woman he loved? He had flung his disability in her face and her imagined desire to find another man. Even at the time, he knew this was totally unjustified. He ached to set it right, to put his good arm around her. She had looked at him for a long moment, but precisely at that time everyone had been called to the tea table.

Everything had conspired to make him angry and confused. It was not just Mikael and his arrogant expression and hateful pro-Greek views. Several other factors played their part: the cool Englishman in his crisp white uniform, who appeared to be yet another new friend of the family, in his mind represented the defeat and humiliation of his own people; the absence of Vahan, who, with his calming and friendly voice would undoubtedly have intervened long before the situation got out of control; even the fact that his new acquaintance, Nicolai, another Christian after all, had seemed so happy and so at home in the company of Sima and the other Avakians. All these factors helped to fan the flames of jealousy in Selim's heart. It was not just sexual, there was an envy about the way all these newcomers fit so easily with this family, while he was the outsider.

Selim lay there unable to explain his reactions, unable to reconcile himself to what had occurred. This was the second time that he had parted from Olga, leaving her in floods of tears. Was this to be their permanent relationship – she to be left in tears at every emotional crisis? Suddenly he recalled those two tentative extensions of Olga's hand reaching out to touch his good hand – that gentle, despairing, pleading, touch; begging him to step back, to stop, to remember his true feelings. She had not been able to say a word, and indeed had not needed to – but he had rejected her. The impatience with which he had snatched his arm away was, as he now realised, more hurtful and meaningful than an hour of abuse. At this point Selim turned his face to the wall and groaned. He could no longer hold back his own tears.

Mikael had turned away and carried on up the hill after leaving the Avakian house, in order to avoid having to walk down behind Selim. He was still seething with anger, as he walked home the long way round. He should never have come. It had all been a terrible mistake.

He was accosted by Nairi the moment he walked back into their house in the centre of Makrikoy.

"Why, Mikael – you're early. What happened, how was it?" said Nairi eagerly.

"Nairi, I don't want to talk about it. It was a God-awful, bloody shambles. You had no right to involve me in this bit of deliberate humiliation."

"Good heavens, my soul, what's the matter, what's the matter? Olga didn't strike me as the sort of person who would want to humiliate anyone."

"It wasn't Olga – though she did make it clear that she had no intention of wanting to see me anymore. She probably thinks I'm too uncouth and vulgar for her precious family. No, it was everyone else, Nairi. They're all a stuck-up bunch of posh, snooty collaborators. Yes, that's the right word – collaborators! Along with the British conquerors and their Turkish friends. I bet their best friends are all those other wealthy Turks with their villas along the Bosporus sucking up like mad to the westerners – there was even one of them there. The Ottoman elite look down on their own poor Turkish peasants, and this lot looked down on me their poor Armenian neighbour. It's all class, not race – bloody class."

"Oh, Mikael – I'm so sorry. Are you sure that was all?"

"Yes. Well, I suppose I had a violent disagreement with an arrogant Turkish guy who called me an uneducated peasant. Can you believe it? Of course they all took sides with him. They suck up to the Turks all the time, desperate not to lose their privileged standard of living. And as for that Olga – infatuated by that arrogant Turkish bastard. She simply wants to be ..."

"Mikael! No! Stop please."

"I'm so sorry, sister, you're right. I'm sorry. Some of the problem is me, I do accept that. I've been restless here ever since getting back from Russia. I really do need to do something."

That night Mikael lay in bed reflecting further. What was he doing here in Makrikoy? Somehow all those years of violence and camaraderie in Russia, first with the Reds and then with the Whites, had left him unable to settle. What, after all, kept him here? He loved his sister, but could not forgive his mother for her rejection of his father, however justified she may have been.

He was not a particularly great admirer of Greek culture or Greek values. He had no sweetheart or even Greek friend, but he had an instinctive feeling that the Greeks and Armenians needed to stick together if they were to survive against the growing backlash of resurgent Turkish nationalism. It was this basic understanding, which so many of the Greek and Armenian leaders did not have, which had caused his outburst at the Avakian tea-party – "Let the Greeks have it."

He had been a soldier for three years – he was experienced, and now, rejected by Olga, he had no ties left in the city. In the end, it was not a difficult decision. The Greek state had an office in the city where they were recruiting volunteers for the army operating in Ionia, where Greeks had lived for millennia. Admittedly, it was set up primarily to persuade ethnic Greeks to join. However, Mikael had no doubt that they would accept him without much question.

The very next day Mikael presented himself at the office situated alongside the Greek embassy. He gave all his details, confirmed all his experience during the Russian civil war claiming that he had been fighting for the Whites and passing over the terrible injuries he had sustained in the Turkish police station – and was duly accepted into the Greek army as a volunteer.

Two days later, he left the city with a small group of other volunteers on board a freighter bound for Smyrna. The future of Greece, indeed perhaps the whole of the Middle East, was to be decided somewhere between Smyrna and Ankara. Constantinople itself was to be the prize. Yet when the Greeks set up their recruiting office in Pera, scarcely two thousand young Greek men out of a population of well over a quarter of a mil*lion* volunteered – and one of them, at least, was an Armenian.

Selim's situation was much more complex. As he looked back, day after day, reflecting on that awful afternoon, he owned up to his own guilt. He did not seek to find facile excuses for his behaviour – but he did begin to question Olga's attitude. Why had she invited him and Mikael together? Surely it must have been to give him a message. As he pondered, he knew that she would never have intended to humiliate him – but it was of course *bey*ond his comprehension that the joint invitation was not her doing. Sima, surely, would not have invited him without Olga's request. He loved Olga; he knew she had been doing her best to restrain him, but why had she created the situation in the first place?

Alongside these feelings was the manner in which Selim, in company with many of his friends and peers, was feeling rejected and humiliated on a daily basis as he walked about the city – his own home and that of his ancestors. There was an open air of Greek triumphalism. The blue and white Greek flag was everywhere. A colossal picture of Venizelos was displayed in Taksim Square. The aggressive new Greek Patriarch required all Greeks to cease all cooperation with the Ottoman government, and was even issuing 'passports' to his co-religionists, as if they were his own 'subjects.'

In addition there was the visible everyday manifestation of British power: 18,000 British and Indian troops: daily meetings between Tim

Harington and whoever was the current Grand Vizier: the Sultan himself continuously bowing to allied, basically British, demands. Selim found himself in a dual emotional turmoil, each mirroring the other. Olga, in tears though she might have been, represented for him in her very person part of the humiliation that was being visited on every Turk in the city. So it wasn't just Mikael that had aroused the anger that had overcome him that afternoon in Makrikoy. The presence, at the same time, of the cool British officer paralleled the political and cultural conflict in the city.

Ottoman or Turk? On the one hand his father's cool rational tolerance of diversity and other cultures, or on the other his mother's steadfast certainties turning to hatred? Tired, multi-cultural internationalism or a vibrant resurgent Turkish nationalism? In the end it was no contest. Like so many others, Selim, with the encouragement of his mother, planned to slip out of Constantinople on a ship sailing along the Black Sea coast to Zonguldak. Selim had chosen. He was off to join those whom the British referred to pejoratively as 'Kemalists,' but who were in reality the new Nationalists. Two nation-states were about to confront each other over the remnants of the old Empire.

And Olga?

Of course she remained in tears after the two young men left the house that afternoon. However, she had a greater confidence and trust in her own judgement about Selim, than he had in her. She had tried to make Mikael welcome, while reiterating that she did not love him. Then she tried to reassure and restrain Selim. The fact that she had failed had left her in tears, but not with the despair that Selim had felt. She loved him, and she was sure in her heart that he loved her. Olga might not be the most perceptive of women but she was totally honest.

She was also unclear in her mind about the meaning of all the crosscurrents of political passion swirling about in the city. She saw Selim only as a man – not as a Moslem, or a Turk, or a Nationalist. She assumed that he saw her only as a woman. It was inconceivable to her that in some section of his mind, he might so analyse the position as to see her as representing a part of his deep feelings of despair and humiliation.

But whether she fully understood the reasons behind Selim's anger or not, she did realise that another crisis had occurred in their relationship. In view of the position with regard to Halideh Hanum, Selim's mother, she was quite unable to visit their home or even send a note. But working in the Turkish military hospital as she still did, she found out soon after the fiasco of the tea party that Selim had joined the lengthening list of young men, politicians and statesmen slipping out of Bolis and joining the Nationalists in Ankara. Olga never thought for a moment that she herself may have been one of the reasons that had led

Selim to this decision.

Before Vahan had a chance to have a word with her about the message he received from Selim about his decision, she had had a conversation with her father, to whom she gave the information that Selim might have left for the interior.

"But my darling father, surely he could have said something – left me a note or something to say goodbye."

"Well, Olga, my soul, stop and consider. He comes to the house and meets here a British naval officer, who admits that he is on General Harington's staff. He overhears, or so I am told, this officer talking about his job and virtually admitting that he acts to keep an eye on citizens intending to go to Ankara. The British have been preventing many prominent people leaving to join Mustapha Kemal, to the point of even imprisoning them. I find it eminently proper that he should not let you or anyone else in this household know of his intentions – which for a Turk I find fairly reasonable."

"But, baba, he knows I love him – and despite all that has happened, I know he loves me."

"My darling, I've seen you together and I do believe that he is an honourable man. I don't doubt your judgement but he doesn't want to embarrass you any more. I don't agree with his view of the political situation, or of the inevitability of the fall of the Ottoman dynasty, and I don't believe that his father would have either – but he must follow his own instincts in this. It's a difficult time for all of us."

"But baba, he knows I love him. What ..."

"Oh, come here, Olga my soul, don't worry – it's all going to come out all right in the end."

And Olga, half sobbing and half laughing cuddled up into her father's arms.

CHAPTER 18

Harry

After Karekin had calmed the atmosphere at the unfortunate Avakian tea party, Harry remained in the beautiful garden, simply enjoying the late afternoon. Haik had taken the weeping Olga away and Sima had gone with them, leaving Karekin, Harry, Nicolai and a subdued Nerissa. Harry and Nicolai, with a single look between them, had decided to leave as soon as decently possible. But once Sima returned, it became obvious that Nicolai was not going to make the first move.

For his part, Harry was enjoying himself in these easy, familial surroundings that he had rarely experienced before. Armineh did not reappear and, as Karekin relaxed, the talk ranged far and wide. After Sima reappeared, confirming all seemed well with Olga, Nerissa perked up.

Harry had been all over the Near East over the last five years, but always in the company of young men of his own class and type. He did not lack conventional social skills; he knew how to chat amenably to young women in a cocktail lounge or at a restaurant table, but had never felt warmth or pleasure in their company. This was true for every relationship he had had with well-bred English girls.

In this respect, there was an ironic similarity in the manner in which English young men of the upper-middle classes were brought up, to the way in which traditional Moslem youth were raised. Without sisters in the household, English public-school boys had no intimate knowledge of the behaviour of young women. This was exactly the same for politer sections of traditional Ottoman society and made Selim stand out so strongly from other Turkish young men. His education at Robert College, and his easy relationship with his sister, had given him straightforwardness in the company of the other sex not enjoyed by many of his peers. This had more to do with local culture than religion.

As the afternoon wore on, the unpleasantness of the earlier hours evaporated. Harry was touched by the bright eyes and almost palpable strength of feeling between Nicolai and Sima. The measured development of Karekin's arguments and ideas, the quick, darting, somewhat humourless comments of Nerissa, and artless chatter of young Seta, did not just charm Harry, it turned his heart over.

For Karekin, the strain of speaking in two languages at once was becoming a strain, and when Armineh finally bustled out into the garden with Haik, it was time to leave. The two young men rose, murmuring their thanks, while Sima also rose and, holding her hand out to Nicolai said, "Gentlemen, shall we take a final stroll in the garden before you leave. Come Nicolai, you can leave from the garden door."

Nicolai hesitated, glancing at Armineh and Karekin – but then he bowed to Armineh, took her hand and kissed it repeating his thanks to her for the afternoon, and with a smile at Karekin who remained seated, took Sima's hand as they walked down towards the orchard.

"Well," said Nerissa to no one in particular, "Come, Haik, Harry, it appears that it has to be the back door for you as well."

Nerissa took Harry's arm as they walked down the stairs into the garden. Making no attempt to catch up with Sima, they dawdled by the orchard, along the old stone wall and through the trees, savouring the scents and saying little. Harry had the hand of this intense girl demurely but firmly through his arm until they arrived at the solid iron door set in the wall facing onto the street, where Sima and Nicolai were standing silently waiting for them.

Some days later Harry reported to General Harington at his headquarters in the Harbiye.

"Well, Harry," said Harington, "how are things in the city? This town never ceases to fascinate me. I attended the Selamlik a few weeks ago with General Chapuy, and that tricky Italian, Mombelli. That day it was at the Santa Sophia. We were up in the visitors gallery. There were thousands in the mosque – fantastic! It can hold so many but, from above, it looks quite small. It was a special service. The old Sultan is not a great horseman, I'm afraid – but rode in on a white horse, and there were great lighted torches all round the animal. It was spectacular Harry, I can tell you."

"You know, sir, there is something particularly meaningful about white horses in this city. Didn't 'desperate Frankie' arrive here riding on one last year."

"Ah well – hm – yes. It all started with Mehmet II, the Ottoman conqueror of the city – they forget nothing these people – more than five hundred years ago, but it's as if it happened yesterday. Right, have you anything to report?"

For some time, Harry and the General discussed technical details around navy-army cooperation. Then Harington genially offered Harry a drink. After the drinks were poured, and the two men relaxed, Harington, said,

"This has been a really great posting. I love it here Harry. The people of Constantinople – all races, Harry, all these nationalities, all mixed up together. They are all so extraordinarily friendly, and there is such a fine atmosphere in the city, don't you find?"

"Well, sir, I'm not so sure that that applies to the Turks at the moment."

"No, maybe not. But I'll tell you something, they may not be quite so happy, but I find them to be an honourable lot. I get on very well with old Mehmet and his entourage – you know we should never have abandoned our pro-Ottoman policy in 1914. A great mistake. That bloody battleship *Goeben*, it has a lot to answer for."

"Yes, sir – but what about the nationalists in Anatolia?"

"You mean the Kemalists? I just don't know. Mustapha Kemal is a real soldier, but he only had a rag-bag of an army a few months ago and last year, I would have argued confidently that there was no way he could have stood up to a well-officered Greek army. However, since then, I understand that he has some sort of deal with the Bolsheviks in

Moscow and they are feeding him arms. They've certainly squeezed the poor Armenians between them. You've heard that a treaty has now been signed, the Treaty of Kars. The unlucky Armenians have even lost their precious Mount Ararat – they really have suffered a catastrophic five or six years – they'll never recover. Kemal no longer has any worries on his eastern front and can turn all his attention to the Greeks."

"Well they are still formidable enough, aren't they?"

"I'm no longer so sure, Harry. Since the return of that Germanophile King Constantine, things have changed yet again. All the previous senior officers have been replaced by new, hopelessly inexperienced Royalist officers. For God's sake, most of them haven't commanded anything for about four years. I found them a cocksure lot, who don't care much for the welfare of their troops – always a bad sign. They strut about dressed in smart uniforms ,which they're very concerned not to get dirty, but in my opinion they don't have much idea about soldiering. I went to inspect their division at Ismid a few weeks ago. The men were fine. Man for man the Greek soldier is as brave as a Turk, though perhaps not quite as mulishly dogged in defence, but – oh dear, the officers! Little motivation and riddled with 'politicals', if you know what I mean."

"Indeed I do, sir. Incidentally I keep hearing rumours round the bar at the Park that the Greeks are considering a move to take over the city."

"I've heard those rumours too, Harry. Listen, I myself believe that it was a terrible mistake of our Welsh wizard to arrange for the occupation of Smyrna by the Greek army. Nothing that we have done during the whole occupation of this city has so helped the nationalists of Ankara to consolidate their support as that decision. But the one thing that the Allied Supreme Council has made quite clear is that they will not allow this city to fall into the hands of the Greek army. So far, for better or worse, Constantinople has been spared the bloodshed and violence going on everywhere else in the old empires and I intend to do my utmost to keep it that way.

I simply can't believe they would be so foolish as to make an attempt on Constantinople itself. The whole situation is amazing – absurd – an aide of the old Sultan actually offered me a force of twenty thousand Turks to help me defend the city. For God's sake I am supposed to be occupying the city against them, and here they are offering me help to defend the city against our supposed allies the Greeks. If it was a Gilbert and Sullivan operetta, it would be too silly. Anyway, I went with Chapuy – he's a good soldier – and we inspected the Chatalja lines, thirty miles away. One of the finest natural military positions in the world. I gave Chapuy the job of holding them, and he has French troops as well as British. No, no, the Greeks wouldn't be so foolish."

"Well, let's hope you're right, sir. If the Greeks were to occupy Constantinople, there could be terrible bloodshed. But, assuming we can avoid that, what is to be its eventual fate?"

"I don't know, Harry. I just don't know All the great European dynasties – Hapsburg, Romanov and several German ones – have all disappeared into the dustbin of history, whereas, here, the Ottomans cling on and remain respected, and yes even loved, by the ordinary people, even though Constantinople is the only European capital ever to have been permanently occupied by a foreign force since Napoleon. Anything is possible, anything, and we have to tread very carefully. The one thing I intend to work for more than anything else is to avoid any harm to this wonderful city."

"I do agree, sir. It would seem to me that the preservation intact of a great thousand-year old city would be a greater personal achievement for any military governor than some ephemeral national or imperial advantage."

CHAPTER 19

Smyrna – the clerics

Innumerable factors eventually led to the terrible catastrophe visited on the hapless Armenian peasantry of the Eastern Anatolian countryside during 1915 and 1916, but the fatal decision of the Ittihad leaders to orchestrate the Ottoman entry into the Great War, facilitated by the escape of the *Goeben* and its dramatic entry into the Dardanelles, was critical. There had of course been many other factors including the sinister and devious character of the corpulent Talaat Pasha, one of the triumvirate leading the Committee of Union and Progress, who ordered the deportations. However, another, was the character and background of each of the Ottoman provincial governors required to carry out the orders sent out by the Ministry of the Interior in Constantinople.

Where the old traditional Ottoman governors were still in place, the decrees were sometimes ignored or avoided. However, where the arrogant new breed had replaced the Governor, imbued as they were with their exclusive brand of nationalism: the one-nation, one-language, one-culture school of thought, the decrees were carried out brutally and with enthusiasm.

In 1915, Smyrna had been one of the vilayets where the old Ottoman governor was still in charge. Rahmi *Bey* was a despot from the old Ottoman elite. He was a tall impressive figure who loved all the good and expensive things in life. Not corrupt, as such, but with a great appetite for luxurious living.

It so happened that at the same time, the Armenian primate was a certain Archbishop Indjeyan. This cleric was a great, fat, jolly gentleman, a medieval clerical figure who also loved the good things of life. Despite his spectacular display of Rabelaisian hedonism, he was well-versed in the arcane subtleties of the doctrinal differences between the Orthodox and Catholic on the one hand, and his own Church's quasi-monophysite beliefs. Did Christ have one divine nature only manifesting itself as human on earth? Alternatively, did he have two natures, human and divine equally? Debate over these subtleties had raged at Nicaea, Chalcedon, Ephesus, and the other early Church Councils all in the area around Smyrna itself. Indjeyan could talk for hours about the true nature of Christ, though he rarely found it necessary; his congregation was not interested, and he himself preferred playing poker.

Rahmi *Bey* and Archbishop Indjeyan soon struck up a useful friendship. Women were excluded from this discourse. The Archbishop, like all the higher clergy of the Armenian church, was celibate, whilst women simply did not figure in the public life of a Moslem grandee. And so, poker games, in opulent surroundings, with plenty of raki and other strong liquors became a regular feature of the relationship between the Turkish governor and the Armenian Primate in the vilayet of Smyrna.

Rahmi *Bey* and his fellow governor of Adrianople on the European side – Hadji Adil *Bey* – were not only both aristocratic Ottomans of the old school, they both men of culture and distinction who understood so much more of the world than Talaat, a postal clerk from Macedonia, ever could. It was crystal clear to these men that the deportation orders, quite apart from their immorality, were fatal for the empire currently trying to fight a difficult and vital war. The new decrees would – at a stroke – remove all the shopkeepers, most of the merchants, the trading middle classes and above all a large class of taxpayers.

In attending the meetings of the CUP in Stamboul, they made it clear that they did not wish to expel the Armenians from their own vilayets. After explaining their reasoning and giving their reports to the minister they stuck to their decisions. Talaat, in the true tradition of a bully, left them alone.

Indjeyan may have been a lover of the fleshpots and neither celibate nor very pious, but he was a shrewd operator, and he understood the importance of keeping on good terms with Rahmi *Bey*. Needless to say the Armenian nationalists of the Armenian Revolutionary Federation did not see it the same way. They, too, were interested in the creation of yet another exclusive, and almost by definition, intolerant nation-state. They saw the unreformed Armenian Church in the cities as almost as moribund as the Ottoman Empire itself, and thought of the relationship between them as one propping up the other.

Meanwhile, the other great clerical figure in the town was Archbishop Chrysostom of the Greek orthodox church – the primate of the Greek community. The Greeks constituted almost half of the population of Smyrna, and had dominated the area for 2,000 years. A more committed Christian than the jolly Indjeyan, he did not have the same easy relationship with Rahmi *Bey*, and was less able to object to the malevolently drafted decrees. Above all, he was not nearly as effective in defending his flock from Rahmi, who sanctioned a few arrests and deportations to keep his masters in Constantinople happy.

An imposing figure, he stood tall, with piercing eyes and a handsome bearded face. He was by nature histrionic. When he raised his hands to bless the congregation, everyone present, Christians and cynics alike, felt personally touched. But he could articulate little about the nature of Christ or of the doctrinal differences between the many different Christian sects within the Empire.

Indjeyan's understanding with Rahmi could not last. Sooner or later the puritanical Armenian nationalist leaders in Smyrna were going to get rid of him. He lacked the commitment to Armenian nationalism they required. To make matters worse, he found the ardent young revolutionaries somewhat ridiculous! Members of the ARF took themselves very seriously indeed. They could tolerate their political opponents, who were as serious about their beliefs as themselves – but to be laughed at by a corpulent priest who hobnobbed with the 'enemy' was too much to bear. Like all ardent young revolutionaries, they were insensitive to the saving of life. The fact that this medieval bishop had saved countless lives by his intercessions with the governor meant nothing to them. For them, the more innocent blood shed the better and they worked successfully to organise the removal of the jolly bishop.

And so, instead of the tolerant, easy-going, luxury-loving prelate, the Armenians now received a new puritanical, abrasive primate – one Archbishop Tourian. Levon Tourian, a relative of a well-loved earlier Patriarch of Constantinople, had been the bishop in Adrianople, from where he had fled to Bulgaria during the war, even though there had been no deportations or arrests there.

The handsome Tourian had never had an easy relationship with anyone. Wherever he went, turmoil and strife tended to follow. He was not outspoken on the nature of Christ or the main Christian message, but his political views were well-defined. By the time of his arrival, Rahmi *Bey* had also been relieved. And so it was, as Smyrna slowly became the focus of all the tensions and problems of the dying Ottoman Empire, the *dramatis personae* of the principle officers in the town changed. Instead of tolerant and easy-going ever-so-slightly corrupt lovers of life, there were now two puritanical bishops.

During these last days of empire, the position of the Christian churches in the Ottoman world was anomalous. For the Ottomans, dividing the Christian Raya into its religious 'millet,' a system which had lasted for five hundred years, was a natural way of government. Islam was a single unit – or so it might wish to appear in an ideal world – but from the start, the Sultans recognised the many divisions into which the conquered Christians were divided. For the Sultan and the Imperial government, those divisions were religious not political. Accordingly, for them, the Orthodox constituted one group to be headed by the Greek Orthodox Patriarch in Constantinople.

By the end of the nineteenth century, the Orthodox community was no longer exclusively Greek. Nationalism had struck creating Serb-orthodox, Bulgarian-orthodox and many other nationalities. None of these were prepared to be led by the Greeks alone.

It was an extraordinarily complex situation. The clergy throughout the Empire increasingly tended to their own flock exclusively – the Armenian Church for the Armenians alone; the Greek Patriarch no longer with power over all the Orthodox, now tending to the spiritual needs only of the ethnic Greeks; the Bulgarian exarchate for the Bulgarians and so on. In so doing, they were in fact pandering to what in another context they referred to as 'the new and destructive principle of nationality.'

At the same time, they were also aware that in one sense their power over their own flock was bound up with the continuation of Ottoman power. Their real enemy, when they thought about it at all – was the young secular nationalists.

This applied equally to the Moslem spiritual leaders who issued fatwa after fatwa against the secular nationalists of Ankara. They too saw their advantage bound up with the continuation of the Ottomans and not with those wishing to break up the Empire. It was, of course, easier for them – their religion and their empire coincided. For the Christian priests it was more difficult. If they rejected 'the destructive principle of nationality' on the grounds that it was basically secular, their flock would see them as 'collaborators' with the Turk.

A sophisticated merchant from Bolis could see the difference between 'Turk' and 'Ottoman' – a simple villager from the Smyrna vilayet could not.

And so the scene was being set for the great confrontation between an intolerant Turkish nation-state based on Ankara, and a Greek nation-state based on Athens. In between these two overgrown nationalist villages, the great Imperial city of Constantinople – whether Ottoman or Byzantine – was about to be squeezed. And neither the Orthodox Patriarch, heir to over a thousand years of spiritual power, nor the Sheik-ul-Islam, religious leader of the most powerful Caliphate in Moslem history, could do anything about it, even though the end result, whichever way it went, was going to end their own power forever.

CHAPTER 20

Selim and Vahan – a question of nationality

Selim had not in fact slipped away without a word to anyone. As Karekin thought he had been worried as to how exactly Harry had fitted into the Avakian family. The British occupation authorities were making great efforts to prevent the seepage of Turks to the Ankara alternative government, and had spies all over the city watching out for such moves.

There was, however, one person whom he knew he could trust completely to pass on information to Olga, without endangering his project by giving information to British Intelligence or to the Ottoman government in Stamboul – his good friend Vahan. And so it was that on the day before he said a final farewell to his mother and sister, he had walked down the steep little road that led from Taksim to the Bosporus seafront and knocked at the door of the Asadourian's terrace house. Ara opened the door.

"Buyurun, *effendi*," he said in his old-fashioned way, recognising Selim and opening the door wide with a smile.

The Asadourian house was small. The main entrance door led straight into a small dark marbled hallway, with its tiny barred window looking out into the street. The sitting room ran from the front to the back of the house on the left side of the hall.

Ara looked into the sitting room and said from the door, "Vahan, brother, your friend Selim *effendi* is here."

Selim smiled broadly as Vahan came bounding out of the door

"Selim, Selim, come in – come in. Both Raffi and my dad are here. They would love to see you."

"Of course I would love to see them, but first I would like to talk to you alone if I may."

"My dear fellow, of course, of course. Come, let's go into the dining room. Ara, my soul, could you bring in a couple of coffees. Oh, yes, when you go back to the sitting room, please tell our father and brother that we will join them shortly."

And so it was that Selim sat at the heavy table sipping a tiny cup of strong Turkish coffee without sugar, while Vahan sat opposite him sipping his heavily sweetened cup. Selim quietly told Vahan all that had happened at the Avakians, making no attempt to hide his own bad behaviour, but neither dwelling on it. Eventually, Selim came to the point of his visit –

"Vahan, my friend. I know your views. I know that you have no wish for Stamboul to be taken over by Athens for instance and that you are an Ottoman supporter and disapprove of the national movement in Anatolia. But Vahan, I can't support the Ottomans anymore. The Sultan is entirely under the thumb of that British general – Harington. It is a national disgrace; and to cap it all they send in the Greeks to occupy Smyrna. I can't bear it – I can't bear it! I am going to leave the city and join the men in Ankara."

"Selim, I don't agree with you, as you know, but I do understand your feelings, but have you ..."

"Vahan, I am leaving tomorrow morning. I came to tell you this, not to discuss my decision, but simply to let you know so that you can tell Olga. Oh, Vahan, I only ever seem to bring her grief. This is the third time we have parted, and my abiding memory of her is in tears."

"Selim, I won't attempt to change your mind about the politics, but about Olga, listen to me. I have no idea who this Mikael chap is, or what his relationship with Olga ever was. But please take it from me – you know I wouldn't lie to you – I am quite certain that there was never any intention in Olga's mind to humiliate you. Look, Olga is not the cleverest of young ladies – but Selim – no – no – she isn't the sort to practice deception. It's not in her nature. If she wanted to break up your relationship, she would tell you so to her face. Please, Selim, don't make any decisions based on what appears to have been an unpremeditated incident."

"I know, Vahan, I know. I am not proposing to join the nationalists because of that, though it has triggered my decision. Over two years have passed since the Armistice was signed and during all that time I have drifted about without purpose. Olga and I see each other fleetingly and never at my own home due to my mother's refusal to see her. I don't go all that often to Makrikoy either, as Olga's own mother, whilst always polite, makes it clear that she disapproves of me."

"Not of you, Selim, of the relationship."

"Yes, well, don't quibble, Vahan. The point is that I suddenly feel

I must act. I believe in the Turkish 'nation,' and I am going to go and work for it – even with this useless stump of an arm."

"My friend, I have already said I am not going to try and change your mind. Go and join Mustapha Kemal – it is clearly your destiny. But I do insist on repeating my views about the whole concept of the 'nation.' It is not, nor has it ever been, anything more than an idea – a theory. A State? Well we all understand what that is – simply a geographic area within certain boundaries in which people follow the same laws and submit to the same government. An ethnic group – there again we all understand that – people who share the same music, eat the same food, speak the same language, marry in the same way, one could go on and on.

"But the so-called 'nation' is not the same as either of those. I ask you, who ever even thought of 'the nation' before the last century – it is an idea dreamed up by intellectuals and academics, the teachers of language and literature in particular. What is it? People with common blood. What nonsense – where the hell is common blood? My God, think of all those harem girls who bore innumerable Sultans, where did they all come from, scarcely a Turk amongst them."

"Vahan, hold on a moment, no one believes in that common blood stuff anymore do they? You're raising an issue just to knock it down."

"Well, Selim, take it from me that some people still do. If they don't talk about common blood anymore, nevertheless they feel that the 'nation' is a sort of spiritual concept. It's all in the mind Selim, there is no reality to it."

"But Vahan, there is such a thing as a common language, and a common memory."

"The state is what matters, and the question is how do you draw the boundaries of an area where there are so many different peoples living together. What applies to the lands of the old Austrian Empire, applies even more to us here. We had Serbs, Bulgarians, Vlachs, Albanians, Turks, Greeks, often of different religions, all living fairly amicably under the Ottomans, however inefficient and imperfect they may have been. How many so-called nation-states do you want to create to accommodate them? You have to lump many of them together to create any sort of viable state, and if you then refer to the result as a nation-state, the dominant ethnic group will oppress the others in the mystical name of 'the nation.'"

"Vahan, diversity is all very well, but people are afraid of differences – it all creates friction between neighbours."

"No – it is perfectly possible to love one's own language and literature, one's own food and dances, ones own music and customs and yet still be part of a state that doesn't directly participate actively in all these things. Look at the United States."

"Vahan, my friend, you know you talk too much. You sound just like my poor old dad. I'm not going to argue any more. I feel 'Turkish' and I know what I mean when I say that, even if others don't. I am not in the business of wanting to dominate others – I don't want empire any more – just a new, modern Turkey."

"Very well, very well – forget the Armenians or the Greeks – what about the Kurds – Moslem but non-Turk."

"Poof – the Kurds? They're certainly not a nation, they're just a sect of Turks!"

"Ah! Selim, there you are, you've articulated the problem in that one sentence. Oh dear, we're never going to agree are we? Never mind, my good friend, I wish you all the very best in your adventure and may you be always fortunate. I will tell Olga, discreetly, of your decision – but to be on the safe side, I'll wait until you are well away. Come, let's join my family."

Vahan stood and came round the table. For a moment they stood staring at each other – then Vahan moved forward and held Selim tight in his arms for a long and significant embrace. They then broke apart without any embarrassment, grinned at each other and went out through the hall and into the sitting- room.

"Hello, father, you know Selim of course," said Vahan.

Since his arrival in Bolis over three years ago, after his enforced and dramatic wanderings in the Syrian desert and cities, Garabed had slowly built up a new small business in the great covered bazaar; at first living in the two rooms at the top of the Patakis house in Stamboul – Ara and Vahan in one room, and he in the other. They had lived, to all intents and purposes, on Vahan's salary from the Electricity Company. Garabed used what little savings he had, and added to it the payments, honourably discharged, from merchants, both Turkish and Armenian, who owed him money from the days before April 1915. He could never have enforced these commercial debts, nevertheless, the old Ottoman honour system of mutual obligations and duties, especially in the commercial world, still prevailed and many of the debts were honoured, at least in part.

And so Garabed had bought a shop in the Grand Bazaar where he sold fine textiles and cloths of many different kinds. When Raffi finally arrived out of the interior, the business had begun to thrive, for Raffi was an energetic hard-working young man, strong and able to lift and carry, and with a sharp business mind. Vahan was helpful in writing letters and in other languages, but he just didn't have the same ruthless drive. He assisted, and as the business expanded, became increasingly involved, but it was Raffi who did the hard physical work. Frenchmen appointed by the allied occupation authorities had replaced the

German directors of the electricity company. Vahan continued to work there for some time, but had now left to join the family business.

Garabed got on well with Selim, and had welcomed him as a friend of his eldest son. Garabed could not speak Armenian. He had missed out on the great nationalist movement of the 1870s and 80s, when Armenian intellectuals, teachers and academics, educated in Western Europe or Bolis, had flooded into the schools and institutions of the Armenian villages and towns in Anatolia in a frenzy of idealism, to teach the language, poetry, history and culture of 'the nation.'

But he knew how to run a commercial venture – and he could do it better than all his educated competitors. He also knew how to relate to the Turks, and Selim felt this, and in his many visits to the Asadourian house had come to look up to Garabed as a father figure.

As they sat down and joined the family, Vahan carefully kept the talk away from the matter of the nationalists in Ankara. But in his care to avoid that subject he overlooked another matter which he had not wanted raised. Before he realised what was happening, Selim and Raffi were talking about the Avakians.

"What's that – you mean Karekin Avakian of the market here," said Garabed pricking up his ears.

"Yes sir, certainly – I'm sure you know his daughter," said Selim, while Vahan was chatting to Ara and not really listening.

"No, no, I don't," said Garabed. "They have a large house in Makrikoy I believe. I don't know them."

"Yes, yes, I was there a few days ago, and I saw Nerissa. I am sure that you know her, Asadour *effendi*. She is the girl who goes dancing so much with Vahan."

Raffi tried to think of something to say quickly but could not manage and mumbled some indistinct words. Selim knew that Nerissa and Vahan often met and went dancing and to tea in the late afternoon after the university day ended; indeed he had sometimes accompanied them. However, it had simply never occurred to him that Vahan had never told his father. He now felt a rising tension; Vahan and Ara had stopped chatting after hearing Selim's last sentence. There was an anxious silence.

What Selim now saw was the man he so respected staring at him and then, leaning heavily on his stick, slowly rising from his chair. Vahan had gone white and was looking at the floor. Raffi had gone bright red and was looking helplessly at his father. Ara was clearly terrified, for no reason at all as far as Selim could see.

Garabed was a man with a hasty and overwhelming temper who had always had to keep tight control on himself. The disappearance and elimination of all the women in his life – all his daughters and his gentle wife, who had done so much to help him curb these moods – in the slaughter of the deportations, had not helped, and he lived on a knife edge of anger. He felt real shame that he had been exposed as a man who had no idea what was happening within his own family. The knuckles of his hand whitened as he gripped the stick.

There was in fact only one person who could help to prevent a shaming outburst, which would have disgraced the old man worse than anything that had been said. Terrified though he was, Ara stood up and in his countrified way, in the awful silence, went and knelt before Garabed now standing upright. Taking the hand that was not gripping the stick, he raised it to his lips and said, "Father, my father, we knew about my brother's interest, but did not wish to disturb you until my brother could make his mind up as to his real feelings."

Garabed looked down at the boy kneeling before him, and took a deep audible breath. He then gently drew his hand away and laid it on Ara's head for a moment. Always aware of what had taken place all those years ago at Ara's home and to his parents, he could never raise his voice at the boy. He had indeed been angry at the thought of being kept in the dark, but, in the end, it was just a matter of pride. Now it suddenly all dissipated. He stopped scowling and smiled at everyone in the room, pulling at Ara's arms to make him get up.

"Come, come everyone – it's a bit of a surprise, but well this is the twentieth century, but see how it has taken a Turk to tell me what my own sons are doing. Thank you Selim, my boy. Now I insist on only one thing – Vahan. I know there is no woman in the house, but we can get round that I'm sure. I want you to invite this young lady to visit us here – perhaps with her mother, or a sister, next Sunday or as soon as possible after. Selim, perhaps you can come too."

Selim stood, as did everyone else.

"Asadour *effendi*, I'm afraid I will be going away on a short trip, so I will not be able to accept your kind invitation – but I wish you all well. May Allah be with this house and with you all." Selim and Vahan looked at each other for a long searching moment – both knowing full well that there was every chance that they might never see each other again. Then Selim turned, smiled at everyone and left.

He set out next day on a small freighter bound for Zonguldak on the Black Sea.

CHAPTER 21

Sima and Haik in Prinkipo

The weeks were passing and still there appeared to be no decisions in sight on the question of the fate of the great Imperial city of Constantinople. The British had been in occupation now for three years and it was beginning to look as permanent as the 'temporary' occupation of Egypt. The nasty and bitter war going on in the mountains, valleys and villages of western Anatolia rumbled on. Young men, Greek and Turkish, were dying on both sides in terrible conditions. But, neither the Royalists in Athens, nor the Nationalists in Ankara were likely to call it off. Pure pride and vanity and a craving for glory had captured the king. Constantine might have retired gracefully from the Smyrna debacle at the point that he had taken over from Venizelos, but he missed his chance in the general euphoria.

The Greeks continued their small offensives, often meeting with minor local success; but the basic strategic position hadn't changed and made absolutely no sense. What could they capture that would end the war? The capture of the little tin pot village of Ankara could not have made the slightest difference. The king turned up at the front, attended by a Staff "completely ignorant of war" as Tim Harington himself put it. The Greeks shouted "To Angora! To Angora!" almost as mindlessly as Turkish mobs shouted "*Giavour, giavour!*" The king was photographed riding splendidly on a white horse in front of a parade.

Meanwhile, in Constantinople itself, it all seemed remote and far away. As the spring days passed and summer arrived, the city simply ignored the events going on in the hinterlands.

When the newspapers reported an insignificant Greek local victory – "Kemal repulsed at Buyuk somewhere or other," excited Greek youths would rush around the city in the new open-topped 'otomobils,' waving their flags and singing songs. If the same newspapers then reported an equally minor Kemalist victory – "Greeks retire at Kutchuk somewhere-or-other" – the cafes along the Bosporus would fill with Turks smoking their narghilehs, smiling and nodding at each other, and making significant finger movements across their throats to show what would happen to the filthy *giavours* when the Kemalists finally arrived. Both events, all but forgotten on the next day.

Harington *effendi* was in charge. Large French and British battleships, with their huge guns, were in the harbour dominating everything. Everybody, regardless of race, was making money. It was party time. Constantinople was intact, thriving and prosperous. Unlike the other great imperial families of Europe – Hapsburgs, Hohenzollerns and Romanovs – the Ottoman dynasty was still in place.

Sima, who had been seeing more and more of Nicolai, accidentally surely, at snatched moments at the Pera Palace, did not consider herself to be 'in love.' That was nonsense, fit only for the romanticism of her sisters. She was sensible, she was going to marry good, reliable, podgy George. They would have a fine house in Bebek and lots of children, and she would be happy and content.

At their last meeting, Nicolai had invited Sima to visit him on Sunday, for his day off, at his home on Prinkipo island, where he was still living with his mother and brother Alexei. Sima had accepted with alacrity, for it was just a day's outing to the beautiful islands of the Marmara. The usual summer picnic trips of the Bolsetsi to the islands, and particularly Prinkipo, had been somewhat curtailed this year, due to the continuing heavy presence of Russian refugees still living in houses requisitioned by the government after the arrival of Wrangel's army.

So why now the hesitation? Sima decided that she could not go alone. She shook her head as if to clear it of all these fuzzy thoughts. Though years had passed and the whole social climate had changed, so what need of a chaperone. Ridiculous! Nevertheless she remained unconvinced by her own arguments. One thing was certain, she was certainly not going to go with Olga or Nerissa, but Seta was also impossible, as that would entail getting parental permission.

Suddenly it was obvious – the one who would really look forward to a trip to Buyukada on a Sunday would be Haik, so it was arranged for the next week. Sima treated the whole matter very lightly; it was just a summer trip to the Princes Island. Nicolai would be meeting them at the boat station on the island and Haik would keep her company on the way out and the way back. She thought that they would be having a picnic in the woods. And why not? Haik was finishing at High School and might soon be going with George to Smyrna with a view to opening a new branch office, so this might be a last chance for him. It was all so natural. Everyone agreed.

Only Armineh was not quite so relaxed and at ease; she sensed feelings in her eldest daughter that Sima herself did not recognise. Thinking of what Karekin had said about the meeting he had witnessed at the Pera Palace, she was beginning to worry – not so much for Sima herself, as for all Karekin's well-laid business plans for the connection with the house of Levonian.

It was a wonderful Sunday morning when Haik and Sima strolled down to the Cobancesme station and took the train to Sirkeci. They both took this same train journey almost daily, but somehow the holiday excursion atmosphere made them more conscious of the glories of the simple trip. The train skirted the Sea of Marmara and then entered through the great city walls at the fortress of Yedikule, passed all round the Topkapi Palace grounds along the sea walls, finally turning the promontory and ending alongside the entrance to the Golden Horn at Sirkeci station.

Sima and Haik rarely did things together unless they were part of the whole family group. There was seven years between them and the difference between a marriageable young lady over twenty-four and a young man who was still only a boy, was enormous. But somehow everything about this day was light and joyful. The atmosphere in the city was without tension. The station was busy, and as they walked down to the Galata bridge the crowds were festive and relaxed. There remained a greater police presence than before the war – but then there were now more rowdy foreigners in the city, and the police, under the control of Harington *effendi*, were polite and helpful.

The boats to the islands, running about every half-hour on a weekend day of such brilliant summer sunshine, were full. Haik managed to get them onto the second boat that pulled in and they found seats at the edge on the upper deck, though they had to wait 30 minutes after the first boat left. Haik was feeling sentimental and his heart suddenly became full of love for his eldest sister – feelings which were normally reserved for Nerissa and Seta. Sima was usually too grand and remote – too much like a second mother to him. Haik was sensitive; he always had been, and he felt warmth and an anticipatory happiness emanating from Sima.

The ferry hooted and pulled away from the quayside. Haik, excited and happy, grabbed and held onto Sima's hand. And thus it was, sitting on the upper deck of the white ferry, hand in hand like when they were children, they watched as the boat slipped away and turned towards the south past the green expanse of the grounds of the old Byzantine palace, the high walls and kiosks of the Ottoman Topkapi Saray, the thousand year old sea walls and moved out to sea. Looming behind them was the wonder of the Aya Sophia and the Sultan Ahmet Mosque. Finally the ferry turned away from Europe and headed towards Asia.

They had both seen all this many times before. Picnic excursions to the islands were a favourite of the Bolsetsi throughout the summer. But today was different. Haik knew it was different, and he also knew that the difference lay in some quality in his sister. She was looking so beautiful and relaxed as she held his hand, just like Nerissa would have done.

For her part, Sima was simply enjoying a beautiful day out – or that's what she thought. What a joy it was to sit in this boat, staring across a flat blue sea, with the incomparable Constantinople skyline as a back-drop and with her only brother sitting alongside, holding her hand. Why hadn't she done something like this before? Haik was such a good boy. Everything looked and felt so wonderful. The boat at last pulled in past the red cliffs to the pine-covered island of Kiraliada. She saw the little seaport promenade filled with happy, jostling people. Sima smiled and, for no apparent reason, squeezed Haik's hand.

The boat stopped there for only a few minutes, then pulled away setting course for the next island, eventually reaching their destination, Buyukada, the principal port of the largest island – Prinkipo.

Haik and Sima got up as almost everybody began shuffling down the stairs and onto the gangplank to the quayside. Waiting at the end of the quay, with a broad smile was Nicolai, and by his side his young brother, a washed and scrubbed Alexei.

"My little brother – Alexei," said Nicolai as they walked up. He took Sima's hand and bent down and kissed it, then straightened up but still held her hand.

"Miss, I'm so happy to ... gosh, you are pretty," said Alexei, taking Sima's hand away from Nicolai. He then leant forward, although only just fifteen he was as tall as her, and kissed her firmly on each cheek Haik watched, amazed that his sister had not pulled back nor shown any embarrassment. Far from it, Sima was laughing with pure pleasure. He was then about to shake hands with Alexei, as Nicolai introduced him, when he found himself being grabbed round the shoulders as Alexei leant up, for Haik was quite a few inches taller, and kissed him also on both cheeks. Alexei, grinning widely then danced away and said – "A carriage, Nicolai, a carriage, there are plenty still available – what fun."

A few steps away from the quayside was the centre of the little town – an oddly shaped, almost circular square, round which were several two-horse carriages ready to take all the passengers to their favourite spots for the afternoon, or just for a long ride round the island.

"Oh, Alexei, please can't we walk, it's so beautiful," said Sima with a quick smile.

They all walked along the lane, still and lazy with the heavy scents of summer blossoms – the pines and other trees at the sides providing a lovely dappled shade. There were no cars or lorries on the island; only the clip-clop of the horses and the bells of the carriages to accompany the idyllic walk. Covering the hills on either side was an abundance of bougainvillea, mimosa, jasmine and honeysuckle, some in bloom, some not. The place was alive with flowers, and with the heavy smell of a high summer's day.

Haik's senses reeled. Led by the hand in an artlessly natural way by this fair-haired, enthusiastic, 15 year-old lad, who appeared to have no inhibitions of any kind, was a delight. As Alexei turned off the road onto a path going through the trees still leading him by the hand Haik stole a quick look back. Nicolai and Sima were themselves walking hand in hand behind. Sima looked flushed but her eyes were sparkling.

As they walked on, now well ahead of the others, Alexei continued to prattle on with great warmth and spirit, not that Haik was paying much attention. But then suddenly Haik stopped. His thoughts had swung from Sima to Paramaz, and the way he hassled young Seta, and the distaste Haik felt for it all.

Alexei let go of his hand, and looking up at him said, speaking French, his more natural language, for the first time – "Monsieur Haik, my friend, you are troubled about something, what is it?"

"I was just wondering whether my reaction to something might be because of jealousy only."

"Jealous? of whom – of my brother's love for your sister?"

"No, no, someone quite different – it would take too long to explain. But wait a moment, what do you mean, your brother's love for my sister."

"Well, come, come, Monsieur Haik, you must have noticed."

Switching back to English, Haik said - "First Alexei, for God's sake stop calling me Monsieur. Then, what are you implying about Nicolai and Sima?"

"Of course, Haik." Calling him 'Haik' seemed to make Alexei a little shy for the first time that day. Nevertheless, taking up Haik's hand again he spun him round to face back up the path weaving down through the trees.

"See, they haven't turned the corner yet, and we've already been standing here for many minutes. I must say I do like your sister already, though she is a bit solemn – but when she does smile it's like the sun coming out. Hey – you do swim, don't you? I'll take you swimming after lunch to my own private swimming spot. No one knows of it, I swear."

At this point, Nicolai and Sima did at last come round the corner and walked up to them still hand in hand but now silent, no longer talking animatedly as before.

The sheer animal spirits of Alexei had communicated itself to Sima. The sight of Haik and Alexei walking ahead of them, hand in hand, and the way Alexei ran alongside the long-striding Haik, looking up and chatting, dashing from right to left and picking flowers and weeds, and holding hands all over again, charmed and disturbed her. Nicolai, meanwhile, was holding her own hand tightly throughout.

After leaving the road and taking the path down the hillside, Haik and Alexei were well ahead and had turned the corner. Nicolai stopped. Everything conspired against Sima and her sensible ideas of propriety.

It was indeed a conspiracy – a conspiracy of nature. The sun was at its highest, shining through the thick trees in a sort of shimmer while birds flitted about; otherwise it was companionably silent. Sima stood still and Nicolai drew her into the shade of a tree at the side of the path. He held her for a moment. Sima knew what was coming – she also knew that just a little step, even a slight movement away on her part, would be totally sufficient to prevent..... Instead, she closed her eyes!

Sima wasn't a flirt, nor had she ever been. There was nothing contrived about what was happening. It made not a jot of difference that the kiss developed from a soft, light touch to a passionate embrace. The moment Sima closed her eyes and let herself relax in Nicolai's arms, she had made a conscious choice and she knew it. They looked at each other for a further half minute, and then, silent for the first time in the whole walk, they strolled on and turned the corner hand in hand.

The Countess Natalya Androvna was sitting in the garden of the villa requisitioned by the government for the use of the Russian refugee families, and which the Androvs had shared since their arrival from Sevastopol. The allied administration was no longer providing free food and many of the families had already left. General Wrangel had been offering the services of his ever-dwindling army around the trouble spots of the world, and already a sizeable force was in the process of leaving with him.

The Countess had married Nicolai's father surprisingly late in life. She had been nearly thirty, and as it had taken a few years before Nicolai was born, she was now approaching sixty. Her hair, which until the recent events in Russia had been black, was now quite white. Neatly but no longer fashionably dressed, she was petite with pale, fair, rather pinched features. Her mother had been Italian and Hungarian, related to the Countess Berchtold, the wife of the Austrian foreign minister at the moment of the outbreak of the Great War.

Natalya was a lingering survivor of that large pre-war international aristocracy that would meet each year at Baden-Baden, or Marienbad or on the Scottish grouse moors, and who managed European state relations between them, though, in the case of Count Berchtold, it had of course been a matter of mismanagement.

Natalya had been the youngest sister in a large family of girls brought up in St. Petersburg. Like all her class, she spoke English, French and German, in all of which languages she was probably more fluent than in Russian. She sat on a low rickety cane chair that Nicolai had acquired, and on the grass alongside, a white tablecloth was laid out with bread, cheese, olives, tomatoes, cucumbers and some fruit, together with two bottles of wine.

The day was warm and Natalya Androvna drowsed in the sun and wondered why this picnic had been arranged. She had heard about Sima of course. Although the Androvs were not as obviously open and talkative as the Avakians, nevertheless Nicolai kept his mother and young brother up to date with everything going on in his life. So she was well aware of the developing friendship, but it seemed to her there was no way that a wealthy merchant family of the city would give their daughter to an impoverished, dispossessed Russian aristocrat. She knew that just as marriages within the Russian landed aristocracy were usually to do with adding estates to each other, so within the upper merchant classes they were often to do with business mergers of one kind or another.

She looked up as the two boys and Nicolai and Sima came out from the path in the trees. Nicolai walked up to his mother and said, still speaking in English, "Mother, may I present Miss Sima Avakian and her brother Haik."

Haik looked on, proud of his sister, as she gave a sort of curtsey and then without hesitation leant down and kissed the old lady on her dried-up cheeks.

"Countess, I'm so pleased to meet you."

"Thank you, my dear. My name is Natalya and I would be pleased if you could call me Natasha."

The afternoon had got off to a wonderful start. They all sat on the warm grass draped round the Countess. They drank indifferent but warming wine; Natalya recounted stories of her childhood in St.Petersburg; they talked inevitably about what was going to happen here in Constantinople; Nicolai spoke nostalgically about his own childhood. Then, as the food finished, Nicolai brought out his violin, and Sima, accompanied by him, sang some old French ditties. The language went back and forth from English to French, but never in either Armenian or Russian.

Eventually, as Natalya's eyes closed for a while, Alexei grabbed Haik's hand and dragged him off for a swim at his famous favourite spot off the rocks just above the sea. They dived, swam, dived again and eventually lay side by side, naked and glistening, sunbathing and dozing off.

Sima and Nicolai did not leave Natalya's side. They also lay next to each other, sometimes on their backs and sometimes on their stomachs, talking quietly or just looking at each other or at the sky. Sima felt totally comfortable and completely at ease. It was all exactly right, and she never thought about what she ought to be doing or thinking – and so the summer afternoon wore on.

Back at the rocks above the sea, facing the Asian coast several miles away, the boys had dozed off. Haik was the first to awake as a slight sea breeze ruffled his hair. He stretched his arms and legs, and then became aware of Alexei, who had turned in his sleep and was now sleeping with his head tucked against Haik's side, and with his upper hand flung across and resting on Haik's chest. Here, there was no silence – the sea was continually washing against the rocks below, and the birds, silent earlier in the midday sun, were now chirping.

Haik lay still, loathe to wake the youth lying alongside. His mind turned to Paramaz, and he realised with a sense of relief, that his aversion had nothing to do with jealousy but brotherly concern for Seta. Paramaz had no real feelings for Seta; he seemed to be toying with her and it was up to himself to warn him off. For heaven's sake, he thought, I have more feelings towards this young lad here, than Paramaz has for my poor sister.

At this point, Haik sat up, allowing Alexei's head to flop back. Alexei stirred and gave a lazy smile before scrambling to his feet.

"Oh, my God, Haigushka, we've got to go."

They pulled on their clothes and were back with the others in less than ten minutes. Alexei, doing three fast somersaults on the way, ran laughing up to his mother and embraced her. Haik, feeling himself so much older for once, walked sedately up and sat cross-legged on the grass. A samovar –was brought out, and everyone had tea. The afternoon was now turning into evening and, for the first time that summer, there was a very slight chill in the air. It was time to go.

Sima was in a state of unadulterated joy as she first said goodbye to the countess and then walked silently back to the little port, hand in hand with Nicolai, under a night sky full of stars. Haik, walked along behind them, with his hand on Alexei's shoulder, marvelling, as they chatted, at the naivety of this youth. Nicolai walked along knowing that he loved this girl and that he was going to do something about it, while Alexei, refined and aristocratic, but without any formal education, simply knew that he loved everyone, and particularly those around him here.

In the central highlands of Anatolia, the slight chill felt in Bolis was a fierce, cold blast down the valleys. Two armies, a Greek nation-state force and a Turkish national force faced each other across and near the banks of a meandering Anatolian river – the river Sakarya. The Greeks were only seventy miles from the capital created by Mustapha Kemal – the provinicial village of Ankara. This was going to be the great breakthrough – the final fruition of the megali idea – the triumph of the equally éprovincial little town of Athens. Young men were going to die in agony on both sides for the fulfilment of this dream.

But, in Constantinople, the great Imperial capital which had controlled and dominated both these two brash little towns for over a thousand years, it was still party time.

CHAPTER 22

Nerissa and Seta at the Asadourians

It was at one of their afternoon meetings at a 'thé-dansant' at Tokatlians that Vahan eventually got round to asking Nerissa if she would like to come to Taksim one day and meet his family. In all the years that they had known each other and been good friends, this was the first time that such an invitation had been broached. Nerissa had been surprised. Vahan had been a fairly frequent visitor to the Avakians ever since that fateful day – the 24th of April 1915 – the day of the arrest and deportation of both Karekin and Garabed – and the assault on the 12 year-old Haik. However, whilst they now met often in the city, Vahan had never once invited her to his home.

As the years had passed, their relationship had developed. Nerissa had enrolled at the University of Stamboul – one of the earliest women students there – studying English literature. The two shared a mutual enjoyment of the new music pouring in from America and the west and the spirited and joyful dancing that was sweeping sophisticated Pera. Vahan and Nerissa were extraordinarily well-suited to each other. Both were of an intellectual turn of mind, not taking much pleasure in gossip or small talk. Neither were fashion conscious or fond of large social occasions, and Nerissa's sisters thought of Vahan as boring,which would annoy Armineh.

The relationship carried on and Armineh even discussed the matter with Karekin, though he could hardly have failed to notice that Vahan was a fairly frequent Sunday guest.

"Karekin, my soul, what do you think of Vahan?"

"Well, I like him if that's what you are asking. He is polite, respectful and really intelligent. His ideas are a bit ..."

"Karekin, my love, you know perfectly well what I mean."

"Yes, yes, yes, very well my dear. I have heard about his father from several acquaintances, and I have looked into the background of the family. Garabed is a provincial from Caesaria. He was arrested on the same day as me, and he too escaped and survived.I don't know the details of course. He eventually turned up here in 1917 sometime, with scarcely a penny to his name. At first, he and a boy, called Ara, an orphan he looked after during the catastrophe, lived with Vahan on Vahan's salary. However he managed to get back into the carpet and textile trade – he had been a fairly well-known carpet entrepreneur before the war."

"Karekin, my soul, I am really impressed. You have looked into it all without having to be prompted. I must ..."

"Well, listen then and stop interrupting. In the last three years or so he has built up a very flourishing business. He has become one of the principal exporters of fine carpets to Europe. His younger son also survived the massacres and rejoined the family here in 1918. But my friends tell me that while the father is a consummate old-fashioned merchant, your Vahan, the quiet-spoken young musician, never known to raise his voice at anyone and without any specific commercial training, is now the brains behind the show. He left his salaried post and joined the family firm. My friends tell me it is he who has turned a small bazaar outfit into an internationally recognised carpet house."

"Oh, Karekin, my love ... and I never once asked you ..."

"Yes, well, I'll amaze you further by saying that I believe he would make a great husband for our Nerissa – there that took you by surprise."

"You really think so, my soul. But you know he has no mother or sisters or any female relations – they were all slaughtered in the catastrophe."

"What difference does that make?"

"Well – they are not going to know how to start. Vahan himself is shy, and I suspect the father is old-fashioned and fairly ignorant of the sort of conventions required."

"Oh Armineh, forget it for the moment. Nowadays, I see the children are making their own decisions; leave it to them, we can always take the initiative later on. Above all don't start pushing her. Being who they are, I suspect that the more we approve of anyone, the more they are likely to react against them."

"You're quite right, my soul, what totally silly geese my daughters all are."

It was fairly shortly after this conversation between husband and wife that Nerissa received Vahan's shy invitation to come to the Asadourians for lunch. Vahan had extended the invitation to include Seta. Nerissa had promised a note back immediately.

Nerissa was undoubtedly the cleverest of the Avakian children. She was not only very intelligent, but being well-read, she was knowledgeable as well. However, her emotional insights into people's feelings had not kept up with her intellect.

Her comfortable relationship with the modest and diffident Vahan, begun five years ago, had been developing as she herself grew up, and they had been seeing each other quite a lot in the last two years since the end of the war. However, throughout this time, Nerissa was only engaged with the fascinating discussions they had together about what was going on in the city; the politics of the Ottomans; was the Empire dying or recovering; the Russian political experiment; British policy and so on. She loved the dance afternoons when she got out of her classes and they met at Tokatlians. She was happy in his company. But she was not aware that Vahan was becoming emotionally involved.

The fact of the matter was that she was not in love with him, so it simply did not register that he might have those feelings for her.

Accordingly, her reaction to the unfortunate events of the tea party, now some weeks ago, had been to dismiss the two young men without a single thought for what may have been prompting their anxieties and feelings. It was her own numbed reaction of helplessness, her sympathy for Olga, her reaction to her father's intervention that counted. As for Vahan, it never crossed her mind, that had Vahan been present, the whole fiasco might never have happened, so good a diplomat was he at smoothing ruffled feathers.

So it was without any great feeling of excitement or anticipation that she set off on a Friday afternoon with Seta for the Asadourians, only a few days after Sima's trip to Prinkipo. She was curious rather than excited. Seta was dressed in her best clothes, bubbling with joy at the prospect of a trip to the city without her parents.

Vahan was waiting for them at Sirkeci, though Nerissa had said that it was not necessary. To Seta's unalloyed joy, Vahan insisted on taking a carriage. After crossing the Galata bridge he asked the driver to go round the coast road via Karekoy, and then take one of the steep roads up to Osman *Bey* and back alongside the park to Taksim and the house. Vahan and Nerissa were quiet – Nerissa because she had nothing to say and indeed never felt any need for small talk with Vahan – and Vahan, because he found himself having complicated and contradictory feelings.

On the one hand, he was savouring the pleasure of this moment. He did not often come this way, or for that matter take a carriage. On the other, he was fearful that this sophisticated girl was going to be put off by his family's rough and ready, all-male household.

The door was opened by Ara with a great flourish. He was dressed for the occasion – the first formal appearance of two young ladies of good family at the house. Dressed à la russe in a loose frilled shirt which Raffi had bought for him, loosely belted over his own long tight trousers tucked into high black boots, he had primed himself for a formal welcome. However, on seeing Nerissa and Seta he just smiled broadly, shouted "welcome, welcome," and waved them in with a bow, somewhat spoiling the effect by grinning at Seta and giving her a great big wink.

Nerissa went in, taking off her hat and gloves and putting them down on the little table in the hall.

"My adopted brother – Ara," said Vahan as they shook hands. Nerissa saw a boy, a little younger than Paramaz and Haik. It seemed to her that he had the kindest, most sympathetic eyes she had ever seen on a young male – her own brother excluded of course. Seta saw a young man, two or three years older than herself, with an infectious grin, warm eyes, but not as darkly good-looking as Paramaz.

The little group moved on into the sitting room. Here there was indeed a little awkwardness for the first time. Garabed had no experience of dealing with a young woman of twenty who was not a member of his own family. Before the war, a social gathering of this sort in Caesaria would have been both unlikely and managed entirely by his wife. Indeed he might not have been involved at all in such a gathering, not even coming into the women's part of the house. That would have been *haram*, 'forbidden.' Nerissa did not in fact have the sophistication that Vahan imagined she had, and which he saw in abundance in Sima and Olga. She felt almost as shy of this stern old man sitting upright on a chair as he was of her.

Nevertheless, she managed to bob a sort of curtsey at him, and with that impeccable instinctive Bolsetsi understanding of what language was appropriate, gave her greetings in Turkish. Garabed's eyes lit up – all the time, what he had been worried about was that he would have to try and welcome her in his hopelessly inadequate Armenian, and would make a mess of it. He replied with a welcome in an effusion of flowery Turkish compliments.

Everyone sat, and at this point Raffi bounded in and took Nerissa's hand. Keeping tight hold of it, he said, "Aha, the lovely Nerissa, we meet at last and, my God, not a moment too soon. I am Raffi, and who is this?"

"My sister Seta."

"Welcome, Seta, welcome. Listen everybody, the British military band have decided to play this afternoon in the park. Why don't we all go for a stroll later and listen to them."

And thus the conventional afternoon passed. Garabed exerted himself to being charming to the two girls. Ara brought in coffee and made funny faces at Seta when no one was looking, while Raffi hovered round Nerissa, saying nothing very much, just prattling on.

Vahan relaxed, it was all going to be all right. He knew his brother very well, and he had been just a little bit anxious in case Raffi took a greater interest in Nerissa than he would have liked. However, he was relieved to recognise that Raffi was not, despite all the male bluster, the slightest bit interested in Nerissa, either to talk to, or as a woman of his own age. His father was being charming. He knew that Nerissa herself could not stand the sort of prattle Raffi was indulging in and so they all went out for the proposed walk in Taksim park and to listen to the British military band.

Seta would have preferred to walk with Ara, but she had to walk with Raffi, whose strong male presence, after she had taken his arm as she had been taught to do, slightly disturbed her. In front walked Nerissa and Vahan, arm in arm, talking earnestly together.

They listened to the Band. They looked down onto the Bosporus and the busy lanes of shipping. They strolled some more and then re-turned to Garabed and some tea. Vahan got hold of another carriage, and this time they rode down the Grande Rue – Seta absolutely agog – across the bridge and to the station from where they took the train home.

A fairly satisfactory day then – the Asadourians had got over their awkwardness at a lack of any female in the house. Raffi, though a bit bored, was pleased that his father had behaved and that Vahan had been happy. Vahan now felt he was ready to make more moves. He considered that he could now approach Nerissa directly to ascertain her true feelings. Once he was sure of her, he would approach her father. No need to rush – all was going well, and he had no eyes for anyone else.

Seta, confiding in her diary that evening, had been overjoyed at the day. She told her diary how well she had comported herself. How she had not embarrassed her sister in any way.

And Nerissa?

Being Nerissa, she did not spend much time analysing or consider-ing Vahan or Raffi's feelings. Only her own reactions interested her. Eventually, as the night wore on she dropped off to sleep – but during the whole night she did not dream of Vahan.

CHAPTER 23

Mikael at war

Mikael held no romantic notions on war or the glamour of the soldier's life – but once accepted as part of the Greek army, a sort of peace de-scended on him. He was easily able to conceal the weakness of his kid-neys and liver when enlisting and made no reference to fighting on the side of the Red Army. His age and experience of fighting with Denikin during the Russian civil war had resulted in almost immediate promotion to the rank of volunteer sergeant.

This was fortunate, as, once he arrived at the front he found himself attached to the 42nd Regiment of Evzones, which had fought with some distinction in the Ukraine alongside a French intervention force operating from the port of Odessa against the Bolsheviks.

The 42nd Evzones were commanded by Colonel Plastiras, a thin, small, dapper man with jet black hair, deep penetrating eyes, thick black eyebrows, sporting a black moustache with sharply pointed ends. The regiment, after arriving in Smyrna some time after the first landings, had already taken part in several battles. The Greeks had taken Afyon Karahissar, and along the coast had captured the old Ottoman capital of Bursa, and had then advanced north as far as Izmid.

That, of course, had been in the days while the Kemalists were still disorganised and disregarded by all, including by someone as dispassionate and professional as Harington himself. However, by the end of 1920, King Constantine was back as a result of the monkey's bite. Here, suddenly, was a chance for the allies to back-pedal on their obligations to the Greeks. Constantine was looked on as being pro-German and anathema to the allies, particularly to the French. Accordingly they took the opportunity of his sudden reappearance to distance themselves, week by week, from the Greek position. Ironically it had also been an opportunity for the Greeks to back out gracefully from the whole megali idea, a chance they failed to grasp.

Led now by inexperienced new commanders, the Greeks pushed forward on all fronts. By keeping a fairly low profile and not involving himself in politics, Colonel Plastiras, though a republican, was still in command of the 42nd. Facing them were Turkish forces getting stronger by the day, led by Mustapha Kemal's friend Ismet Pasha. Two battles had been fought during the first few months of 1921 in and around the village of Inonu, one of the railway halts on the main railway line to the important railway junction of Eskishehir.

When Mikael finally made it up to the front line, he reported to the officer in command of the unit and received his general orders. The line was fairly quiet and, apart from the usual daily patrols, not much was happening. King Constantine had turned up in Smyrna on his white horse, surrounded by his beribboned and smart looking staff, understanding little of the developing situation.

This was totally different to the ferocious Plastiras and the ordinary Greek soldiers who were surprisingly knowledgeable about the strategies of the campaign and what was happening at the front. Mikael felt completely at home; he not only knew how to talk with these companions, he enjoyed doing so. He was totally at ease in this world of male endeavour:

"To turn as swimmers into cleanness leaping,
Glad from a world grown old and cold and weary,
Leave the sick hearts ...
And all the little emptiness of love."

Mikael did not think like Rupert Brooke, but he felt it in a practical way. He had experienced the horrors and sordid side of warfare. He knew what it meant – the blood – the shrieks of pain and agony – the filth – and the continual fear. But he was still able to revel not only in the camaraderie, but also in the physical activity. Once in their confidence, he quickly found out from his men, almost all four or five years younger, what had been happening. And thus one evening shortly after they had settled into their front line, as they gathered round the fire, Mikael had asked,

"Makis, look here, tell me exactly what happened then, when you attacked in January."

"It was a bloody ..."

"I think that what ..."

"No, no, lads. Let Makis tell it, and only interrupt if he gets it wrong."

"Well, Sarge, it was like this. The Turks were entrenched all along the railway line. They had some artillery in the Inonu railway station, nothing very big mind you, on either side of the building. We were led by that old fox Plastiras – the Mavros Kavalaris, and he was up at the front with us and ..."

"Which is more than a lot of those Royalist smart-asses do, skulking in the rear most of them."

"All right, Costas – get on with it Makis," said Mikael.

"Well, Plastiras got two sections to attack the trenches where they thinned out a bit with some woods behind as an escape route. We raced across – it was bloody murder, but we broke through and ran on into the woods, where we cleared out some more Turkish soldiers. We then turned and formed a line ourselves and began firing back on the entrenchments and the station itself. This resulted in the Turks turning their artillery on us – even though we were pretty well camouflaged in the woods. Once the guns were committed against us, the other sections swung down and made an assault on the station buildings themselves."

"Fine, and then what happened."

"Well, Sarge, the Turks didn't retreat – you know how bloody good they are in defence – but we now had the station, and they had lost their four artillery pieces, and we were behind their lines in the woods in this one sector anyway. So, that night they retreated and we took the village."

At this, some of the other young men joined in, and Mikael sensing the mood indicated that Costas should continue.

"Right. We knew – we bloody well knew for certain – that we could have advanced and taken Eskishehir there and then. Plastiras looked through his German binoculars and could see their troops evacuating the guns on the road to the north. He saw that our troops on the right could have moved in, captured the guns and ...' He was right, Sarge, he was right, but that old woman Papoulas ..."

"A little more respect, Costas, General Papoulas to you."

"Yes, well, what actually happened was he ordered a retreat, so we bloody well had to give up our positions across the railway line which had taken many of our comrade's lives to capture in the first place."

"Yes, well, he could have had his reasons, Costas. Perhaps some of the sections on your flanks had retreated, and you might then have been out-flanked in advancing."

"Don't you believe it, Sarge. We've talked to the others since. Sheer lack of nerve on his part, and frankly none of them know what they are doing, strutting about on prancing horses and having their photos taken ..."

Mikael thought about this. Battles always looked so different to the men at the sharp end from those at the rear pouring over their maps. He himself had only ever seen the active end, but in the tiny Denikin army, the men had always accepted the necessity of difficult decisions at the top, which might not appear entirely reasonable. He said –

"Look, you all talk about a second battle. What happened next? Makis – please continue, but without all the political comments please. What happened?"

"Yeah, well – Papoulas decided to make another attack on the same position – that is on the Inonu railway station. But by this time, after we had been ordered to retreat, the Turks had taken a hill, which dominated the whole section of the line. They had planted some bloody great guns on the summit. We had to take that hill first, before we could break the entrenchments round Inonu all over again.

"They sent us up – it was the whole of the 42nd under Plastiras. He's not the sort to throw men, at an enemy position. He infiltrated us up the slopes through the woods, different sections at a time. But the bloody Turks were tough and we lost quite a few in those fucking woods. But then, eventually, once we were near the top, all we could do was charge. It was all a bloody shambles. I don't know what everybody else did, but I just dashed forward, firing without aiming, yelling ... and blow me, they upped and ran down into the woods on the other side."

"And what about the big guns – did you take them?"

"I don't know? I just collapsed behind a raised embankment, and sighted my rifle down the hill in case of any counter-attack."

"Sarge, the answer to your question is yes and no." called out Gianni.

There was a roar of laughter. Gianni was the youngest man present. The men did not believe that he was really eighteen, he certainly looked much younger, and they patronised him shamelessly – particularly as he had foolishly, but honestly, admitted that he was still a virgin. Gianni grinned but gamely continued – "We got some of the guns, though they had been half spiked. However it had taken us quite long time to get up the hill, and they had time to get most of them away."

By now there was a really warm and excited atmosphere amongst all these young men. Ordinary country Greeks from different villages and islands all over the Peloponnese or Thessaly – certainly from old Greece – with nothing much in common except their youth, their language and their pleasure in a shared experience. They smoked; they drank their ouzo if they had any; they thought about their families at home; they lolled about under a warm Anatolian night sky. The last thing that they actually ever thought about, was the megali idea, or any other idea dreamed up by the academics – whose nationalist passion had sent them to this Anatolian valley. They fought and would, if required, fight again the next day, because that is what men did, with their comrades beside them. But for the glory of the 'nation-state? Never.

"So, did you capture the railway station again then?" said Mikael to Makis after a short silence when Gianni had finished.

"Well, Sarge, we were reinforced. Plastiras knows his job all right – and a few days later the Turks tried to do to us what we had done to them. They filtered through the wooded hills on the other side and came at us, blazing away with everything they had. We held out – didn't we, lads? We had no big guns to worry about and we just peppered away at them. Hundreds of the poor buggers died – but they didn't shift us. That black rogue Plastiras was with us all the time on that occasion – he should have been in charge of the whole army; if he had been we would have finished them by now."

"Look, Makis, you never know. The sort of spirit and courage that you need as a Colonel in the thick of a battle, is different to the sort that you need as a General."

"That was Gianni's first major fight, wasn't it guys. He was terrific, really fucking great. Blazing away at them without the slightest hesitation." There was an increasingly sleepy cheer from the rest. "But when we all arrived back at our lines in the rear, the poor lad threw up for a whole hour."

Mikael put out his own cigarette, checked that the sentries were all in place, and huddled down under his greatcoat, looking up dreamily at the night sky full of stars. His mind was clean and clear. He didn't think of Olga, or of his sister Nairi, or of anybody else at all.

But neither did he spend a moment's thought on the glory of Greece.

CHAPTER 24

Selim at war

In the end, Selim hadn't had any trouble slipping aboard a freighter bound for Zonguldak on the Black Sea. Once he arrived, a found a well-oiled system for dealing with men escaping from British-held Constantinople. Decrepit lorries regularly plied between the port at Zonguldak and Ankara in the mountains. After being interviewed and debriefed, Selim found himself on one of these lorries, on his way into the interior.

Ankara was as small and insignificant a little town as Athens had been when modern Greece first achieved its independence. Mustapha Kemal, and his entourage, had commandeered one of the few substantial stone buildings in the town as their military headquarters, but for living quarters they were dotted around the town in houses belonging to the local population.

Imperial Constantinople had so dominated the whole of the lands of the Ottoman Empire for so long, that almost all the other cities of the Empire appeared insignificant by comparison.

Ankara was no more than an overgrown village. The now swollen population were crowded into the little town; men sleeping up to eight to a room, without furniture or any domestic necessities.

The local inhabitants did not mix much with them. It was more like an army of occupation. The six or seven innkeepers in the town served indifferent food and let out sleeping space in all sorts of nooks and crannies in their inns, even on the stairs, which were numbered so that each new arrival felt there was some spot where he could lay his head.

Selim had fought in the festering swamps of Mesopotamia, so sleeping on a stair in the company of several other men, none of whom had much access to soap or running water, held no terrors for him. As it happened, he had been assigned a clothes cupboard, and, by keeping the door open, he could stretch out with his legs sticking into the room *bey*ond. An interview had been arranged for him, even before leaving Zonguldak, for a few hours after his arrival.

He had been worried that his lack of an arm would be a great impediment to his getting worthwhile employment. However, it turned out that it was of no concern for the Colonel who interviewed him. Selim was ideal material: a regular officer of the old Ottoman army, who had served with distinction in the campaign against the British on the Tigris, and who, in addition, was not tainted by too close a connection with the previous Young Turk regime, now wholly discredited amongst the Kemalists.

He had left the army, when invalided out, with the rank of Captain. He was immediately reinstated with that rank, and sent as a Staff Officer to join General Ismet Pasha's army facing the Greeks along the Eskishehir – Ismid railway line. Selim had requested a front-line post and went forward to join Lieutenant Colonel Fethi Pasha, who held an important section of the line, protecting the western approaches to Ankara.

Fethi Pasha was another old Ottoman officer, who at a very early stage had shifted his loyalty to the Ankara regime. He served with them in the east fighting against the Armenians who were desperately holding on to their crumbling Republic against the rising Turkish tide on the one side, and the Bolsheviks on the other. This sector, to which Selim had been posted, was currently quiet. Selim finally arrived at his posting by a mixture of ox-cart, overloaded carriage, and plain foot-slogging, and reported immediately to Fethi.

"Welcome, young man, welcome. You're Doctor Nazim Kemal's son, aren't you. I remember him well – served with Halil Pasha against those Armenian fanatics in Van didn't he?"

"Yes sir," said Selim, still standing to attention.

"Ah – sit down, sit down. Yes I remember him – a very proper man, but my God a stickler for form. When those military doctors railed on about personal hygiene, only your dad had the guts to go out and do something about it, raising a squad of men, and personally seeing to the digging of latrines, and then insisting they be used properly."

Fethi roared with laughter, and beckoned Selim over to the table, where they both looked down at a good map of the sector at which they were based.

"You are going to operate as my Intelligence Officer, and to pass on orders to individual sections, so I had better fill you in as to what has been happening here in the last few months."

Fethi paused and shouted out for some coffee. The two men then spent the next hour over the map, analysing the movements of the two armies around the little station of Inonu, and the capture and loss of the hill of Metristepe. They marked on the map where some units had gone forward and others had been forced back, and discussed the strategic mistakes made by Papoulas.

And this was how all the sweat, blood and effort expended by Mikael and his lads looked to the men in tents and rooms, where their moves were planned and plotted. As drawn on a map, it all looked so neat and simple. Selim, for one, however, was not fooled. He knew the difference between little arrows and flags on a map and the reality.

That night, when Selim retired to his quarters at the back of the headquarters building, he had the whole of the two battles clear in his mind, or so he thought. For, however experienced a soldier you were the view of a battle held in the mind of the planner could never be the same as that of the soldier on the ground.

There was no easy rest for Selim, as there was for Mikael. He thought of Olga. He remembered for the fortieth time the sequence of events at the Avakian tea party. He thought of his sister Yasmin and of his widowed mother. Selim would certainly never think of his relationship with any of these women as "the little emptiness of love." But while Mikael had come to the war to forget – to cleanse his spirit – to recover his self-esteem; Selim had come to remember, to face up to his feelings and to ponder his future and the future of the society to which he belonged.

Selim came to Anatolia, because he could not bear the humiliations of the British occupation of the city – his city. But this was not reflected in a passion for the new nation-state that he was helping to create. He would do his job well, precisely because it was his job. But for Glory? My country right or wrong? To hell with all that stuff!

CHAPTER 25

Sima decides

Sima's first thought, whenever she found herself contemplating a relationship with a man that might lead to marriage, was children and the creation of a stable family unit. She had never doubted that she would eventually marry a man chosen first by her parents, and then approved by herself; trusting her parents implicitly to introduce someone with an eye to her own security and that of her future children.

But mingled with these old- fashioned beliefs, Sima had an honesty and integrity in her own mind, she was never going to deceive anyone, except maybe herself. That day in Prinkipo had been miraculous. Everything had conspired to make it a perfect. It was not only the pleasure she felt when she recalled the attentive and loving Nicolai; she had also been charmed by the old Countess and the boy Alexei who like Cherubino was in love with everybody and everything, and even the loving attention and support of her young brother Haik, all conspired to confirm her feelings for Nicolai.

The very next day, Sima went into town in the late morning and called in at the Levonian offices in Pera. George was always pleased to see her but on this occasion, somewhat to his surprise, Sima did not want to wander along the Grande Rue de Pera, nor go to the cafes of the Pera Palace, the Park hotel, or Tokatlians. She told George that she just wanted to go and sit in the park at Taksim. George sorted out the office, and they walked out together up to the square. Sima and George had never held hands, but Sima tucked her arm into his arm, like an old married couple.

George had discarded the fez, and now wore a panama straw hat with a brim. He carried a stick and always wore gloves. The wearing of hats with brims had become a symbol of Christian independence – practically a political statement. At the same time, the wearing of the fez by a Greek or an Armenian was equally significant as a sign of support for the Ottomans and Sima reflected that her father had not discarded his fez, continuing to wear it fairly ostentatiously in public. The Turks almost all kept strictly to the fez, but then there were those who now wore caps, or no hat at all, thereby making a Kemalist statement. It was all very confusing to anyone but a Bolsetsi.

They strolled through the gates and into the park, and eventually sat on a bench under the trees.

"Well, my dearest Sima, you've manoeuvred me here for a purpose, no doubt. You want to tell me something. I'm right, aren't I?"

Sima looked at George, then down at the ground, and found that she was lost for words. She wanted to ask him if he loved her, but could not bring herself to say the words. She suddenly wondered what she would have answered if George had asked her the same question. Neither she nor George had ever talked together about love, in the whole of the three years of their relationship. In the continuing silence, Sima thought how her own family chattered on about love all the time, and since the end of the war, it was a subject that you should have been able to discuss with anyone.

"Sima, my soul, what's on your mind," said George again.

"George, it has been over five years since we were first introduced to each other. You remember that day that we walked together through the garden and the orchard in Makrikoy – ah yes and with Haik and Tamara in tow." Sima giggled, and George smiled, nodding his head at the shared memory.

"I suppose it was about three years later, after my father escaped and came to Bolis, that we began going out together. So, George, one way or another, we've been walking out together for over two years. Yet in all that time you've never spoken to me about your own feelings."

"But Sima, my soul, how many times have I … hasn't my father approached yours asking for a date for a formal engagement, and how many times have we been told it was not the right time?"

"You are right, of course. But George, even before the war, a couple like us, both well into our twenties, would be discussing our future, our feelings for each other, our hopes and plans, but one way or another you and I have …"

"Sima, I …"

"No, let me finish George, please. This is difficult for me, but I have to let you know before I speak to anyone else how I feel, just the two of us. Oh, George, look, I think … no, oh God, I know … that you are a good man. Kind, considerate and gentle – but George I can't marry you. It wouldn't be right for either of us."

There was a very long silence. Sima sat quietly, realising that now that the words had irrevocably been uttered, how right her decision had been to say them. George was completely stunned.

Sima continued to look down at the ground, and then turned and stole a look at the man sitting alongside her. George, on the plump side, with his unfashionably clean-shaven face, hands resting on his walking stick; George, reliable, rather dull solid George, always a little too anxious to please everyone; George, staring straight ahead, and oh God, with tears silently seeping out of his eyes and trickling down his cheek.

Sima moved closer on the bench, again tucking her arm through his, sitting without a word being spoken. Sima was almost in tears herself but still, even in that moment, it never crossed her mind to take his hand in hers. Like all the Avakians, Sima was good at analysing her own feelings, but not so good at seeing the depth of feeling in others, and she was taken aback by the tears.

"Sima, I know I don't articulate my feelings. Perhaps I don't even have feelings as strong as other people seem to have. I don't know. I certainly don't have your education. I have worked with my father ever since I was sixteen. I do tend to follow what he says and act almost always as he wants me to behave.

I have seen how your family are, and how they react to each other and to the world around them, and Sima, my love, it excites me, though it frightens me a little as well. But Sima, on top of all that, over these last three years I have come to appreciate all your qualities, all your good sense and your discretion. I want to live with you – not just to have you as my wife and the mother of my children. Oh God, Sima, I have come to love you. In my own mind I have been planning for a future and you are always there, plumb in the centre. Sima, my darling, to hell with all the family arrangements, this is me – George – with all my imperfections. Marry me – marry me – not to join two merchant houses, but for us, just for us ....

That was what he felt. But in fact George said not a word. He just sat there in misery, staring straight ahead. He felt Sima's warm hand tucked into his arm – but he said nothing. It was all too late for him.

"George, I'm so sorry, I'm so sorry. Please don't think too badly of me. I am sure it is right for me not to enter into a permanent relationship when I am so unsure. It is better for the two of us to make a clean break now, rather than letting it drag on in uncertainty."

"Oh, Sima ... I'm sorry too." George did not turn towards her, although Sima was looking at him directly, willing him to turn his head.

"George, I haven't said anything to anyone. I felt I had to tell you first. However, I will be telling my parents tonight. I know that they will be angry. I know that I have not acted very honourably. But George, I think that I am right for both our sakes. We have been good friends, haven't we George?"

Sima was beginning to get desperate for a reaction. The tears had been genuine, Sima knew that, but what did they mean? Were they tears of disappointment, tears of frustrated pride – who could say? Or were they tears for a love that had gone for ever? Sima could not say, and the chances were that George could not have said either.

Sima realised she had made her decision long before this scene and she felt it was pointless to drag it out any further. She took her arm out from George's arm and stood up. Bending down, in the middle of the park, heedless of all the people walking by around them, she kissed George on the lips, lingering for that moment more than just a peck and looking straight into his amazed eyes. Then straightening up, she said –

"I'm sorry George ... I'm truly sorry ... goodbye."

Adjusting her large summer hat, she turned and walked towards the park gates without a further word.

"... don't leave me, Sima, don't leave me" whispered George, as he watched her walking away.

As Sima walked away, she knew she had not been entirely honest with George. She had thought of mentioning Nicolai, but at the last moment realised that that would not make things easier, either for her or, so she argued to herself, for George. The sight of George's tears had unnerved her. Somehow she had assumed that all the feelings were only on her side. She walked across Taksim Square and down the Grande Rue de Pera, before ultimately making her way to the Pera Palace.

There, she had to wait impatiently, sipping a cup of tea, as the orchestra played on. The great social changes brought on by the War had not lessened the difficulty for any young woman to sit alone in a public place and she could not avoid the curious looks flashed in her direction, nor the occasional 'gallant' approach. Her heightened sensitivity, and her contemplation of the recent scene, made the wait even more arduous. She had to call on all her reserves of poise, but she stuck it out.

Nicolai was round in a flash the moment the morning music ended and the tables were being laid for lunch.

"Sima, my darling, what is it, you look upset."

"Oh, Nicolai, I'm sorry, I had to see you. I've just broken off my understanding with George. It was very difficult. I feel awful, he was so upset. I never imagined for a moment that he would feel like that. Oh God, I am so selfish – I'm so selfish."

"Sima, Sima, calm down. You know that you never ever loved him. You entered into the arrangement to please your parents. It would have been a terrible mistake to continue – for him as much as for you. Remember what you told your father on that first occasion – that you could never love him."

"Oh, Nicolai, what has it got to do with love. It's all just ..."

"Sima – stop repeating that like a mantra. It's like a Pavlovian reaction every time the word 'love' is mentioned."

"Nicolai, let's get out of here. I feel like a butterfly stuck on a page, with everyone looking at me."

"Nonsense, Sima, but come, we'll walk down to the Golden Horn and stroll along the quays and the houses in the direction of Eyup."

They walked out of the hotel and down to the north side of the Golden Horn into a fairly ramshackle area of boat-builders, fishermen and porters. Once away from the hotel, Nicolai took Sima's hand as they walked down to the shoreline. At last, standing on a tumbledown jetty at the end of a little cobbled street, staring across at the great mosques of the hills of Stamboul on the opposite shore, Nicolai turned, took Sima into his arms and they kissed, long and lingeringly. All Sima's fears and doubts, even her guilt, flowed away from her. It was not, after all, the trees and the sweet-smelling flowers of Prinkipo, which had turned her head, Here, in the middle of the smells of tar and pitch, rotting fish and decay, it felt just as completely right as it had been on the island.

Still, this was not Pera. There were a few muttered oaths from some men sitting about mending nets and pots. The oaths were directed plainly at them for so blatantly flouting the conventions of the place. Nicolai broke away, took her hand despite the dirty looks, and they walked slowly back, twisting and turning in the narrow streets to the Galata bridge.

They understood each other perfectly – it was now up to Nicolai. No more passion – Nicolai bent and took Sima's hand and kissed it, holding so tight that it hurt. They looked at each other, then Sima turned and walked back across the bridge and up to the station to go home. Nicolai watched for a few moments then turned up the hill back towards the Pera Palace for his afternoon work.

"Armineh, my soul, in fairness I have to bear in mind that she did tell me all those years ago after that first meeting, that she could not marry him."

"But Karekin, my dearest, how can she marry that Russian count? They haven't a penny between them. Heaven knows in what circumstances they are living on that island. Who are they after all, who are they?"

"I know, my love, I know. It's almost as bad as Olga, though I assume that that at least is a dead duck now that he's gone. I just don't know what to do. Really Armineh, your daughters are such a stubborn lot."

"Oh I see, they're my daughters now are they? Look she may see some sense yet, but I'll tell you one thing, she's burnt her boats as far as George Levonian is concerned. Karekin, you're going to have to speak to Hovannes. Do you think that this is going to scupper the proposed merger and the opening of the branch office in Smyrna."

"No, no, my love, you can forget about that. That, at least is one thing we don't need to worry about. I don't know what George's feelings may be, but I'll tell you that in his heart Hovannes will be relieved. He'll make an enormous fuss of course, and wring some more concessions from the Avakian side, but believe me deep down he'll be glad to get rid of the proposal. It was noticeable that he had stopped pestering me for an engagement date quite a long time ago. Meanwhile, I've told Sima that there is to be no talk of any engagement or understanding with the Russian boy, until I've got Hovannes sorted out."

It was later at night after this conversation between husband and wife that Karekin, musing in bed, said sleepily – "I wonder, Armineh, my soul, did I make a mistake with believing in a modern education for girls? Have I brought it all on my own head? You always warned me that I was wrong."

"Oh, Karekin, my love, don't think like that for a minute. I know I'm an old-fashioned village girl with not a scrap of education except what you gave me after we got married. Our girls may be stubborn, too noisy and a bit immodest – but they are all honest and caring, and I wouldn't have them any different. We'll just have to wait and see .... Karekin?"

But there was no reply. Karekin was fast asleep.

CHAPTER 26

Olga and Selim's family

Following her experiences in 1915 and her decision to go to work in the Turkish military hospital, a change had taken place in Olga's character. She had become more decisive, more ready to rely on her own opinions and instincts. Of course she was still the same person, impulsive and emotional and not much given to introspective self-analysis. So far as the rest of the family were concerned, no one considered she had suddenly acquired ideas of her own about the current political situation. Nevertheless, she had changed.

Ironically, it was now Nerissa who went dancing with her boy-friend, taking advantage of the new permissive atmosphere in the city and enjoyed the new American rhythms regularly played at Tokatlians tea room. Meanwhile, it was the former fun-loving Olga who worked herself to the bone in the hospital and returned home too exhausted to go out in the evenings.

Olga had been working at the Scutari military hospital now for over four years. She was appreciated both by the doctors and most of the staff, and had reached a fairly senior position, despite being one of the few Armenians still working there. This seniority was partly due to the fact that female nurses were still not given much respect in Ottoman society, even though this particular hospital was the very same hospital at which Florence Nightingale had practised only 60 years before.

Olga had never entertained any feelings of ethnic exclusivity or superiority. In Olga's eyes, every person was a jumble of purely personal physical needs and emotions. The fact that their circumstances were conditioned by their ethnicity simply passed her by. Selim believed that her mind was too pure and uncluttered. Nerissa, on the other hand, said that it was because she simply didn't think about it at all.

It was only a few weeks after Selim had left Constantinople that his sister Yasmin appeared at the hospital one afternoon. She had to wait in the sombre and somewhat depressing waiting room for some time before Olga was free. The hospital was not anything like as busy as it had been during the war and many of the cavernous wards were almost empty.

"Olga – hello – I thought I would take the opportunity to come and visit you. I hope you don't mind."

"But Yasmin, my friend, what a wonderful surprise. Come, let's go for a walk – I've been stuck indoors for two days. It's lovely to see you. Let's stroll through Uskudar – maybe we can pick up a hot bun or something."

Olga took Yasmin's hand and led her out through the main entrance, and they wandered down into the old town.

Ever since Yasmin had first come to the hospital all those years ago, when Selim had arrived more dead than alive, with his infected arm, back from the fighting on the Tigris, she had had an easy rapport with Olga. They would certainly have had even more contact if Halideh had not done her very best to prevent it. The five-year difference in age between them had ceased to have any significance. When Olga had first taken Yasmin round the large and busy hospital, she had been a young woman of eighteen, while Yasmin had only been thirteen at most. Now Yasmin was eighteen, had filled out and appeared to be the more mature woman of the two.

"Olga, I came to ask if you have had any news of Selim. We heard that he arrived safely, and has already been moved up to the front. But we have heard nothing further, and thought that perhaps he may have written to you."

"Oh, Yasmin, my dear, I really know nothing. Selim has not written a word to me, and I don't expect that he will."

"But why, Olga, why – do you know why he left so suddenly?"

"No, Yasmin, but his friend Vahan told me that he had been contemplating the move for some time, and they had discussed it together."

"Well, yes, I know, but it all happened so quickly. Ana and I had no idea that he was doing anything more than just thinking about it. It all happened in such a rush, soon after your sister invited him to come to tea at Makrikoy. He did come, didn't he?"

"Yes."

"Did you have anything to do with his decision, Olga?"

"Yasmin, I really don't know. It was not a happy or successful tea party, and he was angry and upset when he left. Oh Yasmin, I just don't know. Vahan said not, but I fear that it might have been the trigger that set him off. Did he say anything to you about it?"

"No, he said nothing at all, either to me or to mother, except to tell us simply of his decision to join Mustapha Kemal Pasha – and only on the day before he left. My mother is in a state of some distress, and is desperate to know more. She is in a state of confusion, because she is secretly proud of his decision at the same time.

"Did he say anything about the tea party itself?"

"No. I did ask him but he wouldn't talk about it. We don't know what to think."

And so the girls wandered round the old quarters of Uskudar. They walked along the steep, winding, streets, still one of the oldest quarters of Constantinople after Stamboul itself, and still recognisably Ottoman, picturesque but dirty, ramshackle and crumbling. Eventually they wandered down to the Uskudar ferry station, and waited for Yasmin to board, for the trip back to the Galata bridge.

"Olga, I know it is a lot to ask, but would you come to our house one afternoon, perhaps on your way home, and talk to mother about Selim."

Quite spontaneously and without thinking, Olga replied, "Yasmin, of course, of course. But look, are you quite sure that that is what your Ana really wants. You know Halideh hanum's attitude towards me. She has made it clear many times that she wants nothing to do with me, or my family. Yasmin she hates me!"

"Olga, it's not you – it's ... er ... what you stand for."

"But I don't stand for anything except myself, so it is me."

"Oh, Olga, don't be difficult – you know what I mean – you're Armenian."

"So what, I'm still just Olga."

"Don't be so simple. You are Olga, and you are an Armenian, the two are inseparable."

"Here is your boat coming in. My dearest, of course I will come if you think it might help. However, you must promise to send me a note cancelling it if your mother shows the slightest disinclination."

And so it was left, as Olga turned and waved goodbye at Yasmin as she passed the ticket barrier. Olga began walking slowly back up to the hospital.

The city seemed to quiver throughout this long, brilliant summer of 1921. The sea was awash with warships of all shapes and sizes. The British fleet was of course paramount, with the old battleship – *The Iron Duke* – doubling up as the headquarters of the British resident Admiral. However, there were also some French and Italian warships and the American navy was also present with two warships. Trade was booming, and freighters of all kinds plied their trade. However the ubiquitous Russian grain ships, such a vital part of pre-war traffic, had totally disappeared.

After four or five years, her work as a nurse at the Scutari military hospital was coming to an end. Most of the big old-fashioned white-tiled wards were increasingly empty, as the war-wounded either died, or were released to relatives able to care for them. There would always be a smattering of long-term patients – soldiers who would need care on a permanent basis, together with any new civilian patients. However, the great hospital was winding down, and Turkish girls of fairly good families were now beginning to take up careers there.

On her last day, as arranged, she called in at the Kemal's apartment, and was welcomed by Yasmin. The two women went into the sitting room, which had scarcely changed since Nazim had died; basically western style, but with thoughtful and beautiful touches of the orient – Nazim's impeccable taste. Coffee was served almost immediately in exquisite Ottoman cups. On the heels of the departing maid, Halideh hanum appeared at the door. She came in and stood for a moment looking at Olga and Yasmin, as Yasmin stood up. There was a momentary silence and Yasmin then said – "Ana, you remember ..."

"Of course, of course," said Halideh, before Yasmin could give any name. "Excuse me please," she continued, hurrying forward to a small side table by the window. There, still without a word, she grabbed at a cigarette case, took out a cigarette, lit it and started saying, "Please tell nurse Avakian that I am happy ..."

"Mother – you promised!" called out Yasmin.

But this was no longer the same Olga, who had left Halideh's home in adolescent tears all those years ago. Olga now stood up herself, and looking directly at the woman nervously drawing on her cigarette by the window, said very firmly –

"Halideh hanum I was asked to come here and give you what news I might have about your son. I understand your feelings, but I was led to believe that my talking to you might be of some comfort but I am not prepared to be talked to through a third person. You must either address me directly – and my name is Olga – and talk face-to-face frankly and openly, or I intend to leave."

There was a silence as Olga looked at Halideh, and she looked at the cigarette in her hand. Then, quite suddenly, Halideh sighed deeply and tears began to drop soundlessly down her cheeks. She moved forward and sat down heavily at the end of the sofa, facing the two chairs on which Olga and Yasmin had been sitting, tears still flowing helplessly down her cheeks. Yasmin came out of her stupor, jumped forward and took the still smoking cigarette out of her mother's hand and stabbed it out. She sat down on the sofa and held her mother tight. All Olga's firmness and anger melted away, and she too found that she had given way to tears, which she hastily wiped away. She knelt on the carpet, where she stood, and looked up at the still silently weeping woman.

"Yes – thank you Yasmin, you can let me go now," said Halideh wiping away the tears with the back of her hand, and pulling away, firmly but affectionately from Yasmin's clasp.

"Miss Olga, please sit down. I am afraid I cannot say Olga, not because of any pride but simply because that is how I was brought up. It was very wrong of me to start again so badly. It was wrong on many levels, but in particular, Yasmin, your father would have reprimanded me, above all, for sheer bad manners. Oh dear ... Oh, no ..."

The two girls said nothing as the tears started again, as Halideh's thoughts turned back to her long-dead husband, always so correct in his lifetime. Once again, however, she quickly and impatiently wiped away her tears.

"Miss Olga, you know that I lost my Nazim *bey*, shot by Armenians at the siege of Van, and now I am going to lose my only son who will be shot by Greeks. I am bitter and confused."

"Halideh hanum, I do understand, but madam can we talk freely and frankly. You know that I love your son." Olga turned towards Yasmin as she said this, as instinctively she did not want to be looking at Halideh or to see her reaction. But Halideh simply sighed and said – "Yes, yes, Miss Olga. we have to sort it all out eventually I suppose, but please tell me what happened to send Selim off so suddenly?"

"Madam, firstly I would have moved heaven and earth if I had known how to persuade Selim to stay safely at home, quite apart from the general danger. Oh God what made him do it?"

"Olga," said Yasmin, "it must be you – somewhere down the line it must be you, it ..."

At this point, in a strange reversal, Halideh put her hand on Yasmin's arm as a restraint, but Yasmin shook it off. Olga suddenly remembered Selim's similar gesture.

"No, Ana, we are talking frankly and freely, remember. You should face up to the fact that if it is not Olga – then it is you!"

Now it was Olga's turn to look horrified and wide-eyed at this comment, though it did not seem to surprise Halideh. Yasmin continued –

"For, mother, if we accept, as I do, that Selim also loves this woman, then a reason for his sudden departure could be because of your stubborn refusal to contemplate marriage or any relationship between them."

"I know – Allah is my witness – I know. But how could I contemplate his marriage to an Armenian, you Armenians shot my husband in Van."

"But Halideh hanum," Olga interrupted, "I didn't shoot your husband in the same way that you didn't arrest my father. They are not 'your' Turks any more than the citizens of Van are 'my' Armenians. I no more represent Armenians than Selim represents Turks."

"Miss Olga, of course you are Olga, and Selim is Selim – but you are part of a culture and tradition which is 'Armenian.'"

"But Halideh hanum, we are, I hope, still talking frankly, if a person with black hair had shot your husband, would that mean that you could no longer talk to any person with black hair."

Halideh became impatient, and shook her head, suddenly aware of the great difference in age between them. She said, "No, of course not, come, come, there is a huge difference between the being an Armenian and the having black hair."

Olga was about to reply when she had the sense to realise that she should stop. She had not intended her last remark to be taken literally, but only intended to illustrate that stereotypes of all kinds were responsible for hatred in the world, where surface differences became the grounds for racism and genocide.

"I am so sorry, Halideh hanum, please forgive me. I did not mean to trivialise anything. Could I say, reverting to Selim, that you should not have too many worries about his handicap. Having only the one arm is likely to keep him out of real danger. They would not send an experienced officer, like him, into the front line. I am sure of that. Please, I am not saying this just to comfort you."

"Yes, mother, yes, Olga is right."

"Furthermore, Halideh hanum, I don't believe that either you or I need reproach ourselves with the thought that Selim might have acted in response to anything we might have said or done. He is a good patriotic Turk, and he went because that is what he believed in."

And so, at last – plainly and simply, Olga realised that she was telling a lie. As the discussion between them had proceeded, she had become more and more convinced that Selim had indeed left precisely because of her own failures at the awful tea party, and because of the long-term effects of Halideh's continual refusal even to meet her. 'Good patriotic Turk' she had just said – what rubbish! No, Selim had left because she, Olga, had totally mismanaged the situation at the tea party and because he could no longer bear the continual nagging opposition of his mother. Olga suddenly found it all so clear – it was Selim's relationship with herself and with his mother which had decided him, not any abstract political ideals. However, she knew she could never say so to Halideh.

But she also really did believe that Selim would not be sent to the front lines. Both Yasmin and Halideh found themselves in full agreement with her on that point, and for Halideh the further comment about Selim's patriotism was yet more comfort for her.

Once they were in agreement, there was little further to discuss; Halideh reiterating her opposition to any union between Olga and her son and her continued determination to do her utmost to prevent it. However, Olga was in future welcome in her house, as a friend of Yasmin, and in her own right..

What none of them were aware of was that there were even more dangerous positions in an army than in the front line.

CHAPTER 27

Karekin takes control

The business affairs of Avakian Levonian et Cie were developing by leaps and bounds. There was now a formal partnership, and the two merchant houses were cooperating with great success. Karekin imported British textiles from Lancashire to cover the requirements of the British quartermasters to provide the allied forces. Hovannes suggested his small branch in Smyrna should be expanded to supply the Greek military in Smyrna. His plan was to get the contract for the Greek forces for uniform replacements, blankets, linens – all to be supplied from Bolis by the firm of Avakian and Levonian at considerable savings for the Greeks.

Karekin had been right when he told Armineh that Hovannes would not be unduly concerned by Sima's decision about George. His amour-propre, as head of the family, had soon been satisfied by some minor shifts towards the Levonian side in the current business arrangements. As for George himself, the new circumstances seemed to have made no difference to him either.

George soon agreed that he would be happy to take over the management of the Smyrna branch. Despite the lack of any formal engagement, the marriage understanding was well-known among the bigger and more affluent Armenian merchant families and the break-up was beginning to cause gossip and speculation. George was sensitive to this sort of public scrutiny and felt the need to get away for a time. He could see his mother already totting up all the eligible young girls available, who might be suitable. At this terrifying thought, George felt that a year or two in Smyrna would be a welcome break.

In the course of his business dealings with the Avakians, George had developed an affection and respect for Haik, from the moment the boy had joined the firm. Haik had been the only person in either family who appreciated that George had been devastated by Sima's rejection.

As the plans of the firm matured, George began pressing for Haik to accompany him to Smyrna. His argument was that it would be a good experience for Haik to help in setting up the new branch, and that he would need the additional help. It had been Karekin's plan to send only Paramaz. However, as letters passed between the firm and the Greek military suppliers and businesses in Smyrna, it became clear that there was indeed a great commercial opportunity here, which might well need more work and input than George could have managed on his own and that Haik needed the additional work experience and responsibility away from his father's control.

Karekin pondered all the alternatives, and discussed them with Armineh, when he could get her to pay attention. The fact that it would only be for about eighteen months, clinched his decision. Once the business was set up and operating, it would be unlikely that either Haik or George would still be needed in Smyrna. They could all come back, and the business could then be run locally and supervised from the head office of the firm in Bolis.

On the home front, meanwhile, as the summer days slowly passed, both Karekin's elder girls were now back at home and somewhat unsettled. In Sima's case, her feelings were wholly taken up by Nicolai, and it was also undeniable that both he and Armineh liked the young Russian. But what could the young man do to make a living? – where could they live and on what? In the end Armineh had pointed out that in the circumstances any move had to come from them. Sima had made her own feelings clear, and after all, where was the harm in exploring the situation a little further.

And so it was that at last the Androvs had been duly invited to a Sunday lunch. The arrangements had been complicated, but had worked out well. Nicolai himself was unable to get away before the afternoon and was arriving later with Vahan, and so Sima and Haik had gone in the morning to the Russian Orthodox church in Stamboul, and there met the countess and Alexei, who had arrived earlier from Prinkipo. All four had then returned to Makrikoy for lunch after the service.

The whole excursion was a fascinating experience for the countess, who had never ventured further than the church in Stamboul since arriving and settling on the island. The train ride from Sirkeci; going through the great walls at Yedikule; the little station at Cobancesme; the carriage ride up past the Vali *Effendi* racecourse with all four squeezed into the one carriage; lunch on the veranda looking out on the great garden.

The conversation was a mixture of English and French, with the occasional Turkish to explain something for Armineh's benefit. Karekin, whose English was improving, went out of his way to be charming to the old lady, to whom, in any event, he took an immediate liking. She found the mixture of deep formality and warmth of Karekin's character very satisfying.

After lunch, the party had split up. Alexei, Haik, Paramaz and Seta, accompanied by Nerissa, set up a makeshift outdoor badminton court on the grass at the far end of the garden, leaving Karekin and Armineh sitting at the table with Natalya Androvna, sipping their coffees. Sima, who was restless, moved back and forth between them and the kitchen.

While Sima wasn't present, Karekin, now totally relaxed with the countess, but not yet on 'Natalya' terms, said –

"My dear countess, I think we are in a position to speak openly about what appears to be a budding relationship between your son and my daughter are we not? Tell me, do you have any plans for your family?"

"No, monsieur, I am bound to be in Nicolai's hands. I have lost touch with all my husband's Russian relations, most of whom have disappeared, one way or another, during those awful civil war years. My own immediate Russian family have all died. I myself have Austrian relations on my mother's side still in Vienna, but they are in as difficult circumstances as we are. I believe they are planning to join the Italian branch of the family who still have their estates in the Veneto, but I don't know... I just don't know. In any case I have an immediate problem to think about and that is where we are going to move to right here and now. We are going to have to leave Prinkipo soon, as the allied authorities are no longer in a position to allow us to stay."

"Countess, for the moment your life is here in Constantinople. You not only have the immediate problem of your accommodation, but what about your younger son? He must be sixteen or thereabouts. No hope of any further education, but already with a lot of accomplishments. What do you want for him?"

"My dear sir, I have no idea. Social polish, a facility for languages and youthful charm does not go for much, I suppose." Karekin shook his head and said,

"Madam, I can see that as well as those accomplishments, there is in him also a directness and integrity. He reminds me of my own son Haik when he was that age. Look countess, times have changed. Your son is not going to inherit anything, nor have access to an army or state bureaucracy. Assuming you can solve your accommodation problem, would you consider suggesting he come and work as an apprentice at the offices of Avakian Levonian et Cie?"

Armineh, who had been following all this with some difficulty, looked at her husband in surprise. But Karekin's proposal did not come out of the blue. He had already been considering that if the Smyrna plans went through as now proposed, he was going to lose two young men from his office and storerooms. He needed a replacement for Haik's literary qaulities and also the strenth and enthusiasm of enthusiastic young man.

Karekin had liked Nicolai right from the start – Nicolai's combination of warmth and aristocratic formality was very much his style. Then, as this day progressed, who could fail to connect to his lively younger brother. However, he wasn't sure what attitude a Russian aristocrat like Natalya might have towards the taint of commerce. Running a factory on a country estate was one thing – but mercantile trading ... that was perhaps a step too far.

The countess understood what Karekin meant. Furthermore she was sensitive to his slight embarrassment about the offer. She smiled at Karekin and turned to Armineh and said in poor Turkish – "Armineh hanum, I know your husband would not make such a kind offer without sincerely meaning it. I am deeply touched."

Then turning back to Karekin, she said, still in halting Turkish – "Karekin *effendi*, you must just give me a moment to reflect on what your kind offer may mean to us all."

Just then Sima returned, laughing from having taken Seta's position in the badminton game for a few minutes. She plumped herself down on a chair and put on her straw hat as Karekin nodded at Natalya in reply.

A whole cultural revolution went through Natalya's head as she sat staring at the garden and contemplating the family around her. Her past life seemed to pass before her. The glorious Edwardian/Wilhelmine summers of her youth; those early years in Vienna and Venice; the great European spas, country houses and grouse moors; the elegant hotels and bathing resorts throughout the continent; eager young men and innocent romances; followed by a Russian count and a marriage in St. Petersburg. How certain the future seemed then. Any connection with 'trade' would have been unthinkable for all her friends and relations.

But her move back to Russia had changed all that. Her husband had had somewhat advanced views about managing an estate. It was not just going to be growing and cutting down timber. He had built and begun to develop a paper factory, and employed western engineers to help in his investment. He had had the usual labour problems, but on the whole his innovations had been welcomed in the local villages, where the work and the additional cash economy had proved popular and they had socialised with well-to-do peasants who were beginning to invest and trade on their own account.

In the end she did not hesitate for long in making up her mind about Karekin's offer.

"Monsieur, I would like to repeat how grateful I am for the honour you do to me and my family. I will certainly speak to Alexei, and of course Nicolai will have to be consulted. But for my part I cannot see anything but positive value coming from my boy associating himself with you in the way you suggest. I am truly grateful."

Sima stared at them all, not having any idea what was going on. Then when it was explained to her, she gasped, stood up, sat down and then stood up again. Not being as demonstrative as Olga, she just looked at them all. Then, as the three elders waited for her to say something, the front doorbell rang. Nicolai and Vahan had finally arrived.

Sima bounded out to get to the front door before anyone else.

The afternoon had been as great a success as the earlier tea party had been a terrible failure. It was Vahan who had finally come out with the last piece of the jig-saw – accommodation for the Androvs. Nicolai and Sima joined the makeshift badminton party at the far end of the garden. Vahan wandered down with them, nodded at Nerissa and sat watching. The game was taking all sorts of bizarre turns as the players tried out variants to accommodate six people wanting to join in. Vahan seemed to be the only person who was aware of an undercurrent of unpleasant competition between Haik and Paramaz. He soon tired of the entertainment and returned to sit with the parents.

Everybody finally arrived for tea as the afternoon wore on. Paramaz left to help in the kitchen as Talin passed plates, cakes and cups of tea. Conversation was general and swung between English, Turkish and a little Armenian. Karekin's offer had been made public, though by instinctive mutual consent it was not to be discussed until the Androvs had had a chance to discuss it between themselves. Alexei, however, was already bubbling with enthusiasm and had difficulty sitting still. It was then, as the first slice of cake was being cut, that Vahan had his brainwave.

"Listen everyone, I have it. Ever since my father, Raffi and I moved into our new house in Taksim, Christina Patakis and Maria have been living alone. I occasionally pop in to see them. All their spare rooms are still empty, but I know they could do with some rent. Surely this could be the answer. I would have thought that with Nicolai's wages and the little extra that Alexei might now be able to contribute, you would be able to manage. Nicolai – how about it – we could go and see her tomorrow. A bit small, countess, but a lovely part of old Stamboul, and just the usual stroll across the bridge to Pera."

And so it was that so many matters were settled that afternoon, in a flurry of warmth, romance, and nostalgia. During the next two weeks Karekin organised everyone with dignity and unobtrusive control. The Androvs were introduced to Christina and Maria who welcomed them in on generous but sensible terms. Breakfast was to be downstairs and in common, but no other food was provided. Andre's old attic room was to serve as a tiny eating room with a small stove, a table and three chairs. It was all a squeeze, but it sufficed.

Alexei, now dressed in clerkly fashion, in a suit purchased for him with one of their remaining gold coins, turned up at the Avakian offices, wide-eyed and still without many words of Turkish, but proving very willing and ready to put his hand to anything. He adored Haik and looked on him as a real friend. He was slightly overwhelmed by Karekin whose rather stiff public demeanour he found a bit intimidating. However, Karekin was an excellent employer, always teaching as well as demanding service.

Karekin found that he had to hurry. George had already left to look for lodgings in Smyrna, and to organise the new office there. Paramaz and Haik would soon be leaving to join him. Karekin had already taken on a Turkish young man into his employment, and Paramaz and Haik had to train both of them in their respective duties before they left. Karekin insisted that Alexei was to talk only Turkish with Paramaz. At the same time, Karekin mused, here was a boy without formal education, save from his mother, since he was twelve. His French was perfect and his English fair, but he could not write letters like Haik.

Discussing all this with Hovannes, it was suggested that Alexei could take French writing lessons from his wife Yvonne, whose French was impeccable. Karekin wondered whether Hovannes felt manipulated, but decided that the offer was kindly meant.

Accordingly, once or twice a week when the offices closed in the evening, Alexei would return to Bebek with Hovannes and take writing lessons with Yvonne, who knew all the vital nuances in formal French letter writing, and exactly how to finish off any form of letter. Everybody loved Alexei, and on several occasions he was invited to stay over and join them for supper. Alexei was impressed by Yvonne's gossip about Bolsetsi figures, and he liked the corpulent Hovannes of whom he was not the slightest bit in awe. At first Tamara, two years older, was a bit stand-offish, but she too warmed to his open and sunny nature. Alexei, for his part, though obviously smitten by the nubile Tamara, soon found the right teasing approach.

Karekin had manoeuvred everything and everyone to his great satisfaction.

CHAPTER 28

Paramaz

Paramaz never kept a diary or wasted time on self-reflection, but he did have bad dreams, most of which he had forgotten by the morning. They were a terrible mixture of sex and violence, which had become inseparable in his mind. Although crowded into one tiny village house, Paramaz had never witnessed the tender love-making of his father and mother. Then the terrible days of the deportations and the mass killings had caught him just as he reached puberty, and he came to see sex only as an act of violence.

If those lazy days when he tended sheep on the hillsides and experimented with his sexuality with other boys had continued normally, he would most probably have grown up to practise normal sexual relations. But instead, as his sexuality burgeoned, he had been caught up in the death marches in the wilderness, surrounded by terrified women and young girls, guarded by either indifferent or sadistic soldiers. The subsequent amalgam of sex and extreme violence seared itself on his brain and into his dreams forever.

He witnessed the horror of the rape and killing of his mother and the abduction of his young sister, at the same time living with the ever present fear of his own immediate and sudden death. All these feelings festered in him from the very first day that he had escaped from the marching column, and continued day in and day out with no one to help or advise him.

Although he had not died in the wilderness, the trauma of those desperate days, was immediately followed by the abusive months he spent alone with the Kurdish family group wandering the hills with their flocks. But how could he blame them? They too were victims of their iown culture and circumstances. With the strict separation of the sexes on their long, nomadic journeys, what happened to the fearful pre-pubescent 12 year-old Paramaz was inevitable. Paramaz never thought of it as 'rape.' How could he? It seemed to him to be a natural consequence of his totally subordinate situation.

At no time after the dreadful death of his mother, did he ever feel tenderness or compassion in any relationship. Sex was a matter of domination and lust. It was casual, painful and uncaring. Yet, he was fed, there was occasional laughter, and though almost a slave, no one despised him when they sat round the campfire.

But 12 years-old gives way to 13, and Paramaz was growing up quickly. He could never totally recall what had occurred on that evening about a year or so after he had first started living with the Kurds. He recalled a cave in the mountains on a summer evening when he and the burly horsemaster in charge of the herd had tethered the horses, and had settled themselves down to sleep. He recalled vaguely, as if in a fog, the casual command to 'turn-around' – no speech, no request, just a demand for obedience. Then a red fury – an irrepressible anger – a sudden frightening eruption, but whose? A knife – blood – fear – a guttural scream.

What had happened? He could never remember clearly, but the dreams continued ... lying naked on the ground, a snake slithers up to his body, coils itself round him, and delicately, gently, spits into his lips, pushing its poisonous forked tongue into his mouth. He lies there petrified and feels death creeping up on him. A hand takes up a knife – it is not clear whose hand– and drives it deep into the body of the snake, and blood pours out, red blood flowing all round him. But it is not a snake – it is not a snake – it is his father who stands up and stares down at him. There is no more blood and the apparition mutters – "I'm so sorry, Paramaz, I'm so sorry – I thought it was the right thing to do," and then lifting a large rock above Paramaz's head he ... And then Paramaz would awake, not covered in sweat, but ice-cold and trembling – and oh God, usually with an erection – or the guilty remains of one.

Seta had stopped writing those romantic intimate thoughts about Paramaz and his strong muscular body into her diary. Time had passed and she had become aware of the dangerous suppressed anger in his character. Furthermore, as week after week went by, as her education at the English High School for girls developed, she increasingly found the animal magnetism emanating from Paramaz less enticing. While still fascinated in his and her own sexuality, she found, to her surprise, that she did not actually like him very much after all. Haik's sensitive interventions, ensured that she was not too troubled by him.

Supported strongly somewhat to her surprise by Armineh, who spoke sharply to Karekin about it, Seta gave up the Armenian writing lessons. It had, in any event become fairly clear that Paramaz was never going to be able to take up a 'clerical' position in the office.

Karekin was obsessed with education as the great panacea. For him, every social problem of any kind came down to a lack of education. Karekin was aware of the 'bitterness' in the soul of Paramaz, but he also deeply believed that this could be overcome by education.

Both Haik and Armineh had worked to avoid the danger into which Seta might have fallen. Meanwhile, Paramaz found himself rejected yet again and deprived of having a friendship with the only young girl available. Armineh had no patience with his problems, which she thought were only those of a normal over-sexed and frustrated young man. Her reaction was totally maternal, protective and practical.

Haik, on the other hand, felt more accountable, particularly as he was not quite sure how much of his protective anxiety stemmed from jealousy, not in respect to Seta but his father. He never doubted the love of his father, but there was the matter of his attention. He too, after all, had been abandoned at the age of twelve by the arrest and deportation of his father, and had had his difficulties in this respect – though not approaching the suffering of Paramaz.

As the time approached for the departure of Haik and Paramaz to Smyrna, Karekin congratulated himself that all was going well in the business. Contracts were being negotiated and signed. George was reporting enthusiastically from Smyrna, where he was already in contact with the Greek army suppliers. He reported that the branch now needed Haik's literary skills and Paramaz's strength. Meanwhile, the experiment with Alexei had turned out well, and Alexei himself was a shining light in the office, and was overjoyed to be doing something positive at last.

The war and the revolution had abruptly shattered whatever future Alexei might normally have expected. The old count had always favoured the idea of Alexei attending the local village school until he was eleven or twelve, rather than being individually tutored like Nicolai. To this end he had made sure that the school had a good teacher, whose salary he paid. But the count had volunteered to go off to war in 1914, and by the time that anyone was in a position to think of Alexei's further education, the old count was dead, the Revolution had broken out, followed by the civil war, and there was no longer any question of any further education.

On the one hand, this had left Alexei naïve and without any general knowledge of life. But on the other hand, he had missed the stultifying conformity and depression of the spirit that was so often the adjunct of formal education. This had left him extraordinarily innocent, trusting and open-hearted, characteristics which had survived the hasty departure from his ancestral home and the unthinking taunts of his former village school friends as they were forced to leave. His character had also survived the trauma of the long trek later to Sevastopol and the chaos and panic of the quayside.

He had already been a few weeks at the office, and the time was fast approaching when Haik and Paramaz were due to leave. Karekin was getting anxious at Alexei's command of Turkish and whether he was in a position to take over Paramaz's full duties. Everybody was busy and Karekin decided that Paramaz should stay behind on those days that Alexei did not go to Yvonne in Bebek, and that they should work together – talking Turkish all the time and going through all the routine work of baling and making up the goods orders at which Paramaz was now master. And so it was that a week before Haik and Paramaz were about to board the French boat for the journey to Smyrna, Paramaz and Alexei were in the baling room, at the back of the offices on their own, wrapping up parcels, roping bales of cloth and preparing the equivalent invoices and contents dockets.

That evening, Haik had been invited to visit the Levonians, and had been pressured by Karekin to accept. He had accordingly left early to pick up Hovannes at his office and walk with him down to the Galata bridge for the ferry to Bebek. By now it was the height of summer and the ferries up and down the Bosporus were not crowded. The Levonian house was straight up the hill from the ferry station and was only a short walk, so they arrived fairly early.

On this particular evening, Haik had already arranged to spend time with some friends in the Pera district. There were several night-spots, quite apart from the Pera Palace or Tokatlians, to which one could not go without a good suit in the evening, and he had accordingly brought one in to the office to change into later when he got back from Bebek.

Haik was not worried about his father's wish for him to spend an hour or two with the Levonians. At the back of his mind he thought of possibly asking Tamara if she would like to come with him to Tokatlians for a supper/dance, and persuading his friends to join them there. His relationship with the luscious Tamara was a bit tricky. He had never overcome the feeling of timidity towards her from their initial meeting.

Even though Haik was now considerably more mature, he still blushed at the recollection of this – his first major arousal – and he knew that she too remembered the occasion well. However, they both saw it now as a little adolescent adventure and that they were not really suited to each other, despite any family or business pressures, she was clearly too old for him.

Yvonne gushed, and they all sat around in the cool white sitting room, with the white muslin curtains waving in the ever present Bosporus breeze, hiding the views of the blue waters of the straits below, but keeping the room, heavy with summer blossoms in vases all around, pleasantly cool. The Levonians were more subdued than usual; it was clear that George was sorely missed.

In the end Haik decided not to ask Tamara out and after some tea and a cake, Haik said goodbye, and turned to go. Tamara came to the door with him and chastely kissed him on the cheek. She then mischievously switched her lips lightly to his lips looking straight into his eyes. Then she pulled back and giggled – Haik smiled, gave her a wink and went out striding down to the ferry station to get back to Galata to go to the office and change for the evening.

It was a hot afternoon. There was no window in the baling room at the back of the offices. Both Alexei and Paramaz had long since taken off their coats, ties and shirts, and had been working stripped to the waist. Paramaz was wielding the big knife, cutting the ropes as Alexei finished binding. Alexei was clambering about getting hot and dusty, rolling up the bales of cloth and other goods, tying them up, and then preparing the documentation as Paramaz called out the serial numbers.

It got hotter and they regularly flopped down on the unfinished bales, and drink glasses of water. Alexei continued to chatter in Turkish, asking Paramaz for the words he wasn't sure of, and getting him to laugh at his mistakes. He could not keep still. In truth he was enjoying himself. He might not want to do this for the rest of his life, but it was purposeful work. He saw an end product and he was helping people he liked. He studied Paramaz, who appeared so strong and agile.

The sweat was running down their backs, and their trousers were dirty and dishevelled but they were nearly finished.

"Come, Alexei *bey*, that's enough. We need a rest and to freshen up before we go home. Go and fetch me a glass of water, there's a good lad, and come back and we will rest a little."

"Very well, Paramaz *effendi*," said Alexei grinning, copying the ironic formality of Paramaz's remark. He went out to the washroom and returned with two glasses of water and a towel. On his return, he found that Paramaz had taken off his trousers, which he had hung up on a hook, and was laying back on the unfinished cotton bales, clad only in his long white cotton shorts. Paramaz looked over at Alexei with an odd expression,which Alexei could not understand, but even he was aware of the suddenly sexually charged atmosphere in the room.

"Here, Alexei, come and lie down here and have a rest. Why don't you take your trousers off and then we can dust them down. It won't be nice to go out like this."

"Well, no, Paramaz. I'm fine as I am thanks," said Alexei.

Nevertheless, he happily flopped down beside Paramaz and closed his eyes. Paramaz lazily turned towards him on his side, looked at the half-naked Alexei and lightly touched his chest. Alexei smiled sleepily and held Paramaz's hand saying nothing. Paramaz was already excited. Anything could have happened if only Paramaz could have shown some tenderness, some affection, a touch of the lips perhaps, something easy-going and ultimately harmless.

But for Paramaz, sex had become domination. He held Alexei's head between his hands and called out words in Turkish which Alexei did not understand. Alexei had no idea what was happening. He felt himself being pressed hard against Paramaz's chest, which was heavy and sweaty. He became aware of Paramaz's erection, and now in increasing fear, he felt Paramaz violently pressing his head further and further down. Suddenly, he knew in a flash what Paramaz wanted him to do. Paramaz was very strong and heavy, but Alexei was wiry. He tried to twist away, but failed. However he did manage to release his lips, and he shouted out – in Russian now – at the top of his voice –

"Nyet – Paramaz – no – stop, stop."

Paramaz, for whom the violence and the fear of the victim had almost become an indispensable part of the sexual act, went on top of Alexei pressing him down – and then ...

Haik, only partly dressed himself in a shirt and the trousers of his suit, barged in from the office next door, where he had been changing, and where he had heard the muffled cry from the baling room.

"What the hell is going on," he shouted as he took in the scene as best he could in the gloom of the back room.

Paramaz jumped up, leaving Alexei lying staring up at them both.

Paramaz was furious and grabbed the rope knife which was on the floor beside him. He turned, eyes blazing, with the large knife, held like a dagger in front of him, clearly ready to attack. Haik and Paramaz stood staring at each other.

Silence in the room – for a few seconds only, but also a lifetime.

Staring – Haik saw the young man to whom his father had paid so much attention, who had undoubtedly tried to seduce his sister and who was now... .

Paramaz, also staring, with a red veil in front of his eyes, saw the spoiled son of this elitist family, someone who had crossed him at every turn, and whom he hated – yes hated – for his easy charm and natural happiness. Alexei had no idea what to think. He was now more afraid of Paramaz, and the sight of his flushed face, smouldering eyes and the knife in his hand, made him an alarming figure.

But he liked Haik – he loved him like he loved his brother. And, by God, he was a Russian aristocrat! He saw the mounting fear in Haik's eyes as Paramaz began circling towards him and Haik backed away. Then the silence was broken as Alexei jumped up.

"Paramaz, for God's sake stop! Nothing has happened – It's all right both of you – it's all right. Paramaz, please, please put the knife down – just give it to me – please."

Still fearful, but moving very calmly with his eyes fixed on Paramaz's twitching face, he took a step or two towards him, and held his hand out for the knife.

Another moment passed and then Paramaz threw the knife down at Alexei's feet. He turned abruptly, grabbed his trousers and shirt from the hook behind him, and without another word, ran out of the room.

Haik began trembling uncontrollably in delayed reaction to what had occurred, but Alexei felt elated with an unaccountable sense of empowerment. Although the knife had not directly threatened him, he had had to conquer real fear in averting a possible tragedy. He was not so innocent as to have been unaware what Paramaz had wanted, nor whether he might have acquiesced had he shown the slightest touch of tenderness or affection.

Alexei stepped forward, clasped and hugged Haik and said

"It's all right my friend, it's all right. It's all over, it's going nowhere, nowhere. Nothing has happened, and nothing will."

But there, he was wrong.

CHAPTER 29

Olga arrives in Smyrna

By the summer of 1921, Olga had worked as a nurse at the Scutari military hospital for over four years. After the meeting with Yasmin and Halideh, she had taken the final decision to resign and return to a home life. However, once home, she began to feel at a loss. She found that she could no longer stay at home in the traditional way, helping her mother with Seta or with domestic matters. She saw the normally more serious-minded Nerissa going into town and to dances, enjoying the new freedoms of social interaction. She watched as Sima's relationship with Nicolai blossomed, and Sima herself seemed to bloom.

She was really happy for her sisters, but inevitably she could not help but contrast the way in which Sima was being indulged by her parents with the way they had dealt with her. All she could see was that Selim was in every way as good and caring a man as Nicolai. Furthermore, Selim came from a good Ottoman family, which had been living in Bolis for generations. He undoubtedly had the sort of prospects of which Karekin surely must approve. Nicolai on the other hand, was a stateless, impoverished refugee with no prospects at all. Why, then, should he be tolerated as a possible son-in-law, but never Selim, never Selim.

Olga had no intention of complaining but she did confide in Nerissa, who in many confidential chats tried to help her to come to terms with the difference as she saw it.

"Olga, my soul, you must see that marriage between you and Selim is quite impossible if you intend to remain here in this city. It's not just the past centuries of difference in culture and history but the burden of the events of 1915. The Armenians would look upon it as a betrayal of the hundreds of thousands who were slaughtered, while the Turks harbour a deep belief that all Armenians are their implacable enemy, unable to forgive."

"But Nerissa, my soul, I am not proposing to marry a community – what do I care what people think."

"Oh, Olga, we've gone over this so often before. You're not going to live on an island. Then there is the matter of religion ..."

"Oh, come Nerissa – Selim is deeply secular and agrees with Mustapha Kemal's position in despising all the sillier nonsenses of Islam. And don't tell me that our father cares two hoots for all that Christian mumbo-jumbo either."

"Don't be silly Olga, I did say 'religion' admittedly, but it's culture and history not religion as such. Look, Olga, for God's sake, you need to get out more and start having some plain good fun again. There are many good men around."

Olga was always swayed by Nerissa's arguments but the fact was she could not get Selim out of her mind. Where was he? Was he safe? Was he coping with his amputated arm? Did he think of her?

Quite apart from her continued obsession with the memory of Selim, she was finding it impossible to drift back into the warm but enveloping embrace of her family in Makrikoy. It was in this rather restless state of mind that she received two letters, both arriving by pure coincidence on the same day. One was from the executive director of the Uskudar military hospital, whom she had known of course during her work there. Knowing her dedication and great sense of service he wrote to inform her that the Imperial Ottoman Hospital in Smyrna, a well-established old institution, was badly in need of good trained nurses. The current situation in Smyrna meant that Greek girls were no longer willing to work there, while the old-fashioned Turkish Smyrniote population had always been unwilling, unlikke Stamboul, for their daughters to become nurses. He wondered if she might be interested in taking up a post there.

The second letter, which arrived on the same day, was from an administrative officer of Sourp Pirgic, the Armenian hospital in Constantinople. He replied to the effect that there was in fact no shortage of nurses in Bolis, but that he had been asked by the manager of the Armenian hospital in Smyrna if he could recruit some experienced nurses for service there for a year or two. There was, it appeared, a serious shortage of nurses in Smyrna, as so many of the Greek nursing community had volunteered to go to the interior with the army.

Olga was excited and intrigued. She wrote back and forth to the two hospitals, and after a flurry of letters and telegrams, she agreed to take both jobs, arranging a three-day-week contract in each hospital. Admittedly this did not give her much free time, but she felt that she would not really need much, living as she would be in a strange city.

Karekin was against the whole idea and was considering refusing to allow it, until Armineh eventually persuaded him. She argued the proposal fairly passionately –

"Karekin, husband, please consider these points. She is moping about here. She can't seem to get that Turkish boy out of her mind. She goes nowhere. She shows no interest in any young men. My darling, a complete change of atmosphere will do her a lot of good."

"Yes, but ..."

"Then, my love, consider that for the first time she will be going to work in a purely Armenian environment. The doctors there will all be

Armenian. With a bit of luck she will start meeting young men with her education and background. And meanwhile, Haik is going to be there at the same time."

"But, Armineh, what about the political position. Anything could happen. We are still in a state of ..."

"Politics – schmolitics! Rubbish Karekin. The whole sea is simply bristling with allied ships. You have already made it clear that if things turn at all awkward, they must all come back at once. It's going to be really good for her, believe me."

And so it was that the whole family, or what currently remained of it, went up to Karakoy to see Olga off on board an American destroyer – the USS *Lawrence*. It was Harry, in fact, now a fairly regular visitor to the Avakian household, who had introduced Olga to a Major Davis, a senior member of the American Red Cross. He was on his way to Smyrna, where he would be in charge of the Red Cross operations there. He had agreed to escort Olga and make sure that she got to the Armenian hospital.

Smyrna, always referred to by the Turks as 'the *giavour* city,' was still a cosmopolitan town, though not in the same league as Constantinople. Smyrna was a trading merchant city. The people lived well, socialised, made money, gambled and did not dabble much in politics. The deep water of the bay came right up to the quaysides, allowing ships to land their wares right opposite the warehouse doors. English, French and Italian traders not only came to do business, but often ended up living there in some style.

Each community had their own quarter, although over the years these areas had begun to overlap, with class differences adding to the mix. Running parallel to the coastline, a few short streets in from the quaysides, was the area known as the 'Frankish quarter', with the main street called the Rue des Franques. This was where the western Europeans had their luxurious homes, and to where the wealthier of the Turks, Greeks and Armenians had now moved. Further in from the Frankish quarter came the Greeks whose area ran all the way up to the northern Point, sometimes called the Punta. The Armenian quarter lay along the railway line going east up to the Caravan bridge station; and finally the small Jewish quarter lay by the side of the bazaars in the centre of town. As was usual in Ottoman cities throughout the Empire, the Turkish quarter went up to the highest point, straggling up the hillside in a maze of jumbled winding streets to Mount Pagae and the old ruined Byzantine castle at the top. The town was an extraordinary amalgam of Ottoman and western. Delightful suburbs, with western colleges and hospitals, tennis courts and clubs, mixed with labyrinthine crooked streets a few miles away with old men smoking their narghilehs. Modern goods to be sold in the interior were landed on the quayside, while old-fashioned camel caravans loaded with figs and other fruit arrived almost daily, swaying along the back streets of the town. These caravans crossed the Caravan bridge then plodded north to the Point to deliver their cargoes.

The atmosphere enchanted Olga the moment she stepped off the launch in the company of Major Davis. They took a carriage with her luggage, crossed the Rue des Franques and arrived at the Armenian Hospital, located where the Armenian and Greek quarters intertwined. There she thanked the Major and said goodbye.

Waiting for her inside was Haik. Olga was absolutely delighted as they hugged each other, and found herself already looking forward to contented and fruitful months of interesting work and carefree days. Haik filled Olga in with all that had happened to him in the few weeks since he had first arrived.

As the days passed, he showed her around – took her to his lodgings in the heart of the Armenian quarter where he and Paramaz lived with a modest family – the Kapamadjians. Slowly Olga settled in to a routine of work, three days at the Imperial Ottoman Hospital, three days at the Armenian Hospital and one day free. She found herself joining in with the whole party atmosphere of the town. She saw George and Haik and went out with them together or separately occasionally, and she acknowledged Paramaz, who had another smaller attic room in the Kapamadjian house.

In the days that they had remained in Bolis since the incident with Alexei, Paramaz and Haik had maintained an icy politeness towards each other. Haik conveyed clearly to Paramaz that he knew that Paramaz had been hassling the young Seta, and informed him he must desist. It was as if the Alexei incident had settled in him any doubts about his true duty where Paramaz was concerned. As it happened, Seta's infatuation had been lessening ever since her day with Nerissa at the Asadourians, but Paramaz believed that Seta's increasing cheerful indifference towards him was due entirely to what he saw as Haik's jealous interference.

Paramaz loved the work in Smyrna – the camaraderie of the quaysides where he made friends with other porters and clerks, as he checked the bales under George's supervision. George always appeared to him to be friendly and tolerant, and had what Paramaz considered to be reasonable views about life, unlike the stupid liberal Avakians. Haik worked in the office on all the invoices and letters and their paths did not often cross at work.

Paramaz would often wander off when he had the time, to go and watch the camel caravans coming in. The whole atmosphere was much closer to the childhood he remembered before the deportations. He continued to despise the sophistication of the western-style life around him at the grand hotels just down the road. He was indifferent to Olga, who tended to ignore him anyway. But he hated Haik with a virulence which increased the more easy-going charm Haik demonstrated.

Krikor Kapamadjian, the paterfamilias of the house in which Haik and Paramaz lodged, had a small shop selling dried fruit and nuts in the main bazaar on the edge of the Jewish district. The family had two sons – Ohannes who worked at the Greek orphanage and Levon who worked with his father in the shop. There was also a married daughter, Tamara, who was only nineteen. Neither Haik nor Paramaz ever discovered what had happened to her husband, who seemed to have disappeared about six months previously. Tamara had a six-month-old baby boy, whom Krikor's wife delighted in looking after. Both Haik and Paramaz ate their breakfast and evening meal with the family.

Olga was soon in a fulfilling routine. Her experience was valuable and much needed. She worked three days a week at the Imperial Ottoman Hospital, near the government headquarters – the Konak – currently presided over by the Greek governor who had been administering the town now for over two years. She had a tiny room there, and also a similar room at the Armenian Hospital. On her one day off she took trips out into the countryside, accompanied by young doctors, saw Haik or George, or just walked about the town. However, contrary to Armineh's reflections, she never forgot Selim.

And so life in Smyrna went on, revolving round the Opera House, the tea dances at the Kramer Hotel on the seafront and the Casino, where one could gamble or dance all night. Then there were the quaysides, busy with all the merchants and traders going to and from their work, the tally clerks checking on and off wooden cases and bales of cotton, the porters heaving and sweating with huge loads, and finally, the well-dressed customers in the cafés sipping coffee.

Who cared about the war going on in the mountains, which had been going on for over two years? Meanwhile there was money to be made, fun to be had, and, anchored in the great bay were the large allied ships with their great guns pointing at the shore.

CHAPTER 30

Mikael and Selim at war – the Sakarya

It was the height of summer in 1921 when the Greeks resumed their much-heralded offensive. The capture of the important railway junction town of Eskishehir had left the army poised only 80 miles or so away from the Nationalist capital of Angora.

"To Angora – to Angora!" was the mindless cry of the mob in Athens. This was not a whit more sensible or reasonable than the cries of '*Giavour, giavour!*' of the Turkish mobs. General Papoulas, who had now been in command for over six months and had begun to understand the limitations of the Greek position, wanted to dig in at Eskishehir and let the Ankara government bring the fight to him. But the King was in favour of a final drive on Angora in the ridiculous belief that the capture of this unimportant village would break Turkish morale. The King prevailed, and the Greek advance finally resumed on the 13th August.

The 42nd Evzones, as always, were at the forefront of the offensive. Tired, badly fed and with a chronic water shortage, they spent several days marching from the gentle, green valleys of western Anatolia into the forbidding highlands that started not far from Eskishehir. The army had no large tankers for the storage of water and in the height of summer, not much was available on the route. There was of course the railway line coming out of Eskishehir and heading for Angora, but the roads were either completely non-existent or were so bad as to be virtually useless for anything but animal transport.

The old army lorries, and indeed even the new ones, shook to pieces as they tried to negotiate these primitive paths. Sooner or later they would either be abandoned or sent back. The army had to rely on donkeys and camels for their supplies. The great loop of the river Sakarya itself ran through a series of deep gorges with precipitous banks on either side, giving no sustenance on either side; it irrigated no green fields in any of its meanderings.

It was the searing heat and the lack of water that the men had to contend with now and not the cold and the blizzards that they had faced in winter.

"To Angora – to Angora!" Mikael and his men marched on, dust in their eyes, poor food and the effect on morale of the perpetual lack of water – and not just for drinking. The ability to splash your face at midday, to wash yourself at the end of a day's march, or to boil a tin to have a shave, were all important morale-boosters in which they could not indulge.

Mikael understood this from his experiences in the Caucasus. Early on in the offensive, he had come to the conclusion that it was more important to get more water than more food. So whenever the company settled for the night and set up camp in the middle of the harsh, hot rocky desert, he would send the old sweats – Makis and Costas – with extra buckets to grab as much water as they could, using all their wiles and experience to get that important extra bucket or two. Getting food was left to Gianni or one of the other younger men. This often meant that the men would have to make do with fried maize, as the bread would have gone by the time they pushed to the front of the queue.

As the days went by, conditions got worse. After passing through the little town of Siva–hissar they finally crossed the river Sakarya to the south, as it flowed from west to east. So, some ten or twelve days after they had first set out, the whole unit found itself on the other side of the Sakarya at the foot of a long ridge called Mangal Dag.

All that day, they lay in sparse woods at the bottom of the hill, resting in what little shade there was. They were hot, dusty and fed up with all the marching but, thanks to Mikael, were cleaner and more cheerful than most of those around them. At midday, Colonel Plastiras himself rode up with a bevy of officers and called the sergeants and the Company officers together to explain their position. He promised to arrange another delivery of water for everyone in this sector.

"Well, boys," said Mikael when he got back to his unit, "It's going to be a night attack."

"You can't mean it, Sarge. It'll be a bloody shambles – they always are," said Makis.

"Why is that Makis?" said Gianni. "Surely if it's night time, the enemy have more difficulty in seeing you."

"Well, Gianni, stop and think. They may have more difficulty seeing you, but then you have more difficulty in seeing them. All they have to do is sit tight in their trenches or dugouts and blaze away at anything that moves in front of them. But you have to feel your way, moving forward towards something you can't see, making sure all the time that you are keeping in step with those around you. You can't see a fucking thing, you stumble over things, you can't keep up or you get too far ahead. Just trust me – it's always a shambles!"

"All right, all right boys, settle down. This is the position as the old man has outlined it. We go up the hillside, following that dried-up stream that you can see over there leading down to these woods. We will have Company C on our right, and the 33rd on the left."

A loud groan was followed by some rather explicit sexual references to the parentage of the men of the 33rd.

"Yes – yes – but listen, they have been reinforced by some boys from Nauplion."

"Oh, God," shouted Costas, "that makes it even worse."

"Well, anyway, we kick off at about ten o'clock, and they reckon we should be at the top soon after midnight. Now, get some rest. There'll be more water being delivered at the beginning of the evening, so we can use up some of our reserves to clean up – those who want to – and be sure to take a full water bottle with you – it doesn't cool off at night much these days."

Mikael knew that night attacks were indeed difficult and the incidence of failure was high. The important thing was training and to keep calm. The White Russians had used the tactic quite a lot, as small bodies of disciplined and steady men could, by a night attack, sow panic in the raw recruits facing them. However, unmotivated Red workers from some Russian city factory were not the same as tough Anatolian peasants, well known for their dogged defensive capabilities.

However, it was of course a shambles, though it ended up being a successful shambles. Mikael kept a tight control on his own three groups, but once the fighting started and the men began racing forward, all semblance of control by the rear staff was as lost. The top of the ridge was well defended, but after a battle which went on most of the night, the Turks began to withdraw. As the sun rose in the east, they retreated down the other side of the ridge, until they were all back on the north side of the little river by the ridge that ran down into the Sakarya.

The hill of Mangal Dag was now Greek.

Selim, as the intelligence officer in charge of keeping all the maps for the area, was stationed at Polatli on the railway line running from Eskishehir to Angora. Here, for the first time, he at last met the legendary Nationalist leader, Mustapha Kemal Pasha, who had fixed his forward headquarters in this town, not too far from the river Sakarya. Much to Selim's surprise, Mustapha Kemal was wearing the simple uniform of an ordinary soldier when he entered the map conference room with a bevy of other officers.

As all the officers gathered, Selim muttered to one of his fellow Intelligence officers, "Ferid *effendi*, why doesn't he wear his proper uniform? He is a full general isn't he?"

"Well, Selim, the fact is he isn't. He has been dismissed from the Ottoman army by those idiots in Stamboul, so officially he has no rank at all. No doubt if we can survive this onslaught, the National Assembly in Sivas will appoint him to a new rank."

"What, then do you think that they ..."

But at this point, the hurried whispered conversation was cut short when Mustapha Kemal turned his penetrating deep blue eyes on to Selim and called out "Captain Selim, I have some officers here from the Erzurum sector, sent by Kiazim *bey*. Could you outline exactly for them what our position is, and what has been happening over the last few days?"

Selim nodded, put on his uniform cap and went over to the large-scale map hanging from the wall. The group of officers, all from the eastern sector, gathered round. Watched carefully by the eagle-eyed Kemal, Selim pointed to the map, tracing the movements with his stick as he explained the position on this section of the front.

"And so, gentlemen, we have lost hills, we have regained hills and we have lost them again. The Greeks have moved painfully on, hilltop after hilltop, and now finally here they are at the foot of Chal Dag. The whole line has swivelled round and everything now depends on whether we can continue to hold Chal Dag. If Chal Dag falls, the enemy can then take Haymana from Mangal Dag, and Angora would be open to conquest."

Mustapha Kemal grinned, chuckled and called out from the back – "They won't take it – and even if they do, they'll be so exhausted I'll have them in a vice. Meanwhile, come everyone, we are moving my headquarters nearer to Ankara on Mount Alagoz. Thank you, Captain Selim, you will continue here. We will meet again, inshallah, assuming Chal Dag holds."

"Sarge, it's been one bloody hill after another. It's all so pointless. They keep telling us that Angora is just after the next mountain that we are ordered to attack. We attack, several of us are killed, we get to the top of a bloody hill – and still no Angora, just another mountain further ahead."

"Well, yes, Costas, that is indeed how it looks – but we are getting closer on a daily basis. We are, after all, at least twenty miles closer than we were when we took Mangal Dag," said Mikael.

"You can't fool me, Sarge," called out Makis. "You don't believe in the strategy our poncy king has ..."

"Watch it Makis!" called out Costas.

"Well, whatever. It simply doesn't make any sense. And now we are being told that this next mountain or ridge, called Chal Dag, is the last big one and we have to take it. What do you say, Sarge?"

"Look. Makis, I do appreciate that we have been storming one hill after another – but for God's sake what can we do? I have no idea what the plans of our General Staff might be, but I, and many other volunteers, are Ottoman citizens technically and if we are captured, we are likely to be court-martialled and probably shot for treason. So, we have no choice but to press on."

"Don't be silly, sergeant, do you think that those of us from Greece have any better choice."

The next day, the 42nd and a greater part of the rest of the Greek army stormed up the Chal Dag. The fight for this God-forsaken rocky ridge in the middle of nowhere, lasted a full four days. Mikael's unit got to the top, but were then chased back by a counter-attack. On the third day the fighting on the hillside became even more intense and units lost all cohesion. At one moment in the heat of the noon day sun, Gianni found himself with Costas lying face down on some scrubby grass, lapping up some fresh water miraculously still flowing from a spring near the top of the hill. Almost opposite them, but to one side, were another couple of soldiers also slurping up the cool liquid with their heads in the flowing stream, all four gasping with their efforts.

Of the four of them, Gianni was the first to raise his head with a grunt of pleasure.

"Oh my God, Turks!" he shouted.

"Where, where," yelled Costas trying to clamber up.

The two soldiers, drinking from the same stream, hearing the Greeks, also scrambled up. They all just took off in opposite directions running back to where they thought they had come from.

The fourth day was the turning point of the battle. The two armies had fought each other to the point of complete exhaustion and stand-off; the Greeks failing to take and hold Chal Dag were unable to enter Haymana. The shortage of food and above all water began to tell. The Greeks were without shells, without reserves and increasingly without hope. But the Turks, who had held them along the Chal Dag, were not in much better shape. They mounted a counter-attack on Duo Tepe and Kara Dag on either side of the railway. But now it was the Greeks who were defending, and the Turks failed to break through.

The result was on a knife edge, but either way, would be decisive. Both armies were totally exhausted after twenty-two days and nights of continuous fighting – perhaps the longest, single, pitched battle in history until then.

In the end, however, it was the Turks who held out longer. On the 9th of September, Duo Tepe was at last regained by the Turks and the Greek army began to retreat. By the 12th September there were no Greek units left on the east side of the river Sakarya. The battle had ended, and the two armies collapsed in the same positions from which they had started.

CHAPTER 31

Harry

Harry's last interview with Harington took place at the Harbiye, just as the news arrived that he had again been given command of a ship. After giving his final report, Harington said –

"Thank you, Harry. Actually I'm not too sure that even if they succeed in taking Ankara, that would be enough to end the war. In any case, we will soon find out as I'm told that the Greek advance has begun. I understand you are to be given command of another ship. Congratulations!"

"Thank you, sir," said Harry.

And so it was that he finally abandoned his little flat in Taksim to take command of a large destroyer – HMS *Lion* – lying at anchor close to the British flagship – HMS *Iron Duke*. The Admiral in command of this battleship and all the British naval forces in the straits was Admiral Sir Osmond de Beauvoir Brock. From the start, Harry never achieved the sort of easy relationship with this man, his true superior officer, as he had with the tolerant and easy-going Harington, and this led to a series of misunderstandings, destined eventually to be significant.

Although Harry had given up his small flat, he continued to make a point of seeing Nicolai and the Avakians whenever he came ashore. There he saw that despite the fact that Nicolai had no real prospects, both Karekin and Armineh had become reconciled to a formal engagement with Sima. Meanwhile the presence of the cheerful and irrepressible Alexei at the office put Karekin in a good humour, and left him

more open to the whole idea of a more permanent union with the Androv family.

So the second visit between the Avakians and the countess Natalya
finally arrived, intended as a formal confirmation between the two
families of an acceptable arrangement. Anxious and nervous about the
meeting, Nicolai arranged to have Harry invited as well.

Unlike the first meeting with the Levonian family in Makrikoy six
years ago, a war had intervened, and nothing was the same, socially, or
in the respective situations of the principle characters involved. Sima,
then not quite nineteen, was now approaching twenty-five. Now, instead of the only son of another wealthy well-known Armenian merchant family, Nicolai was a young impoverished Russian, a year younger than Sima herself.

In the course of the twenty minute train ride to the Cobancesme station, Harry was charmed by the countess, whose English was impeccable. From the station, they made their way to the Avakian house. It was
a splendid afternoon. Karekin, whose English had improved considerably, went out of his way to be gallant to the old lady. Alexei's Turkish
was good enough for him to pass a few words with Talin after lunch, but
he was shy with Seta, even though their temperaments were so similar.

Armineh, confident in her own household, managed to have much
more contact with the countess than on the first occasion, though neither quite reached the first name stage. The absence of Olga was barely
noticed; but both Karekin and Armineh felt deeply the absence of their
only son Haik. It was this that explained why Alexei had fitted in so well
at Karekin's office, and why he was so welcome at the family home.

At the end of the visit, though it was well into autumn, the evening
was fine, and Harry and the Russians decided to walk back down to the
station, rather than arrange for a carriage to come up, and Sima and
Nerissa accompanied them. In the hall as the party moved out, Alexei,
the last to leave, bowed and took Armineh's hand and kissed it, as he
had seen his brother do. This was his first formal Russian salutation and
he did it with great panache. However, when it came to saying goodbye
to Seta, he took her hand also, but then leant forward and kissed her on
the cheek and hurried out.

Christmas 1921 came and went. Haik had returned and then gone
back again, leaving a tearful Nerissa clinging on to him as he tried to
board the ship taking him back to Smyrna. Karekin, keeping up his
normal reserve, embraced his only son with misgivings in his heart, but
without any real fear. Like everyone in the city, he was aware of the increasing difficulties facing the Greek army in the interior after the battle
of the Sakarya – but with the immense fire-power represented by the

combined allied fleets that were at anchor both here in the Straits and in the great bay of Smyrna, what could possibly go wrong?

Harry, meanwhile, had become one of the Admiral's main subordinate Captains. Even though they were only on cool and polite terms, Harry, was often invited to attend the dinners that Admiral Brock had to give to a range of Allied officers.

On one unfortunate occasion Harry found himself contradicting the extraordinary prejudiced views of Admiral Mark Bristol, the American High Commissioner in Constantinople, who at one formal dinner on the *Iron Duke* made the following speech –

"The whole myth about the massacre and deportation of the Armenians is a tissue of western European propaganda. My own understanding is that in 1915 the Armenians were being moved to the most delightful and fertile parts of Syria where the climate is as benign as in Florida. Furthermore all this was being done at a great expense of money and effort by a benevolent government."

Not only Harry, but all the other junior British officers present, simply stared, aghast, at this quite extraordinary statement, attested later in a written report, coming from the lips of a supposedly high-ranking American official. The French admiral, another guest that day, hid behind his brandy glass pretending that he had not heard anything. To Admiral Brock's displeasure, Harry continued to demur as the American Admiral went on with the most outrageous racist opinions about all the minority peoples of the Ottomans Empire. Although Harry soon forgot this unfortunate episode, he could not have been aware that for Admiral Brock it was yet another irritation, confirming his already low opinion of Harry.

Harry enjoyed his new command and whenever he was stationed in Constantinople, he paid visits to Nicolai and to the Avakians. Meanwhile HMS *Lion* moved round the whole of the eastern Mediterranean, calling at Alexandria, Haifa or Smyrna from time to time, but always returning to Constantinople and mooring alongside the *Iron Duke*.

CHAPTER 32

Selim

The collapse of the Greek offensive in the summer and the final failure to break through along the river Sakarya in August was decisive. The

Greeks had done their best, but they had failed, falling back to their original lines along the Berlin-Baghdad railway. Both armies settled down for the winter. Athens still confronted Ankara, but by now it was no longer an equal contest. The Greek troops were months in arrears of their pay. They were over 3,000 feet up, entrenched on a windswept plateau, in increasingly bitter winter conditions. They were without winter clothing and insufficiently supplied with blankets and tents, despite every effort of the firm of Avakian, Levonian et Cie to provide them. The problem was that the country was almost bankrupt. The return of the King, always suspect in the eyes of the Allies, gave the bankers and governments of the west the perfect excuse to refuse the extension of old loans, or the granting of new ones. In one way or another, the country had now been continuously at war for over ten years, and could not continue.

Of course, so had the Turks, but with a population five times that of the Greeks, they were better able to support the war effort. The Turks were in a sense fighting for their survival rather than an expansionist dream. Their army was led by an energetic and charismatic leader, who was a professional soldier. Ironically, a Greek collapse was going to result in the simultaneous fall of their original conquerors – the Ottomans.

It was not long after the battle of Sakarya, as the cold weather began to take its grip on both armies, that Selim was summoned to his commanding officer's headquarters.

"Ah! Selim *bey*. I don't know what it means, but you have been summoned back to Ankara. I believe that the Gazi, Mustapha Kemal Pasha himself, wants to see you."

"Could you give me any idea, sir, what it's all about?"

"Not really, my lad. All I know is that he requires you for a special task of some kind."

Selim travelled in some comfort for once, on the branch line leading back to the provincial town, now the capital of the nationalists, which the Greeks had been unable to take. There was still the same chaos and lack of accommodation in the town, but things were improving. Eventually, Selim found himself at attention, facing Mustapha Kemal himself, who said as he saluted,

"Sit down, Captain. Do you smoke? Would you like a drink?"

"No thank you, sir," said Selim, overawed by this man whom he had only seen twice, but of whom he had heard so much. His first thought, as he watched his superior light a cigarette and pour himself a glass of raki, adding only a touch of water, was how much smaller he looked when seen close up. But then, the stern pale blue eyes, sharp and gleaming, and the sense of control and command began to dominate, and he forgot the small stature.

"Captain Selim, I was very impressed with your grasp of the whole military situation when I saw you at Polatli. You not only had the whole strategic position at your fingertips, but you explained it very clearly to everyone."

"Thank you, sir," said Selim, inevitably relaxing in the warmth of his superior commander's praise.

"The lack of your left arm doesn't appear to have affected your capacity to operate on the front line at all. Does it ever hurt?"

"No sir, I was lucky with my surgeon at the Scutari military hospital. He did a good job, and I had some excellent nursing," replied Selim, smiling at the recollection of Olga.

"Good. Good. I have a dangerous task that I need carried out – one which requires not only courage, but also a sharp mind and military knowledge. Soon, in the new year, we are going to mount an attack on Smyrna. It's not a great secret. The Greek army is in a bad shape, and I have little doubt that this time I will drive through them without any difficulty. Preparations are already under way. But this will be the first attack on a major city that my troops will have attempted. I cannot be sure that the Greeks will not make a last stand there, assuming that we break through their lines in the first place, and assuming that they retire in good order."

There was a pause. The Gazi was watching him with eyes that for a moment looked hooded and sly.

"Yes – well – it would be worth a whole extra division to me to have a capable intelligence officer in the city, checking out what is going on there at all times. I need to know the mood of the civilian population, the movement of troops in and out of the city, the state of the harbour, and in fact all the militarily valuable information I can get."

With anyone else, Selim would have stood aghast, but he had been brilliantly manipulated and he simply stiffened, sitting as it were to attention, and blurted out –

"You want me to be a spy, sir?"

"Well, if that's how you would like to put it – yes. Instead of standing on a hill with binoculars studying the movements of the enemy and reporting your findings to your commanding officer, you would be standing on a street doing the same thing."

"Yes, sir – but not in an honourable uniform."

"Honour be damned! However that is precisely why I need someone with exceptional courage and intelligence."

The amputated arm floated like a mirage between them. Mustapha Kemal wanted Selim to understand that the lack of his arm, making him perhaps less useful in the front line, was not the reason for this appointment, while avoiding implying the obvious fact that it was actually a great asset for the operation Kemal wanted him to perform. A one-armed man, would cause so much less suspicion wandering about the streets of Smyrna, and this was precisely the reason that Kemal had chosen him. In fact, Selim was the ideal man for the job.

But would he agree? This mission could only be carried out effectively by a genuinely willing volunteer. The commander knew that he had to play it very carefully.

"My dear boy, I really do understand your hesitation. You feel perhaps that your lost arm might cause you difficulties. If you do feel that, please don't hesitate to say so. You know that you can return to lighter duties on the line without any reproaches on my part. You have already proved your courage, my son, in many fields, and you don't need to do anything more to establish that. My boy, do you want to go away and think about it?"

"No, sir," said Selim, at last relaxing back into his chair. "I'll go."

"Now, my boy, I insist – a drink." And the Gazi poured out a second glass of raki, and added water. "To your success!" he called out smiling.

They drank. The leader stubbed out his cigarette, and immediately lit another. The whole interview had only taken fifteen minutes. A few moments later, Selim saluted and went to report, as requested, to Mustapha Kemal's personal secret Intelligence officer.

Ali Ahmet pasha was a sly and secretive man. Few people knew of his existence. Although not one of Kemal's friends, he was nevertheless indispensable to the commander's operational method. Mustapha Kemal was surrounded by recognised military intelligence officers, who were all very competent as indeed Selim himself had been. Furthermore Kemal was a master at sifting these Intelligence reports and plucking out those of significance. But for all his more devious requirements: keeping an eye on what the Ottomans were doing in Stamboul, infiltrating and reporting on Kurdish movements and watching and fomenting Greek political divisions, he relied on this man who operated behind the scenes in total secrecy.

Selim remained with Ali Ahmet for almost a week. He learnt all the little tricks of the trade – how to keep a low profile – how to blend into the background – how to recognise danger signals. He was taught to operate a fairly primitive radio unit. He was given the names of men already in Smyrna who were fully committed to the Nationalist cause on whom he could rely. At the end of his training period he was given papers which showed him to be one Selim Nazim Kemal, born and bred in Smyrna, a loyal soldier in the Ottoman army, who had been honourably discharged, having lost an arm in Mesopotamia. The spymaster believed in keeping to the truth in these details as much as possible.

In due course Selim was ready to leave. A small suite of rooms in a house in the Turkish quarter, just *beyond* the Ottoman hospital, had been procured for him. He took a long route, first southward away from the two opposing armies, then via Adalia, eventually entering Smyrna on a fishing boat. In the chaotic conditions of the Anatolian interior, it had been an easy trip without incident.

He carried nothing of an incriminating nature with him. The tin case containing the radio machine would be delivered to him after he arrived. A leather suitcase containing his Turkish Army uniform, which he had insisted on having available, would also be brought by yet a third person. Even fairly innocuous items like his binoculars were brought separately.

While Selim never felt completely comfortable in his new role, he found it exciting and Smyrna was an exhilarating town. He wandered all over the town every day, until he came to know every street and alleyway. Routinely, he would go up through the European quarter, along the Rue des Franques and up to the Point at the tip. Here lay the freight harbour, where one of the two railway lines coming into the town ended. There he befriended an old man who regularly sat by a low table selling nuts and sweets to the workers on the docks. Sitting next to him, leaning back against a stone wall, he watched and noted the stores being unloaded for the Greek Army. He kept a careful eye on all the troop movements in and out of the port and reported it all back to Ali Ahmet.

Selim often followed the daily camel trains carrying the famous figs of the interior, as they crossed the Caravan bridge and then plodded through the dusty side streets to the freight harbour. Once there, he would settle down alongside the old man as the camels knelt and allowed themselves to be unburdened. He adored the ragged old women, sitting waiting for the figs, who shouted out ribald comments at him, referring without embarrassment to his missing arm and his hidden member in many ingenious ways. As soon as the camels arrived, these women would set about dipping the figs in great buckets of water, then piling them all up on the quayside, while barefoot children ran around and even over the piles of figs. Selim loved it all – the dirt – the life – the curses and the kisses – and even the crude references to his manhood.

A morning at the Point would be followed by a stroll down the great seafront road to the main harbour. Here, Selim would sit and take a coffee or two in one of the cafes under the awnings, as the varied population of Smyrna passed in front of him. He recognised them all – the Greeks strolling by in great confidence – the Armenians hurrying along on their business affairs – the Jews, a good deal poorer and shabbier than their prosperous compatriots in Salonica – and the Turks. The Turks were sharply divided between the *effendim* in their western clothes, now living in the European quarter, and those who lived in the little twisting streets of the old Turkish quarter with their baggy trousers and their veiled women, walking a step or two behind their man.

Selim's small apartment was in an old Ottoman house at the edge of the Turkish quarter – a maze of picturesque but squalid crooked alleys and lanes that ran up the side of the mountain that dominated Smyrna to the south, at the top of which was the ruined Byzantine fortress.

Selim kept very much to himself. He was often invited to join the games of tavlu at the café, but he would always politely decline. There were not many young men about. The Greeks were at the war, while many of the Turkish young men had also slipped away to join the nationalists. Even amongst the Armenians of Smyrna, which had not been badly affected by the deportations of 1915, there was also a shortage of young males. Kemal's instinct was proved right. The one-armed Selim could pass in places where a healthy young Turkish male would have stood out.

Every other evening, sitting at his desk, out would come the tin case, and he would tap out his report to the desk of Ali Ahmet Pasha; a report which would take pride of place among all the other reports to be dissected by Mustapha Kemal, as he and his friends meticulously planned and prepared for the final great offensive.

CHAPTER 33

Olga and Selim

As the spring of 1922 finally turned into summer, it was inevitable that Olga and Selim would meet. Selim passed the Ottoman Hospital at least twice a day and, on occasion, went by the Armenian Hospital on his way up to the Point. However, Olga worked hard during the days and it was not until one of Olga's rare days off that they bumped into each other.

Olga had begun to enjoy the wonderful life in Smyrna. She soon became a desirable companion for the young Armenian doctors at the hospital. She never had any shortage of men seeking her company on her days off. Whilst there was nothing approaching the thé-dansants of the Pera scene, there were elegant dinners in the moonlight on the café terraces along the corniche. An Italian opera group was in town throughout that summer, playing favourites like *Rigoletto* and *La Traviata* at several venues. Sterghiades, the Greek governor, imposed a curfew, but the guitarists and fiddlers played and sang in the cafés till the last moment.

It was late afternoon on a Sunday as Olga was walking down the Rue des Franques in the company of a doctor from the Armenian hospital; part of a group of four, the other two being another Armenian nurse, escorted by a Greek naval officer in his smart and distinctive uniform. The street was filled with Greek soldiers released from their barracks and were strolling round the shops of the European quarter.

This little group had just passed the French consulate building, and were turning down towards the sea, planning to sit on the terrace of the Grand or Kraemar hotel. They were arguing good-humouredly which to choose, when round the corner walked an unkempt young Turkish clerk with an amputated arm.

Selim stopped dead in his tracks recognising Olga immediately. He felt a surge of adrenalin, as he saw the group she was with, including a Greek naval officer and realised the great danger he was in. He should have immediately stepped off the pavement, kept his head down and walked on, but the totally unexpected sight of Olga created such turmoil that he was not thinking straight. At that moment, Olga looked up and their eyes met. They were not much more than ten yards apart. Selim had stopped, but the other four were walking slowly towards him. Four years previously, Olga would probably have called out 'Selim!' and he would likely have ended up in front of a firing squad. But now, there was a moment of silence as the party moved forward, while Selim said not a word, just staring into Olga's eyes.

It was a matter of seconds, and then Olga, turning her young man round towards the nearest shop, said in a strangled voice which she tried to make joyful, but which came out as a sort of loud croak – "Look, look, Dikran! Look everyone."

Everyone turned to look at the shop window which by chance happened to be a rather ramshackle establishment selling old-style Turkish slippers, of no interest to anyone. They all looked back at her and said – "Well, what – what Olga. What is it?"

She said as loudly as she could -

"You know that I am working at the Imperial Ottoman Hospital – well some of the older staff there wear 'pabouches' just like those."

Absolutely red in the face, Olga didn't dare look round to see if Selim had heard or whether he was still there. Instead she continued to stare at the bedraggled slippers in the window.

"Come on, Olga, what's the matter with you. What's so interesting about some old slippers," said Dikran taking her arm and continuing their walk to the seafront. There was no sign of the man with the amputated arm as they walked on for the evening's entertainment.

But Selim had certainly heard before hurrying away, and it did not take him long to arrive at the Imperial Ottoman Hospital, after a quick change at his home only round the corner. Talking impeccable upper-class Ottoman Turkish, he easily discovered that Olga worked there and had her own room. Selim calmly walked up, found Olga's room which was not locked, walked in and stood waiting – knowing that Olga would make her excuses and come soon. It was a tiny room, like a cubicle, containing only a bed and a chair. Selim just stood there for an hour and waited until Olga ran in.

For Selim, all hesitations, all doubts, all fears were over. He stepped forward, held Olga tight with his one good arm, and bent down and kissed her – at last fully, passionately and without holding back. Olga leant back, closing her eyes, and slowly but with certainty twined her arms round his neck and shoulders.

It was never quite clear whose foot it was that leant back and shut the door with a click, but it was probably Olga's. They fell back onto the bed and, at last, after six years of their tumultuous relationship, their love was finally consummated. Selim, unlike Olga, was not a virgin, but this was his first act of love-making as opposed to mere satisfaction of desire. There was of course fumbling and some tears – but it was love.

Selim and Olga spent the whole night together. In the morning they both knew that they would never part again, whatever family or culture might demand. Regardless of wars, regardless of politics, regardless of history, there could be no turning back.

As it transpired, this was Olga's last day of her three-day stint at the Ottoman hospital, and she was due to leave at midday and for her three days at the Armenian hospital. As they lay together in the early morning, she never gave a single thought as to why Selim was in Smyrna. This was always Olga's way. She lived on her instincts without the desire for analysis. She thought how Nerissa would have immediately wanted to know everything. Olga shook her head and smiled – it was early days, and she would find out soon enough.

Olga was to be on duty at 8.00 that evening. They lingered for a short while until Selim went off to complete his usual morning routine, arranging to meet at the coffee bar of the hotel Kraemar opposite the harbour, at six o'clock in the evening. Selim was in a daze of happiness. It had happened, and all his doubts and frustrations lifted from him as he went about his usual routine. Throughout the day he was in a state of complete euphoria, without any thought to possible consequences.

Olga was also in a state of certainty about her feelings and those of her lover. But it was she who first began thinking of the practicalities. She realised there must be some clandestine reason why Selim was in Smyrna. She wasn't concerned about what he might be doing, but she wasn't prepared to continue further furtive meetings in tiny hospital cubicles. She had been thinking for some time of finding herself a small apartment outside the hospitals and this new situation triggered a decision.

It was touch and go where she might have ended up. As it was, she walked away from the Imperial Ottoman Hospital with her little overnight bag. If she had strayed into the small Jewish quarter, or had considered the narrow twisting streets of the Turkish quarter, everything might have ended differently. But in fact, and perhaps inevitably, she walked on towards the Armenian hospital and entered the Armenian quarter. Not wanting to go too far, she confined her searches to the area near the Armenian cathedral of St. Stephen. She spent the whole morning looking at houses with rooms and suites to let advertised in the windows. Finally, in a little street only a hundred yards from the church, she found what she was looking for – an old Ottoman-style house down a side street owned by a widow – Digin Hasmig Derounian. She was offering two rooms on the first floor, with a delightful balcony overlooking her tiny garden at the back, with a bedroom at the front overlooking the narrow street. No food, no complications. She lived on the ground floor and Olga would be free to use the kitchen.

Olga was enchanted. She had never cooked; indeed she had rarely seen inside a kitchen; but she could always learn. She muttered something about her husband. Madame Derounian nodded, but made no comment as they discussed terms. Olga paid her first month's rent there and then, and took the key to the front door. Hasmig Derounian agreed to provide sheets and towels and to make up the bedroom for that night.

Although Olga had spent all day on this venture, she did not feel the least bit tired. As she hurried the half mile or so down to the harbour and the hotel Kraemar, she was in a state of complete bliss. She realised that Selim might have his own views as to where he wanted to live – but even if he did not want to join her at the Derounian house, it was still ideal for her.

While waiting for Olga on the terrace of the hotel, Selim, too, began thinking about the situation. Olga, though thoughtless, was no fool, and he wondered how much he could tell her. He was certain that he could trust his life with her – the way in which she had handled their first meeting in the street, showed that. But he had his duties to carry out. All these thoughts disappeared in a flash as Olga almost ran into the coffee bar. Selim jumped up, but keeping carefully to the conventions, simply took her hand and kissed it Russian style.

Olga excitedly told him of her find and her decision to take the two rooms. Sensing a slight withdrawal on his part, she immediately added – "But Selim, listen, I have been contemplating a move like this for a long time. This is something I've been intending to do for myself anyway. It's a lovely old house, and there is only a widow – a Mrs Derounian – living there."

"Um…Yes, well Olga if you are quite sure. I'm not certain that I can stay there all the time, but if …"

"Selim, I will give up my room at the Armenian hospital, which is only round the corner. It's also only a mile or so from the Imperial hospital so though it might be a little difficult if I have to come home in the middle of the night, it should be fine. Selim, my darling, you'll love it. It's very central so it should be handy for whatever you are working at here in Smyrna."

It was the moment that Selim had been anxiously anticipating since they had met.

"Yes, Olga, I must now tell you what I am doing here even though you may not like it. I …"

"Selim, my dearest, please understand that I don't care what you are doing. I love you. No, it's more than that, I honour you as well. Whatever it is, I know you are only doing what you consider to be your duty, and Selim you need only tell me what you think I need to know … and wait, not here. Come, let's away to Hasmig Derounian, Selim … I'm not on duty after all until 10 o'clock."

Olga's eyes shone and Selim stared back at her, understanding immediately what she meant.

They left, and strolled back arm in arm to the house. Madame Derounian said nothing as they passed her in the tiny hall. Selim gave her a Turkish greeting, with his hand to his heart and forehead. She nodded but said nothing as they went upstairs and into the bedroom of their little suite of rooms.

At half past nine, they left hand in hand. Hasmig came to the door; Olga had explained that she worked at the hospital and that her hours would be very variable. As Olga passed down the stairs, she was in such a state of euphoria that she leant across and gave the old lady a hug. They both walked out into the street, Olga turning to go on to the hospital, Selim moving away to stroll back to the Turkish quarter.

As these wonderful days of summer passed Olga came to understand that Selim was sending information of the situation in the town to the nationalists in Angora. What did she care! Her man was upright, virtuous and brave; she loved him and who cared about all that history? Haik of course had to be told, and Selim agreed with that. However he suggested that their hideaway at the Derounian home should be kept to themselves. "Olga, my love, Haik is of course totally trustworthy, I know – but there is that fellow Paramaz – I don't like him much and I find him odd."

"Yes, I know, I know – but what do you suggest?"

"Tell Haik all about us. Let's meet and do things together, but let him think that you still stay at the hospitals. After all, you do sometimes stay at the Ottoman Hospital at least, overnight. That way, this place will be just ours."

"Oh, Selim, Selim!"

With his arrival in the Armenian quarter, Selim decided to change his outward persona a little. He shaved his moustache and bought some western clothes, though he continued to wear the fez. He was still going every other evening to his room in the Turkish quarter, where under the bed was the little tin box containing the radio, together with another case with his army uniform and medals. But increasingly he didn't stay the night there, going back to be with Olga.

And so the summer days passed. Day by day, Hasmig's sensibilities about her lodgers were overcome, and she mellowed. Oddly enough it was not the fact that Selim was a Turk that bothered her so much as the fact that she was sure that they were not actually married. But whenever she enquired, Olga always answered gaily – "My lovely mamoushka, Hasmig, of course he is my husband."

As well as the Opera, the town's four theatres were full every evening with well-dressed customers, mainly Greek or westerners, but also with some of the wealthier Turks, now living in the Frankish quarter. George told Haik and Paramaz that he hoped soon to wrap up the organisation and leave it in the hands of his cousin, whereupon they could all return to Constantinople. Haik, who had in fact been told about the apartment at the house of Madame Derounian almost immediately, went about once a week on sorties and excursions with Selim and Olga, and regularly visited them in their little home. Paramaz continued to wander about the town when he wasn't working.

August approached and it was on a day at the beginning of the month that Paramaz, while out in the streets, saw Olga and Selim. They were walking hand in hand, and as he surreptitiously followed them out of curiosity, he saw them enter an old Ottoman-style house near the cathedral.

Olga and Selim – a former Turkish officer? Paramaz pondered.

CHAPTER 34

Mikael – the beginning of the end

By the midsummer of that year, all the signs pointing to a Greek collapse were present. Ever since the decisive failure to break through at the battle of the river Sakarya, the morale of the Greek army had been falling day by day. The Greek state, no longer able to float any loans on the international markets, was approaching bankruptcy. The Greek people had been at war with scarcely a break for nearly ten years.

Although the Turks were on the face of it in the same position, they were fighting on their own soil for survival. After their victory at Sakarya they were thoroughly rested and re-equipped with weapons purchased from the Red Army in Crimea and ready for a final battle. Greek attempts on Constantinople and the straits were foiled by General Harington, who even got Turkish gendarmes, to help him hold the Chatalja lines against his supposed allies the Greek army in Eastern Thrace.

The situation was totally ridiculous, but somehow the Greek establishment, without the genius of Venizelos, were unable to resolve it.

Meanwhile, Mustapha Kemal plotted and prepared for his last offensive in great secrecy. All troop movements were made at night, while during the heat of the day the men were rested in the villages and in the shade of the woods. Whilst pretending to mount an attack in the north against Eskishehir, his real objective was Afyon, the centre of the Greek defence in the south, and of course ultimately the capture of Smyrna.

In the last week of August the great offensive began. The Greeks were caught totally unprepared. As the days passed, one unit after another was overwhelmed, surrounded or forced into a humiliating retreat. By the end of the month, only five days after the start of the offensive, almost half the Greek army was annihilated or taken prisoner, while the other half were in total disarray, abandoned by many of their officers. Leaderless, there was a panic-stricken flight to the coast. Apart from a few outstanding units they no longer constituted a recognisable fighting force.

Caught up in the terrified flight, the 42nd Evzones was one of the few regiments left with any cohesion. Whereas hundreds of officers – mainly the Royalist political appointees – simply fled, abandoning their men in their desperate haste to reach the coast, Plastiras and his staff moved forward rather than back, seeking to rally those of their men who had survived. In this way, Mikael and his men who had held fast, were able to keep a semblance of order as they marched back, heading towards Smyrna. These men were among the few disciplined troops who were attempting to slow down the fast advancing Turkish cavalry, as they chased the retreating Greek army.

The disintegrating army of Greek soldiers ahead were retreating through an area of prosperous villages and small towns, some Turkish and some Greek. Without organisation or command, they had become a mob of individuals fearing 'the wrath of the Turk' and indiscriminately burning the villages through which they passed – Turkish or Greek.

As Mikael and his men plodded through village after burning village, they and the rest of the units still commanded by Colonel Plastiras rallied broken men from other units, and fought off the Turkish cavalry moving up fast behind them. At the same time, they urged on and protected many thousands of the Ionian Greek population, helping them to leave their often smouldering homes and make their way to Smyrna.

Mikael looked back at his tired and dispirited men as they marched on. Gianni – no longer a boy in any sense of the word. Makis and Costas, no longer bickering about politics, no longer teasing Gianni, just plodding doggedly in retreat. They had by now been separated from the main Plastiras group which had headed for the Marmara. At last the evening came when Mikael finally camped with his small unit in the fields just outside the suburbs of Smyrna.

It was the 5th September.

The whole shoreline of the city was a perfect beautiful crescent. Outside the inner harbour itself, at anchor in the bay, clearly visible from the shore, were at least twenty-two allied warships – British battleships, French and Italian battle-cruisers and even three American destroyers. Apart from all this tremendous firepower trained on the city, the harbour itself was massed with an enormous number of vessels of all sorts, shapes and sizes, carrying the flags of all the Mediterranean seafaring nations.

Except Greek!

The quayside was becoming more and more congested – piled high with all sorts of crates, trunks, the carpets rolled around family possessions. Already whole family groups, the uprooted villagers from the interior, were squatting on the pavements beside all this jumble of baggage. Carts used to carry some of this baggage down to the harbour were lying about while donkeys wandered about the streets adding to the clamour with their doleful braying. Men were milling about helplessly and in a daze, villagers of the interior who had abandoned their houses in the wake of the panic-stricken Greek soldiers. The men stood or sat, a pace or two away from their families, crushed and unable to think what to do or where to go.

Surprisingly, the population of Smyrna itself had thus far been relatively unaffected. The presence of the smart Greek military, together with the allied naval power massed in the bay, seemed to lull the inhabitants into a state of inertia. On the 1st September the news of the great defeat had begun to filter through. The British consulate started to advise British citizens living in the outlying areas to leave. The wealthier Greeks and Armenians decided over the next few days to lock up their homes and take holidays abroad – leaving discreetly on one of the many scheduled boats, paying large inflated sums for their tickets.

But then the wounded and defeated Greek soldiers began pouring into the city; stumbling in on foot, riding in on half-starved donkeys and mules, on ox-carts and broken-down trucks pulled by camels or hoses. They came in trains packed so tightly that many lay on the roofs of carriages. The walking wounded clambered off the trains and out of the station, wearily making their way out of the town towards the tip of the peninsula that juts right out into the Aegean. The badly wounded were pushed on carts; all aiming for the embarkation point at Cesme, only a few short miles across the sea from the Greek island of Chios.

The flight was massive and disorganised. The trains or vehicles contained dazed, frightened men with lacklustre eyes. Though hungry and in shock, nevertheless they located the Greek quarter, and knocked and banged on doors begging for food. They were handed bread, cheese and olives by the inhabitants, and then stumbled on.

Following on the heels of the fleeing army came the fleeing hordes of uprooted villagers, infected by the same sense of panic, desperate to leave the land of their forefathers but with no idea of where they might go. By the evening of the 5th of September, thousands had poured into the town, mostly on foot, with their children, their pack animals and their shabby suitcases.

They wandered about the streets of the town, a lucky few going to relatives or friends, but the majority just camping out on the streets, in the parks and in the cemeteries. But all eventually drifted down towards the quayside, which was getting more and more crowded by the hour. The wealthier of them besieged the shipping company offices clamouring for tickets or descended on the foreign consulates looking for visas. Though they were ethnic Greek, most of them could speak only Turkish. They were Ottomans in spirit, they and their forefathers had lived in the area for centuries and they had no idea how, or indeed whether, they would be accepted in Greece.

Finally, on the morning of the 6th of September, Mikael and his men, now a group of about twenty, marched into the town, crossed the Caravan bridge, and came to a halt nearby on the river bank. Mikael reflected, as he stood getting his breath, how ever since he had fled to Russia in 1917 he had been fighting in one war or another – and somehow always on the losing side. Now, for the first time in almost two years, his mind went out to family and friends in Bolis, and thoughts of peace and warm normal relationships. He shook his head, he still had things to do.

The men had not flopped down on the grassy bank as they normally did when they stopped. There were no more cigarettes. Though exhausted, they were not hungry – they had carefully hoarded food in their knapsacks. They all looked at Mikael. They knew he was going to tell them what they were to do. Mikael cleared his throat – he had already decided days before.

"Men, this is the end. I've just heard that the Greek civil administration and the Governor himself will be leaving either today or tomorrow. You have to move on immediately today – yes today – to Cesme. It's about a days march away. This is where the bulk of the army is being ferried across to Chios where you will all be safe and will eventually be repatriated to Greece."

"But Sarge, aren't you coming?"

"No Gianni. I am an Ottoman citizen. My family still live in Polis. I might not even be allowed into Greece – but anyway I have to take my chance here and try to get back to Constantinople. Now listen all of you. I am putting Makis in charge. Try to stick together. You have all seen how a disciplined body of men will always fare better than a mob of individuals. But boys, listen, you must be out of here and on the road to Cesme before midday. Don't go down to the quayside, it's bound to be crowded there – just straight on to Cesme. Good luck all of you."

If Mikael thought that that would be the end of it, he was mistaken. The men crowded round him; addresses in remote villages in the Peloponnese were exchanged; the men hugged and embraced him and swore eternal friendship. But eventually they left – marching in step and by God singing – with two reluctant donkeys loaded with knapsacks following behind.

Mikael at last flopped down on the grass by the river, and watched for some time the flow of people and animals moving into the city across the Caravan bridge above him. As he lay on his back, staring at the sky, he found that he was no longer thinking just of his own survival. He remembered the days when he had twisted and turned simply to save himself. He had now spent too long looking after, advising and caring for younger and less experienced men. He felt an urge to be responsible for someone other than himself.

He rolled over and felt for his haversack, which contained his few personal possessions, together with some dry bread and fruit. He searched about and found the piece of paper he was looking for, took it out and studied the address he had scribbled down almost two years ago on the deck of a freighter. The address of Elena and the two children – what were their names – to whom he had become the 'father' for a night and a day, as they all fled from Sevastopol with the remnants of another shattered army.

What made him do it? It had been a very short relationship. Furthermore, he was well aware that his chances of survival were much higher if he was on his own. Still, he wanted companionship, a friendly face, and felt an inchoate desire to act for others and not just for himself? He took up his haversack and walked into the town.

Away from the quaysides and the roads leading down to them, the town was quieter. There was no sense of an impending disaster as yet. Mikael walked through the Armenian quarter, past the hospital and into the Greek quarter. Within minutes he was at the house he was seeking. A few more minutes after that, he had been welcomed and taken in by a large Greek family, for whom his Greek army uniform and the insignia of the 42nd Evzones was a passport. Elena was thrilled. Mikael went to bed within half an hour and slept for the rest of the day and the whole night.

The next day was the 7th of September.

CHAPTER 35

The arrival of the Turkish Army

On the 7th September, which was a Thursday, Harry's boat – the HMS *Lion* – slipped into the bay of Smyrna and moved alongside the *Iron Duke*, which was already at anchor having arrived a few days previously. Harry immediately paid a courtesy visit on Admiral Brock who discussed the situation with him cursorily, making it clear that British policy was to remain strictly neutral. The harbour itself was filled with warships of all kinds, continuing to calm the Smyrniotes, whose initial fears seemed to have subsided.

At the Konak – the government administration building on the waterfront – the Greek High Commissioner announced that the three-year-old Greek civil administration would be coming to an end that very evening. Greek policemen had been continuing to patrol the streets, albeit somewhat nervously, these last few days, and they had been effective in keeping order throughout the city, amongst both Christians and Muslims. Now they were finally leaving and High Commissioner Sterghiades – a stern and on the whole very fair man – was the last man to leave, carefully locking the door behind him. He handed the keys to the French consul and walked down the steps at the front of the building leading to the square, where a small crowd in the square watched him go. There was much hooting and shouting as he walked away, but nobody molested him as he arrived at the quayside and was ferried out to the last Greek ship in the bay.

The next day, the eighth, was a Friday. Everything was quiet. The Greek police had all left. However, there was no panic or disorder, despite the presence of all the Greek refugees on the seafront. Everyone kept to their own quarter and businesses were closed, though many shops were open. The whole city waited.

Both George and Haik were natural optimists; George, because he lacked imagination; Haik, because he always felt that everyone around him was naturally reasonable. They shared that general inertia that impels people to carry on, even in the most dramatic of circumstances. Right up to the last moment of the Greek administration, business continued as normal. Boats came to and fro to the quayside with goods of all kinds. The firm of Avakian, Levonian et Cie worked on despite the refugees clogging the streets.

George was aware that many of the wealthier Greek and Armenian merchants had bought tickets for belated summer holidays. On Thursday he had purchased, just in case, six tickets on a steamship leaving for Constantinople on Sunday, and had telegrammed his father accordingly. It had been his intention to arrange matters with Haik and Paramaz at the office the next day, but overlooked the fact it was a Friday, the start of the Ottoman weekend. George lived in rooms above the office on the quayside and had only a hazy idea where Haik and Paramaz lived, though of course he had their address. He managed to find a courier to take a message to them urging them to contact him as soon as they could. There was after all no urgency.

Paramaz had a quite different attitude to what was unfolding around him from his greater contact with the working Turks of the harbour and he was much more aware of the cross-currants and underlying hatred amongst the crowds. He had long since acquired a good serviceable revolver and the ammunition to go with it, which he kept carefully hidden in his attic room. But even he, a pessimist in these matters, did not believe that there was going to be more than a little unpleasantness when the Turkish army finally arrived.

All work on the quayside had stopped by midday. More and more refugees were pouring down to the waterfront, making it almost impossible to continue any further commercial activity. The refugees parked themselves on the quays in a daze rather than a panic with their pathetic bundles grouped all around them. Those with some money gathered round the offices of the shipping companies clamouring for tickets of one kind or another. The consulates nearby were being besieged for visas. Every hour the quayside became more and more crowded with bewildered families.

On this, the second day after his arrival in the town, Mikael, took the two children with him and strolled across the now quiet Rue des Franques, with some of its shops already closed and shuttered, down to the seafront. The scene was reminiscent of the waterfront at Sevastopol.

He stood and stared, with each child holding a hand on either side. There was still no panic, but there was a sort of miasma of fear hanging over the whole scene. Mikael hurried back to the house.

For Olga and Selim the situation was different again. Selim could not contain his excitement; at last his nation were going to strike back at everyone who had wanted to destroy the Turkish people for ever. As it became apparent that the Greek army was finished for good, and that the Turkish nationalists would soon enter Smyrna, he stopped bothering to send any more reports. It was over – it was just a matter of waiting. But Selim too, active energetic officer though he was, was affected by the same inertia. After weeks of living comfortably, in love and at ease with himself, in the middle of the Armenian quarter, it did not cross his mind to move himself and Olga to the little room he still had in the Turkish quarter.

Selim's military service during the Great War had been with the old, fairly well-disciplined Ottoman army. He had no experience of the large numbers of guerillas and irregulars included in the nationalist forces. As far as Selim was concerned, the forthcoming arrival of the Turkish army would fill a dangerous power vacuum, increasing stability in the city, so he did not expect much to change for Olga and himself though, like everyone else, they stayed indoors as the city held its breath and waited.

It was Saturday the 9th and at last the Turkish army arrived. Mikael again went out in the morning, taking with him Anya and Andreas, both of whom had been cooped up inside all afternoon the previous day. Elena's extended family continued to squabble endlessly over what to do, ending up doing nothing. He stopped and watched as a mob of terrified women were pushed back from the entrance to the American consulate by a squad of American sailors who had been landed from one of the destroyers in the bay. He held on tight to the children and hurried past aiming to get down to the seafront. Then just as he arrived before the quayside, he saw a column of Turkish cavalry, riding slowly down the shorefront road in perfect formation.

Their trot was slow, dignified and disciplined. However, their curved sabres, glinting in the sun, were fully drawn and were held high in their right hands. They looked like every European's nightmare of Mongolian or Scythian hordes advancing out of the steppes of Central Asia. Panicked refugees, who had been squatting, some for days already, on the quaysides, shrieked and scattered in all directions as the horsemen trotted by, clearly heading for the Konak in the south. The horsemen themselves took no notice, only calling out, "Korkma – korkma! – Fear not!" as they passed.

Mikael was impressed. He recognised discipline when he saw it. He hurried back to the house. Behind this cavalry detachment, the Turkish infantry began to pour into the town for the whole of the rest of that Saturday afternoon. Although dressed in an incredible assortment of different uniforms, they arrived in fairly good order, marching in with some discipline. This was a triumphant conquering army, not a retreating one, and it was met on the streets by crowds of cheering Turks, themselves pouring down from the heights of the Turkish quarters but as the infantry began to be taken to their billets, losing the cohesion of the march, their discipline began to weaken.

At the American consulate, where earlier in the day Mikael had watched as the crowds had been scattered by American marines, the Greek Primate had arrived. Archbishop Chrysostom – he who had raised his hands and blessed the arriving Greek troops so dramatically three years before, called to see if the Americans could not do something to protect his people. Consul Horton was sympathetic, but had already received firm orders from the repulsive Admiral Bristol in Constantinople that he had no authority to help any member of the minorities, Greek or Armenian, if they were born as Ottoman citizens. He shook his head sadly and confirmed that he could do little to help.

"Your Eminence, The French Admiral has arranged for a marine escort to collect you and take you out to one of their battleships in the harbour. They are already waiting. I urge you – I beg you – to accept their offer. I can arrange to have them with you at the bishopric within the hour."

"Mr Horton, I do appreciate the offer, and I understand that the French, in particular, are doing everything in their power to help, but I cannot abandon my flock. I must take my chances here with them, whatever happens."

Archbishop Tourian of the Armenian community, had already discreetly slipped away for Athens, some days previously, flock or no flock.

As the day turned to evening, bands of soldiers together with small groups of civilians from the Turkish quarter, roamed into the wealthier parts of the town and began looting. They broke into shops on the Rue des Franques and on finding that neither the few Turkish military patrols now operating nor the French and Italian sailors still on patrol were taking any notice, they became bolder and more aggressive. The looting soon included armed robbery, as bands of soldiers held up any Greek or Armenian still foolish enough to be on the streets and took whatever they could find.

At the Kapamadjian house, deep in the Armenian quarter, Haik sat listening as they sat round the dining table. Ohannes and Levon, the two sons, tried to calm everyone down by insisting that there was no need for the current jitters. They too had witnessed the disciplined arrival of the Turkish cavalry, and they kept repeating the news that

Mustapha Kemal had issued an order to the army that no unarmed civilian was to be molested on pain of a court-martial.

Haik said little, but did add that his own father had always insisted, even after his experiences during his arrest, that the Armenians within the Empire had to be prepared to work with the Turkish authorities; Haik adding that he believed Kemal had no quarrel with the Armenians. This war was against the Greek state and army and not against the Ottoman Christians. Someone mentioned the allied warships sitting in the bay and this relieved some of the tension for the moment.

Paramaz, too, was sitting and listening and did not agree with any of it. What generals ordered at one level was quite different to what occurred at street level. Paramaz decided to see what he could get for himself out of the situation. He excused himself, went up and took his revolver which he slipped into the capacious pocket of a pair of baggy trousers. He took up his battered fez and slipped out into the street.

Looking like any of the other Turkish riff-raff roaming the streets, he walked along carefully observing the groups of soldiers who were becoming more and more brazen as shops were broken into and looted without any reprisal. Avoiding eye contact as much as possible, Paramaz wandered through broken shop doors and picked out small objects which he thought might have some value. Eventually arriving at the more elegant surroundings of the Rue des Franques, he stopped and watched as a Greek jeweller, standing in front of his shop, brought out a rickety stool stood up on it and began trying to fasten a red Turkish flag over the doorway. Two soldiers passed at just that moment. One of them pulled the man down from his stool and began kicking him as he lay sprawled on the pavement. The other tore down the flag, and smashed the window with his rifle butt, exposing watches and precious and semi-precious stones.

Paramaz, with his hand on the revolver in his pocket, sidled forward.

Selim had gone down to his little room in the Turkish quarter earlier in the day. There, he decided that it was now time to get out his Turkish officer's uniform, which had been in a case in the cupboard ever since he had first arrived. He decided to leave the little tin case containing the radio. Selim was already back in their apartment near the Armenian hospital as the evening closed in so missed the first signs of the deteriorating situation in the town. He hung up his uniform and waited for Olga's arrival.

As she hurried back through the streets after coming off duty, Olga saw shop break-ins going on in the Armenian quarter. She saw shutters going up, shouts and shrieks and the corpses of males, shot or stabbed, lying on the roads and pavements with women wailing and trying to staunch wounds, but most just lying abandoned and dying in pools of blood.

"Oh! Selim – it's terrible. There is looting going on everywhere. Soldiers are breaking into the shops and stopping people on the streets, robbing them and shooting people."

"Oh come on, Olga, I'm sure it isn't that bad. They all marched in in good order. Look, my dear, there is bound to be some disorder in situations like this; officers can't be everywhere. Soldiers capturing an enemy town will always ..."

"No, no, Selim, my love – I saw people who had been shot ... and, oh Selim, in the street just round the corner here, I saw some soldiers actually breaking into a private house, not just a shop."

Olga was distraught and so Selim now became upset, though he thought she was surely exaggerating. It was a situation *bey*ond her experience which he knew was bound to be messy. It would soon pass. However, he decided that he would go out and see for himself. He wasn't going to skulk indoors any longer. Impressing upon both Olga and Hasmig not to open the door to anyone until he returned, and ignoring Olga's protests, he went out. He thought for a moment of changing into his uniform, but decided that that would have been equally fraught with danger in this, the first day of the occupation. He strolled through the streets of the Armenian quarter, becoming more and more horrified at the increasing instances of shooting, brutal robbery and haphazard killing.

He made his way towards the Rue des Franques, and arrived at the same corner with the Greek jeweller's shop where Paramaz was standing, just as the two Turkish soldiers stopped kicking the hapless shopkeeper lying on the pavement. Selim noticed to one side a figure, a Turkish civilian, who seemed vaguely familiar, sidling up towards the smashed window. Stunned by what he was seeing, he watched the Turkish soldier who had torn down the shopkeeper's Turkish flag, calmly turn his rifle down and shoot the figure moaning on the pavement in the head. Blood and brains splattered all over the road as the two soldiers turned away and disappeared around the corner.

Selim couldn't remain silent. He shouted out after the two soldiers, who either didn't hear or chose to ignore him. Selim was shaking with anger at the whole senseless scene and shouted out again as he saw the Turkish civilian – Paramaz in fact – who had rushed forward as the soldiers had left and had begun grabbing jewels and watches through the smashed shop window, thrusting them into his baggy trouser pockets.

Selim had no idea who the looter was. He was in tears of frustration. He could do nothing about the two soldiers who had already disappeared, but he was certainly going to do something about this scum who was about to take advantage of a tragic situation. He shouted again and began turning towards the looter. Paramaz stopped shoving the jewels into his pockets, turned and saw at once who it was who was shouting at him. He turned back again to run, pulling out his revolver as watches and jewels scattered in the road.

Paramaz had never used a gun before. Armenian shepherd boys in the Anatolian uplands did not possess guns. On the other hand he had no scruples. He was certainly not going to stop and argue with someone he knew to be a Turkish officer, despite the civilian clothes. Already the cooler more practical side of Selim's character was reasserting itself as he realised the dangerous situation he was in. But it was too late. As he ran, Paramaz turned and aimed his revolver at the figure in the dark. He squeezed the trigger twice. The revolver spat fire and Selim stumbled and fell. Paramaz felt a great surge of power and elation as he ran on with a view to getting back to the Kapamadjian house as quickly as possible.

Selim had been shot with one bullet in the ribs, and one in his knee shattering his kneecap.

It was still Saturday the 9th; brutality, robbery, looting and senseless violence was in the air. But for the moment none of it amounted to very much more than the experience suffered by all cities over the centuries occupied by conquering soldiers. Selim staggered home clutching his ribs to stem the flow of blood, eventually crawling as a result of the intense pain from his shattered kneecap.

For the second time in his life he stood at the door of the home of this Armenian girl waiting to be admitted as blood flowed from a wound in his side. But this was not only a different Selim than seven years ago in Makrikoy, it was also a very different Olga, as the door opened and Selim at last passed out right into her arms.

CHAPTER 36

Sunday the 10th September

It was Sunday the 10th. The day was sunny with a cloudless deep blue sky. The Turkish infantry had been in the town for a full day. Mikael, who had not yet seen the deteriorating situation in the Armenian quarter, left the house early in the morning to look around. Elena's extended family had been arguing over their options almost ceaselessly for the whole of the previous day and he couldn't wait to get away from the prevailing atmosphere of hysteria.

Mikael had experienced the looting of cities during the civil war in Russia, and was reassured by the lack of violence so far, but he hadn't seen the smashing of shop windows or the shooting or stabbing the night before. For the moment, he saw little sign of attacks randomly visited on the hapless Armenians in their quarter.

Throughout the night, the streets had never fallen silent. The Greek quarter was closed up and all the windows of the residential homes were shuttered and the doors heavily barred. This morning, as he passed warily through the streets, he could see that both the windows and doors of many shops were smashed in. There were bands of looters, soldiers and civilians, wandering about. The civilians were mostly riff-raff from the south, though there was also an occasional Christian. When Mikael got to the quayside, matters had deteriorated further. Now individual bands of Turkish soldiers were roaming around and grabbing whatever took their fancy; demanding money from whoever looked as if they had some. Girls were being dragged away and raped and shots were fired when helpless males tried to intervene. But these were only isolated incidents. The predominant mood was that of utter despair. The crowd appeared to have lost its will to do anything but sit on their wretched belongings waiting to be told what to do.

Mikael began walking up towards the Point, his eyes darting everywhere as the crowds thinned out the further he got away from the inner harbour. He was about halfway up when he found what he was looking for. A Smyrniote, almost certainly a Turk, was sitting on the quayside, legs dangling over the edge with his bare feet already in the water. He was fishing! At his feet was a small rowing boat tied up to the bollard against which he was sitting. Mikael knew he would find one somewhere sooner or later, but he was lucky to find it so early.

He had come out with all his hoarded money, comprising by now about twenty gold liras. Wisely, he began by slowing down, sauntering up to the man and starting a slow conversation with the man.

"May Allah give good fortune to your endeavours. Have you caught many fish?"

"I have, *effendi*. See, there, still alive in this bucket. You wish to buy?"

"No, no, my wife, inshallah, is already preparing our midday meal but I would be interested to see them," saying which, Mikael lifted the tin lid of the bucket and peered inside to see several fair-sized fish thrashing about at the bottom in the water. They talked for a short time about the 'good news' of the arrival of law and order in the form of Kemal's soldiers. They considered the difficulties of making ends meet as a fisherman, and examined from all angles the particular problem of managing a rowing boat and fishing at the same time without a son to help. Then at last, after Mikael had ascertained the man's name –

Ahmed – and the fact that he had only daughters, came the moment that both men knew was looming.

"Ahmed *bey*, I do understand that your fishing excursions only brings you in a few kurus or drachmas a day – would you consider leasing me your rowing boat and your services for the whole of next week."

"*Effendi* – so long as I remain in charge of the boat – I might consider this."

"Of course, of course, Ahmed *bey*. Indeed, I might not even ever need to use your services at all. What I would require is for you to come to this spot every morning and wait here from morning until dusk for the next week, fishing as usual. I will pay you now six gold pieces just for you to do this. If the day comes when I need your services, you will get another ..." Mikael hesitated for just a second, then continued "... another twelve gold liras."

The old fisherman gasped in total disbelief. But Mikael, clear in his mind, immediately produced all his gold pieces letting Ahmed see them as he counted out six. Ahmed had probably never seen so much money, even on his wedding day. Mikael knew he was taking a risk. It was perfectly possible that the man, a total stranger only minutes before, might walk off with the six gold liras and never be seen again. It might also turn out to be totally unnecessary expenditure and that the current crisis would be over within a few days. But he relied on the fact that he was not asking a great deal of the fisherman who could come fishing as before for a week, and who would be eager to earn the further twelve gold pieces. And if the boat never needed to be used at all, well that was fine too.

The two men shook hands. Ahmed sat down again after carefully stowing away the gold in his baggy trousers and continued to fish. Mikael turned and strolled back down the waterfront. He picked his way carefully through the family groups huddled round their belongings. He was particularly careful to avoid any eye contact with the soldiers and ruffians wandering amongst the dazed refugees.

He turned away from the quayside, Mikael made his way towards the Armenian quarter, with a view to stepping into the cathedral for a few moments silent prayer. But as he arrived he saw at once that the situation here was quite different from the rest of the town. The walled courtyard of the cathedral was crowded with hundreds of local inhabitants seeking protection from the soldiers wandering about the streets who were beginning to break into homes. Mikael stood on the pavement outside and stared as the public crier passed by him crying out that all Turkish civilians must leave the area immediately, and almost in the same breath proclaiming that anyone caught concealing an Armenian male in their house would face a military court-martial. Mikael shuddered and turned away.

As he walked quickly, but carefully, back towards the Greek quarter, he saw groups of soldiers, assisted by ill-dressed louts, randomly breaking down the great iron doors – robbing – taking valuables – raping – and chasing the population into the streets. Every Armenian in Smyrna had at a stroke become a refugee, no different to the villagers crowded on the quayside. Mikael, however, seemed to have a charmed life. There was something about his bearing – he looked more Turkish than Armenian – that meant that he was not challenged as he hurried home.

Once home he spoke softly and earnestly to Elena and made his intentions clear. The rest of the family could still not make up its collective mind as to the best course of action. But Elena, who was now contemplating fleeing for the third time – having fled first from Odessa and then from Sevastopol – decided quickly. Yes! She would throw in her lot with this man, should the situation deteriorate even further.

Back at the home of Madame Derounian, Selim remained unconscious the whole day. Olga spent the time carefully binding up the wound in his ribs, staunching the blood flow and keeping it clean. She could not however do anything about the broken knee except to prepare some carefully retained pain-killing drug for use when he regained consciousness. She was amazed as to how he had managed to get back through the streets the previous night. Her nurse's experience confirmed how that painful effort had made a bad situation worse. Selim could no longer move under his own power. It had taken her and Hasmig half an hour to drag him up the stairs to bed. It would be agony for him even to get to the door of the bedroom.

The sounds of shooting and screaming in the streets outside came up to Olga as she sat patiently by Selim's bed, wiping the sweat off his forehead as he lay unconscious. Like any good nurse, Olga had a store of morphine and other emergency medical supplies and she worked all day on her lover's health. She knew he would not die.

Olga could not go out, but she could hear the terrifying sounds from the streets around. Whilst competent and clear-headed when it came to nursing a badly wounded man back to health, she was not so sure of herself in their present situation. Unless they were very fortunate, the chances were high that soldiers or civilian ruffians would eventually break into the house, looking for loot or sexual gratification. She went down to buttonhole Hasmig Derounian who was in the kitchen. As Olga went in she saw that she was sitting listlessly on a kitchen chair staring at the blown-up formal photo of her former husband on the wall.

"Hasmig, listen, you may not know that my ... er ... husband – Selim *effendi* – is a Turkish officer. He has his uniform with him. Please you must come up and help me to put it on him. He is unconscious and I can't manage to do it on my own."

Hasmig stared at her apathetically. But then, as if Olga's words had triggered a decision in her mind, she jumped out of her chair and ran to the locked cupboard near the door. Without saying a word, she opened it, and feeling round to the back of the top shelf, she brought out a tin box, which clinked with the sound of coins as she pulled it down. Thrusting it into her handbag, she ran to the front door. Completely taken aback, Olga stared at her from the kitchen door, as she turned and cried out –

"If you stay here, you are going to end up being slaughtered or worse. Our only hope is either one of the foreign consulates or the Cathedral. I know that our Archbishop has contacts with the Turkish authorities – he will help us. Oh, Madame Olga, come with me – I'm going to the cathedral – we may be safe there until law and order is restored. Come. Come."

"But Hasmig, my dear, Archbishop Tourian has already fled – didn't you know?"

"Nonsense child, nonsense. He would never abandon his flock. Just come."

"Impossible – but listen Hasmig you're taking a great risk going out into the streets. They can't enter every single house – we might still be safe here until my husband regains consciousness. Then he will protect us. Listen Hasmig we ..."

But Hasmig had already slipped out into the street leaving the door ajar. Olga hurried forward to lock and bar it again. Taking up some bread and olives, she went back upstairs to sit next to Selim for the rest of the day and night.

On board the *Lion*, Harry spent the day sweeping the quayside with his binoculars, and making sure that the ship's boats were prepared and ready to be launched at a moment's notice. The men were appalled as they all watched as the seafront filled up with more and more people, mainly women, children and old men. Small boats were already moving alongside with people on board begging to be taken aboard. The instructions from the admiral were however clear. No one – no one at all – was to be allowed to board any British ship. Eventually at midday a cutter arrived from the *Iron Duke* with a request that Harry should join the Admiral. Harry was taken across, piped onto the flagship and went immediately to report to the admiral. Harry was apprehensive over why he had been summoned, but Brock put him at ease immediately.

"Sit down, Bridgeman, sit down. Listen, we have a severe problem here. I tried to go ashore yesterday to have a word with the new Turkish governor, Noureddin. But some Turkish soldiers on the quayside fired at our flag. Disgraceful! I felt like shooting straight back at them. Anyway try as we might we couldn't land. I had to turn back."

"Is this happening to everyone, sir?"

"No, damn it! The French admiral – Dumesnil, or whatever his name is, has already gone ashore and both French and Italian patrols are in the city right now protecting their nationals. Anyway Dumesnil told the governor what had happened to me, and I've now been told that I can go and visit him today."

"Yes, sir – that's good. We need to see what we can do to help people in the situation."

"Rubbish, man, that's not the issue at all. I'm not in the business of helping anyone, except very clearly British citizens."

"But, sir, if ..."

"Harry, don't argue for God's sake. I've asked you to accompany me on this meeting because of your experience with these people – but keep your mouth shut unless you see anything you need to tell me about urgently."

And so it was that Harry accompanied the admiral on this second attempt by the British Commander to get ashore to see the new Turkish Governor – General Noureddin.

Harry stood to one side in the grand Ottoman reception room of the governor as the two men talked through an interpreter. The Turkish general started by somewhat cursorily apologising for the way in which his soldiers had fired at the admiral's boat, but making it clear that he considered England to be Turkey's enemy, and when Brock demurred, said,

"How the hell did the Greek army arrive in Smyrna in the first place? It was escorted in by British destroyers. The bloody Greeks would never have dared to make such a move if they hadn't been given the go-ahead by your government."

"No, sir ... no, sir. We are not your enemy. We believe ..."

"Rubbish, sir – nothing has taken place within this country or indeed the whole of the old Ottoman Empire in the past four years without your involvement. Did you know that thousands of my people were slaughtered here on the day that you allowed the Greeks to invade?"

At this point, with Noureddin getting more and more excited, Harry thought that the talks were going to break down. He waited for Brock to deny the ridiculous suggestion about these deaths and then to rise and leave. However, the admiral with that stubborn persistence of his class and background, but also exercising a certain amount of diplomatic tact said –

"Well, sir, you must accept that we had no part in that. Come – I am only interested in sending a small patrol ashore to protect and bring back British nationals and British nationals only. I give you my word, sir, that in every other respect we are entirely neutral in this situation."

This little speech pleased Noureddin, who stood, shook hands for the first time and said,

"I accept your assurances, Admiral. One naval patrol then, for British nationals only. I will issue the necessary orders."

Admiral de Beauvoir Brock stood, saluted and with an appalled Harry in tow, marched out and went back to his battleship.

In Constantinople, several hundred miles north, it was also a cloudless day. Karekin had invited the Levonians and the Androvs – Nicolai, Alexei and the countess – to a day in Prinkipo. The Androvs had not been back since they had moved to Stamboul. It was a perfect day as the party of twelve sat on the terrace of a delightful tree-shaded restaurant looking out over a beautiful blue sea towards the shore of Asia.

There was only one reference to the members of the family in Smyrna, as they began on their opening mezes. Hovannes said, "Ah – the news from Smyrna sounds a bit alarming. Thank goodness I heard from George a few days ago that he had arranged passage for their safe return. He gave no details, but I was under the impression that they might be leaving today."

"Good," said Karekin, as he dipped into the djadjik in front of him – "though I did hear yesterday that the Kemalists are disciplined, and that there is no fighting as the whole Greek army has fled. Nevertheless I am pleased that they are probably on their way back."

But in Smyrna, George had failed to find anyone, and no one had embarked anywhere.

CHAPTER 37

Smyrna on the edge

George simply could not understand why his messages to Haik, and through him to Olga, had not resulted in their arrival at his rooms on the quayside. The six tickets he had purchased a few days ago were now useless, but he could see that even in the face of what looked like a developing human catastrophe, business was still going on in the port. Freighters belonging to many different nations were lying idle at the Point, waiting to load figs and dried fruit, carpets and tobacco, which only a few days before had been pouring into Smyrna in the usual way. George had plenty of contacts with the captains of these ships, if an urgent departure became necessary. So his first task on Monday morning, once it was clear that none of the Avakians had yet made it to the office, was to walk up to the docks to check the position with one of these captains of a freighter tied up at the Point. Money changed hands. However, the captain made it clear that he was loading tobacco and that he would be leaving at the very latest by noon on Wednesday the 13th. George nodded, mentioned the possibility of as many as three more passengers, and returned to the offices.

George had little idea, even after all this time, of exactly where Haik lived, and no idea at all where Olga might be if she was not at the hospital. He felt it best to stay in the offices so as to be on hand when they all turned up. Once he came down from making arrangements with the captain, he began wandering down the seafront back to the harbour and his rooms. He saw the swelling crowds, but did not then realise that for the first time these were not only villagers from the interior, who had already been there for at least two days, but also a few Greeks and Armenians from Smyrna itself. As a result, he wasn't too concerned. Despite the deteriorating situation in the Armenian quarter, there were few Armenian Smyniotes yet on the quayside and scarcely any local Greeks, so he had no conception of problems arising in the back streets of the city.

George, wise enough not to look too much like an *effendi*, wandered down the corniche. He passed many boats of all types and sizes as he strolled on. Here, the boats were loading up with people; most were already dangerously overloaded. The whole scene was one of indescribable confusion and George did not dwell on it. He had to concentrate on avoiding the soldiers wandering about looking for valuables and things to steal and people to rob.

At the French consulate, he saw frenzied people outside pressing to get in. The French were handing out laissez-passers and visas to almost anyone who could speak a little French, and who claimed to be French. The British consulate, by contrast, was barred, admitting nobody who could not produce a British passport. George continued down, and it was then that he began noticing Smyrniotes from the increasingly troubled Armenian quarter joining the crowds.

George finally reached the Watchtower square and the Konak. By now it was noon and he walked over to join the back of the large festive Turkish crowd gathered in front of the colonnaded building, which Mustapha Kemal himself had visited only two days before.

That very morning, the implacable General Noureddin had sent for Archbishop Chrysostom. The Archbishop's staff urged him not to go, but to slip away immediately to the French consulate where even at this late stage he could probably get refuge on one of the French battleships. But Chrysostom would not abandon his people. Arrayed in his full black ecclesiastical robes, he arrived at the Konak, going up the wide steps to an accompaniment of jeers and catcalls from the crowd. He had been whisked up into the same large reception room at which Noureddin had seen Admiral Brock, and which had a large balcony overlooking the square.

"God be with you, Governor *Bey*," said Chyrsostom, moving up slowly to where Noureddin was sitting at his desk, and extending his hand.

But Noureddin leapt up, his face dark with suppressed anger and shouted –

"You pig! Do you think I'm going to touch that hand stained with the blood of my people."

Chrysostom began to stammer a reply, but this seemed to enrage the naturally irascible general even more.

"You are a man condemned to die in all circumstances, and I only called you today to make certain that that sentence is carried out. Now get out – get out – I hope never to see you again."

The Archbishop turned away, there was nothing more that could be said or done. No one in the Konak accosted him or prevented him leaving as he walked down the staircase to the main door. Blinking a little from the bright sunlight as he stepped out, he began walking down the marble steps.

George had arrived a few minutes before and had not seen the arrival of the Archbishop. He had joined the excited crowds milling about in front of the portico of the building meaning to stay only for a moment or two. Then he saw the dignified figure of the Greek archbishop walking slowly down the steps as the crowd began jeering again. Like everyone else in the crowd, he looked up as Noureddin himself appeared on the balcony. Quite beside himself with anger, his voice bellowed out over the suddenly quiet mob – "Treat the *giavour* pig as he deserves."

The crowd rushed forward with George carried along with them, though struggling to get away. Shrieking with an animal passion, the crowd pulled the unfortunate cleric away, raining blows on him the whole time. They dragged him up the street leading back into the town from the square. George watched appalled but unable to get away. He then saw, with some hope of relief, at the far end of the street a small detachment of French marines.

However, just before the crowd reached that end of the street, they all saw a barber's shop, with a scared-looking barber standing in front watching, as the crowd approached.

"Give the bastard a shave – give the *giavour* pig a shave!" they shrieked as they dragged the man into the shop, pushing aside the barber. Grabbing all the razors they could find, they hacked away at his beard, gouged out his eyes and began cutting off all the extraneous parts they could reach. Blood was flying everywhere as the animalistic cries of victim and torturers merged. George had managed to avoid being pushed into the shop and he saw several of the French marines, turn white and start forward hands on guns, but the officer in charge, though red in the face with suppressed emotion, shouted at them to stand still. George managed to turn away and elbow himself out and away as the unfortunate cleric finally expired. George became physically sick, vomiting out his breakfast at the side of the road. A man at the back of the crowd, who not a moment ago was swearing and calling out the most bloodthirsty threats of against the poor cleric, came over and gently asked George whether he needed any help.

George straightened up and managed a smile – a grimace really. He politely thanked the man for his concern, said he was fine and walked away through the now empty square and back to his rooms where he sat shaking for the next hour, suddenly aware of what could happen in this town.

Back at the Derounian house, Selim was drifting in and out of awareness until he finally regained full consciousness in the early morning of Tuesday, just as Olga, ironically, succumbed to sleep. She had been sitting up both nights trying to shut out the screams and fearful sounds coming from the streets and houses around her, all the time mopping Selim's brow, cleaning him and trying to feed him when he came round for a brief moment.

Selim's uniform lay on another chair, but Olga had given up trying to dress him. She did try to get the trousers on, but as she clumsily tried to lift one leg while pulling at the trouser, the wound in his chest opened and she had to stop.

When Selim awoke, he looked across and saw Olga fast asleep in the chair next to the bed. With consciousness came pain. He had not only lost a lot of blood as a result of his shattered ribs, but the pain of the bullet in his knee was excruciating. So, as he moved for the first time, the pain was overwhelming and he gave a cry. Olga woke instantly and put her arms round him. She was very gentle, and after a long embrace, began carefully checking on the bandages and on the shattered knee as best she could.

"My darling, you have been unconscious for over 24 hours – but thank God I think you are through the worst. It's a question now of getting you to a hospital as soon as possible."

"Ah Olga, my love. Olga. Olga!"

"Bear up Selim – it might be difficult, but I will continue to look after you until we can get away."

"Why, Olga, what is happening?"

"Oh Selim, I'm sorry, but it is going from bad to worse. If you listen you can hear, even with the shutters tight closed. The soldiers are going round systematically forcing people out of their homes, raping and robbing."

"Olga, are they really Turkish soldiers?"

"Oh Selim, I'm so sorry to tell you, my darling, but they are soldiers."

Olga saw the sadness on Selim's face, even in the midst of his pain, and hastily added, though she had actually seen nothing.

"But, Selim, they are largely all those chette guerilla types. My sweet, Hasmig has already fled, hoping to find sanctuary in the cathedral. I had no one to help. Selim, you have to get into your uniform. Here – I've got it all laid out for you. I'm afraid there is blood on your trousers. My dearest love it's only your blood. I tried to ..."

"Oh, Olga don't cry. Come let's have a go."

During the next hour, with sweat dripping down his face, Selim struggled to squeeze his leg with its shattered knee into his trousers. Then he had to get his bleeding body into a shirt and his tunic over ribs which, despite all Olga's professional care, began oozing blood again. Selim lay back exhausted on the bed, as Olga finally thought of food and ran down to the kitchen. This had taken all morning, but at last Selim lay on the bed stretched out in his Turkish officer's uniform.

Back at the Kapamadjian's house, which had also not as yet been broken into, Haik and Paramaz now faced their own decision. No message had got through to them from George, but they felt that he would have made some arrangements. However, Haik could not contemplate leaving the area without first checking on Olga. Bands of soldiers were moving from house to house, unchecked by the few officers in the streets, smashing down the strong iron doors with crowbars, and breaking in. Women and girls found cowering inside were raped in the house or dragged out into the streets, where they were picked up by other groups. It was totally haphazard as some houses were entered several times with all occupants slaughtered, whilst others were not entered at all.

However, every Armenian in Smyrna had now become a refugee, and this was slowly beginning to effect the much larger Greek quarter as well. The Kapamadjians were now at last facing up to the situation. It was only a matter of time, unless they were very lucky, before their house would be broken into. But it was not all that easy. There was an elderly mother and father, the two sons, and then there was Tamara with her baby. They began to make preparations to move out, and they decided to make for the Point, rather than the quayside and the harbour.

Haik acted more quickly. He told Paramaz to collect up his things – no clothes, just money and any valuables. He himself ran up to his room and took his reserve gold pieces, together with his money belt and ran into Paramaz's attic room. There, Paramaz had already stashed away in his shabby but capacious baggy trousers all the stolen jewels together with his reloaded revolver. He watched as Haik, in a state of great excitement, filled the belt with such gold and cash that he still had, and then put it round himself next to his skin under his trousers.

They ran down the stairs, and found the family still wandering about in the hall, getting together things they suddenly felt they could not do without. How could they leave that portrait of grandfather? Didn't the baby need spare diapers and food and ...? That carpet had been with the family for generations, how could they leave it behind? What documents did they need? Haik tried to say goodbye, but no one was listening. He and Paramaz slipped out at the back of the house.

By now it was beginning to get darker. Haik and Paramaz worked their way from the back of the house, through some gardens and eventually into the street. Avoiding all eye contact, and trying to look like all the other looters and rioters wandering through the Armenian quarter, they crept on. Dead males lay about in the streets, but no women. It soon became apparent that this was because when a house was entered the men were immediately slaughtered and their bodie thrown out into the street, while the girls and other women were raped and then often killed inside the houses.

Paramaz and Haik crept along and eventually found themselves in the street near the cathedral in where Hasmig Derounian's house stood. There were only a few soldiers wandering about here. Haik knocked on the door, but there was no reply. Paramaz looked at Haik. "For God's sake! What's the matter with you Haik? They aren't going to open the door for that. Here, let me."

He then banged hard on the door, shouting "Olga, Olga!" at the top of his voice through the letterbox. After some moments, Olga finally appeared and let them in.

"Oh, Haik, my soul, my soul, thank goodness you're here. Look we have to get Selim to the hospital, he's been badly wounded. We can't take him to the Armenian hospital round the corner it's too dangerous – it will have to be to the Imperial Ottoman Hospital. But oh God, he can't move, we'll have to find some sort of conveyance – or a stretcher or..."

"But Olga, my dearest, how can we. The streets are full of soldiers killing anyone they think might be an Armenian. You wouldn't be able to get far."

"Look, Haik, no arguing, quick, come and help me get him downstairs at least."

Haik and Olga dashed up the stairs. Paramaz knew that Selim could not have recognised him or he would have certainly told Olga, nevertheless he didn't want to take any risks and he remained hovering about downstairs in the shadows of the hall. At Selim's bedside, Olga and Haik saw at once that Selim was in no position to go anywhere. Olga looked at Haik desperately. Her face was pale, she hadn't slept or fed properly for days. Her hair was awry and her usually elegant clothes were dirty. She was clearly at the end of her resources. Haik considered for a moment and then said, "Olga, what we need is a cart or a barrow. Even a donkey would do it."

"Oh, Haik, that's nonsense. How can we find anything like that in this terrible situation?" She was nearly hysterical.

"Look, listen sister. I've seen several mules and donkeys abandoned in the street – and flat carts, just lying about."

"My God, Haik – do you think it's possible."

"We can try. He certainly can't be carried by the two of us in that state. Look, you wait here and Paramaz and I will go out and see if we can find something. But listen, don't, whatever you do, go out in the street."

Haik gave his sister a quick kiss. She clung to him for a moment, but he pulled free, smiled at her, and clattered down the stairs.

"Paramaz, where are you? Ah, there you are. Listen, we have to get hold of a cart or a donkey or something. Selim can't move. He will only survive if we can get him to a hospital. We've got him fully dressed in his uniform – this will get us through the streets to the hospital in the south."

"Haik, it's idiotic. We've got to get away. Now! What do you think is going to happen to us if we are seen pushing a wounded Turkish officer through the streets on a cart? And what about Olga? There's no way that she could be anything but an Armenian."

"Oh belt up Paramaz. There's no way I am going to abandon Selim."

"Why not, why not for God's sake. He probably stands a much better chance of survival on his own without us around and certainly without Olga. Listen – you dirty your clothes, put mud on your face – we grab Olga over our shoulders, as if we have just taken her, and we make off."

"Paramaz, listen to me. Olga won't leave without Selim, and I won't leave without her. Just shut up and come on. This is the best time. It's dark, but there are still people around – we won't be too conspicuous."

Paramaz looked at this thoughtless, privileged young man, surely half his age in maturity, and the bile rose in his throat at the way he was being ordered about. But he shrugged and followed Haik out of the front door.

The street was almost empty. One or two ruffians, looking out for things to steal from the houses already broken into, were hovering shiftily further along the road. A solitary Turk, sporting a clean fez and a smart coat was walking close by looking about him with obvious curiosity. He nodded at the pair as they came out of the house, and strolled on as if all was normal and he was just out for his evening walk. And there – at the far end of the street, with its two long handles stuck up in the air, outside the open front door of a house on the other side of the street, was a two-wheeled flat cart. Haik turned and gave a great big joyful grin at Paramaz.

"There, there Paramaz – look, see, you have brought us luck. Come on."

Haik began hurrying up the street, but Paramaz was suspicious and hung back, moving slowly behind him.

Suddenly, there was a terrible shriek from the house with the open door, next to which the cart was standing. Haik was only about ten yards away. He stopped as three soldiers came out of the house. Two of them were carrying some clothes and two carpets which were obviously destined for the cart. The third was still doing up his trousers.

Everything then happened at once, all within a very short space of time.

The soldiers immediately saw Haik, who at the sight of the three soldiers had stopped and stood still in a fatal moment of indecision. It all might have been different if he had had the sense just to go sauntering on, or turned away nonchalantly – but that moment of hesitation, and the look that must have crossed his face was fatal.

The two soldiers dropped their bundles and began pulling their rifles off their shoulders, whilst the third just gawped, still trying to do up his fly-buttons. The Turkish gentleman who appeared to be simply out for his evening stroll stepped back against the wall of a house and stared at the scene unfolding before his eyes so fast that he did not yet have time to react or to be afraid. There was only seconds available as Haik turned to run back. His eyes met those of Paramaz, as he took his first desperate steps away from the three fumbling soldiers.

Paramaz pulled out his revolver and fired three shots up the street.

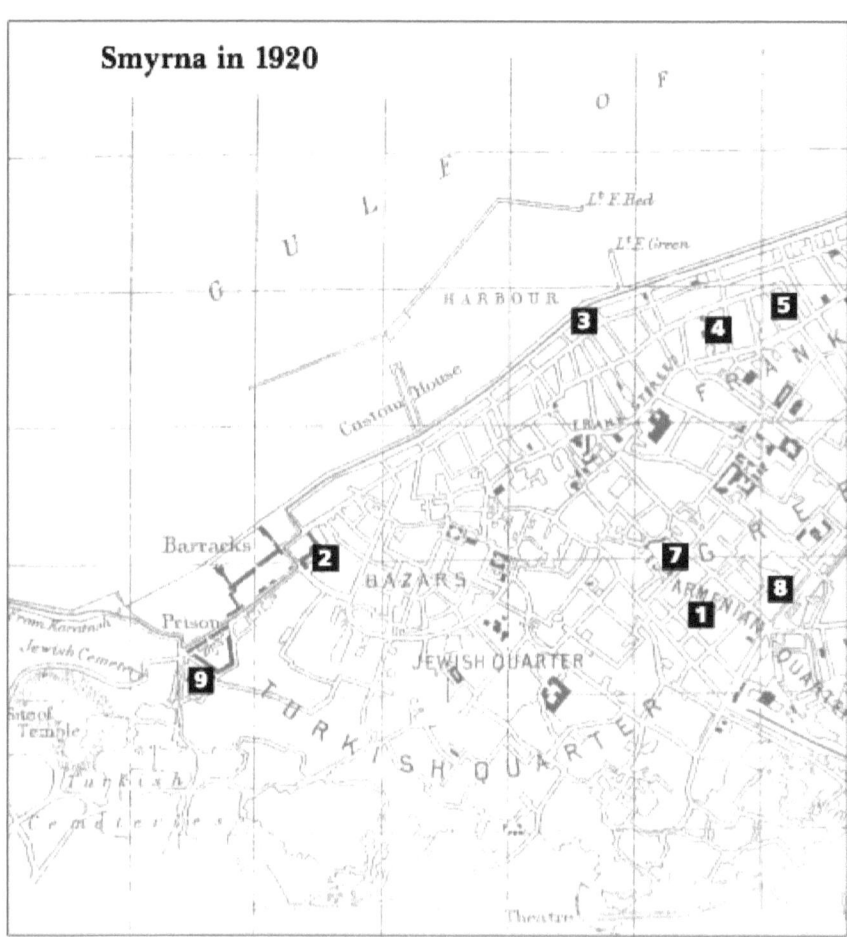

Smyrna in 1920

1   Mdme Derounian's House
2   Konak – The Govenor's Residence
3   Offices of Avakian Levonian
4   The British Consulate
5   The Fire Brigade
6   The French Consulate

7   The Armenian Cathedral
8   The Armenian Hospital
9   The Imperial Ottoman Hospital

It is about one mile from the top of the
map to the bottom.

CHAPTER 38

The burning of Smyrna

The Fire Brigade

Over the whole of the previous few days, wagons bearing drums of gasoline had been seen moving through the Armenian quarter, where they were distributed to the more disciplined groups of soldiers, notably those with junior officers still attached.Meanwhile, the scenes of pillage, together with the looting and haphazard shooting of males over the age of fourteen, were continuing. Bodies lay uncollected in the streets. But in all this chaos there was no sign of any fires anywhere.The Turkish army had now been in the town for nearly three days.

Then, just before midnight of Tuesday the 12th, the wind, which had been blowing gently from the north for days, veered and began for the first time blowing from the south away from the Turkish quarter – the one incontrovertible fact amid a smokescreen of rumours and counter-rumours, claims and counter-claims, panic and conjecture.

Within only one hour of the wind turning, a number of separate fires broke out in the Armenian quarter. The records of the Smyrna Fire department for that night showed that seven separate fires, all starting at different spots inside the quarter, were all reported and logged at the department within one hour of the change of wind direction. The records also show that at each fire to which the fire brigade were able to attend, there was evidence of the smell of petrol.

The Smyrna Fire Department, which was composed almost equally of Turks and Greeks – all dedicated fire fighters – rushed from one reported outbreak to another. But by early daybreak, the firemen had to give up. The whole of the Armenian quarter was by then ablaze and the fire was totally out of control. The wind blowing from the south and east got stronger and the fire began to spread to the Greek and foreign quarters. The fire brigade chief for the local area gave orders that an attempt had to be made to keep the growing fire within the bounds of the Armenian quarter. He himself went down into the streets ordering his men to hose down buildings as yet untouched outside the Armenian areas. He was personally directing water onto a Greek restaurant, which had already been looted, when he saw four soldiers enter the building carrying tins of petrol. The chief rushed inside to witness the men throwing the petrol about.

"For God's sake man, stop ... stop. We are trying to put out these terrible fires to prevent them getting out of control – whilst you are trying to make them worse."

"Well, *effendi*, you have your job to do. Go ahead and do it, we're not stopping you. But we have our orders too, and we are simply carrying them out. Bloody well bugger off."

Paramaz

It was still early in the evening before the fires began, that Haik and Paramaz had slipped out into the street to look for a cart or a donkey to take Selim to the hospital. There were still a few hours to go before the wind turned.

Paramaz was never clear in his own mind what he had actually intended when he pulled out his revolver and shot three times up the street. Was he intending to shoot the three soldiers or had he intended something else entirely? Surely the reason that he fired three times was because he was shooting at three soldiers. Surely?

The fact was however that Haik had turned and stared directly into his eyes and he had stared back for not more than two seconds before shooting the three bullets up the street, every one of which had slammed into Haik's chest. There was no screech of pain, no dying cry, no accusing glare, Haik simply collapsed onto the street and died instantly.

Paramaz did not make the same mistake that Haik had done; he immediately ran forward as the Turkish soldiers finally got their rifles up. Reaching Haik first, he gave the body a kick, and grinned at the soldiers, who, now much relieved at the turn of events, grinned back. Paramaz hesitated at this point, but decided it might be too risky to try to keep all Haik's gold coins to himself. Instead he made a show of searching the still warm body, and then finding the belt.

"Aha – these *giavour* pigs – they always have money hidden somewhere about their stinking bodies," he said, as he undid and pulled down Haik's trousers, revealing the belt wrapped round his middle.

The three Turkish soldiers were regulars not guerilla types. They were simple Anatolian peasants. Paramaz was lucky, he had complete control of the situation. He took off the belt, handed the three men a handful of coins, while he pushed the belt with all the rest of the gold into the deep pockets of his baggy trousers. The Turkish civilian – an *effendi* of some sort with his fez and smart coat – who still retained the air of being a mere bystander, came up and looked at Haik's body, but shook his head when Paramaz offered him some coins as well.

Up to this point, Paramaz always claimed to himself that he had acted without malice. Surely he had never had any conscious intention to kill Haik. The Turkish soldiers would have shot him in the back before he could have run away. Weren't the three shots up the street an attempt to save him? With little knowledge of firearms, was it his fault that he had missed with each shot?

But now he heard himself saying, as the Turkish soldiers did not move away with their grins beginning to fade -

"See, friends, what good quality are his shirt and trousers. Why don't you take them, they'll surely fit you, and if not they will fetch a good price."

The men relaxed and laughed out loud, nodded, and began stripping the body. Paramaz took the chance to slip away without another look at the body or any of the soldiers. The Turkish civilian stared hard at him as Paramaz walked away and disappeared round the corner, then raised his hand in an ineffective gesture to stop the soldiers pulling off Haik's clothes.

Haik's body now lay almost naked in a back street of Smyrna, ignored alike by soldiers or civilians who hurried by. Just part of another statistic to be denied. Within only an hour or two of his death the wind turned and the fires began.

Paramaz, by now an adept at slinking through the streets looking like another looter from the Turkish quarter, walked back through the Greek quarter, still surprisingly quiet despite all the looted shops. He crossed the Rue des Franques, and finally made it to the quayside just north of the French consulate where there appeared to be a large crowd round the main door, though he could not see as he passed, whether it was open or not.

At last the quayside. It was by now even more crowded, as Smyrniotes, both Greek and Armenian, were now being driven to join the original refugees from the interior. The atmosphere of fear and desperation remained, but for the moment there was no panic. Picking his way carefully between all the people sprawled about, some asleep, some just sitting and staring into space, Paramaz at last arrived at the offices of Avakian, Levonian et Cie.

Olga and Selim

Left alone with Selim in the house after Haik and Paramaz had slipped out to look for a cart or donkey or some means to carry Selim, Olga gave way to despair. She had in these last few months in Smyrna found love and a deep fulfilment, which she had worried she would never achieve. But her lover was in a critical condition. Strong as he was, could his body stand up to the battering it had suffered.

She made some food and took it upstairs. Selim was sitting up on the bed, leaning back against the wall. The morphine had obviously helped and he picked delicately at the food Olga had prepared.

"My darling, you'll have to cook better than this if you're going to come into a Turkish family."

"Oh, Selim – let's only get through this, and I'll do anything – anything you want of me."

"Come, come Olga – bear up my darling. Look, even if Haik can't find any sort of transport, I can always stay here. I suppose sooner or later from what you are telling me, it is likely that soldiers are going to break in to this house. Listen, my sweetheart, if you are downstairs you must run straight up here if you hear anyone trying to break in – and we'll face them together. The important thing is that you must make sure that this door is left wide open, so that I can see them as they come up – and they will be able to see me when I shout at them. With a bit of luck I will be able to persuade them to take us to the hospital. Who knows."

And so, as the evening wore on, Olga sat by the bedside, and they planned first what they were going to do. This inevitably turned to what they were going to do when they got back to Constantinople. All the same old problems were there, but they felt sure now that they would be able to surmount them. There would be children, of that they were both sure, but neither of them saw any problem with their upbringing. Their discussion helped to keep the terrors at bay.

But as time went on and Haik did not return, Olga began to become fearful despite all attempts by Selim to keep the conversation going. She never expected that he would find a donkey or a cart quickly, but surely by now he should have returned if only to report his failure. A stomach-churning knot of fear began to overwhelm her. For the moment she kept up a brave front as Selim continued to talk.

But then, the wind turned.

Within a matter of two hours, many streets were ablaze, and slowly all the separate fires began to join into one huge conflagration. The street on which the house of Hasmig Derounian stood was already getting hot, though no fire had taken hold of any houses on either side. On the other side of the street, behind the line of buildings on that side, flames and smoke were now rising into the air in great sheets and clouds. Stone buildings in the distance began to crash down, whilst the many wooden buildings simply disappeared in a rush of flames.

Olga and Selim, bound up with each other, and shut up tight in the house, remained unconscious of the noise, flames and smoke for some time. Then suddenly the noise of the fire rather than the heat impinged on their senses, and Olga screamed out –

"Selim, oh my God, Selim – there is a fire nearby."

She flung open the shutters, and stared out directly onto a great sheet of flame lapping up against the houses on the other side of the street.

"Selim – we have to leave – now. Now! My darling you have to try. Oh, my God where is Haik? Oh God – move Selim, move please."

"Keep calm, my sweetheart. Listen you just go, I'll try to struggle down."

"Oh Selim – come, come."

Selim tried to get up, but the moment he put his foot on the ground he doubled up with pain. With Olga following him from behind, he began crawling out of the bedroom. His ribs began bleeding again before he even got to the top of the stairs. The heat of the coming fire could now be felt through the walls.

"Olga – my darling – Olga – I love you – please I beg of you – go now run – run."

Olga said nothing but stood on the second step of the stairs, beckoning him down. Selim crawled on in considerable pain and then launched himself headfirst down the stairs, using his hands – still the strongest part of his body – to break his fall, with Olga helping to slow his headlong descent. When he arrived at the bottom he again passed out temporarily.

Olga was by now almost hysterical with fear and grief. She tried lifting him, but it was hopeless. When she had first opened the shutters in the bedroom, she had noticed, after the first shock of seeing the flames, that there were still some soldiers, and even a civilian or two in the street, despite the approaching fire. She recalled this now, and leaving the semi-conscious Selim at the bottom of the stairs, she ran to the front door and out into the street.

Even in the stress of that moment, her eye took in the dead bodies in the street, including that of a young man left almost naked in the gutter nearby. In front of the house were three young soldiers, their tunics loose and with sweat running down their faces, busy tying up a bundle with a cart beside them piled up with carpets and clothes of various kinds. Beside them was an older man, who appeared to be a Turkish civilian from the south side, who was watching them standing to one side, but not offering any help. The soldiers were obviously in a hurry to get away. Olga was distraught and almost incoherent as she ran up to the group and cried out, "A Turkish officer – the house – in there – wounded. You must help me, he can't move. Come – come – please quickly."

Mikael

Further to the north and west of the now burning Armenian quarter, Mikael, whose senses were sharply alert, was the first to arise and realise that somewhere nearby there was an fire raging. When he ran out into the street he could see smoke billowing up from the Armenian quarter to the south, and he could already feel the intense heat, even though the fire was still half a mile or so away. He knew at once that the crisis he had feared had arrived. He ran back into the house, where everyone was now up, milling about and collecting whatever they thought was important to take with them.

Mikael sped up the stairs to find that Elena had kept her head and had already dressed the two children in as many clothes as they could reasonably wear. She had also already packed a bag. Back in the hall, the whole Pantelis family was gathering with cases and bags in their hands. As Mikael came down holding Anya in his arms, leading Elena and Andreas, he did not join in the arguments that were still raging, but went straight out into the street without hesitating for a moment.

The noise of the approaching fire could now be clearly heard by everyone. The rest of the family took one look, gave up their fearful discussions and followed Mikael and Elena out into the street. They could see the flames, now only a street or two away, rising above the low houses. Everyone could hear the walls crashing down, and suddenly, throughout the whole Greek quarter the whole population began pouring out into the street, some with cases, others clutching bundles of things that they had grabbed at the last moment.

"Thalassa – thalassa!" – the sea! This was not the exultant cry of Xenophon's troops, but the despairing cry of their descendants desperate to get away from the flames. The fire behind them was like a great wall pushing everyone in its path towards the quays. On the northern and eastern edges of the Greek quarter, there were indeed some individuals, still capable of calm rational thought, who realised that there would then be nowhere further to go when they did get to the seafront. But when they tried working their way to the East, they were stopped by volleys of gunfire from Turkish troops ostensibly guarding the railway line. The effect, was to prevent people from fleeing back out into the eastern suburbs.

Mikael hurried his little family along, away from the flames to the quayside like everyone else. After crossing the Rue des Franques, he found his way frequently blocked by others fleeing haphazardly in panic. He zigzagged through the narrow side streets, passing the British consulate, tightly locked and guarded by a squad of sailors. Here, a naval officer was standing at the door behind the sailors, refusing to allow anyone into the building who could not produce a British passport. Desperate people were waving letters and other dubious papers clamouring for visas, but were being turned away.

Mikael hurried past and working his way north, came to the French consulate. Here, there was an even larger crowd, again pressing up against a squad of French marines guarding the building. In front of them was a mob of Armenians, already there before the Greek exodus had begun. However, on this street the official attitude was different. As Mikael looked back, while he wended his way through the crowds, he saw that anyone who could talk any French at all was being let into the building one by one.

He pressed forward, followed by Elena and Andreas; Anya had her face buried into his shoulder. Suddenly there was an announcement relayed through a megaphone wielded by a bearded French marine;

this called out, in French, that everyone had to leave immediately as the building was about to be evacuated. The fire, he bellowed, had now reached the Rue des Franques, and another office had already been set up on the quay alongside the harbour, where papers authorising passage onto a French naval vessel would be handed out to any 'French' citizens.

By now, Mikael, Elena and the children had already passed the crowd and were heading down to the sea, arriving within minutes at the exact spot where the French marines had set up a table in front of an Insurance office building. As they passed, Mikael saw that the harassed French officials were falling over themselves to try not to turn anyone away. Mikael didn't hesitate, although he did indeed have a smattering of French. He felt that what was important at this stage was not papers authorising passage on a ship, so much as the means to get aboard one. He was not aware that the French admiral had already ordered boats to start moving to and fro to pick up those refugees who had got papers and ferry them back to his ships.

The quayside was now crowded with panic-stricken people. The noise of the approaching fire was terrifying. The stone buildings on the quayside – the Kraemar hotel and all the adjoining offices were higher than the houses in the town – thus for the moment shielding the horrified population from the sight of approaching flames. However, the thick smoke rising up behind the waterfront offices and restaurants could be seen like a great monstrous genie poised to strike.

Mikael hurried his little group up towards the Point, to where he had arranged that Ahmed should be waiting, seated with his back to a particular bollard, and with his rowing boat alongside.

The bollard was empty. There was no sign of Ahmed or any rowing boat.

The whole quayside was now throttled with people all the way from the Konak in the south to the Point in the north. The flames had crossed the Rue des Franques and could now be seen licking their way down the little streets connecting the town to the waterfront. The heat coming from the huge wall of fire was now intense, and what was going to happen when all the buildings along the seafront finally caught fire. The Greek and Armenian population of the city they had lived in for generations were caught between the fire and the sea.

Meanwhile, out in the bay, lay the entire allied fleet; French battleships: Italian cruisers: US destroyers: ships of all sorts and sizes: the *Iron Duke* with Admiral Osmond de Beauvoir Brock himself aboard. Boats from some of these ships were coming across to pick up 'nationals' waiting to be evacuated. Mikael stared uncertainly, as an American boat from one of the US destroyers came up alongside with a small party of marines all with levelled rifles. Waiting patiently on the quayside at just this point was a small group of about ten American couples and families. As Mikael watched, a small tarpaulin covered truck pulled up. He reflected that it must have been one of the last vehicles to get through the fire. Out jumped an American woman, waving the flag of the American Boys College which was in one of the northern suburbs. She pulled back the tarpaulin, beckoned inside, and out jumped nine boys aged between eight and eleven, clearly Armenian orphans, each carrying a little stick with an American flag attached.

Then, just at that moment, Mikael, who had for a short time almost despaired, saw Ahmed in his boat bobbing up and down in the water only a hundred yards or so offshore. He waved and shouted until Ahmed saw him and began rowing towards them. Gathering his 'family' round him, Mikael moved as close to the armed American marines as he dared, waving to Ahmed and pointing to where he should approach the dock. He watched as the American Boys College teacher produced her passport and began a fierce argument with the American lieutenant in charge, while the nine young boys looked on with huge, frightened, wide-open eyes.

"Madam, I have my firm orders. Only Americans can be picked up."

"Lieutenant, these are all my sons – and as such they are Americans," yelled the lady, almost jumping up and down in a frenzied dance.

"Oh yes ma'am – come on – come on lady. I might have been able to accept one or two, but nine of them all the same age. Come, no more nonsense. I can take only Americans."

He beckoned to the waiting families to begin boarding at which point the lady grabbed each boy one by one and running up to each couple and family and begged each family to 'adopt' one boy as their own. Each American mother did so without a moment's hesitation. The young lieutenant looked away as family by family, nine American families got on board, each holding the hand of one 'adopted' Armenian orphan.

Ahmed, meanwhile had drawn up close alongside the quay, and Mikael handed down Anya, and began helping Andreas and Elena into the boat. Ahmed pulled away and they all felt the lessening of the intense heat as he rowed them out. Not many more than a few minutes passed before, looking back, Mikael and Elena saw the first of the buildings on the waterfront suddenly catch fire. Almost immediately all the buildings then burst into flames at once. The whole seafront, along almost two miles of buildings was suddenly ablaze. If ever there was a vision of hell this was it.

There was one great terrible drawn-out scream from the whole terrified crowd, standing between the fire and the sea.

Harry

Harry had risen early as soon as the news had been given of the huge fire spreading towards the seafront from the city. All the officers on HMS *Lion* watched through binoculars as the quays began to fill up with tens of thousands of terrified and panic-stricken people.

So intense was the heat that Harry could feel it even out here in the bay. Everyone could see the crowds surging away from the burning buildings as they caught fire. The water in the bay of Smyrna comes right up to the road only six inches below the edge. As the crowds surged away from the terrible heat, many jumped or were pushed into the sea. Boats, not protected by armed marines, were swamped, overloaded and then overturned right there in front of Harry's eyes.

The whole bay was now filled with a mixture of floating bodies and desperate swimmers trying to board boats standing in the bay. Boats from the French battleships were continually plying between the ship and the shore, ferrying so-called French nationals to the ships. Meanwhile, as he watched, Harry saw sick and aged people being brought down to the quayside on stretchers, as the town behind them burned more and more fiercely.

"Sir, can't we lower the boats and take some of these people aboard?" said a young midshipman, who was on the bridge on duty. Harry did not reply, but ordered his radio man to signal the *Iron Duke* requesting permission to take on board such refugees as could be saved. Everyone on board the *Lion* then turned their eyes and binoculars on to the British flagship, but they could all see with their own eyes that sailors on the *Iron Duke* were throwing buckets of water down onto rowing boats trying to moor up alongside the great ship and directly onto frantic swimmers trying to hold on to cables and ropes hanging from the side.

Admiral Sir Osmond de Beauvoir Brock had issued his orders. Not a single refugee, whatever race he might happen to be, was to be brought onto any British ship. British neutrality, he claimed, was at stake. This answer was signalled back to HMS *Lion* by a direct message addressed to Captain Bridgeman directly, reminding him of the promise given to General Noureddin to remain strictly neutral. It was, as always, touch and go as to what might have happened. Harry's second-in-command warned him that the men were getting restive, and that he might have serious trouble on his hands. It was the wonderful insubordinate, bloody- mindedness of the ordinary British seaman which resolved the situation. A boat which had been trying to get alongside the *Iron Duke* overturned. One of its occupants, a young girl of no more than fourteen years of age, came swimming towards the *Lion*. Everyone watched. She was clearly exhausted and in difficulties. Suddenly a seaman shouted out – "Bugger this!" – kicked off his boots, removed his jacket and jumped overboard. He swam up to the girl and held her up, treading water. Harry no longer hesitated.

"Lower all boats!" he shouted, unnecessarily loudly. There was no cheer or any outward manifestation – the men simply jumped to it, and the boats were lowered in record time, while the men waited for further orders.

"Right men, stay near the ship. Don't go near the shore, there is nothing we can do there now. But pick up any swimmers nearby who appear to be in distress."

Harry made a quick calculation and then called out – "William, you're in overall charge of this flotilla. No more than a total of … two hundred, at the absolute outside. Use your discretion. Off you go."

Harry was well aware that his order constituted a court-martial offence. He also knew that saving 200 people was likely to be a mere drop in the ocean, but he had no regrets. He went down to the radio room and radioed the following to Brock –

"There is no breach of neutrality in saving any human beings, regardless of race, in distress in the sea. Three hundred years of Royal Navy reputation requires us to save even enemies from drowning, when we can."

The answer from the *Iron Duke* was a terse signal to the effect that his action constituted disobedience to a direct order and would be reported and a court-martial recommended.

Olga

Olga was so hysterical as she gabbled at the three Turks in the street outside the house, that in the end all she was saying was "Turkish officer! – Turkish officer!" and pointing back at the house.

Who knows what might have transpired if she could have explained herself better – or if only one of the three could have been from Stamboul and understood her Ottoman Turkish dialect. Perhaps if Selim could have reached the street and shown himself? But what with the approaching wall of fire threatening to engulf them all, the soldiers understood nothing.

Olga was totally distraught, her hair all over the place, her clothes already turning black from the advancing smoke – but alas, she was still beautiful and she was rather obviously Armenian. She screamed as one of the soldiers struck her sharply across the cheek. He then struck her again and made to grab her. Olga bit his hand and struggled as he tried to hold her, whereupon he struck her in the face with his fist so hard that she passed out and fell to the ground. The fire was close by, the heat was becoming intense, the two others pulled at their angry companion as he began pulling at his rifle, urging him to forget her and move on.

And at last, the middle-aged Smyrniote civilian, the same man who had been present at the death of Haik and who was now hurrying home, decided to take a part in the action. Winking at the soldiers and shouting – "She will serve me tonight," the man lifted her across his shoulders like a fireman and grinning at the three soldiers, ran off just in front of the advancing fire towards the Turkish quarter to the south. Olga was mercifully unconscious as the man trotted past the now totally naked body of Haik sprawled in the gutter at the side of the street, where his body had been kicked.

The fire raged up the street as the houses on the other side began to crash down. Selim, still lying at the bottom of the stairs never regained full consciousness. The first part of him to catch fire was his Turkish Army uniform. Haik had died only yards away from where Selim, the Turk who had probably saved his life seven years before, also now breathed his last. Both bodies were burned *beyond* any possible recognition, as the great fire passed over them on its way to the seafront.

The beginning of the end

From their boat, Michael witnessed the sailors from the *Iron Duke* throwing water at the refugees, and directed Ahmed to make for the Italian ships lying a little further out in the harbour. Once alongside and making great play with the two children, he managed to persuade the Italian marine on duty at the top of the gangplank to fetch an officer. The fire, having reached the waterfront the previous hour, was now at its height. The light from the flames lit up the whole bay to make everything as clear as daylight. The children's eyes, large with suppressed terror, looked up at the young officer when he arrived and looked down.

The young Italian officer, under orders not to allow anyone else aboard, fought against his natural instincts, but with the two children looking up at him it was no contest. The 'family' clambered aboard and into safety – but not before Mikael gave Ahmed the rest of the gold coins as promised. Ahmed, like a rock of calm in the midst of chaos, touched his forehead and said simply – "May Allah go with you and your family always." Then without another word he turned and rowed away to the south.

Meanwhile, Paramaz, who had still not seen the fire starting behind him when he had first arrived at the offices of Avakian, Levonian et Cie, persuaded George that he had to move, and to move immediately.

"What about Haik?" said George.

"I'm sorry George *effendi* to have to tell you that Haik is dead, shot by a Turkish soldier who had come to loot the house."

"My God, what ..."

"He died instantly, and I'm sure there was no pain."

"Oh no, oh no – what am I going to tell his parents? But what about Olga?"

"Well I don't know for sure. But you do know that she was with Selim all this time, don't you? I'm sure he will have got her away to the Turkish quarter. There is nothing more to be done. We've now got to get away."

George was ready – indeed he had been ready for hours if not days. He was not too sure whether the arrangements he had made with the freighter captain at the Point would stand. In any event they both hurried up, past all the crowds on the quaysides and reached the Point early in the morning. It was then that they became aware of the flames and smoke rising behind them from the city.

As they arrived, George looked up eagerly, but the quay at which the ship had lain was empty – it had already sailed. The crowds had thinned out as they had gone up the corniche, but here they had thickened again. George and Paramaz stood about uncertainly, not knowing quite what to do. The crowds were getting so dense that movement was becoming difficult. They moved back down the corniche a little. The crowd gasped as the fire down at the inner harbour suddenly caught all the buildings on the seafront at once and the terrifying scream rang out. Out at sea, all sorts of boats, barges, improvised rafts, crowded with people, were floating about from ship to ship in vain. Terribly overcrowded, they often overturned adding to the bodies floating in the water.

The heat during the rest of that day was so intense that down at the inner harbour, the pathetic bags and bundles people carried spontaneously combusted, adding to the shrieks and screams of the crowds. Up at the Point, the heat was not quite so bad, and the panic had died down.

George had started ministering to a pregnant Greek woman holding an infant. She was nearing complete exhaustion and had sunk to the floor. As the crowds surged back and forth, Paramaz by sheer will power and brute force kept the mob from trampling over her. The baby clung to the woman, and Paramaz would gently take it up every so often and jiggle it up and down as he had seen his own mother do in the distant past.

Turkish soldiers were still wandering about among the crowds robbing and snatching girls. Night had now fallen, but the night was as light as day as the whole of Smyrna blazed.

The crowds wailed and moaned all night – and then over the hiss and crackle of the fire, which continued to devour everything in its path, there came the incredible sound of a Strauss march. True to the traditions of the Senior Service, Admiral Brock had ordered that there was no reason why the naval band of the British flagship should not play as usual in the evening to keep up everyone's morale. So it was that Strauss waltzes played out from the *Iron Duke* for almost two hours, while the city burned, and the wretched people moaned and prayed. The entire city remained ablaze and the fires and smoke could be seen from miles out to sea with the thousands of now homeless Greek Ottoman citizens continuing to surge up and down the quays.

In the early morning the pregnant Greek woman, whose name Paramaz never knew, died on the pavement. Before doing so she held up her one-year old baby who had at last fallen asleep on her breast, handing him to Paramaz, saying nothing but just looking up at him until she died.

It was at just exactly this same moment in the early morning that at last Admiral Brock relented and reversed his orders. His Chief of Staff had warned him that the men were getting mutinous as they saw the Italians and the French taking on board refugees and desperate swimmers. He finally ordered "Boats away!" with instructions that anybody of any nationality could be saved. The men released at last, raced to carry out the orders, and moved back and forth from the quays to the ships adding a touch of calm efficiency to the quayside.

Paramaz, now fiercely holding onto the baby who was too exhausted to cry or even whimper, carefully checked where one of the oncoming British boats was going to land. Then, holding the baby up on one arm against his shoulder as if he had been looking after babies for years, he grabbed hold of the dazed George with the other, and manoeuvred all three of them into a position where they could get aboard as the boat arrived at the quay. The boat rowed by strong willing English sailors, captained by a young midshipman, who looked no older than Paramaz himself, pulled up right at the point Paramaz and George were waiting. The baby was handed across and George and Paramaz clambered aboard.

Smyrna dies

Apart from the Turkish quarter in the south, and the warehouses and installations at the Point, Smyrna burned down to the ground. By the next day the city was a charnel house, with the sickly odour of burnt flesh mixed in with the faint but unmistakeable smell of gasoline indicating how the fire was started. The Konak and the Imperial Ottoman hospital remained intact, as did the whole of the Turkish quarter, where not one house was burnt. Smoke continued to rise up in wisps from the charred and burning rubble to which the whole of the rest of the city had been reduced.

In the middle of the Turkish quarter, a little way up the hillside, not far from the hospital, in the squalid stable of one of the larger houses lay Olga, exhausted, mentally wounded, raped, but still alive. Her only consolation was that the man who had saved her from the fire in carrying her off but who had raped her during the night, had told no one else of his acquisition, thus saving her from the brutal repeated rapes to which so many other female *giavour* Smyrniotes had been subjected.

Olga wept and wept – but not for herself, not even for her predicament or her ravished body – but for Selim, her Selim.

"Oh Selim – Selim – my love – my rose. My hero of the East. Oh Selim... Selim ..."

Constantinople

Bad news travels fast. The total collapse of the Greek army, at first regarded with complete disbelief, soon became a certainty. Rumours then began spreading round the city, becoming more and more alarming. The steady advance of the Turkish army and the reports of the burning of both Turkish and Greek villages on the way – regardless of who was carrying it out – added to the atmosphere of apprehension. Finally, bursting on the city like an enveloping cloud of fear, came the confirmation by telegraph of the great fire which had consumed Smyrna, this second city of the Ottoman Empire. As more details of the great fire emerged from several European consulates, who were getting their information by telegraph from their respective capitals, Constantinople seemed to shudder with fear.

In a flash, all the allied firepower of the fleets sitting at anchor in the straits, counted for nothing. Overnight the panama hats and the trilbies disappeared, and the fez was back on every head. Where were all those raucous Greek lads who had been driving excitedly round the city in new-fangled motor-cars? All the Greek flags hanging from first floor windows disappeared. Now there were similar cars driving round the city, but they were festooned with flowers, sporting portraits of Mustapha Kemal and filled with entirely different young men singing songs of triumph.

If Smyrna had indeed burnt down, and the *giavour* population slaughtered or expelled, what might not now happen in this city, once the triumphant nationalist army arrived on the opposite shore?

Karekin, of course, had no need to rummage in his chest of drawers for an old fez wrapped in tissue paper like so many others, who had thought they would have no further use for one. He had continued to wear his fez both as a sign of his support for the Ottoman imperial idea, and to show his disapproval of the triumphalism which had been displayed so openly by the Christian races of the city. He was not prepared to join in the frenzied speculation about what might or might not have happened in Smyrna. For almost everybody, not only for Karekin, two aspects to the crisis had to be faced; there was the political issue as to what the triumph of the nationalists portended for the city, and there was also the agony for the Avakians as for so many other families, as to what had happened to family members who had been in that city.

Sima found that she was unable to sit quietly at home. Once Karekin had risen from the breakfast table and left for the station, without saying a word about what might be happening in Smyrna, the hopeless speculations between all the women would immediately begin. What could have happened? Why had George and the others not arrived, as the telegram to Hovannes Levonian had intimated? Was Olga safe at the Imperial Ottoman Hospital? Where were Haik and Paramaz and why no news? Within an hour of this hopeless speculation starting, Sima would flee, and make her way to the Pera Palace hotel. There she would sit alone for hours in front of her one pot of tea in whichever salon Nikolai was playing. Whenever he had a moment to join her, while the orchestra were taking their break, they would sit quietly together, holding hands quite openly without exchanging a word, until it was time for him to return to the orchestra.

Both of them were aware of the tense and febrile atmosphere of the bars and other public rooms of the hotel, formerly so animated. Allied officers still stood about and chatted, but the arrogance and the certainty had vanished.

For her part, Nerissa went mechanically to her classes at the university which had just reopened after the summer break. She could not get out of her mind her last desperate embrace of Haik, as he had left on the ferry to Smyrna after Christmas. She could concentrate on nothing until she could be sure of what had happened to her brother. She loved her sister, Olga, of course, but somehow she had always felt that Olga could look after herself. Throughout her life she had always been the elder sister who had looked out for her little brother Haik, and she could not get him out of her mind.

On top of all that, sensitive as she was to atmosphere, she was aware that the whole carefree light mood of the city that had existed over the last two or three years, an ambience in which she had herself blossomed, had suddenly darkened. The Christians had overnight become fearful, no longer wanting to dance the nights away. The Turks for their part, were not only for the first time beginning to turn against their Ottoman rulers, but were also turning against what they saw as the hedonism and frivolity of the bars and nightclubs of Pera. A new sense of puritanical righteousness was in the air, and Nerissa could feel it all around her.

Seta just cried and cried, as they all waited for news. All her teenage hormones, mixed up with all the emotions of everyone around her, left her drained and heavily dependent upon her mother.

Armineh stood like a rock in the middle of all this emotional turmoil. However, at the same time as having to comfort Seta, she had to cope with a husband who refused to talk about the situation at all, but who was suffering agonies of anxiety, as only she could see. She managed to cope by bustling about on all her domestic chores, torn between wanting to join the girls in their interminable speculations about what could be happening, and her preference not to think about it at all until there was more certain news.

The citizens of Constantinople – ruled by a Christian power for the first time since 1453 – had been endlessly speculating for the past four years as to what the city was going to become. Ideas and plans had been discussed back and forth by governments, churches, the elite and the people, all to no conclusion. And now, the second city of the Empire had gone up in flames, a revenging army was on its way, and all the theories as to what was to become of the Imperial city died away. Constantinople waited in dread for certain news of what had actually happened.

Then at last, HMS *Iron Duke* and the rest of the British fleet from the Bay of Smyrna steamed into the straits and anchored in front of the city.

End of Empire 1922

CONTENTS

Book 3: End of Empire

?

CHAPTER 1

Spiro

"Oh my God – Spiro! Spiro, my son! Wake up!"

Spiro woke up with a start and looked up at his distraught mother. As soon as she saw he was awake, she stopped shaking him and hurried out of the room. For a moment, he simply sat up and rubbed the sleep from his eyes, but then he smelt the unmistakeable odour of smoke and fire and became aware of cries and shouts in the house from different members of his large extended family.

Jumping out of bed, he grabbed his pants and shirt. Hopping about on one foot and then the other, he pulled up his trousers. He glanced out of his tiny window that faced into the courtyard and nothing appeared to be out of the ordinary. However the smell of smoke and burning was beginning to pervade everything.

Just as he slipped on his sandals his elder brother, Costas, came running in.

"Spiro – grab what you want to take with you and come down fast. We have to leave right away. The fire will be upon us within the hour. Come on, come on!"

Spiro could not take in what was going on. 'What fire?' he thought. However, at not quite 12 years of age, he was used to doing what he was told by his elders without question. He looked round the little room, which had been his alone for as long as he could remember and wondered what his brother had meant. What should he take? He didn't have anything, did he?

But Spiro stopped wondering as he heard the disturbing sounds of the family shouting and yelling in the hall downstairs. He shook his head and took a quick look round. He snatched up his thick sheepskin coat, a recent gift from one of his uncles; then with one last look at the room he ran down the narrow stairs.

In the spacious hall of the house which had been the Pantelis home for generations, Spiro saw the whole of his extended family milling about arguing, shouting, gathering up indiscriminate items and putting them down again. Babies, unchanged and yelling at all the turmoil that they sensed around them, were shoved into the arms of young girls or their mothers. Some of the women were crying and standing about helplessly, others were bustling in and out, piling up things by the front door – blankets, pots and pans, a clock, a small carpet, a picture. The heavy iron door, locked and bolted against the Turkish soldiers who had been roaming the streets for the last few days, was now wide open and Spiro could see out into the street. His eyes opened wide with anxiety and for the first time that morning, he felt fear as he saw great billowing clouds of thick black smoke moving towards the houses on the other side of the street.

No one took much notice of Spiro as he stood by the side of the door clutching his coat and trying to make sense of the chaos. The sight of all the adults in his life rushing about was more frightening than all the smoke and flames. He had to pee – it was beginning to trickle. He ran back into the courtyard and relieved himself.

Smyrna was burning!

Only a few days before, after the defeat and total collapse of the Greek army in the Anatolian interior, Spiro had seen the ragged and exhausted Greek soldiers as they arrived and fled westwards. He had looked on as individual soldiers had knocked at his mother's door begging for food. Bread, cheese, olives and fruit were handed out unstintingly to any soldier who requested it. Spiro was old enough to know that his mother's family had lived in Smyrna for generations. He lived in the middle of the Greek quarter – his friends and all his neighbours were Greek. He went to a Greek school, attended the Greek Orthodox Church on Sundays and spoke Greek. But he also spoke Turkish. All the men in the family, including his own father, wore the fez, symbolising that they were all Ottoman citizens, part of the population of a polyglot and multi-cultural empire which had ruled the whole of this part of the world for centuries.

Spiro had never experienced ethnic or religious discrimination, though he knew that the official religion of the state was Islam and his family were, to that extent, second-class citizens. His spoken Turkish was not the refined Ottoman Turkish of the great capital city of Constantinople, but was fluent and adequate to communicate with everyone, regardless of race, who lived and worked in the streets and the busy quays of this great port. Christos Pantelis, Spiro's father, was a fairly affluent and successful merchant exporting dried fruits from the region. He was the paterfamilias of a large house in the Greek quarter on the other side of the Rue des Franques, not far from the quayside. The household not only included his immediate family - his wife Agape and his two sons, Costas, just 17, and Spiro, almost 12 – but also several relatives and their children, unattached aunts, old nannies and aged servants.

Two years earlier, when he was only nine, Spiro had been present on the quayside, with almost the whole of the rest of his large family, for the arrival of Auntie Elena, the wife of a deceased uncle he had never known, together with her two small children. They were refugees of the Russian civil war and were from one of the fast disappearing Greek communities around the Black Sea coast. As often happened in large extended families like his, he had been required to look out for these two little cousins. Andreas, though four years younger, was cheerfully tolerated and allowed to join in with all his friends who played around the quays. He ignored the little girl Anya, though he never refused to carry her when necessary.

About a week ago, while watching the retreating Greek soldiers pouring through the town, a Sergeant from the 42nd Evzones had called at the house in the afternoon and had been welcomed with great excitement by Auntie Elena. His name was Mikael. During the next few eventful days Spiro had come to understand that Mikael, who was sleeping in the same room as Auntie Elena and his little cousins, was an Armenian. Spiro knew a number of Armenian boys though they lived in a different part of the town immediately alongside the Greek quarter, and they went to a different church. Spiro did not think too deeply about all the different ethnic groups that lived in his town: the Jews, Turks, and Europeans – but if challenged, he would have said that the Armenians were a sort of 'Greek' who spoke a different language and went to a different church. Armenian priests and Greek papas looked very similar and had the same musty incense smell about them. Centuries of sterile arguments raging between these clerics about the nature of Christ meant nothing to Spiro.

Although he had been born an Ottoman citizen, for the last three years he had been living under a Greek administration. Since 1919, at the invitation primarily of the British Prime Minister, a Greek army, escorted into the harbour by a British destroyer, had occupied the town. War had raged between the Greek and Turkish nationalist forces in the interior ever since, while the hapless Ottoman government in Constantinople had watched with ever-increasing impotence. But here in Smyrna, the population had ignored the war and life had gone joyfully on. For Spiro, the police in the streets were Greek, the holy days were orthodox and the military ships in the bay were friendly allies.

Spiro was an observant lad, sensitive to the somewhat contradictory signals coming from the adults. He was aware that a crisis was brewing in the family even before the Greek soldiers came swarming through the city, followed immediately by desperate refugees from the interior. He found it difficult to comprehend the creeping fear and panic he sensed among the adults as the Turkish army poured into town. Sheltered from the sight of the looting and smashing of shop windows in the Rue des Franques, the rape and break-ins in the Armenian quarter and the haphazard killings everywhere, he only knew that he was being kept strictly indoors and not allowed out for any reason. He resented the fact that Sergeant Mikael took his two little cousins out with him twice. How could he begin to understand why an innocent, good-looking 11 year-old boy, uncircumcised and an obvious *giavour*, would be at such risk in streets filled with inflamed and undisciplined Turkish soldiers.

Meanwhile, the adults argued among themselves incessantly, and had seemed to be divided into two contrary groups. One group argued –

"We are Ottoman citizens aren't we? We've lived here for generations. Since 1908 we have even provided soldiers for the Ottoman army. Why should...."

"We've lived alongside each other for four hundred years, haven't we? An occasional bit of unpleasantness but...."

"Kemal Pasha has said that no one is to be harmed...."

Meanwhile there were others in the family who said totally different things –

"But, they're likely to seek revenge for the unfortunate incidents which took place when our army landed...."

"These soldiers in the streets are not like the old Ottoman regulars, many of them are guerrilla thugs and...."

"For God's sake! There are dead bodies lying in the streets of the Armenian quarter already"

But now, Smyrna was burning.

All argument had ceased and the family were preparing to leave. Spiro had already seen Mikael leave the house, holding a weeping Anya in his arms, and Aunt Elena, holding Andreas tightly with one hand and with the other clutching the same shabby leather suitcase she had held two years before when she first arrived. The noise of the approaching fire could now be heard drowning out everything else around him. Spiro felt that he had been standing by the front door for hours, though it could only have been a few minutes. Costas and his father, carrying an assortment of things haphazardly picked up from the items deposited by the women, hurried to the front door and shouted out to everyone that they all had to leave – "Now! – Now!"

Spiro went out into the street and saw for the first time that hundreds of others were also running out of their houses and making for the quays and the sea. The terrifying sight of the smoke and flames, moving inexorably towards them from the south and east, overshadowed the screaming and the chaos. Agape came running out of the house as Costas and his father kept shouting to everyone still inside to leave, in tears and clearly distressed. In one hand she had a bundle of blankets; in the other, she was also holding a short skirt, a headscarf and a faded yellow blouse. She thrust these into Spiro's hands, then, grabbing his other hand, they began running up the street, followed closely by Cristos and Costas and the rest of the family. Mikael and Elena had already disappeared.

Spiro was now very frightened. He urgently needed to pee again, even though it was only a few minutes since he had last done so. His mother hurried him along the streets. The fire behind them was advancing implacably – with hundreds running ahead of it like a flock of sheep, or a horde of lemmings, all moving towards the seafront. It was pure chance that drove the family towards the Point in the north.

The fire was by now moving due west directly towards the harbour. The buildings along the seafront, taller than the town behind, were not yet alight and were screening the sight of the approaching flames from the thousands already milling on the quayside between the buildings and the sea.

As they reached the seafront, Spiro and his mother sank to the ground by the roadside catching their breath. With curiosity overcoming fear, Spiro stood up again and sidled over to his brother. He looked back at the quayside to the south with its crowds of people and, at that moment, a great penetrating scream rang out. He involuntarily wet his pants as he grabbed hold of Costas' hand. Spiro saw with horror that all the buildings on the seafront had almost simultaneously burst into flames. All around him the watching crowd moaned and shrieked, surging back and forth in terror.

The entire city was ablaze, burning for hour after hour, for the rest of that day, the whole of the night and the following day, but all that Spiro could take in were the shrieks of the women and children and the wails of the crowds further down the corniche, who had nowhere left to go save to fall or be pushed into the sea. The heat down near the harbour was at times so great that some of the pathetic suitcases and bundles spontaneously combusted.

The families clustered near the Point in the north could see that the fire was not going to reach them and the tension eased somewhat. Bodies were floating in the sea – swimmers were still desperately trying to get to boats lying idle in the bay, though most were refused access, slipping away from the trailing ropes and adding to the bodies in the water.

Spiro huddled against his mother with Costas holding him tightly on the other side. Two whole days passed like this during which Spiro lay half asleep for much of the time, his mind numbed and overwhelmed by the sights and sounds around him. They had no food and only a little water carefully brought by Costas. Spiro could scarcely take in what was happening. Turkish soldiers, no longer with any discipline, wandered through the crowds, particularly at night, robbing and picking out girls, raping them and slaughtering any of their menfolk who tried to intervene.

The weekend finally arrived. The smell of the fire and burning flesh still hung over the remains of the city, mixed with the faint odour of petrol, proving indisputably that the fire had been deliberately started in the first place. The entire Greek and Armenian quarters of the city, together with most of the European quarter, were a mass of rubble and cinders from which wisps of smoke still rose. A quarter of a mil*lion* people stood, sat, or lay slumped on the ground on a narrow strip of roadway between the sea on one side and the smouldering ruins of the city on the other.

The crowds milling about on the quays, hungry and exhausted were now faced with a new crisis. That weekend, a proclamation issued by the Turkish authorities was posted all along the quayside. From a small solitary aeroplane, leaflets rained down over the many thousands still huddled on the seafront.

"All Greek and Armenian males of, or approaching, military age, are to be treated as prisoners of war and driven into the interior. All remaining Greeks or Armenians, old men, women and children, must be gone within two weeks. If not departed by then, they too will be driven into the interior."

Driven into the interior! Deported! Everyone knew what that meant in practice – death marches. So they had to be gone within two weeks. But gone where and how?

CHAPTER 2

Olga

Olga never learned the name of the man who had first rescued her and then raped her. His fortuitous presence in the street outside the front door had saved her from one of two equally terrible fates. As she had run from the house trying to get help for her stricken lover Selim, she would certainly have been shot by one of the three soldiers to whom she had appealed if this Turkish civilian had not picked her up bodily, thrown her over his shoulder like a sack of potatoes, and carried her away. He had also saved her from the fast approaching flames, which in the end destroyed the whole of Smyrna with the exception of the old Turkish quarter. The flames had burnt her Turkish lover, Selim, to death, and had consumed the broken body of her brother Haik, lying dead in the street a short distance away.

After the Turkish Smyrniote *effendi* had left her lying broken and ravished on the straw in his stable, Olga had wept and wept. She sobbed not for herself, not for the pain and humiliation of what had happened, but for the final and irrevocable loss of the man she had loved for six years, and with whom she had at last discovered fulfilment and a deep happiness.

But tears can only be shed for so long before eventually giving way to numb acquiescence. She didn't sleep for the rest of that terrible night, but as the dawn light found its way through the wide cracks of the stable door into the ramshackle wooden shack in which she lay, Olga's tears finally dried up. The Avakian spirit began to stir in her and she sat up and looked around.

As she had been unconscious, she was not entirely clear where she might now be. However, it was apparent she was in an outbuilding in the Turkish quarter of the city. This meant that her rescuer – or abuser – was likely to be a fairly substantial householder. Now that she was beginning to think more clearly, she recalled that he had been fairly well dressed.

However, the reawakening of her spirit did not mean that she had recovered her strength. She had not slept all night nor eaten anything for hours, and she realised that she was getting thirsty. She fell back on the straw and into a troubled sleep, which lasted most of the rest of the day.

As the afternoon of the second day began to come to an end, Olga finally found the strength to stand up. Her dress, soiled and crumpled, was still intact, but her underwear was torn and cast aside. Olga made no attempt to recover these, but smoothed her dress down as best she could before trying the door. It was locked, but the whole structure was so flimsy and worm-eaten where the door was attached to the framework, that it would not need much effort to break it down. But it would probably make a lot of noise and in addition, at this stage, she didn't have the energy to try.

A rusty dripping tap in the corner, provided her with some water as she lapped at it – though this only seemed to increase her thirst. Sometime in the late afternoon, she heard movement outside for the first time and could hear some conversation, but it was subdued and soon the sounds moved off into the distance. Striving to hear through the cracks in the door, Olga realised there was a change in the background noise of the last 24 hours – the continuous crashing, hissing and rumbling of the huge fire could no longer be heard.

Olga decided that even though she might well have to suffer another night of shame and humiliation, it would be fatal to break out during the day when she was more likely to be seen. She would make her escape in the early hours of the following morning.

As night fell, Olga lay waiting with nerves stretched to breaking point, listening for every sound that might herald the arrival of the man. She was almost dozing off again when there was a rattling at the door and a creak as it was slowly pushed open. It was dark outside and Olga could see nothing. She waited in an agony of suspense, her body quivering in anticipation of what was coming but nothing happened – nothing moved.

There were some more mysterious sounds that she could not place and then, with the same creak, the door seemed to have shut again. The suspense was terrible. She waited for almost 20 minutes before she plucked up the courage to crawl to the door, carefully feeling her way aided by the many cracks in the wooden walls.

Standing just inside the door was a pottery pitcher of cold water and an old earthenware plate on which was a loaf of bread and some wizened olives. Olga never knew who it was who had both rescued her and then raped her. She never knew what had persuaded him to leave her alone that second night, to give her some sustenance, and then to leave the door unlocked.

The relief released another flood of emotions and Olga wept again. Then she ate the food, drank the water and waited for the dawn.

As the sun came up, Olga quietly pushed the door ajar and looked out. It was very early in the morning but was already quite light. She saw a courtyard with a fairly substantial two-storey wooden house, some trees and a bedraggled hedge. On the far side of the courtyard opposite, she could see a narrow cobbled street with a line of ramshackle houses.

Olga took a deep breath. There was nobody about as far as she could see. There was an unusual smell in the air. She sniffed and recognised the distinctive smell of burnt wood and cinders and another sickly smell she could not place – somewhat like the smell of charred bad pork. She had difficulty taking the first step out of the old shed, as if she could not bear to leave the spurious sanctuary of the shed.

In the Avakian household, rape had been discussed in the abstract. The general consensus had been that women subjected to such an experience felt soiled and suffered the guilt of the victim. But Olga found that she had no such feelings. She was ashamed to be naked under her crumpled dress, but her emotions were so bound up with Selim's death, that the rape had totally lost all meaning. This was complicated by her knowledge that the man who had so casually violated her had also saved her life.

She finally took her first timid step out into the open, but then began walking quickly through the courtyard and was almost running when she came out into the little street. She did not know exactly where she was. She knew the Turkish quarter of Smyrna straggled up the hillside to the ruined Byzantine castle at the top, so all she had to do to get to the town centre was to walk downhill.

As she walked down the twisting, narrow, cobbled street, though her mind was in a turmoil, she was no longer reflecting unduly on her own horrific experiences, and she began looking about her as she passed others who were also up early. She was by now so bedraggled that no one gave her a second glance. The twisting street turned sharply right, for the first time leading straight downhill, and it was at this point, as she turned the corner and looked straight down on the town, that Olga stopped and stared in horrified amazement.

The whole of the rest of the town stretching right up to the Point in the distant north lay out before her, including the great bay filled with ships of all kinds. The city was a mass of rubble with smoke rising in wisps from piles of charred timber and stones. The strange smell Olga had noticed before struck her again and, in a sudden flash of recognition, she knew what it was. It was the smell of burnt human flesh.

Feeling faint, Olga went over to the side of the street and leaned against the wall of a house. She could not make out any landmarks – only the flattened city and the ships in the bay *beyond*. She could not see the thousands upon thousands huddled along the quays stretching all the way from the inner harbour right up to the Point. It seemed to her as if there were no more people left in the town, yet Turkish men were still going about their early morning business and muttering 'salaams' as they passed. This in itself was unusual. Unveiled as she was, shamelessly standing in the street in the heart of the Turkish quarter – on any other day she would have attracted disapproving looks instead of muttered morning greetings.

Olga stood there for some time. The increasing numbers of townspeople in the streets were subdued, silent and apprehensive. The academics, poets and politicians might be glorying in the triumph of the national principle: Turkey for the Turks, but the ordinary people were dazed and anxious. They were already missing the Greek grocer down the road, the Jewish baker, everything they had known and been comfortable with for years. Faced with the direct consequences of this enforced ethnic cleansing, to their own surprise, they were quiet and saddened. These people had a strong residual respect for the old tolerant multi-cultural Ottoman ideal. However, nationalist propaganda and the shrill teaching of the academics would soon be setting them straight.

Looking down, Olga saw at last where she had to go. At the bottom of the hill on the edge of the Turkish quarter, still completely intact, was the Imperial Ottoman Hospital – her old employer. Desperate now that she had a clear destination, worried for the first time that she might be arrested or worse before she could reach the hospital, she hurried down the hill.

The hospital was the first place she had seen which was busy with a sense of normalcy, despite the emergency atmosphere. It was now the only functioning hospital in the city and it was crowded and in a state of noisy confusion. Nervous and harassed staff scurried about, while crowds of people accompanying relatives with major or minor burns tried to get their attention. There was not a single Greek or Armenian amongst them; they were either Turks or Jews, but Olga saw only people hurting and in need. She was soon recognised and a uniform of sorts was found for her. No one questioned her appearance.

Olga threw herself into the work, refusing to take more than a few hours sleep. She questioned nothing and did not bother to find out what may have been happening elsewhere in the town. She bandaged, she sewed up wounds, she made up beds, and she held people's hands as doctors operated with the minimum of drugs available. She cleaned up urine and excrement; she comforted complete strangers and even found herself sharing the occasional joke.

But however hard she worked, however hard she concentrated on her patients, she could not hide from herself the knowledge that she was pregnant. She knew with certainty that the baby growing inside her was Selim's. It was not, nor could it possibly have been, the issue of the unknown Turk only a day or two previously. She could work out the days easily enough. She knew that she was carrying Selim's baby.

CHAPTER 3

Paramaz and George

Paramaz held on tight to the baby entrusted to him by its dying mother on the quayside, as one of the ship's boats from HMS *Iron Duke* pulled up at the point where he had carefully positioned himself. He leant over and handed down the baby into the arms of the stunned sailor without giving him a chance to say anything, and then clambered aboard himself, pulling the dazed George after him. The young midshipman in charge of this boat called out from the front, "Are you British subjects?"

Paramaz, who spoke no English, but only Turkish and Armenian with a smattering of Greek, said nothing, simply taking the now squalling baby back from the sailor. But George at last came out of his stupor and called out,

"Certainly, sir ... Cyprus ... but no documents, all gone in the fire."

The young officer nodded and began asking the same question to the others crowding up to the boat, desperate to get on board.

As the great fire of September 1922 raged unchecked, Italian and French warships had sent out boat after boat to pick up survivors and as many of the people trapped between the fire and the sea that they could safely take on board. The French consulate had even set up a small desk on the quayside with officials handing out visas and passes to anyone with French connections.

Aboard his flagship HMS *Iron Duke*, Sir Osmond de Beauvoir Brock was adamant that no ship under his command was to offer shelter or space to any refugees, insisting on the promise of neutrality he had made to the new Turkish governor. The men of the British fleet had become restive and almost mutinous as they watched helplessly while the city burned, forcing the fleeing Greek and Armenian population onto the long, but mercifully wide, quayside of Smyrna.

At the moment of greatest horror, under orders, the sailors had, thrown buckets of water onto a rowing boat that pulled alongside *the Iron Duke* to prevent any one clambering to safety. The boat had overturned, immediately drowning almost all the occupants. One young girl, exhausted and about to expire, arrived near the destroyer commanded by Captain Harry Bridgeman. A grizzled old sailor jumped overboard to rescue her and then Harry ordered all boats away with orders to pick up any survivors in the vicinity in danger of drowning.

The Admiral was furious and promised a court-martial; however by morning, with the waters filled with dead bodies, he had finally relented and, persuaded by his executive officer, he changed his orders. With over 200,000 people along the corniche, the ships could only take a limited number.

Now on board *the Iron Duke*, squeezed into a crowded mess-room, Paramaz sat on the floor cuddling and rocking the baby. The clothes in which the baby was wrapped were filthy, but Paramaz held the baby tight, rocking and crooning as he had seen his mother do with his long-dead baby sisters all those years ago. He seemed to need the infant as much as it needed him.

Eventually, a sailor appeared with a cup of warm milk. George, lying dazed and exhausted alongside, thanked him and handed the cup to Paramaz. For some time Paramaz was unable to get the baby to drink and finally hit on the idea of dipping his little finger in the milk and letting the baby suck on it. It was a tedious and lengthy process, but Paramaz, normally impatient, managed to get the baby fed.

The same sailor who had brought the milk came back some time later to see how the 'mother and child' were faring. With George translating, Paramaz asked for some water to clean the infant. The water arrived, and the sailor stood watching, with curiosity and concern, as Paramaz unwound the sodden rags in which the baby was clothed. When the baby was finally naked, the three of them discovered that it was a boy and Paramaz set about washing the baby boy with the cold water, paying no heed either to the baby's lusty yells or the fact that he was himself getting wet. George had no need to translate. Off went the sailor, returning quickly with a pile of moth-eaten, but clean, woollen vests and a large drawing pin – begged borrowed or stolen from the ship's stores.

George lay still, slowly emerging from the daze into which he had fallen from the moment the great fire had started. He took no notice of the people around him, but went over and over in his mind the events that had led to this point, including his failure to arrange for the escape of his staff, even though he had been aware of the approaching crisis. It was he who, over a year ago, had persuaded his father's partner – Karekin Avakian – to dispatch the two 19 year-olds, Paramaz and Karekin's own son, Haik, to Smyrna. And now Haik was dead – and it was he who was going to have to explain, even though he didn't know how it had happened.

Then there was Olga! He was not, of course, responsible for her presence in Smyrna and he had no idea what might have happened to her. Nevertheless, he was the one who would have to tell her parents something. How were they going to cope? They would be facing the certain loss of their only son and the uncertainty of what might have happened to their second daughter. George had difficulty in articulating his feelings, and was acutely sensitive to the thought of pain to others. How was he going to communicate the death of Haik to his family?

His thoughts turned to Sima, the eldest of the four daughters of the Avakian family to whom he had almost been engaged, and with whom he had fallen in love at the very moment she had rejected him. Then, again, the image of Haik – a young man he had been deeply fond of – would invade his thoughts, bringing silent tears. The loss of the offices, and the complete destruction of the warehouse and all its goods, belonging to the family firm set up by his own father and Karekin, never crossed his mind. Both families were merchant-adventurers. This sort of financial catastrophe was part of the stock-in-trade of any active merchant house. But the loss of an only son – a cheerful, friendly boy with all his life before him – that was different.

At last the fleet passed through the Dardanelles and arrived in the waters facing the city of Constantinople – the capital of a great Christian empire for over a thousand years, then the capital of an equally great Muslim empire for almost five hundred, the seat of the longest-lasting caliphate in Muslim history, now under the administration of a third empire – the British – at the height of its own imperial reach.

Admiral Brock could not wait to tidy up his flagship and be rid of the refugees he had reluctantly taken on board. Ironically, this was one of the small advantages for the assorted mixture of civilians huddled in various corners of the ship. The Admiral – commander of all the British warships throughout the eastern Mediterranean – was in a position to demand immediate attention from the local authorities and their British advisors – and so it was that *the Iron Duke* was one of the first boats to start off-loading all its dispossessed humanity.

George and Paramaz stepped off the launch at the Eminonu quayside, rather than at the busy quays under the Galata Bridge, and were whisked away immediately by a small group of polite Ottoman policemen and led into a temporary building. This was manned by a line of Ottoman bureaucrats sitting behind desks. Behind them were two British army officers. Paramaz and George, neither of whom had been in Bolis for over a year, noticed a subtle change in the relationship between the British and the Ottoman civil servants; the Turks a bit more assertive, while the British officers seemed less sure of their authority.

The baby had begun squalling again and, perhaps as a result, George and Paramaz found that they were among the first to be interviewed. Unafraid for themselves as George had had the foresight to grab his papers before fleeing from the office, they knew they might have difficulty with the baby.

"I see – Paramaz Avakian and George Levonian. Are you from Stamboul?"

"Yes sir," George did all the talking. "Here look, you can see that I was born in Bebek."

"Excuse me, *effendi*" – old Ottoman officials were always unfailingly polite – "I can see the papers, but we are faced with people presenting forged or stolen documents. You may only remain here if you are Ottoman citizens born in this city."

"My parents are here and could vouch for me if necessary."

"Very well. Your papers are clearly in order. What about you sir?"

Paramaz, rocking the baby to and fro, unable to quell its continued wailing, stared back at the official. George said quickly in his upper class Turkish dialect, which had already impressed the official –

"He is the adopted son of Karekin Avakian, one of the important merchants of the city."

"And why can't he answer for himself?"

"I am having difficulty with my baby – I'm sorry – but yes that is indeed so. I live in Makrikoy."

The official immediately recognised Paramaz's Anatolian peasant accent. Only a few months ago his lip might have curled in good-natured contempt, but times were changing. As Mustapha Kemal's nationalist armies of Anatolian peasants were closing in on the old city, the words 'Anadolu Turk' were for the first time in 500 years no longer pejorative. The once-mighty city of Constantinople, which had effortlessly dominated Asia Minor for centuries, was fearfully awaiting the arrival of this avenging Anatolian army. The official nodded at the baby who continued to cry out in that high-pitched scream guaranteed by evolution to upset every human within earshot –

"And the baby?"

George again quickly intervened.

"Oh, *effendi bey*, his wife died during the evacuation of Smyrna and he has been distraught ever since as you can see, and he has had to look after the baby all this time on his own without the help of its mother's milk."

Paramaz marvelled at the speed and clarity of George's answers. He looked at the official who was clearly looking for some excuse to refuse entry at least to this Armenian peasant.

The British officer who had overheard George's last remark as he passed, had stopped behind him. Paramaz, meanwhile, suddenly thought of the wife George had conjured up for him and who had died a terrible death in Smyrna. Without knowing quite why, Paramaz began weeping silently. He wept not only for the baby's mother, but also for the wife he never had.

The British officer murmured something to the official who shrugged.

"You may leave *effendim*."

Wearily, they walked out into the sunshine. Paramaz, who had been unable to weep at the rape and slaughter of his mother or at his sisters' deaths, and whose tears had dried up forever all those years ago, wept silently, tears running down his cheeks. He held the baby tightly to his chest, until the baby's cries subsided.

All around them the life of the city pulsated. They saw the Galata Bridge – still one of the great crossing bridges of the world. As Paramaz's tears at last dried up, George considered what he had to do first. He wanted above all to go home to see his mother and sister, or at least to go to the Levonian offices in Pera and be enfolded in his father's arms. But the matter of Haik's death and Olga's uncertain fate had to be dealt with first.

"Paramaz – are you all right? Good. What will you do now?"

"I'll go home – the only home I know – to the Avakians."

"And the baby?"

"He is mine," replied Paramaz fiercely. "I will look after him. I will see to him."

"But for God's sake – how?"

Paramaz was silent, looking down at the now sleeping bundle. Then without a further word, he stretched out his free hand, touched George gently on the shoulder, held it there for a long moment, settled the baby firmly on his hip and turned with the clear intention of walking back up to Sirkedji station.

If George wondered, fleetingly, how Paramaz was going to pay for the trip back to Makrikoy, he said nothing, but simply watched as Paramaz turned to go up to the station. Emotionally drained, George stood for some moments longer, ignoring all the busy crowds around him, but then making up his mind, he hurried after Paramaz.

At Makrikoy, alighting at the Cobancesme station, Paramaz and George took a carriage up the hill to the Avakian home instead of walking. It was midday, the baby was at last asleep. Of the family, only Armineh was at home when Paramaz rang the bell. Talin opened the door, took one look at Paramaz and screamed out loud. Armineh and Marie bustled out into the Hall as Paramaz walked in – dirty – dishevelled – hungry, and with a fierce look of despair in his eyes. He was followed by George, who was unable to look anyone in the eye, but simply stared down at the floor. Armineh took one look at each of them and realised the worst at once. She did not need to be told. Haik was not with them, so….. Her heart pounded, and she could scarcely stand up. Marie, equally distressed, came forward and held her.

"And Haik, Paramaz, – my son Haik? – my son?"

"I am sorry, Armineh-hanum. I am so sorry. Oh God, your son is dead – shot – and then surely consumed by the flames."

Armineh stood still. She did not faint, though her heart was beating so fast she was almost overcome. She couldn't take it all in – there was a mist before her eyes. She swayed and almost collapsed, but was held tight by Marie – her son, her only son.

And at last Paramaz, who had gone through so much and was still only 19 years-old, gave way to the sheer horror of what had happened and the terrible things he had done. In his mind, he had almost satisfied himself that the shooting of Haik had been an accident, but he was now reminded that that did not apply to the shots he had aimed at the shadowy figure of Selim.

He burst into deep throbbing sobs. This triggered something in Armineh, who began howling, almost like an animal in pain. This went on for some moments as Marie looked on helplessly, herself distraught at the thought of the fifteen years she had helped to look after the boy, who she would never see ever again; but then at last all the noise woke up the baby, who began screaming. Armineh stopped at once and her eyes cleared and focused on the bundle in Paramaz's arms.

"For God's sake, Paramaz, what is that?"

Paramaz stopped sobbing, pulled himself together and looking down at the screaming bundle in his arms said,

"A baby, Digin Armineh, a baby. I have to look after it – it's a little boy."

Paramaz stood looking at the women, and then for the first time bent forward and kissed the child. He slowly rocked the little boy to calm him down, all the while explaining how he had come to look after him. Paramaz was no fool. He knew that in the long run he would be unable to care for the child in his arms without help. As his voice finally died away, he waited. He thought about Haik and Selim and his part in their deaths. He remembered his mother and his two little sisters and the way they had died. He waited in the long pause that followed the end of his story, continuing to cradle the baby in his arms while the silence dragged on.

Then, Armineh shook her head and tried to dry her tears with the back of her sleeve. She walked forward as if in a dream, freeing herself from Marie's support, and taking the little boy from Paramaz's arms, she looked at him with tears still running down her face. She had not cradled a child for over ten years. Holding herself stiffly upright, she passed the baby over to Marie and said,

"Come along Marie, this little man needs a good bath, some nice clean clothes and a warm drink."

Armineh turned to go up the great stairs of the Avakian house, but it was all too much, even for her *indomitable* spirit. As she set foot on the first step, she sagged, her eyes shot up into her head and she fell back in a faint into the arms of George, who had been a silent witness throughout, and anticipating what was about to happen, had rushed forward to catch her.

CHAPTER 4

Harry

Harry had never thought of himself as being particularly sensitive. His father, Colonel William Bridgeman, always careful to hide his own feelings from his son, had encouraged him to remain cool and detached in all circumstances, and avoid any demonstrative display. The product of a 19th century upbringing, his father had only ever kissed his son when asleep; looking down on the sleeping boy, fearful that he would awake and catch him in a moment of weakness.

The minor public school Harry had attended – a 19th-century imitation of Eton – had reinforced this attitude by encouraging self-sufficiency in its young boys. This was achieved by inculcating a strong, muscular Christianity, backed up by liberal thrashings. This had the desired effect of persuading the boys to despise tears and any sign of weakness.

Harry had the innate strength of character to stand up to this regime without turning into a bully himself. As he grew physically stronger, he opposed the atmosphere of bullying and contempt for the weak and vulnerable, which was such a feature of his schooldays. Boys were regularly beaten, in order to ensure they became God-fearing Christians, prepared to fight for King and Country without question. Harry received his full share of punishments, but it had not changed his basic nature. He conformed not because he had to, or because it was more comfortable to do so, but because he had worked out for himself that it was a fairly reasonable philosophy if kept within bounds.

Having become a naval officer, despite opposition from his father – an Army man through and through – Harry had seen active service through the war and the immediate years following the different armistices of 1918. From the start of the Gallipoli campaign of April 1915, he had been stationed with the fleet in the Eastern Mediterranean. He had been with the fleet delivering the army onto the beaches of the Dardanelles. He had been present at the harrowing scenes of the evacuation of the White Russians from Sevastopol. He had witnessed the effects of modern warfare in a variety of situations, but had never seen anything like the burning of Smyrna. As the captain of the destroyer HMS *Lion*, lying with the rest of the fleet in the great bay, he had disobeyed orders and picked up as many survivors from the sea, as his ship could safely carry. He and his men watched helplessly while the city burned for two more days. The quaysides filled with thousands and thousands of despairing human beings, mostly women and children, while some of the ships of the large allied fleet stationed in the bay, continued to stand idly by.

The smell of burning wood and other building materials, mixed with the unmistakeable odour of burned human flesh, was seared into his memory. For the further two or three days that the British fleet remained in the Bay of Smyrna, Harry, together with all the other sailors, had to listen each night to the moans and prayers of the crowds in their thousands milling about the seafront with nowhere to.

Once night fell, the undisciplined Turkish troops began their orgy of rape, slaughter and robbery, moving at will through the helpless crowds while the sound of screams and shrieks went on for hour after hour and could be heard on the ships in the bay.

Eventually the Admiral had relented and allowed ships from his fleet to take on those in danger of drowning together with a few refugees from the shore. As the fires at last began to die down, the Allied ships began to leave and the British fleet steamed away heading for Constantinople. As the bay emptied, Harry, already in a state of considerable emotional turmoil, looked back and saw the line of Ottoman citizens along the shore, numbering at least 200,000, raise their hands in a pointless gesture of supplication as the ships slowly turned away and headed out towards the open sea.

A cry of pain from one person is a tragic enough sound. The same sound from over 200,000 desperate souls makes a noise that carries a long way, a sound any sensitive human being would remember all their lives – and so it was with Harry. This cool British naval officer, brought up in the best traditions of duty and service, a model of calm and discipline, an inspiration to the men under his command, began to have fearful nightmares. Years of service and training came to his aid, and his command was handled impeccably, but his mind would not rest.

Once the British Admiral of the fleet had reversed his orders on the third day of the fire, swimmers had been picked up by many of the British captains, who had also sent boats to pick up some of the destitute from the shore. The fleet now held a large number of refugees from the dying city of Smyrna – a mere drop in the ocean but, nevertheless, some lives had been saved.

When HMS *Lion* arrived in Constantinople, the ships' launches carried their few survivors to the shore, off-loading them at the Eminonu quayside where the Ottoman authorities had set up a reception area, supervised by the British occupation administration. After the two hundred people were safely on shore, he ordered a major clean up of the ship.

Harry had clashed once before with his commanding officer – Admiral Brock – when he had dared to question the racist and xenophobic attitudes of the American High Commissioner at a dinner the Admiral had been hosting on *the Iron Duke*. He knew that he would be court-martialled for his decision on the night of the outbreak of the great fire in Smyrna, but he was quite calm and sure in his own mind that he had acted correctly, not only as a human being, but also in the traditions of an officer of the Royal Navy.

He thought that weeks might well pass before he heard about the court-martial but he was wrong. On the very day of the arrival of the fleet in Constantinople, Admiral Brock had gone to pay a visit to the American High Commissioner at Constantinople – Admiral Mark Bristol. Bristol was an outspoken American whose anti-Semitic jibes, and racist remarks about the Greeks and Armenians, pained the aristocratic British Admiral, though his own views were on the whole fairly similar, the only difference being that Brock was more diplomatic.

"My dear Bristol, I have to confirm that the whole thing was a terrible affair. There were still thousands of refugees on the seafront with the whole of the city burning behind them."

"Admiral Brock, I am quite convinced that the depiction of events by those returning from Smyrna is totally unbalanced, both as to who was responsible and the numbers actually killed."

"Well sir, I won't argue with you, but several of my officers quite clearly saw Turkish soldiers, even officers, pouring petrol on properties not yet burned – and even on the quaysides amongst the civilian refugees."

"Rubbish, man, rubbish! The burning of the city was an accident. My own opinion is that after the Turkish army entered the city, as a totally disciplined force, some Armenians and Greeks decided to burn their own houses so they couldn't be occupied. All this nonsense about petrol is a total fabrication, take it from me. Anyway, it was only when the wind arose that the whole city went up in smoke."

In fairness to Admiral Brock, he did not agree with the opinionated Bristol, whose prejudices about the subject races of the Ottoman Empire were well known to all, but he was not prepared to argue. He had gone to seek Bristol's cooperation for a possible joint approach to the Turkish nationalists regarding the refugees still lining the seafront at Smyrna and needed to play along with the man's prejudices. In this he failed, but in the course of discussing the matter further, Harry's name came up and Brock inadvertently let out the facts of Harry's decision to pick up survivors from the bay when he had been given clear orders not to do so. Bristol was emphatic –

"My dear Admiral, you cannot allow the matter to rest for even a day. I remember him – an argumentative troublemaker, I seem to recall, without any idea of the real issues at stake here. I suspect he's the type ready to spread lies about the events in Smyrna and to inflame the press on the matter. I would muzzle him immediately, before any other of your officers get ideas above their station."

Admiral Brock came away from the meeting without any support from the American for a joint approach to the Kemalists over the situation in Smyrna. He had an instinctive aristocratic distaste for Bristol's bourgeois vulgarity and bigotry, but where Harry was concerned, he thought that Bristol was probably right. It was necessary for Harry to be removed here and now from command, even before any court-martial was convened.

Within another day, Brock had radioed the Admiralty in London setting out briefly the circumstances and recommending, indeed insisting on, an early court-martial, either here in Constantinople or in London. The answer from London was immediate. As so many of the witnesses were likely to be stationed in Constantinople, the court-martial would be held there at a venue to be decided and a senior officer would be appointed to preside. Meanwhile Captain Bridgeman was to be on suspended leave with full pay, without any loss of rank or privileges.

Some days later, Harry's replacement, nominated by the Admiral, was piped aboard. Having folded up all his uniforms and placed all his personal belongings in several suitcases, Harry shook hands with all the ship's officers and left on the ship's launch. This landed Harry at the Galata Bridge, where he hired two porters and walked up the iron stairs onto the bridge.

The Galata Bridge!

This bridge across the entrance to the Golden Horn, connecting old Stamboul to Pera and Galata was the hub of the Ottoman world. It was filled with all the races of the empire crossing from one side to the other; mostly veiled Turkish hanums but some in western dress with their faces uncovered; Armenian and Greek merchants now wearing the fez again after three years of trilbys and panama hats; elderly Ottoman Turks unfailingly polite and wearing the fez; young Turkish men swaggering triumphantly, all sporting Enver-style moustaches but, ironically, no longer wearing the fez; peasants from eastern Thrace riding donkeys; British officers; Kurdish porters, Jewish rabbis, Albanian riff-raff, former Russian soldiers, donkeys, camels, trams clattering across and more and more motorcars. Harry had seen it all before. He loved it, but he had important things to do and couldn't linger. Deciding against the Pera Palace Hotel, he ordered the horse cab to go to the Park Otel on Taksim.

Harry's first thought was to do something about his nightmares. The keenest impression that remained with him from his days by the Bay of Smyrna, was a deep, abiding feeling of shame. This was not the horror of fighting at the front or of bodies broken and dying – he could cope with that – he was, after all, a seasoned officer experienced in the terrible realities of modern war. But Smyrna was different. He couldn't analyse it. There had been four fleets in the harbour – British, French, Italian and American – all staffed by healthy and active young men, of whom he was one. Meanwhile on the seafront, there had been women, children and babies in deep distress and with no young men to help them.

Harry did not hate or blame anyone – he just felt deep shame for being one of those who, to all intents and purposes, did nothing – nothing at all. He felt he had to do something – if necessary, return to the scene of the crime in Smyrna – to get rid of this sense of shame.

Harry acted quickly and decisively. He obviously couldn't get on any British ship but over the years, Harry had made contacts with many shipmates and captains. Within a few hours of arriving at the hotel, he checked up on a series of possible freighters, but none of their captains were thinking of going back to Smyrna. By the afternoon, he heard that an American destroyer – the USS *Lawrence* – was planning to leave the city for Smyrna the very next day to check if there were any more American citizens requiring evacuation. Still in uniform, Harry hired a private motorboat and had himself taken alongside. He knew the captain from previous encounters at the bar of the Pera Palace. It did not take him long to persuade the man to let him travel on the *Lawrence* as an observer – promising to come aboard in civilian clothes.

Harry arranged to come aboard the next afternoon just before the ship sailed. He had the whole of the next morning free so he decided to go and visit his friends, the Avakian family, in the suburb of Makrikoy.

CHAPTER 5

The Avakians in Crisis

Armineh had fainted at the news, but once recovered, she took control of the situation. First, she made sure that Marie and Talin would look after the baby, then went upstairs to her own bedroom, lay on the bed and gave way to her grief. "My son – my only son – oh my darling boy, my son, my son," repeated over and over again. The thought that she would never see his cheerful smiling face was devastating and her tears flowed.

After almost two hours in this state, the tears dried up and she began to think of the rest of the family. Sima would surely be all right – she had the love of Nicolai to fall back on. But what of Nerissa! How would Nerissa manage? She had to be strong for her. Seta, on the other hand, was young, she would bounce back, but Nerissa could collapse completely if not treated with care. Armineh got up, washed and began to think, realising that she could manage her children, but what could she do for her husband. He would not say a word or let on how he was suffering.

How would Karekin react? And Paramaz himself – how had it happened that Haik had been shot while Paramaz appeared to have got away without a scratch? Could she bear never knowing for sure what had *really* happened? And where was Olga? Her mind raced back and forth as she lay back on the bed again and at last sank into a merciful hour's sleep.

When she awoke, she got up, brushed her hair and dressed, care-fully avoiding black and then went downstairs. Paramaz, Marie and Ta-lin had clearly been listening out for her and stood by the dining table outside the kitchen door.

"Now, Marie, what's happened to the baby?"

"Madame, I've put him in the old nursery – he's fast asleep."

"What's his name, Paramaz?"

"I don't know, Digin Armineh, I just don't know."

"Talin – pull yourself together girl. Go and fill some bottles with warm milk, Marie will show you how. We must wait until Karekin re-turns to decide what should be done about the baby"

"I won't let him go – I won't let him go," Paramaz cried out.

"Paramaz, you can't just take a baby into a family without registering with the necessary authorities. Karekin will know what to do."

Armineh was able to get some small comfort from slipping into her role as family manager. She hoped that activity would help push the reality of her son's death to the back of her mind, but these thoughts were only just below the surface. And then – oh God what about Olga?

"Paramaz – what about Olga – what happened to her, do you know?"

"I really don't know; but I can tell you that in those last terrible days she was with Selim and ..."

"What was Selim doing there?"

"I don't know – Oh God, I really don't know... I..." and Paramaz covered his face with his hands.

Armineh had never warmed to Paramaz. She had always been suspi-cious of him and knew he had once caused distress to Seta. But now she could see that he was in a state of genuine anguish, and she decided not to press him further.

"Now listen carefully Paramaz. I want you to go round to Karekin's office. Listen carefully. Don't see him, and if by chance you do, say noth-ing – just leave a message that his wife needs him and asks him to come home as soon as possible. Now – go. Don't worry about the baby, we'll look after him."

Armineh had it all worked out in her mind. Sima would be back soon and once over the shock, she would help with Karekin once he arrived. Armineh waited. She knew that Karekin would know at once what had happened the moment he entered the house.

It is not necessary to chronicle in voyeuristic and harrowing detail all aspects of the Avakian grief, person by person, over the next two days. There was Sima, who, like all eldest sisters in large extended families, had had to hold Haik's hand from when he was a few years old, had helped him to take his first fumbling steps, had relieved her mother from time to time carrying him and had taken him to school during those terrible days in 1915.

He had been closest to Nerissa with whom he had played when they were both little. She wept and wept as she recalled that only he had listened patiently when she needed someone to pour out all her teenage angst. Then there was Seta, mercifully too young to suffer long from grief. Finally there was Karekin. Mixed in with the terrible anguish over the death of his only son, was the inchoate guilt of the survivor – "Asvadz, asvadzim why did I survive in 1915 only to send my only son to his death seven years later."

Above all, the whole process of grieving was made more difficult, not only because there was no body to mourn over, but because there had not been a coherent account of how Haik had died. For two days Karekin stayed at home, and they all sat round the table for hours talking about Haik, remembering him and even arguing over when events had taken place. Armineh and Karekin dozed in each other's arms and slowly the family came to terms with the death.

Then on the fourth day, Karekin gathered the family round the dining table after breakfast. He invited Paramaz and Marie to sit down as well. When everyone was seated, Karekin turned to Paramaz and said –

"Before we talk about the baby, I want to hear from you now the exact details of my son's death. I want it all in detail please from the moment you and he left the Kapamadjian house."

"Karekin *effendi*, I must explain that the situation in the Armenian quarter during that day and the following night was terrible. It was not only shops that were being broken into and looted. Bands of soldiers were breaking down the doors of private houses – particularly the larger houses – rushing in, killing any males they found and raping and then often killing the girls and women. Then they would leave, taking with them anything of value they could lay their hands on."

"We heard that the Turkish army had been well-disciplined."

"Maybe at the beginning when the cavalry entered the town – but once the infantry poured in, with all the guerrillas and hangers-on, it was a different story."

"The American High Commissioner Admiral Bristol said the murder and looting started the moment the Greek governor and police left and before the Turkish army arrived. He said that their arrival relieved the situation."

"That's simply not true, Karekin *effendi*. I saw with my own eyes that after the Greek administration left and before the Turkish army arrived, the streets were completely quiet and orderly. Businesses were open and there was no animosity between the ethnic communities. The port was operating normally and tobacco was being loaded right up to the moment of entry of the Turkish army. There was no rioting or killing or looting of any kind."

"Ah well, never mind – please go on."

"Haik and I decided that we had better get to the harbour and meet up with George, who as you know lived in a flat above the offices. But first Haik insisted that we go to pick up Olga – or at least make sure that she was all right."

"Yes, yes – he would," muttered the family.

"Where was Olga living?" asked Karekin. "Wasn't she at one of the two hospitals at which she was working?"

At this point Paramaz hesitated for the first time. It did not need a shrewd appreciation of his character for it to be clear to all that he was measuring his next words carefully.

"Karekin *effendi*, I was not aware at the time but it seems that Haik knew Olga had taken a small suite of rooms in a private house near the Armenian hospital."

"Very well – get on with it."

"Er – it's a little difficult to explain, sir, … but when we got to the house Olga was not able to come with us directly…."

"Why, Paramaz, why for god's sake? What the blazes are you trying to say"

"Because Selim was with her and he was badly wounded and couldn't move or be moved."

"Selim – Selim – what are you talking about, lad. Selim…" Karekin spluttered and could hardly speak.

Armineh, who together with both Sima and Nerissa, had already worked out for themselves that Olga had been living with Selim in those last days of Ottoman Smyrna, looked directly at her husband and said –

"My soul, my dearest – Selim Kemal – Olga's friend – you must re-member."

"But what the hell was he doing in Smyrna, or did he arrive with the Turkish army. Oh God where is she now – Paramaz for God's sake, tell me."

But now Paramaz had again become distressed. Tears came to his eyes as he blurted out,

"I don't know – I just don't know!"

Karekin calmed down and looked at Paramaz, who cast his eyes down muttering apologies.

"Well go on."

"Haik and I went out to find a cart to help take Selim to the hospital. There were many lying about in the streets abandoned by refugees. Haik saw one further up the road, and before I could say anything he ran forward to get it. But it turned out some Turkish soldiers were loot-ing the house outside which it was standing. They came out just as Haik was running up to it. The soldiers dropped their loot, pulled out their rifles as Haik turned to run back. But it was too late – too late. Three shots rang out and I saw Haik fall dead. I had been walking forward too, but I turned to run. They chased after me, but I got away through some back streets and eventually found my way to George."

There was a long, drawn out silence as everyone tried to imagine the scene.

"And what about Olga?"

"I don't know," said Paramaz. He put his head into his hands and began crying. No one had ever seen Paramaz cry like that before, except Armineh who had already been surprised by his tears on the first day of his return.

Karekin stared at Paramaz. He wanted to strike somebody – anybody – and Paramaz was the closest to hand. He felt Armineh's hand touching his arm lightly. He swallowed his anger, took a deep breath and nodded at Armineh to confirm that he was in control of himself. However he felt sure as he stared at Paramaz that there was something lying unsaid between them.

"Well – let's now talk about the baby. What do you know of him Paramaz? I understand that you don't even know his name or whether he has been baptized yet. I presume that it was an Armenian mother to whom you were talking. Speak up boy, speak up, I can't hear you."

Paramaz was now in a state bordering on hysteria. Lie upon lie was ensnaring him as he muttered –

"Yes, *effendi bey*, I think so…I think so…"

All his contempt – even hatred – for this elitist family, who had come to his rescue, lay in ruins as his mind swirled round and round the events of those last few days in Smyrna. It was an accident, wasn't it? An accident, resulting in his being the hand that had shot the only son of this family; a family that had shown him nothing but kindness. Now he looked away from this man whom, in his ignorance, he had dismissed as a liberal weakling.

Karekin could hardly contain himself. Everyone was uncomfortably aware that there was more to the story than Paramaz was disclosing. But both Armineh and the two elder girls thought that it was an unusual delicacy on his part. Maybe Paramaz was trying to avoid making Olga's liaison with Selim too clear to Karekin. Armineh intervened at this point, saying –

"Karekin, my soul, what are we to do about the baby?"

"My darling, he is to remain with us of course. I don't even care if he turns out to have been a Turk. I am proposing to register the boy as an Armenian orphan, whom I am adopting as our son."

There was another long silence as everyone looked into their hearts at how this decision might affect them. Paramaz, unable to control his tears stood up, walked to the end of the table in the silence that had

followed and knelt on both knees by Karekin's side. He got hold of Karekin's hand and tried to lift it to his lips in a gesture of humility and respect. But Karekin pulled it away before he could complete the gesture.

"Karekin *effendi*, I want you to give the wages you pay me towards
the cost of looking after this baby."

Karekin was about to refuse, even to laugh at the absurdity of the
suggestion, when he caught sight of Armineh. He knew that look and
he immediately held back the cutting remark he was about to make.
Armineh got up from her chair and said quietly –

"That is generous of you Paramaz, we will think further and…." But
at this precise moment there was a ring at the front door.

Talin ran out of the kitchen and went to open the door. In walked
Harry in civilian clothes. He passed his hat to Talin with a smile and
then walked forward as everyone stared.

Harry could see at once that there was an atmosphere of crisis and
that the family were in conference. For a start, it was unusual for Karekin to be at home at this hour. He said at once –

"Oh dear, I am very sorry everyone. I've come at the wrong time I
can see. Please excuse me."

"No, no, my boy. Come in, come in" said Karekin, who was relieved
that the distressing family business could now be set aside for the moment at least. Giving Harry no time to refuse, he said – "I think it would
be a good time for some coffee don't you think? Shekerli?"

Harry mumbled his thanks and then went round to shake hands
with Armineh. Seta, whose eyes were red and who had clearly been
crying, jumped up and ran into Harry's arms. Harry lifted her and she
hugged him, but then started crying again and ran out of the room
as Harry put her down. After all this time, Harry was no longer the
slightest bit embarrassed at the emotional excesses of the Avakians. He
smiled and nodded at Sima and Nerissa on the other side of the table.

By mutual consent, all sat down again round the table as Paramaz
and Talin left, and Marie went into the kitchen to make the coffee.

It didn't take long for Harry to be told the dreadful news about
Haik in Smyrna. Harry had always been a good listener and he did
not interrupt as the story related by Paramaz unfolded. Then, to everyone's amazement, he told them of his own experiences – the voyage
to Smyrna of HMS *Lion* to join the fleet already there – the events that
had occurred in the bay – and his witnessing of the terrible fire, which
had engulfed the city. Finally he came out with his second surprise of
the morning. "You know, I am going back there this very afternoon or
tomorrow at the latest. I am haunted by the sight of all those people lining the seafront, waiting. I am going to do what I can."

Harry had said nothing about the pending court-martial or his own
predicament, whilst none of the Avakians thought to question him.

Meanwhile everyone round the table was quick to realise what this revelation might mean. They waited for Karekin to speak.

"Harry, my boy, I wonder if you could do something for us if you get the chance. Olga, too, was in that ill-fated city a week ago. She was working three days a week at the Imperial Ottoman Hospital, and three days a week at the Armenian hospital. We have had no news of her at all. Paramaz saw her on the last day before the fire broke out but can give us no further information about what may have happened to her. Please if you have the time, could you kindly make some enquiries as best you can at both hospitals and see if you can find anything out."

"But my dear friends, of course, of course, I will consider it my primary task."

Harry soon took his leave as the gharry had been called for him. The girls came and kissed him warmly. Harry shook Karekin's hand, and then for the first time in their relationship gave Armineh a chaste kiss on the cheek.

Harry boarded the USS *Lawrence* that same afternoon. The ship left for the Dardanelles and the Aegean Sea some time after.

CHAPTER 6

Waiting for Ships

Nothing in Spiro's short life could have prepared him for the ordeal he now faced, lasting over ten days, huddled on the quayside at the Point in Smyrna. He spent a lot of the time with his head buried in his mother's lap, not wanting to see too much of what was going on around him. He slept a lot during the day from a mixture of hunger and exhaustion.

For two whole days the fire burned on uncontrollably. The entire city was ablaze. On both those nights, Spiro found it difficult to sleep as the whole harbour was lit up, bathing the bay in a sinister daytime glow. Thousands of homeless citizens surged up and down the quays. Spiro heard the shrieks and screams of the women and children unable to get away from the heat – a heat that had forced the allied ships to move further away from the shoreline.

By the weekend, the fires were beginning to burn themselves out, but the brutality and random killing by the Turkish soldiery continued unabated. Any male between 14 and 50 was grabbed and marched off, or executed on the spot. Spiro couldn't help but watch a group of uniformed soldiers and an officer, fall on a man and club him to death not more than 50 feet away from him. Spiro could hear the bones snap; the body nonchalantly kicked into the sea, after it was searched for any valuables. "Ermeni" ('Armenian') said one of the men to no one in particular, as if that, in itself, was sufficient explanation – and the group moved on.

It was shortly after this incident that Agape, almost hysterical with fear, produced the short skirt and blouse she had grabbed before leaving the house.

"Spiro, come here and stand behind me against the wall. Take off your shirt and pants and put these on."

"Mama – no – why?" and Spiro backed away from his mother whose wild eyes and dishevelled hair scared him.

"Listen, it's your only hope. Can't you see that they are killing all the men. Do it, just do it!"

Fortunately at this point Costas, who was sitting, trying to keep as low a profile as possible, saw what was going on and called out –

"Mother, don't be so ridiculous. It's dangerous enough for him being a young boy – but if he becomes a girl, he'll be taken aside for certain."

Spiro did not understand what his mother and brother were going on about – but he pulled away from his mother's grasp. She burst into tears afresh, unable to make up her mind what was for the best, finally dropping the bundle on the ground.

Shortly after that, both his brother and his father were finally singled out by a party of more disciplined soldiers, led by a competent officer, and were grabbed. Agape jumped up and clung on to her husband, crying out unintelligibly. She was roughly pulled away as Spiro's father, head down, a look of shame crossing his face at his inability to resist, was led away. This had given a moment for Costas to lean down and embrace Spiro and to whisper – "Goodbye, little man – look after our mother." Then he too was pulled away and they both joined a group of males – all Greeks – and marched away. Costas managed to look back just before they turned the corner. Spiro, whose eyes were glued to him the whole time saw a little smile, a wave of the hand and then nothing.

The days passed. Now the crowds of 200,000 souls – mostly women and children – waited, huddled in desperation, squatting, lying and leaning against the remaining walls, which by now had lost their terrible heat. No food, precious little water and above all no ships. Mustapha Kemal's ultimatum was shortly due to expire. Once it did, all that would be left was deportation to the interior – days and weeks of weary trekking to nowhere with little food and no hope; the Armenian deportations of 1915 all over again.

Meanwhile the whole of Greece was in deep mourning: the main buildings in the cities draped in black with black sheets hanging from windows and black ribbons tied round carriages and people's arms; flags flying at half mast and normally lively restaurants stopped playing music. The atmosphere on the streets and in the cafes was feverish and explosive. The King did not emerge in public and the government was on edge.

There was not a soul in the kingdom unaffected by the plight of the quarter mil*lion* surviving Greeks waiting for rescue from the ruins of Smyrna and the sea. But where were the ships? Where was the political will to do something about it? The Greek state had the largest merchant marine capacity in the entire Mediterranean, while the Turkish nationalists did not possess a single ship. Nevertheless, no ships appeared in the bay of Smyrna.

As if to underline the lack of any initiative from Athenian officialdom, at some time on the Monday, after Costas and his father had been marched off, never to be heard of again, a small freighter manoeuvred its way into the harbour, flying the flag of the defunct Tsarist empire. Calmly sailing down from Constantinople into Smyrna, past the increasingly irrelevant might of the British and French fleets, ignoring the profitable produce on the dockside, the Captain, whose nationality no one ever knew, took as many of the desperate refugees as the ship could safely hold, and sailed away to Piraeus. Meanwhile, the Greek administration finally made an announcement that at least saved the honour of the bankrupt state. Despite the desperate situation the country was in, Greece would accept within her borders any refugee from the Anatolian debacle, including any former Ottoman citizen be they Greek, Armenian, Jew or any other nationality. In contrast to this noble declaration, the richest country in the world turned back many of the Smyrna refugees who managed to make their way to Ellis Island.

But for now there were still no ships!

Meanwhile, the victorious Turkish soldiers had clear license to rob and rape, almost as if it was part of official policy to reward them at the end of a hard campaign. Appeasement was pointless, for when those troops wandering the quaysides were withdrawn, fresh soldiers arrived repeating the previous excesses with renewed vigour. No girls between the ages of 13 and 30 were safe, and by the end, very few in that age group survived. Robbery, too, continued unabated until there was nothing left to take.

A certain amount of food arrived, organised by American private citizens – working for organisations like the Red Cross, the YMCA and other relief groups, whose acts of kindness and charity, just managed to save the honour of the United States, which Admiral Bristol was doing so much to besmirch. Contrary to all the reports that he was actually receiving from his own officers, on the 22nd September, Bristol sent the following cable to the State Department –

"The killings in Smyrna are only by individuals or small bands of rowdies. During fire some unavoidable deaths by drowning as people attempted to swim to boats in the harbour – but few. People massed on quay to escape fire are guarded by Turkish troops. Total deaths not exceeding two thousand."

Meanwhile, at the sharp end of such weasel words, repeated by the US media, Spiro had no idea what the world's great leaders were doing to end a tragedy that was growing daily to epic proportions. He was nearly 12 years old and well aware of the menace implicit in the soldiers' proximity. He could hardly recognise his own mother, who seemed to have aged ten years in under a week, and whose staring eyes barely concealed approaching insanity. There were no longer tears for her husband and her eldest son – the matter of survival for herself and Spiro took precedence.

Still no ships and over a quarter of a mil*lion* people standing or lying along a two-mile stretch of seafront – waiting – waiting – with less than a week before Mustapha Kemal's ultimatum expired.

Early on the Sunday morning of the 24th September, less than nine days after the fire had burnt itself out, Spiro rose from another night of restless, troubled sleep. The seafront had become a reeking sewer, but the water system was miraculously still operating, and there were stand pipes from which water could usually be persuaded to trickle.

Agape also awoke, parched and in need of water. Spiro borrowed a tin can from an old woman lying alongside them, and rising up out of the mass of still sleeping bodies lying around him, he went to fetch some water for his mother from a standpipe right by the sea on the other side of the quay. He could see some allied military ships in the great bay fairly far out, all at anchor. There was one ship arriving – an American destroyer surely, as Spiro could pick out the Stars and Stripes.

Picking his way carefully between sleeping and, in some cases, lifeless bodies, he approached the water pipe. And then, out of the blue, a figure that he had not noticed before, who had been crouching as he ferreted through an old tin suitcase, stood up. It was a Turkish soldier, but Spiro had no idea whether he was an officer, guerrilla, regular infantryman or chete irregular. But he immediately saw the man's gleaming eyes looking directly at him, and turned to run. Too late – the soldier jumped forward, grabbed him, with an oath on his lips, and in so doing, tore off Spiro's threadbare shirt, which came away in his hands. Spiro didn't scream – he was terrified but somehow his vocal chords didn't work. He wriggled in the man's grasp and tried to pull away. However, though he himself did not scream, a scream did ring out. Agape, distraught, dirty and dishevelled, until then lying exhausted on the ground, jumped up and flung herself across the road right onto the pair, pulling at Spiro to drag him free.

Who knows what the soldier had intended in tearing off Spiro's shirt – but in any event, the intervention of Agape changed everything. With another violent oath, the soldier let go of Spiro and pulled out a pistol. As Spiro staggered away and turned to look back, the soldier shot Agape full in the face from only a foot away. Frozen to the spot, Spiro saw his mother's face blown wide open, blood and gore splattering over her and the people all around. Without another glance, the soldier turned back towards Spiro. Nearly senseless with fear, and now almost naked, Spiro turned in the only direction left to him and jumped off the quay straight into the sea. More shots rang out. Spiro tried swimming underwater as long as he could. He could hear the sound of bullets pinging into the water around him as he swam – but he was going to have to surface soon.

CHAPTER 7

Admiral Jennings

Throughout those terrible days when no government authority appeared ready to undertake a relief effort, a handful of American citizens were doing their best to fight the nightmare, which was threatening to overwhelm the whole of the Greek and Armenian communities still caught on the quayside of Smyrna. Against the clear and specific orders emanating from the U.S. High Commissioner in Constantinople – Admiral Bristol – these private citizens handed out American flags to parties of Armenian orphans, young boys and girls, protecting them from predatory soldiers. Time and again, at some personal danger to themselves, they handed out food and offered personal protection to elderly Greek widows.

One of these civilians, Asa Jennings, originally an ordained Methodist minister from New York, wrote in his diary –

"*I have seen old men, women and even children whipped, robbed, shot, stabbed and drowned.*

It seemed to me as though the awful, agonising, hopeless shrieks for help would haunt me forever."

For Admiral Bristol, this comment was just another exaggerated claim from an hysterical man on the spot. But in fact, Asa Jennings was a quiet, dispassionate man, not given to exaggeration or hysterics.

Jennings was a frail and unassuming man, only just over five feet tall. He seemed doomed to stand in the shadow of others more boastful and arrogant than himself. He had given up his position as a Methodist minister, but he had not lost his faith. He was not a missionary, but he was driven by the same moral imperative to act. This moral certainty was allied to a calm certainty as to how human beings should act towards each other.

After leaving New York, Jennings joined the YMCA and had been working for them for some time, taking up the job of Secretary of the Boys Section in Smyrna some months previously. As it happened, with both his superiors on leave, he had been left in sole charge at this dramatic and vital moment. As the great fire finally burnt itself out, Jennings witnessed everything that was happening. Although safe during the fire in one of the northern suburbs, he had seen how the Turkish occupation had turned so viciously on the population. Jennings was by nature friendly with everyone and had become ,acquainted with a wealthy Greek property owner with the foresight to take his family on a belated summer holiday as soon as news of the Greek army's defeat was known. Before leaving, he had offered Jennings one of his large houses at the Point for use as a centre to feed the refugees from the interior, already beginning to pour into the town.

The fire had left most of the buildings at the Point intact and Jennings had immediately taken over the building and stocked it with all the provisions he could find, acquiring another Greek-owned building next door, which he also stocked. Jennings hoisted the American flag on each house as an added precaution against the marauding soldiery. Within hours, this resulted in the American vice-consul rushing down to confront him,

"You can't raise the American flag here – we have orders to remain strictly neutral. Take it down, I absolutely insist."

"Yes, of course I see that – I am so sorry. However this is my house and if I wish to fly the American flag over it, I will do so."

"This is an order from your government, you stupid man – haul it down!"

Jennings turned away, leaving the assistant consul, spluttering and almost apoplectic with rage. Defeated by Jennings' intransigence, he returned to the temporary quarters where the consulate had been relocated, and sent a telegram to Bristol referring to Jennings' activities as 'totally irresponsible'. Bristol telegraphed back stating that the US government required Jennings to cease his activities.

Jennings quietly ignored them both – the food continued to trickle out, and Jennings began to take more and more personal responsibility for dealing with the events unfolding around him. Soon the two houses, proudly flying the Stars and Stripes, became a centre for pregnant women and for children who had lost their parents.

American sailors, still patrolling ashore after the other allies had left, also intervened, where possible. If they saw Turkish soldiers leading away a young girl, they would claim the girl was a girlfriend. The Turks would often let the girls go. After all, there were plenty of others and the sailors would bring them to Jennings' two houses, which eventually held more than a thousand souls.

This practice was deeply frowned upon by the US officials still in Smyrna – but in every case the naval officer in charge of the patrol would look away, pursuing some other matter until the confrontation had ended.

Jennings had always deferred to authority, but the certain knowledge that he was totally right and morally justified in his actions, and that his government, in the person of Admiral Bristol was wrong, gave him an ever-increasing determination as the crisis unfolded. He found that he was now giving orders to all and sundry without a moment's hesitation. On the fourth night after the fire had subsided, he accepted an invitation to dinner from the captain of an American naval vessel in the bay. As he arrived and was being directed to the captain's cabin, some shots were heard coming from the shore. Everyone went to the side and looked out. In the ship's lights, lit for the arrival of the ship's launch carrying Jennings from the shore, a figure could be seen swimming towards the ship. The lights were making the swimmer a target for Turkish soldiers on the quayside, and the sailors immediately turned them off. The swimmer could however still be seen by everyone, obviously exhausted and still some way from the ship. No one moved. Jennings called out – "For God's sake, why don't you lower a boat?"

"Sir, of course we would normally, but without specific orders we don't dare, in view of government policy."

"Then go and get some orders – get on with it man."

"But sir, it's no use – no officer could give the order."

"Then damn it – I'll give the order. Now – now – push off the boat and quickly!" Jennings' anger and agitation was obvious from his choice of words – words he would never normally use. Much to his surprise, the men jumped to it. The boat was lowered and rowed out to the swimmer, now clearly in difficulties, and returned with a young girl of about fifteen. She was somewhat unceremoniously dumped on the deck at

Jennings' feet. At that point an officer on duty walked by, saw at once what was going on, turned and strode away in the opposite direction.

The girl was gently wrapped in blankets and eventually she opened her eyes to see a whole line of strange young men gazing down at her. Once realising that she was among people who would not harm her, she began softly crying. The men averted their eyes and looked at Jennings who said before being taken down to the Captain's cabin –

"Please look after her till I go back – Don't worry She will be all right with me when I return."

These were all single episodes, mere drops in the ocean of misery. Unless the world's governments, or at least one of them, took a decisive step, a tragedy of immense proportions was about to occur. Jennings prayed. Everyone was praying. Ships! Where were the world's ships? The whole mass of humanity lining the seafront, now beginning to die from exhaustion and lack of food, waited – and Kemal's ultimatum was due to run out within the week.

Then on the Wednesday morning – the day Harry was visiting the Avakians in Makrikoy – Asa Jennings woke up with a desperate urge to save at least the thousand or so women and children now under his care in the two commandeered houses. He had become friendly with the captain of another US destroyer in the harbour, and managed to persuade him to lend him the use of a manned ship's launch to look for accommodation on those ships still remaining.

As he went round the great bay, he eventually came alongside an Italian cargo liner – the *Constantinopoli* – a good name, he thought. Jennings shouted up –

"Do you have any refugees on board."

"No, sir, we are empty."

"Can you take in some refugees?"

"Wait sir, let me go and fetch the captain."

Jennings waited and began thinking of what he could say to the captain when he appeared.

"Good morning, sir, I am the captain. I am under orders to pick up what cargo I can and sail to Constantinople, where a consignment is waiting for me. I have no orders to take on refugees."

"Captain, I am prepared to pay you the equivalent of any cargo to take about a thousand refugees to Mtilini, which is on your way," said Jennings. He hesitated a moment, then added – "And I'll pay an extra bonus for your personal trouble."

"I would, sir, willingly – but I can't without specific orders, or at least some official confirmation that I won't get into trouble."

"Well, would you accept such confirmation from the Italian Consul here in Smyrna."

"Yes, if he can also get permission from the Turkish authorities for me to move alongside."

Jennings worked all the rest of the day and through the night, getting the necessary orders and permits, arranging the docking of the ship, packing up all his thousand charges, moving them on board, paying the captain from the dwindling money of the Association and then finally coming on board himself. On the following morning, the *Constantinopoli* pulled away from the quay with all Jennings' refugees from the two houses on board, together with quite a few others who had managed to infiltrate themselves into the groups going up the gangplanks. Turkish soldiers stood by, even at this last moment grabbing any valuables and dragging out any young male who looked close to military age, but otherwise not impeding the process.

Jennings himself collapsed in exhaustion onto the bunk in the cabin the Italian captain had allotted to him. There, this little man, this unassuming Napoleon of the waves, gave way to tears of joy or grief or simply plain exhaustion and fell fast asleep.

When the *Constantinopoli* reached the Greek island of Mtilini, it was already late in the afternoon. All the refugees hurried down the gangplank. On shore they were welcomed by the Red Cross, which had already been telegraphed by Jennings from the ship confirming their arrival. As the liner prepared to move on to the city for which it had been named, Jennings also left the ship. Refreshed by six or seven hours sleep, he now saw another chance. Lying in the harbour were twenty large transport vessels, all moored alongside each other. These were the ships, which the Greek government had chartered to evacuate the remains of the Greek army, as it fled to the coast a few weeks previously.

Jennings approached the Greek general in overall command of the fleet and accompanied him into the his office. Jennings, no longer overawed by officers of any rank, said –

"Couldn't all these ships be sent to Smyrna to take off all the refugees stranded along the seafront? If those people are still there when Kemal's ultimatum runs out they will simply be marched off into the interior, and you know what that means."

"My dear sir, I have no idea where your authority lies, but I would be prepared to send say seven – one-third of the fleet – if I had a written guarantee that they would be safe, and that the Turks would not try to grab them for their own use before the refugees boarded."

"General, the US is prepared to escort the ships in and out of the harbour"

"But see here – er – Mr Jennings, that says nothing about protection in case the Turks try to seize the ships once docked."

"General, I will personally accompany the ships in and out of the harbour."

"Er... Mr Jennings – I don't want to appear difficult, but I don't really know who you are or what authority you have. I simply can't take the responsibility."

Jennings fumed. To him it all looked so simple. Here were 20 empty transport vessels – there, were over 200,000 miserable people waiting for ships. Without them, they were likely to die. Jennings had no authority but he did have deep compassion and enormous determination.

There followed a series of wireless messages sent in Greek naval code, back and forth between Athens and Mtilini, which when looked at coldly as they appeared in the official register, read as follows –

"In the name of humanity send the 20 ships now lying idle here in Mtilini to evacuate starving Greek refugees standing on the quayside in Smyrna." Signed Asa Jennings.

"Who the hell is Asa Jennings?"

"US citizen – Chairman of the American Relief Committee."

Jennings always claimed that this was not really a lie, as he formed the Committee as he spoke, and as the only US citizen on the island he was of course its chairman.

"Please note – Prime Minister has called a cabinet meeting and will reply further shortly." was the   reply. Then about an hour later

"What protection is offered?" Signed Prime Minister of Greece."

"Two American destroyers are in the bay and will escort ships in and out of the harbour." Signed Asa Jennings.

"Will American destroyers protect ships if the Turks attempt to seize them."

"No time to discuss details – stated guarantees should be more than sufficient."

Jennings knew that he was on shaky ground. He had discussed the situation with the captain of the USS *Edsall*, one of the American destroyers in Smyrna, who had confirmed that he saw no conflict of orders in escorting ships of any nation in and out of the harbour for humanitarian purposes. But to intervene in a conflict that might break out on the dockside – that was different. As the exchanges continued it soon became clear that the Greek cabinet was not prepared to take the risk.

It was then that this small, self-effacing citizen, defied all the complacent bureaucratic governments of the world and took a major personal risk. The next two messages read as follows –

"If no favourable reply received by 6.00 pm this evening I will wire openly so that all wireless stations throughout the Mediterranean will pick up the message that Turkish authorities had given permission, that American navy had guaranteed protection, yet Greek government would still not permit Greek ships lying idle in Mtilini to save Greek and Armenian lives awaiting almost certain death in Smyrna."

The reply coming well before the 6.00pm deadline read –

"All ships in the Aegean placed under your command for the sole purpose of removing refugees from Smyrna."

Jennings had – to all intents and purposes – just been made Admiral of the entire Greek fleet.

By midnight, Jennings had chosen one of the captains of the 20 transport ships as the lead ship. Ten of the others were ready to sail immediately. Jennings arranged for this lead ship to haul down its Greek flag and raise an American flag. And so it was that Jennings led his mercy fleet of a further ten ships out of Mtilini heading for Smyrna.

About halfway to Smyrna, some hours out of Mtilini, the fleet was met by the USS *Lawrence* – the destroyer from Constantinople on which Harry had managed to get a place. Harry had been unable to sleep and was on deck as the *Lawrence* came alongside the transport ship, sporting an American flag from its topmast. Both ships stood to. Harry heard the following exchange over the megaphones –

"Asa Jennings – can you hear me. I've heard of your mission. Would you prefer to ride the rest of the way with us? We will be there much quicker."

"Thank you sir. A very kind offer. But I have given my word to the Prime Minister of Greece that I would be with the first ship to enter the harbour. I will see you there. Go with God."

The ships parted and the *Lawrence* sped away on its course for Smyrna.

The Greek transport fleet entered Smyrna late the next morning, an hour or two after the *Lawrence* had arrived. Dark clouds still lay over the town and the smell of the fire was still strong. As the convoy closed in, all that could be seen of the city were the gaunt remains of buildings, their black and charred debris silhouetted against the hills behind. Then in the front, at the water's edge between those remains and the sea, lay a long line of suffering human beings, waiting, praying for the arrival of ships. As the fleet approached Jennings saw that every face was turned towards them. Sick people had struggled to stand upright. Women held up small children, and every one of them – every single one – held out their hands towards the lead ship with Jennings on the bridge, as if willing with their hands to guide the ships in.

There was a long moan, the last of the terrible sounds that had arisen from this crowd over the last ten days, and at the sound Jennings coul;d take no more and struggled down to his cabin and wept as the boat approached.

Jennings took off 15,000 refugees from Smyrna that day. After offloading them in Mtilini, he returned two days later with 17 ships and took off another 43,000. And finally, shamed by the initiative of this quiet, private citizen, a huge cargo fleet chartered by the British government arrived and took off the remaining 120,000.

CHAPTER 8

Harry and Olga

After the meeting in mid-sea between the USS *Lawrence* and the first Jennings fleet, Harry had still been unable to fall asleep, but he saw at once how he could be of help. When the Jennings' fleet reached Smyrna, there would be quite a problem of loading and unloading. He had no idea what the attitude of the Turks might be, but whatever happened, there would need to be organisation as the ships docked one by one. Harry knew that he would never forget the nightmare of those two days of fire, nor the screams and distress from the people he witnessed massed on the quays, but now, as he anticipated the practical help he knew he could provide, the cloud of hurt and shame began to lift.

The *Lawrence* sailed into the great Bay of Smyrna and towards the Point. The fire had not reached as far north as this and the buildings, including two houses ostentatiously flying the Stars and Stripes, were still largely intact. Harry gripped the rail and gazed at the same piteous sight of massed crowds lining the seafront.

As the ship came to a halt about two hundred yards from the shoreline, Harry and a sailor beside him heard a faint cry below them but it was just enough to make them both look down. There in the sea, swimming aimlessly round and round, and clearly at the end of his strength, was an almost naked boy. Harry shouted out to drop a line, but the sailors had already begun dropping a line to the struggling figure. They shouted down at him to grab the rope and hold tight as willing hands hauled him up and dumped him on the deck. The boy wore only ragged pants and was shivering with cold and in a state of shock. It was Spiro.

Sometime later Harry heard Spiro's story. After diving into the sea he had begun swimming towards the ship he had seen that morning coming into the harbour, but he had miscalculated the speed at which the *Lawrence* was approaching, not taking into account that it would be slowing down. His remaining strength, already sapped by the days of deprivation on the quay, began to give out just as the men on deck saw him.

A sailor hurried up with a thick coarse blanket, which he handed to Harry. Harry knelt and wrapped it round the child who had still not said a word. Making sure that there were no officers in view, they signalled to Harry and, without speaking, pointed to one of the lifeboats slung along the side. Harry lifted the child, who seemed to be much lighter than his age suggested, and carried him to the lifeboat. One of the sailors unloosened a corner of the tarpaulin covering the boat. Harry gently lay the child inside. Bending down and speaking in his poor Turkish, mixed with a bit of Public School classical; Greek, he indicated that he would be safe there for the moment and that food and water would be brought. It was unlikely that Spiro understood much of Harry's Turkish and certainly none of the classical Greek but the sympathetic body language showed through. Spiro was exhausted from the emotional turmoil of the last few hours and days, and within a few moments he had fallen fast asleep.

Harry carefully closed the tarpaulin on the inner side of the lifeboat, then stretching over, he lifted and pulled back the corner of the tarpaulin on the seaside, where it could not be seen from the deck. The men watched silently. Harry turned and facing them said firmly –

"I take full responsibility for having placed the boy here. Any help that anyone gave me was under my personal order."

Within two hours, the Jennings fleet turned up and the lead ship made it to the quayside. Harry was already ashore and was one of the first up the gangplank. Although wearing civilian clothes, ten years as an officer in the Royal Navy gave Harry a natural authority, which he exercised to the full. He asked for Asa Jennings as if he was a personal friend.

"Where is my friend Asa, Captain? I understand that he is aboard this ship."

"Yes, sir. He has been with us throughout, but he went down to his cabin shortly after we entered the bay."

"Why? He's not ill is he?"

"No sir, I believe it may have been the sight of all those desperate people on the quays that undid him."

"Well, well. Can I take him down a mug of tea from your galley?"

"Tea! Tea! – all you English ever think about is tea. Look, come and get some whisky from my store."

Some minutes later, Harry made it down to Jennings' cabin with a mug of hot tea and a tumbler of whisky. Jennings was already up. He had wiped away his tears and had dressed as formally as possible in order to face the inevitable bureaucratic difficulties, which he believed were unavoidable. Harry had been right – a hot strong tea was just what

Jennings needed to face the many hours of negotiation that were now needed.

Harry introduced himself and after ten minutes, he and Jennings had divided up responsibilities between them. Within another 20 minutes, Harry was already directing lines of refugees and helping them past the barriers that the Turks had raised. The danger was for any male who looked more than 14 or younger than 40. Any suspects were dragged out and led away to the screams and entreaties of their female relations.

Neither Harry nor Jennings lodged a single protest against this. The Turks had always made it clear to Jennings that they would accept the embarkation of all the old men, the sick, the women and children – indeed they were now positively anxious that they should go – but not any menfolk. These were to be treated as prisoners of war. Neither Harry nor Jennings saw any reason to jeopardise the rest of the mission for what, from the Turkish point of view, was a reasonable position.

The taking of girls and young women was another matter. As Turkish officers were present, Harry appealed to them when the girl chosen looked particularly young. The response was one of unfailing politeness in the old Ottoman manner, rather than the arrogance of the new nationalists, but despite this he only 'saved' a handful, though there were fewer and fewer of this age group of women amongst the remaining refugees.

Harry worked all day without rest: carrying babies, directing people to water, helping old men who could scarcely walk, comforting children who had lost their parents, all the while speaking in poor, but at least understood, Turkish. On one unforgettable occasion, he even helped to ease the passage of a baby into the world, comforting the woman and assuring her that he would get her back on board a ship whatever happened.

Two elderly women joined him to help as the baby was born into these extraordinary surroundings. "A boy – a boy." Harry grinned and laughed out loud. Once all was settled and the baby washed and in its mother's arms, Harry personally escorted the woman back into the shuffling line, through the guards and onto the gangplank of the next ship. Weak though she still was, she struggled up, desperate to get on board.

"What is your name sir?" said the woman shyly, clutching tightly onto her squalling baby, as she turned to him before stepping onto the deck.

"Harry, Madame."

"My boy's name will be Hari," she said as she stepped onto the deck and out of sight.

It was already late in the afternoon when the boats could take no more. Jennings was as exhausted as Harry, but both men were on fire with adrenalin and sheer delight in what they had achieved over the last ten hours. They shook hands as Jennings clambered up the gangplank of the last ship, confirming that he would be back within a day or two at the most. At the top, as the gangplank was drawn up, Jennings turned and raised his hand in a modest friendly salute. Harry could not help himself – he stood firmly at attention and saluted in a military manner as the last ship pulled away.

That night, Harry took a short stroll as far as he could go into the burnt areas of the city. His mind turned to the promise he had given the Avakians. As he picked his way through the ravaged Greek and then Armenian quarters, he soon saw there was simply no way that anyone could have survived there. The cathedral was a blackened shell and no building resembling what may have been the Armenian Hospital stood anywhere nearby. That night, Harry slept in one of the two Jennings safe houses, still supposedly under the protection of the Stars and Stripes, despite every effort to have it pulled down by the US vice-consul here in the town and Bristol back in Constantinople.

Exhausted but content, Harry had his first undisturbed night's sleep in ten days. In the morning, as everyone waited in the hope that Jennings would get through again soon, Harry decided to try the Imperial Ottoman Hospital in the south. He knew he couldn't face the long walk to the Konak, through the miserable humanity on the corniche, but movement inland from the Point was now open to all, so long as they were not Greek or Armenian. Harry got the Captain of the *Lawrence*, by now a close friend, to persuade the American consul to lend him the consulate car and a driver to take him through the eastern suburbs and back down to the Konak.

When they arrived at Watchtower Square, Harry arranged for the car to pick him up at three o'clock in the afternoon from the same spot – a time well before Jennings could possibly have returned with any more ships. As the consulate driver departed, Harry turned and stared at the Konak with its great red and white nationalist flag hanging from the balcony. He recalled how only two weeks ago he had attended upon General Noureddin with Admiral Brock in this same building, when they were asking for permission for British naval patrols to land – and that was surely only a few hours before the city was torched.

Standing in the middle of the square, Harry suddenly felt conspicuously aware that there were eyes all round watching his every move. Probably not true, but in the nervous, feverish atmosphere of the town, with the looming tragedy on the seafront still not played out, it was perfectly understandable. Harry hurried to the side of the government building and into the cobbled, straggling streets leading up to the Turkish quarter. Picturesque but squalid, with many old Ottoman houses, their wooden latticed balcony windows and their graceful lines still intact, it presented a dramatic contrast to the burnt charnel house that was the modern city, with its European, Greek and Armenian quarters completely razed to the ground.

Harry walked through this part of the city, which he had never visited, savouring the quiet and the normality of a town seemingly untouched by the terrible events that had taken place less than a mile away. But Harry was no longer the cool, emotionally reserved British officer of even a month ago. He noted that almost all the Turkish inhabitants who passed him had the same sadness in their eyes. Harry was aware there had been no love lost between these same people and the Greeks and Armenians of the modern city below, yet there was no triumphalism in the eyes of these citizens.

Something of the spirit of the city had been irrevocably lost. Though that lost spirit might have been partly *giavour*, these people, not yet brainwashed by the fanatical adherents of the one-people nation-state concept, seemed indescribably bereft.

Harry walked to the Imperial Ottoman Hospital – still fully intact and flourishing – and made his way to the reception desk, manned by a veiled Turkish lady. Politely, Harry asked after a Nurse Avakian. The receptionist, Harry could not tell her age, looked somewhat cursorily at a list and then shook her head.

"I'm sorry *effendi* there is no such person on our staff."

"Please madam, could you look into this further as I know that she was working here for three days a week for the last year."

"Ah, yes – here she is – but *effendi* she left on the 9th September to attend her next three day duties at the Armenian Hospital, and well... er...well... you see ...."

"I'm sorry Madame – I do understand. I won't trouble you further."

Harry turned away, thinking of what he would have to report to the Avakians once he returned. Then, reflecting that this receptionist was probably quite new and had not been working here prior to the arrival of the Turkish army in the city, he turned back and tried just once more –

"Madam, it might be that she is here under the name 'Olga hanum'."

Again the veiled lady shook her head – but just at that moment a nurse was passing. She overheard Harry repeat the words 'Olga hanum'. Speaking impeccable Ottoman Turkish – probably from Stamboul herself– she said to Harry –

"Oh! Are you looking for Olga? She is on duty, but if you wait here, I'll get her to come down when she has finished."

Harry was already in a state of euphoria. His 12 solid hours work yesterday, helping 15,000 refugees board the transport ships, had already given him a happiness he had not known for weeks. Now, he experienced an overflowing sense of joy – not so much at locating Olga, as with the enormous relief and pleasure he would bring her suffering family, who had befriended him so unstintingly. Sitting in the hospital waiting room, he was basking in this warm, almost self-congratulatory mood, when Olga ran in, breathless with joy at seeing a friend from the past for the first time since the end of the fire.

Harry stood at once as Olga ran straight at him and held him tight. There, in the middle of the busy waiting-room, in the midst of people hurrying in and out, Harry brought up his own arms and without thinking, enfolded this extraordinary girl, squeezing her to him, as hot tears ran down Olga's cheeks, dropping onto his neat white shirt collar.

It didn't last for more than a moment. Olga was shaking with quiet sobs. They were not akin to the many tears she had shed since the death of Selim. All the emotional turmoil, lying repressed and dormant since she had returned to work at the hospital, came flooding out. It was the first instance of happiness she had experienced since that terrible moment when she was forced to abandon her lover to the terrible flames of the Great Fire of Smyrna.

Harry stood back and held Olga at arm's length, smiling as her tears of sadness and of hope, continued to flow, while Olga dried her eyes and began to laugh. She squeezed Harry's hand and telling him to wait, hurried off to get permission to leave for an hour or two. They walked out together and she took him to a café, still intact and miraculously serving coffee, in a side street a little way up the hillside. They had a lot to tell each other and it all came tumbling out, but it was not just the facts of what had happened. Harry poured out all his feelings about the great fire, about the plight of the countless refugees still milling about on the quaysides and about his own efforts. He did not refer to the court-martial. For her part, Olga talked about Selim, about the arrival of Haik and Paramaz and about the horrors of the approaching fire and her rescue by a passing Smyrniote Turk. She did not refer to the rape.

They could hardly get their words out fast enough as they interrupted each other. Aware of the passing time and the imminent return of the embassy car to the Watchtower Square, Harry tried to persuade Olga to pick up her things and go back with him to the Point that same evening. But she said she could not just walk out without making proper arrangements. She thought they would probably be quite happy, even relieved, to let her go – she was perhaps the only Armenian left in Smyrna and definitely the only one in the hospital. As they prepared to leave the café, it was agreed that she would accept his invitation to go back with him to Bolis on the *Lawrence* when it left in a day or two.

Harry paid the bill and they left the café to walk back to the hospital. Olga's eyes were shining as she began to imagine a return to normal life. She didn't think of the baby she was carrying. But the knowledge that she would soon be seeing her mother made it all seem possible. As they approached the hospital gates, when everything had been settled, and all the necessary arrangements had been made for their next meeting, she finally said –

"Oh Harry, what about Haik and the others, do you know what happened to them?"

In all the elation, Harry had temporarily forgotten about Haik. He was going to have to tell her the truth and to repeat to her what he had been told when he had gone to the Avakians. He hated spoiling the euphoria, but he knew it was necessary.

"Olga, walk down to the Konak with me please – while we wait, I'll tell you everything I know."

As they waited for the car, mercifully late, Olga heard the news. But she had already expended all her tears, so as Harry talked, she simply bowed her head and stared at the road. When he was finished, she looked up at him and said –

"I knew it deep down, I knew it all the time. Whatever happened, Haik would have come back to me if it had been physically possible for him to do so. I knew he would never have voluntarily abandoned me – only death could have prevented it."

Olga stretched up, gave Harry a little kiss on the cheek, smiled, and walked away back to the hospital as the consulate car finally arrived.

CHAPTER 9

Satenig – Rehia

One of the consequences arising from the strict separation of the sexes in wealthy Moslem households was the physical division between public areas and those that were 'haram' – forbidden to all males except the husband. This cultural attitude often applied also to wealthier Christians in the interior of the Empire. As a result, only the husband had any idea of what was going on amongst the women.

Vahan's mother and all his aunts and elder sisters had disappeared in the second wave of deportations and massacres that had struck Caesaria – Kayseri – the family home for generations.

Matters in the town had gone from bad to worse after the family had been saved from the first wave of deportations as a result of Vahan's commission in the Ottoman army. Within the year, further deportation orders were issued, involving all the remaining Armenians left in the town and the previously spared Protestants and Catholics. Without the help of Raffi, who had run away from the clutches of the police many months before, the women had been forced to join the last wave of Armenians on a death march, setting out in the winter months of 1915/16.

This particular group did not even make it as far as Malatya, which was the assembly point for most of the death marches. Most people ordered out of the homes they had lived in for centuries, simply disappeared as they walked through the empty spaces of Eastern Anatolia; dying of hunger, thirst, mindless killings and exhaustion as they passed. This was the first planned extermination of a whole people in the twentieth century.

Neither Vahan, living in Constantinople throughout this terrible period, nor his brother Raffi, living incognito and hand-to-mouth in the interior, nor Garabed who had survived and managed to reach Aleppo, had any idea what might have happened to their womenfolk. And now in the fourth year of the peace, following the Armistice of Mudros, they still did not know for certain and had no expectation that they ever would.

The situation in the Asadourian house in Caesaria for the two weeks immediately prior to the arrest and deportation of Garabed in April 1915, had been tense and full of foreboding. Garabed, in any case, had had to stay at home as he recovered from the beating he suffered at the hands of the police. It was during those troubled days that he and Mariam had sought solace in each other's arms more deeply than ever before, and when confidences were privately exchanged between them.

In that month, Mariam was already three months pregnant, but she had not yet told Garabed, who hadn't noticed. Mariam was small and had never shown until about the sixth month. Mariam's last child had been born ten years earlier. Mariam was over 40 years old, and an odd feeling of shame accompanied the realisation that she was pregnant, so she had hidden the news for as long as possible. In those last two weeks of their life together, she whispered the news to Garabed. To her surprise and pleasure, Garabed was delighted, though more than a little worried whether she would be able to cope.

On the day before the landings in Gallipoli and only three days after he heard the news, Garabed was arrested. He was sent away the next day and he never saw his wife again. Mariam was already six months pregnant when Raffi was forced to flee.

Unknown to all three men of the family, Mariam gave birth to a little girl, a little prematurely, in the autumn of 1915 at the family house in Caesaria. The infant was about seven or eight months old, healthy and already weaned, when the last round up took place. With no time to prepare – no carts – no donkeys – no young men – only a few possessions and some rolled-up bedding, the women and young children began the dreary, deadly trek out of the town towards the east, heading for Malatya, and ultimately for the Arab vilayet of Syria.

But this final pathetic group, guarded by a disorganised, undisciplined rabble, was not destined to get further than a few days march from the town. On the outskirts of a small village halfway between Kayseri and Burgan, the few 'gendarmes', mostly criminals let out of prison for the purpose, herded the women into a circle and murdered them. Mariam held her little girl to whom she had already given the name – Satenig – tight to her breast as the shooting began. Although she was standing in the middle of the shivering group, she was one of the first to die, sinking under the bodies of those falling on top of her.

But Satenig never got a bullet.

The guards who carried out this particular slaughter were violent, uneducated, petty criminals, who had never intended to go more than a few days walk from their home town. They were also slipshod and careless in carrying out their murderous task, never finishing off the twitching bodies of their victims. And so it was that even though the baby was howling feebly, buried under the dead bodies, they left with their loot and their blood lust assuaged. These killers had not only been brainwashed by the race hatred spread by Talaat's ministry, but they also harboured class hatred as well.

However, not only the baby survived but, also, one of the women, Digin Arabian. She had fainted in sheer terror as she saw the rifles raised and the bullets fired. She fell and, like little Satenig, found herself buried beneath dead bodies.

After half an hour spent quaking with terror, only just able to breathe, and soaked in blood, Nouritza Arabian crawled out from under the bodies and looked around in a daze. Flies were already gathering around to feast on the terrible carnage. It was then she heard the crying of the baby. Fearful as she was, she could not ignore the cries and forced herself to search amongst the inert bodies, finally prising the crying baby out of the arms of Mariam, still holding her tightly in the rigor of death.

Satenig had been the only baby on this particular death march and Nouritza knew who she was and who the parents were. Holding Satenig tight and trying to soothe her increasingly plaintive weeping, she staggered away as fast as she could from this place of death. As she stumbled on, the moment came when she was at the end of her strength, unable to go another step carrying the child. The path she was blindly following was clearly used, surely someone would come by and rescue the child. Riddled with guilt she lay Satenig down on the path by the side of a bush. She could see a large village in the distance down the hillside. Still covered in blood, traumatised by what she had witnessed, not thinking clearly she stood up and staggered down the hillside.

This was still an area of settled habitations and indeed some time later a shepherd, grazing the village sheep, came by. Satenig was crying again and moving feebly. The shepherd – a Turk rather than a Kurd – looked down at the child, now being gently nuzzled by one of his sheep. He was a simple man who honoured Allah. He realised immediately that the baby must have been a *giavour* abandoned on one of the death marches, but, first and foremost, it was an innocent child.

He picked her up, managed to give her some sheep's milk and carried her down to his village - Chehan, - which Nouritza had seen down in the valley. Before delivering the sheep to their owners, he laid the baby down on the steps of one of the small town's two mosques. Satenig was now more than just bedraggled. Her clothes were wet and stinking and she lay there mewling feebly. She had a plain wooden cross with a blue stone hanging from her neck, and this, together with her clothes, identified her as an Armenian.

Chehan was a large village, almost a small town, unusual in having two mosques, and many people did pass by, glancing away from the child lying on the steps. In due course, someone reported the matter to the local gendarmerie. Omar, a married man of about 40 years of age, a sergeant in the police force, put on his belt and sauntered down to see what was going on. As it happened, Omar and his wife Gulmaz had not been able to have any children. He looked down and Satenig looked up at the looming face of Omar peering down at her and raised her arms towards him. Omar was touched. He too saw only a child not a *giavour*. He bent down and picked her up, stinking and dirty as she was. As soon as Satenig found herself in a man's arms, she immediately stopped crying.

Omar carried the child back to his home, where a spirited conversation took place between himself and his wife.

"My revered husband, what exactly do you want me to do with this child?"

"Gulmaz, we have no children. This is obviously an abandoned baby – couldn't we look after it?"

"I am nearly 40, husband, I am far too old to look after a baby. My mother is no longer alive and I wouldn't know what to do. No, no it's impossible."

"Very well, very well – but at least for tonight. I can't take it back to headquarters at this hour. Come Gulmaz we can't leave it out during the night."

"Of course not, Omar. But listen it is a *giavour* child – look at that cross – I'm not going spend my declining years looking after a *giavour*. But very well, just for tonight. Go and speak to Vicdan hanum next door and ask her to come in so that she can help me. She has had lots of children. I wouldn't know where to start. It might help if she could bring some of her children's old clothes, if she still has some."

And so it was that that night, Satenig, the daughter of Garabed and Mariam Asadourian of Caeseria was fed, cleaned and clothed and fell asleep in the house of Omar the police sergeant of Chehan and his wife Gulmaz.

The next morning, Omar left to report what had happened at the police station and to get instructions about what should be done with the infant. Gulmaz fed the child with some porridge but took care, as she explained to Omar, not to hold her or show any sign of affection. Satenig could sit up and even manage a spoon. After drinking some water she sat and stared at Gulmaz with huge brown eyes. Gulmaz took her out into the street. It was still winter, but it happened to be a warm sunny morning presaging the coming spring. Gulmaz sat herself down on the top step as usual taking in the sun, putting the child down in the dusty earth-packed street. Her neighbour Vicdan, who had done most of the work the night before, came out and sat across on her own front steps as the little girl crawled about playing with the stones on the street between the two women.

It was no more than half an hour later, as the two women chatted and watched the little girl that two policemen arrived.

They had been sent by the officer on duty to pick up the little girl and bring her back to the police station where they were still discussing what was to be done.

The two women said nothing as the two men came up. But Satenig, who had been sitting playing with the stones, gave one look at the two uniformed men and, with surprising speed, crawled over to Gulmaz and crept under her long black skirt. Then holding on tightly, she peeped out at the two men. Gulmaz, at first taken aback, looked down at the child hiding under her skirt. She then grabbed up the little girl and cuddling her for the first time, glared at the two uniformed police-men, both of whom she knew very well.

"Well. What do you two want?"

"Gulmaz Hanum, your respected husband has asked us to come and collect the child, abandoned last night on the steps of the mosque. We are to bring her back to headquarters."

"Nonsense. I will be looking after the little girl. Since Allah has seen fit to send her to me, I will bring her up in the true faith."

"But Hanum" said one of the two, thoroughly confused, "you told your husband that you didn't want to look after a *giavour* child and that … ."

"Rubbish. Go and tell my husband and your officer that the child is ours and that her name is… er… is…Rehia."

The two men departed in bemusement. As they turned away, Gulmaz lifted Satenig to her lips and gave her a kiss. Vicdan too waddled across and gave the child a hug.

And so it was that Satenig became Rehia and was brought up as the little daughter of Omar, the town's police sergeant, and Gulmaz his formidable wife. She was loved and mothered and had the best of food and clothes. She called her mother Gulmaz 'Ana' of course, and, when she started speaking, spoke only Turkish. Her father, Omar, was fiercely protective of her and delighted in the child. Omar, was not particularly pious, but the rituals of the house were Muslim. As the years passed and Rehia grew, she knew only that she had a loving father and mother who doted on her. She knew and accepted as natural that they waited for the call to evening prayer from the nearby minaret before they could sit down to their evening meal.

This would have been the end of the story of little Satenig/Rehia except for one further matter. Nouritza Arabian, against all the odds, had also survived. Staggering into this same village a day or two later, she had managed to find shelter and some food for a day or two. Although known to be a refugee from the big city, she had been able to find a lowly domestic post with an up-and-coming Turkish family. They wished to have a mature woman who could read and write and teach their children, rather than a village girl, and Nouritza was ideal as well as very cheap.

Not much was secret and private in this small town and Nouritza soon came to hear about the arrival of the *giavour* baby, found under a bush near the village and adopted by the village police sergeant. She watched from afar the growth of the child – now known as Rehia. This had all happened early in 1916 and Nouritza remained silent as six years passed and the world outside changed.

CHAPTER 10

Constantinople on the Edge

The world's desire – Micklegard – the largest city in the European world for centuries – the Imperial capital of three Empires – the Eastern Roman – the Byzantine and the Ottoman - was in a state of fear and turmoil. The total collapse of the Greek forces in Anatolia was worrying enough for a substantial number in the city; the fall of the second city of the empire which followed was worse; but the total destruction of Smyrna, in one of the great fires of history, together with the looting, rape and killings gave rise to wholesale panic.

The Imperial city had arrogantly lorded it over the peasants and humble farmers of Anatolia for over a thousand years. All their wealth had gone to feed the rulers of the city – from Roman senators to Byzantine Emperors and Ottoman Sultans. Now the city faced an avenging army, which had already shown its complete disdain for the great urban centres of culture and civilisation by the sacking and burning of Smyrna.

As the facts of what had actually happened at Smyrna became widely known, the supposed protection of the allied fleets gathered in the Marmara Sea and at anchor in the straits, suddenly seemed irrelevant. For 20 years, the Great Powers of Europe, had spent a large proportion of their military budgets on expensive battleships. Now, the victorious Turks, marching north from the great debacle in Smyrna, were about to show up the limitations of sea power. As this avenging army marched northwards, it seemed increasingly unlikely that any of these big ships would be able to prevent it from crossing the narrow straits and pouring into the city. Yet the Turkish nationalist forces did not possess a single military vessel.

Throughout history, the straits not only formed the sea passage between the Euxine world and the Mediterranean, but represented the bridge between Asia and Europe. Constantinople, dominating those straits and symbolising centuries of civilisation, now waited, like a tired and raddled old painted lady, for the mayhem to come. Rape she could contemplate, but not the destruction of all the goods she owned, her buildings, her infrastructure, her ancient beauty, her traditions and culture. The city trembled.

It would all be decided in a matter of days. Everyone in Constantinople was on edge. Even the Turkish population felt anxious in the midst of the triumph of their forces. Turkish nationalist flags were everywhere, streaming in the wind from all the windows. Their elders, meanwhile, sat in the cafés smoking their narghiles, thinking nostalgically of the dying glories of the Ottomans. Like so many Stamboulis they too worried in their hearts about what might happen when all those unwashed Anatolian peasants were let loose on their beloved city.

Karekin in Makrikoy could grieve no longer. He remained dissatisfied with Paramaz's recital of what had happened in Smyrna, but he could not put his finger on the cause of his doubts. Realising the importance of ritual in these matters, even though he thought it was mumbo-jumbo, he arranged for the family to have a private mass heard, and the very next day he went back to the office.

The whole basis for the operation of the business partnership of Avakian and Levonian had disappeared with the defeat of the Greek army and the destruction of Smyrna. The earlier ending of the 'arrangement' between his eldest daughter Sima and George, the only son of Hovannes Levonian, added to the likely estrangement of the two families. But for the moment, there were too many other problems looming for any decision to be made. Karekin simply threw himself into work in order to distract himself from his personal worries.

Despite the fact that he had been one of the first of the prominent Armenians to be arrested and deported in April 1915, Karekin had never been an active Armenian nationalist. He considered the Armenian Revolutionary Federation (ARF) irresponsible and mindless. They repeated their nationalistic platitudes without any thought as to whether their demands were suitable or achievable in the present circumstances. He believed that as a political party, they had totally disregarded the peculiarly vulnerable position of the Armenian peasantry of the interior, where Armenians were everywhere in the minority with only a few exceptions.

Karekin had always been a supporter of the old Ottoman ideal of a multi-cultural, multi-ethnic Empire based on geography and economic convenience, rather than on any one exclusive ethnicity. Having talked several times to Selim, he knew it was likely he would have been in complete agreement with Nazim, Selim's father, if he had ever had the chance to meet him. However, even Karekin could now see that the current Ottoman government, totally dependent on the British military presence, was inevitably moving towards the dustbin of history. Almost all the possibilities for the city, seriously considered only a few months before, were no longer feasible. The hope of a reformed, liberal Ottoman revival, perhaps with Mustapha Kemal as the power behind the throne, was fading fast. Turning Constantinople – a city situated both in Europe and Asia – into an international city, perhaps the seat of the new League of Nations, had long since been dismissed by the Eurocentric western powers and Kemal had already decreed that Ankara would be the capital of the new nation-state that he was creating. Over half a mil*lion* Greeks had already fled from the old Ionian coastline. What about the half mil*lion* Christians of the city – was it all going to end in a tragedy similar to Smyrna?

Karekin was in a quandary. It was not just a matter of politics. His own daily life and the welfare of his family were going to be directly affected by whatever happened. If the Greeks had to leave, what about the Russians, like Sima's beloved Nicolai and his young brother Alexei who was still working in Karekin's office? What about the 100,000 Armenians of the city – were they to be dealt with like the 20,000 Armenians of Smyrna? Surely impossible, there was no such thing as an Armenian quarter in Bolis, but what... then?

If there was to be a Smyrna solution, shouldn't he take his family away. But where could they go? There was too little time. And so, like everyone else, Karekin did nothing. He continued going to work, remaining calm and rational, as far as his family was concerned. He refused to call on a God in whom he didn't believe, and joined his talkative family in discussions round the dining table. He took great care to soothe the fears expressed by Nerissa and Seta, who brought back lurid tales about Smyrna from university and school, but he did not try to hide anything, ignoring attempts by Armineh to shield the girls from the realities facing them all.

The problem for Tim Harington, the British commander of the allied forces occupying Constantinople, was quite different. He had to balance two different agendas. As the representative of the British government, he was required to carry out as best he could the imperial requirements of British policy, but he also felt a personal responsibility for this unique city, which he had come to love over the years of his mission. When the Greek Royalist government had made a tentative move to take over the city only a few months previously, Harington had not waited for any instructions from London. He acted immediately and decisively to prevent it happening. He had appreciated how catastrophic an attempted Greek military conquest of the city would be. It was not a question of who would win in the end, it was the certainty of the terrible damage that would result. Any modern military campaign would spell doom to this architectural and cultural jewel.

At the same time he was responsible for the ordinary soldiers under his command. Following the unexpectedly complete defeat of the Greek army, the road to Constantinople now lay wide open to the nationalist army. To all intents and purposes, there were only two obstacles standing in the way. First was the continued presence of the large British fleet under Admiral Brock. But what precisely could this huge fleet do except bombard everyone, it could not take or hold any ground? The second obstacle was Harington, himself, in command of about 5,000 men.

Positioned astride the route coming up from Smyrna, sitting in the town of Chanak on the Asiatic side of the Dardanelles, was a small British garrison. The French and Italians had already made their peace with the Turkish nationalists and had withdrawn their small contingents. From the 14th September onwards, almost 40,000 highly motivated Turkish troops began to move north from Smyrna. These forces would shortly be in a position to attack both the small British garrison at Chanak and, ultimately, Constantinople itself.

Harington did possess one of the important qualities necessary in any military leader – unflappability. He immediately started to strengthen the garrison, backed up by the guns of the fleet behind, to withstand any attack, short of an all-out offensive by the whole Turkish army. He called on reinforcements to be sent from Egypt and Malta. But he could see how perilous the situation had become. Officially his task was to make the tactical 'on-the-spot' decisions, but the vagaries of the telegraph system, and the speed at which events were unfolding, often meant that he had to make strategic decisions as well. The exact opposite was happening in London. The existence of the telegraph tempted the decision-makers to interfere with tactical decisions that could only be made on the spot, rather than concentrating on the urgently necessary strategic ones.

In London, the collapse of the Greeks and the destruction of Smyrna had led to an immediate political crisis, which steadily worsened as the triumphant Turkish army drew closer to Chanak and Constantinople. The principal players in London were Lloyd George the Prime Minister, Lord Curzon the aristocratic foreign minister, and Churchill the architect of the original Gallipoli campaign.

Lloyd George based almost all his views on affairs in the Eastern Mediterranean on a mixture of a Gladstonian dislike of the Turks, and ideas taken from the bible, particularly the Old Testament. While he had been unhappy with the Greek Royalist government that had ousted his friend Venizelos, he had no time at all for the Turks. Curzon and the officials at the Foreign Office, though less anti-Turk, were currently angry at the abandonment of the alliance by the French and Italians, and their support for the Turkish position, which they viewed as verging on treachery. Churchill, who was in no way anti-Turk, resented the challenge to British prestige, and believed that to restore its credibility, the government had to act boldly in the Straits and be seen to do so. All agreed that firmness of purpose had to be demonstrated. Churchill, and the others who thought like him, believed that to back down in the face of an Asiatic, Moslem army would be fatal for the prestige and power of the British Empire.

Finally, there was the all-important matter of the demands of the Turkish government in Ankara – for such it now was. Despite every British effort to put some backbone into the rump Ottoman government in Constantinople, it was evident that Mohammed VI, and his court of aging ministers, now counted for almost nothing. The real issue was what Mustapha Kemal wanted on the issue of Stamboul.

Contrary to the puritan image he promoted in public, Kemal had always enjoyed the life in Constantinople, frequenting its bars and other places of entertainment, even becoming an accomplished dancer of all the latest western dances. He was not a bigoted prude.

There was in fact no longer a real question of who was going to have Constantinople. Once the fatal decision had been taken to let the Greeks land in Smyrna, the resulting Turkish backlash, and the nationalist revival in Anatolia, meant that the city was going to become Turkish again, sooner or later. The real problem now was the issue of the minorities. What was to become of the half-mil*lion* Greeks, Armenians, Jews and others in the city?

Kemal was adamant on most of the issues still outstanding between nationalist Turkey on the one hand and the allied powers on the other. When a peace was eventually negotiated to bring the state of war between the Ottoman Empire and the Allies to an end, there were certain matters on which he would stand firm. The hated 'capitulations' had to go – Eastern Thrace and Adrianople on the European side had to return to Turkey – all foreign troops had to leave Constantinople – above all, Kemal was not prepared to allow any of the Ionian Greeks who had fled from Smyrna and its hinterland to return. Kemal may not have been personally responsible for the decision to burn down the Christian quarters of Smyrna, but like the pragmatist that he was, he was happy to profit from the new situation resulting from it.

But on the matter of the Armenians, Greeks and Jews of Constantinople, the attitude of Ankara and Kemal, hung in the balance.

Only the British Empire, with Harington as its representative, stood between Kemal and all he wanted. If it came to a military confrontation, the chance of a 'Smyrna' solution was high. On the other hand, if the British simply backed down and retired, it could surely herald the beginning of the end of their own Empire.

Meanwhile, the Avakians and all the rest of the citizens of Constantinople waited.

CHAPTER 11

Vahan's Decision

When the end of the Great War came in the closing months of 1918, it took quite some time before the changed circumstances and attitudes penetrated into the remoter villages and small towns of the interior.

Inertia in human affairs is strong, and Nouritza Arabian was no different in this respect to those living around her. Her lowly work with the Kazim family had given her a measure of contentment. Of course she would never forget the past, her previous life in Caesaria and the horrors of the final deportation orders, or the terror of the three-day trek, culminating in the final slaughter, which only she and the baby daughter of Mariam Asadourian had survived.

But she was grateful for the shelter she had been given, and slowly, as the Kazim children grew, life settled into an acceptable routine. She taught them the Arabic script of the Turkish language and looked after them whenever their parents were away. As the family became more affluent and acquired more servants, her status in the family improved and she became a sort of honorary grannie.

All this time, she kept an eye on little Rehia – the adopted daughter of the town's police sergeant Omar and his wife Gulmaz hanum. Apart from making an effort to become acquainted with them, she was careful not to say anything about Rehia's past, but three separate but connected occurrences changed all this.

The first event, which was the catalyst for her eventual decision, occurred in the winter of 1920, when the friendly and popular police sergeant caught a bad chill. He lingered on for a few days and then died, surrounded by his grieving neighbours and his wife, attended by his only child – Rehia.

Within the next year Gulmaz hanum, left alone as a wealthy widow, married again – this time to a younger man, Orhan, a soldier in the old Ottoman army who had retired after the war. Orhan had married a young village girl by whom he had already had two children, but the old Ottoman law allowed Muslim men to have more than one wife. So there was nothing to prevent this young man from taking Gulmaz under his wing, and marrying her for her money and property. Gulmaz was no fool; she was perfectly aware what lay behind the offer of marriage. In the end, the life of a second wife was preferable to that of a widow. It was a trade-off: male protection in return for sharing her property.

Gulmaz remained a warm and good mother and to Rehia, Gulmaz was always her 'Ana' – her beloved mother. But inevitably things changed. The new father of the family wasn't interested in this precocious little girl. The first wife wasn't a problem; if anything, she looked up to the well respected Gulmaz, but she had her own two children, and there were inevitable tensions between them and Rehia, a strong-willed child, somewhat spoiled by Omar's doting affection.

All the townsfolk knew that Rehia was an Armenian infant found abandoned by the side of the road, yet such was their basic goodwill, no hint of this had ever been given. So Rehia had no idea where she had come from or who she really was, believing herself to be the beloved only daughter of Omar – the policeman.

Orhan was not a hard or unreasonable man, but he felt the need to establish his position vis-à-vis his new second wife. It was necessary to make it clear to the village community that he was the head of his household. Unfortunately, the point of contention between him and Gulmaz was nearly always little Rehia, and the whole town was aware of it and so was Nouritza Arabian.

The final event which triggered her decision, was hearing about a law, passed by the Ottoman government in Constantinople, that any Armenian orphans taken in by Turkish families during the terrible events of 1915 had to be returned to any relatives who made a proper claim. It was one thing to pass such a law, quite another to enforce it in the lawless conditions of the Anatolian interior. Either way, it wouldn't have crossed Nouritza's mind to do anything about it if Omar had still been alive. But in the chamged circumstances, these events coalesced in Nouritza's mind and she decided to act.

As a 'gesaratsi' from the previous Armenian community of Caesaria, she knew the well-known and well-to-do Asadourian family. She was aware that their eldest son had been in Bolis at the time of the deportations. She had no idea if any of them had survived, but she had been with Mariam throughout the dreadful trek, helping her to carry the baby Satenig, and talking with her until the end.

Although she had achieved a measure of ease with the Kazim family, she missed her people, her community, her religion and the customs of her youth. Accordingly, she had warned the family that as soon as the improving political allowed her to travel, she intended to go to Stamboul and seek out any of her own surviving relatives. So it was that she came to write a letter addressed to the Asadourian family. She sent it care of the address of the Armenian Relief Organisation in Constantinople, known to all Armenians still left alive in Eastern Anatolia, for assisting in the recovery of Armenian children. The letter read –

Sireli Asadourianer

My name is Nouritza Arabian and I live in the village of Chehan, on the road between Kayseri and Burgan. I was with your wife/mother Mariam when we were forced to leave Kayseri six years ago. I am sure that you know that she and all the rest of her family were killed only three days after we left.

Out of our whole group only I survived, as did your baby daughter/sister – Satenig. She had survived the shootings by the guards and I was able to take her out of Mariam's arms after the soldiers had gone. We eventually came to this town. Here the baby was taken in and adopted by a good man – Omar and his wife Gulmaz. I myself took work with another family and I have watched as the little girl, who was given the name Rehia, grew up. She is now about six years old. No one has ever told her that she is an Armenian – but all the rest of the village knows and Gulmaz hanum still has the wooden cross which was round her neck.

Omar, the father, who doted on the child, has died and Gulmaz hanum has remarried a man who has children of his own.

I don't know if any of your family has survived. Mariam told me that her eldest son – Vahan – was living in Bolis. I am myself proposing to come to Bolis once the countryside is more settled. My address here is at the top of this letter and if I get any reply I will try to persuade everyone that Rehia could come with me if you should so desire. Although Gulmaz hanum undoubtedly still loves the child, she may be prepared to let her go in view of her remarriage and the new law on Armenian orphans.

However I would warn you that Rehia has no knowledge at all of her ante-cedents. She loves her Ana and believes that she is her child. I doubt if I myself could persuade her to accompany me. Although she does know me as an Arme-nian, in order to protect the general village consensus, I have never approached her on this matter.

I await hearing in the hope that one of the family is alive."

This letter was eventually delivered to the little house in Taksim where the Asadourians lived, arriving on Saturday the 16th September, the same day the Avakians were told by Paramaz of the death of Haik. The family had informed Vahan and had asked for his help in comforting Nerissa.

When Vahan arrived home that evening he was met by the bomb-shell which had burst on the Asadourian home. The family gathered in the little sitting room. The four men sat: Garabed on one side of the fire, which had been lit despite the fairly benign weather; Vahan and his younger brother Raffi sat on the other side; 18 year-old Ara, sat near the door. Garabed slowly read out Nouritza Arabian's letter again.

"Baba – could this possibly be true?" said Vahan once he had taken it in.

"Impossible, brother, impossible! I was there, remember, for at least two months after baba had been deported and I saw no sign of mother being pregnant. It's nonsense – some sort of attempt to get money out of us...." said Raffi.

"Enough boys, enough" said Garabed looking down at the floor. Mariam told me only a week before my arrest that she was pregnant."

"But baba, it's simply not...."

"Enough Raffi – you were only 16 at the time and you are not known, even now, for being very observant of other people. Mariam was certainly pregnant in April 1915. This lady could not have known that Mariam had already told me. Her story rings true. It seems that I have a daughter and you, my sons, have a sister who has miraculously survived."

Everyone sat, silently absorbing the implications of the letter and the information, which Garabed had kept to himself all these years. Then at last Garabed slowly got up and said –

"I am tired. Tomorrow is Sunday and as you know, I will be away until Monday. This is a matter we must all think about before deciding what to do. I am sorry, Vahan, to hear about the distress in the Avakian family. I never met their young son, but by your accounts he was likely to have turned into a good man. I understand that you have already invited Miss Nerissa, to come here after University classes on Tuesday. I have no objection to her being here when we decide on this matter. I have always found her very understanding. It might be a good thing for us to have some female insight into our problem."

"Very well, father."

"So, everyone, we'll talk about this on Tuesday. Meanwhile Raffi, it will be your task to find out if it is physically possible for anyone to travel to this town. You, Vahan, will look into the legal position and also whether there is any way we can send money to this woman. Once we have all the facts, we'll discuss it further when I get back on Tuesday."

And with that the family meeting broke up.

Nerissa was still grieving on the Tuesday she had agreed to go to tea at the Asadourians, but she had returned to her classes the day before, and was no longer breaking down into sudden floods of tears. There was still no news of Olga, which added to the worry, as she tried to contend with her grief for Haik. But she was looking forward to her outing to the Asadourians, recognising that it would take her mind off her own troubles. She had never quite got over her awe of Garabed *effendi* – but he was always so charming to her, that she always ended up totally disarmed by him.

When she arrived, only Ara and Vahan were at home. Ara opened the door to her and welcomed her in his normal effusive manner. Vahan came bounding down from his room and gave her a chaste kiss on the cheek. In the sitting room, Nerissa sat on the edge of a chair. After a few short words of explanation, Vahan handed her Nouritza's letter. Nerissa read it through quickly, then looked up at Vahan with eyes wide open in surprise.

"It's quite true my sweet, it seems that baba knew that mother was pregnant when he was arrested in April."

"But…"

"Listen, I believe I can hear Raffi and father coming in now. Please read it again slowly and carefully as we are going to discuss it together."

Ara already had tea prepared. Conversation, which had been in Armenian till then, switched immediately to Turkish once Garabed came in. For some time, the talk ranged over the uncertainties of the current political situation. Garabed had noticed the letter in Nerissa's hands when he came in, and eventually, as Ara cleared up, he raised the issue facing the family.

"Now, what are we going to do about this little girl – Satenig?"

Raffi immediately burst out without any hesitation –

"Father, there is no difficulty in travelling. It is perfectly possible now that the nationalists are in full control of the whole of Anatolia to get through to Kayseri. From there, whoever goes can easily hire horses and get through within hours to this little town. One of us must go at once and rescue this little girl."

"Baba" said Vahan, "I am not so sure. Her name – the only name she has ever known – is Rehia. Since she was six months old, she has only known this woman, Gulmaz, as her mother. She has been brought up as a Turkish girl in a little Anatolian town in the middle of nowhere. Imagine the distress it will cause if she is dragged away from the only mother she has ever known."

"How can you say or even think such a thing," Raffi interrupted excitedly. "She is an Armenian whose mother was murdered by Turks. Are we now to leave her in the hands of other Turks, as if rewarding them for slaughtering the rest of her family?"

"Raffi, you can't group people together like that as if they were all the same. The Turks who murdered your mother aren't the same people who saved and brought up your sister," said Nerissa, speaking for the first time.

At this point, partly to forestall Raffi who was getting excited and about to answer back, Garabed intervened.

"Well Miss Nerissa you may be right, but what then do you suggest we do."

"Garabed *effendi*, I have no doubt that Vahan is right. Rushing off and taking the little girl away from the only mother she knows is going to be very distressing for her. According to this letter, she has no idea that she is a foundling and that Omar and Gulmaz are not her real mother and father. However, young children are very resilient. She will weep, she may rage, but in the end if she finds new love and tenderness she will recover."

"She is Armenian, she is entitled to know her own people and her own culture," shouted Raffi.

"Oh for heaven's sake brother, forget all that stuff. As of this moment, she is Turkish – all her culture is Turkish and even her name is Turkish. Instead Raffi, say to me – 'She is my sister, the only sister that I can ever have'."

Raffi looked at Vahan for a long moment and then nodded finally saying –

"One thing is clear. There is no way this little girl is going to leave with this Nouritza woman. One of us will have to go and bring them both back. I know the area well and I would be prepared to do it."

There was a long silence as everyone thought some more. Garabed, still leaning on his stick, looked at his two sons and said–

"Have either of you considered how we, a totally male household, are going to look after a little girl of six in this house?"

"Oh father, come on, we'll manage" said Vahan. "Love is all that matters in the long run, and that is a commodity that can be given by men just as much as by women. But look – it is impossible for Raffi to go. You know, brother, that you may be more resourceful and practical than me, but you have little tact and a hasty temper. You'll end up alienating everybody and ..."

"Don't give me all that diplomacy nonsense. I've got far more strength in my little finger than..."

"That's enough " called out Garabed, as Nerissa began cringing, as she usually did, when passions took over from reasoned argument.

"We are talking about my daughter...my own daughter. Oh God, the last gift of my wife." Garabed's voice shook for a moment and tears stood in his eyes. Then he continued firmly – "I agree with all of you. Raffi, you are correct that we must move heaven and earth to try to get her back. You, Miss Nerissa, are also correct in pointing out that it needs to be done as carefully as possible, and she is not to be torn roughly from her mother. And finally I agree with you Vahan that you are the only one who can do it. Can you manage?"

"Yes of course. But I insist that I will make my own decision when I see the situation in Chehan. I will force no one."

Then, for the first time, Ara, who had been leaning against the wall, spoke up –

"Father, Vahan will need some help. Let me go with him."

And so it was that two days later, Vahan and Ara set sail for the little port of Mersin, not much more than 150 miles from Kayseri. At the same time, a letter was penned marked 'urgent' to Nouritza Asadourian at the address given at the top of her letter, informing her of their impending arrival, possibly within the week.

Nerissa was escorted back to Sirkedji station by Vahan at the end of the afternoon. For the first time in her life, she considered how other families, too, had love and anger mixed up in their relationships; how other families, too, could be sensitive to each other. Above all, she found herself thinking for the first time of Vahan not just as a family friend, her brother's saviour, and a good dancing partner, but as someone with beliefs and passions, which she found she shared.

CHAPTER 12

Olga Arrives Home

Jennings' second trip with seventeen of the Greek transport ships from Mtilini returned to Smyrna on the 25th. It departed in the evening of the same day with 43,000 souls on board. Harry worked all day, helping to shepherd the now shattered and drearily apathetic refugees through the Turkish checkpoints and onto the ships. Olga offered to help, but she was so obviously Armenian, it would have been positively unhelpful and even dangerous. Harry had lent her some money to buy some new clothes, but as only the Turkish residential quarter had remained untouched by the great fire, there were no shops left in the city. Olga spent the day working as usual at the Ottoman Hospital, whilst preparing to leave the next day when the *Lawrence* was due to sail.

Having cleared the position with the Captain of the *Lawrence*, Harry came with the Consulate car to pick her up the next morning. The USS *Lawrence* sailed out of the great bay at noon and at last, apart from the still unburied, blackened corpse of Haik, there were no Avakians left in the ruins of the once thriving city of Smyrna.

The matter of the naked boy hidden in one of the ship's lifeboats had not, as yet, been resolved. The sailors had carefully fed him and provided water, under the impression that the Captain had no idea what was going on. In fact, there was not a single officer who was unaware of the existence of the boy, and how he had come to be on board. Within two hours of leaving the Bay of Smyrna, the Captain asked Harry and Olga to attend a meeting in the officer's mess together with his own senior men.

"Captain Bridgeman, I have called this meeting because we have to decide a few issues before we reach Constantinople."

"Certainly sir, I understand perfectly."

"First there is the matter of this young lady. Will there be any difficulty in her disembarking when we arrive?"

"Captain," interrupted Olga, "I am an Ottoman citizen, born in, and a lifelong resident of, Constantinople."

"I can confirm this, sir, as I know the family well," said Harry.

"Very well. However, we have a more serious matter to think about. What about this young Greek boy whose arrival on board this ship, against all current standing orders, was largely your responsibility Captain Bridgeman."

"Yes sir – I'm sorry. I seem to be diso*bey*ing orders on a daily basis these days, having followed them scrupulously all my life until now."

"Look, Harry – I don't care about all that. The question is how we are to deal with him when we reach Constantinople. Neither the British nor any Ottoman officials will allow any Smyrniote Greek to land. The issue of the Ionian refugees is a political hot potato."

Various possibilities were considered, though it was agreed that the Captain could not escort the boy ashore in his official capacity, as this would run the risk of involving not only him in an official enquiry, but the whole crew of the *Lawrence*.

One of the American officers said –

"Look, the boy's name is Spiro. We know Spiro can swim, after all he swam out to us didn't he? Let him slip off the boat during the night when we anchor and swim ashore."

"My God Vergil, he's only 11 – what will he do when he arrives penniless on the shore."

"Listen", said another officer, "he's a bright lad, what about letting him stay aboard as a cabin boy. He'll learn English fast enough, and we can let him off if he wants to leave whenever we next touch at a Greek port."

This seemed to be a generally acceptable solution, but then the Captain interjected –

"I'm sorry but that's impossible. As it happens, I've been promoted and have to report for a new assignment when we reach Constantinople. I'm afraid that he is either going to have to swim or to take his chances with Turkish officialdom. After all, the Brits are still there – surely the worst that could happen is that he will be deported – which simply means sending him to Greece."

There was a short silence, broken by Olga, whose female voice took everyone by surprise.

"Sir, I have spoken to Spiro. He is terrified of being handed back to Turkish policemen. He sees little difference between the Turkish uniforms that he encountered during those last terrible days in Smyrna, and the Turkish uniforms that he will have to face there in the city. I will take responsibility for him and say that I brought Spiro on board with me when I arranged my return to my home city; that Spiro is an Armenian relative who has been working as my servant and helper for about a year. I'll bluff it through. He already knows a few words of street Armenian. I'll manage it, gentlemen, and if that fails, the worst that can happen is for him to be deported – but at least none of you will be to blame."

Harry looked across at Olga, seeing for the first time, not just a strikingly beautiful and elegant woman whose company he had always enjoyed, but a woman who possessed a spirited and forceful character, with a morality similar to his own. In the silence that greeted Olga's last statement, he said –

"She will manage, gentlemen."

The Captain stood up.

"That is a very fair offer, Miss Avakian, for which I thank you. Let the boy out of that infernal lifeboat, and arrange for him to be berthed with Miss Avakian in her cabin. And Arthur – for god's sake – get the ship's tailor to make up some basic clothes for him. We can't have Miss Avakian being attended by a naked boy, even if he is only 11 or 12."

And with that, the meeting broke up.

As the USS *Lawrence* slowly moved up the Dardanelles, Harry could see the frenetic activity of the many British naval vessels patrolling the area. As they passed Chanak on the right, and the Gallipoli peninsula on the left, Harry pulled out his binoculars and tried to work out what was going on. But having been away from the centre of affairs now for over a week, he had no idea of the looming crisis that was arising as Kemal's victorious army approached.

The *Lawrence* arrived in the waters off Constantinople on the 27th September. Almost all official business had virtually ceased. Kemal's army had arrived on the Asian shore, and advance parties were even now taunting British troops across the lines at Chanak. In the event Olga had only minimal difficulty in negotiating her entry, once she had established that she was a bona fide Ottoman citizen from Constantinople. There were still no officious Turkish nationalist officers at Eminonu; they were still the Ottoman bureaucrats of the old school. Inefficient they might be, but they were polite and well mannered. Olga explained what was the truth, namely that she had lost her 'nufus' and other papers in the fire; however, she could produce her papers from the Imperial Ottoman hospital, showing that she had been working there until only a few days previously.

The officer nodded and gave scarcely a second glance at the servant boy accompanying her. Like everyone else in the city, his mind was concentrated on the approach of Kemal's army. Harry, meanwhile, had been waved through immediately. He said he would wait for her at Sirkedji station.

From the moment that Nerissa had returned from university on the day that Paramaz and George had returned from Smyrna, she had been in a state of anxious confusion. The devastating grief for the death of her brother had been followed by the alarming reports of the horrific scenes in Smyrna before, during and after the fire. Vahan, her friend and dancing partner, had been on hand at the worst moment, when she was told of the death of Haik, and his presence had comforted her. But what Nerissa really craved was physical comfort. Deep down, she wanted to curl up in her father's arms.

But Karekin could not quite contemplate taking his clever twenty-year-old daughter into his arms as of old. Determined to be honest, and imagining that this daughter simply needed to sort things out in her own mind, he kept his comments about his own fears, to a minimum. Armineh, who had long since given up cuddling her elder daughters, had her time cut out seeing to the 12 year-old Seta and calming her fears fuelled by school gossip.

Meanwhile Vahan wanted nothing more than to hold her in his arms, and not just on the dance floor. Why then did Nerissa hold back? She had now seen her sensible elder sister, Sima, fall head over heels into a romantic attachment with an impoverished Russian refugee. There had been a permanent argument among the three girls, with Olga and Nerissa claiming that what was important in any relationship was that spark of 'love' – they called it chemistry – between couples, while Sima, had claimed that common background, common culture, and mutual understanding had to be the first consideration. Yet, in the end, Sima had rejected the eminently suitable George, the perfect match, in favour of the 'chemistry' she had always affected to despise.

Now Nerissa could see that Sima was deeply happy and content in her relationship with Nicolai, and this reinforced her own certainty that what was important was love – a spark she didn't seem to feel with the shy, introverted, former music student with whom she had been going dancing since the end of the war and she also failed to see that Vahan, with whom she continued to have long and intimate conversations, had fallen in love with her. For his part Vahan, who still remembered the very first time he had smiled at her all those years ago at that afternoon tea at Tokatlians, where Olga and Selim first held hands, could no longer contemplate his future without her. Feeling her coolness towards him, he didn't know how to react.

Only Nerissa was at home when Olga and Harry arrived at the house. Olga, excited and bursting with anticipation, rang the bell. She fell upon Talin with kisses when she opened the door, and then burst into the great hall of the Avakian house.

"Mama, everyone, Mama I'm home, I'm home." Olga shouted out.

Nerissa, up in her room working on an essay on Trollope, jumped up, scattering her papers as she did so, and ran out onto the landing. Looking down over the banister she saw a radiant Olga looking up and alongside her Harry, with a young boy behind. Nerissa flew downstairs, almost tripping and falling in her eagerness, and collapsed with tears of joy into Olga's arms. The two sisters, so different and so often in disagreement, were sobbing with joy. Harry smiled and Spiro gave a little giggle – he of course had seen this sort of thing many times before.

"Where's mother?" Olga said at last.

"Oh Olga, they're all out, they'll be back soon. My soul, what happened, how did you get back, what's the … oh sorry!" she said as she noticed Harry again, and reverting immediately to English said – "Look, we must all sit and have some tea."

Nerissa released Olga and turned to extend her hand to Harry. To her surprise he ignored it, and instead, coming forward, he held her and kissed her firmly on both cheeks. Then, stepping back he indicated Spiro, still standing behind him. Spiro hadn't understood a word, neither the Armenian nor the English. Speaking in his poor Turkish, he waved at the lad with a flourish and said –

"May I introduce my friend – Spiro Pantelis *effendi*."

Spiro did not know where to look; in all his almost 12 years he had never before been referred to as '*effendi*'. He coloured bright red and shifted his feet, but then saw Talin, who was giggling, and immediately recovered, grinning at his own discomfiture. Olga, also now talking Turkish, said –

"Please Talin, sober up and go and fetch some tea and cakes – and look after Spiro and give him something to eat – and no teasing, there's a good girl."

Talin still in a fit of giggles indicated to Spiro to follow her and stalked out to the kitchen. Nerissa saw for the first time that the boy was dressed in an extraordinary outfit, which appeared to have been made out of a grown man's sailor suit.

One by one, the rest of the family came in as the afternoon wore on. Seta bounced in with a great burst of joy when she realised who was sitting at the table. Then Armineh and Sima came in together. Armineh just stood and tears flowed soundlessly down her cheeks as Olga jumped up. They held each other tight and cried together for a long time. Finally Karekin arrived, earlier than usual as if he had had a premonition, with Paramaz in tow. He too stood stock still when he entered. Then he held his daughter tightly to him for a time – for an eternity.

Tea gave way to supper and the family remained at the table. The great fire of Smyrna and all the political events leading up to it were ignored as the house rang with the noise of an Avakian family reunion. The discussion ranged over all the personal matters which had transpired. Paramaz had not joined them, but the baby boy was brought down by Marie and, gurgling happily, was handed round between the women. Nerissa, notoriously uninterested in babies, passed the little boy straight on to Olga. Seta, sitting on the other side of Olga, expected the child to be passed straight on to her, but was surprised to find that Olga held on to him, making all the usual cooing noises and cuddling him. Armineh also noticed this with surprise, but made no comment.

Inevitably, the conversation kept turning to Selim's presence in Smyrna, and then, as quickly, shying away. Olga wasn't ready to go into that part of her life. Ironically, she had had no trouble talking about it to Harry on several occasions as they had travelled together. She kept prevaricating and changing the subject – but these were Avakians she was dealing with and they persisted.

She was going to have to admit the existence of the relationship. She assumed that Paramaz would have told them that she was living with Selim before the catastrophe. But the Great War had not changed conventions that much, at least not in the Ottoman world. She felt she couldn't blurt out the true facts in front of the whole family just like that – there was, after all, Seta to consider - and on top of that, the family would be embarrassed by Harry's presence. They were not to know that he was already aware that a relationship had existed. She appealed to her mother, saying she would tell all about things 'tomorrow', when she was not quite so overwhelmed by the joy of her return.

Armineh, who had long since interpreted Paramaz's prevarications, and knew that Olga must have been living with Selim, intervened. She recognised the element of distress in Olga's evasions and moved the discussion away from this subject. This then was the moment for Harry to get up and declare that he was happy to walk down to the station and did not need the carriage to be called. Reverting to formality while the parents were present, he shook hands with all of them, said goodbye and left.

Olga went up to her room with Nerissa. As they continued to chat together, she could think only of the baby growing inside her. Within a few weeks she knew it would become obvious, to her mother at least, if not to everyone else. She had to decide very soon what she was going to tell Armineh – and more to the point what she could say to her father.

As Olga considered her position, it seemed to her that if she admitted to the baby being Selim's child, conceived naturally and with her loving consent, this might be shameful for Karekin. If, however, she admitted the rape and explained the coming child that way, he would be upset, but not shamed. What should she do?

CHAPTER 13

Chanak

As the Avakians tried to come to terms with their situation, the Turkish army moved out of Smyrna and headed towards the Imperial City. After almost two thousand years of effortless domination over the native peasantry of Anatolia – whether Greek, Seljuk, Turk or Kurd –- the city was about to be brought sharply and painfully to its knees, while the arrogant Western powers waited to see what Mustafa Kemal would do. For his part, he had made it clear that at the very least he intended to take back the city and would chase the Greeks out of Thrace – but standing in his way was Harrington and the British force in the city and the small garrison in Chanak.

On the 23rd September – the day Jennings lifted his first batch of survivors from the Smyrna quaysides – Turkish cavalry crossed into the neutral zone that had been established with the concurrence of the Ottoman government and approached the small British outpost of Chanak. The British position had improved, as Harington had sent in reinforcements, making the little port militarily secure. There were still enormous problems as hordes of Greek refugees, people who had lived peaceably in the area for generations, had been pouring into the Chanak zone daily. With a shortage of clean drinking water, urgent evacuation plans were called for and barges had been hired to ferry people to the European side, but many refugees still remained.

The local commander at Chanak was still short of the full complement necessary for a sure defence. The battleships and cruisers of the Eastern Mediterranean fleet, with the one exception of *the Iron Duke* still in Constantinople, were anchored in the straits outside Chanak. Their firepower would at last be significant if fighting actually started. Harington left the operational control to the local commanders, who understood the importance of convincing the Turks that the British would fight if necessary and Harington had placed troops as far forward in the neutral zone as he could – 40 miles or so inland.

Up rode the Turkish cavalry, fortunately much the best disciplined element in the Turkish nationalist army. Harington had given strict orders that no British soldier was to fire a single shot until fired upon. The situation was tense – a false order, a trigger-happy trooper, could easily have set off hostilities, which would have been almost impossible to stop. It soon became obvious that the Turkish force had received similar orders, and there followed several hours, indeed days, of stand-off.

Instead of concealing their movements from each other, both sides ostentatiously displayed their strength and determination, on almost the same battlefields on which the siege of Troy was fought a millennia earlier, as if they were Greek and Trojan heroes.

It was all shadow-boxing and bluff. But it was dangerous brinkmanship, both on the part of London and of Mustafa Kemal, as a minor incident could, at any moment, set off an explosion. It was doubly dangerous because the ensuing crisis had little to do with Constantinople itself, or with the freedom of navigation of the straits, but a lot to do with the honour and national pride of the two protagonists, the French and Italians having already withdrawn.

This crisis, which followed the burning of Smyrna and the expulsion of the Greeks from Anatolia, had arisen because of British fears that the Turks would cross into Europe, seize Constantinople and chase the Greeks out of Thrace and even further. But by this date in September, it was already obvious that the British were ready to give up Constantinople, and possibly Eastern Thrace and Adrianople as well, to the Turks. That being so, what was all this posturing about?

The reasoning of the British government was complicated, but pressing. Lloyd George took the view, as Gladstone had before him, that the return of the Turks into Europe would necessarily mean oppression, corruption and massacres. Furthermore in view of the events in Smyrna, he was justified in that opinion. Having prevented the Greeks – nominal allies after all – from descending on Constantinople a few months earlier, it was inevitable that his reaction would be similar towards the Turks. But the vital psychological response of the British political establishment was to defend the British flag, flying defiantly at Chanak. They felt it vital to resist any capitulation in the face of an Asiatic peasant army, which would involve irreparable loss of Imperial prestige. Though the British public's appetite for glory, after the blood, mud and disillusion of the fields of Flanders, had disappeared, it still flickered in the Churchillian wing of the political establishment. Furthermore those romantic Imperialists were right in the long run and the events that took place over the next few weeks here at Chanak and in Constantinople did, indeed, spell the beginning of the end of Empire. Before Chanak the British Empire stood at its greatest ever extent. Within less than thirty years it was fast disappearing, while the Ottoman Empire had gone altogether.

The Turkish army threatening Chanak now numbered over 50,000, without counting the reserves moving up all the time from the interior. The split between the British and French widened and their relationship now reached its nadir since the entente was first negotiated 20 years before. The British foreign minister Curzon had met the French premier Poincaré in Paris on the 22nd September, the day before the arrival of the Turkish cavalry in the neutral zone at Chanak.

There at the Quai d'Orsay, Curzon talked of the French having 'abandoned' the British at Chanak. Poincaré, livid with rage, demanded that Curzon withdraw his comments, though they were strictly correct, as the small French contingent had indeed been withdrawn. He shouted out torrents of abuse in the most insulting manner. Curzon – a grandee aristocrat to his fingertips – the once mighty Viceroy of India – was actually trembling and stumbled out of the room, collapsing outside into the arms of the British Ambassador.

Yet, surprisingly, the meeting was fairly successful, once the parties reconvened and apologies were exchanged. A vital seven more days were gained when it was agreed that under Harington's direction a conference should be held at Mudania – another sleepy little port on the Sea of Marmara – with an invitation to Kemal's representatives, to make the necessary arrangements for the Turks' entry into Constantinople. This was yet to be accepted by the Turkish nationalists, but meanwhile the Turks remained within the neutral zone. Throughout this period, British reinforcements were pouring into Chanak and were now in a well-entrenched position with artillery, naval support and air supremacy in the form of a small air force squadron.

This was the position when the cabinet instructed Harington to deliver an ultimatum threatening immediate war unless Mustafa Kemal withdrew from the neutral zone and to notify the Turkish commander outside Chanak that unless his troops were withdrawn, 'all the forces at my disposal will fire upon your troops'. Here at last was the crunch. On the one side, an old Empire supposedly at the height of its power and prestige, facing 'an army of Orientals'. Meanwhile, on the other, a nationalist force heady with victory after the total defeat of their ancestral enemy and the fall of Smyrna, and equally concerned about the possible loss of momentum if they voluntarily withdrew.

Harington received his instructions on the 29th September. At the same time, the Admiralty sent instructions to Admiral Brock to destroy all private shipping moored in Constantinople to prevent nationalist forces from using them to cross the Bosporus into Europe. All was in the balance and once again, Constantinople waited in dread for the denouement.

CHAPTER 14

The Village of Chehan

The Village of Chehan

he will be at the café. He is often there in the middle of the day. You will find the café next to the school just past the mosque – there – down the road." It was not quite accurate to describe Chehan as a village. It had two mosques and a permanently manned and staffed police station, larger than any of the one-street villages that abounded in the area. It had some cafés. On the other hand it was not a town. There was no public bakery, as everybody made their own bread. Some of the citizens still owned and kept sheep and perhaps a cow in their backyards, and shepherds still called to collect the sheep to take them out to pasture.

There was a little school, right next door to the main café, a tiny hole of a building, where the men sat for hours on stools and chairs on the street just outside. There they would sit, smoking narghilés and sipping one tiny coffee cup all morning. In the school in the next building, those boys paid for by their parents came and sat cross-legged in rows in front of a crusty old Hodja with a large old-fashioned turban, nodding their heads and repeating lines from the Koran in Arabic – a language none of them really understood.

Orhan's own little boy was not yet old enough for school so, instead, Rehia played with him all day long running barefoot in the street. In the house, there were servants and what could only be described as 'hangers-on' and Gulmaz only needed to supervise and organise the work and little Rehia was not burdened with household chores, other than the traditional one for elder daughters to look after the next child down.

Orhan was somewhat lazy – he spent a lot of time at the little café playing endless games of tavloo with his friends – but he was not a mean man. He did his best towards Rehia and was never cruel. In the culture from which he sprung, girls counted for nothing, and he considered that Rehia, who had been over-indulged by Omar, was far too noisy and active. She was apt to argue back to adults. If all children should be seen and not heard, it was arguable for Orhan whether little girls should even be seen.

Vahan had left Caesaria (Kayseri) in 1914 to go to University in

Stamboul and had never returned in the years since. Kayseri lay on the direct road from the coast to the village of Chehan. The morning he and Ara arrived in Kayseri, Vahan made a tour of the old Armenian quarter and went to look at the old family home, while Ara went off to find a donkey-master. Unlike Raffi, Vahan had not witnessed or personally experienced any of the traumatic events of the great massacres and deportations of 1915 that had struck his people. He walked through the old quarter where he had gone to school, attended church, and run and played in the streets with Turk and Armenian alike, and was devastated by what he saw.

Knowing what had happened did not prepare him for the reality. From a thriving community of over 10,000 people, not a single Armenian was left. He had expected to see more physical destruction. Instead, the streets were now eerily empty. One or two of the more modest houses had been re-occupied by squatters, mostly Turks uprooted from other parts of the empire preferring the smaller dwellings, while the grand houses of the wealthier merchants remained empty and abandoned.

Vahan walked slowly past the abandoned homes. Tiles were beginning to fall off roofs; windows were broken, shutters smashed, doors broken open revealing the empty rooms *bey*ond. Vahan could remember grand receptions in some of these houses, when as a boy he would come and stand with his friends in the street and watch the guests arriving; and as a shy young man, on the eve of leaving for university, he had himself come as one of those guests with his parents.

Vahan felt the brooding silence of the streets. He could see that the present townsfolk – who seven or eight years ago had shouted '*giavour asiliyor*' '*giavour*! *giavour*!' now avoided going into the empty Armenian quarter; perhaps to efface the memories of the throngs of people who had formed the backdrop to their lives a few years before. It was still hot for September. Vahan sat down on a stone bench and tried to recall his childhood. Surely it hadn't been that bad. He had never felt 'hated.' He went to the Armenian school, but played in the streets with lots of Turkish kids; his mother attended the local 'hamam' with all the other mothers, Turk and Armenian, while his father was a respected 'mukhtar' of the district, and would sit at the cafés with Turkish business acquaintances sharing a hookah.

The more he tried to remember the atmosphere of the old Ottoman days of his childhood, the more puzzled he became. There really could be only one answer – the hatred must have been orchestrated. Class envy exists in all societies, he thought, but this had been turned by thoughtless ideological academics into ethnic hatred.

Vahan gave a sigh, rose and walked back through the narrow, silent, cobbled streets to the main bazaar and back into the bustling life of a Turkish provincial town. Ara had found a donkey-master, one Achmet, prepared to accompany them to Chehan with four donkeys and with spare fodder for the two horses purchased in Marsin for the journey here.

It had taken the old women and children, deported in the early months of 1916, three days to stagger to the point just short of Chehan where they were murdered. It took Vahan's little caravan less than a day, plodding into the village in the early evening. Achmet knew of a family willing to give shelter to visitors, especially those with gold.

It was a delicate situation. Vahan felt that it might be embarrassing, even dangerous for Nouritza Arabian if they approached her first. So, in the morning, he and Ara went to the police station where Omar had been the sergeant. Nationalist unicultural fervour had not yet penetrated this little town and they were met with the unfailing politeness of the old Ottoman police. Vahan asked to be directed to the house of Orhan and Gulmaz khatun, and he was given clear directions. However as he turned to leave Ara said –

"Constable *effendi*, it would be very helpful if you could tell us if Orhan *bey* is likely to be at home."

"No sir, almost certainly he will not be."

"And where, *effendi*, would we be able to find him."

"I believe

As they came out into the sunshine Vahan raised his eyebrows at Ara and said simply,

"Why?"

"Well, my brother, I know these people better than you. Gulmaz might well be the one to have the last word – but for many reasons we must approach the husband first, because that is what would be expected. The little girl will likely reject us and the mother will seek to protect her. We have to go at the matter obliquely – first the husband, then the wife, and only right at the end the little girl."

At the café it was the young Ara who made all the running. His country accent became an asset, where Vahan's Stambouli Turkish was regarded with suspicion. But it was Vahan who ordered the bottle of raki, which went round the few customers and broke the ice. The other men sitting round were ready to follow the lead of Orhan in his response to these strangers. Orhan introduced himself immediately. Neither Vahan nor Ara mentioned the new law regarding Armenian orphans at any stage. The talk, at first lengthy with elaborate greetings and introductions, ever so slowly progressed to the business in hand. As the objective of the strangers emerged, Ara quickly established that Vahan was the little girl's blood brother. This was a relationship everybody understood and sympathised with, and slowly, as Orhan himself contemplated the matter, everyone began to come round to the logic of the situation and the proposed solution. Without making any direct reference to money,

Vahan let it be known that compensation would be offered for the years the family had cared for the little girl. The men nodded and drank up the second bottle of raki. No one mentioned the deaths or the circumstances in which this *effendi*'s little sister had come to be there. Thus the morning passed pleasantly enough.

"You must be totally crazy, husband. Do you think for one moment that I am going to give up my darling Rehia for a few pieces of silver. What are you saying, you must…"

"Calm down, wife, calm down. No one is selling the little girl. Come – come. It is her brother who has arrived. Her very own blood brother. You know this is happening all over the countryside – the orphan children who escaped the death marches are being returned to relatives far less closely related than this."

"Pig! This isn't an orphan child we are talking about – it is my baby, my Rehia, whom I have loved and cared for all her life. I can't let her go to strangers, and I …"

At this point Gulmaz broke down and began weeping. Orhan took her in his arms, saying she was still young enough to have children of her own with him. Gulmaz knew that Orhan did not care for Rehia. She also knew in her heart that just as she had been unable to have children with Omar, she was unlikely to have them ten years later with Orhan. She wept bitterly and would not be comforted, for she knew that though she would put up a fight, in the end unless she could change Orhan's mind, she would have to give in.

It was eventually decided that Vahan and Ara would be invited to come for coffee the next morning. That afternoon, Vahan at last paid a visit to the Kazim family, where he finally met Nouritza. She had already warned the Kazims of her decision to leave as soon as she could – and here was her chance. She arranged with Vahan that she would accompany him back to Bolis, whether Rehia accompanied them or not.

Everyone in the village was now fully aware of the arrival of these Stambouli strangers – Armenians – relatives of the little Rehia. Everyone in the village sympathised with Orhan. Sooner or later Rehia was going to find out about her real roots – indeed it was likely that the other children had already teased Rehia. But they were also aware of the strength of will of Gulmaz. Once little Rehia called out 'Ana! Ana!', no one knew what would happen.

The scene that next morning at the home of Orhan and Gulmaz was distressing – though in the end the person who was most distressed was probably Vahan. It is not easy to grasp fully the mind of Rehia who was now nearly seven years old. She raged and wept and clung to her 'Ana', but she was curious as well. She was not acting when she hid her head in Gulmaz's skirts, but she peeped out, clearly intrigued by Ara who was a master at making funny faces at her behind Vahan's back. She had been aware that there was some mystery in her birth, and had returned Orhan's indifference towards her with childish dislike.

Vahan made no attempt to explain Ara's presence, save to say that he was his younger bother. Gulmaz, facing the combined opposition of almost everyone crowded into the room, raised objection after objection. Who could the little Rehia talk to, she did not know a word of Armenian? But Madam, as you can see, we are all talking Turkish, came Vahan's reply. Who will give her presents, who will clothe and feed her? Then as if in desperation and speaking in real and genuine distress – "Who will love her like I do?"

At this last desperate cry, Vahan, almost in tears himself, rose and came to Gulmaz, and bowing down before her, took her hand, raised it to his lips and kissed it in a gesture of deep respect and emotion.

"Gulmaz hanum, she is my beloved sister, my mother and father's daughter. I will love her like you do all the rest of my life. There, in Stamboul, she will have not only all her family but her own natural father as well. Here all she has to sustain her is you. That is worth a lot of course – your love, madam, shines out from your eyes, but in Stamboul she will be surrounded by family – father - close friends – her brothers – her community – for all of whom she will be like a miracle sent down by Allah. She is seven. She will always remember you as her 'Ana'. Ishallah she will visit you here when she becomes a young lady. I myself will bring her. I know it is hard, but I am sure that you will give her this chance."

There was a long, a very long, silence as Vahan returned to his seat. Vicdan, who had given Rehia her first bath in this village all those years ago, moved across to hold her neighbour tightly. She whispered in her ear. Orhan looked on with wonder. He had never seen his wife listen to someone for so long without interrupting. The silence dragged on. Rehia, looking on with her huge brown eyes, had long since gone to sit with Orhan's young wife. Then at last, as the silence became deafening, Gulmaz spoke, looking down at the floor –

"*Asadour effendi*, would you please arrange to send Nouritza hanum to me later this morning. I know she is fond of Rehia, and Rehia knows her fairly well. I have things to arrange and things to say to them both." There was a short pause. "In private and without all you clumsy men around." Gulmaz glared all round her in a show of defiant bravado – though her heart was breaking. She went out of the room and into the women's quarters, without even looking at Orhan.

Orhan and Vahan quickly came to an arrangement about the compensation for all Rehia's clothes and bedding and everything else that had been done for her. It was clear enough to Vahan that Gulmaz was unlikely to get any of it, or indeed would have wanted a single penny.

Vahan never got to know what Gulmaz said to Nouritza and to little Rehia – but the very next day the little caravan moved off. Achmet had arranged for a double straw pannier to be placed across the back of one of the stronger donkeys. Rehia's bedding, and her carefully cleaned and folded clothes, went into one of the panniers, and Rehia herself balanced the load sitting in the other pannier peeping out over the edge. Nouritza sat on one of the other donkeys, Ara and Vahan on their horses, and the donkey master on the lead donkey with its tinkling bell.

The final parting between Rehia and the only mother she had ever known had been poignant. Rehia cried and clung to her mother, but Vahan could see that the true tragedy was for Gulmaz, who no longer wept, and giving Rehia one last embrace, turned away. Within an hour or so of leaving the village, Rehia started peering out curiously over the edge of the pannier. The little caravan moved all day, for five full days, in order to reach the coast at Mersin. At the end of each day a camp was set up, a fire lit by Ara, who also did the cooking, and a tent put up over Nouritza and Rehia, while the three men slept out in the open. It was all very exciting and Rehia had little time to be sad.

Vahan hadn't brought his violin, but his singing voice was an attractive high baritone, and every night after they had all eaten, he would sing lullabies and sad Armenian songs to Rehia. On the first night, emotionally and physically exhausted, Rehia had called for her 'Ana' and cried herself to sleep. But as each night passed – helping the ever-cheerful Ara prepare the food – listening with wide-open eyes to Vahan's singing – cuddling up to Nouritza, she began to recover her natural high spirits. During the day, Rehia spent most of her time looking out over the edge of her pannier, except when she was lulled to sleep. Ara would occasionally ride alongside and tell her a story.

The little party arrived at the port of Mersin without any further problems. They managed to find a berth on a Bulgarian freighter heading for Constantinople within hours of arriving, selling the horses and paying off Achmet.

Two days later, the great mosques of Constantinople – that incomparable shoreline vista – came into view, as the ship steamed up out of the Marmara to its anchorage.

CHAPTER 15

Burhan Celal

Burhan Celal had lived all his life in the city of Smyrna, the principal port of the Ottoman Empire after Constantinople itself. His father, an *effendi* in the service of the local Ottoman administration, owned a substantial two-storey house in a road running up from the Konak and the harbour to the ruined Byzantine castle perched at the top.

This the Turkish quarter was a crazy patchwork of twisting narrow streets and steps straggling up the hillside. Many of the houses, almost all wooden, had great views over the rest of the city below and the wide sweep of the bay *bey*ond.

The home in which Burhan had been brought up was large and square, surrounding an internal open patio in the middle of which was an old covered well. To one side was a side courtyard opening out onto the street in front. This was separated from the neighbour's equally large house on that side by trees and a high flowering line of bushes. At the back of the courtyard was a line of three decrepit wooden outbuildings where animals had been kept in his father's time..

The whole area had narrow twisting streets with small open spaces containing undersized trees and in a number of cases, fountains, decorated with blue and white tiles, donated in the past by some pious gentleman of means. Every so often there were modest mosques with shallow rounded domes and a small low minaret. There were fewer carriages in these streets than down in the wider streets of the Armenian, Greek and Jewish quarters. All the necessary goods, the furniture and other heavy items, were still largely carried by porters, stooped forward with thongs round their foreheads stretching back to hold the goods on their backs, which they steadied with one hand, as they trotted forward calling out "make way, make way!" They would try not to stop or slow down, allowing the momentum from the weight on their backs to carry them forward.

As the only son of a well-to-do father who was an official of the Empire, Burhan went to school at a modern establishment at the bottom of the hill near the bazaar. Like so many Ottoman citizens, whatever their race or their religion, Burhan and his father had had to face the difficult questions hovering over the Empire at the end of the nineteenth century. Above all, what was the identity or underlying principle of this Empire of which they were all part?

If the Ottoman Empire was not a state whose identity was purely Moslem – then what was it? Clearly it was not a Turkish national state.

Even after the loss of many of its European possessions by the start of the twentieth century, the Turks still constituted barely thirty per cent of the total. Could it perhaps be defined as a geographic entity uniting many lands and regions, all far better off if organised as a single state? The peoples of the empire, from the Arabs in the south, through many races and religions, to the Macedonians in the west, were so intertwined that a single empire managing them all made obvious social and economic sense. If this was indeed to be the basis for the state, then loyalty to a five hundred year old dynasty with a great historic past made as much sense as anything else.

But while very rational it was not very inspiring. Men will die for their religion. They will also die for their nation, for the defense of their tribe. But apply reason, and most sensible people would prefer not to die at all.

Burhan was destined to become a civil servant himself and when he was twenty, only a year into the twentieth century, he was sent to Constantinople to stay with relatives and study law – not Koranic law but modern jurisprudence. He had long since given up any deep faith.

Burhan's studies and his life in Constantinople came to an abrupt end after only three years, on the news of the death of his father. Accordingly, he was already back in Smyrna and married to a girl carefully chosen by his mother when the revolution of 1908 broke out. Like most Turks of his age and background, he considered the decision of the Ittihad leaders to join the war as an ally of Imperial Germany a terrible mistake, but he never wavered in his support for the government. At the age of 35 on the outbreak of war, he was, of course, eligible for military service, but as an official in the administration of the Smyrna province he was exempt, and so during the war he continued to serve under the excellent original Ottoman Governor - Rahmi *Bey* – who had fortunately not been replaced by the Ittihad.

Burhan had never had much to do with the non-Turkish people of the city. All of them, Greeks, Armenians, Jews and Kurds all spoke Turkish and all considered themselves to be Ottoman citizens. Unlike the many Greek Orthodox villages in the interior, where the inhabitants did not speak or know the Greek language at all, those of Smyrna spoke good Greek. However, despite all the nationalist fervour and propaganda directed at them from Athens, hardly a single Greek from Smyrna had ever had the slightest desire to leave the city or the empire to go to the small Greek kingdom on the other side of the Aegean. If the poor thought at all of emigrating, it would have been across the Atlantic, not just across the Aegean.

Like everyone in Smyrna, Burhan went to Greek grocers, he bought his bread as he made his way home from a Jewish baker, he expected the policeman on the corner to be a Turk, he expected the clerk who served him behind the counter at the Bank to be an Armenian, he employed a Kurd to carry home goods he had purchased. His weekend lasted from Friday prayers, through the Jewish Sabbath to the end of the Christian Sunday.

Then, as Burhan was approaching 40 years-old, came the total defeat of the Ottomans and the end of the war. That was bad enough, but then within a year came the single most important event affecting the future of Burhan and everyone else throughout the old Ottoman world, effects which would reverberate throughout the whole of the 20th century. The Greeks of Athens were invited to invade and take over control of Burhan's home town – Smyrna. Led by British destroyers the Greeks landed in 1919 and a Greek governor was installed in the Konak.

Burhan lost his job.

In the end there was never any question of the Greeks setting up another Empire – a new Byzantine empire perhaps - with room for many different people and religions. All they were after in Athens was a Greater Greece. Having lost his job, Burhan felt that overnight he had become a second-class citizen, even worse off than his Greek neighbour had been under the non-nationalist Ottomans. Mehmed VI, the impotent Sultan still under British control in Constantinople, wept without stopping for over an hour when he heard the news. He was right to do so, as the Greek occupation spelt the end of his dynasty one way or another, whichever of the two competing nationalities won the now inevitable war.

Burhan, who had always loved writing, drifted into writing articles for the only Turkish language newspaper left in the city, and he became one of their most active reporters. He was an open supporter of the nationalists in Ankara, but he was never persecuted in any way by what was, by and large, an honest and fairly efficient Greek administration. Month by month he lost all respect for the Ottomans, save for a residue of nostalgic regret, as they became increasingly irrelevant to political developments.

When on September 9th the Turkish army entered Smyrna, Burhan was delirious with excitement. Even though the newspapers had closed down, he was out in the streets making notes on everything he was seeing.

It was on the evening of Tuesday the 12th September that Burhan was out again in the streets. His excitement was intense – his whole body thrilled to the dramatic events being played out in his city. He had experienced nothing like it any time before in his life, and he knew he was going to write a great article for some newspaper. Burhan was not usually insensitive, he was not in any way sadistic, he did not hate anyone enough to wish them ill, he had no thoughtless religious fanaticism; so why was it, as he wandered through the Armenian quarter, that he did not recoil from all the haphazard killing, looting and rape? What was it about journalism that made his eyes alight with animation as his pencil jotted down snippets of impressions as he wandered through the increasingly bloody streets, rather than looking away in revulsion?

He was in this state of euphoric curiosity and overwhelming tension when he passed the house of Madame Derounian, where Olga and Selim had been living. He was present and saw Haik and Paramaz emerge. He actually nodded at them as they came out. However there appeared to be no one else on the street, so he stopped and watched as Haik had run forward to grab the empty cart standing upright further up the street. Of course he had no idea that this was in order to take the wounded Selim to the hospital. He saw the three Turkish soldiers come out of the house carrying looted property, and he saw them grab at their rifles as they spotted Haik. He witnessed the unknown Paramaz pull out his revolver and aim three shots up the street and then watched as the unknown young man died and the equally unknown Paramaz run up and start rifling the body, even offering Burhan himself some coins.

Burhan remained in a state of intense physical excitement. Jotting down this event, he moved on and continued to survey the complete breakdown of any law and order in the Armenian quarter and the idle killing and rape going on all around him. It was a terrible night, and Burhan was trying to take it all in when he became aware of the great fire starting in the streets behind him. He hurriedly began retracing his steps to get back to the Turkish quarter and found himself back on the street where he had earlier witnessed the killing of the unknown young man. The three soldiers were still there with their cart now piled high with carpets and clothes and other items clearly part of their loot. The huge fire was now not many metres away, shielded at the moment by the houses on the other side of the street. Burhan, who could now see the way out at the other end of the street to the south, hesitated for a moment, and it was at that moment that Olga had run out of the house, the same house from which the two young men had previously emerged.

Burhan's senses were aflame – there was real danger present – only a few moments separated them from being trapped by the flames. Death was staring at them all as the young soldier, having struck the girl so hard she had fallen down unconscious at his feet, pulled out his rifle in order to finish off this Armenian girl, who was gabbling incoherently about a Turkish officer. At this point with only seconds left, Burhan at last acted. Aware that even he was in danger from the inflamed soldiers, he shouted out the only words he could think of which established him as an ally and not another Armenian. Calling out "she will serve me tonight brothers," he lifted up the unconscious young girl and ran off with her over his shoulder, just in front of the approaching flames. He did not take any notice of what happened to the three soldiers as they trundled away with their full cart.

Afterwards, Burhan never sought to excuse himself for his actions when, gasping for breath, he finally got home and threw the still half-conscious girl onto the straw in his decrepit old shed at the back of the house. The passions in the streets, the drama, the haphazard killings, the real danger of death all overwhelmed his basic decency. Crouching beside her, he pulled up the already torn and crumpled dress. He dragged off the underwear and then had his will quickly and without any opposition. When it was over, he stumbled out, locking the barn door behind him, and into his own bedroom.

The following day, with the fire raging all day in the city below, and the huge billowing smoke and flames rising into the sky, with his wife - Nefise and his daughters staring out of the window all day, wide-eyed with wonder and anxiety, Burhan sat at his desk. He found that he was unable to write a single word of the famous article about the events of the previous day, that he'd thought would make his worldwide reputation. His notes were all intact, the words were all there, but he could not set down a word. From being a reporter of events, he had become part of the event itself. What had he done? He was a respectable middle-aged man; he had a wife and three daughters, though in a sense all that was irrelevant. His action was despicable whatever his circumstances and regardless of his age. He brooded all day. There was no question of fear – no one would ever reproach him even if he shouted it out from the rooftops – but he remained knotted up with guilt.

When night fell, he waited until it was dark and then went to the kitchen and got a pitcher of water and a plate of bread and olives. He walked to the shed and opened the door, but he lacked the courage to go inside. He knelt and put the pitcher and the plate just inside the door, shut it but left it unlocked, and hurried away.

Burhan did not sleep the whole night. He was at the window at dawn when he saw the dishevelled figure of Olga slip out of the shed and into the street and away. He breathed a sigh of relief – it was over.

But not quite!

Burhan's eldest daughter, an active and lively eight year-old, was playing with her friends a few days later at the edge of the area near the burnt-out former Armenian quarter, when she stumbled and fell into some cinders, still smouldering a day or two after the fire had died down. Screaming with pain she was brought back to the house by a neighbour. Burhan was sitting at his desk, still unable to put pen to paper or to get Tuesday night's events out of his mind. He took her into his arms but saw, at once, that she needed more than a kiss to make it better. He was not going to leave it to anyone else to take her down to the hospital. With the whole Greek, Armenian and European quarters burnt to the ground, the Imperial Ottoman Hospital at the bottom of the hill was the only place where doctors were still working and where wounds or burns could be treated. So with his daughter in his arms, he hurried down the hill.

Burhan, well-off and fairly well-connected, did not have to wait long before his daughter was taken in and her hand and arms treated. Burhan sat and waited for several hours and there, in all that coming and going, in all the confusion and noise of the hospital, he saw Olga, working away grimly and with dedication. He recognised her at once, even in the crisp white uniform. He had no fear, but his guilt, which had never left him, redoubled and became unbearable.

He made a discreet enquiry and discovered her name. He then asked the receptionist whether, if he wrote to a nurse at the hospital to thank her for her help, it would be delivered to her personally. He was told firmly that it would be if she was still with them.

Burhan took his daughter home in the evening once she had been treated and seemed to have recovered. He then spent two whole weeks pondering on the letter he intended to send – anonymously of course – to this woman. This was to be in lieu of the famous article that would never now be written. He intended to set out all that had happened on that terrible day and would frankly confess his shame at how the day had ended. It took him ten days of careful thought to cover everything he had seen and every shabby act that had taken place. The shooting of the young man on the street; the removal of the money belt from the dead body; the things he saw later on the Rue des Franques; the atmosphere in the town; his return to that first street once the fire started; and finally the shame of what had occurred when he returned home.

The letter was a masterpiece of his journalistic art – it was undoubtedly one of the best articles he had ever written. It would, however, be seen by only one person. It was only after the letter had been written, addressed to N. (which he imagined was short for nurse) Avakian, and posted to the Imperial Ottoman Hospital that he was able at last to come again to his wife's bedroom.

CHAPTER 16

The Androvs Consider

The defeat of the Greeks and the burning of Smyrna not only had many consequences that would influence the history of the region over the coming century, but also several minor ones immediately affecting many people at the time. One of these was the atmosphere of puritan reaction against the gaiety and joy of the last few years, which led to the closure of many of the night-clubs and dance halls. The disappearance of almost all the French and Italian military and the allied naval personnel, now confined to their ships, meant that there were fewer people coming to the entertainment centres of Pera.

This, in turn affected the large Russian émigré population. General Wrangel and the remnants of his White Russian army had already departed to various adventures in the Balkans and elsewhere. However, a fairly large Russian civilian element had remained, drifting into employment as musicians, waiters and waitresses, cooks and washers-up serving the entertainment world of Pera, which had been thriving over the previous three years. During most of the British occupation, Constantinople was probably the liveliest of the capital cities of Europe.

Now its nemesis, in the form of an avenging army of Anatolian peasants, was looming. If the army acted as it had in Smyrna there would be a bloodbath. No one wanted to go dancing anymore as the city waited anxiously. The Russian restaurants, the Russian orchestras, the Russian night-clubs and the Russian brothels all began to close. Even the revered Pera Palace Hotel – the centre for Allied officers who had passed through the city on tours of duty – had to start retrenching as the elite local merchants began staying away and visitors dried up. In the middle of the uncertainty and anxiety affecting the Avakians, Count Nicolai Androv, Sima's Russian fiancée, lost his job as a violinist in the Hotel's saloon orchestra. Overnight, the only income coming in to the Androv household was the small amount that 16 year-old Alexei, was bringing in from his work in Karekin's office. His mother, the Countess Natalya Androvna still had a few of her jewels, the carefully saved gold coins and the valuable Rublev icon – but the future looked bleak.

Nicolai knew that Sima, the eldest daughter of one of the major Armenian merchants in the city, had taken an unconventional step in allying herself with him. He was aware that from the point of view of the large Armenian trading community he was only a penniless, now nationless, Russian aristocrat with no prospects of any kind. Karekin's offer the year before of a junior post – an apprenticeship – for Alexei, who was only 15, had been a gesture of support for Sima's choice, but as the political situation began to shift, so did the position of the Androvs. Nicolai had not spent these last two years just playing the violin and basking in the warmth of a budding romantic attachment. He had also managed to get Nansen passports for all the family. But the moment of reckoning over the future of his mother and young brother, both his responsibility, was now approaching as fast as the oncoming Turkish army.

Karekin was a man who had always surprised his friends and his business acquaintances by his unusual views. In particular they all looked askance at the way he had chosen to bring up his daughters, all of whom had as full an education as any boy of the city. But when it had come to the final test of his liberal cross-cultural opinions, he had been unable to accept the possibility that one of his daughters might marry a young Turk. While he had not directly opposed the relationship – that was not his style – he had ignored it and left it to Armineh. Olga had been left in no doubt of her father's inner opposition.

In reaction to the realisation of his own failure to live up fully to his own ideals, he had fallen over backwards in accepting Sima's decision to attach herself to the perhaps even more unsuitable Nicolai. Karekin pondered the matter philosophically. His different attitude to the two suitors of his daughters had certainly not arisen as a result of his opinion on the respective characters of Sima and Olga. He knew that he might have started off trusting Sima's maturity and intellectual capacity more than Olga's, but he had been aware that Olga had grown. Why, then, had he accepted the penniless Nicolai and rejected Selim? Was it in the character rof the two young men? No way, as he had come to like both men. Well – religion? But that was absurd as he did not believe in any religion.

Karekin never fully worked it out for himself; but he had an inkling. The Ottoman ideal was collapsing, and all round him the proponents of exclusive one-nation states were each claiming that their particular people could not possibly live with their neighbours within the same state. He sensed that it was all artificial – deliberate hatred for each other created by clever academics, historians and political philosophers, and then taken up by unscrupulous politicians.

Karekin shuddered, because as he tried to decide why there had been this great difference in his attitude to his two possible sons-in-law, it became clear to him that he too must have been affected by the deliberate espousal of ethnic hatred spewed out by the Department of the Interior led by the venal Talaat, and which had resulted in the great catastrophe of 1915. If he, a well-educated and sophisticated citizen could be so affected, what hope was there for the simple villagers of the interior. In any event it was now too late. Selim was dead!

On the day that Nicolai received his notice and his last weeks wages, whilst on his way home from the Pera Palace to the Patakis house in Stamboul, he had called in at a small Russian-owned bar and restaurant tucked away on a side street leading down to the Galata bridge. Here, countesses of the Imperial Court washed up dishes in the kitchen, and the cook had previously worked for years in the Imperial Palace at Yalta. The waitresses were no less distinguished. Not so long ago, one might have seen a Russian customer rise from his table and stoop and kiss the hand of a Princess who was serving him.

Now, however, the place was empty, but for Nicolai himself, and a sailor from the merchant marine sleeping at a corner table over an unfinished vodka. The staff gathered round Nicolai at the bar staring at the empty tables with anxious eyes.

"What do you think is going to happen, Nicolai – can we survive here?"

"I don't know, Countess, I really don't know. However, I can tell you that I have just been given notice. Today was the last day that I will play at the Pera Palace, and unless I can find a new post, I won't be able to afford dropping in here anymore."

"Oh no Nicolai – I'm so sorry – so sorry," came a chorus of voices from all around followed by a short silence as they all contemplated the fact that, as customers like Nicolai dried up, their employer was unlikely to be able to carry on for much longer, and that they too would shortly to be out of a job.

"We'll simply have to go," said the cook. "There is not going to be any work round here for Russians, even if we are allowed to survive when the city falls. If we stay, the chances are that we are either going to have our throats cut, or we will be left on some seashore waiting to board ships to take us away, destitute and without anything to call our own. Look at what has just happened in Smyrna. This is their ideal moment to get rid of the whole non-Turkish population in one fell swoop – Greek, Jew, Armenian, Russian – the lot."

Nicolai said nothing but he felt that Dimitri's words made sense. Smyrna was a clear example of what could happen here. He sat for a few minutes more, looking at the worried and, in some cases, terrified eyes of the staff. He had already heard stories going the rounds of the bars. It did not really matter whether there was even the slightest element of truth in it or not. It was symptomatic of the feverish atmosphere in the city. Here lay a city of a mil*lion* people over half of whom were waiting in dread for what was going to happen next.

Nicolai got home before dark and immediately started talking things over with his mother.

"You must get away from Constantinople. We don't belong here mother. Why should we stay and suffer the consequences that may be visited on these people? It is only an accident that we are here in the first place."

"Yes, Nicolai I agree. We can go to Vienna, and from there possibly to the Veneto. My mother had three daughters, me and my two sisters. One was the Countess Berchtold – you know, I've told you about her, the wife of the former Austrian Foreign Minister at the time of the outbreak of the War. I am not sure whether she has had any children, but I know she is alive and is still in Vienna. We have been in contact in the last two years. Then my other sister, also obviously your other Aunt, the Contessa Maggi, was married to an Italian Conte who had an estate in the Veneto. They certainly do not have any children."

"Mother, we could send your Viennese relatives a telegram. It shouldn't be too expensive to take the train. We will only need to sell one of your pieces to give you plenty of leeway."

Nicolai was thinking ahead fast - considering all possibilities – when Natalya quietly said –

"And what about Miss Sima, Nicolai?"

There was a long silence. In all his worries during the day about what was necessary for his mother and brother after he had lost his job, Nikolai realised that he had not beenconsidering the position of the woman he loved. Nicolai reflected how during the most tragic of circumstances, when Sima first heard of the death of her only brother, her first thought had nevertheless been of him – her lover. Yet, faced with his own problem, he had put their future life together to one side, while he resolved the question of his mother's safety. Now his mother's gentle reminder brought him up sharply.

"Mother, mother, my mamushka, I thought you understood from the start that I was only talking about you and Alexei."

"But Nicolai...."

"No, mama, there are many reasons why I cannot accompany you. First I cannot impose myself on your relatives' charity – a grown man without any work or income – until you have yourself been welcomed. The position is quite different for you and Alexei."

"Come, family sentiment and obligations do not depend on the age of the...."

"No, mama, you don't understand, the problem lies in me, not my uncles. In any case, I can't abandon Sima – she is to all intents and purposes my fiancée – and there really is no way that Karekin would allow her to accompany me to Vienna or anywhere else, even if we got married quickly. And frankly mama, I wouldn't blame him."

"So?"

"So, mother, I must remain here to face the future with Sima – and you and Alexei will...."

At this point, his cheerful brother rushed into the room; grabbing his mother round her still slender waist, he kissed her full on the lips; then turned and hugged his brother kissing him on both cheeks. He threw his fez at the hat stand, missing it completely. He then collapsed onto the chair with a great beaming smile on his face.

"Well – why the long faces – what's going on?"

Both Nicolai and the Countess suddenly realised that in all their discussions about the future, they had failed to think of Alexei's position. He had been working for Karekin for over a year, ever since the departure of Haik and Paramaz to Smyrna. Karekin had been good to him and it had been a help for the Androv family all round. Quite apart from the fact that they had not thought for a moment of Alexei's possible feelings on the matter – he was, after all, 16 – they had ignored any obligations he might have towards Karekin.

Since coming into contact with the Avakians, the Androvs had fallen into the habit of discussing matters together rather more fully than they had done before. This was increased by Alexei's own growing self-confidence, if not actual maturity, as he grew from a naïve 14 year-old into a lively 16. Now both Nicolai and his mother talked at once, explaining the impact of Nicolai's loss of his job, and their fears about the anticipated arrival of the Turkish nationalist army.

Alexei's own feelings about the Avakian office and his work there had become complicated over the last few days. He had been very fond of Haik and the news of his death had cast a gloom over the whole office, even though once he had returned to work, Karekin had displayed no outward sign of grief before his staff. Meanwhile, Paramaz had returned to the office to take over his former duties. Alexei had long since forgotten the dramatic confrontation between Haik and Paramaz, but the return of Paramaz brought it all back. He recalled the fear in Haik's eyes at the sight of the knife and the burning hatred in Paramaz's eyes as his clumsily attempted sexual assault on Alexei was thwarted. Nevertheless, like everyone else, he sensed a subtle change in the young man. He looked ill and was obviously not sleeping well. Within a day of Paramaz's return, Karekin had taken Alexei off his packing and checking duties, and brought him into the inner office where it became clear that he wanted him to take over Haik's letter writing, filing and general office work. Alexei's French was excellent and his written English was improving the whole time. Two years in Bolis had already given him that Bolsetsi gift of switching between languages as appropriate.

Meanwhile, Alexei saw other young émigrés of his class and background without work or hope of a better future, driving taxis, carrying loads or, even worse, hovering on the edges of the sex trade. He was very grateful to Karekin, whom he no longer feared. Though a cheerful extrovert, Alexei was also sensitive to the feelings of others, and he was aware, without quite understanding it, of Karekin's increasing dependence on his own presence in the office as an antidote to the sorrow caused by the loss of his only son.

Alexei's grin faded as Nicolai began to explain exactly what he and the Countess had been discussing and the plans they were considering. Nicolai stumbled to an end and Alexei immediately said–

"Very well, my brother, I hear you, but Nicolai what about Miss Sima. What are you proposing? Just to leave?"

Nicolai looked at his young brother and thought to himself – 'My God, my light-hearted, thoughtless, young brother has grown up without my realising it'.

It seemed he had two responsibilities – one to do his best for his mother and his dependent brother – and the other to look after the woman he loved. It was also clear to him that the Ottoman-born Greeks, Armenians and Jews of the city had become fearful, not only of a possible massacre when the Kemalist army arrived in the city, but of the near certainty of wholesale forced emigration, as had happened in Smyrna. If Ottoman citizens considered themselves to be at risk, how much more certain was it that the Russian refugees from Sevastopol, without any rights of residence, would suffer an even worse fate. This was the moment for the Androvs to leave and seek out their relatives before there was any chance of a forced exodus, in murderous conditions.

But what about Sima? He was not married to her and there was no way she could leave with him if he left – Karekin would not allow it, and it would be dishonourable of him even to suggest it. So he had already decided that he would have to stay whatever his mother and Alexei did. But doing what? After the short silence which had greeted Alexei's comment, Nicolai finally said –

"You are right – I myself will not be able to join you for some time until things are more settled here, and mother is aware of that."

"And what, brother, are you proposing to do? Come crawling into the Avakian firm?"

"Oh, Alexei please – my love – my brother – we are not competing. I am trying to do my best for everyone."

Alexei looked away for a moment then turned and smiled at Nicolai – "I'm sorry, Nicolai, I am truly sorry – please continue."

"As it happens the thought had crossed my mind that Mr Avakian might offer me a job when he hears of our dilemma, but I couldn't bear the thought of it. It was one thing for you, Alexei, to work for him – quite another for me, the fiancée of his daughter – completely dishonourable."

"Oh I understand you completely," said Alexei

"Well, I don't," snapped Natalya, "It's nothing but male pride. Here in Constantinople the culture is heavily family-oriented. It is absolutely normal – indeed to be expected – that sons follow in their father's footsteps and sons-in-law move naturally into their in-laws businesses. Look, Nicolai, think – suppose you had married the daughter of Count Voroshin – you remember him, our neighbour on the other side of the river. You wouldn't have thought twice, would you, of working for him on his estate."

"That would have been quite different. It would not have been a matter of a weekly salary."

"Well, you are no longer in a position to have such scruples. You can't go on playing in second-rate orchestras all your life – not if you want to get married and have a family. I'm right, Alexei, am I not?"

"I'm afraid you are, mother. I'm sorry, Nicolai – but mother is right."

There was a short silence before Alexei stood up. Putting on a smile to soften what, he was about to say, he said firmly –

"Mama, Nicolai, I am sorry if this makes things more difficult for you, but I cannot just cut and run and abandon the Avakians because things might be getting difficult for them. I understand what you are saying but I just can't run away. I can see what you are thinking but I simply can't walk out on them when they might be facing another massacre."

Nicolai and the Countess now joined forces, while Alexei stood obstinately by his decision repeating that, as he was now 16, he was entitled to make his own decision. Finally, Nicolai came out with an argument that swung the case against himself.

"But Alexei," he said "mother has to go, and one of us has to go with her."

At this point Alexei hesitated for the first time. But now the Countess turned on Nicolai.

"Come – that's nonsense. Complete nonsense. I can see that it would make things easier if I left for the moment and joined my sister in Vienna or my other sister in Italy – but needing to be 'looked after' that's rubbish."

It only remained for the details to be worked out. The Countess would leave for Vienna as soon as possible while Nicolai and Alexei would remain and take their chances for the moment with the arriving Turkish army. Once the situation was clearer, once Sima and Nicolai were able to travel together, and assuming nothing terrible happened, the family would hopefully be reunited. Meanwhile the Countess would be able to look out for any prospects for Nicolai in the west.

Accordingly the very next day two telegrams went out – one to the

Countess Berchtold in Vienna and the other to the Contessa Maggi at an address in the Veneto. Once the decision had been made, there was no need for any further delay. The closer the moment came for the arrival of the victorious Turkish army, the more difficult it might be to get reservations on the Orient Express.

Within a further day a telegram arrived back from the Countess Berchtold, which read –

"Situation here in Vienna still not good – but you are of course welcome. Please send date and time of arrival. Will meet you at the station."

Yet another jewel was now sold and a First Class seat was reserved for her on the train. She was due to leave on the mid-morning train on the 2nd October.

CHAPTER 17

Mikael and Elena

The whole town of Piraeus appeared to be in deep mourning as Mikael and Elena stepped off the launch that had carried them from the Italian Navy frigate lying at anchor outside the port, and which had brought them away from the horrors of the dying city of Smyrna. Almost all the ramshackle buildings surrounding the port had black drapes hanging from windows. Any flags flying were at half-mast. Many of the restaurants were closed and those few that were open had no musicians, no dancing, no joyous groups raising toasts with glasses of ouzo.

There were scarcely any difficulties as Mikael, Elena and the two children – Andreas and Anya – clambered onto the quayside. Greece had made it clear that she was prepared to accept every human being who was a refugee from the new Turkey being born on the other side of the Aegean, regardless of race or religion. The Greek nation state was redeeming itself by a new tolerance born of adversity.

Mikael imagined, as he stepped onto Greek soil for the first time, that he was about to witness the heart of classical Greece; a modern westernised capital, a people looking back to the glories of the Parthenon and the Periclean golden age. Instead, he was taken aback by the provincial aspect of the life he saw around him. Athens would surely be different, he thought, but it was not.

During those first few days, as he and Elena tried to work out what they were going to do, Mikael saw that his ideas of the Kingdom of Greece as the heir to the glorious classical past, was romantic nonsense. It was Byzantium which was at the heart of modern Greek culture, not classical Athens. Mikael had always referred to the city in which he was born as 'Bolis' – the Armenian version of the Greek 'Polis' meaning 'the city'. What he had not realised was that the Greeks of old Greece also referred to Constantinople as 'Polis'. There were innumerable cities in Greece but only one of all these towns was referred to as 'Polis'. If you said in Piraeus – I am going to Polis – you meant Constantinople.

Mikael still had some of his precious gold coins, and even Elena had managed to save a few valuables as she had hurriedly packed her case in Smyrna. This would give them some weeks grace to decide what to do. They managed to find some modest lodgings in Athens, just ahead of the desperate and mainly penniless refugees pouring in from Smyrna and the Ionian coast.

Mikael and Elena had found comfort in each other's arms – but if ever there was a marriage of convenience, this was it. Mikael knew he did not have the same feelings for Elena as he had had for Olga Avakian. It was certainly not a matter of physical beauty or sexual attraction. Battle-hardened soldier as he was – he had been serving in some army or another, starting with the Reds in the Russian Civil War, since 1917 – he had never had a problem satisfying his sexual needs. In many ways, he had more in common with Elena than with the *haut bourgeois* Avakians. Was it, he wondered, because Olga had rejected him while Elena had accepted him too willingly? Did he perversely hanker after Olga, because he could never have her?

Elena, on the other hand, had never known what it was to 'love' a man. She had felt affection for the father of her two children, but it had never really amounted to more than that. The days of intimacy in the bedroom over those few days she had lived with Mikael in Smyrna had been satisfactory enough, but no more than her former life in an arranged marriage.

Yet here they were, inextricably thrown together, forced by the turbulent political situation to sink or swim together; Elena, because she needed someone to help her, Mikael, for the more subtle reason that by helping her and taking responsibility for her children, he was making up for the lack of direction in his own life.

Mikael remained an Ottoman citizen. He still had his old passport and 'nufus' – papers carefully retained through all the vicissitudes of the last two years. On top of that, his mother and sister were still living in Makrikoy in Constantinople so far as he knew. But how was he to get back – and indeed would he be allowed back? Rumours of what was happening in and around the city were raging in the Greek capital.

Kemal's Anatolian army was already at the Straits staring at the British garrison in Chanak, and waiting patiently on the Asian side to enter – or to storm – the city itself. People talked fearfully of another massacre, of a burning and sacking next to which the drama of Smyrna would pale into insignificance.

Mikael wandered the streets. In the gloomy atmosphere in Athens, he found people friendlier than might have been the case normally and ready to speak freely to strangers in the cafés. In the course of his years in the Greek army, Mikael had lost his 'Polis' accent and the Athenians did not recognise him as a 'yoghurt-baptised' one – the pejorative term they were already using to refer to the Ionians fleeing from the Ottoman Empire. He listened to the views freely expressed around him, but in the end simply became more muddled. Forthright and decisive in the past, now he dithered.

There were large numbers of people sleeping on the streets. Whole families, rescued by the Jennings fleet, were completely destitute, sleeping in the ruins of the Acropolis or any building which might be empty. The National Opera house was filled with families taking over the boxes – the orchestra stalls – the grand stairs. Makeshift camps sprang up all round the town, and winter was yet to come.

As September began to draw to an end, a revolution broke out, led by Mikael's old commander, Colonel Plastiras of the 42nd Evzones, and the Venizelists swung back into power on the back of a military revolt. Constantine formally abdicated on the 27th September and was hurried into exile. Venizelos himself was despatched at speed as Ambassador to Great Britain. Mikael thus found himself in the middle of his second revolution. But this was nothing like the events six years ago in Rostov at the start of the Russian Civil war. No one had a good word left for 'Tino' as he fled, and there was no fighting or opposition in the streets, although, in good Greek style, there was plenty of noisy argument, sometimes ending in fisticuffs.

None of this affected Mikael's position directly. He could see that he had no future in Athens; there was no work – no prospects. Only a few weeks ago, he had been a respected senior sergeant. Now, the Greek government could no longer even afford to pay its basic civil servants; but the railways were still running.

The branch of the Simplon-Orient express that ran down to Athens was still operating. This line ran on from Salonika through Adrianople and Eastern Thrace on to Constantinople. Eastern Thrace was still held by the Greek army up against the Chatalja lines manned by Harington's forces. Kemal and his nationalist army was now fully in control of the Asian side of the Straits. Harington's small but significant British forces held Constantinople itself, the European side of the Bosporus, with the small garrison of Chanak on the Asian side. The large and powerful

allied fleet still patrolled the straits, preventing the Turkish nationalists from crossing. Then finally, there was the unbeaten remnant of the
Greek army in Thrace, on the other side of the British.

This extraordinary turmoil had not prevented the administrators of
the Compagnie Internationale des Wagons-lits et des Grands Express
Européenes from doggedly continuing to run their trains from Athens
northwards and from Sofia eastwards into the Imperial Ottoman capital. Thousands of peasants were trudging hopelessly away from their
homes to heaven knows where, but the elite bourgeoisie of Europe still
wanted to travel. The trains ran, but they had to go through many more
checkpoints.

After days of deliberation, Mikael at last made up his mind. He decided to go back to Constantinople. First, he ascertained that he could
buy the necessary tickets travelling third class and then hurried back
and confronted Elena in their tiny rooms.

"Elena, my love, will you marry me?"

It was not the most romantic of proposals. The abruptness of the
sudden question and the rather brusque tone of Mikael's voice seemed
to belie the words, but then Elena had long since realised that she could
not expect 'tenderness' from Mikael.

"What – what are you saying?"

"It's clear enough isn't it. I am asking you to marry me."

"But Mikael, why now? What's the hurry?"

"Elena – you have two children who are entirely dependent upon
you. I am already a raddled 30 year-old. We need to hold on to each
other in a world which is falling apart around us. My suggestion is quite
clear. I think we need to get married officially."

Elena shook her head. Her hesitation was not, as Mikael had thought,
because she hankered after a love affair. She had fled first in fear and
terror from Odessa to Crimea; then from Sevastopol. Finally she had
had to flee in dread and horror from Smyrna to Athens. She longed for
security, for a feeling of safety, but there was something about Mikael's
manner that disturbed her. She had come to understand his reserved,
proud and prickly character, but couldn't he just once say that he loved
her?

"Mikael – it's impossible. I am a married woman and I don't know
whether my husband is still alive or not."

"Oh, that's ridiculous. You can't go through the rest of your life wondering whether Gianni is still alive or not. Look, my dear, I am determined to get back to Bolis. My mother and sister are still there and it
is my home town. Athens holds nothing for either of us. With all the
refugees pouring in, I could never find work. How are we going to live
here? Neither one of us are Greek citizens – you are completely stateless and I am an Ottoman subject. Once in Bolis we have a home, we

have help with the children and I have good prospects for work. I have the legal right to return, but in case of any difficulty at the frontiers and checkpoints, you must be my legal wife. Oh Elena, you do see that, don't you?"

The more Mikael talked the more he was sure of his position. There was a short silence – then Elena said –

"Mikael – I can't do it. You know that for both of us, there is no marriage without a church ceremony, and there is no way that I could take the oath before God that there is nothing preventing us from getting married."

"But – it is the state's marriage certificate we need – not the good Lord's sanction."

Even as he said these eminently sensible words, Mikael, who was himself a devout believer, knew that Elena was right. A church marriage was the only real option open to them and it was impossible.

Nevertheless, he was not going to give up. There was no certainty about what was going to happen or what lay between him in Athens and his goal on the landline to Constantinople. Surely, if the worst came to worst, they would probably be able to walk across whatever frontier might exist and then into the city. Once there, he knew he would be able to manage. Papers? Come, all he needed to say was that the marriage documents had been lost. He knew the Ottoman world backwards – he would manage. But was the world they would be returning to still Ottoman?

"Very well, Elena, if necessary we will claim we are man and wife and that our papers have been lost. As my wife, you are also an Ottoman citizen. But whatever happens we must leave – you do see that."

"Yes Mikael, yes. I am in your hands as indeed I have been since you walked back into my life – my God, was it only three weeks ago? I will get the children ready and prepared for yet another flight. But you must give us a few more days."

"I will need that in any case to get the tickets. Oh Elena, I know this is the right decision for us. You are brave. I love …." And with this last remark unfinished, Mikael and Elena kissed – affectionately and lingeringly. That night they made love for the first time since arriving in Athens, a gentle love in stark contrast to the passionate and violent love of their days in Smyrna.

CHAPTER 18

Harry

Back in Constantinople events were moving fast. In the great game played out between London and Constantinople, Athens and Ankara, Harington and his political masters, and the last Ottoman Sultan and Mustapha Kemal Pasha, every day, every hour brought some new twist, some new possibility.

Yet in the midst of all the turmoil, the wheels of Whitehall bureaucracy continued to turn. The day after Harry returned with Olga from Smyrna, he received notice that his court-martial was to be held on *the Iron Duke*. It had been decided that the case would be heard by a senior officer, sent out from London for the sole purpose of presiding at the hearing, aided by two officers that he would himself appoint from the junior officers available on the station.

When asked by telegram, Harry had replied that he did not feel the necessity for legal representation. He received a further notification that a prosecuting counsel would be arriving with the senior officer appointed to hear the case. This had not changed Harry's mind.

Even with the work he had done with Jennings in Smyrna – an effort he felt was truly meaningful – Harry had not entirely forgotten the crisis looming in his own life. His conscience was clear. The more he examined his decisions, the less he worried about the judgement he had made at the time.

Despite these thoughts, there was inevitably something daunting about the legal proceedings themselves. The cold calculating manner in which the things he had done would be viewed when examined in a public forum, would cause anxiety in the staunchest and coolest of men. Decisions, which may have looked simple to Harry at the time, could easily be made to appear irrational, muddled, perhaps even mutinous under scrutiny.

His worries were aggravated by the fact that he had kept the whole matter to himself. His colleagues in the East Mediterranean station knew of the impending trial, but Harry had not wanted to strain their loyalty by discussing the matter with them. This was almost certainly an error of pride on Harry's part, as his fellow officers would have welcomed the chance to support him.

As a responsible British officer, it never crossed his mind to mention any of this to the Avakians. What did it have to do with them? He only allowed himself emotional release in a long letter written to his father after he had been suspended, before setting off for Smyrna. He knew that his father would be disappointed in him. To Colonel Bridgeman, diso*bey*ing a direct military order would surely be the greatest crime a man could commit. Harry had spent a lifetime trying to win his father's approval. Now he felt he had finally forfeited any hope of obtaining it.

It was not in Harry's nature to try and excuse or mitigate the consequences of his actions – least of all to his father. He had simply written an exact and detailed account of what had occurred from the moment he had accompanied Admiral Brock to the interview with the newly-appointed Turkish governor – General Nureddin – to the moment he had called 'boats away' and authorised the picking up of 200 survivors from the waters of the bay. The letter had taken four hours to write, but had been a cathartic experience. After he had posted it, he had departed for Smyrna in a happier frame of mind.

The notice served on Harry stated that the court-martial would open on Wednesday, the 4th October, and would be heard in the stateroom on board *the Iron Duke*. He was informed that a launch would be waiting to pick him up from the Galata Bridge at nine o'clock on that morning. This was in less than a week's time.

Sitting in his hotel room near Taksim, staring at the telegrams and notices, Harry felt alone and vulnerable. This was irrational as his actions were not a 'hanging offence', and many years of good service would surely count for much. The trouble was that with no one to talk it over with, his mind wandered over remote and unlikely possibilities, which any objective observer would have rejected immediately.

A telegram arrived on the morning of the 29th September. In two or three short sentences it changed Harry's outlook forever. It read –

"Letter received. Am arriving Sirkedji station Simplon-Orient express morning Monday 2nd.
Don't worry son. Dad."

Suddenly, from the unreasonable gloom of the last 24 hours, Harry's mood swung back to the euphoria he had experienced while working with Jennings on the quaysides of Smyrna. Every single word of the telegram meant something to him, even the signature. His father had never signed his letters, even those sent to him at his boarding school, with the word – Dad. Everything about the telegram gave him a feeling of happiness; something from his father that he had been desperately seeking all his life without realising it.

The next day was Saturday the 30th. Harington still had the ultimatum in his pocket. Turkish soldiers were probing the Chanak bridgehead, grinning at the 'tommies' behind their barbed wire, and exchanging ribald sexual innuendo with them. Neither side could understand the other, though the body language was clear enough. More British soldiers were arriving in Stamboul from Malta and Egypt. The British cabinet was murmuring wilder and wilder defiance, while the Turkish nationalist army had already passed Ismid and were camped in lines not too far from the city on the Asian side. The Turkish cavalry had not withdrawn and remained inside the neutral zone at Chanak, while the British cabinet continued to wait for Harington to deliver the ultimatum and for war to begin.

But Harington held his hand. He had already begun preparations to hold the conference which had been proposed at the Curzon-Poincaré meeting seven days earlier, but to which the Turks had not as yet replied

In a sense, Harington's refusal to deliver the ultimatum, carefully prepared by the cabinet, and sent to him with clear orders to pass on to the Turks, was as clear a breach of his duty as Harry's disobedience at Smyrna – though further up the chain. Harington was under just as much compulsion to follow the orders of the constitutional civilian authority as Harry had been, when he defied the orders of his military superior.

On this Saturday, as it became clear in London that the ultimatum had still not been delivered, there were several in the cabinet – in particular Lloyd George – who now wanted to have the ultimatum sent at once directly to Ankara. They were not even prepared to wait for the conference at Mudania due to commence on the 3rd October. They pointed out that the Turks had still not agreed to the proposed meeting.

It was at this time that Venizelos reappeared in London, having been appointed as the new Greek ambassador by the new government in Athens, after the forced abdication of the King. Lloyd George now proposed that the remains of the Greek army still in Eastern Thrace, only hours away from Constantinople, could be called upon to help in repelling the Turkish nationalists. He simply could not accept that his cherished policy of creating a strong new Greece to act as a surrogate for the power of the British Empire in the Eastern Mediterranean had totally failed. In his frustration, there was even a suggestion that General Harington should now be censured and possibly recalled for disobeying his orders to deliver the ultimatum. Churchill and his group, on the other hand, believed with some justification, that to withdraw from a confrontation would be the thin edge of the wedge spelling the beginning of the end of Empire. Only Curzon stood firm against both points of view, convinced that the whole matter was exaggerated and only diplomacy could sort it out. He managed to earn a delay from his cabinet colleagues. No further telegrams were sent to Harington for the moment, and the Foreign Office made further contact with Kemalist representatives in Europe. They immediately passed on his views and his hints as to the eventual outcome for the city and for Eastern Thrace, to Mustapha Kemal himself, newly returned to a hero's welcome in Ankara.

On the other side of the equation, the Turks were in some disagreement with each other. Kemal was being pressed to ignore the Allies. Now that the French and Italians no longer opposed any moves into Europe, the Turkish army of over 200,000 battle-hardened veterans, could pour into Europe. Once across the straits, the small and demoralised remains of the Greek army would surely be completely unable to stop its advance. Not only Eastern Thrace would fall like a ripe plum, but Western Thrace and even Macedonia and Salonika could yet be recovered.

Mustapha Kemal was not impressed. His reply to these advisors was –

"What do you want? Do you want the cry to go up again throughout the Balkans – 'the Turks are coming, the Turks are coming'? No, I am ready to send a delegate to meet with the Allied representatives. Let's see what they have to say. So long as we get no ultimatum, which we could not in honour accept, we can at least see what they propose."

This acceptance was at last communicated to Harington. A conference at Mudania was to go ahead on Tuesday the 3rd October. It looked as if direct war between the British Empire and the Turks might be avoided. But the question of Constantinople remained open.

Meanwhile, Having sent a suitable message in reply to his father, Harry stepped out to visit the Avakians in Makrikoy, with a smile on his face and a light heart.

CHAPTER 19

Spiro's Future

That morning Karekin had invited Paramaz to sit with the rest of the family after the breakfast things were cleared away, to make some final decisions.

Karekin repeated the question he had asked Paramaz previously.

"Do you have any idea whether the baby has been baptized or the name he was given? Are you sure the mother didn't say anything before she died?"

"I'm sorry, sir, I don't have any idea. We were surrounded by panic-stricken crowds. She was lying on the road and I was trying to make sure she wasn't trampled. I never heard her utter a word."

"Very well Paramaz – but how are you sure she was Armenian? When I asked George yesterday he was hesitant. He rather thought she was Greek, but then he said that you would know better as she spoke to you as you were helping her."

Paramaz hesitated, but then began speaking quickly as he saw everyone staring at him.

"She said a few words in Armenian, sir – "

"But you just said that you hadn't heard her utter a word."

"No...er...what I meant was that we didn't have a conversation."

Karekin shook his head. He remained puzzled by everything he had been told about Smyrna – not only by Paramaz but by Olga as well. Armineh, too, whose common sense advice he could usually rely on, had been unable to help him. He knew she suspected that Paramaz knew more than he was saying, but she had not given him her version of the truth behind Olga's reticence and the evasions of Paramaz.

"Very well, we have to proceed on the basis that the baby has not yet been baptized. I have arranged with Father Haroutune to baptize the baby tomorrow after the Sunday morning service. Paramaz, as the saviour of this little lad, you must be the godfather, but who will be the godmother?"

There was a short silence as Karekin looked round the room at his three elder daughters.

"Nerissa, my soul, I think this is a duty you should take on." Karekin did not wait for her assent.

"Now Paramaz – what name would you like? It should be your choice as it is you who have given him life."

"I don't know – I don't know. Can I leave it until tomorrow please? He must at least have the name of Karekin as he will be the only Ava-kian male. Oh God!"

No one said a word as Paramaz turned deathly pale and walked out of the room into the kitchen. The silence was broken by Seta who started weeping quietly, but stopped at once when Nerissa took her hand and squeezed it tight.

Karekin cleared his throat, quite unnecessarily straightened his tie and ended the uncharacteristic silence, by passing on to his other un-resolved concern.

"Now we must talk about Spiro. His situation is, of course, quite different. No, Seta, don't look at me like that. There is no way at all that we can adopt him into our ..."

"But baba, he has lost all his family where ..."

"Baba, you can't just send him away, he ..."

There was an immediate outcry from the four girls.

"Look, my girls, this has nothing to do with race or nationality – it is a matter of practicality and what is best for the lad. He is not a baby – he is not even a small child – he is 11 or 12 and has already been brought up in the Greek culture. He speaks Greek first and then Turkish, and has only a few words of Armenian picked up in the streets. He needs to be with his own kind who can give him the love and attention he needs."

"Oh, father, are you suggesting that we would not be able to give that love and attention?" said Olga quietly.

"Baba," said Nerissa, "he could go to the local Greek school here. We wouldn't force him into any Armenian ways. Come, you yourself said he is not a child, he doesn't have to be adopted – he can stay and live with us, like Paramaz and Talin."

"Nerissa, I don't believe that that would be right for him. He is approaching young manhood. If he had been a year or two older he would have been shot and would not have survived at all. No, I have talked it over with him and have explained that if he remains with us, he will eventually have a crisis of identity, even if he went to a Greek school or a Greek church."

"But, father, you can't just throw him out or send him to one of those awful orphanages," said Sima, as the four looked at Karekin anxiously.

"No – of course not – that's not an option at all. What I've already done is to speak with a couple of my Greek colleagues at the Exchange. They both happened to know of a Greek couple with a farm about forty miles from here on the other side of Chatalja – near Sinekli. The family have lived and farmed there for generations and there is a good Greek school nearby. They have just lost their only son who was fifteen and they have no other children. I am told they want to adopt a Greek orphan and have been looking into this for months."

"But baba – who are they?"

"Oh, come girls! You should give your father more credit. Just listen and stop interrupting for heaven's sake," said Armineh sharply.

"Well – I have arranged take Spiro to meet these people on Monday. It's less than two hours away on the train and they will be meeting us at the station. First, we will see where they live and Spiro can tell me what he thinks. My intention is that unless he hates it, or if I myself have any qualms, I will leave him with them. We can deal with any legal matters later."

"But..."

"No, no, listen. I intend to leave a return ticket and some money just in case. If anything goes wrong he will be able to return. For heavens sake, it's only a couple of hours away. Don't shake your heads like that – the lad is 12, and has been through much more than any problems adapting to a new family and a new way of life. I have decided and…"

At this point the front door bell rang.

"Nicolai" called out Sima and jumped up and ran to the door. Harry, smiling from ear to metaphoric ear, walked in on the surprised Sima and planted a firm kiss on her cheek, no longer surprising anyone by this open show of affection. Two years in the Avakian atmosphere had changed Harry forever.

"See, I too now know where the bell is – that makes me part of the family doesn't it?" said Harry, putting his hat down on the small table by the front door.

"Come in, come in my boy," said Karekin reverting immediately to his rather heavily accented English. "A coffee – yes – yes. But look we have all sat round the table long enough – let's go into the sitting room."

Olga, seemed overjoyed to see him, took his arm and sat him down next to her on one of the sofas.

"We were discussing Spiro's future" she said.

Karekin had taken up his favourite position, standing with his back to the fire with his arms held together behind him.

"Now, Harry – don't say anything Olga – I would really like to hear what you think we should do or advise Spiro to do about his future."

Harry, still in a state of euphoria as a result of his father's telegram, felt the warmth of Olga's arm still tucked through his as they sat together. He loved this family and suddenly – like the flash of an electric spark – it came to him that over the last few days, from the moment he had first met Olga again at the Ottoman Hospital in Smyrna and the hours that they had spent together since then, he…

"Well, sir," Harry hesitated as he saw the three women were staring at him with greater intensity than usual. His natural inclination would have been to try to ascertain what the old man wanted him to say – and then say it. He decided, however, to come out with what he really felt.

"I see the difficulty. However, I would like to say, at once, that this young man does not pose anything like the same problem as that of the baby brought back out of that inferno by Paramaz. Spiro seemed to me to be an intelligent lad who knows who he is and who has already weathered one of the worst experiences any boy can go through – namely the brutal killing of his own mother in front of his very eyes. It is tricky I can see that. He is not quite old enough to be left to make his own way – yet he is too old to be treated like a child.

"Hmm… My own instinct would be to go to the Greek Patriarchate in town and talk with some of the priests there or perhaps one of the administrators. They are bound to have arrangements already in place. There have been droves of Greek refugees coming in to Bolis from all round the Black Sea. Spiro can have a word with them and they could help him decide."

There was a short silence. Both Sima and Nerissa had almost gasped when Harry had said 'Bolis' rather than 'Constantinople'. Olga had not even noticed – she felt comfortable with this man and had hardly heard a word of what he was saying.

She looked up with affection at her father. He continued to stand ramrod straight as usual in front of the fire. It was still only the 30th September and the fire was not lit every morning until October 1st. She wondered idly why it had been lit today. She saw her father start to smile at Harry's words,

"That's it Harry, my thoughts exactly, though there is no way that I would think of leaving the decision to a bunch of clerics – especially that Greek lot. My God, you've seen the way they have treated the Ottoman government from the moment the British took over. Hubris – hubris – they are now about to suffer the consequences once the Kemalists arrive. Passports issued for their flock indeed…"

At this reminder of how the Greek patriarchate had acted in those early years of the British occupation, Karekin totally lost the thread of what he was saying. In any case the three women had now clearly capitulated.

"Nerissa, my soul, go and tell your mother that Harry is staying for lunch. No, no – I insist. Meanwhile I'll tell you what I have decided."

For the next hour, the Spiro situation was hammered out and considered from all angles. Nerissa, not wanting to miss a word, had hurried back, and everyone was eager to give their views. Only Olga remained surprisingly quiet and thoughtful, still clinging on to Harry's arm.

Lunch was served and still the discussion continued, though the talk began turning to the baby and the christening to take place the next day.

After lunch, Olga rose and, before anyone else could say anything, she turned to Harry and said,

"It's a beautiful day, crisp and cold but wonderfully bright. Let's take a walk together in the gardens."

CHAPTER 20

Instincts

Despite the fire in the sitting room it was still September – just – and the weather though crisp and fresh was sunny and bright. Harry tried to recall the last time he had strolled through the trees of the orchard at the bottom of the lawn in the Avakian garden. Olga held his arm as they walked through the French windows out onto the long veranda which ran along the back of the house.

They strolled slowly in the early afternoon sunshine, absorbed in their own reveries. As they walked past the little door set in the stone wall which led out into the street *beyo*nd, Harry suddenly remembered. Yes of course – it was at the end of that awful tea-party over a year ago, when that passionate young Armenian…what was his name… ah yes Mikael, and the good-looking Turk Selim had almost come to blows. It came back to him in fine detail. He had walked this way with Nerissa demurely holding his arm, both of them keeping a discreet distance behind Sima and Nicolai, so they could have some privacy.

And what about Olga – where had she been on that occasion? He looked down at the beautiful girl at his side, clinging on to his arm more tightly than the young Nerissa had, and recalled she had been taken up in tears to her room by her brother as the party had broken up in disarray.

Harry had learnt a lot about Olga and her problems after he found her at the Ottoman Imperial Hospital. Olga had told him almost everything about her life in Smyrna before the fire. They had talked then and at even greater length during the voyage on the USS *Lawrence* as it brought them back to Constantinople. Harry had understood that she and Selim must have been living together during the months before the Great Fire. She and Selim had considered themselves to be man and wife and were intending to marry when the circumstances allowed. Still, they had not actually been married.

The Great War had undoubtedly changed attitudes but not quite so far as social acceptance of impropriety. Harry was not even quite sure what he thought about it. He had not been 'shocked' at the revelation Olga had confessed with unthinking honesty, but his pre-war upbringing accepted that nice girls from good families did not go to bed with men before they were officially married, did they?

They were walking together in companionable silence while Harry continued to muse. The circumstances of Olga's relationship with Selim had undoubtedly been difficult and both of them had clearly shown a long-lasting fidelity to each other. They walked on quietly until Olga saw the bench in a corner of the wall and suggested that they sit for a moment.

Olga had not as yet told anyone about the baby though it was now nearly a month since she realised she was pregnant. In a singular, but surprisingly pedestrian confrontation, she had finally got round to telling Armineh the full events of that 13th September, ending with the death of Selim. Sima was also present as she outlined the circumstances; the arrival of Haik and Paramaz; the desperate attempt to get Selim out of the house as the flames approached; the three soldiers in the street outside; and finally the escape from the flames at the hands of the unknown Turk who had saved her from the advancing fire. She had not said a word about the rape – this she would keep to herself – though she hinted at some brutality before she made her escape. The revelation to her mother and her elder sister of the affair with Selim was both matter of fact and unsentimental. Sima and Armineh could see that the trauma and emotion of those days resulted from the death of Selim, not from the brutality of the events she had witnessed.

But Armineh was no fool. She saw clearly what Sima could not see: that Olga was no longer a virgin when these terrible events happened and that Olga and Selim's love had been consummated. Once that was understood, the rest of the story began to make sense; not only Paramaz's version, but also his evasiveness. Obviously the boy had some merit in him, after all, and was seeking to save Karekin the embarrassment and shame of learning that his daughter and Selim had been openly living together.

It was all so extraordinary. Here was Karekin, a man of deeply liberal views, well-known throughout the city as a freethinker with enlightened opinions on the role of women in society; yet the instincts of his wife and eldest daughter were to protect the fact that his second daughter had been living with the man she had loved for many years; while Olga, who was now carrying her lover's child, seriously contemplated passing off the coming child to her father as the result of a brutal rape, rather than an act of love. In one way or another, it appeared that all three women instinctively believed that Karekin would be unable to accept that his daughter had been openly living with a man without being married.

Olga was weary as she and Harry sat down on the old wooden bench. Added to the physical tiredness, was the mental fatigue of knowing that she was at least one month pregnant, but unable, as yet, to share this knowledge with the people she loved. Living with Selim, knowing that on their return to Constantinople they would be married, she had existed in a state of euphoria, one day at a time. She loved her work, caring for her patients, then returning joyfully to the little first floor apartment. She would lay the little table and there would be a surge of happiness as Selim came in. Whatever she was doing, she would drop it and run to him, and he would enfold her in his arms....his hands... his lips. What did she care what people might think? She had told Madame. Derounian they were married. She had not really been dishonest – she felt in her heart it was so.

But now she was home with her family, it was no longer so simple. Now Selim would never again be there to talk to; but there was his child, and suddenly convention and propriety muscled in. She wasn't frightened, but she was confused. She had only been back a mere three or four days, yet it seemed like ages. She would have to speak up one way or another soon.

"Harry, that was lovely. Do you mind if we sit and talk a bit?"

"My dear, why not?" replied Harry.

Olga sat and curled her legs up underneath her as Harry sat alongside and stretched his out into the path. There was another comfortable silence as they looked around. Then Harry said,

"Look, the trees are just beginning to turn. It'll be a bit longer before the leaves actually begin to fall, but some of the colours are just starting to change. Down here it isn't all that dramatic, but you should see the autumn in England – in a good year it can be extraordinary."

"Harry, you appear to be so happy today – is there any particular reason?"

"Well, well, I didn't realise it was so obvious. There is, as it happens. My father is coming to Bolis and will be here on Monday, and I..."

"Oh that's marvellous. Your own father coming all that way just to see you. How wonderful. Why is he...no, no, why not...Where will he be staying? Oh Harry, I'll tell mama – he must come and visit us here."

"Olga wait – you're so ... well never mind. Aren't you curious why he should be coming all this way after all the years I've been stationed here?"

"Who cares about the reasons. You must be ..."

"No, wait a moment – I must tell you – no more evasions, no more secrets. The fact is, I am facing a serious court-martial, which is due to be heard on Wednesday. You know what a court- martial is? Well, my father heard about it and is coming out to give me his support."

The step had been taken and Harry spent the next fifteen minutes pouring his heart out to Olga. He explained the conditions in the Bay during those fateful days; he spoke of his decision and the inevitable result. Unlike their first meeting in the little café up the hill *beyond* the hospital, Olga sat quietly and listened carefully to every word. As the explanations went on, Olga eventually said –

"And your father's reaction to all this?"

It was like a floodgate opening in a dam and Harry began talking about his father and everything that he had felt over the years. This turned inexorably into what he believed that his father had thought about his only son: the coldness, the lack of physical warmth between them, his continual fear that he would not come up to his father's expectations. He talked about the way he wanted to emulate his father and, almost in the same breath, how he wanted to be very different.

"My God, Olga – even now I crave a hug from my father and to hug him back – imagine, a grown man, an officer in His Majesty's Royal Navy."

"Well, why don't you?"

"He wouldn't understand. We don't do things that way in England – it wouldn't be manly. We would end up being embarrassed with each other."

"All right, all right – but even a handshake can either be warm and full of love, or it can be cold and formal. Harry, I'm looking forward to meeting this baba of yours."

Olga jumped up from the bench, her eyes lit up with enthusiasm, as Harry sat staring up at her, contemplating with wonder all the confidences that had just come tumbling out. Olga held out her hand and grasping Harry's, she pulled him up.

"Come, let's walk on, and now you can listen to me while I tell you about my baba."

They began walking again, arm in arm, naturally, without affectation. They soon came out onto the lawn on the other side from where they had started. They were now facing back towards the house and saw that Armineh and Karekin had come out onto the veranda and were seated at the white wrought-iron table having their coffee. Nicolai was there as well sitting next to Sima. They were holding hands quite openly. Olga stared for a moment as Sima called out to her, but then steered Harry back into the orchard and out of sight.

Now it was Olga who was doing all the talking, matching Harry's personal revelations about his relationship with his father, with her relationship with her own. But in her case, the approach was radically different. She was seeking answers from someone she could trust, having already placed herself fully into his hands in Smyrna.

She wanted to be told what she should tell her father – but she wasn't thinking clearly. She wanted Harry to give her the benefit of his advice, but somehow to give it without knowing the real nature of the problem. As she talked and strolled, they eventually got back to the same wooden bench on which they had been sitting earlier. Olga sat and began fiddling with a bracelet, looking down at her hands. Harry sat down beside her and again stretched out his long legs, putting his clasped hands behind his head. He felt totally relaxed and contented.

Harry had had to make a substantial leap of faith in disclosing to Olga the details of his forthcoming court-martial – something he would not normally have disclosed to anyone outside the Service. In the same way, Olga, fiddling with her bracelet, was now contemplating an equal leap in disclosing something deeply personal to someone outside the immediate family circle.

She had reached the stage where she had to confide in someone before telling her mother – and that someone was going to be Harry.

"Harry, I've been rambling on about my papa and our relationship as father and daughter. I have been going on about it because I need to talk with someone who knows us both. Frankly, I need some objective advice."

"Listen Olga, I've been all ears, but I do urge you not to come out with an intimacy without thinking deeply first. So often people come out with confidences they later regret. I will try to help and be as honest as possible, but I have not had all that much experience ..."

"I know the man you are and I trust you. I want you to know about the problem that has been playing terribly on my mind. I know that I can confide in you."

Harry turned his head, pulled up his feet and brought his hands down in front of him. Now looking straight into Olga's eyes, he nodded and waited.

"You know that Selim and I were living together those last few weeks before the fall of Smyrna. I don't really know what he was doing there and I was never interested in finding out. For me it was enough that we were together, that he wanted to marry me and that we would be able to live together as man and wife. Harry – I was blissfully happy. I had been dreaming about this for six years."

There was a short silence. Harry, who had never experienced such a passionate revelation before, felt a shameful wish to look away. Instead, he held firm and continued to look directly into her eyes. Then she suddenly looked away and staring at her bracelet said –

"I am pregnant. I am bearing Selim's child who will be born in eight months time."

CHAPTER 21

Nicolai and Sima

Nicolai had turned up at the Avakians somewhat unexpectedly after lunch immediately after Olga and Harry had strolled down into the garden. He had kissed Sima hurriedly in the hall and then asked to speak to Karekin. They had talked about this moment many times before and she realized at once what this hurried, unscheduled visit meant, coupled as it was with a rather cold and nervous formality. She blushed for a moment but said nothing, taking Nicolai by the hand and into the sitting room where everyone except Harry and Olga were now sitting waiting for coffee.

"Ah, Nicolai. You're a bit late for lunch my boy. It was 'mantu', my favourite – you missed a treat – but come, come. Coffee of course."

"Well, no thank you sir. I rather wanted to have a word with you in private at some time please, if that would be possible."

Karekin looked across at Armineh, who said nothing and would not even return his glance. Alexei had told Karekin that the Countess would be going to visit their relatives in Vienna but he would not be leaving with his mother. Karekin had passed this on to Armineh and they had already discussed the possible implications of the Androv family decision. They weren't aware Nicolai had lost his job with the Pera Palace orchestra.

Nicolai was always a little more formal in his speech than the Avakians but his manner was now at his most aristocratic. With an involuntary sigh Karekin stood up from the hardback armchair and putting an arm round Nicolai's shoulders, ushered him from the room and into the study.

But, ironically, it was Karekin who was nervous, not Nicolai. Nicolai was worried how Karekin would react, but he was both calm and clear as to what he wanted, whereas Karekin was quite unsure of what he would reply, assuming that he was right about what were Nicolai's intentions.

"Sir, I know that you know of my feelings for Sima – feelings which I believe she shares for me. Your kindness to my family has given me some hope that you might look kindly on the continuation of our relationship."

Karekin stood by his desk, one arm as usual behind his back, the other with fingers splayed on the desktop; then, sitting down, he swivelled his chair round so he could look straight at Nicolai and nodded at him to continue.

"Sir, as I believe you know, my mother is leaving on Monday for Vienna where she will be staying with her eldest sister – the Countess Berchtold. The situation in Vienna is currently as desperate as here, so she might be going on to her other sister who is married to an Italian Count – Count Maggi – whose estate in the Veneto is still intact."

"Well – yes, yes, very well – go on my boy."

"I am not going with her, largely because I wish to resolve my situation here with your daughter. In short, sir, I wish to marry Sima. Whilst I have not yet made any formal request to her, I believe that she knows of my wishes and approves, subject, of course, to what you and Madame Avakian might think."

By this stage, Karekin knew precisely where he was leading. His first thought was that in a family of young girls, all of marriageable age, this was the first formal request for the hand of one of his daughters he had ever received direct from a young man.

A silence now fell between them – both men quite comfortable with it. Now that the question had finally been put, he brought out his beautiful amber beads and began clicking them, not nervously but deliberately – passing them slowly between thumb and first finger. He made a little gesture indicating that Nicolai should take a seat. Nicolai declined, preferring to continue standing. It was now his turn to get nervous as he waited for Karekin to speak.

Eventually, Karekin, looking up, said, as kindly as he could,

"Nicolai, my boy, how will you manage – where are you proposing to live with Sima and what will you live on. You could hardly manage to provide for her and any future family on your wages from the Pera Palace."

At this point Nicolai finally took the chair Karekin had indicated, and sat down, realising that he hadn't even mentioned that he had lost this job.

"Well, sir, I anticipated your question. First, I have already given up my job at the Pera Palace. With the political situation as it is, they simply can't afford to keep up the orchestra in the same numbers as before."

He swallowed, his mouth dry, anticipating some sort of an outburst from Karekin at this revelation. Surprisingly, he saw that Karekin was not the slightest bit disturbed by this news, though he said nothing. Nicolai continued –

"The reason, sir, for my sense of urgency is that I wish to take Sima with me to Europe. I don't suppose that I'll have much more chance in finding good work in Vienna than I've had here. But my uncle has a fairly extensive estate in North Italy, and I have high hopes that he will welcome having an experienced member of the family as an Estate

Manager. He is getting old and will be needing someone to help him soon."

Once again there was a silence as Karekin digested Nicolai's increasingly hurried words.

"I would add, sir, that I have several jewels left to me by my mother, which I am in the process of selling for some starting capital and a cushion in case of problems."

"Have you considered, *deghas*," and here Karekin deliberately used the Armenian word, meaning both 'my boy' and 'my son', "that as my potential son-in-law, you would be most welcome to join the merchant house of Avakian & Co."

Every word seemed to be loaded with significance in this conversation. Nicolai noted immediately that Karekin had not said 'Avakian, Levonian & Co' the current official designation of the firm. However, his reply was quick and decisive –

"I deeply appreciate your suggestion. You have already done a lot for my family – it has been the making of Alexei for a start. My mother told me that you might make this offer and urged me to accept it with gratitude – but, sir, I cannot. I have to try to establish my own future if I can."

"I can't agree with you. I could understand you might feel a gulf between our differing cultural backgrounds – between Russian landed gentry and Ottoman merchant adventurer. But why would you immediately accept an offer of work from an uncle you have never met, as against one from your prospective father-in-law whom I hope you have now come to know?"

The truth was that Nicolai was not at all certain why he felt there was a difference or why he could accept help from one and not the other – so said nothing. Karekin then continued –

"Bear in mind, Nicolai, that you will be requiring my daughter to share the same risk you choose to take by going off to Italy, or anywhere else without any immediate prospects."

At last Nicolai found his voice –

"I would like to add, sir, that in the current situation anything could happen. I doubt that we will actually end up with a Smyrna situation, but who knows? Everything about this city is in the melting pot and at least if we can arrange a marriage quickly, I would be in a position to take your daughter out of it. As you know I have acquired a Nansen passport and depending what happens, such a passport might well be worth more than an Ottoman document, easily repudiated by whatever government is finally established here. I admit I don't think it will come to that – but it might, who knows."

Karekin thought to himself that this was the first really good argument he had heard – there was more to this boy than noblesse and impeccably good manners. He stood up and again using the word *deghas* smiled at Nicolai and said –

"*Deghas*, you are welcome to ask Sima for her hand in marriage – and if she accepts you, you have my blessing for an early marriage – but on one absolute condition."

"Oh my God – what... er ... yes, sir, what would that condition be?"

"I want your solemn word, Nicolai, one on which I can absolutely rely, one in which your personal honour will be at stake, that if matters do not work out either in Vienna or the Veneto, you won't just try to make do in order to salve your pride, but will come back to make your life in this city and in my merchant house."

"I accept wholeheartedly and with thanks," said Nicolai, grinning from ear to ear. "I would never put Sima through penury just to salve my pride as you put it, but all this depends on whether, in a month or two, there is still a city here in which you or I would be welcome and whether the merchant house of Avakian & Co. will still be in business."

Karekin rose from his seat and put away his beads. He walked round the desk and put his arms round Nicolai's shoulders who had jumped up, this time receiving Karekin's embrace without awkwardness. They walked together out into the sitting-room, which was now empty, and from there into the garden to join Sima and Armineh, who were sitting at one of the white wrought-iron tables, staring across at the orchard.

They looked up as Nicolai and Karekin walked through the French windows and onto the veranda. Karekin still had his hand on Nicolai's shoulder as if he was pushing him forward – a rare gesture on his part. Both women immediately knew the question had been put and permission granted, but neither said a word.

Karekin took his hand off Nicolai's shoulder and, nodding at Armineh, he turned and went back into the sitting room without a word as Armineh hurried off after him. Nicolai was now more nervous than he had been with Karekin. He was aware of the weakness of his own current situation and prospects. Even before Karekin had pointed it out, he knew how little he was offering this very practical woman.

Now, suddenly, he was unsure of her response. He was proposing to take her away with him and to throw themselves on the goodwill of an extended family who even he hardly knew. On top of that, he was stateless and had an aging mother to look after. Would she be prepared to join him in building a satisfactory life for themselves, and for any children, far away from her family and the city she had always called home? He moved round the table towards her and then bent and took her hand in his.

"Sima, my sweetheart, my darling – will you marry me?"

There was hardly a second's hesitation. Sima knew what she was being asked to accept. A home of their own was nowhere in sight; the joy of children would have to be put aside until Nicolai could find his feet; there would be uncertainty even in where they would live. Nevertheless, this was the man she wanted as the father of her children – this was the man she loved. She jumped up out of her chair, almost before he had finished his sentence. She put her arms round him and managed to gasp out –

"Oh yes, yes, Nicolai. Oh yes ... yes ... my love."

After Karekin and Armineh returned, in answer to Sima's cries, they all sat round the table; the coffee arrived together with a bottle of Karekin's best champagne brought by Marie, who tearfully embraced Sima. As practical details were discussed, Olga and Harry first emerged, arm in arm, from the orchard. Olga waved at the seated group, and rather hurriedly turned away, pulling Harry back into the trees before anyone could call out. Well, there was plenty of time – there was plenty of time – perhaps.

CHAPTER 22

Confidences

Harry was over 30 and had the self-confidence that came from having been a commander of men for more than four or five years. He was also a product of the British public school system, which produced Britain's future rulers. He believed he had been a good officer and was proud of his record. The forthcoming court-martial had not affected his self-belief. But Olga's quiet confession, put to him without dramatics, left him unable to say a word.

Harry had changed enormously since the end of the war and during the two years of his mission in Constantinople – but not quite enough to cope with something like this. He was an 'only' child. Like so many of his class and times he had moved straight from an all-male boarding school into the military. He had little experience of women and none whatsoever of 'pregnancy'. "I am pregnant," she had told him. What was he supposed to say? Why did no words come from him? At the same time, they had worked together on Spiro's behalf; she had supported him in facing the nightmare of what had occurred on the quaysides; they had talked together for hour after hour on the USS *Lawrence* and ever since. Talk between them had become effortless and meaningful, yet in response to this confidence, he was speechless. He could not think what help or support he could offer. His first reaction to the revelation of her liaison with Selim had been judgmental. These thoughts passed through his mind like a flash – but, as it turned out, she was not expecting any immediate answer, only a sounding board –

"I am happy about it, Harry – I am truly happy and not afraid. I am only sorry that I missed the moment to tell Selim before he died. I did suspect the possibility at the time, but I waited to be sure and then.... and then.... events took over and it was too late."

Harry leaned back against the stone wall for a moment. Then in a gesture of alliance, almost of complicity, he stretched his hand behind Olga's back and round her far shoulder, holding her firmly. He didn't speak, but his mind went through a series of mental gymnastics as he wrestled with the revelation of their liaison before marriage. It was as if the natural outcome – the arrival of another life, a baby, anxiously awaited and looked for – changed his whole attitude. Background, culture and upbringing are paramount in forming opinions, but circumstances and emotions can override them, particularly in the case of men with staunchly independent characters. And this was what was happening to Harry.

"Anyway, Harry, I haven't told mother or my sisters yet, but I will probably tell them this evening. But it is father, Harry, my father! How can I put it to him – what is he going to say – what is he going to think? Already, everyone is scared about telling him I was living with Selim during those two months. If we can't even tell him about that, how will he take the knowledge that I am pregnant. Oh Harry, I am so scared of losing his love."

At last Harry sailed into clearer waters. At last he knew what this girl wanted from him. She needed the sort of reassurance that he wished a loving father had given him ten years ago. As he turned towards her, a new and deeper warmth came over him. The combination of his father's telegram that morning and this girl's confidence in him, was making this a day like no other he had ever experienced.

"Olga, you know that I have no experience with this sort of problem, but on the matter of your father, I believe I have come to know him well enough over the years, to give an opinion. Firstly, my dear, you must tell him soon and not leave it hanging over you. Tell him immediately after the baptism ceremony for the baby tomorrow. And Olga, tell him yourself, don't be persuaded by your mother to leave it to her. And just tell him the truth – no excuses, no hiding anything."

Harry had been talking quickly with considerable emphasis. He was anxious to have his say before he could be interrupted – but for once Olga listened patiently to every word.

"He may well find it a difficult to accept your decision to live together. His generation would undoubtedly have expected you to wait, however difficult the circumstances. But once he has taken that on board – and the circumstances were pretty exceptional – the arrival of a baby will not faze him one jot. It is his first grandchild. He will have wanted things to turn out differently, but the arrival of a baby won't hurt him. Good God, Olga, he'll probably be delighted."

Harry took a deep breath. Olga stood up, eyes gleaming. Then, she bent down and gave him a soft kiss, which lingered for more than just a moment, directly on his lips. Then she straightened up and said –

"Thank you Harry. I knew I could rely on you and your good sense. Come, enough revelations. Let's go in. Thank you Harry – my mind is clear."

Even by Avakian standards the talk, the animated discussions and the overwhelming delight over the news of Sima and Nicolai's forthcoming marriage, was impressive. It lasted for the rest of the afternoon. In Ottoman Armenian circles, an engagement was usually the excuse for an enormous party, funded always by the girl's father. The marriage itself, usually organised by the bridegroom's family, was normally a quieter affair for the two families and their more intimate friends.

However, in this case, the political situation was so tense that a traditional engagement party might have seemed gratuitous. As the conversation rumbled on, Nicolai realised the decision was largely out of his hands. New bottles kept arriving at the table, and Harry and Nicolai were becoming dazed, as the discussion raged. The consensus was much as Nicolai wanted. Everyone agreed that the actual wedding should take place as soon as possible, but practically, this meant a month at least to arrange.

Armineh thought that she would need this much time to send out invitations, prepare for the actual day and for such practical matters as dresses and the reception. Sima knew she needed the time to sort out her own things. She would have to look into the rooms at the Patakis house, for at her own insistence it had been agreed that after the marriage there would be no question of coming to Makrikoy. They would start their marriage together in those rented rooms, as by then, the Countess would have departed. Without anything being said, it was accepted that Alexei should be persuaded to come to live in Makrikoy, but he would have to be consulted.

Karekin was also pleased as he felt that the political situation would be resolved by that time. The question of what would happen to the city and to the dynasty remained unknown – but violence was now unlikely unless the Greek army refused to accept the decisions taken at Mudanya. On the other hand, the dread phrase 'exchange of populations' was already being bandied about, leaving a terrible question mark hanging over everyone in the city.

Olga? Well Olga was as happy as everyone else for Sima, but was distracted by thoughts of the coming evening's conversation with her mother.

The afternoon wore on and Harry and Nicolai, both already more than mellow from Karekin's excellent champagne, prepared to leave. Karekin indicated that he would go with them to see Father Haroutune and start the necessary arrangements for a wedding. Armineh had noticed that Seta had become a little tearful from all the excitement, so suggested that she accompany her father on the trip.

After everyone left, the Avakian women were left alone in the house, which was suddenly quiet. Armineh finally sat down heavily in the sitting room and considered her three daughters.

"Well, my daughters, are you ready for the baptism tomorrow. Nerissa, you will have to hold the baby. Remember, only hand him to Paramaz at the font."

"Yes, mama. You'll be next to me, won't you?"

"Of course – but your father will not be at the font. Traditionally as the father of the infant he will be hovering about at the back."

"Do you know who will be coming," said Sima.

"We will all be there, of course, but I have not invited anyone else outside the family. The Androvs – well they are family now anyway – will be there. And Sima, I'm sure you won't mind, but I have also sent a message round to George. After all he was there with Paramaz when the baby was saved, wasn't he."

There was a short comfortable silence.

Then Olga, who had said nothing for some time, sat up straight on the edge of the sofa and turned to address Armineh directly. She felt an unaccustomed rush of blood to her face and said rather more sharply than she had intended –

"Mama – the word she spoke in Armenian literally translated as 'my own darling mother' – I have to tell you, all of you, something about Smyrna."

There was again a short silence, no longer quite so comfortable.

"You all know that I met Selim quite by chance about six months after I arrived in the city. What I have not said – at least not directly – is that we took a little apartment together in the Armenian quarter and lived together. You know exactly what I mean, my darlings, don't you. We lived happily together right up to the moment when the Turkish army entered the city. Our plan was to get married as soon as we got back home."

"But how…"

"What was…"

"Please wait. Selim had a couple of rooms in the Turkish quarter. I never saw them or went there. He would go there sometimes whenever I was on duty at the hospital."

Sima and Nerissa were enthralled, even though they had both already guessed what she was telling them. Armineh said nothing but stared hard at Olga. She had long since realised that this was the case, but although she wasn't 'shocked', she totally and utterly disapproved. She didn't judge, she didn't blame, but she disapproved. It was against everything she believed in.

Olga could sense her mother's disapproval; she felt the tears springing to her eyes, but she swallowed and went on as best she could –

"Oh dear, this is difficult. My loves – I must tell you what I've been bottling up for days. I'm pregnant. I will have Selim's child, in eight months."

The switch of feelings in the three women who were listening was immediate. Sima and Nerissa suddenly realised the consequences of two lovers living together. Sima immediately saw the cultural and social costs and the practical difficulties to be overcome. Nerissa was equally shocked by the product of this romantic attachment. In the space of a sentence, the talk had turned from romance to physical passion. As always, she was struck dumb by this turn of events.

But Armineh stood up. She still disapproved, completely and without equivocation. She stared down at her daughter, who looked back up at her with silent tears running down her cheeks. But here was a reality that had to be faced. It was nature. Bending down, she took Olga's head between her hands and kissed her on her forehead, saying –

"Oh dear – you silly goose – you silly, silly goose. Are you all right? Have you started feeling sick? Come, come, my darling – we have work to do and we must start planning."

With her tears now turning to tears of relief, Olga bent forward and clasped her mother round her knees burying her head in her mothers long, soft grey skirt. Mumbling into the skirt so that they could only just hear the words she said–

"Oh, mother – I do so want to have Selim's child. I really loved him – and mother he loved me."

"Hush child – calm yourself. Of course you are going to have the child – and look, look at the wonderful aunts he is going to have."

Sima, sitting on her other side, leaned across and hugged Olga, in a rush of emotion. Nerissa sat for a moment, then she too arose and gave her sister a warm embrace.

CHAPTER 23

The Christening

Step by step, Paramaz walked with his two little sisters, each holding on to one hand. The scene was strange and desolate – there were boulders everywhere of all shapes and sizes and he had to lead the two little girls round each one, in some cases having to lift them over. Even at this stage in the dream, he was already afraid, but he had no idea of what.

Suddenly, in front of them as they walked round yet another boulder, his father stood, gripping a sword in one hand and holding up Paramaz's mother who was leaning against him with the other. Even as he stared at them blood began pouring out from between his mother's legs and she began to sink to the floor, despite his father's efforts to keep her standing. Until this moment there had been an eerie silence as he had walked on with the girls – but now he heard the words 'Manchus – manchigus' (my son – my darling son) as his mother sank to the ground with her arms outstretched towards him.

His two little sisters let go of his hand and ran to the man who had been holding on to his mother – but it was no longer his father. His father had somehow become a large distended naked man with an erect penis, who with one sweep of his sword, struck off the heads of the two little girls. Then he advanced upon Paramaz, now with a spear held aloft – the sword had somehow disappeared.

Paramaz shrank away in horror but his feet were stuck to the ground. He could not escape – but now the father/apparition melted away and in his place stood an androgynous figure, with no recognisable features. But Paramaz knew who it was – he knew exactly who it was. Still the figure advanced, sometimes looking like a boy of 17, sometimes like a young girl of 15, indistinct and blurred, but always with a sweet smile which drove terror into his heart. It continued advancing, without appearing to get any closer. Why wasn't it already upon him? But then at last the hands of the figure came up and caressed each side of his face – and the lips of the boy/girl stretched forward for a kiss.

In a frenzy of terror and repulsion, Paramaz found his father's sword was now in his hand. Fearful of the lips touching his, he raised the sword and struck and struck. Blood was every where. He dragged at the clothes of the dying figure, tearing them off one by one – striking again and again – but still the thing smiled up at him. As he pulled layer upon layer away, the body seemed to shrink. Each time he struck again at what was left. At last, the sweet smile had gone – and there before him lay a baby. Dripping with blood Paramaz bent to pick it up, but it was no child – it was a snake spitting venom into his eyes – Paramaz screamed, waking up covered in sweat and cowering in fear.

Night after night, ever since his return, Paramaz had dreamed this dream, or ones very like. Once awakened by the terror, he could never get to sleep again but would lie in his own sweat waiting for the dawn to break. Had he killed his Kurdish abuser in that cave all those years ago, or was that also just a dream? And the brutal rape and murder of his mother on the death march, couldn't he have done something – any-thing – instead of thinking only of his own survival?

Often this last memory brought tears to his eyes, and sometimes he could turn his head and doze. But the repetition night after night of the same awful dreams was leaving him weak and sensitive during the day, to the point where he was having difficulty dealing with even the simplest of tasks set him by Karekin.

It was early in the morning of Sunday the 1st October – the day the baby, rescued from the horrors of Smyrna, was to be christened into the Armenian Gregorian Church as the adopted child of Karekin Avakian. Paramaz had awoken with a start in a state of complete mental panic from the nightmare which had enveloped him.

Armineh was up early this morning. There was no longer the need to chivvy along her daughters or an untidily dressed son. But the organi-sation of any event was still hers to manage. The baby had to be washed and changed. She didn't know the baby's real age, but she presumed he was coming up to one year's old, not a month-old baby christened in swaddling clothes – the children's white christening dresses, saved since Sima was born, were of no use. Coolly and with only a slight shiver, she went to the old cupboards and brought out some of Haik's old clothes. There they lay, smelling of mothballs, lovingly stored away for the use of the first male grandchild. Not a tear dropped from her eyes as she picked out a suitable dress for the new baby.

Even at this late stage, the family weren't sure what the full name of the little boy would be, but the little boy would carry the Avakian surname. The boy's godfather – an important role in Armenian families – would be Paramaz. Nerissa had agreed to be the godmother. In all Ar-menian christenings, it was the role of the godfather to name the child. Normally, there would have been family discussions first, and often, there were family traditions to be observed – but ultimately it was the godfather's decision. The family had indeed discussed it somewhat cur-sorily but assumed that Paramaz would name the child after Karekin. So it was that as the family gathered to go to the church near Taksim, where Karekin's favourite priest – Father Haroutune – presided, no one was quite sure what the full name of the little boy would be.

Despite all the political uncertainty and the worries swirling round the city, the family party was full of joy and anticipation. Two carriages had been ordered from the station. This was the first full day since the tragic news of Haik's death had first burst upon them, that the family had been able to relax a little and turn their minds towards the future. Sima's happiness from the previous day was contagious, and there was a feeling that they were all ready to resume a more normal life. The sorrow over the death of the family's only son and brother would of course remain always in their hearts. The four girls were wearing their best clothes and their most fashionable hats; the weather was getting colder but was still crisp and clear; and everyone was in white, even Seta, who usually preferred blue. Olga was sporting a large hat with a wide brim, but the other three were wearing the currently fashionable 'cloche' hats.

Talin carried the baby. Paramaz was attired in his dark office suit and was the only one not smiling, looking tired and anxious. A few months before, Seta had been given one of the new black box cameras, just coming onto the market. She had been fascinated by it and was going around, taking snaps of everyone. She had already become a good photographer, having learned not to make everyone pose as was the fashion, but snapping away to catch the moment. Everyone was cheerful, smiling at the camera and at the baby, except Paramaz, who turned away whenever the camera was aimed towards him.

The Androvs were already in the Church when the family arrived and filed in. Morning service had ended, but there were still strangers and acquaintances in the Church. Harry, who had never before attended an Armenian church service was there, having already gone to the morning service earlier, out of curiosity. The Levonians, including George and Tamara were of course there. Of all the Church sacraments – baptism is probably the most relaxed and joyous, even more so than weddings, which tend to have a more serious element. Everyone was still smiling after all the kissing, hugging and shaking of hands had been completed.

Father Haroutune was in his full ecclesiastical robes and was assisted by three deacons and a young 'vartabed'. The service began with everyone gathered round the font at the far end of the nave; Karekin hovering at the back of the crowd – the traditional place for the father. As always, all the questions and answers, the prayers and the promises, the ritual phrases, were between the godparents and the clergy.

The baby was held by Paramaz, who rocked the child and kept him gurgling happily as the service dragged on. Armineh was there ready to help if necessary. Nerissa stood by him watching with wonder as Paramaz replied to the rituals, looking down with real affection at the infant staring back at him with big, brown, intelligent eyes. The older girls were close by and the only member of the family anywhere close to Karekin was Seta, who was still darting about taking pictures.

The climax finally came. Father Haroutune stretched his hands out and took the child from the arms of Paramaz. Then firmly holding the infant who looked a little surprised, he turned to Paramaz and said, intoning the words in a full bass voice –

"What shall be the child's given names in Christ." Paramaz looked straight at the priest and said quietly – "Haik Karekin."

Father Haroutune held the child over the baptismal font – dipped his hand into the warm holy water and made a cross with the water on the child's forehead. He called out in his warm and resonant voice –

"I name this child Haik Karekin and I … "

But Karekin no longer heard what the priest was saying. He held himself stiffly upright, his arms hard to his side. He was determined not to react publicly, but he could not help the wetness in his eyes as he stood still. Seta was by his side like a shot and her hand crept into his, as tears came into her own eyes. Poor Father Haroutune – somehow no one now seemed to be paying much attention anymore as the service continued to its predestined conclusion. It was not a resumption of grief, it was just that this congregation all of a sudden went elsewhere, all in different directions. George became distressed; Nerissa looked on with amazement as little Haik was handed back to Paramaz; every member of the family seemed to want some physical contact with a neighbour; Nicolai's arms went round Sima's shoulders; Olga took and held onto Harry's hand gripping it tightly. There were only two people who appeared unaffected – Paramaz, who was calmly rocking the little boy back and forth, looking down into his smiling eyes – and Armineh, who touched no one, but looked at all her family one by one to make sure that none needed her help.

"In the name of the Father, Son and Holy Ghost for ever and always," called out Father Haroutune raising his arms and making the sign of the cross over the whole congregation.

Then the hullabaloo commenced – people gathered round Paramaz and little Haik – there were smiles and tears as Seta ran round taking pictures of perhaps this last occasion when all the family would be present together. Only Karekin was not there. He had turned, blinking away his tears and walked out, slowly but deliberately, before the blessing.

CHAPTER 24

Sirkedji Station

It was the day after the baptism ceremony and autumn had at last arrived. The morning was overcast and there was a steady drizzle of rain throughout the whole of Thrace. The rain poured down on the Greek army on the other side of the Chatalja lines; on the British forces, holding the line against the Greeks at Chatalja and against the Turks, facing them on the other side of the wire outside Chanak; and it poured down on the Avakians.

The family were up early, getting ready for the departure of Karekin and Spiro for Sinekli to meet the Kafides family. Sinekli was less than two hours away on the fast trains out of Sirkedji station heading for Adrianople. The carriage had been ordered and had arrived, and a coffee taken out to Abdul by Talin. Karekin, impeccably dressed as usual, came down the stairs to join the others at breakfast.

Spiro had already gulped down some bread and honey with Talin in the kitchen, and was waiting there fidgeting. He was both nervous and excited at one and the same time. After all the drama and terrors of those last few days in Smyrna, he had found relief and security in this household, and he was fearful of leaving, though keyed up at the same time. He was at that stage in life when he was sometimes a child, tearful at his memories and desperate for physical comfort from adults. But at other times, he was a boy capable of jumping into the sea to save himself, ready to stand up for himself against the world and with the stirring of sexual feelings in his groin, that he could not quite control.

Spiro had arrived in the Avakian family with absolutely nothing except the clothes he stood up in. Armineh had already clad him with clothes originally belonging to the Haik. In her thrifty and careful way, these had been cleaned, ironed and stowed away. What had been in her mind? Male grandchildren, perhaps. Either way, Spiro had worn these and had been walking around, trailing a faint smell of mothballs, for the last week. This morning, before daybreak, Armineh had arisen and prepared a small case into which she had packed more of these clothes, together with a new pair of shoes and at the last moment, throwing in an old child's short tennis racquet and a couple of ragged white tennis balls that had been a treasured possession of her now dead son.

"Good morning", said Nerissa, looking up at Olga as she came running down the stairs. "Why are you wearing those clothes?"

"Because I'm going with Baba and Spiro – and can't you see it's raining."

"What – what's this. What's this," spluttered Karekin looking up from his tea.

"Baba – please don't fuss. I want to see what Spiro is going. I promise I will be very discreet – no talking out of place, or contradicting anyone. But baba you know that I feel responsible for the boy – and anyway it will be company for you on the way back."

Olga, having now arrived at the table, kissed her father and ran into the kitchen so he was unable to raise any objections. She emerged holding Spiro's hand. He had been waiting stoically in dread and anticipation all this time. But Olga's warm embrace, the firm and loving way in which she held his hand and led him out, was all too much. To his intense embarrassment, his lips began to tremble and by the time they were out in the hall, the tears were trickling down his face. While the rest of the family stared at him, he put his arms around Olga, and buried his head in her waist.

As Olga glared at her father and the others as if they were to blame for causing the boy's distress, Armineh quietly rose and, making no attempt to comfort anyone, took up the case, which had been by her side and said –

"Well, well – come, it's time to be going. Seta, go and get your father's hat, gloves and coat. Olga, my love, please be sure to take your winter coat – it's a cold day already and it will be even colder in the countryside. Now Spiro – look, here is an old coat that used to belong to my son, you tried it on yesterday, remember? Good. Do you think that you could also manage to carry this case? Try it. It's quite heavy. I don't want Karekin to carry it if you can do it."

"Yes, hanum, I'm sure I can," said Spiro, swallowing his tears and coming round the table to take the coat. He put it on and then hefted the case, feeling it's weight. All of a sudden he was 12 again, and not eleven. He knelt in front of Armineh, took her hand and raised it to his forehead. Where Karekin might have pulled his hand away, Armineh said nothing thus giving a touch of dignity to what might have seemed an absurd gesture. Instead she let him keep hold of her hand and leant forward and kissed him on the top of his head.

Olga smiled gratefully at her mother. Then suddenly it was all action and within minutes the three of them had gone

In Stamboul, the Androvs were also up and about at daybreak. Even though the Direct-Orient express was not due to leave till just before midday, Nicolai wanted to get to the station early without rushing. There were two large trunks to manage – a carriage to be obtained – and, at the other end, a porter to be hired.

For Alexei this would be the first time in his life that he would be separated from his mother. The Countess loved her younger son, but, for her, this separation was not such a great wrench. In her world, sons left their mothers and went off to serve the state in the army or civil service. It had been normal for her to watch Nicolai go off to war, albeit a different kind of war than what she had expected. Alexei's position was subtly different. He had begun life on the family estate in the traditional manner of the Russian landed aristocracy. His father had arranged for him to start his studies by attending the local village school.

In 1914, when Alexei was not yet eight, the Great War broke out and Count Androv had gone to war himself. Three years later, the Revolution had begun in St. Petersburg, and Alexei found he was no longer welcome in the village school and lost all his boyhood friends. This was followed by the Civil War and Nicolai went off to war, leaving him alone with only his mother. She had fled with him to the family property in Crimea, and there he had remained with her until the evacuation from Sevastopol.

So Alexei had had no father since he was eight, nor his older brother to guide him, until he came to Constantinople and was taken on as an apprentice by Karekin. His reaction to the forthcoming separation from the Countess was similar to Spiro's feelings – a mixture of nervous dread and excited anticipation.

The Androvs arrived at Sirkedji station far too early – but it was at the exact moment that Harry arrived to meet his father, due in on the same Orient Express in the morning. He was dressed in civilian clothes. He waved at the Androvs as he stepped out of his carriage, tipping the driver handsomely to wait for them outside the station.

Sirkedji station had been completed only thirty years earlier, built, in part, for the short-haul local railway line going through the small suburban towns strung along the north coast of the Marmara Sea. This was a busy line, heavily used by the residents of these little towns. Its principal purpose, however, was as the terminus of the various Orient expresses – the Simplon-Orient – the Direct-Orient – the Balkan – and so on. The Simplon-Orient had started its first run from Paris the year before the station was completed, although the breach cut into the great Theodosian walls at Yedikule to make way for the lines had already been constructed.

The building had an ornate oriental façade and included an excellent café, with tables outside, and a good restaurant inside on the main platform. The entrance hall had a great, round, stained glass window at the street entrance, with a polished marble floor and cut-glass chandeliers hanging from the ceiling. The façade had no dome or minarets – which would have been blasphemous – but, nevertheless, the architecture was reminiscent of a mosque – or perhaps a small oriental palace.

When it had first opened for business, it was, for a short time, a fashionable place to sit and have a coffee and watch the arrival of one of the great trains that had travelled three days from the west. But by now, these trains were running frequently and the station no longer held such allure. There was gas lighting and gas heating installed for the winter months – and on this day, the 2nd October – both were functioning.

After all the necessary arrangements and preliminaries had been settled by Nicolai: tickets checked, porter engaged, timings checked and rechecked, Harry suggested that everyone retire to the station café. There he commandeered two tables, which were pushed together. He reminded the Androvs that an Avakian group were coming that morning as well, and that it would be worth having extra chairs available, so they would have somewhere to sit. He thought it would only be Karekin and Spiro travelling – but perhaps Sima might be coming as well, just to the station. The Avakians would be taking the fast local train to Adrianople, and would be without luggage, so it was unlikely they would arrive until half an hour or so before the departure of their train.

Alexei may have been in a state of apprehension, but he was bubbling over with excitement. The atmosphere of an international railway station, with all its comings and goings, lifted everyone's spirits, as they gathered round the table to take their coffee and pastries.

The Simplon-Orient on which William Bridgeman was travelling from London was due to arrive dead on time at 8.30. The local train to Adrianople on which Karekin and Spiro were going to Sinekli for the day would leave at about 10.00. Finally, the Direct-Orient express for Vienna, already at a platform in the station would start boarding at 11.00, to leave within the following hour.

Shortly after the party had settled down, the local suburban train pulled in to the station, a little late but well ahead of the Simplon-Orient arriving behind it. Karekin and Spiro came out of the carriage, followed by Olga. Olga took Spiro's hand, and seeing Harry and the Androvs at the café, came over while Karekin strode off to arrange the tickets. As Olga embraced everyone, Spiro smiled shyly all round, but eagerly shook Harry's hand, pleased to acknowledge the man who had referred to him as 'my friend Spiro Pantelis *effendi*'.

Just then the station loudspeaker announced that the Simplon-Orient would be arriving within the next five minutes. Everyone checked the clocks and their own watches, and it was indeed exactly 8.25. Harry jumped up.

"I've got to go. I'm meeting my father off this train. I'll bring him back to have a coffee after we deal with the luggage, if he's not too tired."

He smiled at Olga and went over to the arrival platform. Karekin finally arrived at the table, kissed the countess on the cheek, shook hands with Nicolai and Alexei and sat down to order a coffee. Olga kept her eyes on the departing Harry. Only she knew how much this meeting meant to him.

The great train, hissing steam and moving slowly, and with immense majesty, lumbered into the station. Already the brown-coated attendants of each sleeping car were opening the door of their carriage from the outside. Turkish and Kurdish porters stood leaning on their trolleys, waiting to be hired as the passengers alighted. People travelled with heavy luggage, and Harry, remembering his own arrival at this station two years ago thought of hiring a porter himself – but then decided to wait and see what his father needed. William Bridgeman, a Colonel in the British army, had served in many colonial wars, mainly in Africa, before he retired. He was used to travelling light if his wife wasn't with him.

With a hiss of steam and a final shudder, the monstrous machine came to a halt, and there was an immediate babble of noise – whistles – shouts. The single sleeping car marked 'Londres' which had started from Victoria station attached to the Golden Arrow Express, was usually the first of the sleeping cars after the engine. This coach would have been shunted onto the rail ferry at Dover. After arriving at the Gare du Nord in Paris, it was attached to the Simplon-Orient waiting at the Gare de Lyons for its three-day journey to Constantinople.

Harry's heart gave a butterfly lurch as he caught sight of a young Naval Lieutenant helping his father down the steps of the first coach. Olga, going over to the newspaper kiosk to get a newspaper for Karekin, watched as Harry strode forward. She saw Harry stretch out his hand and grasp his father's hand. They stood like that staring at each other for a moment. She couldn't hear any words, and was not even sure that they were talking. And then... in the middle of a public place, Colonel Bridgeman sloughed off the habits of a lifetime and clasped Harry round the shoulders and squeezed him in a semblance of a hug. Olga's heart leapt for joy as she saw that neither Harry nor his father showed the slightest sign of embarrassment as they parted.

Harry had been right to wait. Colonel Bridgeman only had a small Gladstone bag, which Harry immediately took charge of, and turned to lead the way. He found that the young Naval Lieutenant was still standing alongside, waiting to be introduced. "Ah, Harry my boy, er... yes. This is Lieutenant Jones of the Royal Naval Legal department. Mr Jones this is my son Captain Harry Bridgeman."

"Good morning sir", said a voice, which could have belonged to a 19 year-old.

"Good morning," said Harry shaking hands, somewhat confused by the reference to the legal department. "But I thought the prosecution team had already arrived – or so I was told."

"Er… well yes sir, that is indeed so – but I am your defending counsel."

"What the…"

"Now, now Harry, my boy, don't let's go off at half-cock. I will explain everything as soon as… But hello who do we have here?" Olga, consumed with curiosity and anxious not to leave before meeting this man, of whom she had already painted a somewhat negative mental picture, had come forward holding her newspaper. Harry turned and saw her and then unaccountably blushed and stammered out –

"Sir, this is a friend, Miss Olga Avakian – Miss Avakian, my father – William Bridgeman."

"Ah, Mr Bridgeman, we have been expecting you. Please come and meet my father and share a coffee with us. I'm sure you must be tired, but we have to leave within the hour to catch another train and it would be a great pleasure if you would join us."

The Colonel was rather pleased that he had been interrupted and if he was surprised at the pure English accent of this beautiful, elegant woman, he did not show it. Instead nodding at the hovering Harry to come along with the bag, he gave his arm to Olga and said –

"Well, well – let's go and have that coffee. What an amazing railway station…"

Harry could only gasp in surprise and trail along behind, with the mysterious Lieutenant Jones in tow, as they joined the party at the café table.

Two previously distinct outlooks were coming together in this meeting between father and son in an exotic foreign railway station concourse. The old Colonel, already 40 when Harry was born, had been unable to show his only son as much affection as the boy had craved. This had not been because William Bridgeman did not feel love – it was because, like so many at that time, he genuinely believed it was bad for a boy to receive overt signs of affection from his father. Only his wife knew that he would sometimes steal up to the young boy's bedroom at night, stare down at the sleeping child and give him a light kiss, fearful that he might awake and catch him out. Harry had left home at an early age for boarding school, university, an early entry into the navy, and then the War had separated him from his father.

Meanwhile, as William Bridgeman had grown older and wiser, he had come to see the rather ridiculous Edwardian ideas for what they were. Now that his son was a grown man, he no longer felt it necessary to hide or suppress his feelings. Well, only up to a point. He was an English gentleman after all.

Olga's excitement, Harry's joy at the arrival of his father, and the obvious fact that the Colonel was not only determined to enjoy himself but was clearly doing so, infected everybody round the table. Karekin, also in great spirits, ordered champagne to toast the Countess. Harry made a few belated attempts to rise and leave, but the Colonel airily waved him aside.

Within minutes, the Colonel knew the relationship of everyone round the table. He fell over himself to be as charming to the Countess as Karekin was – and indeed managed even better, Karekin's spoken English not quite up to the challenge. They sparred away with an old-fashioned courtesy which delighted the Countess, as she sat back enjoying the attentions of the two grand gentlemen seated on either side of her. They, too, found that they were enjoying each other's company as well as that of the Countess – surprising perhaps in view of the enormous cultural difference between them.

The time passed quickly and before long, it was time for Spiro, Karekin and Olga to depart. Spiro, halfway between tears and excitement, solemnly went round the table and shook hands with everyone. This finally broke up the party. Promising to visit as soon as he could, William Bridgeman said goodbye to the Avakians, and he, Harry, and Lieutenant Jones left to pick up the carriage retained by Harry earlier, still waiting patiently in the street outside.

The Androv family watched as the Adrianople train pulled out. Then at last it was the moment for the Countess herself to get on board the Direct-Orient express bound for Vienna, the second of the company to leave the Imperial city forever.

CHAPTER 25

The Mudania Conference

The refusal of General Harington to deliver the ultimatum to the Turkish nationalists, had defused the situation somewhat. The possibility of a new war had diminished, though it had not disappeared. Lloyd George had appealed to the Dominion governments for support at Constantinople in emotional terms – referring to the graves of the dead on the Gallipoli peninsula. There had been some response from the Australian government, but the others – New Zealand, Canada and South Africa - had been distinctly cool and the French refused any support to the British government. Above all, neither the coalition nor the British public in general, were enthusiastic about the renewal of formal hostilities.

Arrangements had been made by Lord Curzon and the French President Poincaré for Harington to go to the little port of Mudania to meet with representatives of the Turkish nationalists. Both the French and Italian colleagues of Harington – Charpy and Mombelli – were to be present. The Turks would not allow any Greek to be present.

Mudania was a typical, small eastern Mediterranean port with a population of about 5,000, half of whom had been Greeks until a few weeks before. It had whitewashed houses straggling up a low hillside, nestled round a small sheltered bay. The little town had old timbered Ottoman houses and cobbled streets. The long wharf, the only pretence to a harbour, was simple and free of any major buildings.

Harington decided to travel in a fairly ostentatious manner on *the Iron Duke*, sailing with Admiral Brock himself. All had agreed there should be no provocation on either side in Chanak, while the Conference was in session, and the Turkish cavalry retired a few hundred yards, though not to the extent of leaving the neutral zone.

The drizzle and overcast skies of the previous day, when the Androvs and the Avakians had met at Sirkedji station, had now turned to heavy rain. As Harington stepped onto the pier from the launch, a furious wind and sea-spray sprang up, soaking his clothing. Generals Charpy and Mombelli had already arrived on the quayside and were sheltering behind a low wall.

The conference was to be held in the former Russian consulate – the only stone building of any size anywhere near the pier. It was bare and cold, though some Turkish carpets had been hurriedly draped about the low whitewashed rooms. There were not enough chairs, so in the end Harington, Charpy and Mombelli were the only ones seated on one side of the table, facing General Ismet Pasha, the Turkish nationalist representative, seated on the other.

Stubborn and wily, deaf when it suited him, Ismet – in touch with Kemal in Ankara by telephone throughout – was a good deal shrewder than he appeared. Whenever matters became difficult Ismet either pretended not to hear or would immediately insist on checking with Ankara, while he considered a suitable response.

The conference went on all day. Harington not only had to consider the requirements pressed on him by London, but found that time and again, the French General was acting as a mouthpiece for Ismet. Constantinople was no longer the top of the agenda; the problem was Eastern Thrace. The Treaty of Sevres, signed, only two years before, by the Allies and the Ottoman government, had given this area to Greece. Greek troops patrolled Adrianople and it was still governed by a Greek administration up to the Chatalja lines. By one of those quirks of historical and geographic development, Eastern Thrace was home to a majority of ethnic Greeks, whereas Western Thrace, now firmly within Greek borders, had a majority of Muslims. This hadn't mattered so long as both parts were part of the multi-national Ottoman Empire; but had now become a problem which the conference was forced to resolve.

The French and Italians were ready to give in to Ankara on every point and the British, too, were prepared to give way on most matters affecting Constantinople. The Turks hinted that for their part they would not press their demand for Western Thrace, which had been given to Greece by the Treaty of Neuilly, so long as Eastern Thrace was returned, insisting on an immediate transfer. Harington main concern was to avoid problems caused if insufficient time was allowed for a trouble-free handover, as would be he case in the evnt of an immediate seizure by the Turks of Constantinople.

On the evening of the first day, Harington left for *the Iron Duke* to retire for the night..

The next day, as discussions dragged on, Harington lost patience and produced a hastily scribbled draft agreement declaring that these were his final terms, that he was proposing to return to Constantinople that very afternoon, returning the next day for the reply. True to his word, Harington left that afternoon, sending a wireless message to General Marden, now in command of the Chanak garrison, warning him that it looked as if the conference was breaking up and authorised him to be ready to open hostilities against the Turks. Once back in Constantinople, Harington ensured that all military arrangements for holding on to the city were also in place in case no agreement was signed. All was in the balance.

The fast local train to Adrianople steamed out of Sirkedji station, made the great loop round the grounds of the Topkapi Palace and out of the city. Spiro sat in the first class carriage with his face pressed against the window, staring out as the little towns, fields and open country passed by. He had seen trains in Smyrna, but this was the first time he had ever sat in one. Karekin and Olga chatted together in Armenian, while Spiro watched the changing scenes go by. After following along the Marmara coast, the railway line turned inland into agricultural areas. There were few roads and those that did exist were merely dirt tracks. The landscape was treeless and would have been completely featureless save for the evidence of careful human husbandry, but to Spiro, who had often gone for family picnics in the lush well-watered countryside around Smyrna, the vista was sad and desolate.

The train passed through the Chatalja lines where Allied troops were still posted in small encampments. As the train moved on, these small camps opened out into the main Greek army camp. Spiro thrilled to see line after line of smart white military tents, with the flag of the Greek Kingdom proudly fluttering from the tops of poles. Spiro knew nothing about the politics, which were fashioning his life, though he was beginning to pick up on some of the attitudes and anxieties of the adults. Although he was an Ottoman citizen, just like Karekin and Olga, he had been living under a Greek administration since he was eight.

He still found it difficult to reconcile those three to four years of childhood security with the 13 days of nightmare ending only a week ago. He was still processing the loss of his father and brother Costas to certain death and the brutal death of his mother he had witnessed. Spiro continued to stare out of the window as the train steamed on through the countryside.

Then the train pulled into its second stop – Sinekli station. The station was a pleasant two-platform affair with only a few people waiting. Most of these clambered onto the second-class carriages at the back. However, standing on the platform, looking up and down the train, was an elderly couple dressed formally in black and easily recognisable as the Kafides family. Slightly behind them, was a fairly elderly man, dressed more colourfully in working clothes. They didn't move as they watched Karekin get down from the carriage and then turn to give his hand to Olga. However, as Spiro clambered down, dragging behind him the precious case entrusted to him by Armineh, they moved shyly forward.

"Mr Karekin Avakian?" enquired the elderly man extending his hand somewhat diffidently, and speaking Turkish.

"Certainly – and do I have the pleasure of speaking to Christos Kafides *effendi*?", replied Karekin smiling broadly.

The man nodded his head, then introduced his wife Saroula, and his neighbour, Mukhtadir, the farmer who tilled the land next to his, and who had driven them into Sinekli in his cart to meet the train. Spiro said nothing as more introductions were made. He shook hands with Mr Kafides and then with the Turkish neighbour – Mukhtadir - who winked at him as he looked up. Spiro smiled for the first time that day and then found himself enveloped in the voluminous skirts of Madam Kafides. Saroula kissed him on his head as she held him to her and then said – in the first Greek spoken that day to Spiro –

"Welcome – oh, welcome, young man. I, who have lost a son – and you who have lost a mother … We'll do – yes, we'll do well."

She took his hand and he relinquished for the first time his grip on Armineh's case, which was gently taken by the grizzled Mukhtadir. The little party moved off the platform and into the dirty, shabby street outside the station. There was still a slight drizzle. Further on, stood a large farm cart drawn by two strong horses. It became clear that Mr Kafides was a little embarrassed by the open cart, and said to Karekin – nodding towards Olga –

"Avakian *bey* – I will hire one of these carriages for you and your daughter to travel in."

Olga immediately replied, for the first tim speaking in Greek - "No, no, sir – I love the rain – I prefer the freedom of open carriages. You and papa go in the closed carriage by all means, but Spiro and I will go with Mukhtadir Bayram *effendi*."

Then, helped by Spiro, she clambered aboard the cart. Saroula had already ensconced herself in the front and was handing back big black umbrellas, which had been under the front seats.

Christos Kafides, a conservative farmer of the old school, had been a little shocked by the way this young lady had interrupted the talk between the two male elders – but considered that this must be how it had become in Polis. He politely extended his hand for Karekin to clamber aboard as well. Dressed as he always was in an impeccably tailored grey suit, Karekin, would have preferred to go in the carriage offered, but he put on his most charming smile, opened up one of the umbrellas handed to him, and sat down with the others. The two horses started off, trundling over the cobbled streets and moving sedately through the town which gave way, abruptly, to the flat treeless countryside.

All around them was the evidence of small well-tended farms. The neatness of the farmyards he passed, and the well-managed aspect of the agriculture, was unlike the usual disorder of the small Balkan farms that Karekin had seen. Looking around him, and later going on a tour of the Kafides farm, Karekin saw that this was the result of generations of tender care by mainly Greek peasants, who had worked the land for centuries. The people had lived under a tolerant Ottoman government, and while it would be an exaggeration to suggest it was benign, it had at least allowed them to manage their own land and worship at their own churches.

The old man may have been irritated by Olga's intervention, but it had broken the ice and they spoke Greek for the rest of the day. Both Christos and Karekin wore a fez; Mukhtadir was bareheaded. After leaving them at the farm gates, he indicated that he would return to take them back to the station in the late afternoon.

Karekin and Christos were awkward in their conversation. Christos was shy and a little in awe of this Ottoman *effendi* from the big city. Karekin, never very good at general chit-chat, remained a bit aloof, until he was taken for a tour of the farm after lunch and found himself interested in the 'business' side of farm management. Christos lost his shyness and Karekin his reserve.

When they returned to the farmhouse, Christos raised a matter which had been at the back of his mind for some time –

"Avakian oglu can you advise me on what is happening in the city?"

"I'm afraid I really don't know. I hope that the Sultan will remain, but one thing is certain, either way Polis will become Turkish again soon, of that there is no doubt."

"And here in Thrace?"

"Again I cannot say – but Thrace was annexed to Greece by solemn treaty with the legitimate Turkish government and the Greek government and the British pride themselves on not treating treaties as mere scraps of paper."

"Well, perhaps, but look what happened in Smyrna."

"Yes – but the situation here in Thrace is different. They'll act like they did over Belgium – that's the sign of a Great Power"

"I am not so sure Karekin *effendi*. Even Great Powers act only in their own narrow interest. I fear... I fear that it is going to be Smyrna all over again."

"I understand Kafides *bey*. I know how terrible it can be when Turks arrive, enraged and bloodthirsty ... Surely it is different here. I lost a son in Smyrna but ...."

Conversations like this, were taking place all over Eastern Thrace as everyone, Christian and Moslem alike, waited to know what the great and good were going to decide. By fairly early in the afternoon, it was clear that Spiro would stay with the Kafides. For their part, they needed some young blood on their farm, while he needed a permanent home within a Greek community. He may have been a bit shy of the formal Christos, but he had clearly warmed to Saroula and she to him. Karekin could see that Olga was happy enough with what she saw. And so matters were settled and Spiro took up his case to the room that had formerly belonged to the Kafides son.

When Karekin and Olga left to catch the early evening train, Karekin pressed an envelope containing some gold coins into Spiro's hand, telling him to keep it safe, and not to open it except in an emergency. Spiro had spent the whole of the afternoon after lunch running about the farm, delighted with the fresh air and the sense of freedom. He loved the animals and was already making friends with the local farm labourer who worked at the farm. He was ready to settle here, desperate as he was to belong somewhere again after all the trauma of the last three weeks. What did he know of the men sitting round a table in a bare room on the other side of the sea? Surely, he was home again at last?

But on the very next day after Harington left Mudania on *the Iron Duke*, he returned on a Royal Navy frigate, leaving Admiral Brock in the city to continue preparations in the event of a military attack by the Turkish nationalist army. Further down at Chanak, General Marden had instructions to begin his attack on the Turkish cavalry at a specific hour, unless contacted otherwise. Harington was also armed with a telegram from London authorising him to contest any military action within the neutral zone, if and when the current negotiations broke down, as was expected. Furthermore, he was authorised to issue yet another ultimatum threatening war if the Turks did not withdraw.

Charpy and Mombelli were waiting for him on the quayside. Once again the three generals, with their interpreters, went into the bare white-washed room in the old Russian consulate, and gathered round the table opposite Ismet Pasha. Once again, matters were discussed, the future of whole peoples, whole provinces, were bandied about from one side of the table to the other. But the atmosphere had changed – there were now only a few points of disagreement left. Ismet paced up and down the room on one side of the table as Harington did the same on the other, while the French and Italian generals looked on. At last, eliciting a quiet sigh of relief from Harington, Ismet stopped his pacing and said loudly –

"*J'accepte!*"

The Convention of Mudania settled many minor matters and left open others to be dealt with later at a conference to be held in Lausanne. But its principal agreement – flashed round the world by telegraph – was that the Turks were free to cross the straits, to enter Constantinople and take over Eastern Thrace. The Greek army was to start evacuation immediately and to retire across the River Maritza into Western Thrace, giving up the whole province and the city of Adrianople at once. Turkish gendarmes, numbering over 8,000, were to enter the province on the heels of the departing Greeks. There had not been a single Greek representative in Mudania at the conference.

Already, men in frock coats were speaking of new concepts, sanitised to sound benign, like 'exchange of populations'. What this meant in practice was cleansing the state of ethnic communities the Turks no longer wanted, regardless of how many centuries they may have lived there, or whether they wanted to leave.

These men believed they were dealing with a problem in a humane and logical manner, but no crazed Ottoman Sultan, however ruthless and fanatical, would ever have dreamt of imposing such a heartless solution on the diverse peoples living within the old Empire.

Meanwhile, Spiro was settling into his new life and home, learning about animals and crops, which he hoped would help his new, adopted parents. What did those respectable men care for the likes of Spiro and his new family? While the Kafides family carried on with their hard-working, everyday lives on land which had been theirs for generations, the statesmen were planning the final conference to settle, once and for all, the affairs of the dying Ottoman Empire; a settlement which would throw thousands more people off their lands, and draw up innumerable new artificial frontiers the consequences of which would still be reverberating a hundred years later.

CHAPTER 26

Harry and his Father

Once the Avakians had left on the Adrianople train with Spiro, Harry and his father, together with Lieutenant Jones, clambered aboard the carriage, which had been patiently waiting outside the station. As it clattered across the Galata Bridge, there was a silence among the three passengers. The cover was closed as the rain continued, though it was open at the front. Sitting next to his father, Harry sat back and let his thoughts wander. The young lieutenant ignored the rain as he leant eagerly from one side to the other, taking in the views of this extraordinary city. The carriage was following the sea road to avoid the steps that climbed up to the Grande Rue.

While Colonel Bridgeman and Lieutenant Jones were looking round and marvelling, as the wonders of the city unfolded, Harry at last had time to consider why this Lieutenant was here at all. Once the formalities of registering at the Park Otel were completed, and he was alone with his father, he asked –

"Father, why is the Lieutenant here with you?"

"Listen, son, don't jump to conclusions. Court-martials are not all that different in the Royal Navy to those in the army – and I have had experience of these affairs in my 40 years in the Service. The atmosphere is intimidating, and one can easily be dominated and overawed by the occasion; that is precisely how they are meant to be. You will be facing a prosecuting officer whose duty is to portray you as totally in the wrong – without malice – but because that is his job."

"Yes, very well father, but you forget that I was involved in one of the Navy's most notorious recent court-martials when Admiral Troubridge was accused of dereliction of duty in allowing the *Goeben* and the *Breslau* to slip through his fingers in such dramatic circumstances at the start of the war."

"Yes, well, that's a perfect case in point. Do you think for a moment that Troubridge would have been acquitted of all charges, as he was, if he had not had an experienced military lawyer to put his case?"

"Well, father, I am not Troubridge."

"No Harry, but you need someone to present your case succinctly and unemotionally and with the professional expertise you inevitably lack."

"And this Jones fellow – he's very young – what experience…"

"Trust me Harry. I have just spent three days and nights with him closeted in a railway carriage. He spent the whole time going through the documents the Admiralty supplied. He may not be the greatest legal eagle, but he knows what he is about."

"How did you find him?"

"Well I just went round to the Admiralty. They told me you had refused their offer of a defence lawyer and I countermanded that by offering to pay for an officer to come with me to act on your behalf – subject of course, my boy, to your agreeing. They agreed and…"

"Father, are you saying that you have paid to…"

"Oh tosh Harry – don't be ridiculous. Now listen, the court-martial is the day after tomorrow – so you only have the one day to discuss it with Jones."

And so it was, that Harry spent the whole of the next day closeted with the young Lieutenant Jones, going through the fateful events of the days spent on the HMS *Lion* in the bay of Smyrna. Now that the actual court-martial was upon him, the thought of all the formalities of the courtroom, the pleadings, the speeches, and the reading of witness statements, caused butterflies in his stomach. He was already imagining his arrival on *the Iron Duke*, dressed in full dress uniform, the curious stares of the sailors, the boardroom where the trial would be held and the salutes, handshakes and false smiles. But it was only his imagination working overtime, for things turned out rather differently.

The next morning – the day Harry was going to spend going through his case with the Lieutenant – as they were all breakfasting together in the hotel, two letters were handed to him by one of the hotel messenger boys. One was a formal note from the East Mediterranean Naval Command. This was short and terse, informing him that *the Iron Duke* had sailed that morning with the Admiral and General Harington on board and would be away on the other side of the Marmara for a day or two. The court-martial was now to be held at the Harbiye – the old Ottoman military academy, the headquarters of the British administration of the city, and the shore headquarters of the Navy. The message confirmed that the proceedings were not scheduled to take longer than a day, as agreed between the prosecuting officer and Lieutenant Jones for the defence. The opening statements would start at 10.00am the next morning and the note was a formal notice requiring Harry to attend at that time.

The second note was from Olga, written the night before.

"*Dear Harry,*" it read, "*we have just returned after leaving Spiro with the Kafides. It all went very well and you will be pleased to hear that both baba and I were happy with the situation. I hope he will be able to make a new life for himself there.*

It crossed my mind that you might be busy tomorrow, dealing with prepara-tions for the trial and your father will be on his own. If it is of any interest to him, I would be happy to show off some of the sights of the city. Nerissa will be finishing her classes in the early afternoon and my father will be at his office all day, but has invited everyone to Tokatlians for tea at four o'clock.

I will quite understand if your father is too tired or would rather stay with you. In any event I will call at the Park on my own at about 11.00am and no doubt we can make any further arrangements, as I hope your father can at least accept my father's invitation. Respectfully yours, Olga."

"Er…father," said Harry after handing him the letter to read, "don't worry, I'm sure you won't want to traipse round the town with this young lady. Really she won't mind a bit, we'll have a coffee together and then she …"

"Good heavens, Harry, stop talking nonsense. I can't think of a bet-ter way to spend a morning. You'll be engrossed with Jones. No – no. But what is this Tokatlians she is talking about."

"It is the smartest restaurant, tea-room and dancing spot in Pera. It's where all the fashionable Armenian wedding receptions take place – they have a church right next door."

Olga arrived about an hour later.

Tension in the city was running high, but neither the Colonel nor Lieutenant Jones was aware of it. Harry had so many other thoughts on his mind, that even he was oblivious. Everybody was aware of the departure of *the Iron Duke* with Harington *effendi* on board. Whether Greek, Turk, Armenian, Russian or Jew, it was common knowledge that four or five generals were going to be sitting round a table at the lit-tle flea pot of a port across the Marmara – Mudania. It was expected that the basic terms for the future of the Empire and the city would be worked out there.

If no settlement was reached, and war broke out, anything at all could happen. The revolution in Greece, and the flight of the King, had given some hope to the Greek community, who were aware that it was Tino's return that had so soured relations between the Greeks and the British. Maybe they might get Polis for themselves after all.

Speculation was rife in the febrile atmosphere of the city. There was no going back on the new situation in Anatolia created by the resurgent Turkish nationalists – but as for Eastern Thrace and Constantinople itself, their fates were still undecided.

Like the perfect host he always was Karekin arrived early at Tokatlians. He took a table for eight in the grand *thé dansant* room. Nerissa was the first to arrive. She often came here – it was a favourite spot for her and Vahan to meet after her classes at the university ended. She saw Karekin sitting alone, and came to join him at the table. After kissing her father, she looked round the salon she knew so well. Despite all the changes wrought by the war and it's aftermath, this room had scarcely changed at all since that day in April 1915 when, as a shy young girl of sixteen, she had chaperoned Olga in this very spot. Here Olga had sat with her, holding Selim's hand under the table, while she looked on dreamily as officers of the army of the Ottoman Empire had danced away the whole afternoon with elegant and well-dressed ladies in their arms. Old Europe dying on its feet, with Gallipoli and about half a mil-*lion* deaths, only days and a few miles away.

The grand room was still much the same – a glass roof with a large and rather vulgar chandelier hanging from the centre of cast-iron struts. Nerissa smiled as she recalled how worried she had been about the relationship Olga was rushing into. Now Selim was dead – dead in the same fire that had burned her beloved brother Haik. A tear came to her eye. She looked away from her father, who was examining the teatime menu, and wished that Vahan was here. She had sent a note to the Asadourian house inviting him to join them all – but she wasn't sure if he was back from his trip into Anatolia.

The next to arrive was Colonel Bridgeman, with Olga on his arm. They floated into the room – the Colonel clearly in high good humour, both chatting away to each other. The Colonel was introduced to Nerissa and they all sat down, while Olga went over all they had done together during the day. The morning's leisurely tour of the city in the company of a beautiful and elegant young woman, so easy to talk to and who charmed him without flattery, left William Bridgeman in a contented state of well- being. The city had worked its magic.

Harry's father mused on the extraordinary sea change in his relationship with his son. He had never, for a moment, appreciated the effect that his telegram would have on Harry when he composed and sent it. From the moment of that first long handclasp, and the embrace that followed, their relationship had changed irrevocably for the better with each discussion bringing a deeper understanding between them.

Last to arrive was Harry, accompanied by Lieutenant Jones, and this made a perfect six. Tea was ordered. William Bridgeman and Karekin drew together and chatted about the options facing Harington in Mudania, the present military position, and where the parties to the conflict were heading. Meanwhile, the others danced. Jones turned out to be a good dancer and Nerissa enjoyed herself. Harry was a good deal more uncoordinated and didn't know any of the new American dances but then neither did Olga. They could do the waltzes and the more old-fashioned dances, and Olga remained unusually quiet in Harry's arms.

When the party broke up, the English group to walk back up the Grande Rue du Pera, the Avakians to take a carriage back to Sirkedji station, Olga leant up and gave him a kiss on the cheek – whispering into his ear – "Good luck, Harry, good luck for tomorrow."

The next day, Harry arrived at the Harbiye military academy in good time. He was dressed in his full ceremonial uniform and accompanied by the trim and dapper figure of the young lieutenant. As they stood at the hotel entrance waiting for the carriage, Colonel Bridgeman had grasped Harry's hand and said –

"Good luck, son, good luck. Don't worry. I only hope that faced with the same circumstances I would have had the moral courage to act as you did. Orders are orders – but sometimes, common humanity must come first. I'm totally with you, Harry, my boy. Totally – whatever happens."

Then, fearing even now that he had gone too far, he smiled and turned away as the two young men clambered into the carriage to the Harbiye.

CHAPTER 27

The Court Martial

Harry's vague ideas of what the proceedings would be like had been largely correct. Lieutenant Jones and the principal prosecuting officer had put their heads together, and quite a lot of the evidence had already been agreed between them, without the necessity of calling all the witnesses. There were three officer-judges hearing the case – the chairman, sent from London by the lords of the Admiralty, and two senior officers from the East Mediterranean station.

There was a lot of procedural posturing by the prosecutor and young Jones. There was the usual obsequious address to 'my Lords', and 'my respected friend'. There was plenty of 'with the greatest respect' when the witness being questioned, or the opposing Counsel, was talking rubbish; or worse, 'with the greatest possible respect'. But it was fairly low-key with little fireworks from either quarter.

The radio operator on *the Iron Duke* was called and gave his evidence, producing the relevant forms and notes made on the day. Two of the officers on the *Lion* gave their evidence in a quiet manner, embarrassed to look at their former Captain. Apart from Harry, Jones called only one further witness, over and above those called by the prosecutor. This was the young midshipman who had been on duty throughout the whole incident. He was called to give evidence regarding the actions of the old sailor who jumped overboard to rescue the young girl, after she had been turned away from *the Iron Duke*.

Eventually, Harry was called to the stand. After taking his service details, Lieutenant Jones asked him to set out, in his own words, what had occurred on that day in the Bay of Smyrna. Harry spoke for several minutes, finishing in mid-sentence, unclear how to continue, but to everyone's surprise Jones simply said 'thank you' and sat down, inviting the Prosecuting Officer to cross-examine.

The prosecuting counsel took Harry through a number of formal matters for the record before asking two or three questions, which stood out in Harry's mind as being fairly significant.

"Did you accompany Admiral Brock on his visit to General Nureddin?"

"I did."

"The Admiral required permission to put a party of marines ashore for the sole purpose of picking up British citizens. Can you recall what was said at that interview? Please tell us in your own words what was said and describe the atmosphere?"

"General Nureddin was in a very excited state, refusing initially to shake hands with the Admiral, and said he considered the British to be the principal enemy of the new Turkey. The Admiral was tactful, but persistent, particularly on the question of the protection of British nationals, pointing out that French, Italian and US boats were already doing the same and assuring the new Governor – 'that in every other respect we are entirely neutral'."

"What did you think of that, Captain?"

At this point Harry hesitated before replying, though this was not recorded in the dry official account, where the reply was simply –

"I find it a little difficult, sir, to set out my personal reaction as at the time it was mixed, and since then I have had time to reflect on it. I believe it would be fair to say that I quite understood and admired the Admiral for the calm and tactful way he was dealing with General Nureddin. However, it was not entirely clear what the Admiral meant when he assured the general with those words. I certainly took them to mean that they applied to the attitude adopted by any patrol that was given permission to go ashore."

"Is that all Captain?"

"No, I must admit that even then I thought the Admiral had gone a step too far. I made no comment and accepted that it was probably the least the Admiral could promise to be sure of getting the permission needed."

"Were you aware, Captain, of the pressures being applied by the government in London?"

"No, sir, I was not – nor would I have expected the Admiral to discuss such matters with me."

Then, after clearing up some more points to avoid any ambiguities, came the final questions –

"Captain Bridgeman, did you see the sailors on HMS *Iron Duke* pouring buckets of water down on swimmers attempting to grab hold of trailing ropes?"

"I did."

"Did you assume that they were acting under proper orders?"

"Yes."

"Were the sailors on the deck of your ship under your orders to remain at their posts?"

"They were."

"Did one of your sailors diso*bey* your orders and jump overboard to rescue one of those swimmers who was swimming away from *the Iron Duke*?"

"Yes, Sir."

"Did you discipline that sailor?"

"No, I did not."

The trial ended shortly after with two short speeches by the Prosecutor and the Defending Counsel. The summations were followed by a short statement from the leading tribunal officer. He confirmed that judgement would be handed down formally within a month, and that Captain Bridgeman was to remain suspended on full pay. The Court then rose and the court martial was over.

Outside in the corridor, Harry shook hands with the officers from the *Lion* and returned to the hotel.

He had remained calm and correct throughout the proceedings. However, the effort of concentrating on the testimony and answering the questions in as truthful a way as possible, had left him mentally exhausted. The moment he arrived back at the hotel he began to shiver and feel the cold. William had been waiting all afternoon in the lobby and jumped up and strode over to his son when Harry walked in.

Harry gave him a wry smile, and William Bridgeman, in public view and against decades of training, clasped his son in a tight embrace. Slowly but surely Harry's shivers, which only William Bridgeman had seen or felt, subsided and still his father held on. What was it about the atmosphere of this city that made it possible for the old Colonel to act so out of character – or was it perhaps his true character emerging after years of suppression. Back in his room, Harry told his father all that had transpired, as well as the gist of the two summing up speeches. Then, with two extra pullovers, he dropped off to sleep, exhausted but still smiling at his father's last words as he left and closed the door behind him –

"Harry, my boy, I'm proud of you – truly proud, whatever the authorities might finally decide. You acted like the honourable man I always knew you were."

The Prosecution Speech

Members of the Tribunal, representative of the Lords of the Admiralty, this case is somewhat unusual in that there is no dispute as to the facts. The facts are clear, and both the defence and the prosecution are in total agreement as to what occurred within the British Fleet in the Bay of Smyrna on the 13th September 1922 – what signals and orders were issued by the Commander of the Fleet – Admiral Sir Osmond de Beauvoir Brock, and were received by the Commanding officer of HMS Lion – Captain Harry Bridgeman, against whom these charges have been brought.

I will not, therefore, repeat the facts which have been carefully considered throughout the day. All you are asked to decide, My Lords, is whether the facts as agreed constitute an offence under the various Navy Acts, and what course of action is recommended.

I am sure that I do not need to emphasise that this is not a Court set up to determine whether the actions of Captain Bridgeman were morally correct or not. We are here simply to decide whether the defendant had the right to ignore the clear orders of his immediate superior.

No Navy or military unit could operate properly if it was not clear that orders should be obeyed immediately and without question. When Captain Bridgeman himself ordered his men to 'lower the boats', in order to go to the rescue of some of the refugees, he did not need to argue his case with them. It did not cross his mind for a moment that his orders would not be obeyed. He could rely on their training to act without question. Without such a certainty, no army, indeed no disciplined body of men could ever function efficiently.

This principle applies with particular emphasis to the Royal Navy. In all ships throughout history, every sailor of whatever rank, depends on everyone else around him. The whole safety of each ship, and indeed that of the whole fleet, depends on the certainty of the chain of command.

Consider, My Lords, how impossible it would be if admirals could not be sure that their orders would be carried out to the letter by their captains, or if captains could not be sure that their orders to ordinary seamen were not equally obeyed immediately.

Though the conditions in this case were not easy – the maintenance of discipline and order is even more important in such circumstances. How could Captain Bridgeman know under what political pressures the Admiral may have been labouring. Regardless of the circumstances, it was not his place to decide how the Royal Navy should react to the events that were unfolding in Smyrna on that day. It was, after all, only by virtue of the British taxpayer, and the British government, that he was there in the Bay of Smyrna at all.

My Lords, this is a simple matter. Did Captain Bridgeman disobey a very clear order issued to him directly by his superior officer. You need look no further than that. If he did, he must be found guilty and dealt with as such.

The Defence speech given by Lieutenant Jones

My Lords, the Prosecuting Officer has in his final address pointed out that there is no dispute as to the facts in this case, and has accordingly not dwelt upon them in any way. However, I feel that I must refer specifically to one or two of these undisputed facts.

Firstly, it has been mentioned several times during these proceedings that Captain Bridgeman was present when Admiral Brock gave General Nureddin his word that the British would remain strictly neutral, and that this personal knowledge of the defendant makes him somehow more culpable. However, I do believe that it is a vital aspect of this case to analyse what was meant by that neutrality offer. I would suggest that the neutrality promised could only refer specifically to the events unfolding in the city. The Admiral had to make sure that the General understood that any patrol the British sent ashore would remain strictly neutral. It was the necessary precondition that General Nureddin demanded from the Admiral in order to allow British marines to operate on the shore to bring off their own nationals, as the French, Italians and Americans had already been doing for days. Neutrality meant not interfering with whatever was happening on shore. No marines were to be landed – no bombardment would be made - to influence whatever was going on in the city.

The Admiral's signal to the fleet, which is the basis of the order which Captain Bridgeman is accused of disobeying, was to the effect that no 'refugees', whatever their race, should be allowed onto any British ship. 'Refugee' has a clear meaning, my Lords; it could only refer to all those unfortunate people milling about on the quayside looking for some way to escape the approaching fire. A drowning man is not first and foremost a refugee – he is simply 'a drowning man'. Captain Bridgeman's actual orders and actions avoided the picking-up of any people, obviously potential refugees, on the waterfront and were directed only to picking up people already in the water in danger of drowning. He specifically ordered his boats not to approach the shoreline, but only to pick up people in distress already in the sea.

I would repeat that a drowning man or woman is not a refugee. When wit-

nessing a man about to drown in the sea you neither consider his race nor his political status.

The signal that Captain Bridgeman sent back to the Admiral may have been a little too firm and perhaps a bit unwise for a Captain to his commanding officer, but it states the position clearly, and I will repeat it here in full. It read –

"There is no breach of neutrality in saving any human beings regardless of race, in distress in the sea. Three hundred years of Royal Navy reputation requires us to save even outright enemies from drowning, when we can."

The only intention of this signal was to make it clear that he understood the promise given to General Nureddin, but that he wanted the Admiral to understand that he considered that his actions did not in any way jeopardise that promise of neutrality.

I accept totally the Prosecutor's argument that it was not for Captain Bridgeman to decide whether the Admiral's policy of strict neutrality was correct politically or not. But, as I have tried to show, the actions of Captain Bridgeman had nothing to do with the policy of strict neutrality, which applied to the situation on shore. I would simply say that the signal sent showed that while he was happy to accept the Admiral's decision in every respect, he believed that picking up drowning people from the sea did not breach that promise or policy in any way.

In lowering the boats to pick up survivors drowning in the water, Captain Bridgeman believed he was acting well within the scope of his orders, and that it was a matter of using his own initiative in difficult circumstances. In this respect, I would add, my Lords, that he had already been warned by his second-in-command that his men, experienced sailors, were getting highly restive as they were forced to watch women and young girls, drowning all around them; and this agitation, as evidenced by the old sailor who jumped overboard, was likely to lead to a loss of morale and was a factor that he was entitled to take into account when making his decision.

Finally, this brings me to that veteran sailor and the failure of Captain Bridgeman to discipline him. Is it really suggested that on saving a drowning young girl, Captain Bridgeman should then have clapped the man in irons – and then what – thrown the girl back into the sea?

I must, therefore, put it to you that Captain Bridgeman's actions were not only morally correct but were not contrary to the spirit of the orders he had received. I repeat that he was most careful to make sure that none of the boats launched from HMS Lion that day were to go anywhere near the shore. In the end he was entitled to use his initiative in circumstances, of which his superior commander might not have been fully aware.

Accordingly I would invite you to treat the matter as one not requiring any further action.

CHAPTER 28

Departures and Arrivals

Two days later, William Bridgeman and Harry arrived at midday at
Sirkedji station. His father was to catch the two o'clock afternoon Simplon-Orient Express. The day after Harry's return from the proceedings at the Harbiye had been spent sightseeing. He and his father spent
the morning going round the city visiting, one after the other, all the
famous sites and monuments, in particular, the mosques.

In the afternoon, the Colonel, anxious to stretch his legs further, and
to put some colour into Harry's cheeks, persuaded him to accompany
him on a full-scale tour of the great Theodosian triple walls. These began in the north at the ruined old Byzantine Palace – the Blachernae
– on the Golden Horn, then across the peninsula and down to the Ottoman fortress of Yedikule on the Marmara coast.

The Colonel had read up all the military manuals and dissertations
about these formidable walls, which had made Constantinople virtually
impregnable throughout the Middle Ages. The great land walls had
never been breached in one thousand years, until the arrival of gun-
powder changed the balance between missiles and walls forever.

On that particular afternoon, it was cold but bright. William, relaxed
and in fine fettle, strode out at a pace which belied his increasing years.
He took notes at all the important places along the wall, where the
manuals indicated particular weaknesses or strengths, the countryside
coming right up to the walls.

There was hardly a single point along the whole stretch which had
not witnessed some dramatic event in the city's history. Almost every
one of its one hundred towers had some myth or story attached to it.
The Colonel noted the famous weak spot where the river Lycus ran into
the city and where the ground sloped down on either side of the valley.
Finally, they lingered at the one place where the walls had at last succumbed to the pounding of the great cannon and had been breached
for the first and only time in 1453 by the Ottoman conqueror of the city
– Mehmet II. This event – above all others – had symbolised the end of
the Middle Ages. The triumph of the 'gun' over the hitherto dominant
'wall.' In that dramatic year the last Byzantine Emperor – Constantine
XI – had died as the Ottoman army surged over the walls. His power
and his empire had by then been reduced to the city alone. Now, nearly
500 years later, as the Colonel and Harry strode along the same walls

that the last Byzantine emperor had defended with his life, the power of his ultimate successor, the current Ottoman Sultan had also been reduced to this one city, all his other power having fallen away.

Perhaps Mustapha Kemal Pasha was right in referring always to the decadent, effeminate and corrupting influence of this half-European and half-Asian city. Could it be that it deserved all that was threatened by the avenging Anatolian army, drawn up on the other side of the straits.

The following afternoon after this military stroll, the Colonel and Harry arrived at midday in good time to have a lunch together in the portico of the restaurant at Sirkedji station. They were comfortable and relaxed in each other's company, perhaps for the first time in their lives. The city had worked its charm as always.

"Harry, my boy, what is going to become of Constantinople? What a city!"

"I really have no idea, father. The agreements at Mudanya will return Eastern Thrace and even Adrianople to the Turks, and that inevitably will include this city. But what the regime will be is still in the melting pot."

"What do you mean – as the Kemalists have won, won't they simply take over?"

"Well that is indeed most likely. However, it's easy to be misled by all the noisy nationalist demonstrations in the streets and ignore the deep-rooted emotional attachment to the Ottoman dynasty by the majority of the people; a pride embodied in their sense of identity for over 500 years."

A quiet voice behind them said –

"I agree with you entirely young man."

Both the Bridgemans looked up startled. There, behind Harry's chair, stood the tall, impeccably dressed, figure of Karekin, already removing his hat and gloves.

"May I join you?"

"Certainly, sir, certainly, with pleasure. I was seeing my father off," said Harry jumping up and bringing over another chair. "What brings you to Sirkedji."

"Why, the departure of your father, of course," said Karekin calling out to the waiter for a coffee. "How could I let such a distinguished visitor depart from my city, my world, without a proper farewell."

William Bridgeman beamed with delight and the three of them drifted into a wide-ranging discussion of the future of the city. The Mudanya conference was still going on and they agreed there was absolutely no 'historical imperative' as to what might yet happen.

Finally, the moment came when the Colonel had to board the train, waiting opposite them on Platform 1. Karekin rose, too, and shook hands –

"Last week I was here for the departure of the Countess Androvna – the mother of my first prospective son-in-law. Now here I am again, Colonel, to see you off. I wonder how many more departures I have yet to face from my town, my birthplace and that of my forefathers."

Karekin smiled warmly as he shook hands in an attempt to lessen the solemnity of this last comment. The Colonel and Harry strode away as Karekin turned and left the station.

Welcomed by the brown-uniformed Wagons-Lits attendant, waiting at the door of his coach, William Bridgeman turned, looked at his son and embraced him again before boarding for the three-day journey to London. Harry turned and walked briskly away without another word.

What indeed was to become of Constantinople? Harington was still occupying the city as Allied Commander of about 5,000 troops. This might have appeared puny, compared to the 80,000 Anatolian peasants facing them across the straits, but this 5,000 represented a still mighty empire. Furthermore an Empire counting more Moslem subjects than any othjer state in the world. Sheltering behind the British occupiers, the Ottoman government still existed with a nominal authority over the city itself. The old Sultan, Mehmet VI, still sat on the throne – not only as ruler of what was left of the Ottoman Empire, but as Caliph, representative of God on earth, protector and ruler of all the faithful – the Moslem Umma over all the world.

In the other camp, was Kemal, opposed to the idea of moving the capital back to Constantinople. As for the concept of 'Caliph', he looked on it as an obsolete relic of a religion in which he himself no longer believed. But he kept these opinions carefully to himself. As matters stood, the conservative and pious Turkish lower classes, together with the elite in the cities, remained deeply loyal to the dynasty. So he stepped softly by introducing the questionable concept of the Sultanate as being the temporal power in the Empire separate from the Caliphate as the spiritual power, a complete misrepresentation of the office. From its inception, the office of Caliph had belonged, by tradition and acclamation, to the strongest ruler in the Moslem world; it had become hereditary in all but name because of the Ottoman hold. Mustapha Kemal was going to confound them all.

By now the Conference at Mudanya had come to an end. The documents had been signed by all parties to the accord. Adrianople and Eastern Thrace were to be returned to the authority of the Turkish state and 8,000 Turkish troops and policemen would be allowed to cross the straits to take control over the area. The Greek army had to make immediate preparations to abandon the province and leave without raising a finger in opposition.

The treaty of Sevres was now consigned to the dustbin, unlike the guarantees given to plucky little Belgium, the repudiation of which had aroused such moral indignation in the British public only eight years previously. The British Empire had begun its slippery slide from its high moral position and in its political reach. It was undeniable that the peace, which Harington had negotiated was most welcome and any armed conflict would have been totally futile. Nevertheless, the retreat over the Chanak affair marked the high-water mark of the British Empire, and was its turning point. From Mudanya onwards it was going to be downhill all the way.

Still the question remained – what was to become of Constantinople? Mustapha Kemal was now in Bursa, halfway between the two wings of his army, one facing the peninsula leading to the Bosporus, the other facing Chanak ready to pounce on the Dardanelles. With the decision taken to hand over Eastern Thrace to the nationalists, Kemal appointed his friend Refet Pasha to be the new military governor of the province, with his headquarters in Constantinople itself. This was a particularly brilliant strategy, well within the spirit of what had been decided at Mudanya, but effectively introducing a high-ranking representative of the Ankara government into the city, right under the noses of the British and the Sultan.

The Galata Bridge again!

Four years after the arrival at this same point of General Franchet d'Espery - desperate Frankie – and his dramatic entrance into the city on that symbolic white horse, another steamer, with Refet Pasha on board, approached. It was the 19th of October, scarcely a week had passed since the signing at Mudanya. The whole harbour was awash with hundreds of small boats sailing out from both the Asian and European shores – all festooned with the red and white flags of the new Turkey. Thousands of people milled about in the streets – the bridge itself was impassable, filled with excited men. At the Stamboul side of the bridge a great cluster of women stood ululating; most were unveiled, with their hair uncovered, and earning not a single look of disapproval in their direction, symbolising what was to become one of the most deep-rooted and radical revolutions in history.

As the steamer carrying Refet Pasha finally drew alongside the bridge the noise was deafening. A huge roar arose from the crowds as Refet stepped ashore. Of course the vast majority of the crowd were Turks – but this was Constantinople not Smyrna. Thousands of Greeks, Jews and Armenians also stood in the midst of the enthusiastic crowds and watched this moment of history, together with foreigners from all over the world. Harington had made sure that there would be no British soldiers present in uniform. Karekin could not have kept away. He invited Hovannes Levonian to walk down to the bridge with him but, fearful and apprehensive, he declined. George, however, was equally curious and agreed to accompany Karekin. After all, instead of the arrival of an army, here was the historic arrival of one man.

Smiling broadly, Refet stepped ashore onto the quayside under the bridge. Youthful looking, with the Ankara style fur kalpak on his head, he looked immaculate and 'modern' in every sense. As the crowd shouted enthusiastically, he was met by the aide-de-camp of the old Sultan himself. No one, outside the officials waiting on the quayside, could hear a word of what was being said – but Refet shook hands with each one, expressing his religious devotion to the Caliph, and the persons representing that office, while carefully refraining from mentioning the Sultanate or the doddering elderly Mehmet VI.

An open topped car was waiting for Refet. He stepped in and stood smiling but standing stiffly to attention, a small and elegant figure as the car drove slowly off. His first stop was at the tomb of Sultan Mehmet – the Ottoman conqueror of the city. As Harington had ruefully been reminded, the people of this city – Greek, Turk, Jew or Armenian – never forgot a single moment of their history.

Refet had come with a personal bodyguard of no more than 20 gendarmes. Officially, he was only the military governor of Thrace on the other side of the Chatalja lines, and had no authority in the city, but such was the emotional atmosphere, it was immediately apparent that all power had finally and irrevocably passed from the Sultan's government. The days of Harington's command at the head of the British occupiers were numbered.

With Refet's landing, and his triumphant procession to the tomb of Fatih, Karekin saw, with his own eyes, the fall of the dynasty to which he had given political loyalty all his life. He turned to George, standing next to him at the window watching the events unfold on the streets below, and said

"Well, George – this is the end of the Ottomans. Sad in a way, I suppose, but on the other hand it looks fairly promising doesn't it – the crowds are in a good humour."

"So it would seem, sir, but nevertheless I have persuaded my father to book a passage for the whole family on a boat leaving in a few days, bound for Famagusta. We haven't had a summer holiday this year and have booked a hotel on the slopes of the Troodos mountains. Don't forget, I saw what happened in Smyrna – three days of discipline and good humour soon turned to riots and eventually bloodshed and rape."

"Yes, but George this is Bolis!"

"So what, sir. All the emotion and passion could so easily turn violent. Look at these crowds, do you think that the small British force here could stand up to a mob intent on breaking into *giavour* homes or churches."

"You're understandably prejudiced after Smyrna, but this city has no specific, defined 'quarters'. A bit of unpleasantness here and there, perhaps, but on the whole, all will be well."

"I do hope you're right sir, however, there's no harm in taking a short holiday now. Our house and our street in Bebek is known to be largely Armenian."

Two days later, George and Tamara left with their parents for their holiday in Cyprus. Before leaving, Hovannes and Karekin quietly concluded several business arrangements bringing their partnership to an end, but also making prudent arrangements for dealing with affairs in the event the Levonians were unable to return, or the Avakians were forced to leave in a hurry.

George's fears were not unfounded, but for the moment the centre held. The pent-up passions of the last three years during which those who supported the Ankara nationalists had kept a low profile, now burst out into the open. The authority of Harington's police force disintegrated, while the old Sultan, holed up at the Yildiz Palace, became totally irrelevant.

A vacuum of power arose in the city. While Ankara had finally and completely prevailed, it was even now uncertain how it would all end. Constantinople drifted into a semi-anarchic state as the various parties involved jockeyed for position, and preparations began to hammer out a final and hopefully lasting peace between the Ottoman Empire and the Allied governments in Lausanne.

CHAPTER 29

What's in a Name?

Nouritza Arabian had been unable to trace any of her relatives, after the little party returned from Chehan to Constantinople. She stayed on at the Asadourian house to look after Rehia during the day. Ara had always left the shop and warehouse earlier than the others, in order to prepare the evening meal, and this arrangement continued, but the little house was cramped, so Nouritza arranged to get lodgings nearby with another widowed lady, arriving at the Asadourian house in the morning and leaving when Ara returned.

From the first moment that the little girl had stepped into the all-male household, she had totally disrupted their routines – her liveliness and continual chatter completely disoriented the four men. Garabed was totally enthralled by his new daughter. He did not spoil her – he remained the conservative paterfamilias of old – but he had noticeably mellowed. The fact that his daughter, like him, could only speak Turkish, had created an immediate bond.

An old-fashioned Anatolian Armenian, Garabed had never concerned himself with the upbringing of his three earlier daughters. They were only educated to the age of twelve, and he had left the details of obtaining husbands entirely to his wife. He remained an Ottoman gentleman at heart. He only spoke Turkish and he had lived his life in the manner and style of an Ottoman citizen of good standing, with the sole exception of religion, though he was closer to his pious Moslem neighbours than they were to the new nationalist rulers.

Of course, he had not remained untouched by the nationalism of the late 19th century which had affected everyone, Turk, Greek and Armenian alike, but he disliked all their glib talk of 'blood', 'martyrdom', and 'national destiny' – the blood to be shed always being that of others, particularly that of the peasants and farmers of the interior. He was wary of all those city-educated, revolutionary academics, urging the farmers on to martyrdom.

Yet he had made sure that his sons received a good education from those very same academics, some of whom, in fairness, had sacrificed themselves to come and teach in the provinces. He was proud that they all spoke good Armenian – that they read Armenian literature and poetry – that his eldest son spoke excellent English and a little French. But for all that, there was a sort of distance separating him from his two sons, a distance which didn't extend to Ara, the farmer's son now his own adopted son.

And, above all, it didn't apply to Rehia.

.

Vahan had been living in Constantinople throughout those terrible months of 1915. He had not experienced what it meant to be hunted down, merely because he belonged to a particular ethnic community. He had no idea of the jumble of emotions, which swirled about in Garabed's head. When he saw the distress in his father's face, he thought it was continuing sorrow for the loss of his wife – and of course he knew nothing of the guilty monthly visits to rooms in the seedy streets parallel to the Grande Rue.

Both Vahan and Raffi adored the little girl and, as so often happened, it was the unthinking Raffi, who treated her roughly like a boy,

who became her favourite. Vahan had come home early on this particular day. He watched as Rehia talked non-stop to the doll, playing
some game of imagination he could not comprehend. This was his sister
– the only surviving daughter of his father. It was a wonder she wasn't
already spoilt, yet it was only a few weeks since she had arrived. Despite
all the turmoil in the city, the news of the Mudanya agreement, the arrival of the dapper Refet, life went on as usual. This was after all sophisticated Constantinople not grim Ankara. Even among the supporters
of the Kemalist nationalist movement, 'kef' still ruled – it could not be
changed overnight. So it was that on this afternoon, Nerissa, with Seta
in tow, was due to come for an early dinner

"My father believes that the Ottomans are at last finished and that
Mustapha Kemal Pasha intends to get rid of them once and for all.
What do you think sir?" asked Nerissa.

The conversation round the dinner table was in Turkish. Nerissa
and Seta were the only ones not entirely fluent, being more at home in
Armenian, English and French. Poor Garabed, even after all these years
in the city, could not get used to a 20-year-old girl openly addressing
him, but he was learning.

"My girl, I cannot believe that he will be able to dismiss them just
like that. The Sultan's government is crumbling, that's for sure. Refet
Pasha is slowly going to take over the city. But to get rid of the dynasty
that has ruled us for 500 years. No, no. It won't be that easy. I think he
will depose Mehmet, the deposition of weak Sultans is well within our
tradition, and make his son, or some other member of the family, Sultan
in his place – but only as the nominal head of state – like constitutional
monarchs in the west."

"It's not only the old guard at Yildiz Palace who are disappearing,
father. The British, too, are being eased out," said Vahan. "Day by day
Harington *effendi* has less and less authority and Refet, more and more.
There may not be anarchy, but there is a power vacuum. Though the
police are still around, they no longer know whose orders to follow. The
old Ottoman officials are slowly resigning, but as yet Refet can't take full
control."

"No anarchy, yes," called out Raffi finishing his soup, "but the streets
are no longer quite as safe as they were even a few days ago. Nothing
racial at the moment, but there are a lot of plain criminals about and
there is a hesitancy in dealing with them, as they hide their criminal
intentions behind nationalist patriotic slogans."

"Are we going to face a Smyrna here then, Raffi *effendi*?" piped up
Seta, shocking the unfortunate Garabed even more – surely the girl was
only 15?

"No, no, Seta, no. I think that at last we can forget that awful episode. Since Mudanya, there will be no more fighting. There will be a triumphal parade on the part of the army, but most of them will be shipped straight across the straits and directly into Thrace. The fear of another Smyrna has passed for good."

There was a murmur of agreement all round.

The light was fading as the dinner came to an end. Madame Arabian took Rehia up to bed and left for home shortly after. Rehia rather clumsily shook hands with Nerissa and Seta and, after kissing her brothers and father, skipped out, not deigning to hold Nouritza's hand. They all moved into the sitting room while Ara went out to make the coffee. The conversation turned to the decisions that soon needed to be made about Rehia.

"Look, baba, surely Rehia is going to go to an Armenian school." Raffi said to Garabed. "If that is so, she should use her Armenian name. She was baptized Satenig – and Satenig is what she should be called."

"Baptized?" said Vahan. "I'm not so sure brother. There were hardly any Armenians left in the town when she was born – and none of the churches were functioning."

"Well, yes, I think you may well be right," said Raffi, remembering how he had been forced to watch the public hanging of all his own schoolteachers, "but it's not relevant. Mother named her Satenig and Digin Arabian, for instance, always knew her as Satenig. Above all, how can we put her into an Armenian girls school with such an obviously Turkish name."

Garabed sat forward on the hard chair he preferred, leaning on his stick with both hands. What was for the best, he simply didn't know. He looked at Nerissa who hadn't ventured an opinion yet. Now, encouraged by his questioning look she said –

"The real problem is Rehia herself, not whether she will have any difficulty in an Armenian kindergarten or school having a Turkish name. Since first learning to speak, she has known and thought of herself as Rehia. The first person Rehia knew as her mother – Gulmaz hanum – called her Rehia. In her own mind she is Rehia. Requiring her to change her name may cause resentment. I would be very careful how you set about it."

"Oh come on Miss Nerissa," called out Raffi. "She's only six – she's a little girl. Possibly a day or two of tears, but then she will be Satenig again, if everyone calls her that. She'll have forgotten Rehia within a few weeks."

"Actually, Nerissa," said Vahan interrupting, "you can't dismiss the school and culture problem. I accept that what the teachers or the other children might think for a day or two is irrelevant – but her name is symbolic of other things as well. Is she going to be a little Turkish girl, brought up in the Armenian culture, or is she to become an Armenian girl, raised as part of the Armenian community?"

"If we're not sure," said Raffi, "she must be baptized. She's our sister, her name is Asadourian, by right and by law. How can we give her a Turkish Christian name – it's a contradiction in terms. She has to go back to the name she was given by her biological mother. Frankly the sooner we all start referring to her as Satenig, the better."

Garabed sat straight up on his chair, his hands folded over his stick, with his chin now resting on his hands. He saw Nerissa's point very clearly – Rehia came easily to his lips. But his dear wife, who had borne the suffering alone in giving life to this little girl, who had died with her in her arms, shielding her with her own body as she fell; her last words were probably a whispered – 'Satenig'. He looked across at Seta and, despite himself, he gave her a smile, inviting her comment. She clearly wanted to say something. However, despite the ease with which she participated in family discussions, she recognised that in this household, she should not express an opinion until invited to do so.

"Oh, sir, I'm sorry to interrupt but I would like to say something – don't look at me like that Nerissa ...."

"Yes, yes – go on, my girl, tell us what you think."

Seta blushed, for suddenly everyone was looking at her. Then she looked up and saw Ara giving her a big wink and that gave her even more encouragement.

"Sir I do think that my sister has a point. Forcing Rehia suddenly to change her name, as if we want her to forget her 'Ana' and her first six years of life, will seem to her unjustified and she will resent it, perhaps for the rest of her life. It's the sort of thing where you end up lying in bed, hugging your doll and thinking my secret name is Rehia. On the other hand – oh dear, Daddy always tells me to try and avoid that phrase – she is Armenian, she is your daughter and your real sister and the problems of culture and community will.... Ah well. Could I ask why shouldn't she have both names? Her baptised name could be 'Satenig Rehia Asadourian'. It can be explained to her that she is a very special girl with two names. Some will still call her Rehia – some can start by saying Satenig, though it would be best if there was some consistency."

Seta ground to a halt, blushing a deep crimson, as she realised that she had stood up in the course of her contribution – and sat down with a bump.

Then at last Garabed raised his head from his folded hands and said –

"Oriort Seta you have settled the problem sensibly. I compliment you. You, Raffi and you, Ara can start calling her Satenig as soon as it has been explained to her that she has two names. I will for the moment stick to Rehia. Everyone else can decide for themselves. She will be baptised next week – Satenig Rehia – and I won't stand for any black-robed priest complaining that the second name is not a Christian one. Eventually, she will make up her own mind over which name she prefers."

He stopped for a moment and looked at everyone in turn. They all remained silent. It was as if by arriving at a decision, he had reasserted his position as head of the family. It only needed a look for him to quell the objection that Raffi was about to raise. Vahan too swallowed what he was about to say. Then he turned to Nerissa and said –

"Miss Nerissa could I request a really great favour, one which might not be easy for you but which I would really appreciate..." Garabed would have blundered on with Turkish-style compliments forever, without getting to the point, but Nerissa cut him short, gently saying –

"Barón Garabed – please ask me, I will happily do what I can."

"Hmph...Could I ask if you would take on the task of explaining to Rehia, in the way I believe only you can do – the coming baptism service and her two names, one named for her by her 'Ana' and the other given to her by ... given to her by ... by ..."

"Her real mother," supplied Nerissa quickly. "Certainly, Barón. In fact, I could come tomorrow after breakfast – but please explain the position to Digin Arabian. I think I would like to start by taking....", she swallowed, but then smiled, almost as stunningly as Olga, at everyone "Satenig Rehia out to look at some of the boats."

Seta beamed with pride at her wonderful sister, as they got ready to take the carriage to Sirkedji for the return home.

CHAPTER 30

Panic in Thrace

Rumour and fear! How is it they spread so quickly? The news of the final decisions arrived at in Mudanya began to spread in this way among the Greek farmers of Eastern Thrace. What everyone heard was that the Turkish army was crossing the straits to return after four years – that same avenging army that had wreaked such a terrible vengeance in Smyrna only a few weeks before.

The Greek army, in fairly good shape here, despite scare-mongering reports to the contrary, was massed on the other side of the Chatalja lines but there was not going to be a last stand. Greece was in utter turmoil. A revolution had broken out and King Constantine had fled. The country was bankrupt and had been abandoned by the British, who had egged them on so disastrously in the first place. Britain, too, had its own form of revolution with Lloyd George the first casualty, his government fell and he left office never to return.

What the thousands – the hundreds of thousands – of the ancient tillers of the soil saw, was the sight of the Greek army hauling down its flags and marching away; away from Adrianople, away from Constantinople, across the River Maritza and out of Eastern Thrace. The rumours redoubled in force, as these people who had lived in the province for generations, whose ancestors and way of life could be traced back centuries, began to hear the dread words – 'exchange of populations'; words which meant new horrors and the abandonment of the only lives they had ever known.

So it was that one by one, and then in their hundreds, and finally thousands – mere statistics to the men in London, Paris and Washington – began to up sticks and move.

"But Kafides *bey*, my friend, why are you leaving? Why? Has not our Ghazi, Mustapha Kemal himself, confirmed that no one is to be harmed. This is your own land. I remember well your father discussing crops with mine, and his clever brother, your uncle, who left and went to the city. How can you leave like this?"

"Mukhtadir *effendi*, I know, but see what happened at Smyrna. There too, the Ghazi said no one would be harmed. You heard what this boy has told us. Do you think he is lying, my friend? My old friend – I do not fear my neighbours, I never have. But it was not 'neighbours' who carried out the murderous attacks in Smyrna. I fear the outsiders who come among us and stir up hatreds that never existed before."

"But Costas *effendi*, everything you have worked for, all your memories, your friends, are here. All you have or have ever had is here. How can you just up and leave?"

"Haven't you heard, my friend, that they are all going to meet in some town in Switzerland? There, they will decide the fate of all the populations living in eastern and western Thrace. Those of Moslem faith will be forced to move either here or to Anatolia, while those, like us, who live here as Orthodox Christians will have to move out. Should I wait to be thrown out and find myself at the end of a long queue – or should I try to keep ahead of the mass exodus to come?"

Spiro stood by the side of his new foster-father. He had been on the farm now for about two weeks and, already, the days spent with the Avakians seemed an age away, whereas the horror of those last two weeks on the quay in Smyrna were returning to plague his dreams. His new parents were kind but firm and Costas urged him to learn as quickly as possible all about the farm and animal husbandry.

The young hired help arrived early every morning and had been told by Costas to wake Spiro if he was still sleeping. Ali shouted at him outside his window and he would immediately join him – milking the cows – leading them out to graze – dealing with the hens – the goats, and everything else that needed seeing to in the morning. Only after three hours of work did they both come in to eat the breakfast prepared by Saroula and ready for all of them round the kitchen table. Costas also grew tobacco, but this was more specialised work and he told Spiro that this would become his particular expertise next year, when he would be taught all there was to know about the growing and marketing of this cash crop. For now, he should apply himself to learning the general principles of running a small farm.

Spiro was essentially a city boy, and struggled initially to adapt to the rigorous work but the routine and physical labour soon came to soothe him and daily, he suffered less and less from bad dreams. Within days he took on strength and looked more and more like a young man, and less like a child. For the first time since that dreadful day of the 13th September in Smyrna, Spiro had begun to feel settled.

But for Spiro, these days turned out to be a mere interlude in the continuing tragedy of the disintegration of the Ottoman empire. On the day after Spiro had listened to the conversation with Mukhtadir, Costas told his wife and Spiro that they were going to leave and join the hordes of farmers and peasants already trailing across the plains towards the old Greek frontier, now destined to become the new one.

As if in sympathy with the tears shed by all the people forced into exile, the heavens opened and the rain poured down. What roads existed – mostly just paths – turned to seas of mud. Neither the hired hand nor Mukhtadir turned up that morning as Spiro and Costas got out the cart and began filling it with the things Saroula put out at the door – mattresses on the bottom – then the better carpets, the sewing machine, a rococo mirror, pots and pans, knives and spoons, the useless old grandfather clock that had stood in the hall, which simply could not be abandoned. Then the clothes and Spiro's own bag, originally packed by Armineh with all the clothes that had belonged to Haik, some barely unpacked, joined the growing pile. Finally the same three umbrellas, which had sheltered Karekin and Olga, were placed on top.

The river Maritza was over a hundred miles away and the question which exercised Costas was 'fodder' for the animals. The horses would have to drag the overladen cart and they needed to eat. Then, there was the herd of cows? He only had five, but they would provide milk on the way and form the nucleus for a new herd but they too needed fodder.

In the end Saroula provided the answer – neither she nor Spiro would ride on the cart. The top of the cart would be covered with such straw and hay as they could gather together. The hens would be settled onto the hay, the tools would be packed in under the straw, as would what food, cheese, olives and bread they could manage. For the two adults, it was heart-breaking as they contemplated their denuded home. For Spiro, mixed with the fear of the future was the sense of shared adversity with his foster-parents.

At the last moment, just before setting out, Mukhtadir turned up. The knowledge that they would probably never ever meet again; the strange feeling of shame and sorrow on the part of those remaining as they said their farewells against the fear of those being forced to leave, was the same for both the Greek-speaking Moslems having to leave the Greek Macedonian countryside and the Turkish-speaking Orthodox having to leave the old Ottoman world.

All over Thrace on the Turkish side and Macedonia on the Greek side similar partings were taking place between neighbours, whom the bright academics and nationalists on both sides assured them, despite all their real feelings, that they had hated.

They said little to each other – there really was nothing left to say. The rain fell unceasingly as slowly, churning up the mud, the little procession moved off: Costas, walking ahead with his scythe over his shoulder; Saroula, following, leading the two horses pulling the creaking cart; Spiro, bringing up the rear, driving the five cows. Mukhtadir stood and watched as the little party went on over the flat plains into the distance. He didn't wave, but watched until they disappeared from view. Then, with a sigh, he turned to the open door of the empty farmhouse to see if there was anything left worth taking back to his wife.

Costas knew where to aim for; that he could not just strike due west to take the shortest way to the Maritza. There were swamps and impassable roads that way, if any roads at all. He had decided to make for the railway line and follow it all the way to Adrianople and, from there, to cross into Greece. Unfortunately, thousands of others had the same idea. So it was that travellers, still riding comfortably on the carriages of the Orient Express, stared out of their windows at line after line of Greek peasants trudging, mostly on foot, with their chickens round their necks, their wheelbarrows and carts heavily laden and soaked through, their animals and all their other worldly goods, passing on each side of the railway lines. The French directors complained both to the Greeks and to the British authorities in Constantinople that all these people were interfering with the efficient running of their services.

Within a few days, Spiro and his new family found themselves part of this long line of refugees, soaked to the skin from the incessant rain. Small children, younger than Spiro, staggered along with any items they could carry draped round their little bodies, some useful, but many not. Their tired eyes looked up with wonder as the trains of the Orient Express passed by in each direction, with the 'haut bourgeoisie' of Europe staring back at them with neither comprehension nor compassion. Even pregnant women walked rather than add their weight to the overloaded carts and the oxen pulling them.

The Kafides party had almost reached Adrianople, not far from the railway and road bridge crossing over the River Maritsa into the old borders of Western Thrace. They were about 30 miles away when the whole line of carts, animals, wheelbarrows and exhausted people came to a complete standstill. Far away across the plains, whenever the rain lifted, they could see the minarets of the old town in the distance. But now everyone and everything was completely stuck on both sides of the railway line.

"Spiro, it looks as if we'll have to stop here for a while. I'll take one of the horses and ride up and see what's happening up ahead. In any case, the horses are exhausted and I don't think we can keep driving them anymore. The cattle have been managing to graze fairly well, and they can digest this poor hay better than the horses. What we'll do is let the horses come with us if they can – but in future we'll get the cattle to pull the cart."

"But can they do it, sir – they're not oxen but milk cows."

"Well, it won't be good for them and they'll be slow, but we can't go any faster than the lot ahead of us anyway. The horses won't survive pulling the cart."

Spiro and Costas untethered the horses and took the two strongest cows and managed to hitch them. Costas kissed Saroula and patted Spiro on the head and rode off, up past the long line of refugees. Spiro settled down and Saroula produced some stale bread and cheese for him. They had already been travelling for over a week. Spiro sat back against the cart, chewing at the bread and looked around him. They had stopped right next to the railway line. The trains that passed were moving very slowly due to the proximity of the people and animals on either side of the track. All along the railway lines and paths, there were now thousands and thousands of exhausted men and women walking in the rain with everything they possessed either in carts or wheelbarrows or on their backs. None of them had the slightest idea where they were going or what they would do when they got there.

There were no relief organisations – no soup kitchens – no medical facilities – it was a picture out of a medieval nightmare unfolding before Spiro's questioning eyes. None of the statesmen whose decisions had provoked this exodus would ever have believed such scenes were taking place in the second decade of the twentieth century. Meanwhile in the midst of all this misery, modern trains full of affluent passengers, emanating from Paris, Milan, Vienna, Bucharest …and Salonika, passed every few hours with brutal efficiency, while thousands of human tragedies took place on either side of the line.

Costas soon returned, trotting back through the fields away from the lines of hopeless refugees. It appeared that all the carts, the cattle, the people and their animals were jammed solid on the bridge over the Maritza leading into Western Thrace and the Kingdom of Greece. No ethnic Greeks were being allowed into Bulgaria further ahead, though Armenians merchants and small shopkeepers from the little towns in the province were allowed to enter. Costas told Spiro to be ready to move, as once the great line shuffled forward again, as it surely would, there would be no time to gather things together.

The rain never stopped. Costas settled down next to Saroula, holding her tight and comforting her as best he could. All three huddled close together, Spiro held an umbrella over his new parents. A train slowly moved up the tracks alongside them. Somewhere between here and Constantinople, something must have blocked the line, as the train shuddered to a halt, steam rising from under the carriages – the whole monstrous machine clanking and hissing. Spiro stared up at the big clean window of a first class carriage. There, a lady dressed in furs with a large brimmed hat looked back down at him. Opposite her sat a gentleman reading a newspaper. Spiro felt embarrassed – after all, he had stared at plenty of ladies like this one in the smart cafés on the quaysides in Smyrna – but now, bedraggled, dirty, unwashed for days, he found he could not meet her eye. He looked away as the train hooted and moved away. Then, suddenly, it came to another shuddering halt.

That very morning Mikael, Elena and the two children had finally arrived in Adrianople. Getting the tickets in Athens, and making all the necessary arrangements, had proved more difficult and costly than Mikael had first envisaged. Everyone was looking for tickets to Salonika and northwards, but as it happened, few people wanted to go on from Salonika to Constantinople. So, in the end, by booking and paying for his ticket right through to the city, Mikael had finally got his four third-class seats.

One of the extraordinary features of these chaotic few weeks was the way in which some aspects of life continued as if nothing had changed for one group of people, while another group would be suffering the horrors of the collapse of organised civilisation. Mikael had seen this contradiction during the civil war in Russia and here it was again in Athens. There was terrible hunger and disease in the streets of the little capital as Greeks from all over the old Ottoman world, came pouring in. Yet at the same time, Mikael had been able to send a telegram addressed to Nairi and his mother, informing them of his survival and warning them that he was trying to get back to their home in Makrikoy.

At last the day arrived when the train left Athens with Mikael and his family aboard. It stopped for a few hours in Salonika, coaches were uncoupled and reattached and then it trundled on, along the mainly one-way track along the Aegean, finally turning north to go along the Maritza and into Adrianople. Already, before the train even entered the province of Eastern Thrace, Mikael could see the enormous difference between his seat in this modern twentieth century train and the devastating sight of the lines of refugees they were passing by outside.

The fearless, brave and even arrogant Mikael no longer existed. He had matured immeasurably. He was now responsible for a companion and her two children. Anya slept with her head in Elena's lap, and Andreas dozed next to Mikael with his head nestling against his shoulder. And Mikael found that he was anxious in a way that he had never been throughout the vicissitudes of the Anatolian campaign, even at moments of extreme danger. He accepted that he had no idea how he was going to get Elena and the two children through to Bolis. He thought vaguely of leaving the train before it entered the Allied Zone and walking into the city.

But the first hurdle passed without incident. The train steamed slowly into the station with signs stating unequivocally 'Adrianopolis'. There had been no frontier post, no guards demanding passports. Mikael did not know it, but he was just ahead of the game. It would not be more than another few days before the signs in the station were removed and replaced by "Edirne". And even before that happened, Turkish gendarmes would already have arrived and set up the old frontier posts, abandoned for the last four years.

The little family party had to change trains here in Adrianople to catch the next train coming through Bulgaria and going on across the plains to the city. Adrianople was in turmoil. The Greek administration was packing up, and the only authority present in the streets were small bands of Greek cavalry riding past, ignoring the population on their way out of town.

Mikael and his little group did not, indeed could not, move far from the station. They gulped down a coffee and some bread at a small café and hurried back into the warm comforting embrace of the train station and took their seats in the only third class carriage on this particular train, coming through Bulgaria from Vienna. Mikael was now almost sick with anxiety. With a lurch and a hissing of steam, the train moved out of the station, out of the town and onto the great flat Thracian plains. Mikael stared with increasing fear and trepidation at the two lines of bedraggled people on either side, as the train lumbered slowly forward, hooting at the donkeys and cattle wandering across the tracks. The train stopped and started, eventually coming to a complete halt and stood still for about ten minutes.

Mikael looked blankly out, registering only the fear that he too might have to join this mass of wretched humanity and trek back into

Greece, if he could not get his charges into the city with him. Then with a sudden lurch, which churned his stomach all over again, the train started moving again between the two lines of refugees, only to come to another shuddering halt with all the carriages clanging into each other. Mikael stared down out of the window at a boy, soaked to the skin, sitting leaning against a ramshackle cart by the side of his mother and father, holding an umbrella over them. The boy looked up at him as the train stopped. For just a moment Mikael thought that the boy looked familiar. He smiled and gave a little wave as the train lurched forward again. This woke Andreas who had been dozing again.

"Who were you waving to Uncle?" he said as the train began at last picking up speed.

"On, no one in particular," replied Mikael. "A little boy who looked a bit like your cousin - Spiro. Come, it's no use your looking out; we've passed him and it couldn't have been him anyway – these are all farmers from Thrace trying to leave before the Turks arrive. Come, sleep some more, we will arrive at the city soon, and we may have to get out and walk a bit."

And with a sigh of escaping steam, Spiro's last remaining relatives, the last survivors of that big, happy, extended family, passed away down the railway line heading for the great city of Constantinople. He hadn't recognised Mikael, who he had only seen for a few days and in the most traumatic of circumstances. Looking up as the train disappeared down the line he saw the line of refugees ahead begin to move forward at last. He hurriedly shook Costas and Saroula who had dozed off in each other's arms. Then for the first time ever, he called out to them –

"Father, mother, get up – get up, we're going at last."

CHAPTER 31

The City Waits

Two weeks had already passed since the Countess Androvna had left the city on the Direct-Orient express bound for Vienna. The Greek army had departed from the province of Eastern Thrace. Refet Pasha lorded it over the city, and British authority was diminishing with every hour that passed. Turkish gendarmes, considerably more than the 8,000 agreed at Mudanya, had poured into the province on the heels of the departing Greek peasants. Attempts were being made by these arriving policemen, hardened nationalists of the new breed, to prevent those who had not already left earlier, from taking their cattle and their farming tools. Admiral Bristol, who had not even been at Mudanya, was nevertheless indignant, claiming that the terms of the conference were such that these 'pesky Greek farmers' were not entitled to remove either their animals or their tools – and he sent telegrams to all and sundry to make his feelings known. Happily, by now, no one of any consequence was interested in what Admiral Bristol had to say.

Fortunately for Mikael and Elena, they had passed through the province a day or two before the Turkish police arrived. These gendarmes had reopened the frontier posts and taken over control, right up and down the railway line as far as Chatalja. The little family could not have timed it better and were sitting comfortably in their express train while the control posts were still manned by the old Ottoman officials, backed up by British personnel. Within days, these officials would be replaced by Refet's men and the British would be withdrawing from the frontier control.

As it turned out, apart from a cursory glance at Mikael's Ottoman papers, followed by a hasty murmur about the loss in a fire of 'his wife's' papers – he, Elena and the children passed through to Sirkedji without a hitch.

The Mudanya conference had not touched directly on the matter of the city itself. All the old questions remained unanswered. What was to become of Constantinople and the variety of diverse communities living there? The fate of the non-Turkish peoples, was unresolved, as was its status as the capital city. For a fearful Bolsetsi, everything pointed towards deportations of one kind or another. Everyone claimed to know a story or piece of gossip relating to the population of the city. With the British about to leave, could the army of discontented Anatolian peasants on the other side of the straits be controlled?

Meanwhile, the dread words – 'exchange of population' brought fear to the minority populations of the city. The 100,000 or so Armenians had no one to be exchanged with, however they knew what deportation, if it came to that, was likely to mean in reality. It was the Greeks, at least 40 per cent of the population, who listened to the rumours and news coming out of the countryside of Thrace. Nevertheless, in the midst of all this uncertainty, people continued to work, to have babies, to eat out at the wonderful restaurants along the Bosporus, to love and to marry.

Sima and Armineh worked together in planning the wedding. It was decided they would be married in the small local Armenian church in Makrikoy, which the family rarely attended. Father Haroutune would preside. It was not going to be a grand affair, though Sima did want a traditional wedding with all the Christian trimmings. She had listened all her life to her father's confirmed, secular cynicism about the clergy and about organised religion and, as a result, didn't have any strong religious convictions. But on this one instance, she wanted it all done in a proper manner and the church was booked for the 1st November, followed by a small reception at home, for which purpose caterers were organised by Armineh.

During the next days Sima went often to the Patakis house, not just to be with Nicolai, but to set about arranging the rented rooms for their coming life together. A letter had already arrived from Vienna. The Countess was living with her sister, the Countess Berchtold, in fairly comfortable surroundings, but she had written to warn that conditions in Vienna were worse than they were in Constantinople. Electricity was often cut during the day and the heating in the apartments was erratic. Vienna, it would appear from her comments, had become a bulging capital city without a country to govern. Bureaucrats, landed gentry and officials from all over the old Hapsburg Empire were returning to Vienna, without anything left to do. There was no work and little joy.

However, she wrote that she had already spoken to her other sister – the Contessa Maggi – and that in Italy, the situation was different. The old Count still retained all his land. There had been no social revolution and it did not look as if there would be. She wrote to add that he had already indicated to her – his sister-in-law – that he would welcome her coming to Padua. Furthermore, he was encouraging about the suggestion that Nicolai might also come, and be employed in the management of his estates in the Veneto.

Meanwhile, Nicolai had found some work with a Greek shipping firm, who required a clerk to write letters in English and French. Nicolai's Greek was non-existent but his Turkish had become more than adequate. There were plenty of Greeks in the city who could speak English and many who could speak French, but those who could manage both were few, so Nicolai got the job.

Despite Harry's advice, Olga had not spoken to Karekin after the baptism service. Karekin had walked out before the end of the service. He had walked aimlessly for a short time up the Grande Rue du Pera, remembering his son yet again, his good spirits, his moments of shyness, and his triumphant ones. Tears prickled – it was all still too soon. He would do his best for the little boy baptised this morning, but he knew in his heart that he could never come to love him as he had his own son. At one level, he was irritated that Paramaz had sprung the name Haik, like that, at the last moment. However, he had seen immediately that all his womenfolk, taken aback at first had been delighted. Eventually he wandered back to join the rest of the family. The Levonians had invited everyone to a grand restaurant on the Bosporus in Bebek. The carriages were ready and they were waiting for him to depart.

Lunch had gone on at the waterside tavern until six in the evening and everyone was exhausted by the time they arrived home. Either way there had been no time for Olga to broach any subject, never mind one quite so sensitive.

The next day had been the trip to Sinekli with Spiro and once again Olga had been unable on the return journey to raise the matter, as she had never been alone with her father. With the passing of each day it became more and more difficult. Meanwhile she was seeing Harry almost every day – either he would come to Makrikoy and would have lunch, or she would meet him in Pera and they would go somewhere together. After the rainy days earlier in October, the weather had brightened again. They passed days wandering round the older parts of the city, the covered bazaar, the various Byzantine ruins, Prinkipo, Rumeli Hissar, and even one, crisp afternoon, following the same route Harry had walked with his father along the old walls.

Like so many people who live in wonderful and historic old cities, Olga had taken it all for granted. She had seen more of the famous sights of Jerusalem, which she had visited with the rest of the family as a tourist before the War, than she knew of her own city. But Harry had become an enthusiast over the two years of his life spent here. He took her to back streets in old Stamboul, the cemeteries of Eyup, villages in the woods of Sultan Su, all of which she had never seen. And every day, without fail, he would urge her to speak to her father to explain what had happened and her current condition. And every day his heart, still filled with the joy of the five days spent with his father, became ever more enamoured. He found himself begrudging the time he could not be in her company. His heart raced with pleasure every time she ran up to him at their rendezvous in Pera, or when she opened the door to him, on arrival at the house in Makrikoy. Harry was 30 years-old. He knew that he was falling in love.

But he also knew, too well, that Olga had been deeply in love, for over six years with another man, who had died only a few months before. Furthermore, he also knew she was carrying this man's child. How could he impinge on her grief? Wouldn't it be insensitive to make his growing feelings known to her? He felt that with a woman like Olga, it was almost impossible to gauge what she might be feeling towards him. Her natural vivacity, her Avakian enthusiasms, and the outpouring of warmth that was a part of her character, aimed directly at him when they were alone together, appeared to be aimed equally at others. It was very confusing, and it was so very un-English. Harry dithered. However, on the matter of her talking to Karekin, he was firm. He could see that she was making herself ill with the thought of speaking to him. So one afternoon, as they sat in a café in Karakoy watching the ferries coming by, before they strolled back across the bridge for Olga to return home, he said –

"Olga, my dearest, this must stop. You simply cannot go on keeping from your father what has happened."

"Oh Harry, I will, I will. It just seems so difficult to get him alone and…"

"Nonsense, you are simply finding excuses. Think, think how much of a strain it must be on your mother, being unable to talk to Karekin about what must be a worry for her. I know that she promised to leave it to you, but that was now days and days ago."

"All right, all right, I'll speak to him soon."

"No, no. That's rubbish and you know it, my dear. You'll speak to him tonight – tonight Olga. I'm coming to Makrikoy tomorrow after lunch. I want to hear about how it went from you, or I…"

"Or what, Harry?" said Olga somewhat mischievously.

"Or…. Oh I don't know." Harry laughed as did Olga. "But honestly Olga, I really will be hurt, I mean it."

Olga looked back into his eyes and their eyes clashed. It was Olga who turned away, but she could see that it would, indeed, wound him, and that realisation brought her thoughts sharply into focus.

That night after supper, she asked Karekin if she could talk to him in his study. Karekin was surprised. Haik had occasionally asked to speak to him privately if he had wanted to confess some misdemeanour, but this had never happened with any of his daughters. He looked across at Armineh, at the other end of the table, but she deliberately looked away, refusing to let him catch her eye. He suddenly felt anxious and took out his amber beads as he walked ahead to the study where he sat at his desk and motioned to Olga to sit on the other side.

"It's about Smyrna isn't it? It's something that I don't know about isn't it, my soul?"

"Oh, father, yes. I haven't told you everything about my life there yet."

Karekin fingered his beads, clicking them as quietly as possible and looked straight into his daughter's eyes. She flushed ever so slightly but then looked straight back. The blood slowly rose to her cheeks as she continued –

"Father, after I had been in Smyrna for some months I suddenly met Selim quite by chance in the street. Father, you knew that throughout those days I loved Selim and that he loved me. Oh, baba, you knew, you knew in your heart that I had not forgotten him... his visits …"

She trailed off. Karekin said nothing but continued fingering his beads. Olga swallowed and looked down, but continued –

"We decided after that chance meeting that despite opposition from both our parents, we were going to marry. I was living at the time in small rooms at the back of each of the hospitals. Selim had a room in the Turkish quarter. We got a small apartment, just two rooms, in the house of a Madame Derounian in the Armenian quarter near the cathedral. We lived together there for about three months right up to the moment that the Turkish army poured into the city. Baba, he was in the city clandestinely. We couldn't have got married there – but we lived together as man and wife."

Coming to the end of what she was saying, Olga was aware that Karekin's attention had wandered for a moment. Then, with a lurch of her heart she heard the beads falling to the floor. She had never seen this happen before and assumed that her father had thrown them down on hearing what she had just said. And so they both sat, staring at each other, both silent and both totally misunderstanding each other.

Karekin despised mere convention. He didn't care a jot about what society might think. He accepted that in the current circumstances, he was taking a risk bringing up his daughters in the way he had. But he was no hypocrite. He would not open them up to liberal influences and then condemn them for acting on the basis of that upbringing.

But his thoughts were in turmoil, edging away all the time to his dead son. He, too, misunderstood the position, thinking that Olga was merely trying to expiate her own feelings of guilt and that she was only seeking some words of penance or atonement from him – something he felt he could not supply with any conviction. The silence dragged on until at last – at last – Olga without looking at Karekin, said quietly –

"Oh father, baba – I am pregnant. I am going to have Selim's child in about seven months time. I am happy about it. I want to hold a bit of Selim again. Oh father, I ..."

Karekin's mind cleared as if a bolt of lightening had pierced a great fog. He rose, kicking aside the forgotten beads, and came round to Olga who till then had not shed a single tear. Lifting her from the chair he enveloped her in his arms. Holding her tight as she began crying, murmuring –

"Oh, my daughter...my daughter...," over and over again.

Nothing further was needed. They both knew that everything between them was going to be fine. Karekin realised that this must be the reason why Armineh had been acting so strangely over the last few days. Olga realised that Harry had been right all along. It came to her that even if her father deep down, disapproved of her actions, the arrival of his first grandchild delighted him, unequivocally ...

Some days later, as October passed and as the day of the wedding approached, Alexei moved out of the Patakis house and came to live in Makrikoy. There was not the slightest hesitation when Armineh arranged for him to move into Haik's old room.

CHAPTER 32

Love and Marriage

Mikael, Elena and the two children arrived at the house of Vartuhi Sarafian in the centre of Makrikoy in a state of high euphoria. Almost up to the last moment, Mikael had worried that an overzealous official would suddenly appear and demand to see their papers. Elena had no papers. She had been born a citizen of Imperial Russia, before fleeing with Wrangel's defeated army from Sevastopol two years ago. Settled in Smyrna with the Pantelis family, sheltered by a benevolent Greek administration, and nurtured in a welcoming extended family, she had never bothered to sort out nationality for herself and her children.

They had been lucky, and now Mikael was determined that he, and his little adopted family, would never again go through such days of uncertainty again. From the moment that he got on to the train in Salonika, to the moment that he finally walked out of the station at Sirkedji and into the hustle and bustle of the Stamboul crowds, he had been in a state of nervous anxiety, far worse than anything he had ever felt in battle.

He was going to marry. Once married, the marriage certificate, coupled to his own papers – the valuable Ottoman 'nufus' – would be enough. It never crossed his mind that the poor peasants he had seen, trekking wearily along the railway line to an unknown future in a bankrupt and poverty-stricken Greece, had legally valid documents. As they talked it over, Elena did not see it that way.

"Mikael, we both want a church wedding, in accordance with our beliefs. We already talked this over in Athens, remember? Can we take vows before God, when I am a married woman and don't know for certain whether my husband is still alive or not?"

"Elena, you parted in the panic in Odessa over five years ago. All sorts of things have happened since but it is inconceivable that he wouldn't have got some news back to his family in Smyrna, if he was still alive. There was a sizeable Greek community in Odessa, and many have been trickling out since the civil war ended. No, no. Listen. We go to a special confession, we see a priest, either here in Makrikoy or at the Patriarchate in Bolis, and we see what they have to say."

There was a silence between them, created largely by Elena.

It was only the second day after their fortuitous arrival back home in

Makrikoy. Mikael's mother Vartouhi was not very happy about a marriage which included two stepchildren but she was so overjoyed at having Mikael back home that she would have accepted any nationality as a daughter-in-law. Nairi was over the moon right from the start – she, more than her mother, was aware of how her brother had matured. So why did Elena hesitate and look for excuses?

She had never experienced love in her marriage, but then she had not expected it. It was her duty though she had expected affection to grow and fill the void and perhaps turn to love. The silence lengthened between them, but before Mikael could come out with any more comments, she said quietly –

"Do you love me, Mikael, or do you just want a ready-made family?"

Now the silence was on the other side. He knew that the all-consuming passion he had felt for Olga Avakian, all those years ago, was quite different to his feelings for this woman. Which of the two was 'love'? Mikael didn't like being confused and this time, anger and impatience came to his aid.

"Elena, my sweetheart, if all that I have done for you over the last six weeks has not been enough to prove my love – then you are not the woman I have taken you for. I am prepared to lay down my life for you and your children. If you had been forced off that train and had to trek back to an unknown future all the way to Greece, you know very well that I would have got off too and shared your fate with you."

Tears came to Elena's eyes. He was surely a good, if brutally honest, man. He was right; no one could have done more; he had saved her and her children. She was going to marry this man and entrust him with her future, but somewhere deep down in her consciousness, she was aware that he had never said – 'Elena, I love you'.

Brushing away her tears, she made her decision.

"Oh Mikael – yes. Let's get married as soon as possible – here in your home town – in the Armenian church. Please, Mikael, as soon as possible."

For the past week, Nerissa had been visiting the Asadourian home regularly, almost every afternoon, after University. She found the task given to her by old Barón Garabed was intellectually more stimulating than she had imagined. Explaining to this intelligent little girl, step by step, the circumstances that had brought her to this house, in this city, was fascinating. She was determined from the start that this was not to be a tale of terrible massacres, of the premeditated cruelty by one section of a population against another. Satenig was not to become an enemy of Rehia. The tragedy of her true mother's death was not to be laid against her affection for her Ana.

In this, she found she clashed with Raffi. He wanted Satenig to be told the facts – that his mother had been brutally murdered, egged on by the ideologues and the authorities; she shouldn't be spared the knowledge that this was only one small incident in a planned genocide, which had largely succeeded.

"Nerissa, I'm not suggesting that you have to frighten the little girl. These are matters that must be clothed in the language a six year-old can understand. But it would be wrong to make them seem anything less that what they really are. Sooner or later, she will find out the truth, and you will be doing her a disservice not to prepare her for it."

"But Raffi, it is not necessary to burden her with that at six years old. How can she reconcile the 'truth' with the kindness and love she received in the village, and the care and security she got from her Ana. There are two sides tom every issue and I....."

"My God, Nerissa – a true Avakian position. Listen – face it - just because there are two sides to an issue, that doesn't mean they both carry equal weight. On one side, we have the planned extermination of over a mil*lion* helpless people, and on the other, we have many, perhaps even thousands of small acts of kindness shown by individuals, often against their own leaders' decrees. There is no bloody equivalence – none, none at all."

Raffi was now getting red, but Nerissa was no longer abashed by the strongly expressed feelings of others. She no longer blushed and looked away, but said quite sharply –

"Raffi, please don't swear – it doesn't strengthen your argument one little bit."

Raffi bit his lip and said –

"I'm sorry Oriort Nerissa, I'm really sorry – but I do feel deeply about this. She is my sister and I do not want her to grow up without an appreciation of what happened to her family and why."

The conversation continued, Nerissa admitting that Satenig would, sooner or later, come to understand the truth of why she had two names, but that six years-old was too early. She only need know that her true mother had died and that her ana had looked after outm of the goodness of her heart. However, when she talked it over with Vahan some days later, she found that she was changing her mind again. When she reported her conversation with Raffi to him, he said –

"Nerissa, my soul, it's inevitable that Raffi takes a one-sided view of these things. After all, he was personally touched by the events of 1915. He was there when I was not. However, he has a point. Surely, you can't take a middle course in describing what happened in April 1915. It has to be simply and roundly condemned, with no 'ifs' or 'buts'. There can be no moral equivalence in this matter and, on that, Raffi is right."

"But Vahan, I don't disagree. I am simply saying that it is not good for a child of this age to be forced to face up to a conflict between the truth of what happened to her biological mother and the love she feels for the only actual mother she can recall. It is too much to take in all at once."

Vahan looked at this girl and he knew that he loved her. He also knew she didn't love him – at least not yet. But for all his quiet and sensitive spirit, he was in his own way as stubborn as his brother Raffi – and he was going to marry her. She did not know it yet – but he did. They were looking straight into each other's eyes and he almost blurted out – 'I am going to marry you, you know'. What he actually said was –

"Nerissa, my soul, you must do exactly as your conscience tells you. My father may be a bit brusque but he has always been an excellent judge of people. He asked you to take on the task of explaining the two names to Satenig, and he means you to do it as you think fit."

That afternoon, when she left to go home, Nerissa not only bent down and gave Satenig a great big hug – but also, for the first time, leant forward and gave Vahan a quick, tentative, kiss on the lips as she passed out into the street. But Nerissa was not thinking – not then – of love or marriage.

Sima, the practical sister; the one who had always scorned her sisters' romantic notions of the chemistry of love; the one who was only going to marry when she found the man who could provide for her; was hopelessly in love with a man who was unlikely to be able to do either of those things, at least for some time. The day of her wedding drew closer.

Olga would undoubtedly have married Selim, if they had both survived the holocaust of Smyrna. She had always taken the line that the only really important matter in considering marriage was love, the overwhelming desire for another person. But ironically, the more she remembered the relationship she had had for over three months with Selim, the more confused she became. For the first time she began to question whether it had just been a physical attraction between them. If desire was all that really mattered, then weren't her parents and society right to expect her to wait have waited until the union could be sanctioned by... by whom? God? Society?

She was incapable of the sort of self-analysis that was second nature to Nerissa. She knew that it was Selim's character which had become the important factor in their happiness together. It was the beauty and wonder of his spirit, his kindness, his roughness, that had made her ache for him to come home and which she thought about during the day when she was not at work – not the beauty and wonder of his body. What did that say about chemistry?

Olga knew that her friendship with Harry was deepening. She couldn't tell how far his feelings for her had developed, but she could see that he went out of his way to seek her company. She was grateful to him for having pushed her into speaking to her father. She was never shy in his company – she loved their trips together all over the city, and they were always cheerful and fond of each other – her shyness was in her own mind. She was glad he knew her secret. But knowing as he did that she was expecting another man's child, how could she encourage him in his attentions? Somehow, it felt morally wrong on her part to openly welcome any advances. But Harry had not, as yet, said anything to her directly. Perhaps she was imagining a problem that didn't exist. It never crossed her mind that Harry might have been having similar thoughts about her.

Olga was not the sort to keep things to herself and as the day of Sima's wedding approached, she and Nerissa drew closer. Sima and Armineh had their heads together, continually, in lengthy discussions about the wedding. She may have been in a romantic daze where Nicolai was concerned, but, as always, she was highly practical. So it was that Olga, who would normally have been more likely to confide in her elder sister, talked instead to Nerissa. They both felt alienated from all the marriage preparations; Olga, with just an element of regret for the wedding she could not have; Nerissa, thinking it was a lot of unnecessary fuss. They both accepted, on a purely practical level, that marriage was a social act in which society had an interest and a sacrament in which the church had an interest. Very well, that too perhaps – but all the surrounding fuss had nothing to do with the church or society.

Olga needed to talk to someone and she turned to her younger sister who had always been critical of her and, what she described as her frivolous attitude to life. But things had changed – life had progressed – both of them were more mature, and so one night in Nerissa's bedroom –

"Oh dear, Nerissa, I am so tired of all this talk about the wedding. Why can't people just give their vows to each other and get on with it?"

"Because, in the end, it is a contract, embodying property rights and inheritance, in which civil society has a stake."

"Nerissa is that all it is? Didn't we used to believe that it was primarily a matter of two people loving each other?"

"You may have believed that – but I only agreed that love is the vital factor in choosing the man. But Olga, once your choice is made, society has the right to intervene, to witness, to register and in the last resort to make the rules.

"And the church?"

"Oh poof Olga, neither you nor I believe in the right of a priest, guru, mullah, rabbi or shaman to prognosticate, bless or condemn. We just go through the motions dictated by them, because that is how society likes to organise these things. I doubt it will last another hundred years."

"And what about me? I'm going to have the child of a man who is dead and can no longer marry me."

"Oh Olga, my darling, my soul, just be thankful that your child is going to be born into a family where he, or she, will receive as much love and security as any child born into a family with their father present."

"Well I suppose so… but have I the right to want another man? Would that not be the height of selfishness? Is it even possible in view of the depth of feelings I had for another?"

"My dear sister, you can't repress genuine feelings you have for another person, just because you once loved another. But Olga, your moral position must, absolutely must, be dependent on the man knowing of your condition and accepting it completely."

"Oh Nerissa, even if he knows all the circumstances, should you allow yourself to indulge in fantasies about him, or encourage him?"

This question was followed by a long and quite comfortable silence, as Nerissa took time to grasp the full meaning of her sister's question. Then she said –

"It's Harry isn't it?"

"Yes. I think he likes me; in fact I think it might be much more than that. He knows about Selim, and about Selim's child. I've been careful not to encourage him in case … Oh Nerissa it's so complicated – I like him – we have fun together. But I worry that my attachment is … I don't know … artificial – as if I am looking for someone to help me out of my current predicament. He saved me from myself in Smyrna, and I know he likes my company but he doesn't say anything. He is so English!"

"Are you sure that it is the English in him, and not that he is worried that he might pressurise you? After all, it is only three months since you were living with a man to whom you were truly devoted. He might be feeling that it would be selfish to press you."

"My God Nerissa, I don't know, my love. It's all in the air. We are all just waiting …"

CHAPTER 33

Olga and the City at the Crossroads

While the Mudania agreement had finalised the basis for an eventual territorial settlement, the status of the Imperial city itself had yet to be sorted out as well as the whole incredible muddle that had befallen the Eastern Mediterranean since the defeat of the Greeks and the burning of Smyrna. Looming in the background was the policy of population exchange, another name for ethnic cleansing, for which tidy-minded bureaucrats were busily creating blueprints.

Surprising though this appears in hindsight, British diplomatic circles had first thought of holding a limited conference, between themselves and the Turks in Smyrna, before the Anatolian army began moving on Chanak. On hearing of this proposal, Lord Curzon observed to a senior foreign office official –

"As to a conference at Smyrna, my dear Crowe, not even Nero held a symposium amid the smoking ruins of Rome."

Then came the Mudania conference, where the men on the spot sorted out, as best they could, the purely military arrangements for the territorial settlement. But a full conference of all interested parties was still needed and, after much discussion, Lausanne was the venue selected. The conference would consider the whole future of the collapsing Ottoman Empire – above all the legal status of the straits and the city which controlled them, a matter of vital concern to the whole world.

Such a conference required the presence of all interested parties, not just the participants in the war. That included the Americans and Soviet Russia, still pariahs on the international stage. The participation of America meant the necessity of including the impossible person who occupied the position of American High Commissioner in Constantinople – Admiral Mark Bristol. His involvement scotched any proposition that America might be given the task of looking after British affairs in the event of hostilities between Britain and the new Turkey; Crowe stating,"*If he were a person less hostile to the Christian populations of the city and less petty and vindictive in his personal attitudes, it might have been a good idea.*"

As the panic-stricken Greek farmers of Eastern Thrace continued to pour out of that province; as the authority of the British occupation forces and the power of the Ottoman administration in Constantinople declined and as Mustapha Kemal imposed his will on the city from the backwaters of Ankara, the delegates began arriving by train at the city of Lausanne on the shores of Lake Geneva.

The wedding of Nicolai and Sima – the first of the Avakian girls to leave home – had come and gone. In Armenian weddings, the best man – in this case Alexei – was required to stand between and behind the happy couple, holding a cross aloft over their heads. It was considered unlucky if the cross drooped or failed to remain permanently over the heads of the bride and groom. This was fine if the best man was tall and strong. But both Sima and Nicolai were tall, while Alexei, desperately anxious not to let his brother down, was fairly short. Fortunately, Father Haroutune did not believe in lengthy ceremonies, and Alexei had kept the gold cross bravely aloft throughout.

Sima and Nicolai had gone straight from the small reception in the family home in Makrikoy, to the Patakis house. The Countess Androvna, now moved from Vienna and settled in her sister's apartment in Padua, had already written with confirmation that the Count Maggi had warmly welcomed the idea that Nicolai should come to Padua with his new wife to take over the management of his estate in the Veneto. Nicolai had started a crash course in Italian. He went every evening, after returning from work, to the little apartment of a somewhat impoverished Italian widow, who had no children and immediately fell for the reserved and well-mannered Nicolai. Nicolai learned quickly, but whether the refined conversations he had with her for two hours every evening was going to be much help in dealing with stubborn peasants in the Veneto countryside, was another matter.

The impending departure of her eldest daughter had galvanised Armineh. She was continuously closeted with Sima, preparing cases, packing and repacking. There was then the question of dividing those items, which had to accompany them from those that could be shipped separately. Karekin took little part – but already bills of exchange were lodged with his agent in Lancashire and his bankers in Milan. Letters of credit in Sima's name were already with her papers. Alexei had spent three whole days at the Italian consulate having Sima's Ottoman passport checked and counter-signed, and Nicolai's Nansen passport issued with a visa. Alexei claimed that holding up the great gold cross at the wedding was nothing compared to the sheer tedium of waiting in the dingy corridors of the Italian consulate.

The movement of some of Karekin's commercial balances out to his European agents and bankers was not just in case Sima and Nicolai were in need of ready capital. There was also an element of prudent insurance against the possibility of a Smyrna solution for the Greeks, Jews and Armenians of the city. Karekin looked on in despair as the Ottoman world disintegrated in front of his eyes. It was becoming clear that no one, Turk or Christian, had much respect for the person of the current Sultan, the garrulous and timid Mehmet VI. Refet Pasha was now the only credible authority in the city and the counterbalance of the British was being whittled away day by day.

However, despite the slippage of authority and the powerful nationalist propaganda; despite the shouts of the students cheering on the Turkish troops marching through the city to join the gendarmes in Eastern Thrace; there remained a residual respect and love for the dynasty that had commanded the city and the Turkish people for centuries. The students, might shout enthusiastically – 'Down with the old rascal at the Yildiz' – but the majority of the patient working people of the city felt differently. Many of them, both Turk and non-Turk, were aware that the heir to the current Sultan, his cousin Abdul Medjid, was waiting in the wings to take over. A robust, honourable man, he had enlightened views, an artistic spirit and was modern in outlook. He was a devout Muslim, but also had sympathy with the nationalist movement.

With the future in the balance, Karekin felt he must to be ready to move in any direction, at a moment's notice, for the security of his family. He had absolutely no wish to leave the city, to move away from the life, culture, memories and friends he had made over 50 years in this beautiful city. Despite the fear and trauma of the events in April 1915, despite the pain that each community had inflicted on the other – Greek on Turk – Turk on Armenian – everyone on the Jews – a residue of underlying respect for the religion and culture of other faiths and peoples, which had maintained the Ottoman dynasty for centuries, still lingered. Karekin had plenty of Turkish friends and business associates who felt the same way, despite all the propaganda directed at them.

The academics in the schools and universities, fabricating lies and myths, and all the small-minded bureaucrats gathering in Lausanne, went about their business of declaring that the peoples of the Empire had always hated each other and been unable to live peaceably together and the only solution was to separate them with lines on a map.

Nationalism! As soon as geography is looked at in detail, the naturalness of a so-called national border melts away, and the horror of ethnic cleansing emerges. Officials and sectarian academics designed this 'exchange of populations',, to ensure that a 'people' and their 'land' coincided, but it was precisely these abstract divisions, which were so unnatural and so cruel. No former Ottoman Sultan, however ruthless or despotic, would have contemplated such a solution.

Harry, waiting in a sort of professional limbo for the decision of the court-martial, had spent almost every day since, either at Makrikoy or visiting favourite sites in and around the city – always in the company of Olga. The continual rain and cold of the first weeks of October, had given way to balmy skies and warm sunny days in November as they strolled over ruins, looked at old castles, picnicked at the Sweet Waters and swam off the islands. There was no constraint between them; they enjoyed each other's company unreservedly, and the easy nature of their relationship, established in such dramatic circumstances in Smyrna, continued. But Harry was quite unable to rid himself of the looming presence of Selim. It was not just the thought that he had been Olga's first love, a love she had loyally maintained and consummated, but that Olga was carrying his child.

Olga was enjoying a contentment that she had believed impossible, following the events of 13th September. The support she had received from the whole of her family now led her to

disregard the social difficulties her present condition would cause, once it became obvious. She knew her baby would be surrounded by love, despite being without a father, and this, at last, overcame her grief at the death of her lover.

Yet, perversely, her joy, radiating from her open, expressive features, became a barrier for Harry. He came to know every nuance of her expressions, and he concluded that she was happy – happy in her memories of Selim – happy for the baby growing inside her – and did not need any further emotional entanglements. But he now knew that he loved this woman and wanted to spend his life with her. He had already been approached by the Admiralty with news that, subject to the results of the court martial, he would be posted to the headquarters of the Eastern Mediterranean fleet in Alexandria, and should begin making preparations for leaving. He began thinking of his own departure from the city, and from the lives of all the people, who, in different ways, he had come to love.

Events now began crowding in on each other. An anti-nationalist ex-minister in the old Ottoman administration was arrested by Refet's secret policemen right in the middle of the main street in Pera. He was dragged away, gagged, put aboard a boat and taken by night to the Asian side and put into the hands of the nationalist army. Once there, he was brought before the local commander, who interrogated him and then had him led in chains, with only a few guards to accompany him, to the local prison. Word was carefully spread of the route he would be taking and he was surrounded by a mob inflamed by propaganda – now shouting 'traitor' instead of '*giavour*'. The guards, forewarned, melted away, and he was brutally murdered by the mob, in scenes reminiscent of the death of Archbishop Chrysostom in Smyrna, two months before.

The Sultan now became seriously alarmed. Memories of the fate of the odious Abdul Hamid, left the garrulous old man in fear for his life. On the 4th November, following one of Mustapha Kemal's lethal speeches before the assembly in Ankara, the deputies had voted in favour of a declaration stripping Mehmet of the title of Sultan, but, for the moment, retaining his title of Caliph. Stating that this would separate the temporal power (the Sultanate) from the spiritual (the Caliphate), Mustapha Kemal hinted that the Caliphate would pass to Abdul Medjid.

It was not that Kemal had the slightest reverence for the title of Caliph. For him it was outmoded, medieval, like Selim had often said to Vahan – 'It's an Arab thing – let it go'.

But there it was, for better or worse, for the first time in the history of Islam, there was to be a separation of temporal from spiritual power. That day – that very day – the National Assembly ended their session with prayers; prayers, which the principal nationalist ministers did not attend, but which, for the first time in history, were recited not in Arabic, but in Turkish.

Since returning from Smyrna, Olga's moods had swung between grief and despair on the one hand, to joy and euphoria on the other. But once she had settled Spiro permanently with the Kafides family in Thrace and after she had brought Karekin fully into the picture, she began for the first time to think of Selim's family – his sister Yasmin and his implacable mother Halideh hanum. After sending Yasmin a note, she heard back that the Ankara authorities had written a cursory official letter to her mother stating that Selim had been in Smyrna with the army as it entered the city, but that he had disappeared and was believed to have died in the fire that had 'accidentally' broken out and destroyed the town. The note had been signed by a certain Ali Ahmet, who no one had heard of, but it was written on paper with the Ghazi's personal heading. Yasmin told Olga that it stated, categorically, that Selim had died a heroic death as a full Major in the Turkish army.

The balmy days of early November continued and at last without thinking it through sufficiently Olga decided that she had to go to see Halideh hanum and tell her of the approaching birth of her grandchild. She did not confide in Harry or anyone else. She simply made an arrangement to meet him for lunch after her visit. Harry suggested that they meet at the Pierre Loti café and then visit the mosque at Eyub. Neither of them knew that this was the spot, five years before, where Karekin had witnessed the death of his great friend – Doctor Manuelian – and had been forced to abandon him in his last moments.

Olga did not send a note to Yasmin, but directly addressed it to Halideh. She didn't think enough about it – happy as she was at the thought of the coming child – secure as she was in the love and support of her own family, but simply charged ahead with her plan. After all, she felt, the child was as much Halideh's grandchild as it was Karekin's.

So, there she was in the elegant sitting room in the apartment block, on the Grande Rue du Pera. It was only after she arrived, and was let in by the maid, that she realised that Yasmin was not going to be present, and it was probable that Halideh had not even told her that Olga was coming.

Halideh came in almost at once, and forced greetings were exchanged between them, until the maid reappeared with a tray of coffee and some pastries. Halideh, who looked pale and was chain smoking, silently handed Olga the letter received from Ali Ahmet *effendi* from Ankara. For the first time, Olga began to question her decision to come to this house of grief and stir up matters which might be better left alone. She could have said some comforting words, remarked on the fact that Selim appeared to have been promoted, and left. The two women sat silently as Olga's mind raced. Halideh thought that she was still reading when, in fact, Olga was facing up to her own impulsive action, everything suddenly seemed to be warning her to remain silent and not add to this woman's grief. Just go, she thought to herself!

But she didn't. Surely Halideh was as much entitled to the truth as Karekin was. She would make every effort to present the truth as kindly as possible. So, leaving out that she had also been working at the Armenian hospital, she told Selim's mother of her appointment to work as a senior nurse at the Imperial Ottoman hospital in Smyrna. She then went on to speak of her chance meeting with Selim in the street, of their love, of their life together at the house of Madame Derounian. She described, as gently as possible, Selim's shattered knee and broken leg, her inability to get help for him, and his death in the fire which swallowed up the whole street.

Halideh never uttered a single word, just staring at Olga, as she smoked cigarette after cigarette. Olga became more and more uncomfortable but at last came to her final words –

"I helped him to put on his uniform at the end, and he died a full officer in the army, which he had joined voluntarily the year before. I have to tell you Halideh hanum that we intended to marry as soon as we returned to Stamboul. I also wanted to tell you that I am pregnant and expecting Selim's child – your grandchild."

There was a long silence as Halideh continued to stare at Olga, who now blushed as the blood raced to her head. Then speaking slowly and deliberately Halideh rose from her seat and looking down at Olga said –

"So, Miss Olga, what you are saying is that my son was in Smyrna on some clandestine mission for the Ankara government. There you met him and seduced him into your bed. No – don't interrupt me. This clearly must have taken place in the *giavour* quarter of the city as the fire did not touch the Moslem quarter. So, if you had not persuaded him to live with you, my son would almost certainly be alive today."

"Halideh hanum …please …I …"

"No. Let me finish. Quite apart from your sluttish behaviour in sleeping with a man before you were married, you then failed to help him when he arrived at your door wounded and in great pain. I don't know, as you have not explained, how you yourself managed to get away from the fire – but it is clear that you abandoned my son to die in the flames that your people had probably started in the first place. You left my son to die and saved yourself. You have only ever brought me grief and pain from the moment I first set eyes on you. Now please leave this house. I never want to see or hear from you again."

Olga, stunned and in a state of complete shock, struggled up from the sofa. There were such barbed elements of truth in what the implacable lady was saying, she could not think straight. In a trance she moved to the door where the maid was now standing, and out into the hall. Then as she reached the front door of the flat a shrill voice called out –

"I curse you, you loose woman; who knows whether my son really is the father of your bastard child. May you both perish together when your time comes!"

And Olga staggered out of the apartment, unaware that Yasmin had arrived very soon after her and had heard it all.

Olga had no idea how she managed to get from Pera down to the Galata Bridge and onto a ferry going up the Horn to Eyub. She remembered nothing of the trip there, or stumbling through the cemetery, up the hill to the Pierre Loti café. Harry was sitting at a small round table for two, reading a book, as usual as she walked up from where the carriage had left her at the bottom of the path, halfway up through the trees of the old Moslem cemetery. Olga had blushed redder and redder as the words of Halideh had burned into her, but there weren't, as yet, any tears. Nor had she cried either on the ferry or in the carriage from the ferry station. But, as she arrived and saw Harry sitting there with his head buried deep in a book, the tears began coursing down her cheeks and she stopped in her tracks.

Oh God, it was true, it was all true. She had abandoned her lover hadn't she? She was a slut wasn't she? Would Selim have got into her bed if she hadn't willed it, wanted it? And above all, it was true that if he had stayed safely in the Turkish quarter he would be alive today.

As Harry at last looked up from his book, Olga sank down onto the little wrought-iron seat on the other side of the table.

"My God, Olga, what is it, what is it my darling – what has happened." Harry jumped up and came round and held Olga tight round her shoulders. At this, Olga finally burst into sobs.

Sobbing, and unaware that Harry was now kneeling beside her holding her hand, she told him what had happened and what Halideh had said. Then in a frenzy of self-loathing, she stood up making Harry who was still holding her hand stand up as well and blurted out in a mixture of sobs and hysterical laughter –

"But, Harry she was right, she was right. I did abandon Selim didn't I. Surely I ..."

"Oh nonsense, Olga, absolute nonsense. You were desperately seeking the only way you could to get him out of the house."

"But would Selim have died if I hadn't persuaded him to come and live with me in Hasmig Derounian's house. Oh God, Harry I am a slut – I did persuade him. Oh God, how will I face my child when he asks after his father?"

"You were both deeply and honourably in love. You were both adults, you both knew what you were doing. How can you be responsible for what occurred in Smyrna later – for the fire and destruction in one section of the city."

"I abandoned him – I abandoned him – she was right, I am a loose woman, yes, she called me that, oh heavens when she cursed me and ..."

"Olga, stop it, you know none of this is true. Here is a woman who desperately needs to blame someone for the death of her son. What does she know of the circumstances in which you were struck unconscious as you sought help? Come, my love, come, bear up, I ..."

And then it happened. Harry might never have been able to refer in words to his love for Olga. However, standing there outside the little café, with his back to the crazy patchwork of gravestones in the cemetery, still holding onto Olga's hand as she tried to wipe her tears with the other, he leant forward and kissed her full on the lips, oblivious to the whole world around him. Standing tall and strong, his lips on hers, he held her tight and his strength and support flowed directly to her in the embrace.

Olga, crying and in a complete maelstrom of emotions, felt herself held tightly by this man, in whose company she had been almost every day for the last month. In one section of her mind, she knew that the inferences made by the relentless old lady were completely unjustified – but it had all been close to a part of the truth. Every event can be seen inhindsight in more than one way – however unjustly. But she thought of none of this consciously. She was after all Olga, not Nerissa. All she felt was the strength of feeling in Harry's embrace. As oblivious to all around her as Harry was, she returned his kiss as they stood there under the trees, for a minute – for an eternity.

CHAPTER 34

The End of the Sultanate and many other things

It was the 17th November, the day before the projected departure of Sima and Nicolai on the Simplon-Orient Express, for their journey to

Venice and on to Padua and the Maggi estate. The weather, which had been so gentle and warm for the past fortnight, had at last broken for good. The rain was bucketing down, as Karekin hurried to the station at Cobancesme, to catch the morning train into the city.

Karekin was becoming worn out by all the events pressing in on him – political and personal. It was Armineh who had been dealing with all the practical details – the trunks that would accompany them on the train, and those which could be sent on as freight by sea, once they had settled in. But ultimately, it fell to Karekin and his office, with the enthusiastic participation of Alexei, to deal with the documentary formalities.

Tired, almost punch-drunk though he was, he revelled in his capacity to deal with it all. He had it all worked out; every detail of the departure of his eldest daughter to her new life in Italy; every detail of how and where he would take the family in the event that Lausanne decreed an 'exchange of population' for the city; a school for Seta in Switzerland.

Only the day before, he had faced up to yet another change in family circumstances. In the morning, as he was dressing before going down to breakfast, Armineh had warned him of the likelihood of a visit he should expect that day.

"My soul, I think that you are going to be approached by Harry."

"Harry? All right, all right, don't glare at me. Yes – yes, the Englishman who has been here almost every day for weeks. What does he want?"

"Karekin, are you deliberately irritating me? It's Sima's next to last full day and we still haven't decided on everything. Surely you have noticed that this young man has been paying a lot of attention to Olga. They have become very close since their meeting in Smyrna. Olga confided to me last week that Harry asked her to marry him – in that café above the Eyub mosque of all places."

Karekin, who had indeed been teasing his wife, pulled up short. He'd been aware, who could not have been, that ever since coming back from Smyrna, Olga had grown close to the Englishman. He understood her feelings and emotions better than any of his other children. He had seen the enormous affection she had bestowed on this Englishman, and she seemed happier in his company. However, he had not seen the same passion as she had shown towards Selim. Olga must have changed in some way that he had not appreciated – was it the coming baby?

"And what, my love, did she say back to him?"

"She has, informally, accepted him."

"But Armineh – Armineh – does he know about the baby. I can't.... we can't....it would be quite wrong....I...."

"Come, come – you've always said that however silly our girls may be, they do know right from wrong, I understand that she told Harry all about her pregnancy even before she told any one of us."

"Good heavens – and despite all that, he still wants to marry her. Does he realise that...."

"I'm going down Karekin. He's a good man. He will make a good father to the child which, to all the world, except just a few, will be his. But of course ... of course, another of our children will be leaving us. They will be here for lunch – could you come early from the office. I will arrange a late lunch for everyone."

And so it was that Karekin found himself sitting behind his desk in his study that afternoon, listening yet again to a young man asking for the hand of his daughter. As he strode down to the station, he reflected on how different the two experiences had been. Nicolai, young, penniless but passionate, and ready to fight for what he wanted; Harry, older, more mature, reserved and secure – equally ready to fight, but coolly presuming that he wouldn't have to.

"Harry, my boy, I do want to be clear on one thing. I understand that you know Olga is now nearly three months pregnant and expecting Selim's child. You only met Selim once, I think, at that awful tea party here in the summer, over a year ago. He was an honourable man. I could have accepted him as a son-in-law, despite the strong opposition of both mothers. Are you prepared to take on my first grandchild as your own? Please think about it – are you sure."

"Sir, I accept the responsibility and I don't need to think further. I believe that my love for your daughter will sustain me in this. It is not only blood that counts in these matters. I will be the natural father of this child when it arrives, for everyone, except for a very select few here in Bolis. I will love the child as much as any children Olga and I are blessed with in the future. Come, sir, I hope you will have many more grandchildren and all will be equally cherished."

"Well, well, Harry, you couldn't have put it more fairly. Tell me what exactly are your immediate plans."

"I'm not entirely sure, sir. I'm still awaiting the verdict of the court martial. It is highly unlikely that I would be cashiered, even if the verdict goes against me. I'm likely to be posted to the headquarters of the Eastern Mediterranean fleet in Alexandria. But sir, with your permission, I hope to arrange our marriage at the earliest possible moment."

"But if the decision does go against you?"

"I cannot say – but these are decisions which I will make with Olga's help. Either way, we cannot stay in Constantinople much longer. Anticipating a favourable decision from you, sir, and knowing as I did that I have Olga's ...er ...love ...er ... consent, I have begun making arrangements for a secular marriage at the British Embassy. We need to move quickly and I'm sorry but neither of us wanted a church..."

Karekin arrived at the station platform smiling to himself as he recalled Harry's embarrassment in revealing that he and Olga wanted a
civil marriage. This had not worried him a bit. What a joy that at least
one of his daughters was going to avoid those meddling priests and
their silly, long-winded rituals.

As it was still raining, he took a carriage from Sirkedji station and
eventually arrived at his office. Alexei was already at his desk, having
taken an earlier train, as were the rest of his staff. He decided that he
would work for the morning, but would then walk down to the Galata
Bridge and over to the Patakis house. He nodded at Alexei and motioned him to come into his office.

"Alexei, finish those letters you are working on and then leave and
go back home. Armineh went out without her coat this morning. Please
get her coat and then go straight back to the Patakis house and lend a
hand there. I will see you there."

"Yes – thank you sir. By the way, a letter was delivered this morning
by a boy from the Armenian Bureau for Missing Persons. It is addressed
to 'N. Avakian' and was forwarded from the Imperial Ottoman Hospital
in Smyrna. Knowing that your middle name is Norair they have assumed it is for you. There is no other N. Avakian in the city. Here it is."

"Very well – thank you", said Karekin lightly, putting the envelope to
one side, "I'll look at it later."

Alexei nodded, turned and, taking his umbrella, left the office to walk
back down to Sirkedji. There he took the next train back to Makrikoy.

It was very early in the morning of the 17th November when Tim
Harington arrived at his desk in the Harbiye. He too, like Karekin, was
reflecting on what had happened the day before. In the morning he
had been sitting at his desk when he was told that the old Sultan's aide-
de-camp was in the building, asking to see him. Harington went down
and found that the man in question was the Court bandmaster, and not
the officer referred to. Knowing that this man was the father of one of
the Sultan's wives, he realised at once that it was likely to be important
and confidential and invited him up to his office, making sure his own
A.D.C was present.

"Greetings, *effendi*. How can I help you?"

"Your Excellency I have come from the Palace at the express request
of the Sultan."

"Yes. I have already been warned that the Sultan might use your
services."

"Your Excellency, everyone at the Palace has become disloyal. The
ministers have all resigned, and yesterday, even his personal doctor,
who has been with him for years, fled without a word. Sir, my master

believes that he is going to be murdered tomorrow at the Selamlik service. He is asking you to save his life by arranging for him to leave the city immediately."

"But what evidence is there? Surely there is no way that Refet Pasha would be party to such an outrage. No, no, your master is surely mistaken."

"Your Excellency I can only repeat that my master is desperate and begs your intervention."

Harington felt he had acted both decisively and correctly in requiring the old bandmaster to go back to the palace and return with a letter, signed by the Sultan himself, setting out exactly what he wanted Harington to do. This had duly arrived and as he sat at his desk, watching the same rain that was drenching Karekin's shoes, he studied the letter. The document had been written by the old Sultan in his own handwriting and under his own personal seal. It read –

"Sir. Considering my life here to be in imminent danger, I voluntarily take refuge with the British government, and request that I be taken away from Konstantiye as soon as possible."

This pathetic note, written by the last descendent of a great dynasty, which had terrorised the monarchs of Europe for centuries, was signed – Mehmed VI, Sultan and Caliph of the Muslim Umma.

Harington had been warned by the British High Commissioner, Rumbold, before he left for Lausanne, that he was to be responsible for the life of the old man. The Palace was well guarded with spies, reporting daily to Refet Pasha. The problem was how to get the last Sultan of the Ottoman Empire out of his own palace alive, and without the intervention of the nationalists, who, in almost all respects, now controlled the city. Harington had spent most of the previous day discussing this with his two senior commanders.

The plan they had finally adopted was that the Sultan and his son should spend the night in one of the kiosks at the far end of the palace gardens. This was not particularly unusual and wouldn't arouse suspicion. The building conveniently adjoined a gate in the wall, leading out into a square, itself bordered by the current barracks of the Grenadier Guards. The plan was that the Sultan and his party should leave from this gate early in the morning. At the agreed time, the Grenadier Guards would be drilling in the square. Two ambulances were to be stationed in the square – Yildiz Square – and parked on either side of the gate. The gate was to be opened at the agreed time by one of the palace eunuchs, or, if necessary, forced open. The intention was for the Sultan and his sons to go into one ambulance, and the rest of his party with the luggage and father-in-law, the loyal old bandmaster, should go into the second vehicle. Both ambulances would drive to the quayside outside the Dolmabahce Palace, where Harington himself, and a naval detachment of at least one hundred men, would to be ready to receive the party. Officers with loaded revolvers were to be out for a morning walk at as many points along the route as possible.

The time had come and Harington could sit patiently at his desk waiting, no longer. He took out his own revolver, buckled on his belt and went out to take his car down to the quayside. HMS *Malaya*, the ship chosen to transport the last Ottoman Sultan away from his capital, coincidentally the only British battleship to have been largely paid for by a Muslim community, already lay out in the straits opposite the Dolmabahce.

Harington arrived well before 8.00 – the two ambulances were not due to arrive before 8.20 at the earliest, even if all went well. He strode up and down with his two aides. But 8.40 came and there was still no sign of either of the ambulances. His thoughts went to the Flight to Varennes and the failed attempt of Louis XVI to flee from Paris and the French revolutionaries, ending in complete disaster. Was this to be a repeat fiasco?

At five minutes to nine, already half an hour late, the second ambulance with the luggage and the servants arrived at the dock. But where was the first, containing the Sultan, which had left earlier? In the pouring rain, the second ambulance had taken a wrong turning and had wandered round on a longer route, hence its delay in arriving. But the first ambulance containing the Sultan should have arrived long ago. It had not, although it had left the Yildiz Square almost an hour before.

The rain poured down. Back in Makrikoy in the Avakian house, Paramaz was looking after baby Haik. He had been given the day off – it was a Friday – and he was lying on his back in the hall letting the infant crawl all over him. He would throw him up and then catch the squealing infant, who was yelling lustily in a mixture of joy and delighted apprehension. Talin was finishing some chores and Marie was bustling around keeping an eye on the idyllic domestic scene. Eventually Talin finished and came to watch Paramaz and Haik rolling about on the floor. It was at this point that Marie made her fatal suggestion.

"Talin – it's been raining for days. This poor child has been indoors all this time. It looks as if it might be slackening. The little lad has not been out in the fresh air for days. Why don't you take him out for a walk in the pram."

"But Marie, it's pouring with rain."

Yes, fine – but I can see it getting lighter all the time. Take one of the really large umbrellas and put the pram hood up and walk on the road down the hill. Paramaz, you go and nail up that coal shed door as Karekin *bey* instructed – and then go down and meet Talin and help her to push the pram back up the hill. Now Talin don't go down as far as the railway, go about halfway and Paramaz will come and join you for the way back."

As it happened, Talin took much longer to get the child ready, whereas Paramaz went straight round to the back of the house to finish the task Karekin had set him. It was therefore about 10.00am before Talin set out carrying an enormous umbrella, with little Haik sitting up in the cumbersome old carriage and staring out. This old pram had been used for all the children, starting with Sima, and somehow had always been overlooked when it came to buying new things. The rain here in Makrikoy was beginning to slacken off, and the air smelt fresh and invigorating. Talin, glad, after all, to be out of the house, trundled the old pram down the road between the fields.

Before the war, Constantinople had always been one of the safest cities in the world. Westerners had always nurtured myths that the city was one of darkened doorways, daggers in the night, the decadent orient steeped in poison and vice. It was a lie going back to the great days of Byzantium when the uncouth and unwashed Anglo-Norman and Frankish Barons passed through the city on one of their interminable crusades. Finding themselves in a sophisticated imperial city, where people wore clean clothes and washed and bathed regularly, they suffered from a deep inferiority complex, inventing the myth of a decadent and depraved city. This story survived and, years later, would be applied to their Ottoman successors.

While the rulers themselves, both Byzantine and Ottoman, cheerfully murdered each other in a welter of blood, over any disputed succession, the ordinary people lived in a city which, until the middle of the nineteenth century was well-regulated and, above all, safer than any other city in Europe. Up until the end of the Great War, no woman, veiled or not, would ever be molested anywhere in the street.

The arrival of the Allied forces and the occupation of the city, changed all that. Drunken sailors weaving through the streets of Pera at night became a normal sight. Women no longer walked alone in the streets after dark. The city became home to criminals and riff-raff of all types and nationalities. However, Harington's police had been fairly effective, once the British took firm control of the gendarmerie. Even the arrival of a quarter of a mil*lion* hard- bitten soldiers from General Wrangel's defeated army at the end of 1920 had been successfully assimilated and accommodated. But now, as everyone waited for the outcome of the Lausanne talks, the city was drifting towards anarchy. The old Ottoman city police force had crumbled; the British presence was vacillating; the Ottoman government was in total disarray while the nationalists did not yet have the capacity to take over the police and deal with criminal behaviour.

There was a power vacuum. What the Sultan had failed to take into account. the collapse of allied will – the criminal classes of the town were quick to see and exploit.

It was not a matter of lawlessness – nor was there evidence of ethnic conflict. There was simply an atmosphere of suppressed excitement and anticipation, and the mood of violence in the city had spilt over, even to the quiet suburb of Makrikoy.

The rain continued to slacken, but there was a fine wet mist in the air as Talin continued to walk down the road. She was about halfway down and approaching the edge of the Valli *effendi* racecourse, when she stopped to wait for Paramaz. She made funny faces at Haik, which had him giggling, when she saw, coming up the road towards her, out of the fine mist, three scruffy young men. They weren't local youths but the increasingly confident and uncontrolled riff-raff of the poorer quarters of the city, and they were looking for trouble and something to steal.

Talin was a brave girl, but she had been through a lot. She had seen her family die of exposure and hunger in the horrific death marches of 1915. She was only 14 and she felt helpless as the young men stopped and stood in the rain staring at her. One of them began rocking the pram violently. Talin gave a scream – a screech really – and leant in to the pram, grabbing the baby Haik and pulling him out. She held him tight, pressed against her wet clothes. The child did not appreciate being yanked out of his dry and cosy shelter into the rain and began yelling at the top of his lungs. Until that moment the young men had been grimly silent, but now one of them shouted viciously at Talin –

"Shut the fucking thing up."

Talin, now thoroughly scared, began rocking Haik in a frantic effort to quiet him down, but he yelled even more. One young man was eyeing the pram somewhat dubiously, while the other was pulling out the expensive linen and blankets. It was at this point that Talin felt the hands of the third man stroking her buttocks, and probing front and back. Holding on desperately to the screaming Haik, she could do nothing but let out a scream herself – not a screech this time but a full-blooded scream.

Then, coming out of the mist further down the road she saw Alexei hurrying up the road from the station. She shouted out – "Alexei!".

The early morning of the 17th November had been spent by the last Sultan of the Ottoman Empire in the Merasi Kiosk at the far end of the garden of the Yildiz Palace, as arranged with General Harington. All night he had fussed about with the servants who would accompany him into exile, packing jewels and other valuables into the trunks that had been left in the kiosk the day before. Everyone carried revolvers and the atmosphere was tense. Portraits of the great Padishahs of the past glared down at him from the walls. What could he possibly be afraid of? What could the nationalists have done to him? Even if the Turks repudiated the dynasty, there was no way that they could have physically harmed the last Caliph of the Moslem world. Mustapha Kemal may well have thought that it was all religious nonsense, but he was a supremely pragmatic realist, and he would not have risked the inevitable odium of harming the old man.

But the paranoia of the atmosphere of the Yildiz Palace – the baleful spirit of the almost demented Abdul Hamid cast its fearful shadow over the last Sultan. He was sure that something tragic and dramatic was going to happen to him.

It was 7.00am. A large detachment of the Grenadier Guards was ordered out to parade for drill on the Yildiz square. The rain poured down, and the comments of these 200 men, regular soldiers of the permanent army, could not be repeated in polite society. To be ordered out to 'drill' in such indescribably bad weather, and at such an unearthly hour, must mean that their officers had finally gone mad. But the drill began – left-right... left-right... about turn... and so it continued as two ambulances drove unobtrusively into the square and parked alongside a small doorway set into the high wall of the palace. The young soldiers had never seen this door opened. Now, as they drilled, from the corner of their eyes, they saw the door open and a party of men came out. Trunks were carried out and loaded into one of the ambulances while the men continued to drill, marching back and forth and making a lot of noise.

Eventually, the first ambulance, into which some men had been bundled, drove off and out of the square. The second ambulance, which was crowded with as many as six others together with all the trunks, finally shuddered into life and turned round the square and followed in the direction of the first and out of sight. The drill continued for another five minutes and then unaccountably stopped, as pointlessly as it had started in the first place.

In the first ambulance, Mehmed VI talked incessantly, smoking cigarette after cigarette. His talk was rambling and incoherent – but the gist was that he was not afraid of dying, but was afraid of being put on trial and being humiliated if he stayed. There was always the possibility of assassination – some fanatic, inflamed by the passions of the nationalists, might end the dynasty with a single shot. He rambled on as the ambulance carefully negotiated the badly pot-holed, road leading down to the Bosporus. There was only ten minutes more to go before they arrived at the dockside rendezvous, when there was a sharp sound like a muffled shot. The ambulance swerved violently and came to an abrupt halt with its front wheels over the pavement in what appeared to be a deserted and narrow street.

No one in the city, except the few directly involved participants, were aware of the drama being played out as the last of the Ottomans made his attempt to flee the city. Certainly Karekin, as he sat at his desk, had no idea what might be happening on the wider political stage; he had enough problems of his own to deal with.

It was a Friday. After Alexei had left to collect Armineh's coat, Karekin found he could not settle down. There was really no point in trying to work. He decided he would close up the office and go over to help with the preparations for Sima and Nicolai's departure tomorrow. He called out to the remaining staff that they could leave for the rest of the day and he would lock up. He looked round to check if he had dealt with everything, and took up the letter handed to him by Alexei.

It was the letter written by Burhan Celal two months previously, addressed by him to N. Avakian, instead of Nurse Avakian. Karekin read it through quickly. It was vivid and well-written prose, and it was only as he approached the end that Karekin realised that it had been meant for his daughter Olga. But by then, he couldn't stop. He read it through again slowly, sentence by sentence, taking in every nuance of meaning. Burhan had been a journalist of repute. His articles had been read by a large readership, who had revelled in his elegant prose, his command of Ottoman Turkish and his great descriptive talent. This letter had been drafted with all the benefit of his notes to take the place of the world-famous article on the Great Fire of Smyrna, which he had never got round to writing, and it burned itself, line by line into Karekin's mind.

Suddenly every event of that terrible day in September became clear to him. Like a stroke of lightening, the whole mystery of those last few hours of the life of his only son was illuminated. So, he had dealt with everything had he? His mind reeled, and he shouted out into the empty office a blasphemous profanity, words which no one had ever heard him utter. He read the letter again and again. He saw himself in the streets as the flames drew nearer. He knew exactly what his daughter had meant when she was gabbling out 'Turkish officer' in the street. And then – the rape!

At this thought Karekin groaned out loud and found he could hardly breathe. What man can hear of the rape of his own daughter and remain entirely sane. Yet she had said nothing – not a word of it to anyone – not to him, nor, more to the point, to her mother. His mind broke down, if only for a moment. He got up and paced round the office, picking things up and putting them down randomly. It was still pouring outside as he stared, unseeing, out of the window.

Then, sentence by sentence, he forced himself to contemplate the violent death of his only son. The son he himself had sent to Smyrna, deliberately sending him there in the company of his murderer. As he read, he groaned out again. Had every decision he had ever made rebounded against his own family? He stopped for a moment – had he perhaps misunderstood? He forced himself to read slowly, word for word, the writer's vivid description in the third page of his letter, of what he had witnessed when arrived outside the house from which Olga emerged.

"This third day I went out again and found myself in a narrow street in the Armenian quarter, not far from their cathedral. The cathedral was filled inside and out in the courtyard with wailing Armenians, mainly women and children with a few old men. They were clearly taking refuge, but from what I could not then tell. Later, as I walked through the Armenian quarter I saw that many houses had been entered and pillaged by the soldiers. Looting and even rape was proceeding in front of my eyes as our soldiers took revenge for some of the sights they had witnessed as the Greek army fled through the Turkish villages of the interior.

I was standing outside a house, by chance the same house which figures later in this narrative, when I saw two young men emerge. They seemed to be Armenians, the only young Armenian men I saw during the whole of that night. I saw the younger one run forward up the street towards an empty cart propped up against the wall several doors down. The other young man hung back. The doors of many of the houses on both sides of the street were swinging open. No one was at any window as far as I could see, though I had the impression that there were fearful and watchful eyes somewhere.

As the young man ran forward, three soldiers came out of the house where the empty cart was standing. They were carrying bundles of carpets and clothes. At their first sight of the young man, they dropped these bundles and began grabbing for their rifles which had been slung across their shoulders. The running boy stopped momentarily and stared at the soldiers and turned to run back. I thought at once that it would be too late – his hesitation had condemned him as two of the soldiers already had their guns up and aiming. But then I saw the second young man pull out a revolver, aim up the road and fire three shots. Each shot went into the chest of the boy who died instantly.

This was one of several incidents but I have dwelled on it as it happened outside the same house, which was later the scene of my own shame. It is one of the surprises of the human condition how quickly civilised behaviour disappears in conditions of extreme duress and danger. I myself had instinctively stepped back into the doorway of a house, and saw the young man who had fired the shots run forward and begin rifling through the clothes of the dead boy. Pulling down the boy's trousers, he found a money belt and took it. He then handed some coins to the three soldiers and offered some to me, which I declined. I gave little more thought to the incident – there were corpses everywhere. I moved on and next found myself...."

Sentence by sentence, word by word, syllable by syllable Karekin read and reread this passage. Once again he could not breathe properly – the bile rose in his throat and he ran to the washroom and thrust his head under the cold tap. It was no use, the heat and fever in him was inside his head and could not be assuaged by cold water. It was he who had set up the Bureau for Orphans; it was he who had introduced this viper into his home; it was he with his liberal values, his worship of tolerance; Oh God! What had he done? – It was all his fault. Oh my son – my son.

As the image of his cheerful smiling son came to his mind, the relief of tears finally arrived as he fell to his knees onto the floor. He stayed there on his hands and knees for many minutes – banging his fist on the floor until his hand began to bleed. He rose, feeling dishevelled and went to tidy himself up. A cold and devastating anger now took hold of him – an anger he had not felt for years. Forgiveness and reconciliation – the very thought made him groan out loud again. His only son who he had loved with a fierce pride – how could he ever forgive? As he paced up and down, his emotions began to overwhelm his whole philosophy of life. Had he been wrong all the time? Perhaps the nationalists had been right after all – why should there be forgiveness or reconciliation towards people who had caused such harm to him and his own.

There was now only one way he could relieve the terrible tension in his head. He would find out exactly what Paramaz would say when confronted and would avenge his son's death with his own hands. Then he would find and kill the man who had raped his daughter. He could not keep still and, at last, exhausted, he locked the office and went out into the city – his beloved city – and walked, seeing nothing.

In a desolate cobbled street somewhere near the Dolmabahce Palace, the ambulance containing the old Sultan and his son Ertogrul had mounted the dilapidated pavement and was standing stationary, halfway down a deserted street. The houses loomed up on either side, but not a window was open – not a soul looked down on the end of a dynasty. Had the old man been justified – was there an assassin lurking somewhere? Not so – 'the world ends not with a bang but a whimper'. The ambulance had simply had a puncture – but changing the wheel was taking a long time. The driver and his officer assistant got out, but the two other occupants remained in the van, adding to the weight. It seemed to take forever, and still no one, not a single person, appeared on the street. It only actually took about 35 minutes, but it seemed like forever. Mehmed, the sixth of that name by the grace of Allah, had at last stopped talking.

Once the ambulance arrived at the dock, Harington hurried forward with relief and escorted the Sultan and his party onto the waiting launch, and from there onto the deck of HMS *Malaya*. In the cabin that had been allotted to the fleeing monarch, Harington said –

"Your Highness, you are now on British territory. You are completely safe, I guarantee it. Where do you wish to go?"

"Harington *bey*," replied the last Osmanli, "I have no idea, no preference – I cannot think of my own future at the moment."

"Well, sir, we were planning for the ship to go to Malta where you will be safe as the guest of His Majesty's government. This would give you the time to make plans for the future."

"For the future – what future? I am abandoning the city of my forefathers. I have no future now, only a past."

Harington said nothing. It was not his problem any longer. The old man was safe and would leave while he would have to face music when news of the escape came out. He saluted and left the disconsolate old man, promising to help send his wives and daughters on after him. HMS *Malaya*, with full steam up, slowly moved away, passed round the point of the old Byzantine palace and the Ottoman Seraglio, and into the Marmara Sea, taking with it the last Osmanli Sultan forever.

Back in the Yildiz Palace, one of Refet's spies, realising what had happened, rushed to see Refet, who had spent a sleepless night, sensing that something was afoot in the Yildiz. Bursting into Refet's room, he reported what he feared had now taken place, anxious, above all, at his own dereliction of duty. Refet smiled and told him to go back to bed and get some sleep, then informed Ankara that they no longer needed to worry about the ex-Sultan as he had left of his own accord. Furthermore, he had done so with the aid of the infidel occupiers, at a stroke destroying any lingering support he might have enjoyed. He sank back onto his bed as the rain began to slacken, and fell peacefully to sleep for the first time that morning.

Alexei could scarcely credit what he was seeing as he emerged from the light mist and saw Talin ahead of him, standing in the road, holding a distressed Haik in her arms, and surrounded by three menacing young men. He heard Talin scream and shout out his name and immediately ran up the road towards the group. The scene froze as the three thugs turned at Talin's shout to see Alexei, a mere boy, running forward and shouting – 'stop … stop … leave her alone'.

Three knives appeared in a flash, glinting in their hands. Talin was still holding the now silent baby, shocked out of his own yelling by Talin's terrified scream. Alexei was brave, but he had no experience in street fighting. Now that they had a clear view of whom they were facing, they began grinning, which chilled the frightened Talin even more, but she had the sense to slowly back away, step by step, up the hill.

The tableau below her had frozen. There was no one about, and events could have gone in any direction. Alexei stood with his rolled up umbrella raised in front of him in a rather futile gesture of defiance, facing three young toughs, any one of whom could have knifed him, before he knew what was happening. Then suddenly it all unfroze as Paramaz came charging down the hill.

Paramaz, far more canny and streetwise than Alexei could ever hope to be, saw at once what was happening. He saw Talin, turning to look back at him with tears in her eyes, holding on tightly to the unhappy Haik – his baby – his godson. He saw the 16 year-old Alexei further down, attempting to hold off the ruffians with an old umbrella. He saw the three hooligans, the stolen bedclothes and the three wicked looking knives. He did not hesitate for a moment but started running down the hill.

It was the 17th November. The weather in Western Europe was not much better than in Constantinople. Lloyd George had already re-signed, his government having fallen largely due to the handling of the situation in Constantinople. At the General Election, which followed his resignation, Gladstonian Liberalism had been rejected and a Conserva-tive government came into power. Lord Curzon was confirmed in his office as Foreign Secretary, and so it was he who left London for Laus-anne, on the same Friday that saw off the last Sultan of the Ottoman Empire from the Imperial city.

The delegates were gathering. The reinstated Venizelos, unques-tionably the ablest man at the conference, was already there, but in a very weak position. Lord Curzon met President Poincaré in Paris and, despite their mutual antipathy, they travelled down by special train to-gether to the Swiss city on the lake. A certain Signor Mussolini, who had only two weeks previously taken power in Rome also arrived by special train for the opening, insisting on meeting his supposed allies – Curzon and Poincaré – outside Lausanne, before proceeding solemnly to the town.

Kemal had insisted that his friend, Ismet Pasha, who had conducted the negotiations with Harington at Mudania so ably, should lead the Turkish delegation at Lausanne. The Turks were convinced that the new nation-state they were creating was immeasurably superior to the multi- cultural empire they were succeeding. As conquerors, they be-lieved they could impose a conqueror's peace. Soviet Russia was their ally; France and Italy had become friendly; and in repudiating Lloyd George's government, the British would no longer oppose any of the new Turkey's demands.

In the event, despite all the odds stacked against him, Lord Curzon did well, and Great Britain emerged with its prestige less dented than might have been expected. The process was urbane and civilised, yet the outcome was the forced 'ethnic cleansing' of the old Ottoman Empire.

Here in the Chateau d'Ouchy, described by an American journalist as "a pile of stone so ugly as to make the town hall of any Hicksville USA look like the Parthenon," a decision was to be taken that raised up rampant nationalism as the dominant creed of the rest of the century. It was to be a decision as ugly in its effect, as the building from which it emanated.

Article I of the convention which was put before the delegates at Lausanne stated clearly and explicitly –

"There shall take place a compulsory exchange of Turkish nationals of the Greek Orthodox religion established in the territory of the Ottoman Empire and of Greek nationals of the Moslem religion established in the territory of the Kingdom of Greece. These persons shall never return to live in Greece or Turkey, respectively."

This convention, enthusiastically accepted as a matter of 'political necessity' by politicians, foreign dignitaries and academics alike, remained, forever after, the greatest example of the crude exercise of the power of the state over the individual.

The criteria for the exchange, was religion – offensive enough some might say – but the rationale was the mystical notion of the nation. Over a mil*lion* mostly Turkish-speaking Greeks, would be forced out of their homes to flood into the already impoverished Kingdom of Greece, together with a further 100,000 or so Armenians. Although not included in the proposed exchange, Greece accepted them without discrimination, requiring the commissioners 'to treat them with the same consideration as Greeks'.

The question of whether Karekin and his family, or the Asadourians, or the Patakis family, would have to leave the only homes they had ever known was also discussed in tones of calm objectivity. For reasons only of commercial advantage to the parties, Article II however proposed the exclusion of Greek and Orthodox inhabitants of the city of Constantinople from the forced exchange.

The convention stated there would be no right of return, in perpetuity, for any of those like Spiro's new parents, who as a matter of a solemn treaty could never ever return to their farm in Sinekli. As they finally crossed the bridge over the Maritza, they had no idea what the future held in store. Yet even they were more fortunate than most of their compatriots. They had two exhausted horses, five milk cows and all their tools. They also had a bright 12 year-old son, who respected them, and had been a great help during their flight, and whom they had come to love.

For Karekin, the beginning of the Conference of Lausanne on this Friday, an event he had been waiting for so long, no longer mattered at all. He walked and walked until he found himself on the Galata Bridge. Leaning against the parapet, he stood and stared down at the ferries jostling each other for the several spots where they were to discharge their passengers. He ignored the fine rain now falling on him and never saw the HMS *Malaya*, as it passed across the mouth of the Golden Horn and into the Sea of Marmara.

He was quite unaware of how much time had passed. Wearily, he turned and began walking toward Sirkedji station. But then the thought of going straight home to confront Paramaz was too much for him. Instead, he began walking up the hill towards his daughter's lodgings. There he would at least see Armineh. His thoughts now turned to his wife, instead of wallowing in his own distress, quickening his pace as he turned into the cul-de-sac leading to the Patakis house.

He was let in by the domestic and walked up the wooden stairs into the sitting room on the first floor. The room was filled with trunks, all open and filled to the brim. Standing in the middle of it all, looking hot and flustered was Armineh, who took a quick glance at him as he entered and said –

"Ah, Karekin, my soul, Sima is out with Nicolai for some last minute shopping and..."

"Armineh, my love I..."

At that constricted cry, Armineh turned and looked at her husband for the first time. They were not a couple given to overt displays of emotion, particularly outside the home, but there was no one else in the room. Armineh dropped the blouse she was holding and ran to Karekin's side, clasping him hard.

"Oh my God, husband, what is it – what has happened?"

"Armineh – wife – I don't know how to tell you. I have found out ... oh, merciful heavens ... I have..."

"Karekin just tell me. Whatever it is, we will both cope better, if it is shared."

Karekin suddenly felt very tired. Without another word, he handed Armineh the letter and sank down on one of the sofas.

It was a long letter – the article that Burhan had felt too guilty to publish. There was a long silence as Armineh read slowly. Her mastery of the Arabic script of the Turkish language, had not been as thorough as she might have wished. But she read on calmly as the description of the events on that narrow street in the Armenian quarter had at first little impact. It was only at the end of the letter, with the appearance of Olga into the road, that the significance sank in. Armineh paled as the realisation hit her. She put the letter down for a moment and rubbed her eyes, then quickly picked it up and continued reading. This brought her to the revelation of the rape, which she read almost with equanimity. When she finished the letter she looked down at her husband – dishevelled, with his head in his hands and in a state bordering on despair.

"My God, so that is what has been eating at Paramaz's soul all this time. That's why he is obsessed with the baby, that's why he named it after my son."

At the words 'my son' she choked and struggled to restrain her tears. Karekin at last looked up and said –

"I know I can undo nothing. I know that I can't bring my son back – but I will have a life for a life. One way or another, I will have my vengeance."

"Karekin, my soul, my love, don't, please don't. How do we know that it wasn't an accident?"

"Nonsense. Look how the writer describes what happened immediately after the shooting. Turk though the writer may be, he saw the rifling of the body and the stealing of the money belt and would have no part in it. But he too will die at my hands. Hypocrite! Rapist! They're all the same – I hate them all."

"No you don't hate them all, Karekin. Stop please. Consider just for a moment that, but for the writer of this letter, our daughter would not be alive today. Has the manner of Haik's death changed everything for you. My darling, if Haik had been shot by the Turkish soldiers, would it make all that much difference to your peace of mind? You have already grieved and are becoming reconciled to the death of your son, as one of the tragic consequences of the death of an empire and a way of life – that still applies, whoever pulled the trigger."

"It's my son, Armineh. It is one thing to face up to the consequences of a national catastrophe and to learn to live with it, but my own son, my only son, that I ..."

"But all the people who died in 1915, they were the sons or daughters of others. Is there no hope of forgiveness? Karekin, you have already lived through your grief – you can't begin all over again – it will tear at your soul and destroy you. You have to let go."

"Oh God, I can't. Help me, I can't. I have been at fault all along. I was wrong with all my liberal ideals – they have only led to my own son's death. My daughters I forced into a liberal western education. What has been the result – one has married a penniless Russian count and is leaving us – and the other has been raped. My ..."

"That's enough Karekin. You are lacerating yourself for no purpose. Not everything is due to you or controlled by you. Now snap out of it!"

At this point, Armineh stamped her foot. And at that traditional sight, Karekin gave a wry smile. He stood up, and they embraced long and lovingly in the middle of the untidy room.

"Karekin, we must go home right away. We will interview Paramaz together and at least find out his side of the story. Whatever he says, I accept that it would be quite impossible for him to remain in the house. But Karekin, while forgiveness might be too difficult, some sort of reconciliation is vital. We have adopted a new son – the baby Haik – it would be condemning him for the sins of others if he too were now rejected. Paramaz will have to go but...."

"And Olga?"

"Karekin, forget your male pride. Olga has chosen to ignore what happened to her on that terrible night. She has chosen not to tell anyone, not even me. Whether she eventually tells Harry after they are married, is entirely up to her. I hope that she does get round to it – perhaps when they have their own first child together. But, Karekin, she must not be burdened with this letter. It seems to me that Olga has coped with it like women have always had to do over the centuries. She doesn't need the burden of your anger or your guilt, as well."

Holding hands as they rarely did, Karekin and Armineh left the room with a message to Sima and Nicolai that they would meet them at Sirkedji for the departure to Venice the next day. Unlocking their hands once in the street they took the usual train back to Makrikoy.

Paramaz, who had immediately taken in the situation on the road below him, charged forward and by the sheer force of his charge ran straight down onto the first youth, knocking him over with a single blow. Alexei, with a whoop of excitement, joined in, swinging his umbrella with a will, but was immediately stabbed in the shoulder. Blood began pouring out. Paramaz turned to deal with Alexei's assailant, striking him hard over the head with the butt of his revolver which he had taken out as he ran – the same weapon which he had fired at Selim and at Haik all those weeks ago, and which he had kept with him ever since, although there was only one bullet left. Then, before that second youth staggered away, Paramaz too was stabbed near the neck – and he too began spurting blood.

Meanwhile, Talin had walked back, step by step, up the hill, clutching the baby tightly to her. The third man saw his two accomplices on the floor crawling away, and assumed that this newcomer must also have a knife. He sized up the situation in a flash, took the necessary few steps up the hill and grabbed Talin, raising his knife and threatening to plunge it into her body – or worse, into the baby.

Paramaz went cold – he did not realize the extent of the blood he was losing. He sank to the ground onto his knees, looking up at the knife poised so close to Talin and his baby – his godson Haik. Then slowly and deliberately holding himself up with one hand he raised the revolver – his hand did not shake – he aimed at the tableau in front of him and shot. The bullet went straight through the heart of the bully holding Talin. He fell to the ground, instantly dead, without a sound, but with a look of pure amazement on his face. The last thought that passed through Paramaz's mind as he too sank to the ground unconscious, was the horrific realisation, which he had never accepted before, that he was, and always had been, a natural good shot. Alexei, holding his own shoulder in an attempt to stem the blood, came and knelt by the side of Paramaz as the other two youths, hearing the gunshot, staggered up and took to their heels down the hill. The rain began again, falling gently as Talin stepped down to join the bleeding Alexei kneeling beside Paramaz, who appeared to be sleeping. Haik had stopped crying and sensing, somehow, that the crisis had passed, was wriggling to be put down. Paramaz opened his eyes and tried to sit up, but with every movement, blood spurted from his throat. He could hardly speak. Young though they were, Alexei and Talin had both seen enough death in their lives to know that Paramaz was unlikely to survive. They bent to listen as Paramaz gurgled out some words.

"Oh God, Alexei, Oh God – it turns out that I was always a good shot. Oh Haik forgive me, forgive me."

"Paramaz – hear me, hear me – there is nothing to forgive," said Talin. "Look here is Haik – see, he is well, he is well – you saved him again."

Talin bent down and placed the infant on Paramaz's chest. He was now lying on his back staring up at the sky, covered in blood. The infant Haik, remembering his play with Paramaz earlier in the morning and expecting more, bounced up and down on the dying Paramaz. The rain began to fall more heavily again, washing away some of the blood. Paramaz tried to sit up a little and finally blurted out –

"Asvadz, Asvadzim – Father – Mother – my sweet sisters – Oh God I never knew it, but I was, after all, always a good shot. Oh forgive me..."

But neither Talin nor Alexei understood a word – it all came out as a gurgle, as more blood spurted out of his throat. Only the baby reacted, creeping forward on the bloody chest of Paramaz, and put his little hands out to touch his eyes as they closed forever.

The rain had stopped when Karekin and Armineh arrived at the Cobancesme station. They were both exhausted and didn't hesitate to wave at Abdul to take the carriage home. Karekin had already calmed his fever, as they arrived, and followed Armineh as they walked into the hall and into the sad situation that confronted them.

None of the four girls were there, but the rest of the household were gathered in the hall. The family doctor had already come up from the town and was still tending Alexei's wounds. Haik, already washed and changed by Marie, was in her arms. The two men who had helped to carry up the body of Paramaz had already departed, and his body lay on the floor at the foot of the stairs covered by a dark sheet.

The explanations poured out, jumbled and frantic. Armineh went forward and took the baby from Marie and cuddled him, much to his gurgling satisfaction. Karekin listened and then, when everyone had stopped talking and everything had been explained he said –

"Poor Paramaz. He had a difficult life, in which nothing ever went right for him, after he was left alone when all his family were massacred in that death march. He coped with it all as best he could, and saved the life of this infant – twice it would seem. We will have a service for him within the next few days."

He then turned and, leaving them all in the hall, went into the sitting room and for a moment, leaning on the mantelpiece, he stood silently staring down into the flames in the fireplace. Then he took out the letter and without a further look, he tore it to shreds and fed them to the flames.

CHAPTER 35

The End of the Imperial City

The next day, a Saturday, the whole family gathered at midday at Sirkedji station. Alexei, already recovered from the superficial wound he had received, went ahead to get a table for twelve at the restaurant on Platform 1. Two porters had been engaged for the whole morning until the departure time. They stood patiently at the grand entrance to the station, leaning on their trolleys and waiting for Sima and Nicolai to arrive. The death of Paramaz had added a sombre touch to an occasion that was already melancholy. Their eldest daughter was leaving them, not only their home, but the city of her birth. The news of the departure of the Sultan the day before was now all over the city, and uninformed speculation was rife, but Karekin no longer cared. He had more than enough to worry about in sorting out his family's affairs.

The carriage containing Sima and Nicolai finally arrived in front of the station. Alexei, who had made himself the master of ceremonies for the whole occasion, came forward out of the entrance hall, extended his arm and handed down Sima from the carriage, as if she was a Grand

Duchess of the Imperial Court arriving at the annual ball. Sima was beaming, flushed with pleasure and heady with excitement and anticipation. Everyone had by then arrived and were all gathered outside the chandeliered entrance hall – Nerissa in a white dress and large floppy hat despite the cold weather – Olga, standing beside Harry, their hands touching – Seta, jumping up and down in excitement. Talin had not come – she was still upset and had elected to stay at home and look after Haik. However, Marie was there – in tears almost the whole time – dressed in her best Sunday clothes.

As Sima, smiling broadly, stepped down from the carriage, the whole party burst into spontaneous applause, clapping as she ran forward to Armineh and hugged her tight. Karekin felt a mixture of pride and sadness. He reflected on the fact that he had been married for almost thirty years, and now his first-born child was leaving home, as would his second girl soon afterwards. Was it all downhill now as his other children left him one by one?

He shook his head, as if to rid himself of cobwebs. The words of Armineh, thrust at him yesterday, as he was about to give way to self-pitying despair, came back to him. She had pointed out that it was a form of arrogance on his part to assume that everything emanated from him and depended entirely on his will. He smiled. He would be reconciled.

As Armineh and Sima embraced, Nicolai, still in the carriage directing the porters to the cases piled up behind, turned and gave a great shout of joy and welcome. Striding up from the seafront came Vahan with what appeared to be a huge bunch of flowers.

"You don't want all these, Sima," he said, "They wouldn't all fit in the compartment."

It wasn't actually one enormous bunch, but four more modest smaller ones. Vahan was no Alexei, but nevertheless he managed to put some panache, for once, into the gesture. He handed one to each of the Avakian girls – including a blushing and extremely pleased Seta. The two porters laboriously loaded their trolleys with the six trunks, two hatcases and several bits of hand luggage, which were accompanying the couple. Then they all trooped into the station and over to the restaurant. No one wanted to go inside, despite the chilly weather.

A table was already laid for twelve, though they were in fact only eleven. Alexei had jotted down the numbers two days before and of course...

Considering the circumstances, it was a surprisingly cheerful party. As often happened in Bolis, the neighbouring tables were sent round drinks by Karekin and even dishes to try. They were invited to join in the toasts, and reciprocated by raising their own glasses to the future of the two newlyweds. Karekin swelled with pride and emotion, and Armineh smiled.

Then the empty train, with the carriages all cleaned and prepared, pulled slowly into the station and alongside the platform and immediately, there was animated activity, although there was still half an hour before the train was due to depart. The brown-uniformed Wagons-Lits attendants were already at their doors with their lists of boarding occupants. The two porters were already on their way up the train. Everyone began to stand at the table and the tears began. Olga and Sima embraced for more than a minute. Everyone hugged everyone – there were no more words. Bolsetsi Armenian 'good-byes' were always notoriously long and over-emotional – but even Harry joined in.

Then, they all streamed out of the restaurant and up to the coach marked for Venice, and on to Milan. With a hissing of steam from under all the coaches – with a great cacophony of shouts and whistles, without which no train was able to start from Sirkedji station – with a great clanging lurch – the train hooted once, and slowly left for the West.

A week later – exactly the same group, but without Sima and Nicolai and instead including some of Olga's friends and also Yasmin who had been specifically invited, gathered in a side room of the imposing British embassy just off the Grande Rue du Pera. Olga, stunning in a compromise between a white dress and a gorgeous Turkish shawl, held Harry's hand throughout as they stood in front of a table completely covered with an enormous Union Jack. Two of Harry's friends, fellow officers from the *Lion*, were present in full uniform. Tim Harington sent a warm note of congratulations. Harry himself was in civilian clothes, looking cool and dashing, but without the impeccable elegance exhibited by his new father-in-law.

The arrangements were carefully organised, and once again it was Alexei who sorted everything out. The lunch, after the ceremony, was in a private room at Tokatlians just round the corner from the Embassy; carriages for everyone for the ride down to the sea-front at Eminonu were ready after lunch; and finally, yet another bottle of champagne as Harry and Olga boarded the launch to the liner which would take them to the start of their new life together in Alexandria. It had all been much to Karekin's taste, though fashionable Bolis viewed it as yet another Avakian eccentricity.

One month later the decision of the court martial held in the Harbiye buildings was published. Harry was found guilty of exceeding his authority and disregarding orders from his superior commander. Extenuating circumstances were accepted, and Harry was given an official reprimand and put back in seniority, though not reduced in rank. On reflection, there was no way that the Court, faced with the standing and reputation of one of the Navy's senior Admirals, could have decided otherwise. The decision was sent immediately to Alexandria, where

Harry and Olga were already settled.

Several months later the politicians gathered in the city of Lausanne beside the clear waters of Lake Geneva passed a final resolution requiring a compulsory exchange of populations between Greece and the new Turkey. The compulsory exchange was to be based on people's religious beliefs; the date of the finality of the decree to be the 1st May 1923. In Article 2, Greek Orthodox citizens registered as living in the city of Constantinople were to be exempted. However, the treaty made it clear that any Greeks who had already fled, would not to be allowed to return.

Who cared about Spiro and his new family, wandering homeless along the Aegean coast? Who cared about the many Turks of Macedonia, who had lived there under Ottoman rule for centuries, and only spoke Greek? Some of them even applied to change religion in order to remain. The nationalists were adamant. No exceptions! This conference, praised for tidying up a difficult situation, ushered in a whole century of other experiments in 'ethnic cleansing', all in the name of the sanctity of the nation.

Nationalism and the nation-state cannot exist in a conflict-free condition. It cannot exist without claims, counter-claims, grudges and resentments. Whenever the nationalism of one group of people raises its ugly head, immediately as if springing up out of the very earth, the nationalism of another group will emerge in opposition.

There are, and were, plenty of other possible solutions. Humanity is capable of many forms of civilised rule. 'But surely' said the gentlemen in their miserable and ugly Chateau, 'they all hated each other, didn't they? – We had better separate them.' People may hate other people for all sorts of personal and petty reasons. But hatred of a whole group is always a matter of deliberate manipulation by a ruling elite, usually supported by propagandists, ready to orchestrate myths shoring up one form of nationalism against another. Hate? The Spiros of this world wouldn't even hate the well-dressed urbane gentlemen of Lausanne who so unreasonably had ordered their lives.

On the very same day that the convention was finally signed Conrad Bridgeman was born to Olga Bridgeman in a nursing home opposite Regents Park, in the imperial city of London.

A year later the last acknowledged Caliph of the Moslem community – Abdul Medjid – the successor to the last Sultan, was sitting in the Dolmabahce Palace reading the Koran, when the palace was surrounded by troops sent from Ankara. He was summarily informed that he had to leave the city at dawn the next day. Mustapha Kemal had already decreed that Ankara was to be the capital of the new republic. After over 1,500 years as an imperial capital, longer than any other city in the world, it had now, at a stroke of a pen, become the second city of a republic. Kemal refused to visit the city. He removed the wily, cheerful Refet and one year after the departure of the last Sultan, he abolished the Caliphate without a murmur of dissent. Early the following morning, at half past five, the Caliph was bundled into a car. Orders had already been sent that there was to be no send-off at Sirkedji station. Two cars, followed by a lorry carrying such luggage as could be packed in the eight hour notice given, drove out of the Yedikule gate and on to Chatalja, 30 miles away.

Six hours after setting off, the party arrived at the Chatalja railway station, cordoned off from inquisitive eyes. The station-master here was Jewish and had been here since 1912. He had witnessed the whole of the political and military events which had lapped round the station. The arrival of the Bulgarians, the counterattack by the Young Turks, the German supply trains, the Greeks, the British and now the nationalists. He had remained loyal, as had almost all the Jews in the city, to the Ottomans throughout. He offered the exhausted Caliph his own quarters while they waited for the train to arrive. It was not due until the evening.

As the Caliph got ready to leave the station-master's little house to wait on the platform, he gave thanks for the hospitality he had received. The good man, disregarding the nationalist officials looking on disapprovingly, bowed and said –

"Your honour, when our ancestors were driven out of Spain, it was your Ottoman ancestors who alone agreed to give us shelter and who saved us from extinction. Only through their generosity and help did we retain our religion, our language and our lives. As their representative at this moment I will serve you always as best as I can."

The Orient Express – it was the Simplon-Orient this time – steamed into the little station to make a special stop. Most of the occupants were already asleep and few of the green blinds were pushed aside to look out as the Caliph, the last reigning Ottoman and his little party, boarded the train into the coach, hurriedly arranged by the new governor of Constantinople the day before. The Caliph tried to smile, as the officials and the local gendarmes gave him his last salute. The Governor who had at last turned up, handed his secretary passports, visas for Switzerland and a wad of money. The doors shut, the train hissed and the last Ottoman left the land they had ruled for 500 years.

Finally three years later, by decree emanating from Ankara, the name of the city founded by the Roman Emperor Constantine, with its myriad of alternative local names, perched half in Europe and half in Asia, was officially changed. It was to be known only as Istanbul. Notice was given that no letter addressed to Constantinople would be delivered by the Republican Postal services.

Constantinople no longer existed.

www.ingramcontent.com/pod-product-compliance
Lightning Source LLC
Chambersburg PA
CBHW030737030726
47497CB00001B/23